To my good friend
George
from Adrian M [illegible]
Blessed Be.
April 2008

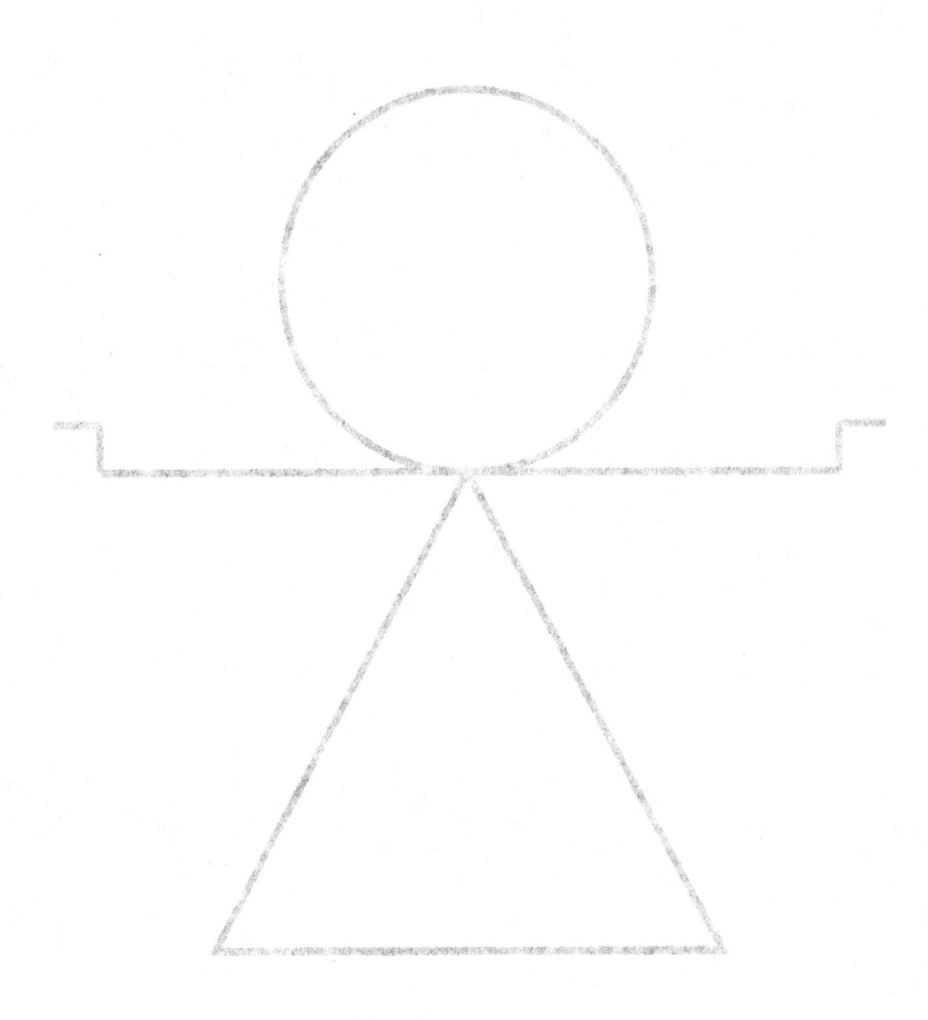

THE PRIESTESS OF TANIT

A NOVEL BY A M SAMPSON

THE PRIESTESS OF TANIT

A NOVEL BY A M SAMPSON©

A STORY OF REINCARNATION

The Priestess of Tanit

Published by Shunava Productions.
ISBN 978-09551323-1-5

For more information or to order your copy send e mail to:
shunavasampson @yahoo.co.uk

Dedicatory Note

This volume is dedicated to George A Foster in recognition of his generosity and unflagging belief in my creative endeavours, as well as his unyielding enthusiasm for life and the creative process.

A M Sampson
Norwich. January 2008.

A NOTE ON THE HISTORICAL BACKGROUND TO THE NOVEL

The Phoenicians were an ancient seafaring people, who, it is believed, rose out of Mesopotamia at least two thousand years before the common era (BCE). We can certainly look to a strong Semitic link for their origins, and there is some genetic evidence that the modern people living in the Levant, and those of ancient Phoenicians before them, have a common ancestry. It is known that their motherland was that of modern day Lebanon. The name they called themselves was *'bani kan'an'* 'Children of Canaan. They only came to be called 'Phoenician', through the Greek *'Phoinike'* (*Φοiνίkη*): 'purple people'. This came about because of the association with the 'Phoenicians' and the trade and production of the famous Tyrian purple dye. Tyre, being the one time capitol of the Phoenicians.

The spread of the Phoenicians from the Levant, west into Tripolitania, to eventually encompass the whole of the Maghreb, and places as far flung as Ireland and Cornwall (at least in terms of trade), also coincided with the expansion of Tanit worship.

The Gaelic word for fire, *teine,* is very sillier to the Carthaginian word *tine:* Fire was a gift of Tanit. The Celtic festival of Beltane is also believed to have Phoenician links in that it is derived from the names of the Phoenician triad of Baal-Hammon Tanit and Eshmun. Tanit is consort of Baal-Hammon. Both Tanit and Baal-Hammon are fertility gods that were worshipped together. Tanit is a celestial goddess who has strong associations with the moon, particularly in her crescent waxing aspect. Tanit is a triple goddess in that she is also associated with the sun through fire as well as the earth in respects of fertility and fecundity. She is linked with other deities of the pantheon such as those of: Ishtar, Ashtart, Astarte and Artemis, and of the Roman goddess Juno Caelestis. Her symbol is not unlike that of the Egyptian symbol for life, the Ankh: a circle supported by a blunt cone, with a straight line dividing the two points. She is also represented by other geometric patterns, for example, that of a Cone supporting a circle in a upturned crescent, above which is a symbol of the sun, a triangle above a square above which is a crescent and a star. Tanit is also depicted on Carthaginian stele as a female figure crowned with an upward pointing crescent, above which is a symbol of the sun; in each of her hands she holds outstretched, cornucopia, from which issues forth fruit and ambrosia: images of grapes and wheat are also shown, all symbolic of her primary role of goddess of fertility, abundance and regeneration. Her symbolic image of a goddess of fecundity meant that her priests and priestesses practised sacred prostitution. Such practices were very common amongst ancient eastern religious cults, such as the cult of Isis and the worship of Demeter, Persephone/Core, in the Eleusinian Mysteries. Both Marries of the bible were very probably versed in the art of sacred sex as initiators into the *mysteries* of such religions as these.

January 2008

PREFACE

The Priestess of Tanit was begun shortly after the completion of my first Shunava publication: 'Lightning Over a Distant Shore', which was published in October 2005. Work began on Tanit sometime in late October or early November, with the working title 'The Priest', the proof copy version being completed in June 2007. The rewrite resulted, as is usual in the revision of any work, with some scenes being added, and others cut, notably the first chapter lengthened and the fight scene in the church tower was told exclusively from Bethany's perspective. The ending was also slightly altered, resulting in the work being lengthened by some forty eight pages. The final copy was completed in early January 2008.

The initial story was a much smaller, somewhat chaotic piece of work comprising some sixty or so pages of double spaced A4, which has now been destroyed. It was begun whilst living in Eastbourne, sometime in 1997. It was never really finished; the plot was confused, but I felt that the idea was a good one. Much of 'The Priest' survives in the first ten chapters of Tanit, although greatly altered in places, while in others the exact words are preserved, where I thought they had merit. Without going in to too much tedious detail, the first twenty or so pages are virtually unaltered from the original manuscript, other examples are the description of Natasha's sordid existence in the London bed-sit.

The High Priestess of Tanit, in its finalised form goes far beyond the original concept of The Priest. It is an esoteric work containing many elegant erotic scenes: it is a glorification of the senses, a spiritual and sensual affirmation of life, in which is charted the rise and fall of our heroin, Karen, who in an earlier incarnation offended the Phoenician goddess Tanit. A high priestess of the Phoenician goddess of fecundity was essentially the holy whore par excellence, who would have practised ritualised sex as an an initiation into the highest level of the mysteries of Tanit. A high priestess variously named: Nachash, Taanach, Shaula, in the novel, became so powerful that she believed herself to be the living embodiment of Tanit herself. Having incurred the wrath of the goddess for trying to usurp her power, the soul of the high priestess is reincarnated down through the ages, each life lived out against the backdrop of sexual vagaries that leave her soul in a maelstrom of mental and physical discontent that always leads to the same ignominious yet always tragic early death. We catch up with Taanach's fated soul in modern times in the shape of Karen, a highly attractive and popular girl, who whilst at high school befriends our hero Julian, a somewhat aloof and less than popular young man, who Karen identifies as a person who, although unconventional, has very solid convictions; he is somebody she feels she can trust, someone who will not automatically try to seduce her, most importantly he is the only person she can confide in about her feelings of dark despair: her 'demon', or 'darkness' as she describes it. Unfortunately her demon gets the upper hand, and tugs her away from the stabilising influence of Julian, to follow a career as a nude model which ultimately leads into a debauched life style that has haunted all of Taanach's incarnations.

Is this the last throw of the dice for this wayward soul? Can Karen, in this life, with the help of Julian and others, put her demon on the back foot and bring the curse of Tanit to an end? These question are what form the basis of 'The Priestess of Tanit', and which, to a large degree are answered in the pages herein.

It became apparent from the early manuscript of 'The Priest', that there had to be some sort of linkage between Karen's wayward soul and some past-life experience which set her on her licentious trajectory. It came to me with such perfect clarity, that this linkage had to be centred around the worship of the goddess Tanit, as to have been spoken to me by the goddess herself.

I very often felt, whilst writing the novel, that it was very much directed by something outside of me, or perhaps within me. It almost wrote itself - it seemed, at times. It certainly seemed to follow its own somewhat circuitous path towards a rather ironic ending. I must thank my muse for this - who knows, perhaps Tanit herself.

Blessed Be.

Norwich. January 2008

I

She called it a darkness. A biding presence that she tried hard to control. She feared that one day it would over power her. She said that it was the cause of her dissatisfaction with life, and the reason why she tired so quickly of people. Whatever its true nature, it had always been there, waiting for the right time to emerge and take control. Yet to see her, one would have never guessed the nature of the demons that lurked below that serene and beautiful countenance.

When I first met Karen she was still at high school. She was by far the most attractive and most popular girl of her senior year. Her obvious good looks, together with a mature figure for her age, made her very popular with the boys, but she paid scant interest in those of her own age, and preferred to date college students who were three or four years her senior.

Karen was one of those people who seem to glide through life without anything seeming to harm them, while all around people were being torn apart, usually by each other. One got the feeling she was invincible: that she rode above the storm. I believed it then, and I still think that it is true. We all have our demons, but in Karen's case, I had no idea just how potent they were. If it had been any body ordinary they would have succumbed to them immediately.

I had known Karen since high school and I suppose, like a hundred others, I had fallen in love with her looks and her cool superiority, but I wasn't like the others. I always found myself on the outside of things looking in. I suppose this aloofness was what made Karen aware of me. To my astonishment she began to acknowledge my existence, first with a look, then a smile, then a greeting. I never had the courage to ask her out on a date, but somehow we began to spend more and more time in each other's company. There were many that thought we were dating. Those that Karen knew thought she had lost her mind, those that I knew, that had first regarded me with derision, now looked on in envy and amazement, perhaps even disbelief, especially when she smiled at me in front of the others, and then gave me the wink. I found it hard to believe myself, that the most popular and most attractive girl in school would wish to seek me out. As I said before, I had no idea then, of the kind of demons that pursued her.

In a sense Karen's problems were an inverse of my own. She knew the power she had stemmed from her looks. She was totally confident and at ease with her body. At the same time she knew that she would never find any rest from the attentions of men. She would never escape their eyes or their wanting her, and so she took refuge in me. Intuitively, she felt she was safe with me.

One night in a kind of desperation she suddenly clung to me. "You are a good person, aren't you?" she asked looking up at me, her lavender eyes wide with expectation. I told her that I thought that I was.

"I hate pretence," she said. "What I love about you is that you don't have an angle. What you say is what you *actually* believe. You don't want what all the others want from me."

I knew only too well what she meant, but I had to confess that I was still a man, and as such only too well aware of Karen's obvious sexuality. And as if she read my mind she laughed. "Don't look so shocked, I know you find me attractive. I know you would love to get me into bed!"

"Well..." I began, blushing, "perhaps I'm not as good a person as you think I am?"

"I didn't say you were perfect, besides which there would be something wrong if you didn't find me attractive. No I wouldn't like that at all. That too would be a kind of deceit."

Sometimes Karen would just take off and I wouldn't see her for days. You see, she gave me the illusion that I knew where she was and who she was with, but the truth was, for most of the time, I hadn't a clue. The time I didn't spend with her, however, seemed worth all the anguish the moment I set eyes on her again.

To me she *was* invincible: strong, unafraid, perfect in every way. I considered myself fortunate, blessed by the gods, that for some inexplicable reason, Karen should choose to spend so much time with me. My parents were pleased too, that I was *normal* at last, that I had a girlfriend, and a very pretty one too. They didn't know the truth about our relationship. My friends, such as they were did not know the truth either - although I was sure some had begun to guess that my associations with Karen were purely Platonic. Oh we kissed, we hugged, but that was all.

"I value our friendship. You understand don't you?" said Karen, one evening, when saying goodnight. I became overly amorous and felt her breast. "Sex," she informed me, "would spoil the beauty of what we shared."

If it meant not seeing her again I put aside my desire for her as best as I was able. I had resigned myself to the fact that my knowledge of Karen would always remain on an intellectual level. A kind of priest, or confidant. So you can imagine my surprise when she called at my parent's one evening without us having arranged to meet. Such impromptu calls were unusual. Her presence in my parent's living room seemed somewhat incongruous. Rather as if a wild creature of the night, a panther perhaps, had strayed in from the cold. She wasn't looking her normal composed self. The moment she saw me she got up and was ready to leave. We quickly said our good-byes, and just like cats we sped off into the darkness.

We tore off down the street, leaving clouds of dust and headed out onto the beach road. Karen always drove fast but I had never seen her handle the car so recklessly. I asked her if anything was wrong but she ignored me. I didn't think it a good idea to ask again! It was obvious that something was bothering her.

We puled up alongside a deserted stretch of beach. The sea was invisible in the darkness, only the sound of waves indicated its presence. Karen looked toward the darkness. When she turned to me, there were tears in her eyes. Suddenly she held me tightly.

"Promise me you won't leave me Julian?"

I felt confused: never had I seen Karen display such emotion before.

"Of course I won't leave you," I said.

"You don't think I am a bad person do you?"

"No, you're beautiful."

Karen made a sound in her throat. "Oh yes, I am to look at. So everyone tells me. But in here," she said, indicating her head. "In here! " she repeated. "What about in here? My mind is full of horrible things."

"What horrible things?"

Karen looked out to sea again. "It doesn't matter. Just promise me you will never go away."

"Of course not," I replied, thinking what a strange request, and one I had no way of promising, since it has always been my belief that nothing in life is ever permanent.

"You are a good person Julian. You underestimate yourself," she said. "You keep the darkness at bay."

There is a part of ourselves in all of us, that we do not understand. With Karen, this unknown aspect to her being frightened her. It made her: 'do things,' she told me. She was afraid of where the darkness would lead her. Clinging to me tightly she repeated: 'I was her only hope.'

Karen began to kiss me in a way she had never done before. She pressed her strong body against mine, encouraging me to touch her breasts. "You can do it to me if you want," she said in my ear. "I know you have been wanting to for so long."

Karen got out of the car and walked down on to the beach towards the sound of the waves. I could just discern her outline in the dimness of the night.

I followed her into the darkness. When we got back to the car we were no longer the same people.

"It probably wasn't a good idea," said Karen, at length.

"I'm sorry," I replied, feebly

"Don't be."

"I'm just not that good, I guess!" I said, thinking of all the other men she must have been with.

"Don't worry, lets not think about it for the moment."

After that night we discovered different vulnerabilities about ourselves, which brought us even closer.

Karen liked the beach at night and we went there often together, usually to just listen to the sound of the waves. I simply loved to be near her, and in time, I came to identify her with the sea, for there was something deep and unfathomable about her, as well as something to be a little afraid of.

It was only a few months before we graduated from high school that we began to see each other. That last summer before we began college were the happiest and most memorable days of my life. We both applied to the same college, and both got accepted. Everything seemed to be working out for once in my life. And then, just a few days before we were to begin the new term, Karen told me the news. She had landed a job with a modelling agency. I don't know why I should have been so shocked, after all, if one took a look at her it was the obvious path for her to follow. I tried to sound happy for her, but I could not keep the edge out of my voice. I felt that the fates had begun to work against us, and Karen's career choice would sooner or later take her away from me for good.

I didn't realise just how quickly it would happen. Within two weeks Karen was gone from my life. The agency was obviously impressed by what they saw, and had quickly signed her up for a fashion magazine in New York.

Of course we promised to do all of the usual things people do when they part. For a time we kept in contact. At first we phoned one another quite regularly, and then after a few months I realised it was me that was doing all the phoning, and Karen sounded less and less like the person I had known. I began to write her long letters instead, which described the desolation that I felt without her. For a time I got replies from her assuring me that we would be together again soon, but gradually the assurances became less, along with her replies. Finally when I suggested meeting up with her there came neither a reply, by telephone or letter. Within a year Karen had disappeared from my radar.

Somehow or other, I managed to graduate from college and landed a job with a newspaper in Los Angeles. It was here, in the world of magazines and tabloid press that I was to be confronted once more with the image of Karen, but this time in one of those soft porn magazines for men, featuring fast cars and scantily clad women. The caption read in large letters: 'Natasha knows how to stop her man from getting away', followed by a short fictitious biography of how she grew up on a ranch in Wyoming including, at the end, her vital statistics: '34D-18-36, which I strongly suspected were the only concession to truth to be found in the short article. She was pictured adopting a provocative pose, her legs spread wide apart, wearing a pair of tight jeans that had been cut to shreds so that they barely functioned as a garment at all, and a denim jacket undone, to reveal a tantalising glimpse of her naked body beneath. She had on a cowboy hat and boots, while holding a lasso in one hand, while her other played with the last catch on her already low-slung jeans.

Her beautiful head was cocked to one side, her left eye closed, in what was to become her trade mark: the wink. To others it might be taken as an inviting provocative gesture of the girl who had seen it all, the girl who was up for anything. But I couldn't help feeling that it was meant specifically for me; that she hadn't completely lost touch with the Karen that I had known at high school. After the initial shock of being confronted with Karen, or should I say 'Natasha,' I began to see this particular form of image as a way of being close to her again. I found her in other magazines and calendars; where she would always be giving me 'the wink'. For the most part they were always tastefully done. One never saw all of her breasts, for example, sometimes her long hair would partially obscure them, or else her hands would only allow a tantalising glimpse of part of a perfect hemisphere. Even so, this kind of exploitation depressed me, and I felt rather disgusted with myself for being in some way a part of the business of that very exploitation. My beautiful Karen and her beautiful body, were held up for every low life to indulge their sick fantasy.

It had been only three years since she had gone away. The girl then had looked a lot different. The later images of Natasha were a lot more raw, a lot more - *louche*. There was a hardness about her body, that was reflected in a callousness in her face. In most of these images she no longer gave me, 'the wink'. She stared out at you, barefaced, hard and aggressive, her chine jutting forward, her lips slightly parted, her teeth clenched. Her arms by her side, while her hands caressed her thigh; barebreasted, bareboned, all attempts at concealment, any overtures to modesty thrown away.

Karen always had a lithe figure, but in some of these photos she looked almost emaciated, but without the accompanying look of weakness that comes from malnutrition. Her skin still retained a surreal glow of health, even if one could easily count every rib in her long body. She retained a sleek muscular look that could only have come from many regular hours spent in the gym. The overall effect was something a bit strange. In these photographs Karen didn't look like the kind of person one might meet in the course of a normal day, that is, if Karen had ever looked ordinary? There was something uncanny, unreal about her look. If one reached out and touched her one might have been surprised to find warm flesh. Instead she reminded me of a kind of yellow marble or ivory sculpture. Only her beautiful living eyes prevented the similitude of a statue from becoming complete.

Natasha was explicit and unequivocal in her sexuality. She was Karen unveiled. On the glossy page of a magazine or a calendar, half naked or baring all, Karen acted out her demonic side. The slut, the whore that she masqueraded as, the sex goddess, the creature of men, and *women's* fantasies was given full expression; but this was not the person I had once known! An image of her in a magazine comes to mind of Natasha topless in a pair of boxer shorts standing astride a muscular man as he lay prostrate, one foot on his chest her arms raised as in the style of the champion, with big red boxing-gloves on each hand.

An incongruous image, one that demonstrated the power she had over the male sex. The caption read: 'Men watch out, the new look Natasha is a knockout winner every time, having been voted in the top ten sexiest girls in America.' There followed a short article on her, wherein she describes the kind of man she prefers: 'He has to be big where it matters,' we are told. 'But I don't think the man that can truly satisfy me has been born yet, but I'm remain optimistic in finding Mr right - one day!' It was predictable hackneyed stuff but it was what was expected of a girl like 'Natasha', and the punters lapped it up, so Natasha gave them what they wanted - and in spades. She pandered to the modern sick obsession with size. She pandered to men's secret insecurities!

It seemed that Karen was growing in more than just notoriety. After having read her vital statistics (yet again), I realised what they meant by the, 'new look Karen': a year on year expansion of her bust size, from a thirty four C in her first year of modelling, to a thirty four double D in her second year, until she ended up with the mind-boggling statistics of a thirty six E bust, eighteen inch waist and thirty six inches across her hips. I wondered, 'was there no end to this obsession with size? How much was there left of the real Karen? Had Natasha completely taken over?'

In the world of the glamour model there was always the pressure from other girls to stay on top. One had to be fit, one had to be strong to last. Natasha was still a fit twenty one year old at the top of her career, but no matter how strong the body, slowly little by little, time was eating away at her looks, and one day, quite suddenly she would be too old for the game. How would she look when she was forty and burnt out? What would she look like without the silicon to buoy-up her breasts? All that stretched flesh! An unpleasant image to conjure with, without a doubt!

Karen as Natasha, was *unequivocal* when it came to selling herself, rating herself as: unsurpassed in history. 'No one has a body that is as perfect as mine,' she claimed in an interview, 'Pamela Lloyd is nothing,' she said of her rival, 'everyone knows I'm better looking than her, she may have bigger tits but mine are firmer; she is clearly past her best.'

Such remarks as these did not help the image of the brand: 'Natasha'. She was seen as too strident in her opinion of rival models, her image too stark. She lacked the popularity necessary to become an iconic figure of female sexuality, no matter how many breast enlargements she underwent.

That Natasha was voted in the top ten sexiest girls in America, stood for very little; the truth was she didn't have the international notoriety that Pamela Lloyd or the English glamour star Vanessa Drake possessed. She had failed to land the big contracts that would have set her on course for international stardom. The truth was there were at least a thousand other girls, equally as sexy as Karen, and each just as hungry for fame and success. Super-models like Vanessa Drake, Pamela Lloyd and other famous names, such as the notorious sex goddess Liza Redcliffe, as famous for her career on the silver screen and stage as she was a model, possessed an aura about them, that went towards a qualitative difference between them and other models.

Natasha looked set to remain a mediocre porn star on the fringes of fame, so I guess she felt she had nothing to loose by striking out in a whole new direction, perhaps what she needed was a whole arena to herself, to this end Europe beckoned. Before she left the States for what was to become, relative obscurity, she left amid allegations in the press of drug addiction and sexual excess. Rather than deny these claims she indulged one half of them, with the boast that she regularly took part in sexual orgies that went on for days at a time, that her sexual powers were, like those of her looks, her figure: unparalleled! What validity these claims held remained largely unsubstantiated, but media hacks were only too keen to speculate, with accounts varying from between fifty to as many as a hundred and fifty sexual partners visiting her bed - in a single session! Perhaps it was all just highfalutin talk, one thing was for sure, Karen, or should I say Natasha, regarded herself as the: '*ne plus ultra* of all female kind.' What a *rara avis*, she was!

It is true she had acquired a small measure of fame, but her notoriety was short lived, the magazines are soon thrown away and the calendars taken down, the latest 'hot new thing' comes to the fore and in its turn recede, but Karen had had her taste of power and it must have swelled her already inflated ego to gargantuan proportions - if only she could live up to it! It must have driven her frantic that the world was not yet ready to kneel before the sex goddess.

In reality, even those that had made it big, like Pamela Lloyd and Liza Redcliffe: the ones who got the veneration, had transformed their great beauty into a commodity. In the final analysis they were just so much meat sold on the market. People bought the product if the packaging looked attractive, what existed inside didn't really matter. To this end Karen was expendable. Her value was her sex, so she had repackaged herself and called the product 'Natasha'. In casting off the skin of her earlier self, she had developed a raw and harder edged sexuality. Yet still some semblance of the Karen I knew remained. The end result was a persona that transmitted a sense of corrupted innocence. This was what made Natasha such an enigmatic figure. One thought one had got all there was of her to get, that she was just another body, her eyes though, indicated that she was holding the best part of herself back, and only those with discerning eyes could see that this was so. Like the times, Natasha sent out an image that was stark and uncompromising. She represented a stark truth about the age. Everything about it had been laid bare. There were no more secrets left. There was no point any more in trying to pretend that innocence existed. Everything, everyone was up for exploitation. Karen looked out of the page at you, her dark stare challenging the onlooker, or else she gave one the wink: enigmatic! Invariably all anybody was interested in were her broad hips, narrow waist, and large enhanced breasts. Whether clothed or unclothed, one could see the ready made relationship she had with the camera. Put a lace shawl over her shoulders, or wrap her brown body in a sheet out of some vestige of decency - it didn't work! The result was always the same, Natasha was the epitome of a game that had all, but been played out.

The love I felt for her was pure and good but somehow, now, it seemed to be sullied and something dirty - to be ashamed of. The Karen I had known at high school and during that briefest of summers was not the person that stared out at me from the pages of these cheap magazines; indeed this person didn't even have the same name any more. The provocative attire she wore, or complete lack there of, and the suggestive pose she adopted, was not echoed by the look on her face, which made the viewer, (at least for me,) feel slightly ashamed. Unlike some of the other girls that appeared alongside Natasha, there was a knowing look, but the look of a very different kind of knowing, it seemed to be a cajoling one - 'yes, go on, take a good look if you want, this is all you will ever know of *me!'*

*

L A, like the rest of the world it seemed, had sold itself so many times that the pretence that it stood for anything other than the exploitation of the market place was now completely stripped bare. The modern world it seemed to me had all the solidity of quicksand. The same vacuous look was on everyone's face. People had stopped believing in innocence and truth. Worse than that, I felt that people had begun to stop thinking altogether. I leafed through yet another lurid magazine, hating myself more each time, but I was promised yet again a view of a girl I once knew. The look in her eye used to keep my hope alive, that she too had not become a victim of the modern world, but with each new level of baseness I came across, I felt the game was up. If I could prod the figure would I find it empty and shallow? The only thing left, it seemed, that was in any sense authentic in the world could be found in one of Karen's poses. There, there existed the look of the prostitute, there, existed the worship of the flesh, and like the society I was a part of, it was meretricious, shallow and two dimensional!

And presumably this was the secret of Karen's success. Looking at her, photographed with her back to the camera, looking over her shoulder giving me the wink, with a mischievous grin on her face, which only accentuates further the suggestion that I was in on a private joke, her legs spread wide apart, with a long sinewy hand covering what everyone wanted to see, no one could epitomise better all the shallowness and licentiousness of a cheap whore, than Karen, in the guise of Natasha. But it was *her* joke, a joke she was playing on the whole darn world. Yet it still sickened me to look at her. To look at what she had become, but then I remembered what she had told me all that time ago, how she was afraid of her dark side. Well now, as I looked at her, and wondered what kind of life she lead, what kind of person she was, I understood suddenly the nature of her demon, and in the same instant I knew what I must do. I had to try and find her. Not because I wanted her, my reason was not sexually motivated, even though I was only too well aware of how gorgeous she was; most men might find that hard to understand, probably the kind that bought into the industry that Karen was a part of. And no, I didn't have leanings towards my own gender either. I guess it was a chemical thing that prevented us from gelling on the physical side. In any case I knew that I didn't satisfy her sexually. No, my reason for wanting her back was quite simply to save her - save her from herself. Perhaps it might sound pretentious. Was it possible to commit the unselfish act? It wasn't out of some noble cause: I wasn't particularly religious, I didn't go much on people that were, or had anything to do with the virtuous. They were the worst kind of all. I simply wanted to help her. Call it compassion if you must - I mean, you wouldn't ignore a cat or a dog if it was starving on the street and in need of a home - *would you?*

As I look at her again in one of her classic poses, her left arm partly concealing her perfect breasts, her head thrown back, a cheeky grin on her face, as she blows her public a kiss, her legs wide apart, her belly thrust forward, while her right hand is placed between her solid thighs - of course I would be lying if I said it did not at first send a wave of desire through me, but this was merely momentary, what persisted was probably the worst kind of emotion of all: I felt sorry for her, and all the other good looking girls that lay between the pages. There was no doubt that she needed saving from her demon.

Using my own connections in the business, (working on a newspaper has its advantages), I was easily able to trace the agency that employed Karen. They were very uncooperative at first when it came to telling me of her whereabouts. Information though, like most things in life, is made more available when money is employed as an inducement. I discovered that she was no longer with the *agency* in New York. The last they had heard was that she was going to travel overseas and that, 'some Spanish guy by the name of Garcia was taking care of things for her.' Where, overseas, no one could say for sure, although it was definitely somewhere in Europe. The agency put me on to a friend of Karen's who would have a better idea of where she had gone. After spending a few more dollars I discovered that she had purchased an air ticket for Rome.

Then the fates suddenly seemed to work in my favour again, although perhaps a bit on the late side, as they could have saved me several hundred dollars. A postcard arrived from Italy. The message was short but succinct: 'I am so sorry my dearest friend, my protector, for letting you down. I need you again. I will be leaving Italy this week, please forgive me. ' It was signed quite simply, 'Karen' and three crosses, followed by the name of a Greek island. Having never heard of it before I looked it up in the Atlas - all that was shown was a tiny dot in the middle of the Aegean sea: the island of Sapphos.

The only way of getting there was to fly to Athens and then travel by ferry. On the days leading up to my flight I didn't sleep well. I couldn't get Karen out of my mind, I imagined her in desperate straits; exploited by this Garcia character, as some sort of sex slave. I had never felt any pangs of jealousy when I had known Karen at high school, or when she left for a career in modelling; it was true that I felt a sense of loneliness, perhaps even despair, but I was never jealous as far as I can remember, so why should I now be exhibiting all the feelings of a betrayed lover? I lay awake afraid sometimes, to close my eyes, for then my own demons would lead my mind astray. I would picture Karen and Garcia together. He would be the kind of man who knew how to get the best out of his woman! And then all the images I had seen of her, together with those of other girls, gathered together to assail my mind. I fought hard against my demons until, unable to stand it any more I rose from my bed, and in a fit of pique, in the early hours of morning, I gathered together my collection of magazines and calendars that featured Natasha, and took them down to the basement and committed them to the flames of the incinerator. The more innocuous images of Karen, the shots of her for the more reputable fashion houses, advertising lingerie, I kept from the flames. She had such a perfect figure, perfect face, why should she want to parade her naked body in front of the camera, when she could easily earn a living as a model - but with her clothes on? But this was not what Natasha did. I know it is naïve of me to think otherwise. It was still hard sometimes to accept Karen as a separate entity from Natasha. She had to be still in there, submerged at times, but still alive! Perhaps I had looked at Karen through the guise of Natasha for too long? Was it that I had allowed Natasha to take control? Natasha was the girl that had evoked feelings of jealousy and resentment in me. I realised that I wanted Natasha in a way I had never wanted Karen. And yet It was Karen who had sent the note from Italy, but it was with Natasha that I saw myself, when I shut my eyes at night.

II

The thought of Natasha with another man drove me crazy. By the time I boarded the plane bound for Athens, the idea of this Garcia character getting his evil paws on Karen, was enough to make me want to kill him. I sat and looked out of the window as the plane ascended, and sipped my Martini. I laughed at myself for having such notions, anyone who knew me would have seen how incongruous such ideas were for me. What disturbed me was that I should have such strong feelings as these in the first place.

Once in Greece I took a ferry from the large port of Piraeus, and sailed to the island of Naxos, the largest of the group of islands known as the Cyclades. There were no official ferry links with the small island of Sapphos my ultimate destination. After a few enquiries I soon discovered that there were plenty of small privately owned craft for hire.

The final leg of the journey took the best part of the morning. Many islands came and went, but finally one stayed in view longer than the others. The captain of our small vessel headed towards landfall at a small, rickety wooden jetty. I stepped out of the boat and the captain handed me my bags. To my surprise I heard the engine suddenly throttle up and the small vessel began to back away from the jetty. I waved good-bye with the feeling of being stranded.

After only a couple of minutes a wooden cart pulled by a tired old ass rumbled towards me. I walked up to the shaky looking vehicle and addressed the old man at the reins. "Garcia...?" I asked. The old man muttered something in Greek and gestured in the direction he had come. He grunted something again in his tongue and I handed him up my luggage which he then threw unceremoniously into the back. I climbed aboard next to the old man. He gave another command, this time addressing the tired looking creature at the end of the reins, and it turned slowly, beginning the journey back from whence it had come, along a single dirt track which, I was soon to discover, lead to Garcia's crazy villa, and my ultimate reunion with Karen.

The dirt track, it seemed, was the only link to the coast and the outside world. My companion said very little, only pointing up the road when I mentioned the name 'Garcia'. The heat of the midday sun would have been unbearable were it not for the constant flow of air of the Cyclades. Stunted bushes and rocky sandy soil slowly gave way to olive groves, then vineyards and, further inland, eventually fields of wheat. Rounding a bend and situated at the top of a small hill was an impressive stone facade, gleaming brilliant white in the crystalline pure air: the old man pointed up ahead with his stick and uttered the name 'Garcia.' As we got closer it became apparent that the structure was a boundary wall which encircled a large area of land, somewhat like a ranch, or perhaps a better comparison would be a Roman villa, with its associated temples and outbuildings.

The main building was surrounded by a portico, with a tiled roof supported by marble pillars. The effect was to enhance the image of a classical Roman or Greek site. Not far from the road to my right, was what looked to be the genuine thing: a small stone structure with a flat roof supported by stone pillars. On seeing these two impressive monuments I felt as though I had distinctly left the modern world far behind me.

The old ass suddenly came to a halt still several hundred yards from the villa. The cart lurched and creaked. The old man motioned for me to get down, he then unceremoniously ditched my luggage out, landing at my feet. He gave a sharp motion with the reins and the old ass started into life again and, with a slight falter, the cart and its driver slowly went on their way. I looked on, somewhat bemused by the spectacle of my slowly vanishing transport.

I scratched my head and started to consider my options. There seemed nothing for it other than to make my way on foot. As I stooped to pick up my bags I heard a rustling come from the bushes adjacent to the road. Appearing at my side came an old man of about seventy, with silvery grey hair and a short silver beard, accompanied by a more youthful figure with closely cropped hair. The youthful one in particular reminded me of a Buddhist monk, as both men were attired in long white gowns. The younger man stepped purposefully over to my bags and picked them up. The old silver haired man stretched out his hand to me. "I am Garcia," he said, "welcome to my island."

"Where is Karen?" I asked, after removing my hand from his deathlike grasp.

The old man smiled. "You are very direct. She is perfectly safe." He said, putting his hand on my shoulder. "You must be Mr Julian! Come." I followed Garcia off the road through an avenue of tall hedgerows, while his younger companion had gone off down the track towards the villa with my baggage. At the end of the avenue was a brilliant white colonnade of stone pillars as well as statues of what I took to be classical Greek Gods and Goddesses. Beyond the colonnade was a beautiful blue shimmering pool set in white marble, and laying upon the cool stone were two long naked dark female bodies. As we got closer I recognised the lighter toned one of the two; unmistakably it was Karen. The image of her in a hundred or more provocative poses came flooding back. Both girls were oblivious to our presence, they gave the impression of sublime indolence and ease. The statues of the goddesses, might have reason to look on with jealous eyes at the site of so much perfect mortal flesh. Both girls, like the ancients themselves depilated their bodies. Dare I say it, even Venus would have been envious. Her obvious allure perplexed me. There before me, on full display, was the abode of her daemon and the font of Natasha's notoriety.

The other girl had a definite Mediterranean look about her, which probably accounted for her much darker skin. Their long snake like bodies glistened in the sun. The one with the deep chestnut tan bent forward to apply a red coloured oil to her skin. She handed the bottle to Karen who then began to massage the other girl's back with the oil. It was then that Karen looked up and saw me standing next to Garcia. In a fit of exuberance that was so typical of Karen, she leapt to her feet, forgetting the other girl, and ran over to me, calling my name.

"You came! You came..!" she said, throwing her arms around me and pressing her greasy face against mine. She kissed me hard on the mouth. Aware of strongly smelling aromatic oily flesh, I was reluctant to put my hands on her body. I must have communicated this fact of slight repulsion because Karen cut short her embrace and glanced down at herself.

"Forgive me," she said, "I completely forgot, but here on the island we often go around like this."

"Do you really?" I said, glancing at Garcia.

"We are all lovers of beauty and nature here." he said. "Oh but do not worry, you will not have to do the same if it makes you uncomfortable."
Karen's friend who was now dressed in a silk Kimono style robe, came over and helped Karen into a similar form of apparel.
"Well I will leave you to get reacquainted," said Garcia, and looking to Karen. "Come up to the villa for drinks when you are ready."

Garcia's villa was built in the style of a Greek temple. The stone from which it had been constructed, he informed me, had been collected from various locations on the island and each piece had once been part of a much larger temple that had been destroyed in the ancient past. Its location was exactly where the present building now stood. All that remained of the original building were the foundations and some mosaic tilled floors, which had all been lovingly restored by Garcia. The inside of the walls were plastered and decorated with gaily painted murals depicting various scenes from Greek mythology. The atmosphere of the place gave one the feeling of having stepped back in time to ancient Greece. I could tell that Karen was enchanted by the place. I watched her in the presence of Garcia - she was enthralled by him, she hung upon his every word, she hung upon him, quite literally.

Garcia's villa, with its surrounding ornate walled gardens, orchards and olive groves, was at the heart of a small community that was totally self-sufficient. Water was drawn from a well that was fed by a spring, the grain from the fields was used to make various pastries and bread. Oranges and other fruits were grown, even grapes were cultivated and made into wine. Sheep and goats that grazed the fields in various parts of the island supplied milk and cheese, and the animals themselves, as Garcia explained, were slaughtered to provide meat, but this was done only on certain days of the month. What he was alluding to, of course, was their ritual sacrifice.

There were non of the modern entrapments of luxury and convenience, although there existed luxury and opulence of a different form. But of the twentieth century there was a distinct absence in the way of electricity and communications. Even my ride up to the villa, and the surrounding settlement, had been made on a rickety old cart pulled by a tired old ass.

Garcia proudly declared that he, 'no longer had need of the modern world,' and that he had, 'totally turned his back on it!' He lived the life of an ancient Greek scholar, a philosopher, a priest. In modern eyes we would say that he was either mad or just a harmless old eccentric. Garcia, though, took himself very seriously. He believed in *his* way of life as passionately as he believed in the various gods and goddesses that he sacrificed to. He lived almost exclusively on the island with just a handful of his devotees. There were about fifty of them, that attended to the crops and the livestock and various other jobs that kept the small community functioning. This was a non evangelical movement. Everyone who laboured on the island did so purely out of love for paganism and Garcia's dream. The dream of course was for a world republic, based upon the ideals of paganism. He wanted to open the mind of modern man to the folly of the modern world and its obsession with control over nature. Garcia rejected the fundemental premise that the modern world is founded upon, namely that constant technological innovation and change, equates to progress. 'In a world that is constantly undergoing change, how can there be any notion of progress? *all one has is a state of flux,'* he pointed out.

I can say all of this with such exactitude because during my time with Garcia this was all I ever heard him speak about. Garcia was a man of passion. He believed firmly and unquestionably in his ideas, and it always sends alarm bells off in my head whenever I encounter those that believe, with a passion, that they and they alone have the answer. But perhaps Garcia was one of the few men whose ideas did not fill me full of dread. In some respects I agreed with him. I too thought that things had gone too far concerning mankind's dependence on technology. After all it was, one way or another, destroying the planet I lived on. Garcia was no idle boaster: he was a man of means, and the small number of people who lived and worked on the island, in short, practised a way of life, the pagan way, were only the tip of an iceberg. Many came to the island, learned of Garcia's ways and then left to set up other communities in other parts of the world. But this was not just another hippie colony, and Garcia was very adamant that he should not be compared with a hippie, a 'drop out!' The main difference, of course, was the religious aspect: the open worship of the old Gods.

But what kind of man, dear reader, have I portrayed? Have I given you the wrong impression of him I wonder? He was not, and I feel fairly sure of this, some mad despotic ruler who had plans to overthrow the world order, although he might have had such ideas. Who can say what goes on in the depths of the mind of mankind? In all the time I spent with him, and we had many intimate conversations, not once did I detect anything like conceit or the love of power. He seemed on the whole almost afraid of the idea that he may be seen as arrogant. Garcia simply was! It was as if he wished to eradicate the ego, sublimate it to a strange kind of humility. I suppose when you really know in your heart that you have the answer, such stupid posturing is no longer needed.

He went about his strange world in a kind of daze. Often he would pass me in the corridor, nod to me, while all the time muttering to himself in Greek or Latin. At such times I wondered what strange daemon he was consulting with. Was he mad? Who can say? I do know he was inspired. He had read the classics, everything that existed in print, and some things that were only known to Garcia. His inspiration also came from what he saw around him. The modern world convinced him that a better way had once existed and needed to be reasserted: a way of life that was benign and in harmony with nature

It was to the past, and the world of ancient Greece and Rome that Garcia looked. He saw this period, from around 700 BCE, up to the time of the Christians, around 400 CE, as the pinnacle of civilisation. After this period he regarded everything as a decline into barbarism and inhumanity.

"No one is greater than mother earth," he said to me one day. Stooping down, he gathered a handful of sand. "We must revere even the humblest plant and animal, even the soil we walk upon."

He opened his fingers and let the sand fall from his grasp and be carried away by the warm wind. And then, in one swift movement, he stretched out his arm and pointed at a large statue of some god or other, (perhaps it was Zeus). "There," he said, "is the reminder of who we are and what we are. We are but grains of dust in the eyes of the gods. There is the reminder of mankind's limits. It is at his own peril that he defies the gods, defies the laws of nature, for he is bound to them just as the stars that move in the heavens."

One question, though, kept returning to mind: if this pagan way of life was so perfect why did it collapse? Garcia laughed when I put this question to him.
"The gods," he said, "have never gone away. Mankind has simply turned his back on them. Man is really a very stupid ignorant creature that is easily lead," he said with another loud guffaw. Garcia put his hand on my shoulder to steady himself, I looked at him somewhat bemused as another paroxysm of laughter ripped through him. "He really is so very stupid, you know, you have no idea just how stupid he really is...!"
Garcia puled himself upright and cleared his throat. He seemed to have gained control of himself again. "Yes anyway, " he went on soberly, "where was I? Oh yes, the old ways, yes you see the old ways were lost because those that ruled the empire listened to the wrong people. The poisonous words of the Christian priests subverted the ruling families - easily lead you see. The disease ran rife among the slave culture of Rome. It was therefore able to slither its way into the bosom of the empire. It wasn't brought down by any invading army, Rome and Greece rotted from the inside, just as surely as if a maggot were eating its way through the core of a healthy apple. Rome had lasted for more than twelve hundred years when the statue of the goddess was removed from the senate and the sentiments of the pagan senate was overruled by Theodosius.
"Which goddess?" I asked, feeling that Garcia would chastise me for not knowing something that was so obvious to himself.
"Why Victory of course. The last of the great deities to be openly worshipped. The very ideal for which Rome stood for. When she was removed in the year 381 of the common era, the final collapse of the western empire followed almost immediately. A mere forty years on and the Goths sacked Rome, after that the world fell into a dark age from which we are yet to emerge. We turn our backs on the Gods at our own expense Julian, this is what one must understand."

We carried on walking in silence when suddenly a strong gust of warm Cycladic air, threw up sand and dust from the dirt track down which we were walking. I shielded my eyes and face from the dust that was thrown in my direction. I was able to glance towards Garcia - he seemed to be totally impervious to the dust storm that momentarily raged about us. He nonchalantly kicked small stones along the path. He suddenly stooped to pick up a particularly large specimen and hurled it with great force into the adjacent field. "So you see Julian," he said, suddenly ranging round at me, "in the long history of the ancient world it took no time at all, once paganism was abandoned, for the whole fabric of society to fall apart."

"Put like that - no." I replied. "It seems such a shame that so many beautiful temples and building are now just ruins. The ravages of time..." I mused.

"Ravages of time be damned!" Shouted Garcia. "The rabble, the Christian's emperors, Gratian and Theodosius are what did for the ancient world and the splendour of its architecture. Christians, Romans and Greeks, were the protagonists behind so much vandalism. The Vandals got the blame." Garcia paused a moment, and shook his head and smiled wryly to himself. "The poor Vandals..." Turning to me, "It wasn't conquering armies that destroyed the temples and the statues and other pagan symbolism, it was just ordinary misguided people who nominally called themselves 'Christian.' They did not know what they were doing. So we must forgive them I suppose? But here, here on this little island I have begun to re-establish sanity and order through the return of the old ways."

After this discussion between myself and Garcia, I began to look upon the statues of the gods, and the pagan rites with more reverence. My respect for Garcia also grew. There was no doubting the man's zeal and passion for what he believed. He had a powerful charismatic appeal. I must confess, however, that this aspect of his character frustrated me. He seemed to be able to charm people with a simple smile, particularly it seemed, the women. Something I was only too aware of that was lacking in myself. But even though Karen and her friend Rachine had fallen deeply under his spell, one could not help loving old Garcia.

When we sat and listened to him expound his philosophy, quoting the ancient myths and the stories of the gods, with just the firelight and the sound of the Aegean in the background, we wanted the moment to go on forever. We were always disappointed when he said he felt tired and had to retire. We would look at one another, not knowing what to say, each trying to hold on to the afterglow of the dream he had so vividly brought to life. In a sense the dream, so long as we remained on the island, was a tangible thing and there was every possibility that the dream, would spread to other islands in the Aegean, even other parts of the world.

I had been on the Sapphos for nearly a fortnight and I was beginning to get impatient to understand what was behind Karen's presence on the island, and why she had invited me to join her after having not being in contact for so long. I felt instinctively that it must have something to do with whatever it was that haunted Karen and forced her to flee towards Natasha.

I was becoming increasingly restless. I had explored most of the island, aware that there was no way off, it was then that I felt somewhat like a prisoner. There was the crystalline clear Aegean in which to swim, or else we would lounge about the pool; then of course there was Garcia's huge library to look through. Works of philosophy, literature, plays and novels, histories and letters, by all the great names, such as Socrates Plato, Parmenides Cicero, Longus, Arisophane, Menander, to name but a few, as well as works by authors that I had never heard of before.

To my surprise I met Rachine one day in the library. "Fascinating isn't it." She said. She caught me off guard. "Oh the books you mean. An amazing collection. Truly amazing."

Rachine was looking at a book of Greek poetry. She looked down and carried on reading. She was dressed in a small bikini top and a sarong. I took out a book at random and pretended to read (the book was in Greek), I looked toward Rachine now and again, I couldn't concentrate on the book. So much dark skin, a woman of such overt sexuality seemed wrong in a place of books and study. An ambiguous place for a creature of the light to inhabit. A creature more readily associated with sunlight and surf.

I turned to replace the volume and take another down. I could feel her eyes on me. I was about to come out with some trite comment when the door to Garcia's private study opened. He nodded to me, "I see you read Greek Mr Julian."

"Well...just a little," I stammered, with embarrassment at having been caught out. I paused when I saw Karen follow Garcia out of his study. I thought she looked incredible, dressed in a red, tightly wound satin kimono.

I looked at her in surprise. "I never took you for the bookish sort." I said.
"I was consulting with Garcia over a private matter," she replied, with a detectable tone that indicated her annoyance.
"It's a fascinating collection you have here." I said, addressing Garcia and then looking towards Rachine.
"Come into my study, and I will show you the book that first put me on to the idea of all of this," said Garcia, casting his eyes about the vast collection.
He took some keys from his desk, undid a drawer and produced a small volume bound in olive green leather. He laid it on the desk and slid it over to me. The title, in simple gold block read: *Lightning Over a Distant Shore*. I picked it up and leafed through it.
"I've never heard of it." I said, "or the author." I was unimpressed quite frankly, and put the book down. I expected some ancient text, instead the book was a first edition and only a few years old.
"Oh him." Said Rachine, who I suddenly became aware of standing beside me.
"You've read it then." I said.
She picked it up and leafed through a few pages. "Well some of it." She appeared equally unimpressed. She laughed to herself. "He does have some very strange ideas, it has to be said. I met him we he was in Rome.
"At my request," Interjected Garcia.
"Such a strange young man. Very self-effacing. Analisa was quite taken by him if I remember," concluded Rachine, handing the book back to Garcia.
It was plain to see that Garcia had great admiration for the work, by the reverent way he handled it. He placed it down upon the desk in front of him and gently lay his hand upon it. "Yes it was from his ideas, his critique of modern society that I came to this island and put into practice what is loosely described in this book."
"Well I've never heard of him?" I reiterated, shaking my head.
"No I don't suppose you have, but one day everyone will know of him. His unassuming character hides a genius. Any one with perception can see it in his words, his ideas. He is someone who can see through the morass of lies and hypocrisy that so clutters the modern world, and prevents mankind from rising above his ape-like mentality. This man," Continued Garcia tapping the book

with his fingers, "Can see to the quick of things, the very core of the human condition."

"Indeed!" I replied. "A remarkable feat."

"A remarkable young man! Most remarkable. *His*, is an appeal for a better world based upon pagan concepts and ideas concerning the nature of god. Like him I was dissatisfied with the modern world. Its greed and corruption, leading towards the rape of a planet for its resources, *without any care - any care whosoever*," went on Garcia, waving his arms about frantically, "for life on this planet, *all life*. I was not prepared to wait for 'the world republic,' that the author describes. I am no philosopher you see. I am a man of action. I wanted the world republic here and now. So I took myself off and turned my back on the modern world. "Throwing his hand over his shoulder, "let them keep it! Let them have all their junk of technology. I want non of it - non of it, non of it here, I won't have it. Not here, not on this island. No I won't." Garcia leaned across the table at me. I must admit I was a little afraid of him when he became so *passionate*. "Let me tell you something! When I came here, to this island I came alone. There was just me and the goats, gradually though like-minded people got to hear of what I was attempting, and so...so they joined me." Garcia straightened himself. "You see unlike my writer friend I was not without some influence. I had money and therefore power."

I picked up Garcia's sacred book and read part of the introduction. "It says here he is influenced by thinkers such as Max Weber and Nietzsche. Is he some kind of Fascist Marxist?"

"That is always the danger of a truly great mind, of being misinterpreted by fools such as yourself. He uses their ideas as a platform on which to build and base his critique of modern culture. Each of his epigrams and essays are like a block of stone built one upon another, just as I and my companions rebuilt this temple. His temple was of the mind, and I have recreated it in time and space."

I handed Garcia his book back and let out a heavy sigh. Garcia's highfalutin ideas, his moral posturing had started to depress me.

"Indeed - well it's all very impressive Garcia, but you can never stop progress. You have simply turned your back on the modern world. Your philosopher friend here, knew enough to simply write about it, and there is nothing wrong with having ideas, but this is just one tiny island, and a few individuals; the world is run by governments. It's a business Mr Garcia, and you won't change that!"

"Well put Mr Julian! I admire a man with opinions who is not afraid to express them."

He picked up the green volume and placed it back in the draw to his desk and locked it. "Now I am afraid I must ask you all to leave. It has been most interesting to here your opinions Mr Julian, but now I have some research to catch up on. "

"I hope the old boy is all right," I said, when the three of us were outside. "I hope I haven't upset him."

"Garcia? No - he'll be fine. Besides its about time someone challenged his ideas for a change," observed Rachine.

"This book that Garcia has taken as a blueprint for his new world order? Have you met its author?"

"I don't know if I would call it a *new world order*, but yes - yes I've met him," replied Rachine. "I don't know what to say about him? I do know that Analisa was quite taken by him," continued Rachine, turning to Karen

"Yes and we can guess why, "interjected Karen. Both girls laughed. "But didn't her sister think he was an idiot?"

"She didn't like him because of his ability to see right through a person's pretensions. He was like a mirror that he held up to you, it forced a person to face themselves and often, as in Anastasia's case, they didn't like what they saw. He could see straight off how meretricious Anastasia was. It was rather sad really," mused Rachine.

"Sad ! Why sad?" I asked.

"Let's sit here," interrupted Karen. The three of us had wandered on to a terrace that overlooked the garden and swimming pool as well as the statues of scantily clad men and women depicting the various gods and goddesses of the Greek and Roman pantheon.

"It was sad," continued Rachine, "because Anastasia liked him a lot."

"Yes but those two always competed over their men," put in Karen.
"True, but I think she would have been good for him, as it was he was in love with this other girl, Beth, or Bethany, her name was. She was a pretty little thing. Short but big in other ways - powerfully built. Always boasting about how strong she was, challenging *men* and *women* to arm wrestling contests. She always beat the girls and sometimes the men too. Our author friend was completely besotted by her; of course, with a girl like Beth, he didn't stand a chance."
"No, he wasn't a bonehead, from what I can gather?" observed Karen.
"No, definitely not a bonehead. See that girl over there? The pretty one by that statue," said Rachine pointing, with a long finger.
"What about her? I said, following her finger.
"That is Alisiya, Garcia's current favourite."
"She's only eighteen." said Karen.
"Well Alisiya is the spitting image of Bethany. Now, I ask you, what could our bookish writer do with a creature like that?"
"Not being a bonehead." repeated Karen
"Not being a bonehead," reiterated Rachine, "She lead him a merry little dance. Which is why I said he would have been better off with Anastasia - with a girl like *that* you at least know what you are getting."
Suddenly Rachine lent over the parapet and yelled at the top of her voice, waving frantically: "hey you there, you - yes you, come up here!"
The pretty girl looked up startled. "Come here." About five minutes later the young girl was standing in front of us. "Wine, bring us some *wine!*" Commanded Rachine. Alisiya just shook her head. "Its no good the creature doesn't speak English. You ask, Karen, my Greek is terrible."
Karen spoke rapidly to the girl. Immediately Alisiya smiled and nodded, and then began to laugh, putting her hand to her mouth in embarrassment.
"Why did she laugh? What did you say to her?" I asked.
"I don't think it's *what* I said, more the way I said it. I only speak classic and archaic Doric forms of Greek. But they get the drift."
I looked at Karen in disbelief. "It's a long story..." she concluded.
About ten minutes later one of Garcia's lackeys arrived with a large pitcher of

wine and three earthenware beakers. He poured the wine and then stood to attention a few feet away. Rachine gave him a hostile glare and made a motion with her hands. The young man quickly took the *not* so subtle hint to be gone.

"I do hate it when they hang about like that," said Rachine.

"So that was Alisiya?" I said.

"What did you think of her?" asked Karen.

"Very - beautiful." I replied. "If Beth looked anything like her...well!" I reflected a moment and began to feel a certain affinity with our sensitive author. "You mean she was unfaithful to him." I said.

"Well it's a long story, " Continued Rachine. "There was a guy in England she was in love with."

"The bonehead," interrupted Karen, knowingly.

"Precisely! But what was worse, was that Garcia took quite a liking to her himself."

"What Garcia wants he normally gets," said Karen.

I glanced at her nervously. "Does he now!"

"As you heard him say, he was enthralled by the work of the young writer, but sadly, equally enthralled by his travelling companion," continued Rachine. " He wined them and dined them. Bestowed lavish gifts upon them, particularly the girl. He even took them up to his villa and stud, in Tuscany. All three of them had heated debates long into the night about religion and morality, which Bethany in particular took very seriously. Beth you see was a devout Christian and this infuriated Garcia. He tried hard to convince her of the error of her ways, but she was as stubborn and headstrong as she was physically strong - as strong as an ox. He was confounded by her high morals, eventually though as he always does in the end, he got his way with her by getting her heavily drunk; and then there was revealed quite another side to Bethany altogether."

"My god!" Exclaimed Karen, and all this under the nose of a man that Garcia was supposed to admire?"

"I'm afraid so. He can be quite merciless if he sets his mind on something. Once Bethany's resolve had been broken she became quite depraved. She had an affair with one of Garcia's assistants, there was even rumours of bestiality. Although these may have been started by Garcia, prompted by his brief but intimate knowledge of her. He was truly perplexed by her. She was a conundrum. Such a small girl, you wouldn't think there was much to her, but there was more than met the eye! And yet she had all these highfalutin ideas concerning chastity and morality. In the end she spurned Garcia's advances, she rejected anything to do with him or his ideas. He begged her not to leave, I never saw him fawn over a woman the way he did around Bethany. He was obsessed by her, he even had her pose nude for a statue. This she found quite acceptable, she was quite the exhibitionist, although I can't understand what Garcia saw in her! Yes she had a very pretty face but she really had no cause to be as conceited as she was about her appearance. Her breasts were quite small she had no real figure to speak of, a nice ass I suppose and she *was* quite powerfully built. As she would say, 'as strong as an ox.' "

"I suppose she had what all men are after?" I said.

"According to Garcia. He said that there was something not right about her. She wasn't like other women...I never knew what he meant by that." said Rachine, furrowing her brow. "In the end, her high minded Christian principles and her sexual exploits were more than he could stand. If *he* couldn't have her no one would. Analisa, myself, Anastasia and another girl did for her. Together we quite messed up that pretty little face of hers. And she acted as though she was so tough! Anastasia virtually took her single handed. She hardly put up any resistance at all, despite her great strength and all her boasting and arrogance she had no fight in her. We got her in the end where it hurt the most.

"Good. I would like to have been there." Said Karen, her face twisting into a snarl.

"What happened in the end to our poor writer?"

"Karen shook her head. "The poor bastard. "To have been in love with someone like that, and to get nothing back!" Karen gave me a lingering look that was not with out a tinge of guilt.

"The poor bastard! " I reiterated.

"Well Bethany went limping back to England, probably to the bonehead of a boyfriend, and our writer ran after her. As far as I know he is still running after her, apparently not put off by the condition we left her in."

We moved down to the pool, it was late in the evening and we were expecting the appearance of Garcia quite soon. Karen suddenly got up and began to undo her Kimono. Underneath she had on just a tiny thong. She stretched showing off her *own* well defined musculature, particularly her lower body, which had come from hours of dedicated workouts, driven by the constant pressure on her to, 'look good.' "I could have taken her." She said, before plunging headlong into the expanse of cool blue water.

"Ha! " I smiled wryly. "The hard, hard world of men and women. What chance did a writer of epigrams and poetry have against a *bonehead* and a man like Garcia?"

Rachine looked at me squarely. I felt her hand on mine. I looked at her suspiciously. What she had said had affected me deeply for some reason. For a while I even found myself getting caught up in the vitriol that both girls displayed towards Beth. Where had it all come from? It was evident to me that Bethany must have posed a threat. She was to other women competition, and she clearly possessed qualities that went beyond just having a pretty face. I speculated that Bethany was of a different type, a different species of womankind altogether, and therefore could not be tolerated, and so had to be destroyed. 'Poor Bethany,' I thought, and secretly hoped that Rachine and her gang had not done irrevocable damage to her.

"Was she badly injured?" I asked, tentatively.

"Who, Bethany?" Rachine smirked, "One hard hit from Anastasia and Bethany went down. She was nothing. Even I could have taken her." Rachine laughed. All her posing and boastful talk came to nothing. The rest of us were there because Garcia wanted her badly hurt, but we weren't really needed. As I said, Anastasia and her sister did most of the damage. I never got involved myself. I quite liked her, I admired her independent nature. A pity, really - perhaps they went too far...."

"How far? - I mean, was she badly hurt?" I said, trying to keep my voice steady.

Rachine looked at me soberly, "She had to be hospitalised. She was in a coma for about a week. I suppose her face would heal over in time, but she would never be the same again. Had it been anyone else I doubt they would have survived." Rachine shrugged her shoulders, "hah, I guess she was tough after all!"

Each one of Rachine's admissions, it seemed, dealt me a similar sort of blow, as my hopes of Bethany getting off with only minor injuries receded.
"I doubt very much whether she could ever have children." Rachine added, nonchalantly
I lite a cigarette to hide the panic, and violent hatred that suddenly swept over me.
"And Garcia, was he there?"
Garcia! He just stuck around and phoned for the ambulance," replied Rachine. She leveled me with a dark obsidian gaze. "Why all the concern?" she asked, slowly."
"I don't know," I replied. "I hate violence I suppose."
Rachine took this as sufficent, and leaned back to take a long draught of her wine. She peered over the top of her drinking vesel, keeping a steady jet black gaze into my eyes. "Don't mess with Garcia. That's what I learnt from that little episode. You are either with him, in which case it's fine, but if you stand against him," Rachine shook her head, *"boy oh boy....*poor kid!"
"Silly wabit, she should have known, tricks are for kids," said Karen, coming up behind me, her exiguous form glistening and dripping with water.

III

Garcia was more than just a lover of beauty in stone. There were, apart from Karen and Rachine, many women on the island who were of outstanding beauty; who seemed to do little more than lounge around the pool most of the day, while others, dressed in long flowing robes, waited on Garcia and guests, such as Karen and myself. When the great man himself appeared they came to life and gravitated to his side. Everyone on the island, it had been explained to me, had a function. There were those that toiled in the fields, others that worked the land, there were those that went out fishing in the small boats that were kept in a special wooden boathouse on the far side of the island. And then there were others, whose only task, it seemed was to wait on Garcia's *every* need. One girl would bring the wine, another serve him food, all of them beautiful, all of them dedicated to Garcia's happiness. I saw the look in Garcia's eyes, when a particularly good looking girl bent over him with a tray of fruit. He was a man who had it all.

Yes, everyone had a function, the question was, what was mine and Karen's? And despite all these distractions I could not help but feel, as time went on, more and more of a prisoner. There were days when I thought of escaping with Karen on one of the small fishing boats. One day Garcia caught me looking round the boathouse. He asked me in a stern voice what I was doing there. Without trying to be convincing I told him that I was interested in the design of his boats. He laughed. "You know you are free to go whenever you wish."

"I am?" I replied, somewhat embarrassed.

He opened out his hands and stretched out his arms expansively, in a manner that indicated that the whole world was already his. "All those that you see here on this island are here of their own free will. They are here because it is their wish to be here, they share my dream, and yet may leave whenever they wish - but why?" he said, pointing a finger skywards, like Zeus. "Why would they want to, why would anyone want to leave paradise?"

"Why did you invite me here? Why is Karen here?" I said, not allowing myself to be put off any more by his shenanigans.

Garcia nodded, and came over to me. He put his big arm about my shoulder. "I can see there is still much of the impatience of the modern world about you. You know one day, and one day soon, the day will be upon us, the day of eternal truth - fear not," he said, as he led me back to the Temple - Villa complex. We walked on in silence for a while. He breathed a deep sigh, and shook his head, "But surely you might have guessed why I want you here?"

"No." I replied, "I guess it has something to do with Karen?"

The old man smiled ruefully, "In a manner of speaking." He looked at me out of the corner of his eye. "Why, it is for Natasha," he said, as if it were obvious. "It is for Natasha - Natasha you understand. It is for her you are here."

"How so?"

Garcia shook his head and made a sound with his lips, "All will be revealed in good time. When it is right."

"But when?" I persisted.

He looked at me with a poker face. "Well - when it's right of course."

Then, out of the corner of his eye he saw something move, something that one might only expect a cat to see. "Wait!" he said, holding me back. "There, by that old piece of masonry. Look there, an Oleander Hawk-moth!"

I followed the old man's gaze, but could see nothing. He went over to a piece of ancient masonry beneath a bush. On it was a beautiful winged beast. He looked at the bush his nostrils twitching like a big rabbit.

"Smell that? The scent of Jasmine. They love the Jasmine, and of course Oleander."

"It's beautiful," I said, looking at the tiny creature's iridescent wings, as it slowly opened and shut them. "Is it a good omen, do you think?"

Old Garcia looked round at me sharply, "I don't know - is it?" he said, keenly.

I shrugged. "I have no idea."

"Oh..." said Garcia, sounding disappointed. "I thought for a minute you might be able to tell me."

"I thought you were the expert on such matters."

"Oh - I know some of the art of augury." He looked at the moth quizzically and scratched his head. "I don't know the meaning of this little fellow though. Sometimes a moth is just a moth. I was caught by its great beauty." he sighed, "we let so much that is beautiful pass us by, just because we are in too much of a hurry, especially small things like moths." He smelt the Jasmine and encouraged me to do the same.

"What do you think? Sweet - hey..!"

"Hmmm...sure is a sweet smelling flower.".

"Now of plants I know a little. Does it remind you of any one?"

"Jasmine! Yes its Karen's favourite." I said, putting my nose into the flowers. "hmm, yes it reminds me of her."

"Hot and sweet, hey Mr Julian. A truly passionate plant. Sacred to the Hindus of India you know. The god Vishnu - I believe."

"Fascinating," I replied.

"To western paganism it is associated with Artemis, goddess of the moon, and the hunt. In her saffron robe, armed with her bow - what a sight! Beautiful but deadly."

I shook my head, "all of that, and from just a little flower." I observed.

"Its oil can be used as an aphrodisiac as well.." added Garcia, with a little chuckle. I gave him a shrewd look. He knew as well as me, that the combination of Karen's obvious erotism and the heady aroma of the Jasmine was enough to drive even the most dour of men wild with desire.

Garcia had opened my eyes to the smell and the sights and sounds of nature that abounded. We walked on stopping now and then as Garcia pointed to some small beetle or flower.

Garcia is best described as a collector, but not of insects. He collected objects of great beauty and beautiful people too. When he set eyes on Karen at a fashion show he decided that he wanted her too. The idea of a glamorous woman in glamorous clothes - well I suppose it was too much for him to resist. And so Karen became *acquainted* with Garcia. He spent amazing sums of money on her. He gave her an apartment of her own in Florence. He was the kind of man, that if he fancied your wife, would invite you to a meal in order to seduce her over the hors d' oeuvres, and if that didn't work he would calmly ask what was her price. If Karen had been my wife I would have enjoyed listening to his sales pitch and how much he would be prepared to offer, before telling him, among other things, to get lost. And then I thought, 'well would I really. After all everyone and everything has its price, *doesn't it ?*' But I am sure this was what Garcia believed. And then again, people like Garcia don't even need to ask *permesso*, before taking your wife. I thought of Bethany, and admired her for not allowing herself to be easily bought off. She was also a lesson in what can happen to those that resist the Garcia charm.

I woke early one morning, and unable to go back to sleep I left my room and made my way down towards the sea. The sky was quite light but the sun had not yet risen. An ambient glow shone silvery white over the water.

I noticed a shape moving through the waves close to the shore and excitedly I thought it might be a porpoise, but as I strained my eyes I became aware that it wasn't a sea creature at all but a man. Some moments later I saw that it wasn't just any man, but Garcia. His dark shape came out of the sea - he stood erect before me. Rising from out of the water he turned to face the sun which had begun to rise, a blood red disc on the horizon. He stared, eyes transfixed on the fiery ball, and then as it slowly grew brighter, he knelt down and bowed. He stayed like that for several minutes before getting to his feet. It was only then that he acknowledged my existence. Garcia was naked and quite unselfconscious, prideful even. He was a very big man, powerfully built in every quarter. Even though I was younger than him by several years I felt he was the stronger, the more powerful, more dominant, male. He stood in front of me, his silvery white hair glistening like a halo against the rising sun; water running down his face, dripping from his big dark body. He was the alpha male. He had the power, the power to choose. The power of selection and rejection, but even he, I recalled, had been rebuffed, and had been forced to assert his power through his physical superiority. He seemed to intimidate me simply by his obvious maleness, and lack of shame. He had every reason to be proud, and I, every reason to hide away. I had no desire to face him and turned away, but he had seen me. His deep voice pulled me up.

"Wait, wait Mr Julian."

He caught up to me, I looked down, thankfully he had produced a towel from somewhere.

"Don't be in such a hurry Julian, me boy. Come with me, let me show you something splendid, something from another world, something from *my* world." And like a child, or perhaps a lamb to the slaughter, I of course followed him.

I followed in Garcia's footsteps along a narrow higgledy-piggledy track, that wound its way through thickets of dense scrub. Eventually we came to a small shack.

"Wait there a moment." He said. I waited. A few moments later he came out wearing his customary white robe fastened round his waist with a purple cord, in his hand he was carrying a large bunch of keys. Without saying any more I followed Garcia around the shack and along the track which became quite precipitous. At the peak of the only major incline on the island were a set of ancient stone steps which lead to a large court yard at the centre of which stood a pagan temple. Judging from the colour of the stone, and the general appearance of neglect I concluded that it must have stood there for many thousands of years, it was plainly not one of Garcia's reconstructed efforts, this was the real McCoy. It looked quite neglected; weeds grew between the flag-stones and scrub encroached all around, threatening to submerge the ancient building, erasing it from the view of moderns. Some of the original blocks of stone had been replaced by new, sharp clean white ones. Indicating that some attempt had been made to forestall its departure from the present. Garcia went up to the building and unlocked a wrought iron gate which stood in front of the portico. Beyond this was a large wooden door which he also unlocked and which gave entrance to the temple. Garcia instructed me again to 'wait.' He was soon lost inside the blackness of the interior. I began to experience an inexplicable feeling of trepidation as I stood in the portico surrounded by the craftsmanship of the ancient Greeks; a people so distant in time as they were in their customs, that they might as well have come from another planet! It was as though I stood on the threshold of the ancient world. One way, towards the light of day down and down the twisting path stood the modern world, the other way stood a very different world.

I peered after Garcia and beheld a tiny glimmer, and I could just about discern his white robe, as he fflitted about the interior like a spectre, lighting up one oil lamp after another.

"Come," he said, in a quiet voice. My heart began to race as I crossed the threshold, and entered into another world, one that it seemed, had all but perished from memory. The first thing that hit my senses was the pungent aroma of incense. There was a special kind of stillness that wrapped around one, insulating one from everything - *out there*. I could only hear my feet as they clicked over the marble, and even though the temple was dimly lit by a dozen or so oil lamps that were attached to the walls, it was possible to detect the red colour of the marble, which was used to decorate the columns and interior walls. The guttering lamps cast long airy shadows, the most unsettling of all was that of Garcia's and what I took to be another living soul standing next to him.

Garcia stood to one side as I got closer, and I saw that the other shadow was cast by a statue that resided at the rear of the building. A large torch burned behind it, bathing it in a of halo of pinkish light. The statue was that of a girl fashioned in white marble, placed as she was on a plinth which itself stood on a raised dais, her overall height was about eight feet, although the figure itself was only about five feet tall. The whole structure was housed from head to toe behind finely wrought bronze bars, effectively imprisoning her.

"Come - behold," said Garcia, when I had stopped dead in my tracks, spell bound by the vision my eyes beheld. I came a little closer, slowly, reverently. I stared up at the statue, and looked. What I saw was the most beautiful face of a girl I had ever seen.

One gets a feeling, after a time of what is an original classical Greek or Roman statue, and what is modern, but even though *she* was new, she could still hold me with that incomprehensible *aura*, which one only usually finds in an ancient piece.

Garcia stood at my side and put his his large hand on my shoulder. I looked round at him and saw that there were tears in his eyes. "Isn't she remarkable!"

"Yes, " I replied, and I felt my own voice choke with emotion, "Yes...truly she is..."

Garcia moved off a little bit, each aware that such beauty could only truly be appreciated alone.

And just what am I supposed to say? How is one to relate such beauty in mere words? Yes I can give you a description of her face but that will not relate the aura she cast over us. Recognising my duty, I can tell you she had a small oval face with a pretty slightly turned up nose, all her features perfectly proportioned. Her look: very elfin, distinctly *mischievous.* Her beautiful head was supported by a strong neck which itself was supported by powerful shoulders. Her whole body conveyed an impression of vigorous sensual vitality, also a sense of inner calm, pure and resolute, was she. The artist, whoever it was, was exemplary in their skill, to so painstakingly elevate from the raw material every muscle on her back, her arms and her shoulders, her thighs, to convey in stone such silent strength.

Her pose seemed to indicate that she had been captured at the moment of disrobing. A long flowing garment trailed in her left hand. There was the air of nonchalance about her, of quiet confidence, that we may look if we wish, and one got the impression, (I don't know where from) that she wanted us to look, to feast our eyes upon her nakedness. Her wonderful head was slightly turned to one side and elevated about ten degrees so that she did not confront one's gaze but if one placed oneself before her face she would always be looking into the distance. One felt, therefore, she was always beyond you, the viewer: you whoever you are, would always be an irrelevance to her. *She was beyond one, and would always be looking far off into the distance...*That mischievous face, as mischievous as the pose she strikes, with one broad hip thrust out to one side, confronting the viewer at eye level.

One will never know where her gaze is directed, but there is little doubt where the gaze of earthly man will fall. I could not fault her figure, although her breasts were not large, they were two perfectly domed hemispheres. In terms of female sexual hierarchy she had to be close to its zenith. I walked round to her rear and beheld the same level of sublimity of form. Her hair was in plaits and hung the length of her back ending just before the cleavage of her ripe buoyant buttocks, seated atop towering pillared thighs.

I came back again to the front of the statue. Garcia opened an invisible gate set in the bars, he knelt and tenderly, as if she were a living being, laid his lips on her small bare feet. He then lit a candle and placed it before the object of veneration and caught up in the emotion and magic of the moment I too lit a candle, but felt it inproper to go as far as kissing her feet, although I felt strongly inclined to do so. Garcia backed away, and muttered some words of a prayer, before silently closing and locking the gate. Finally he tended to a single Orchid that had been lovingly placed in a tall fluted glass vase, situated on the dais before the goddess's gaze.

While Garcia busied himself with the floral arrangement, I stood back to admire her once again, the image of sublime beauty, of grace and vitality. I felt the blood surge in me, as I regarded her elfin features. The artist had faithfully reproduced every facet of her female anatomy; her right hand, in a tentative display of modesty covered the point at which her big thighs bifurcated. The artist, or the model clearly wanted us to be fully appreciative of her, as a sexual creature. But was such a creature possible? Was she perhaps only an invention of the artist's imagination? For how could mere cold stone cause such a painful reaction of desire in one, from what were no more than a few curves and deep furrows cut into marble?

I considered myself to be privileged to look upon such a work of art, I also appreciated how much more privileged the artist was who had created it. Not just for his ability as a sculptor, but to have actually borne witness to the subject in flesh and blood. What an eye he had for detail, every muscle and sinew, even down to the veins in her wrists, faithfully reproduced. And was it he or perhaps the model herself, who suggested the provocative pose? Whoever it may have been, a quality in *her* would always suggest that *she* was beyond the judgement of mere mortals; her gaze was always directed towards infinity, she had no concerns for our baser instincts. Her body and looks were merely coincidental with man's lustful imaginings. There below her right hand, almost touching, guarding cautiously, that eternal and perplexing mystery.

"Come let us leave her now", said Garcia breaking the spell that had been cast over me. One by one he began to stop-out the light from the oil lamps, until just the two candles were left burning, casting airy flickering shadows over the pristine marble. Reluctantly I turned my back on the figure and made my way towards the entrance. Garcia opened the door and I turned to take one last look at her before leaving the dim light of the old world for the harsher light of the modern.

I stood in the portico squinting in the brilliant light of the day. Garcia was at the entrance, his back to me. He whispered something I couldn't quite hear and then he slowly closed and locked the heavy wood door. Shocked to be in the land of mortals again we silently descended the path we had taken only an hour or so ago, but which now felt as if it had happened many ages ago. The world itself, ordinary plants, even the sky and the sea no longer seemed the same any more.

*

For several days after visiting the temple I went around in a kind of daze. The world, even Garcia's world full of beautiful things, seemed dull to me. Nothing could compare with the beauty and magic I had beheld. The image of the statue haunted me. I saw her in my dreams, and then she would get down off her pedestal and I would hold her in my arms, but not as cold stone but living palpitating flesh.

Karen quickly picked up on my mood. I felt reluctant to speak about what I had seen. It felt as though I had been unfaithful to her, but I could keep nothing from her, so I told Karen all about my meeting Garcia, and my visit to the temple.

"So you've met her at last!" replied Karen knowingly.

"Met who?"

"Why Bethany - of course!"

For a second my vision went blurry and I was back in the twilight of the temple.

"Are you all right? You look pale - like you've seen a ghost."

"Perhaps I have," I replied, and shakily I lit a cigarette."

Garcia's veneration for the statue, the loving way he kissed it's feet, the tears he had in his eyes, it all suddenly made sense. What he had whispered before he left the temple, sounded like - *sorry.*

"He had her shipped over from Italy. Made from the finest Italian marble."

"Have you seen her?" I asked.

"Me!" Exclaimed Karen, "No - he won't let any one go there. Only Garcia has the key's. He says it is sacred to the Goddess of the island, 'the temple of Fortuna.' " Karen looked at me wistfully over the top of her wine glass. "I'm surprised he took you up there?" she paused a moment before continuing."Well you are very quiet! Thinking about her? She must be very beautiful...Is she better than me? Does she have a better body than me?"

"listen to yourself! You sound ridiculous Karen. Comparing yourself with a lump of marble! "

"Yes but it is based on a real living body."

I put my drink down and looked at Karen squarely, "yes and didn't Garcia have that body broken!" I said, finding it hard to keep the passion out of my voice.

There was silence for a moment. Karen looked at me demurely. "Well, so what, if he did. What is she to you? You blame me for being jealous and yet you act as if you know this girl personally. Its like you love her or something!"

Karen shook her head and laughed. "It's just like you, to fall in love with a statue."

"What do you mean by that?"

"Oh come on! You know how you love to look." Karen stretched her long body showing off her svelte, rackish form. She levelled me with her lavender eyes. "See, you're doing it now," she said, laughing.

"It's you, you love showing yourself off."

Karen looked away. "I shouldn't worry, Rachine said Bethany was a tough cookie. I dare say she will mend - in time."

I found in Karen's words a curious sense of solace. "What kind of man would do a thing like that?" I said.

"Well there's a bit more to it than that." Karen paused a moment as if unsure she should go on.

"You know Garcia has this belief in the old gods."

"Of course."

"Well it wasn't just the book that put him on to all of this. For a long time he believed firmly in reincarnation. As soon as he set eyes on Bethany he became convinced that he had known her in another life. He hypnotised her and put her through what he calls, 'past life regression.' "

Given all that I had seen and what I knew of Garcia, I wasn't surprised in the least by this fact. I simply nodded.

"Well..." Karen paused again.

"Tell me." I insisted.

"This is what Rachine told me," began Karen, in a hushed earnest voice. "In this other life, which was in the days of ancient Rome, Garcia was very much the man he is today - that is, he was rich and powerful, except perhaps more powerful then. He had many slaves and there was one in particular who had stolen his heart."

"Bethany!" I exclaimed.

"Yes - except she went by a different name then. I can't remember what Rachine said it was. Mariana, or something like that. Don't you think it's romantic? - Anyway, Garcia was madly in love with her, so much so he *must* have her. I suppose he was then as he is now, used to getting what he wanted - and so he bought her her freedom, so that he could marry her, but she didn't come to him in the way he expected. She was in love with another you see, and besides that, she was a Christian, when the religion was still in its infancy. He solved the problem of Mariana's boyfriend by having him executed. This of course was hardly going to win her affections but at least he could take her as his wife, even though he may never have her love. Yet he became frustrated by her constant rejection of him, infuriated by her, holier than thou, Christian sense of morality, as Garcia put it. Finally he gave up hope of ever winning her love. The mere sight of her drove him crazy. So he decided that if he couldn't have her no one would."

I nodded. "So history repeated itself. He had her beaten up I suppose?"

"Worse than that! He gave her over to the authorities, which meant that she, along with many other Christians of the time, was fed to the lions. Sounds familiar doesn't it! I mean, except for the lions.

"So she spurned him, instead of repaying him with her gratitude for giving her her freedom. It must have driven him mad. It does sound familiar, except she didn't die this time round."

"No, but she very nearly did, if Rachine's account of what happened is to be believed. Once, in another life, Garcia had her head cut off, in another she was stoned to death, and so it goes on down throughout the ages."

"Poor Mariana."

"Poor Garcia, to constantly fall in love with the same woman, yet never to have that love returned. Although, according to Garcia, the fact that she didn't die this time, is evidence that the effects are lessening with time?"

"No thanks to Garcia, by all accounts." I observed.

"That's the thing with destiny, you have no control over your actions, especially where love is concerned."

"People say its a kind of madness." I said.

Karen looked at me demurely, and chose not to comment.

"It's a fascinating, and as you say, *romantic* story Karen - but you don't believe it do you?

"I don't know. But I do think Garcia has some kind of special knowledge of the future. You think that is incredible, just wait until you hear what he has to say about us."

IV

It so turned out that I didn't have long to wait before finding out why he had brought Karen and I to his island. Two days after my visit to the temple Karen and I came upon him sitting at a table on the terrace, talking to his eighteen year old nymphet, Alisiya. She raised her beautiful head and looked toward us, and a wild spasm of hot lust bubbled up in my veins. It was as if for a second my dream had come true, that the statue had stepped down off of her plinth escaped her golden cage and the twilight of the temple, for the stark light of day. So taken was I by the sudden shock of her nymphean beauty, that my footsteps faltered. Karen stopped and looked at me askance.

"Whatever is the matter with you?" she said, grabbing hold of my hand.

"Nothing, I just got something in my eye." I replied, hoping to avert Karen's inquisitive nature. Although I think she guessed that I was suffering from a terrible case of *nypholepsy*. Garcia made a tiny gesture with his hands, and fortunately the gorgeous creature got up and disappeared before we got any closer. Garcia rose to his feet to greet us. His hands held high, his deeply tanned face glowing with vitality, his blue eyes shining brightly, madly, and on this particular morning, a bit more intense than usual.

"Ahh! - my friends, my friends, there you are Mr Julian and the beautiful Miss Karen. We meet again this wonderful god given morning! Come, come please, please sit and partake with me of this wonderful herb tea."

"I didn't know the ancients drank tea?" I said, taking a seat opposite Garcia.

Garcia chuckled to himself. "Tea, tobacco, we had it all me boy. But this herbal remedy is particularly good. And miss Karen as beautiful as ever! Don't you think, Mr Julian?"

"As ever..." I replied.

"Yes indeed, such beauty!" reiterated Garcia, tutting and shaking his head, "my, my, my - what beauty!" he went on, whilst looking unashamedly at the copious swell of Karen's bosom, wrapped tightly in a green silk Kimono."

"Alisiya is very pretty too." put in Karen.
"She is, she is. I am a fortunate man - you my dear" he said, patting Karen's hand, "have a very different sort of beauty. I fear Mr Julian is the more fortunate of the two of us."

Karen looked toward me. "I don't think Julian would agree with you."

"No - I think señor Garcia is right," I replied. "I am the fortunate one."

Karen raised her head a couple of centimetres and turned it, presenting me with her arrogant profile. She looked like one of those girls on a Greek vase painting. She had a proud nose that followed a straight line from her forehead, her strong jaw line clearly defined. As if to underline the point she wished to make, without uttering a word, she threw her shoulders back and pushed her chest out. Old Garcia looked at me and then furtively towards Karen.

I suddenly got the jitters and knew that my *nympholepsy* had struck again. Perhaps it was contagious because for a second the old man didn't know what to do with his hands either. Finally he had to look away. Breathing heavily he clapped his hands together and rubbed them vigorously.

"Well then, let us get down to business," he said, his words breaking the animal tension. "First partake of the herb tea," he said, pouring Karen and myself generous cupfuls which he dispensed from a large pot.

"Do you ever think of the deeper questions of life?" he said. Without waiting for a reply, he chuckled to himself and went on: "I do - all the time. The universe," he said, suddenly looking up at the clear blue sky, "where do we fit into it all? We do you know! Everything that exists has a part to play in the great drama of existence. Except its only a drama if you see it that way. Take time for instance."

"About quarter past ten," I said, looking at my wrist watch.

Karen put her head on one side and looked at me with a bored expression.

"Yes, very good Mr Julian," said Garcia, waving his finger at me. "You know that's - ah - very good. You see that is the typical modern response to such a question. Modern people - such as yourselves, seldom ponder the deep metaphysical problems, such as the nature of time. It is taken very much for granted. Our perception of the universe you see, all hinges around a mistaken belief that time runs linear. Moment to moment, with the past stretching back and only the future in front of us. Take this pot of tea for example. Is it the same pot of tea that was brought to the table earlier?

"Well no," said Karen, "it was probably full when it was first brought out, and now I guess it's half empty."

"Ah! - so you are saying it is not the same. But what if I were to tell you that the teapot is full and empty at the same time! What if I told you that the history of this teapot is not something that happened in the past, but is still going on from moment to moment! What one must cultivate is a more flexible view of history."

Karen and I both stared at the teapot.

"Yes - yes, go on, help yourself to some more tea," prompted Garcia. "You see the thing is, the common notion is to regard what is considered events in the past as being immutable. A moment that is gone forever."

"Like Julian drinking his tea and now he is standing his cup down with a shaky hand," said Karen.

Garcia gave me a funny look. "Precisely, Miss Karen. The important thing to remember though is the drinking of the tea, or for that matter any event, is an event in *time*. If one were to assert that it no longer took place, it must be an event outside of time, but since we have already asserted that it took place, then the event must still be happening. Must still be *real*. It is simply that the event is no longer running concurrent with our own *perception* of time."

Karen, who had looked somewhat pleased with herself, was now looking perplexed, and I have to admit, I felt the same.

"The common notion of history, " continued Garcia, " tells us that certain events occurred in the past: history then is a science of looking back over ones shoulder. Its only concern is the interpretation of events, perceived as having taken place in the past. It does not say anything more about them, except that they happened. But history is constantly being made - right now, at this very moment. Where my view departs company from that of the historian, is that I do not believe that once those events become the past, they remain immutable because of that."

Garcia picked up his cup and threw his head back so as to drain it of every last drop, he then put it down with far more force than was required: sighing heavily like the man who knew it all, and found its explanation rather tedious, he reached across the table with his big hand for the teapot, and filled his cup up to the brim.

"I do not look over my shoulder," proclaimed Garcia, looking over his shoulder, and then back to me and Karen, "I am not a scribbler of notes of things that have happened, then regard it as dead and gone in the way that history does. Such a view presupposes time as being linear in nature." Raising his head and looking into the distance, he went on: "No - instead I can stand back and look at not just what was, but what will be, and when I do this I can see that both the past and the future are linked - rather like a wound-up piece of string, or to use a modern analogy, the tape on a tape recorder." Garcia silently mused a moment before continuing, "But it is more than this, since I can see that this analogy still bears some of the linear framework. Instead we must see both the past and the future as one whole, an organic whole, that is constantly being made and remade in untold different ways."

There was an uncomfortable silence for a moment. Karen self-consciously drank some of her tea. It was obvious Garcia was expecting some kind of response from us: a pat on the back for such a profound exposition. I could see that Karen was not going to offer up anything constructive. I felt one of us should humour the old man, especially since he took these ideas so seriously.

"An organic whole," I said. "You mean that the past and present are all some how interlinked, that they are a part of each other?" I said.

"Yes in a sense that is what I mean."

Karen gave me an odd look from across the table.

"The past no more exists independently from the present, as the present does from the future. They are all happening exactly at the same moment. It is just that we can only interpret our universe on a three dimensional level, but physics has already shown that there could be seven or, eight different dimensions at the subatomic level."

"Ah - but that's science. You are using science to aid your argument." I said, imagining I had found a weakness in his thinking, but Garcia waved his hand in a dismissive manner.

"I'm not concerned with winning arguments, or where I take my proof from. Its all grist to my mill Mr Julian. It alters non of my beliefs whether science has proven these things or not, I merely appeal to the modern way of thinking. That is that science has all the answers. Ironically science will prove that it is I that have all the answers. I have already been there and seen it." Expansively waving his arms about: "Science comes along the path *that I* have already trod. I walk along the river bank and see the river flowing, but I also know that - I, the river bank, and the river are one."

Karen and I looked at one another, and I wondered if she was thinking the same as me: 'that the old boy had finally flipped.' And then Karen perked up brightly and said: "So what you are saying is that these other dimensions exist outside of our awareness, but that is no reason why they should not exist! It's just that we live our lives from a linear perspective!"

Karen looked at me and smirked.

"Quite so Karen," replied Garcia, nonchalantly, "and if we say that the past is as real as the present, then of course the future is just as real. What we were, what we are, and what we will be, all is just as certain."

"So there is nothing we can do to change the outcome of events, if they have already happened? It's a bit of a bleak view if that is the case?" I observed.

"The way modern people view it it is, but why should it be bleak! It only seems like that because moderns are obsessed with control. They find it especially hard to accept the idea, that the thing they thought they had most control over, namely their own life, is purely illusory. The idea that they have control couldn't be further from the truth. You would be surprised by the outrage such an idea as predetermination, engenders among the ignorant young of modern society. They fly into such a rage! Some have even turned physically violent, when I have pointed out that they have about as much control over the outcome of their pathetic little existence, as does an ant, or any other insect that toils away in a colony: 'dumb and blind to their fate are men and insects alike.' "

"If you put it to them like that, then I'm not surprised they get outraged."

Garcia chuckled to himself. "Quite so, Mr Julian." And then banging his fist hard on the table so that our cups rattled in their saucers:

"You think I have got time for such idiots, their heads filled with rubbish; arrogant that their modern world has all the answers....Huh! They couldn't be further from the truth; ignorant even, of what or who they are. Modern society, as my friend *Felix* pointed out: 'is full of cardboard cut-out people, who lack any substance. People with one dimensional thoughts. They have no belief in anything except power if that can get it, and money. They are the living dead."

There followed a stunned silence. Garcia tipped the teapot and found that it was empty. He snapped his fingers and momentarily a young boy of about fourteen came over with a fresh pot of herb tea. His features resembled that of the nymphet. The same delicate bone structure, the turned-up nose, the same dark eyes full of gravity. He gave me a look as he went, a quick turn of the head, and for a second I saw the face of the statue superimposed on that of the boy. After he had gone I asked if he was related to Alisiya. I was told that he was not. I felt puzzled by that, since everyone on the island, it seemed to me, had the same elfin features. I stared at Karen, even her features seemed to be growing more and more elfin-like. I looked down at my brimming cup and felt my head swim.

"Drink some more of the herb tea, especially you Mr Julian, it relaxes the nerves."

"Yes Julian you seem very tense," enjoined Karen.

I looked up and I saw the girls face again but this time superimposed on Karen.

"Stop staring Julian. Whatever is wrong with you!"

I shook my head. For a while my vision went blurry and then Karen came into focus, as she screwed up her face at me.

"Do not be too harsh on him Miss Karen. It is only natural he should be taken by such beauty as yours." Garcia turned to me. "Are you feeling all right me boy?"

"Yes I think so." I said. My vision still playing tricks on me. I sat back in a kind of daze, occasionally taking sips of my tea, the effects of which slowly caught up on one. It was a bit like being drunk but more subtle. If anything, ones thoughts and sensations became more finely tuned. The voice of Garcia gurgled on in the backdrop of my mind, while I conjured up the beautiful image of the nymph. I found I could make her appear at will. That any person, or object, for that matter, could become her.

"What is that you find so amusing Julian?" said Karen, breaking the spell.

"Nothing," I said, all innocence and wide eyes. I quickly rounded my thoughts on Garcia's words, and it struck me, how claustrophobic his ideas on time and destiny sounded.

"If you are right and we have no control over our future then it is very serious. It makes everything rather futile - don't you think?" I said, taking a good draught of my herb tea.
"Futile! Why do you say that?" replied Garcia.
"Well, why bother striving to achieve anything, if its all preordained?"
"But that's just it." interrupted Karen, "we are still inclined to live the life we are destined to, I mean if it is your destiny to strive, then you'll strive, you can't do anything else except what you are destined to do... And the thing is, no one, not even Garcia can know for certain the way any of our lives will turn out."
"Well I wouldn't quite say that," interjected Garcia. "It is possible for some of us to effect a change."
I shook my head. "No...no..." I began, excitedly. "You said earlier that everything is preordained, and now you seem to be saying that there is an element of chance."

Garcia raised an arm. "Not chance exactly, although I do believe it is possible to change ones fate and have some control over the way our lives turn out, but one can only gain this knowledge if one tries to open ones mind. One must see life as having every possibility within ones grasp. Not to live always for the future, or engrossed in the present. One must have the wider view. While we run frightened of death, through greater and greater levels of distraction, be it in work or the entertainment industry, then the vast majority of people will live out their tawdry little lives again and again, always repeating the same mistakes, fighting the same wars. What is required is a completely new perspective on life - and all existence. Mankind needs to revaluate himself - his whole *gestalt*."
"And how is that to be done?" I said, reaching over for the teapot. My eyes wide as I replenished my cup, until it brimmed over.
"The thing is to understand what our true nature is. We must be conscious all the time, that we are not our body. The only thing that is eternal and gives life to the body, is the soul. Also we must be aware that *all* existence's are interlinked. No body, no thing, exists independently of itself. The actions of one person effect those of another, like ripples in a pond. We are all time travels Mr Julian - all of us."

Just as Garcia stopped speaking the tall dark presence of Rachine came up from behind me. She was wearing an orange silk sarong, and a black translucent blouse.

"You are just in time Rachine, please do sit and join us," said Garcia, indicating a vacant chair.

"Ah! Is it the herb tea Garcia?" observed Rachine, clapping her hands with glee.

"Yes, please just help yourself. "Garcia snapped his fingers and a few seconds later the young boy returned with yet another pot of tea. My eyes went all misty again, as the boy looked at me with his black eyes, full of gravity. 'God its rough when you're suffering from the *nympholepsy!'* It was only the import of Garcia's words which drew me out of my hallucination.

"It is important Julian to know why you are here - I mean in this particular body, this particular incarnation of your soul. You have come to this island for a purpose Mr Julian, as has everyone, especially Karen here. Yes - this life Julian is one in which you play a very important role. What you do will effect the life of those around you, especially one who is particularly close to you."

"You mean Karen?"

Garcia nodded.

"You see Julian." said Karen, smiling vaguely, "Garcia has told me things about myself that I have been trying for a long while to deny. He found me, he has brought me here in order to try and save me from myself, but there is only so much he can do." Karen reached over and touched Garcia's hand. "You don't know how grateful I am," she said, turning to him.

"I can only do so much. You see Julian, there are those whose task it is to act and those whose role it is to advice. For my part I can only try to help through the advice I give and what shelter I can offer Karen from the outside world, but she cannot stay here forever; she must confront her demons," he said, looking into her eyes. "I have certain knowledge of events that are yet to unfold. There are many of us scattered around the world who have the power to see, as I see. It is our task to show the right course of action for those who are wandering in the thick of the wood. I can call out to you from my vantage point and hope you will take the right path, but whether or not you heed the call is up to you. Sometimes two people my be wandering down the same path, but only one of them may be able to heed the call, and guide the other to safety. If the one that does not hear, looses sight of the other, then that soul may wonder off into the ever darkening regions of the wood."

"You can look into the future?" I asked, with a note of incredulity.

"To a limited degree - and with the aid of such devices as are used in fortune telling. Beings, such as I are gifted with a second sight, given to us by the force in the universe which created us all. Some call us witches or magicians, and many of us have been persecuted down through the ages. I have a duty to perform that is all I know, and that is to guide those that need help through the twists and turns, of the rights and wrongs of their actions. Numerology, Necromancy, and other such methods, such as the Tarot and Palmistry, are rudimentary skills. In order to see clearly one must take oneself above the corporeal level and look out on the tangled web that is life, the tangled web that makes life so complicated and seemingly incomprehensible. Incomprehensible because the web has been woven since the beginning of time, stretching in every direction - what you may call the past and the future.

"An organic whole." Put in Rachine.

"Quite so, my dear. I have been teaching Rachine some of my knowledge. It is innate in all of us, but in some more developed than others."

"I'm confused! - If only you could tell me what it is I must do in order to help Karen," I said, beginning to feel quite fretful. "I have felt so often that she has been trying to shut me out."

"I haven't. At least I never meant to."

"Karen is afraid that is all. She is aware that the door to one part of her life has been slowly closing, and as it closes she feels herself being drawn closer and closer to her fate. And in following her destiny she has tried to close the door. You Julian are the light behind the door. Your love for Karen is the only thing that is stopping the door from closing. You are already doing all that you were meant to do, simply by being here. It is true that Karen was lost for a time, but through my knowledge I have brought her back on the safe path - at least for the time being."

"You must never stop loving her Julian, even when it is painful to do so," added Rachine.

"I don't think I ever did, even when she left me to follow her career. But often I have felt completely superfluous to her existence. For example her modelling career. She has made the big time both in the States and Europe, I'm happy for her in a way, even though some of the stuff she has done....Anyway I guess I felt that she didn't need me around."

"I never stopped thinking about you Julian. I hated what I had become, I am ashamed, of some of the things I've done."

"This is why it is so important Julian," said Garcia.

He reached over and took both our hands in his. "It is difficult I know, but believe me when I say that you need each other. Karen, you are just a victim of your own fate. You need faith now in order to place yourself along a completely new spiral of destiny, and in so doing break the curse that has hovered over your soul for millennia and the tragically fated lives that you have lived. Where gradually the licentious aspect of your being came in the end to dominate and eat away at your very soul - your very existence. But enough of that, I will speak more of Karen's incarnations later." Sounding optimistic, Garcia continued, "But it will come, it will come right this time I am sure of it, with the help of all of us."

Rachine reached across the table and took hold of my other hand, and so the three of us formed a link around the table. "We are all here for you Karen, and you Julian," said Rachine, "we can guide her out on to an entirely new life that is not fated, the way her last lives have been; driven by excess and bent upon their own destruction."

I looked across at Rachine who shifted position so as to face me almost square-on. Her hand was long, the skin burnt dark by the sun. The veins were prominent over its leathery surface, distended with blood, promising hidden reserves of strength. Her body was lean and hard, her large bosom sat up stiff beneath the flimsy fabric of her blouse. Intoxicated as I now was by the herb tea, which seemed to accentuate ones sensual awareness, I wondered if they were authentic and felt a compunction to test their resilience against the soft material. I felt bemused, since I had never previously been aware of such intense feelings for Rachine, or come to that - any woman apart from Karen.

I felt her obsidian gaze on me, their black discs seemed to cut to the quick of me. I was certain she could read my every thought.

"It will be all right," she said, encouragingly. Rachine moved away a little and looked across at Karen, who was talking to Garcia. Rachine smiled faintly with her mouth, her black eyes remained inert. I looked down and saw that her sarong had fallen open to reveal a large area of deep chestnut brown thigh, when she saw me looking, instead of covering herself, she pulled it further back so that all of one leg was naked. Still with a firm grip on my hand she pulled it down beneath the table. I felt the firmness of her thigh, and the sudden shock on discovering that the sarong was all she had on.

"Don't worry, everything will be all right," she intoned, in her dark Latin voice.

I looked at the dark girl unable to speak as she guided my hand to her wide hips. Her pupils dilated: she returned my gaze, an inky blackness that threatened to swallow the sun. Rachine's obsidian eyes were not enough though to swallow the lavender light that came from Karen's eyes. Karen was on her scent and she fixed Rachine with a cold silver look. The pressure she was exerting on my hand faded and I moved it out of there damn fast.

"Don't worry Julian," said Karen, "Garcia knows what must be done."

"I'm sure that he does. I just find it all a bit confusing," I said.

"The organic structure of time can be difficult to picture. Imagine it though, as a spiral, each cycle of destiny spiralling round itself," said Rachine."

"You mean like the orbits of the planets," said Karen.

"Yes, yes similar to that. Each persons destiny follows kind of a path that crosses over the path of others, and just when a planet crosses the path of another, it effects the orbit of that planet through its gravitational pull, so it is with individual destinies."

"But we do not just go round and round," interrupted Garcia. "Through these interactions we are swayed this away and that, and for a terribly fated person one can be lead far from the light of eternal being. If we continue our stellar analogy and say that God is at the centre just as the sun is the centre of the solar system, then some souls reside close to the One - and such a soul is very pure, very just. But just as there are planets that are so far away from the sun they hardly receive any warmth or light, so to there are souls that are remote and cut off from the warmth of the One. And then there are other souls that can be compared with the lonely wanderings of comets, that travel so far from their primary that they are not seen for thousands of years. Sometimes they wander so far away that they become lost altogether. A soul such as this is a very irresolute entity that only looks to its own misguided self for direction."

"And what of Karen?" I put in.

"We hope she will not wander any further from the light of eternal being than she already has. Destiny does not run straight but in a great arc so that eventually one may come back to the point one started from," said Garcia.

"It almost sounds as if our lives are like a train that can only follow the tracks that it rests on!" I said.

"That is a very good analogy Mr Julian. Imagine though, that just a few miles along the track is equivalent to a life time and that there are many thousands and thousands of miles of track, then you can see that it will take many thousands of life times before a soul can return to the point from which it began." Garcia raised a finger, indicating as was his wont, a further caveat to his discourse. "But just as tracks have points which enable a train to transfer from one track to another taking it to a different destination, so to the soul on *its* journey, as a corporeal entity, can veer off along an entirely new course as well."

I nodded and smiled, as I at last began to grasp Garcia's ideas concerning time and rebirth.

"But of course," continued Garcia. " The real nature of time, that is, its form and structure is nothing like that at all."

I slumped forward and rested my head in my hands. "Oh no," I groaned. "You are too much *mister* Garcia!"

The old man chuckled to himself. "This analogy is very good in order to demonstrate the dynamics of time and the course of destiny, but we must remember that it is still dependent on a linear type, three dimensional world. We must bear in mind, as Rachine pointed out, 'time is an organic whole.' "

"*En block*," pronounced Rachine.

"And just when I was beginning to feel happy with the idea!" I said.

"Our task is to understand Karen's predicament," continued Garcia, in serious tone of voice. "We must guide her towards a new path, a new *track* in time - if you will."

"Or else she may run out of time altogether," observed Rachine, with a certain amount of misappropriated glee.
"Oh my God!" said Karen, putting her hand over her mouth. "You never told me that!"
Garcia put his arm about her, in a fatherly way. "I'm sure it won't come to that, I think Rachine is being a little bit too alarmist!"
Garcia looked for a moment menacingly towards her.
"Yes I'm sure it won't come to that Karen. I sometimes say the stupidest of things," explained the other girl.
"I won't just disappear from life will I Garcia?" said Karen, fretfully
"No, that's is why we are here. Why you are here. We won't let that happen."
"No, we won't I won't let it happen," I endorsed.
Karen tried to put a brave face on by smiling, but it was obvious she was generally spooked by the concept of non existence.
"Don't worry *hon...*" I said, reaching across the table for her hand. "I won't let anything happen to you."
"You won't?" replied Karen, in a feeble voice.
"Not ever..." I said.
For the first time I had been on Sapphos with Karen I felt close to her. It was like we had at last made the connection that had been missing since LA.
"I think I might go and lay down a while," she said.
"That might be a good idea," replied Garcia.
I rose out of my chair, but Garcia indicated for me to sit down. "No I need to explain more to you Julian, concerning in particular the pattern of Karen's incarnations; in other words the different people she has been: the past lives she has lived. Karen already knows about it." Turning to the darker skinned girl, "Rachine can accompany Karen. And mind you don't say anything to upset her further," warned Garcia.
"Don't worry she will be OK with me," replied Rachine. As she turned to leave with Karen, she gave me a long lingering look. "I'll see *you* later Julian - adieu my friend."
Garcia chuckled to himself again. "My, but she is a one that Rachine! You have to watch'm you know. Especially that one. But what a beauty! - Ne?"

"Yes remarkable, but it's only Karen that I care about..."
"Of course it is me boy. Let us have some wine Julian," said Garcia, raising his hands and clapping them together. In a moment a young girl appeared about the same age as the boy. At least I think it was a girl, such was the androgynous look of these elfin creatures. Of course she was stunningly beautiful, her skin was dark, her black hair was cut short adding to her boyish look, with only the hint of breasts beneath her shimmering satin gown. She set-down before us: silver drinking cups, and a large silver pitcher that contained red wine, from which the girl poured copious amounts into our cups. Old Garcia followed my eyes. He looked up at the girl when she had finished pouring. Her dark eyes searching out mine. Garcia coughed.
"That will be all, Urania." The nimble footed creature slipped away. "Now Mr Julian, if you can take your eyes off of my servants for a moment, is there anything you want to say, before I continue? - You seem to understand the principles by now, which hold sway over all our lives!"

The ethereal creature sat on my shoulder as I mused with Garcia's concept of time and rebirth.
"Well - you talked about time being continuous, and everything happening at the same moment, and I think I can just about grasp that, but just now you or rather Rachine, eluded to the disturbing conclusion that time for some may be running out."

Garcia raised an arm. "I am sorry please forgive me. How clumsy it was of our friend to put it like that. Of course time itself is relative to the dimensions of space and so on and so forth - and so long as the universe keeps ticking over then notions of time will go on. The point Rachine rather clumsily made was that *existence* within the framework of time, charted by continuous death and rebirth, *is finite* - as she said. Remember we spoke of spirals of time - lines of destiny spiralling inwards towards the creative force, as the Neoplatonists refer to it, 'The One' - well at the same time, the paths of destiny spiral outward as well, toward the darker regions that are remote from the light of truth, which emanates from The One: the eternal life giving force of the universe. If a soul wanders too far from this *truth*, towards a place that is cold and dark, it will eventually loose its way. It will become confused and slowly loose its cohesion as a discrete entity and dissipate into the fabric of the universe lost in the noise of space."

"And is this going to happen to Karen's soul?"

"It could happen - yes."

"But how? How can you know?"

Garcia took a large gulp of wine, as if in preparation to my question.

"When the soul has no time for repose. When the space between each new incarnation becomes increasingly small. The soul has no sooner sloughed off one body to regain another. The soul needs time to gather itself. To prepare for its next incarnation as a living being. It is an extremely traumatic experience for the soul to find itself united with matter, to exist corporeally. You see Julian, for the soul to exist on the material level it ideally requires a body. That is why I said, we must not think of ourselves as our body. It is merely a shell, a husk that is cast off at death. The soul is a traveller Mr Julian, it travels through space and time, but life is a journey that all souls must embark upon. But it is not the souls true nature, which is why life is often so full of pain. It is in every souls destiny to be united with matter, to experience the pain and the ecstasies of life. Along the way some souls are overcome by this experience and may never find their way back to the light of eternal being. And when a soul is terribly fated like this, there is little time to break free of its destiny before death comes to the body and the soul returns again, each occasion with less and less time in between each new incarnation."

"It sounds terrible to be such a soul as this, " I remarked.

We both sat back and drank some wine and reflected a moment upon Karen's fate. "So, no sooner has she cast off one life, than Karen is plunged back into another." I mused, "but how quickly does this happen?"

"It is hard to say - time is different for a soul unalloyed with the body, but here on the material level, perhaps only a matter of months or years. At least this is what my research has shown."

"No wonder then she retains memories of her pervious life! Of course - this would explain the use of her alias: 'Natasha!' " I said, with surprise.

"Quite so."

"And so when there is no space between death and rebirth...?"

"then there is neither."

"Non existence!" I said, looking off into the distance.

"In a manner of speaking. Her soul may remain forever in darkness and confusion, cold and dark - until eventually after an incalculable period of time it will eventually perish, although essentially soul is considered incorruptible, it will dissipate into the universe as a confused mass of energy indistinguishable, from the background radiation of the birth of the universe itself."

Solemnly: "How long does she have? How many rebirths before...?

Garcia sighed and shook his head. "Its hard to say with any certainty. May be one, may be two - perhaps this life is her last. Its hard to say for sure. I have been doing some research," he continued, more optimistically, "I have discovered who this 'Natasha' was. In understanding the fate of her pervious life, it can give us clues to the obstacles we must surmount in her present incarnation as Karen. Always the same pattern is followed, but it is the minor variations that we must exploit. You see everyone we meet in this life, even casual acquaintances, we have known in previous lives, but each person in a different life may have a different role to play. Some who we know, perhaps only by sight, in this life, may have had a more important role in a previous one."

I do not believe Mr Julian that forces for the good were ever exploited enough in Karen's previous incarnations, and you yourself are such a force as this."

"Which is why you brought me here."

"Quite so - in all probability your friendship with Karen would have ended when she left America. She would then have been left to her fate."

V

I listened, fascinated as Garcia went on to describe the many past existences that Karen's soul had known.

Natasha, as with all of Karen's reincarnations, had followed more or less the same tragic path. A path that lead back over three thousand years to one known as Taanach: a high priestess of the goddess Tanit: the principle deity worshipped by the Phoenicians. Famed triple goddess of fecundity, of birth, death, and rebirth, as symbolised by the three phases of the moon. Taanach the terrible, Taanach the glorious: all subsequent incarnations would be lived out in her long dark shadow. A shadow that Garcia had begun to dispel by uncovering layer upon layer of personality that had gone before. The more he searched the more he understood the terrible truth of Karen's daemon. It seemed that long ago Karen's soul pivoted between light and dark. The dark arrogance and wantonness of Taanach, on the one hand, and that of the serenity and innocence of one called Chloe, on the other, a young girl who lived a life of purity and innocence as a shepherdess and later became associated with the priesthood of Hestia. Most recent of all was Natasha, who was born in Stockholm in 1950, to a rather middle class family. But she was never satisfied with the mundane or the ordinary. The shadow of Taanach fell long and dark over Natasha. *Ofisiodeis*, as she was also known, meaning 'serpentine', had plunged her fangs deep into her own soul, its head deeply rooted in the past, its long body snaking its way down through the twists and turns of destiny, on and on down through the ages.

"She never was, she never could be satisfied," said Garcia, energetically, she felt the tug of fate puling at her from a very early age. Pulling her away from the safety of her family. Fate snatched her up, snapped at her heels, waiting for her at every turn. Do you not see Mr Julian, what hope did she have? What hope do any of us have - my God!" Proclaimed Garcia, shaking his head. He paused a moment to gather himself.

"Forgive me - it is just that I know each one of Karen's incarnations, but in many ways it is Natasha that I feel closest to, because she was alive at the same time as myself, yet fate did not bring her close enough for me to help her. Nevertheless fate led her abroad when she was just seventeen. Fate took her from the bosom of her family, even her country of birth. It led her to the places it best knew - the places that had seen the drama of her past lives played out towards their miserable end, a thousand times over." Garcia shook his head again, and sipped some of the wine. "She knew, of course, from her youngest days that she was special, and that her beauty, even in a land notorious for beautiful women, her own beauty was something classical, and rare. It wasn't enough though for her to be content with just being beautiful, she felt that she had something to prove to the world - that she, Natasha, was the best. She soon slipped into her old licentious ways, inherited from Taanach's bitter pride: "As if her body was the expression of her true beauty!" said Garcia, scornfully.
"So Natasha left home when she was very young." I observed.
"Yes at the age of seventeen. She was but a child still, and incredibly naïve. But her looks, her body were a lot more developed."
"I see." I replied. "Not a good combination."
"In her case disastrous. Take Karen's beauty for example, imagine that, in the hands of an immature young girl of seventeen; for Natasha was all of Karen's beauty, and perhaps even more."
"Are there any photographs of her?"
"There are a few - mostly nudes, I will show you them later. They can be quite disturbing, especially to a young impressionable man like yourself...She was easy prey to those who exploit women for their bodies - for their sex."

Garcia shook his head again, as in a man in despair. "I mean, what can be done! Oh the evil - the beast in the heart of man!" he said, his hands open, beseechingly.

I said nothing. What reply was there to such a statement. Again he fell silent a moment, drank some more wine and then continued his narrative of Natasha's life story: "She found her way to Germany, Berlin in fact, and had no problem getting a job as a dancer in a sleazy club, where she was paid a few Marks for taking her clothes off for a lot of drunk American and English servicemen.

Germany in those days was full of foreigners, all manner of types looking to make a profit. And this is the worst of it," said Garcia, rubbing his head. "I was one of them - but please don't ask me anymore about it."

By Garcia's behaviour I guessed that he had probably slept with Natasha, or in some other way, had contributed to her downfall. Feeling somewhat embarrassed for him, I looked away and concentrated on my wine.

"She had only been at the club for a few months," continued Garcia, "when a man, an Englishman, of some wealth and importance saw Natasha. He was immediately struck by her unusual beauty and decided to make her his. He had the power, the money to take her away from it all. The son of a self-made millionaire who had made his fortune through shipping; one might have thought that through Jon Kindell Natasha had found a lucky break - that Kindell had come along just in time to save her from a life of sin and debauchery, but Julian you will see how fate intervenes, to bring down around her ears a future that promised to be so bright, and turn it, as with all of her incarnations, towards misery and eventual destruction."

Garcia poured himself some more wine and sat back expansively, his silver chalice in hand. "All this I found out through extensive research," he went on, "I also used less orthodox methods such as divination: Tarot and the I Ching, for example, the details of which I won't bore you with now. Eventually though I formed a picture of Natasha, as accurate as it is possible to be. I know her character, her behaviour, as if she were my own daughter. It is important that you do the same with Karen. In the end I failed to save Natasha and only came to know her when it was too late - but you my boy, together we *must* save her this time."

"I don't understand," I said, "this Kindell character sounds all right to me."

"Jon Kindell is best described as an overgrown schoolboy who never had to do a days work in his life. A lazy decadent good-for-nothing. He collected people and used them for his entertainment as though they were mere objects. Of course his new favourite object was Natasha. An overgrown boy who used the world as a playground and people as *toys* to play with. He was a sexual homunculus, a sexual failure, a sexual weakling, a monster full of pent-up sexual frustration that found its expression in violence and sexual perversions of every kind imaginable. He was a weakling, a failure as a man who needed a sexy young girl to prop up his flimsy ego..."

Garcia broke off, in order to take a well needed gulp of wine. "Excuse me," he continued, "but you have no idea Julian just how much Kindell disgusts me, how much his filthy rotten type disgust me. I hate them, all those that are weak and feeble but use their money and power to get them what ever they want, which in normal circumstances would be far beyond their scope. They are overreachers, who intoxicated by their own power, eventually become unstuck, but for me it can never happen soon enough."

Garcia flicked his fingers. *"Más ve, más ve,"* he shouted. Almost immediately the young nymph appeared, the one he called, Urania. She placed a fresh pitcher of wine on the table; again her coal black eyes lingered over me. Garcia looked up at her and addressed her quickly in Greek. Not taking her eyes off me she assented and spoke softly and quickly.

I enquired after the nature of their brief conversation. The old man smiled mischievously.

"I asked her if she wanted you. She said she would very much like it if you came to he room one evening."

"Señior Garcia! You know that I can't." I looked at the girl again. Her deep black eyes sent out streamers of intense sexual energy so much so that it scalded my eyes to look at her. Her lithe elfin form hovered patiently. "She is extremely beautiful but I don't think it would be right."

Garcia raised his arm. Urania leaned over smiling, to take the empty pitcher, in so doing affording me a view down her loosely fitting gown. Her breasts rose from her bony chest like twin pointed pyramids. She lingered over me letting me take my fill. A heavy aroma came from her of essence of bergamot, sharp and intense, she overloaded my senses. She was like Karen in so far as one identified her through her smell. In Karen's case it was always Jasmine. Urania moved off lithely, turning to give one last lingering look with her night black eyes, as if reminding me of what a fool I was. If that wasn't enough, her scent lingered in the air as a further disturbing reminder.

"I know her mother well. She has taught her everything she knows of the art of love making. She is still very young but she surpasses every other on the island

may be even my Alisiya. Don't dismiss the opportunity out of hand."
"I am a lover of beauty Garcia, that is all. Besides there is Karen to think of."
"Being a lover of beauty is all well and good Mr Julian, but there comes a time when a man must make love to beauty, as well as stand back and admire it. A man must take what he wants," he said, "especially if it is offered the way Urania offers herself," Garcia added, aside.
"But what about Karen?"
"What of her! Urania is discrete. A man must act, must follow his passion! If he wants something - a woman say, then he must take her, regardless of what others think. Regardless of the consequences even."
"What if you can't always get what you want?" I said, thinking of what he had had done to Bethany.

Garcia looked at me with cold blue eyes, and I saw the merciless composure of a man who was used to getting what he wanted.
"I never consider it an option," he replied icily.

His beady steel blue eyes darted about madly in his head. "Now let us speak more of Natasha. Ah...Natasha! - Natasha!" He shook his head, going off into a reverie. "What an incredible young woman she was! Never was there another such as she! One whose passion burned as intensely as the surface of a star. But not just any star, a star that was black and cold and distant. A star that takes everything into it, making it denser and denser; so it was with Natasha's soul. It grew heavier and heavier, and darker all the time, until she no longer existed in her own right. Like one of those black stars, that astronomers are always talking about - they know its there because everything is drawn toward it. It was the same with Natasha. Men were drawn to her for one thing. In this sense alone, Natasha existed for them as much as for herself, and then ironically, she was often too much for them. In the end weighed down by the immense weight of her soul, she proved to be even too much for herself - or, at least for mortal flesh to bear."

Hearing him talk about her in almost reverential terms it was strange to think that all the time he was, in another sense referring to Karen. I therefore concluded, given all that I knew of the man, that if he had known Natasha intimately, he was sure to have the same knowledge of Karen. I bit my lip, and choose to remain silent over the issue.

Replenishing his cup he went on: "But I don't want to paint too gloomy a picture for you. For the first year or so she lived a fantastic lifestyle, travelling to exotic places around the world accompanied by her rich boyfriend, except he wasn't a boy, in anything other than his outlook. He was older than Natasha by more than forty years. Yes at first she had a great time of it; she wasn't in love with Kindell of course, and I think he knew that, but she was young and sexy, and fun, and it made him look the part. They got married in Buenos Aires, only a year after he found her in the strip joint - she was just eighteen. They travelled around for a while after they were married, eventually making their way back to Europe. Kindell had a villa in Spain and it was during their stay there, that I was first introduced to Natasha.....I was a young man then Mr Julian, not much older than yourself. At the time I thought Natasha was the most exquisite creature I had ever seen. There were a lot of parties, I remember that, and Natasha always seemed to go through the motions only, of enjoying herself. It must have been around about this time that she began to have affairs. I doubt if Kindell had ever really been able to satisfy her sexually. A girl like that needed to feel loved, needed to feel wanted and valued by her man." Garcia nodded: "and yes, before you say anything, I was privileged to *know* her in that way, but I like to think I did so honourably, from the standpoint of an artist."

"Oh - I see." I interjected, "if you're an *artist* its OK to screw someone else's wife?" I immediately regretted what I had said but I couldn't help it. The arrogance and the pomposity of the man had become too much for me to remain silent any longer.

I was a little afraid of what Garcia might do. He looked at me with a perfectly straight face. "But of course!" he said, "only an artist could truly appreciate a young woman, as special as Natasha. Except she wasn't so much a woman as a wild untameable creature. In ones arms - my word! then you saw her demon. A wild thing, when you got right down to it. You would think the very *Furies* themselves had been let loose." Old Garcia suddenly looked up, coming back from his reverie. He slapped me hard on the back and guffawed loudly, "Oh but, my - my Mr Julian, you are a card - really you are! I like that about you, you're not afraid to speak your mind."

I found it perplexing. Despite everything about him, despite the fact that he had very probably screwed Karen, in the end, I couldn't bring myself to hate him.

More soberly he went on: "You know perfectly well Mr Julian that where my actions with Natasha are concerned, I did what I did in good faith. I wasn't out to exploit her or, anybody. At least I respected *her* I valued *her,* which is more than that vermin Kindell ever did. At that time I thought of myself as another Picasso. I offered to paint Natasha, *she* of course was only too eager to pose nude for me. What you have to understand is that Kindell didn't care if other men slept with his wife, he was twisted, warped like that. He derived some sordid pleasure from knowing that she came to him, from another man's bed. But it wasn't like that with Natasha and I, we connected in some spiritual way. I could see she wasn't really happy with her lot. When Kindell suspected that there was something serious between Natasha and myself, he took her away. He could never tolerate any body getting too close to her.

"I'm sorry to hear that Garcia." I said, trying to sound sincere, "it seems you would have been a positive influence."

Garcia spied me wistfully. "Would I Julian? - I wonder. Anyway," he said, waving his hand dismisively, "it was not destined, that is all one can say of it. Kindell took her back to his native land so that he could show off to his peers, his beautiful bride: prove to them that he was a man. Then everything started to go wrong for both of them. He tried to keep her as one might keep a pet, except Natasha was no pussy-cat, she was young, a wild thing - as you know Karen to be. You yourself, Mr Julian thought you could keep her as a tame creature. But she is not, and neither was Natasha. She could not bear to be pent-up; she hungered all the time for excitement - excitement of any kind, and if she couldn't find it through travel, or sex, she would find it some other way. Kindell should have realised that the walls of his mansion could not contain someone like *her.*"

"What happened?"

"She turned to the worse kind of escape there is - drugs Mr Julian..."

I shook my head, appreciating the grim outlook of such a remedy to her frustrations. I had seen enough 'Kooks' on Venice beach, flying high on the superman trip! And then the other side of it on the streets of LA: the panhandlers, the pushers, the filth and the vermin, that was the drug culture. Drugs provided no escape at all, but were in fact a, *cul-de-sac:*

"But where could she have got them?"
"She must have got them from a servant. They lived in a large house set in several acres in the south of England. A county called Surrey. She was never allowed out on her own, except to walk in the extensive grounds. For a time she found a brief distraction in one of the gamekeepers who worked on the estate. A rather shady character by all accounts. It was very probably him that got her started on her addiction. As soon as Kindell got wind of it he was given the sack, along with a succession of other male staff that were of an age, that they might still know what to do with a sexy thing like Natasha. Kindell was a typical English upper-class snob. He drew a line at her doing it with servants, but amongst his own kind, there had been times when he actively encouraged it.
"Poor girl," I reflected, "shut away like that, and with a man like Kindell. It must have driven her mad!"
"Even a sadistic monster like Kindell eventually saw that his beautiful young wife was wilting away in front of his eyes. Her emaciated and gaunt appearance bore testimony to her deep unhappiness. He knew that he alone could not make her happy, in fact the reverse was true. Some light must have gone on in that convoluted mind of his, that what she needed were people, so he decided to hold a large party in her name. Natasha, needless to say, was the centre of attention. Handsome, wealthy young men zoomed in on her from all over the country. Natasha of course responded by doing what she did best, which was to flirt with all these eligible young men. Kindell simply sat back and watched, knowing that there was nothing he could do. The pretence of living a descent normal life went out of the window that night. He must have realised that it was impossible to keep up the charade. So rather than try to control her wanton ways, he indulged them instead. That initial party at their Surrey residence was the first of many - really it never came to an end. Tales of what went on there filtered back to me, in Spain. I of course was never invited, and even if I had been I don't think I could have brought myself to go. To witness what Natasha had now become." Garcia paused a moment, and closed his eyes..."When I think about the things she did, or rather, the things she was encouraged to do." Garcia's eyes flittered open, heavy and saturnine: "it was said that men would queue up outside her room to take their turn, and these

parties would go on for days. But Kindell always kept a watchful I on his male guests, and any young man who took an interest in Natasha, for more than just sex, found themselves no longer included on future guest lists. News of what went on behind the tall iron gates of Jon Kindell's estate, began to filter out to the general public. A national Newspaper reporter managed to get himself invited. Not long after, it became a national scandal. Allegations of drunken orgies, drugs - all manner of 'activities', alarmed the establishment, not least because, very often it was those very pillars of the establishment that were being spotlighted in these allegations."

I had to laugh at this. It confirmed something I had long believed. That it was always those that held the highest positions of power in society, those so called 'servants' of democracy, those that presented themselves as the bastions of etiquette, those 'holier than thou ' types, that had there minds most firmly rooted in the gutter. They could afford expensive clothes, live in luxury, drive around in expensive cars, on the surface look so clean and sharp and yet their minds, their inner lives, were festering swamps of lasciviousness and corruption. I was not surprised then when Garcia went on to explain how, in order to throw the media off the scent, Kindell befriended the local Priest.

"He did what all rich people do when they want to be approved of by the masses, he made generous donations of money, this time to the church fund; he even got himself on the committee, his fatal error was to get Natasha involved. Perhaps he even thought that a good dose of God worship would do her good. As debased as Kindell was, some of Natasha's behaviour was even shocking to him. Kindell was one of the most ungodly, unspiritual men that ever was, and in his naiveté he did not regard individuals such as the local priest to be *real* men, which is ironic really, since Kindell himself could hardly be considered as a *real* man: the homunculus that he was, the twisted example of perverted humanity that he was!

"Natasha took one look at the priest and fell in love. In many ways he could have been her ideal partner, her soul mate."

"Do you think there is such a thing?"

"Oh, of course there is Mr Julian, there is always that someone special; sometimes it doesn't always work out in a single life time, but when people talk of love at first sight, it is simply the soul remembering that special affinity it had with that other person from a previous life. Sometimes when a soul is very confused it does not recognise, or rather, it forgets what it had known from a previous incarnation. Natasha's life could have been saved then, but where the soul of Natasha is concerned it is never that simple."

"At least her soul recognised the priest." I said, optimistically.

"Yes but it wasn't enough. Fate stood in her way. To begin with he was a Christian priest, consequently he was carrying all the guilt that goes with that dismal religion. But love as we know is a powerful thing and after all, the priest what ever else he may have been, was still a man; so he could not help but be tempted by the danger of her beautiful body. I think he must have been one of the few men who could ever really have satisfied Natasha fully. Her body and her soul became like fire in his arms,"

"You should have been a writer Mr Garcia." I interjected.

"I know it may sound hackneyed, but I am sure that is how she must have felt with this man. Obviously I am using what is known as 'artistic licence', but think back Mr Julian to when you were in love with Karen, when you held her - was it not like fire?"

I nodded, understanding exactly what he was trying to convey. "Like fire - yes just like fire! But didn't Kindell suspect anything?"

"Why should he! After all it was his idea that she should get involved with the Church. That she went so often - well I suppose he must have concluded that she had found religion, when in reality she was getting a lot more than spiritual guidance."

"I suppose you could say that the priest was putting god into her."

"Quite so, in the months that followed she saw the priest regularly, but as I said before, the priest had to contend with centuries of dogmatic teachings: slogans such as 'renounceth the flesh' and a hundred other, 'thou shalt nots' - and with all this mumbo jumbo going on in his head, he found it increasingly difficult to continue the affair. He tried of course, to stop seeing her, but she would go to him and he would relinquish at the sight of her, and each time their desire for one another burned that much more fiercely." Garcia shook his head again: "When I think of what must have gone on in the vestry!"

I could not help but have a good old laugh at this last comment of Garcia's.
"One would have thought he would have had more respect for his God? "I said.
"Yes one might, but remember he was a Christian, the most hypocritical breed there is. Besides, they were in love, and what man could deny Natasha. But it was obvious, even to Natasha, that they could not go on as they were. Kindell by now was also beginning to have his suspicions. So it was decided that if they were to have any future Natasha must go to her husband and confess her adultery."
"From what you said about Kindell, he surely wasn't the kind of man to accept that!"
"Indeed not, and Natasha must have seen the futility of the gesture, but the priest was adamant."
"The selfish bastard!" I suddenly spurted. "Why couldn't have Kindell have stepped aside, he must have seen that the priest and she were in love? If he loved her at all and knew she was not happy, he should have done the manly thing, the right thing, and stepped aside."
"I agree, but you and I are upright, which is why I trust you with Karen. I know that *you* would do the right thing. But creatures such as Kindell are not the same as us; they are cowardly papier-máché characters - cardboard cut-out people without guts, without integrity. Predictably Jon Kindell refused point-blank to grant her a divorce. He flew into a rage and forbade Natasha ever to see Paul again. He threatened to poor down on him the full weight of his power and influence and have him defrocked. He would make sure he never worked again. But Kindell, as with most despicable types was quite clever. He decided to leave him there, in his Church, where he could keep an eye on him."
"Imprisoned by his own faith." I said.
"Indeed that was exactly what he intended." Garcia sighed heavily, he was looking quite tired and strained.
"You know you don't have to go on Garcia." I said, tentatively.
He lifted the wine pitcher and replenished his cup once again. "Its all right me boy." he said, "its just that I find the whole damn thing so wearisome. Natasha seemed doomed from every angle. If Paul the priest had been more positive, if only he had stood up to Kindell and called his bluff! In the end his precious

Church meant more to him than Natasha. The man was a fool in my opinion, since who would have to think twice about devoting ones life to a girl like Natasha - given the choice between her and the grey dismal world of Christianity! - still there you are."

"One would have to question whether he was ever in love with her." I observed.

"For the likes of you and I - we know what we would have done, but to be fair there is no counting on the way an individual will behave under pressure. Perhaps Paul the priest *was* thinking of Natasha when Kindell had threatened to ruin him. They would never have found any peace. Jon would never let her go. Natasha though - well she is something quite different. She knew what she wanted - after all she had been searching for it, for long enough."

"The anguish of it all, to know that the man she loved was a mile or so down the road but she could never be with him! This Jon Kindell is a disgustingly cruel individual." I commented.

"She knew only one thing, she could not live with her husband any longer. When he locked her in her room she climbed down a drainpipe and went strait to Paul the priest; when he turned her away it was the final straw."

"She must have felt terribly alone."

"Absolutely alone," said Garcia gravely, "she told her lover that she was going to run away. Paul found some money for her, and in just the clothes she was standing in got on the train for London, and disappeared into its dark grimy interior."

"It doesn't sound good. A girl like her in a big city all alone. Without the priest what would become of her?" I mused.

"Indeed so Mr Julian. She needed a man who was decisive, but Paul's religion had sucked all the natural desires for living out of him."

"Natasha must have been bitterly disappointed. I thought you said she had found her soul mate in him? The one who would save her!"

"Finding ones soul mate is one thing. It takes two to realise the truth, and even then there are no guarantees that everything will work out in the end. One thing is for certain, she must have been in great despair. It must have felt as though that dark cloud that had haunted her for all her life was drawing nearer, threatening to surround her - swallow her up: that dark cloud was London, and as she boarded the last train, she must have looked back a moment and saw how horribly fated her life was."

"I can't believe Paul the priest could so easily let her go!"

"Who can say! May be he said he would come and get her later, but Jon Kindell made sure that he stayed in his parish. He had a hell of a time of it, the gossip must have been rife in the village."

With some trepidation I asked Garcia of Natasha's plight after arriving in London. He looked very solemn, and before he spoke he took a deep breath:

"She just disappeared as so many young people do in that city - in all big cities. It just swallowed her up."

"And that's it! She was never heard of again?"

"She was found dead in a mouldering apartment in a part of London known as Peckham. I believe it has been condemned now."

"What the apartment?"

"No the place - Peckham! I went there once, when I was researching Natasha's life. The most dismal place on gods earth; if it isn't condemned it should be. I imagine she hung around such places as, Brockwell Park, Dulwich, Peckham Common, Peckham road, and other dismal places, Notting Hill or, was it Black Heath, and Lucacs Gardens! I forget now. But I think she must have felt at home in these places because of the total sense of abandonment of hope, the abandonment of spirit, that was to be found there - in the buildings and in the faces of those that lived there."

I felt my own soul recoil in horror at Garcia's description of this part of London.

"She was found gagged and badly beaten. She had died from internal injuries. The corona registered death by misadventure. She was a prostitute, what can you expect! Someone went a bit too far with their sick fantasy, who can say?" Garcia sighed heavily: "Yes, after just four years of leaving Kindell she was dead - probably murdered for a few pounds, its not difficult to peace together the way her life went after leaving Kindell and the priest. She was of course drawn to her dark daemon. She probably got very little money from the men she took back to her rotting bed-sit. What she did get was plenty of the pent-up aggression that these people, who go to women like Natasha, harbour inside themselves. They would use her body like so much prime beef, until their tiny passions burned themselves out between her powerful thighs, and afterwards crush a few pounds into her hot little hand. It perhaps didn't particularly bother Natasha what they did to her, so far gone was she now in her despair. It must have seemed like the final justification for her existence - that there was no way of escaping her fate! Even her beautiful face and body was horribly mutilated by deep scars."

I bowed my head and shook it. It pained me to hear Garcia describe what *they* had done to her. How *they* had spoiled her looks. How *they* had done for her, and not just those that came to her in order to act out their sordid fantasies, but all those that should have helped her; especially when they professed to love her.

"Shall I go on?" asked Garcia, observing me intently.

"I..I don't know." I replied. We sat in silence for a moment. "They must have scared her."

"Who must have?"

"Pimps." I replied, absently

"Yes perhaps - or other women jealous of her beauty. She was very proud, she would have seen herself as simply surviving - not just a common whore. Who can say what went on Mr Julian, in the kind of world she had entered. But you have not heard the worst of it."

I looked at Garcia, wondering what more could be said that was worse.

"I discovered some years later that the priest knew of her whereabouts. He sent her money and food parcels but never came to see her himself."

"If that's the case why did she choose such a life?"

"As I already said: she was proud, she rejected it, she rejected it Julian, rejected it all. Even Kindell knew of her plight, but when he saw what had become of her - the level she had sunk to, he washed his hands of her for good. And don't ask me how I know, but an associate of Kindell, a man by the name of Greythorpe was implicated for a time with her death. It is known that he went to see Natasha several times. He had always secretly admired her, but knew how jealous Kindell could be of any one who displayed genuine affection towards her. But people like that, people with money and power, can get away with all sorts of things."

"Did Greythorpe kill her then?"

"I'd rather not say. It is known he had a temper. He would take her over the common, or drive her to a secluded place. Remember, Greythorpe was one of Jon Kindell's set, he was therefore use to getting what he wanted. He shared the same kind of perversions that go with these type of men - so it doesn't take a lot of imagination to guess what went on."

"He wasn't put off by the fact that she had lost her looks?"

"In many ways the scars were the ace that she held, and it can be conjectured that Natasha also derived a perverse kind of satisfaction, in knowing just how warn her features had become over such a short period of time. He didn't love her, he didn't want to marry her, he just wanted to use her body. He bought her expensive clothes and jewellery, but they only covered the horror beneath. If Greythorpe was every inch the sadist, then Natasha accommodated him inch for inch as the masochist."

"She must have been!" I said, "Why else would she reject the help of Paul the priest, and yet accept Greythope's slimy advances. May be she had met her soul mate after all?"

"I think you have identified Natasha's dark daemon. It seems that all her actions were oriented towards her own destruction. The fragments that are left from a journal she kept, point to this aspect of her character. I will show you it later."

"What happened to the priest?"

"He did what all priests of that religion should do. On hearing the news of Natasha's death he hung himself Mr Julian. At least that is one theory..."

"Oh I see - of course! And Kindell?"

"He lived for a while. He was planning on getting a divorce, but when Natasha died he got married to another young girl who was old enough to be his daughter. In the end he drank himself to death. As for Greythorpe, he was convicted of raping a young girl on Wimbledon common. Shortly after being released he was sentenced to life for murdering and sexually assaulting another girl in her teens. As far as I know he is still doing time. But of the priest no one really knows for sure what happened to him."

"Oh I see."

We sat for some time in silence. It was late afternoon by the time Garcia had said all he was going to say, concerning Natasha's brief life.

"I will leave you now Mr Julian to your thoughts, for you will have much to think upon, I am feeling very tired, I shall lay down I think."

"Yes - yes of course Garcia."

"No don't get up. Oh, and drop by a bit later and I will show you a copy of Natasha's journal."

"Very well. I think I'll find Karen in a moment. And thank you Garcia."

Garcia bowed slightly and departed, leaving me feeling quite alone, with just - *my thoughts.*

FRAGMENTS FROM NATASHA'S JOURNAL

I had the nightmare again last night. The same thing. It starts with me running away from something, first across fields of green, its quite a nice sensation at first, even though I know something is after me. Then the ground grows bogy and then suddenly I'm stuck and the thing, whatever it is, is about to get me, and there is nothing I can do. The sky grows dark, suddenly I'm surrounded by darkness. Sometimes I'll be running through fields and then suddenly I'll be in a town and I'll be running down endless streets until I end up at a dead end. I turn round and see the blackness again, blacker than the night. At that point I wake up bathed in sweat.

Perhaps the darkness is not out there but in me. Its always been there, ever since I can remember, even when I was a little girl I would have the same bad dream and mother would come into my room after hearing my screams.

I know that one day the blackness will get me, and it won't be a dream. Even my waking life is like a nightmare.

Perhaps I am evil. Why do I do the things I do?

I've always felt hunted, but now I can really feel it. I hate it hear and yet I feel this is where I belong. My nightmares are coming true. Every morning I wake with a feeling of impending doom. No, its more like a terror. Like, 'Is this real? am I really living this life?' I feel the emptiness in me. Its like I am a shell, with nothing inside me, except blackness, a blackness that goes on and on forever.

I thought I would write my feeling down so that I could make sense of them but the reverse is true, it just makes me more aware of how lost I am. I know it can't go on like this. It will end, its just how and where.

Am I evil. Why do I do the things I do? In my heart I don't feel as though I am a bad person. I don't even enjoy the sex, well most of the time, but there is this gnawing emptiness in my guts and its the only thing that can stop it. *

* Undated extracts, probably written not long after Nataha's arrival in London.

September 2nd 1975

Steven Greythorpe came to see me. I thought he had been sent by Jon to bring me back, but he said he had come because he was concerned for me. I recognised that look in his eye, the look men get when they want it. I knew what he had come for.

He said he always thought I was the sexiest thing he had ever known, and that Jon had never appreciated me, that he would take care of me from now on. I asked him if he thought I was ugly now that I've got a scared face. He said he liked it and that I shouldn't bother with lots of make-up, which I usually do. He liked me as I was, that the scars were a 'turn on,' for him. So I got undressed in front of him there and then. It had been a long time since I had been with Steven and I had forgot how big he was - there had been so many. It was most pleasant. I could tell he liked what he saw, as did I.

As a lover he is very aggressive, it was like he wanted to kill me or something. He asked me how I got the marks on my body. I told him a guy I knew tied me up recently and did some weird stuff to me. I got the impression that Steven would liked to have done the same kind of thing, but somehow felt inhibited. I told him he could do anything he wanted to me, that there were no limits as far as I was concerned.

Afterwards we went for a drink in the country. On the way back he drove down this quiet country street. He parked his Jag and we went into the woods. He ripped the clothes off of me. He was very impatient and aggressive again. I realised that I was completely at his mercy, which scared me and turned me on at the same time. I got caught up in the madness that had come over him. Most exhilarating.

Since that first time with him I have seen him two or three times a week. I was right about the weird stuff!

He always gives me money and has bought me some expensive clothes. It means I don't have to rely on X, or any of his druggy friends - or for that matter go with any of those smelly old men - for a while at least.

October 2nd

Steven telephoned to say that he would not be able to make it this weekend. I am beginning to wonder if I will see him again. May be he didn't like me after all? I dream about him. I feel like I'm burning up inside. Its only been a week, but already I am feeling weak. I think there must be something wrong with me. Steven is everything I want. He is a bit of a brute, but I like that. He is a real man. Paul was too soft, always worrying if I was all right or not. Got another food parcel from him the other day and some money. Why does he bother, doesn't he know that it is him I need not his charity! Oh well, another donation for the Salvation Army.

Steven rang again to say that he has to go away on business for a time. He didn't know how long. I hoped he would offer to take me with him, but he didn't. I know he sees other women. I cried for hours last night.

X came round again. Wanted the usual. What could I do. He was odd, wanted to know who I had been seeing. I told him no one but he didn't believe. He called me a lying slut and hit me in the mouth and then left, only to come back again a bit later completely out of his head. He was in a state! I said he needed to see a doctor. In the end he just passed out on the bed.

Despite how violent he gets sometimes I sort of love him. At least I care about him. Is that love?

I hope Steven comes back soon so that he can take me away from all of this. X worries me a lot. The other day he beat me up again bad. Think I've got a broken rib or something - it hurts every time I breath and I cough up blood. I ache all over. And yet still I can't say no to him, how odd life is!

I woke in the early hours. The worst nightmare ever. The blackness was all around me and I couldn't find any way through. There were black tentacles around my body pulling me down.

October 7 1974

I hated it when X left the other night, but sometimes I hate it just as much when he is here. Sometimes he makes me feel so alive. He said I was the best. That he couldn't live without me. We did some drugs together, not that I enjoy it, but he likes it when I join in.

Got a call from Steven. He said he wanted to come over. Bit concerned. Said I would meet him at Waterloo. He got angry on the phone, said why did I want to meet him there. He called me a whore and hung up. In the end he came over. I was kind of spaced out and I think he could tell that there had been another man in the place. He said he had better things to do than waist his money and time on a slut like me. He hit me in the face and left. I can't blame him.

I told X not to come back. Now he is pissed with me as well, but I am sure Steven will come back tonight some time, I know he can't resist me in the end, He'll never find any one like me - non of them will....

Excerpt from the: Peckham and Dulwich Observer. October 11th

Natasha Kindell, formally Tomlonson - 22, the estranged wife of playboy and shipping Tycoon was found dead on October 9th at her London flat. Her body was found by a friend. She had been badly beaten. A Police spokesperson said that her death was being treated as suspicious.

Miss Tomlonson, who was born in Sweden came to this country after marrying the son of the late shipping magnet Keith Kindell. Her marriage to Jon Kindell was tainted by allegations of drug abuse and promiscuity, ending in an affair with a local priest.

After a lavish lifestyle the last few years of her life were spent in relative poverty. It is believed that she worked as a prostitute to supplement a dependency on drugs.

Jon Kindell said he was saddened by the news of her untimely death, describing her life as 'tragic.'

VI

I was being asked to believe this fantastic story that Karen had once been this other person, Natasha, and that even further back she had been someone called Taanach, a high priestess of Tanit, the Phoenician goddess of fecundity. It was this high priestess who had set the whole pattern for future incarnations of this most misguided of souls. I was being asked to believe that the tragic end of Taanach's life had coloured subsequent incarnations down through the mists of time: the most recent of all being Karen. And that if nothing was done to alter the pattern, Karen's life would follow the same trajectory as all the others that had gone before; culminating in a tragic end. In every life, the soul of Taanach, or her alter ego Chloe, as well as Natasha, and now Karen, had its existence in a body that was always sexually provocative. Ritual sex was at the core of Tanit worship. It was the duty of every high priestess to emulate the fecundity of her goddess by coupling with as great a number of the opposite sex as possible, especially during certain Phoenician religious rites: such as Beltane, or at the new and full moon. These occasions were marked by ecstatic outpourings of sexual licence and promiscuity, that was not always confined to the opposite sex. It was obvious that one had to have a certain licentious predisposition to become a high priestess of such a religion, based on sexual excess, and to this end Taanach had be chosen at an early age and groomed in the 'special' duties of a priestess of Tanit. As with every high priestess, Taanach was no different than any other, in that she was exceptionally beautiful and took her duties with the utmost seriousness, but non that had come before had taken them to such extremes. The celebrations of Beltane became legend under her patronage, where it was said men - and women too, would come from all over the provinces of Phoenicia to lay with Taanach. She had many names: El Nachash, for her serpent qualities, Taanach'Shaula of the scorpion's sting, Taanach'Ówlam the everlasting - high priestess of Tanit. Her sexual exploits became famed in the ancient world, throughout: Mesopotamia, Egypt, Greece, from Carthage to Etruria. The more her fame and power grew the more she became convinced of her goddess status. Taanach believed herself to be the flesh and blood incarnation of Tanit herself. It was this very licentious aspect of soul that Taanach passed on down throughout the ages to come. Such a soul as this was unable to identify itself as anything other than the body that it occupied. The soul of all these incarnations had lost its own identity; it was unable to appreciate the true nature of its own being, which was something quite different from its corporeal form. Such were the praises that had been heaped upon it over the centuries, that Karen's soul had become completely narcissistic. Her soul saw itself as an expression of the perfect female physical form. It had become so entwined with the love of itself, as this expression of existence, that it had become blind to all other possibilities. It no longer saw itself as a discrete entity: soul and body had been joined in an intimate embrace, destined to repeat forever the same dance of life; except Garcia had shown that the music of the dance was wearing thin and its time upon the stage was growing less and less, with each new incarnation.

I remember asking Karen how she had come by her professional name of Natasha. 'I don't know,' she said, 'it just came to me. It seemed perfectly natural that I should call myself by that name. I didn't have to think about it.'

It was as though Karen were giving expression to a part of herself that she had previously tried to deny. But this - other self, was too powerful to ignore or push aside. I remember too, Karen speaking of what she called her 'dark side,' and her: 'demon' that always seemed to be goading her on to new things, making her bored with people and places so easily. The same demon, no doubt, that had forced Natasha to leave the safety of her family and friends at a similary young age. The same darkness that she felt was hunting her down. Yet there remained the possibility that Karen had chosen the name 'Natasha', out of coincidence, that it was coincidence, too, that Karen had a licentious character, that had caused her to live a similar wanton existence. If that were the case, then Garcia and perhaps myself, as well as a lot of other people were completely mad. My intuition, however, told me otherwise. As eccentric as Garcia appeared to be, he also seemed a man of deep convictions as well as passion. His followers seemed to believe ardently enough in his ideas. If it was the case, that what he was saying was true, then it had astonishing implications for us all. It meant that my soul and that of Garcia's, that all human existence was bound by the same laws - that we were all destined to be born again as another person when our present existence had run its course. If it was true, it had profound implications that went far beyond the current issues of Karen's present existence. It meant that one must fundamentally rethink ones whole ideas concerning the nature of life on this planet. The idea that Garcia might be right made me shiver. It meant I no longer knew for certain who I was, since I must also have been somebody else in another life, and perhaps not all that long ago!

With this knowledge burning inside of me, I suddenly had an overwhelming need to be with Karen. I felt a tremendous new feeling of compassion for her. A desire to be with her, an urgency to express this new kind of love and understanding, I had of her. A love I had only gleaned the light of, in a partial sense, now the full brilliance of that love was clear to me, since now, I understood my role in her life. No doubt Karen had been told this already by Garcia, but I was like one of the newly converted, I must share my truth - but not with just any body, but with the one that mattered the most to me.

Imagining Karen was still resting I went straight to her room and knocked tentatively on the door. So full with the excitement of good will and love was I, that when there came no reply I went straight in. The sight I beheld left me mesmerised for several moments. Both Karen and Rachine were naked on the bed, their dark limbs entwined about each other. Suddenly I became aware of two coal-black eyes staring back at me. I mumbled something that sounded like, 'sorry' and left the scene as fast as I could. My nerves all of a jangle, I found my way to my room, and sat down on the edge of the bed. A few minutes later and there was a sound at the door. I asked who it was, Rachine let herself in.

She came over to where I was sitting. She was dressed in a red silk kimono that she had wound so tightly about her sumptuous form, that her large breasts gave the impression that they were about to burst through the delicate fabric. I looked up at her sensuous face, her black eyes tried to engage mine but I refused to look at her, keeping my gaze to the floor.

"Are you all right?" she asked.

"I had no idea!" I said, "you and Karen...."

"That we are lovers!" she gave a little laugh. "Why not! You are so naïve Julian. You need to open your mind more, I think - no?"
I heard a kind of, soft swishing sound and saw the red silk robe lying at my feet. I didn't want to look up, but some sort of automatic response took hold of me. She stood before me naked: her body, long, thin and dark. She pushed forward with her abdomen, her body arching snake-like, her heavy breasts that were much bigger than Karen's, hung an inch or so from my face. Again a strange automatic response came over me and I found my hands being drawn to her waist and her angular hips. I pulled her to me, at last fulfilling my wish to feel the resilience of her breasts, and they didn't dissapoint. It was Incredulous perhaps, to think that they could be god's work! I felt her hand on my head as she pressed me hard against them. I wanted to devour them. I had never felt such madness before, such wanton recklessness. Then some other part of my mind took hold and I thought of Karen. I found myself pushing Rachine gently away.
"What are you doing?" she said, looking somewhat bewildered.
The sight of her was too much for my eyes, I had to avert my vision. My fragile senses though, were still overwhelmed by her. I could smell the erotic scent of some type of oriental perfume on her. I focused on her robe and picked it up, a scent of the Lotus flower hit me and I was for a moment, overwhelmed.
"Please - put it on." I said, holding it out to her, my eyes shut tight.
"Do you not like what you see Monsieur?"
"That's just it. I like too much."
"You are thinking of Karen perhaps. She will not mind."
"Yes but I will. Please - put on your robe."
"Is it because you are afraid of me? You lack confidence! Karen told me."
"What did she say?" I said, loosing my patience.
"Oh - just that you were reluctant to be her lover." Rachine paused a moment, in an effort to put forward something she was obviously unsure about. "I mean if it is that you are not very big," she looked, down at herself, her gaze directed at her powerful thighs," I have much skill in these matters - you need not be ashamed..." Looking back at me with her coal-black eyes I suddenly felt her hand on me. "Hmmm....I think though this will not be a problem."
"No," I said, turning at last to face her, my hand on hers.

"You say one thing, your body another."

"No, its no good. It would be no good. Just cover yourself."

There was the same swishing sound, as Rachine petulantly put the robe about her shoulders. "Hah - you are crazy," she said.

"Look, I don't wish to offend you. You are very beautiful, and I am sure very resourceful, but its a personal thing between me and Karen. After what Garcia has told me, Karen needs me more than ever before. She needs guidance away from this sort of thing." I said, watching Rachine as she wound the silken kimono tightly about her lovely body.

"Well, it is your loss. You will never find another that can offer the kind of pleasures that I alone can give. Pleasures that you could never dream of existing."

"May be not, but I love Karen."

"*Idiota!*" blurted Rachine, her throat thick now with her own tongue. "Hah! - if you knew only half of what she is capable of - well, I then wonder Monsieur Julian, I wonder then if you would say you love her?"

"If you mean her career as a nude model: the videos - I've seen most of them. I already know what she is like."

Rachine looked at me, giving me the full impact of her obsidian eyes, now full of venom. "Who are you!" she said, derisively. "What do you know! You know nothing of the kind of person Karen is."

"I think I do. One has to have faith." I said, unconvincingly.

Rachine laughed. "Why don't you go back to America and leave Karen to her fate."

"You think I would abandon her to the likes of you..!"

"If you ask me, Garcia is wasting his time too. I have told him, her soul is *damned*."

"You don't know the kind of person she really is, only the person she has become." I said. "Preyed on by a sick society, and led astray by people such as yourself."

"Huh! How stupid - how naïve you are Monsieur. She needs no encouragement from me." Rachine laughed in my face. "You have no idea what you are dealing with - do you? You poor fool. I should pity you, perhaps?

"That's something I don't need - *your pity!*" I said, realising that I was yelling. "You perhaps can't understand this - but *I* love Karen. I would do any thing for her. She needs help." I continued, in a more even tone of voice.

Putting her nose in the air and looking at me with contempt, as if I were a tiny creature that she could squash at will. "And you think *you* are the one to help her?" she replied, derisively.

"Well someone has to guide her along the right path!"

There was another swishing sound as Rachine turned swiftly to leave. "You can try, you can try, but remember the leopard - remember the leopard and her spots Monsieur Julian."

After Rachine had gone I I laid down, and weary of the days proceedings fell into a deep sleep. It was evening when I was awoken by the presence of Karen, sitting at the end of my bed.

"Hello there," she said.

I looked at my watch and calculated that I must have slept for a good two hours. "How long have you been there?" I asked, bleary eyed.

"I don't know. May be an hour."

"An hour?"

"I wanted to look at you, as you slept."

"And how did I sleep?"

Karen shrugged her shoulders, "I d'know just asleep. Although you do grind your teeth - did you know that?"

"Yeah, so I have been told. It's due to inner stress." I said, being aware of a certain unspecified resentfulness. Perhaps from being observed.

I got up and went into the bathroom and splashed my face with some cold water. When I came back Karen was stretched out on the bed. She was wearing a beautiful green Japanese style vest that double-buttoned down the front, and cut just above the knee. Over her legs she wore blue fishnet tights. She stretched and luxuriated like a big cat. I sat on a chair opposite the bed and regarded her, as one might, a potentially dangerous animal.

"Don't you want to join me on the bed Julian?" She patted the space next to her.

"No I'm all right here, thank you," I replied, the image of Rachine still fresh in my mind.

"Oh well - " she said, half to herself. A serious expression came over her face, as she sat up and adjusted the pillow behind her head. She looked down at her self and smoothed out the creases in her silk jacket. The garment fitted her tightly about the chest, and displaying a certain level of discomfiture, she undid the top three buttons. Karen looked over at me in a seemingly unconscious manner, yet still displayed a certain sort of frankness, that seemed to say, 'well here I am! A sexually desirable woman laying on your bed, adjusting her clothing, and you do nothing!'

I got up and went back into the bathroom and poured myself a glass of water.

"Now what are you doing?" Karen called.

I promptly came back into the room and sat down again. "Water!" I said, holding out the glass to her. I took a large gulp, and prepared myself.

"I saw you," I said. "You and Rachine."

Karen looked down at her self again, straightening her top, but this time self-consciously.

"I see - " After a pause she went on, in a slightly irritated tone: "And what do you want me to say? So what! You saw me in bed with Rachine! - It doesn't mean anything."

I had to laugh at that. "You were both naked." I said.

Karen pushed her hand through her thick golden hair. "For god's sake Julian, you know me by now. You have seen me naked with men and women before!"

"They were just photos in a magazine or a film. I thought it was just an act?"

Karen laughed. "Oh, Julian you are so silly sometimes. Surely, by now you must know the kind of person I am! You've seen the videos of me. That *girl* in them *is* me - it's how I am. I am Natasha the sex goddess. I can be anything that men want me to be. You can't do those kind of things, if its not a part of you."

Karen looked away and carried on speaking, more to herself: "God knows what's wrong with me! I guess I am more like the Natasha that came before me!"

"You are *Karen* not Natasha."

"Natasha - Karen - Natasha...I don't know who I am any more." She slumped head head down, and stared up at the ceiling. I went over to her and took her hand.

"We need to find the real you. The real Karen."

Karen just looked at me, kind of vacant. "Be a sweet and get me a cigarette will you."

I sat down on the edge of the bed and looked at her as she drew heavily on it. Even the simple act of smoking a cigarette was erotic in Karen's hands.

"I suppose, I am bisexual," Karen ventured. She breathed in deeply. "Although I don't like to think of myself as anything - I'm just me. I hate labels. There are some girls that really do it for me - you know!" Karen exhaled a cloud of smoke in my direction. "Rachine is one of those girls. I like her. She's strong and sexy as hell. She has great boobs, I wish mine were like hers - they're real too! Don't you think she's sexy...?"

"She's sexy for sure." I replied, perplexed by the thought that Rachine's breasts could be a natural phenomena.

"You don't know how relieved I am to hear you say that, because if you didn't...well...! The thing is she is like me in lots of ways. I guess that's why she's here. Why she is one of - Garcia's women!"

"And are you one of Garcia's women?"

Karen took a long drag on her cigarette, and swung round to face me. "That's not important now. What you have to understand is the kind of person I am. I am a sexual creature Julian." Karen picked up the ashtray and crushed out her cigarette. "To the core - to the very core of me Julian."

There followed an uncomfortable silence. I began to fully appreciate what Karen was telling me. I started to realise that even after all the nude images and scenes I had seen of Karen, even after Garcia's exposition of the character of Natasha - still a part of me had refused to except in totality, the true nature of Karen's being, which was that ' to the core,' she was a licentious creature.

"Come on lets go down, its nearly time to eat."

"Just one thing. I think you ought to know that - well Rachine..."

"She came here - to your room..." interrupted Karen.

"Yes, how did you know? Did she tell you?"

Karen laughed. "No - I guessed...She probably saw you when you came to my room and decided to pay you a visit herself. Did you sleep with her? I wouldn't mind if you did."

"Of course not." I replied. "That would be just the kind of thing she would want,

so that she would have have something over us. I just don't trust her."
"Oh, I know you care about me," replied Karen, reaching out her hand to me, so that she could get another cigarette. "There really is no need to worry."
I shook my head. "I just don't see how you could do a thing like that, straight after what Garcia had said?"
Karen sat back in bed and gave me a hurt look. She put her finger to her mouth like a naughty little girl. "I don't know..."
"I don't mean to get mad at you. I care about you. Heck I love you Karen," I said squeezing her hand. I looked at her gorgeous face.
"*Shucks Julian* - don't!" She wiped away a tear.
I looked at her gorgeous face amazed at how innocent and vulnerable she could look at times. I wanted to tell her the rest of what Rachine had said, regarding her soul, but it was impossible.
I went over to the bed and she flopped her arms around my neck and clung to me like a rag-doll. I heard her muffled words as she spoke into my ear: "You are so sweet - mad but sweet but I'm glad you love me."
I pushed her down on to the bed and began kissing her, and started to undo her tunic, suddenly though something again stopped me from going any further. I guess Karen sensed the same thing. She flicked the hair out of her face and sat up. "Come on, let's go down, I'm famished," she said, doing up her vest. Suddenly the madness had gone. At that moment our relationship, it seemed, had lurched, yet again in another direction.
Karen put her arm in mine as we left. "Don't worry Julian, everything will come good, so long as I have you around to keep me safe."

We normally ate our meals in the large dinning hall. There would be about a dozen or so at the long table, made up of Garcia's favourite girls and right hand men. The girls were always brightly dressed in silks, the men were all clean shaven and wore the long white robe that Garcia wore, the only difference being in the colour of the belt that each man wore, in the form of a long length of chord tied around the middle. Garcia was the only one to wear a purple belt, some had blue, others green, the man who had accompanied Garcia on my first day on the island had a length of red chord tied around his waist. All this had something to do with rank I imagined. As for me, since I was a guest on his island I was allowed to wear pretty much anything I liked. I usually livened-up these formal occasions by wearing one of my bright Hawaiian shirts, together with Bermuda-shorts. Sometimes I would put on one of my dazzling Vegas winners jackets - much to Karen's chagrin.

Garcia would always reside at the head of the table. His favourite girl, like his most high ranking man would be seated closest, but we as guests usually sat only a few places away from the great man himself. He was the focal point of the proceedings, usually relating some story or other from Homer or else propounding his philosophy on life, or else that of someone like Plato, which amounted to the same thing. On this particular evening he was most conspicuous by his absence. The food was served and after the initial surprise on seeing his seat vacant, conversation disintegrated into a private affair with the person seated opposite. Servants dressed in brightly coloured tunics, both girls and boys, brought to the table each lavish dish, and wine as always was supplied in an uninterrupted flow. Gradually each person, having had their fill of food and drink, took their leave. The men bowing briefly in our direction, the girls nodding sweetly in their assent: Garcia's absence seemed to make us the focal point.

After what had transpired between us earlier, the conversation between myself and Rachine was limited. 'Perhaps she had a conscience after all?' I surmised. She excused herself and left before Karen and myself. There were only a few left now at the table. We paid our respects to those that remained, and were about to leave the hall when a young boy of about twelve, who was Greek, judging by his accent, came up to Karen and I, to inform us that Garcia wished to speak with us; we looked at each other: Karen wide eyed. The boy waited by the door so we assumed that he was also to be our guide. We followed his nimble feet through a large door situated at the far end of the villa, which lead to a wing we previously had not known the existence of, but which we were soon to discover, comprised Garcia's private quarters.

We entered a kind of inner chamber, with lots of bronze and marble statues; in the centre was a fountain around which was situated a marble seating area. The floor was sumptuously decorated with fine mosaics, depicting scenes from

Greek mythology. The boy opened another set of doors that let in the cool of the night air. He remained standing, and gestured that we go on ahead.

Garcia sat, a lonely dark figure at a table, a few feet away beneath the portico. I looked at Karen, she grinned, trying to suppress nervous laughter, and pushed me on ahead. The boy, remained some way off by the door. We must have made more noise than I realised because I saw the dark figure move and languidly raise an arm in a beckoning fashion. "Come - sit," called the figure.

I went on ahead of Karen, who for some reason, hung back. It was, I suppose, rather daunting to approach the great man in his private quarters. It had an airy atmosphere - silent but for the sound of the water from the fountain, as it plunged into the marble basin. The place was subdued, lit by oil lamps which could also be herd guttering and spluttering. The great man sat with his back to us as we approached, which I suppose made for a somewhat unusual aspect: his broad back bent over the table. When we sat down opposite him, his face darkly lit, he seemed all of his seventy plus years. He also seemed more than his usual enigmatic self. Some how aloof - brooding, as though he had been thinking about stuff an awful lot, and it seemed to way heavy. He looked at me and then to Karen, his face inscrutable.

"I must apologise for seeming mysterious, and of course for my absence at the evening meal," said Garcia, breaking the awkward silence, "it is just that I have had much to think of. Yes, much that has to be considered," he ruminated.

Garcia raised his arm and waved it a little. Seconds later the boy who had been our guide, came up to the table and poured some wine into the beakers that had been set before us; his task complete he then retreated back into the shadows. "Let us have a toast, what shall it be?" said Garcia

"How about the future?" proposed Karen.

"Yes - yes my dear, what a marvellous idea." Garcia reached over and patted Karen's hand." Yes - yes the future, trust her, trust our Karen to think of that, hey!"

Karen smiled vaguely, and then looked at me and gave me one of her 'winks'. I could tell she wanted to laugh.

"The future," we all said in unison, before taking a drink. Garcia emptied his beaker in one draught. Sure enough, before we knew it, the boy was back with the pitcher of wine, to attend to Garcia's requirements.

"But do tell me, how was the meal? was it to your liking? All of it is produced here you know, on my island."

'Here we go again.' I thought, preparing for another outburst. Garcia though was if anything, but predictable.

"It was lovely," said Karen, filling in the silence. Then wrinkling her nose in a cute way whenever she was quizzical about something: she added, "what was in one of the dishes towards the end, like rabbit, you know Julian, but smaller - tiny rabbit I thought!"

"Oh - yes, that would be dormouse," replied Garcia

"Hmmm, very good I thought - tasty, but not much of it," she replied.

"It is, of course, a delicacy."

"I thought you were a vegetarian Garcia?" I said.

"Well - you know how it is me boy, we all have our weakness', I must admit I am quite partial to lark."

"Oh - lovely," chirruped Karen, and then suddenly unable to contain herself any more, burst into fits of laughter.

I looked at Karen and thought her quite amusing, so I added, "well yes - nothing like a good bird or rodent for dinner." This had the effect I hoped it would, and propelled Karen into further hysterics.

Garcia looked on disapprovingly. "I think the Miss Karen has had too much wine," observed Garcia.

Karen quickly gained control - and fanning herself: "No - it's not that, just nervous laughter."

"I think I understand. We'll have some more wine any way," proposed Garcia.

As if by magic the boy was at my side again. "You can leave the pitcher here - be off now." The servant bowed swiftly and was gone.

"It will soon be time for my young birds to fly the nest," said the grey haired old man. He opened his wide arms and embraced both Karen and myself. When he sat back, even in the dim light we could see that there were tears in his eyes.

"Don't worry Garcia, everything will be all right," said Karen, getting up and hugging the old fellow. Looking over to me, with another 'wink', "I have Julian to protect me."

"I know - I know my dear.... I have every confidence in Mr Julian here, and I am sure that like Natasha, your heart is good."

"Any way - we can stay here, can't we Julian?"

I looked at her in surprise. "I suppose so." I said, not relishing the prospect.

"My dear..." said Garcia, "you can't hide away from life. You cannot hide from your destiny. You cannot deny what you are! But that does not mean that your fate will be the same as that of Natasha's. Now, I have told Julian most of what happened leading up to her death. Here are copies from her journal, and the newspaper clipping which reported her death." Garcia put his hand on my shoulder. "You must ignore these," he said pointing at his eyes, "these are just tears of an old man who has allowed himself the folly of sentiment."

"That is such a sad and tragic life." said Karen, after having read the journal fragments.

"Yes it is, and that is why we must not fail, or else Karen's life will have the same tragic end," said Garcia. "You need to know the facts Karen, and the point I wish to make is that the time difference between Natasha's death and your birth is not that great at all, which makes it all the more important that we do not fail this time round to push your soul onto a completely different line of destiny. One that is not so dismally fated." Looking at me, Garcia continued, "the exact date of Natasha's demise, as you might be able to discern from her journal, was 7th of October 1974. Karen was born in the early hours of October 9th 1974."

"Little more than a day later." I observed.

"Precisely! And thinking ahead to the worst possible scenario - and I know this is disturbing for you," said Garcia, stroking Karen's hand, "but I cannot guarantee that all the right circumstances will come together, as they seem to have at present, in Karen's case. The next time around.... what I mean is, if we fail this time - there may not be another...." He looked down. "Dissolution," he mumbled.

Karen let out a little gasp and shuddered. I put my arm about her, and she laid her head on my shoulder.

"I'm telling you all this because you need to be aware of just how desperate the situation is. I tried to intervene to save Natasha, but my knowledge and ability in these matters then was not as advanced as it is now. Although I was too late to

save her, I learnt much about her - in other words, much about you, my dear."
"How is it Garcia, that you know so much about Natasha? I don't get it..." I said, scratching my head.

Garcia smiled broadly.

Pointing a finger at Garcia: "Unless ? *you* were the priest!"

Garcia guffawed. "Me boy! Oh dear me, me boy..me boy." he said, banging his hand down on the table, "there is hope for you yet!" Then he looked at me seriously. "No I am afraid to disappoint you, I was not him, but wouldn't it have been an interesting piece of intrigue - but wouldn't! That is not to say, however, that I did not make his acquaintance." Garcia paused to take a drink. "I know what I have said so far must sound like a cheap novel, but please spare me that much."

"It does sound fantastic." I said.

"I think it's tragic." said Karen, leafing through Natasha's journal again, "not cheap at all. Goddamn tragic!"

"Goddamn tragic!" said Garcia, repeating Karen's words. "Perhaps one might call it, a bloody tragedy!" he said.

I realised that everyone had been skirting the issue so far, but that some one had to ask the question, and as usual it would fall to me to confront things head on. "So," I began, "how much time does Karen...do we have?" I asked.

Garcia looked at me, then towards Karen, and sighed heavily. "You must understand, I cannot say with any certainty. Natasha died when she was twenty four. Going as far back as Taanach, or Nachash, as I refer to her, for she had many names, it seems she was struck down by some sort of wasting disease brought on by her excesses, but she could not have been more than thirty when she died. Other incarnations have died between the ages of eighteen and thirty. You see, each life is unique, effected by subtle differences; these differences the soul has no real control over. This is why it is called, a souls 'destiny'," concluded Garcia. And then in a more optimistic note: "until *now* - at last, through my research it may be possible to effect a change, that will not result in Karen having to live out her life doomed to repeat the same thing again. You are still but young, barely twenty-one are you not? I caught you just in time. I can only reveal certain truths to you. It is up to you to act upon the knowledge I give you. I cannot say for certain that you will outlive Natasha and the others, it could be that my very meddling in your life may send you on a more ruinous path."

"You mean that what ever we do, she is destined to die anyway?"

"We're all going to die someday Julian," Karen pointed out.

"I know that. I meant, the way you die..."

Karen put her hand to her mouth and turned away. "Oh please don't. I don't want to die like that."

Karen laid her head on Garcia's shoulder and broke down in a flood of tears.

"I'm sorry. Me and my big mouth."

"It's all right Mr Julian. Death is a difficult subject to talk about at the best of times."

"But I don't want to die like poor Natasha. Alone in some horrible place. I don't want to become *her...*" sobbed Karen..

"Calm yourself my child," said Garcia, holding her by the shoulders and looking hard into her eyes. "You must be brave. There is no reason why you should end your days like Natasha. To begin with, you are not her." and then aside: "Although in another sense you are," continuing to address Karen: "Your life is Karen's life. It is completely different to that of Natasha's. You see that don't you?"

"Yes - yes I think so," said Karen, in a little voice. She wiped the tears from her eyes.

"Besides which, you have me and Julian on your side. Poor Natasha had no one."

"Yes," I said, going over to her. "I won't let anything happen to you."

Karen looked from Garcia to me. "You won't? Promise?"

"I promise," I said.

Karen put her finger to her mouth like a little girl. I drew her to me and kissed the side her face and her lovely neck, allowing her heady scent of Jasmine to permeate my senses, and percolate on into the depths of my mind. I knew then that I would have her in my head forever. "I'll never leave you." I whispered.

Karen clung to me tightly. She puled her head back and gave me a strange look, her lavender eyes, unusually bright and big, brimming with tears.

"I know you won't," she whispered, "and I'll never leave you either." Her eyes narrowing.

"I was getting close to Natasha," said Garcia.

We both looked over to the old man, who was now sitting at the table his hands spread open. My eyes wondered back to Karen's face. I felt distracted. Her words sounded more like a threat than a promise.

"If she had lived another year I might have been able to reach her. But everything that she did, everything that *was* Natasha, insured that would never happen," continued Garcia. "Had it been the case, then we would not be having this conversation. Karen would most probably not exist and *Natasha* would still be alive." Garcia replenished our beakers with wine. "I did manage to make contact with her lover," continued Garcia, in a matter of fact tone, "I told him my theory, that one day Natasha would come back, but he thought I was mad." Garcia chuckled to himself and I saw that familiar look of mania come in to his eyes. "When I think about the kind of people she knew. She had a knack for finding the most rotten examples of humanity you can imagine. The filthiest types, from swindling playboys, the clergy, on down to filthy dirty rotten drug addict types: the worst kind of all; who only wanted her in order to satiate their sick depraved egos. Huh! - they are not even men. Worthless scum! What she saw in him I cannot imagine."

"You mean, Mr X? I commented.

Garcia gave me a shrewd look. "Yes, and I think, for certain reasons that I won't go into, it should stay that way. Either way he was a drug addict, in other words an homunculus, and an alcoholic to boot."

"Perhaps that is how she saw herself?" I ventured.

Garcia waved his hand in a dismissive way. "Perhaps." he said, seeming unimpressed by my explanation.

Karen looked at me askance. "I'm not sure I like the sound of that, she was me you know."

"She was you and not you," I said, trying to extricate myself. "As Garcia said: each life is subtly different."

"Quite so me boy. The fundamental pattern remains the same, only the colours change. A fascination with sex and dangerous men is indicative of her character, but the circumstances are never exactly the same, or else Karen would have lived exactly the same kind of life as Natasha, but Karen was born

on the other side of the Atlantic, and at a different time."
"Well I can't help being what I am!" said Karen, frustrated.
"No one is blaming you - Garcia and I are here to help."
"I know", Karen replied, laying her head again, briefly on my shoulder.
"I think our Miss Karen has been very brave, do you not Mr Julian? *That* is one of her souls more finer qualities."
"I agree," I replied.

Garcia looked serious again. "I brought you both here tonight because there is still so much you do not know, and yet the time for you to go from here, is close at hand. It is perhaps a little too complicated to go into in detail, but it is important that certain astrological alignments are taken advantage of, but do not worry, everything begins and ends at exactly the right moment. There is no set date for you to leave, no wave to catch that will send you safely up against some distant shore; all will transpire as and when it should, but a helpful nudge is sometimes appropriate."
"I think we understand Garcia, we don't want to out stay our welcome." I said.
"Oh, but I so love it here. I feel safe here," said Karen. "I know you are bored though."
"Well, I am a bit," I confessed.
"You know of course, that when it was confirmed that Natasha was dead I went to that other lover, who was really no better than the drug addict she was hanging out with in Peckham..."
"You mean the priest." I interjected.
"Quite so. I went to him and I told him more or less what I had told her boyfriend: that one day Natasha will return, and that when she does she will try to get in contact with him. He being a priest of *that* religion had a bit more of an understanding of these things, and I feel that it is half possible he took me serious, although like most of his kind, he would have had a misconception of what it means to be 'resurrected'; so it is possible he might not have understood after all. With hindsight I should have never have gone to him at all, but there were things that were not known to me then. Now tell me Karen, and this is most important, has a priest of that fowl religion ever contacted you or, have you heard of one trying to get in contact with you - say perhaps, through a friend?"

"Well not being particularly religious, I mean come on: *in my line of work* - hardly likely!"

"Think carefully Karen," cautioned Garcia.

Karen shook her head. "*Nope* - don't think so. Over the last few years I have met so many different people."

"Are you sure? It is very important you remember. It could have been just a casual acquaintance. Someone of a spiritual nature, apart from myself. Have they for instance approached any of your friends? Anyone at all?"

"Well now let me think," said Karen, resting her chin lightly upon her forefinger. "Well - now I think of it, several months back I remember Rachine went to Scotland on some photo shoot or other, and when she came back she said she had met some interesting people, including some middle aged guy who was into religion in a big way - Christian I think. He ran some sort of commune."

Garcia nodded, and looked at me gravely. "Scotland is not that far away," he said.

"I was supposed to go with her, but I can't remember now why I didn't; something else came up."

"Are you sure you don't know..?" prompted Garcia.

"But of course! it was *you!* - it was your fashion parade. That was how we met!"

Garcia just smiled broadly.

"Do you think it means anything? do you think it was him?" I said.

"Fate me boy," he said, slapping my back. "Let's drink; we are ahead of the game."

We drank plenty. Garcia seemed less perplexed but still very edgy. It had obviously been a close run thing, which meant that it had probably less to do with fate that Karen had not gone to Scotland, and more to do with Garcia's shepherding of Karen's life. Then again, the way Garcia described it, whatever way you looked at it, it was all down to fate in the end.

"Have you told Julian about the others?" piped-up Karen, all of a sudden. "Did you know for instance that I was tried and found guilty of witchcraft, not once mind, but on three different occasions - I mean lives; did you know I lived in the court of Rome, as the emperor Caligula's play thing, and because of jealousy I was murdered by his sister Julia. To think I have been all these people and many many more besides. Garcia took me back through hypnosis, and I felt all the things that they - or rather, I felt; just as real and as clear as I see you. Some of it was very painful."

"Past life regression," said Garcia. "I'll do you one day, if you like."

"No thank you Garcia, I would be afraid of what you might discover. I might be the reincarnation of Hitler or Ivan the Terrible, knowing my luck."

"I doubt that very much me boy. I would not wish to conjecture the fate of a soul such as theirs. But yes, Miss Karen's soul has had a remarkable existence. Natasha, and now Karen, are the last links in a chain that stretches back more than two thousand years."

"To look at me you wouldn't think I was that old, would you!" said Karen.

I looked into her grey eyes, there was something about them at times that seemed to confess the age of her soul. There was something very uncanny about the way she sometimes looked at one. Was her soul crying out for it all to stop? So tired, so weary of the game!

Now though, there was something mischievous in her look. She undid her kimono a bit further so that it revealed part of her bosom, and the black lace bra she had on. Perhaps the wine had made her horny or something, because she slid her hand inside her top and began to touch herself; with her other hand she reached down and lay it on my thigh. She was like a wild creature really, that one has tried unsuccessfully to tame. It needed to be fed plenty and often, but in its domesticated state it could never get the right kind of feed. She had come to my room, but I had been unable or, unwilling to give her what she really came for, and now she had a gnawing hunger, as keen as Natasha's, that required satiating. For a time her advances blocked out my senses, suddenly I became aware of Garcia talking - seemingly oblivious to her behaviour. Perhaps he had seen it all before?

"And so," Garcia concluded, " for simply living as a recluse, and being attractive to men, she was taken by a delegation lead by the clergy, striped naked, beaten, and then bound to a steak and burnt as a witch.

"To think, they did that to me!" said Karen, "but it wasn't exactly like that was it? on one occasion it was much worse. Not satisfied with simply burning me, they had to ensure that I experienced every once of pain. That was how sadistic they were."

"What did they do?" I said, wondering what could possibly be worse.

"They bound my naked body with wet rags where my vital organs were, and wound a wet cloth around my head too. That way, lived long enough to see my skin seared by the flames, to feel most of my body burn to the very bone. Do you know what it is like to wish with all your heart to die, and yet not be able to!"

Karen ran her fingers through her thick hair and then curled her hand into a tight little fist and banged it hard down on the table. "*Bastards!* - How dare they do that to me!" Turning to me, her eyes fierce on me. I hardly recognised her. She ran her hand over her body groping her big breasts: "Can you believe they did that to me? To me!" she said, writhing around as if the flames were at her feet again.

"No," I said. I took her hand and she put it beneath her kimono, sliding it up her thigh. Her sin was smoother than the finest silk; silkier smooth even, than the material that was used to make her beautiful green kimono.

"That particular regression was a very traumatic experience for all concerned," explained Garcia, "but in so doing, by bringing these memories to the fore, it lessens the hold fate has over Karen's soul. It is little wonder, carrying around such pain and trauma, that when Karen first came to me she described herself as: 'living in a daze, and thought of herself as 'evil'."

"To think that people are capable of doing such things? To spoil something that is so perfect as you." I said, whilst my hand remained under her expert tutelage. I allowed her to take me where she wilt, moving upward over the contour of her thigh. I felt my fingers negotiate the meagre little undergarment she had on.

"And that was done by Christian's," said Garcia, the mania beginning to flare up again in his eyes. "I hate them for what they did to this child. I hate them," he repeated, banging furiously on the table with his big fist.

Karen suddenly straightened herself, her back stiffening. She sighed heavily and looked at me a second, as if pleased and shocked at the same time, then she gave me the wink. I could feel the intense heat of her body. She gasped, and I felt the pressure of her thighs on my wrist.

Karen looked at Garcia, her eyes wild looking, her pupils madly dilated.

"I never did anything to them - did I Garcia?" she said, in a little voice.
"Of course you didn't my dear, it is simply you are not of them, you are better than them, and if you are not for them, then in their eyes you are against them. It is the same today. There is little tolerance to be found in this world for those that think deeply, for those that are special. I curse their narrow mindedness, the way they pick on any body that is different from them; their lack of appreciation for the beauty that exists in the world. It goes deeper than just inflicting pain on others, they have marred the mind of mankind with shame and guilt and self loathing, for all that is natural in man. Now there is only cold efficiency and the worship of money; they cannot accept that there might be a middle ground. Sensitive souls just get squashed. This world undervalues passionate souls and lovers of beauty - but mark this," said Garcia, holding up a judgmental forefinger, "they ignore us at their own peril, for what will be left for *them* when they have turned the whole world into a rotting sewer full of filth, fit only for vermin?"
"So, if they - the powers that be, saw that your ideas were catching on..." I said.
"Why - they would not think twice about invading this island, of arresting me, of *disappearing* me," interjected Garcia, "like Karen's poor soul in that other life, although we harm no one, they do not trust those that seek a different path. They label what they do not understand as communist or subversive. They are ignorant and lack any compassion. The culprit is organised religion: Christian Muslim, Hindu, even Buddhist's, call them what you like, they only teach man one thing, and that is to destroy anything or, anyone that cannot be understood by them, or that cannot be appropriated by them. "Garcia paused a moment: "That is why I have asked you here, to be on your guard when you leave my protection, especially for this priest who knew Natasha."
"Why yes, he would be middle aged by now, if he is still alive," remarked Karen.
"And there is every reason to suppose he is."
"Julian will keep me safe - I know it."
I looked at her and she leaned towards me and whispered words of a carnal nature in my ear. Her lascivious movements were becoming more desperate, more overt. The pressure of Karen's thighs was such that it felt as though my wrist and metacarpals would break.

Garcia looked over at Karen. Some invisible signal seemed to stream between the two of them.

"My beautiful child - your perfect body, your skin without blemish of any kind. My child - my beautiful child." lamented Garcia, his hands aloft and shaking. "They must not win again."

Karen stretched her hand across the table and Garcia took it in his big fist. The three of us were connected, Garcia and I through the fulcrum of Karen.

"Don't worry Garcia, they won't get me again," intoned Karen.

"That's my girl. What a girl - hey! Mr Julian."

Her kimono had fallen open from her earlier groping and writhing. The old man was staring at her lovely orbs as they nestled in her bra, and Karen seemed not to care. She looked down at them with pride, and then back to Garcia and gave *him* the wink. Then she turned to me, her face flushed, and brought my hand up to her lips.

"I think our Miss Karen is trying to tell us something. I talk too much in any case," said Garcia. "Go in peace my children and heed well my words of warning."

"We will," I replied.

"Come on," said Karen, already standing and tugging at my arm, "Lets go back to my room. I want you..." she said, between clenched teeth.

Garcia hailed the servant and he came to escort us back to the main part of the villa.

"You go on ahead Karen, I just want a quick word with Garcia.."

Karen lingered a moment. "All right, but don't be long, I'll be waiting in my room for you."

I went back to the table where Garcia still sat. He looked up in slight surprise, and filled my beaker with what was left of the wine. "What is it, Mr Julian?

"There is something that I think you should know."

"Indeed ?"

"It concerns Rachine. When you asked Karen if she knew of anyone who had come into contact with the priest, and she said Rachine had met such a person..."

"Your point Mr Julian."

"Well I know for a fact that Rachine despises you, and thinks that Karen's soul is damned, that we are all wasting our time trying to save her."

Garcia chuckled. "I'm ahead of you. I understand your concerns. Miss Rachine is a very outspoken young person. I am aware of her scepticism concerning my beliefs, but it is good to have people such as her around, also she is highly attractive - would you not agree?"

"That's another thing! " I paused, embarrassed by what had happened. "Earlier this evening she came to my room. She wanted to have sex with me."

Garcia laughed. "Oh that Rachine, she is a mischievous little creature. But tell me, me boy, did you? Not an opportunity to miss, I can tell you. Of all my girls she is probably the best. She could even show the Miss Karen a thing or two I don't doubt!"

I shook my head in disbelief. "But did you know I saw her in bed with Karen earlier?"

Garcia rose to his feet, leaned forward and pattered me on the back. "Don't let it worry you me boy. You have to let her enjoy herself. I thought you *knew* her nature by now? But fear not, I am well aware of the risk Rachine represents. If I have her here, in my sights, what can she do?"

"But what if she alerts the priest?"

"Let me worry about that. Now come with me, there is something I want to show you. It might even help you understand Karen a bit better. I am sure you will find it quite revelatory."

I followed Garcia through his sumptuous rooms through a maze of corridors, which finally lead to the atrium, and the library. Sitting outside on an ornately styled couch was Garcia's favourite, the nymph Alisiya. She raised her elfin face as Garcia bent to receive a kiss from her. He spoke to her in Italian; she smiled, and obediently waited outside the library.

"It seems all our women must wait for us tonight Mr Julian. I'll try not to keep you long, but I am sure what you will see will explain much concerning Karen's temperament, and remove any doubts you may still have of her origins. Garcia puled down a large volume from one of the shelves. It was a fairly modern book full of photographs of classical Greek and Roman sculpture. Finally he came to the page he was looking for. "Here," he said, spinning the book round so that I may look at it. There were three photographs of the same sculpture but viewed from three different angles, one from above, and one from either side. It was the sculpture of a young girl laying on her front, so that from above, all one could see was her lovely shaped back and behind. The idea of the sculpture seemed to be one of shock; for me it was to be doubly so - to see the face of Karen on a sculpture that was over two thousand years old.

The idea was that the viewer of the three-dimensional object would see the face of a very beautiful girl, appreciate her well formed feminine body, and then walk round to appreciate her from the other side, only to be confronted with the fact that she was not a she, but an hermaphrodite; and as hermaphrodites go, one that was as well endowed in terms of female beauty, as it was in its singular male quality.

The male organ that grew from her loins, hung limply at her side; in human scale it would have been nearly twenty centimetres in length, and perhaps as much as six centimetres thick. The face of the girl was captured as she slept. She seemed like any other beautiful girl, quite natural, although the position of her limbs and the tangled bedding around her feet, suggested that it had been a somewhat troubled sleep.

Beneath the larger of the two photographs, the one giving the view from above, read the caption: 'Hermaphrodite. From an original bronze, probably attributed to Polycles. This example from the Borghese collection, restored by Bernini in the sixteenth century.'

"But Karen, isn't an hermaphrodite, "I said. "I would know a thing like that, I mean look how big she is."

"How big, *it* is!" corrected Garcia. "In the hermaphrodite, exists the third species: one that had not been cleaved in two, still united in it's male and female aspect...but Mr Julian! - you look quite pale, sit down a moment."

"It's her! It is Karen. But without the huge male organ. Could there have possibly been such a person - a thing, as that?"

"Yes it's possible, but the girl may have been just a model. We may never know. In any case, I am sure you have not encountered such a thing with the Karen of today!"

"No," I replied, "I think I would have noticed."

Garcia slapped me on the back and roared with laughter: "Ha! Ha!..ah-ha-ha-

ha-ha-ha! Ha-ha-ha-ha! My, but you are a wit Julian me boy....Ah,ha-ha-ha-ha!"
"Has Karen seen it?"
"Oh yes! It was the first bit of evidence I presented her with. It was when we were in Rome. I took her to see her in the flesh, so to speak."
"What was her reaction?"
"Surprisingly, she was not totally convinced of the likeness. However she most certainly was impressed by the hermaphrodite's male proportions. She thought it quite right, that as an hermaphrodite she should be one of the most imposing of her kind."
"That's Karen all over." I put in.
"Now, we must not keep our women waiting any longer. I'm sure you can hardly contain yourself? My word, what a night you'll have with Karen! What a girl she is!"
I found myself lingering. The sight of the hermaphrodite with its huge male appendage distinctly unsettled me, adding to the concern I already had in that direction.
"About that." I said.
"Yes - yes me boy, what is it? What's on your mind?"
"You know how Karen is! How experienced she is in matters of sex!"
"Yes!"
"Well I'm not sure I can live up to her expectations, if you know what I mean?"
"Come now! What is all this?" said Garcia, knitting his brow. "Why, you're a man aren't you? Hey! hey!" he smiled, and slapped me hard on the back, knocking me nearly off my feet.
"Well yes, but..."
"Give it to her, me boy," he interrupted. "I'm sure you won't disappoint the miss Karen? I'm sure you have what it takes....?" He looked at me sceptically. "By the gods! I hope I haven't misjudged you? I take it you do like women?"
"Oh yes, I find Karen incredibly attractive."
Garcia put his hand on his heart. "Thank goodness for that. For a second there I thought I had misjudged you completely. Even if the Greeks did indulge in homosexual activity, I take a dim view of it myself."
"I don't think you need worry about that on my score." I replied.

"Well! What's the problem? Give her what she wants."

"That's just it. I tried once, back in the states; for some reason it didn't work out. I see her more as a friend. I guess, I think she is too good for me! She needs a real man."

Garcia shook his head. "I'm sorry I don't understand. You're a man! What can be the problem? Give it to her. It's what she wants. There's nothing complicated about it. It's the most natural thing in the world."

"You'd think so wouldn't you," I replied, realising that talking to a man like Garcia about such concerns, was a waste of time.

"I'm sure it will work out," I said, making to leave.

Garcia put his hand on my shoulder. "Not so fast, young Julian." He was smiling broadly, like he had just seen the joke. "You don't have to be a great lover Julian, to satisfy a girl like Karen. She will show *you* what to do. Just go with the flow...." He looked hard into my eyes and glanced down again to *that* place. My face burned. I wanted to hide away.

I felt the weight of the big man's arm about my shoulder. He spoke in a conspiratorial tone: "Look, I know that not all men are the same, they are not all endowed the same. A pity though - a girl like Karen..." he mused. "A girl like Karen...well she grows accustomed to a certain type of man. You get my drift? She will just have to make do - that's all." He chuckled to himself.."Ahh-ha err ha-ha! It must seem a bit daunting for you me boy, a girl like that. But you'll soon get use to it. You'll find she is very resourceful - very resourceful indeed." The big man stood back, as one admiring his handy-work. "And if she starts to complain, come to me, and I will have a word or two in her ear. No..no, it's all right me boy, we will keep it just between us," he said, giving me another pat on the back. "Just between us - ne! - but you are the man, you are the man, no matter what your deficiencies may be in certain areas, you are the man for her."

I looked at Garcia, speechless as he went on: "You just lack confidence...it's understandable, but pretty soon you'll be having the time of your life! - Now come, we must get back to our women, and the nocturnal proceedings."

He kept his big arm about me in a fatherly fashion as we strolled down the corridors of his villa, all the time imparting advice as to the best way to please a woman. In conclusion he said: "You know Julian, I like you, the only trouble is you worry too much."

VII

On my way back to my room I almost literally stumbled into Rachine. She smiled at me fiendishly.

"Sorry," I said, trying to be pleasant. Momentarily distracted by the sway of her hips as she went by, I failed to ask her what she was doing so close to my room, when her rooms were on the other side of the villa.

"Aren't you going to ask me where I've been Julian," she called.

"Where have you been then?"

Rachine laughed. "I've been enjoying Karen's company - what else!. You know, you really shouldn't keep a girl like Karen waiting."

I walked over to her, unsure of what I was going to say or do. "Why don't you just go away - leave us alone!"

"I would but its her. She just can't get enough." Rachine looked me up and down. "If you ask me, I doubt you have what it takes to keep a girl like Karen happy. I doubt you are any *blady guood,"* she said, her accent showing through.

I clenched my fists, I would have loved to wipe the smirk permanently off her sexy face.

"You're goddamn sick." I said, and walked off before she could goad me any more.

"We'll see then, shall we, I *know what she is,* remember that!" called Rachine, as she swayed arrogantly away.

I stood outside my door a moment to gather myself. I already felt highly discombobulated after what had occurred in the library, without bumping into Rachine. Just as I was about to enter, Karen opened the door. She had on just a flimsy silk blouse, mostly unbuttoned, and a pair of skimpy black knickers.

"So there you are! Where the hell have you been? "

"I just saw Rachine."

"Oh yes, she just popped by," replied Karen nonchalantly.

"Yeah I bet." I said, under my breath pushing past Karen. I went to the bathroom to freshen up, when I came back Karen was laying on the bed. She looked so

sexy lying there, and yet still somehow, I couldn't bring myself to touch her.
"So what did you see Garcia about?"
"I talked to him about Rachine," I said. "I don't trust her one bit."
"Oh, you mean that thing about the priest that Garcia was going on about." Karen waved her arm dismissively. "Don't worry, I asked her myself and she assures me that it was nothing. She didn't even remember until I reminded her. She said he was one of these born again Christian types who had tried to get her into bed - you know their sort. Anyway, Rachine hates anything to do with religion, so they had nothing much in common. So you see there's nothing to worry about."
Karen stretched out her hand to me. " Now, come on silly we're wasting time. I want you."
I resisted the temptation to take it, instead I just watched her as she writhed and twisted her long body like a snake. She thrust out with her strong legs and lifted her back off the bed.
"Come on Julian! don't you want me?"
"Are you sure it's a good idea? You know how it was last time!" I said, and then repeating to myself: '*no blady guood,*' the way Rachine had said it.
"It'll be different now, you'll be great, you'll see! - I mean how can you not, with me?"
'That is just the problem,' I thought to myself. 'You're too darn good.' And then there was the image of the hermaphrodite. There was something about it that I found extremely disconcerting: Karen the hermaphrodite, the embodiment of the perfect female form, combined with the potency of the *alpha male*, whose aspect hung limply across its thigh, at least twenty centimetres long. The effect: startling, shocking, provocative in every sense.
The face of a beautiful girl, with her eyes closed, dreaming fitfully of whatever hermaphrodites dream of, remained oblivious to all the looks of shock and cries of outrage that had rung out down through the ages. This seeming unconcern, only seemed to add to the overall shock-effect of the subject. The image of which had impinged itself on my deep unconscious. I found Karen's sexuality intimidating as a normal female, now it was doubly so. I was unable to go any further with her, until I confessed to her, what I had seen.

"Garcia showed me a photograph of a sculpture." I said..
"Oh!"
"Yes, he said it was of you: 'The hermaphrodite.' "
Karen suddenly burst into laughter. "Really..! You didn't believe him - did you? What did he say? Did he say I was an hermaphrodite?"
"No, he implied you may have been."
Karen shook her head. "So he still has that crazy idea! He was convinced that I had been an hermaphrodite." Karen had another good old laugh: "Ahh! ha-ha-ha-ha-ha-ha! Ahh! ha-ha-ha-ha-ha Ha! ah Ha-ha-ha-ha!" Her laughter gurgled on in her throat, gradually bubbling away.
"I'm sorry," she said, dabbing her eyes. "It's just your face. You looked so serious."
"But it *was* you! Your face!"
"He tried to convince me of the same. He took me to see the real thing, not long after I met him. He tried to convince me that it was a two thousand year old sculpture of me!....I suppose there is a certain resemblance. She has a good body like mine, but that's as far as the similarity goes." Karen laughed again, looking at me. "It is big though, isn't it!" she said, proudly. Her hand wandered down to her groin, perhaps in her mind she was looking for that missing part.
"Did you think it was a good likeness - I mean the face?"
"I thought it *was* you. The body, the face!.."
"Julian, you're as bad as Garcia, always jumping to conclusions. But if I was her - I mean the hermaphrodite, I would be like that. One of the best. The best female aspects, combined with the best male aspect. But who knows, may be you really think I am? Perhaps you should check, and find out for sure?"
Karen thrust her pelvis upwards further, and in one quick movement ripped off the tiny garment that covered her there. Although I had seen lots of shots of her nude, nothing prepared me for the real thing. She was so much more vital, so much more animate and voluminous in the flesh.
"You're perfect." I said.
"I know I am," she replied.
And it was true, god had set the bench mark higher, when it came to Karen's physiology.

"You see, no surprises there," she said, before going on to have another good old laugh, but I felt it was less spontaneous, and more at my own expense.

"You *are* a big girl, Karen!" I said, looking down on the spectacle.

My words, pulled her up-short. She eyed me sharply, her hand going down defensively, to cover her prodigious *Venus mons.*

"I know. It's what Garcia said. It amazes them all..."

'So Garcia has been there,' I thought. I suddenly wondered about all the others that had been there. Those - *other* men, those *big* men. All those that had been there before me! How would I compare with them? I felt myself physically shrinking away from her.

"What is it? What's wrong? What's wrong with you? Don't you like me? Come on Julian!" She spread her hands over herself in self adoration, flexing her sinewy frame like a snake. There was a lot of the *snake* about Karen.

"What's wrong? Is it Garcia? If it is you don't have to worry about him? It's you that I want - you Julian. It's always been you."

'Always you, always been you,' she continued to moan. I tried to think of her as a normal girl, but the image of the hermaphrodite kept coming into my mind. I did not want to fail her again, so I did what the colossi suggested: I closed my eyes and let Karen take control. Quickly I found myself melting into her. The cloven beast was cloven no more. The only question that continued to nag away was: 'was I enough for he?' When I opened my eyes, the look on her face was that of someone in a trance - a state of wild stupefaction, and yet the doubt remained.

Karen stretched luxuriously. "Hmm - that was good Julian. You see, there is nothing wrong with you. *Nothing at all.* You know you are very lucky. Men have given much to be with me."

I sat on the edge of the bed and looked over at her. Her body glistened slightly with sweat, reminding me even more of a serpent. She was absently stroking her body. I thought how vain she was. How in love she was with herself. There was something about her actions, her lasciviousness, that excluded me. I could only look and *marvel.*

I went to the refrigerator and poured myself a small glass of beer and lite a cigarette, and stood and looked at her.

Come here. I want you," she said.

"Give me a second." I replied.

"Is there anything wrong?"

"Its just something Garcia said."

Karen sat up in bed, and puled the sheets about her in a token gesture of modesty. "Oh yes!" She looked over at me, derisively. "Give me one." She held out her hand.

I leaned over and put a cigarette in her mouth and lite it for her. Karen drew heavily on on it. Everything she did was in some sense provocative. "Well what did he say?" she said, with an air of exasperation.

"Its just this whole reincarnation thing. You know - Natasha?"

"What about her?"

"Just, the kind of person she was. The life she lead! You see, sometimes when I look at you, it strikes me, that you're not a whole lot different from her?"

"Well thanks a lot Julian!" Karen looked askance.

"You know what I mean."

Karen stubbed out the cigarette. "I don't know," she said, pausing to look at me long and hard. "You know what I've been Julian. What my life was like. May be we're not that different - Natasha, and I! If you don't like what you see, you don't have to stick around."

"I do," I replied, lamely.

Karen eyed me with derision. I put my drink down and came and sat down next to her on the bed. I tried to put my arm around her but she shrugged it off.

"I don't.. I don't know what to believe?" I stammered. " The whole thing, is just crazy. I'm so sorry Karen." I pushed my hand, through my hair in frustration, "I don't know what to believe any more?" I repeated, to myself.

Karen turned away from me and groaned. I put my hand on her shoulder and asked if she was all right. When she looked at me there were tears in her eyes.

"Look Julian, you mustn't believe everything Garcia comes out with. Its like that stuff about me being this statue, and the whole hermaphrodite thing! Sometimes I think he is quite mad."

"Don't you at least believe you are the reincarnation of Natasha?"

Karen wiped her eyes. "Who knows? What does it matter? We're all going to die some day." Karen shrugged her shoulders. "If I am her, then I don't remember that much about her, except what Garcia helped me to remember. But whose to say it's not just part of a fertile imagination? All I'm saying Julian is try to keep an open mind. If I believed everything he said, I would be a nervous reck, too afraid to do anything. That's how it has got me, at times. I think we *should* leave the island, and soon."

I was relieved to hear Karen say that she wanted to leave, but confused about everything else. She rolled over on her side, her breasts pushed against one another. Her abdomen twisted like a snake, accentuating her broad hips and narrow waist. I marvelled at the spectacle of her. Although I had seen lots of shots of her nude, nothing could have ever prepared me for the sight and smell of her, in the living palpitating flesh. I put my beer down and went to her. I touched the firmness of her body. Her greasy skin was taught over her spare frame. Bareribbed, barebreasted: her body was hard to the touch, even her breasts were stiff, heavily laden as they were, her skin distended, by copious amounts of silicon.

"They're perfect." I said, as I traced the circumference of her stupendous orbs.

She looked down at herself appreciatively. "Aren't they, though! Do you think I'm better than Rachine?"

"Of course you are. You are the best."

"I am, aren't I! - but aren't I the best! Tell me again, tell me how good I am." Thrashing her head from side to side: "Tell me I am the best, better than all of them." she said, in a kind of delirium.

And so I told what she wanted to hear: 'that she was the best,' and she was, quite probably right. She went kind of crazy, clawing at herself, leaving long red weals. I grabbed hold of her hands and pined her down, I had the feeling it was what she wanted me to do. I felt she had the strength in her, to push me away if she wanted. She was breathing hard, her body flexing all the time. Her muscular diaphragm expanding and contracting rapidly with every deep breath. Her big thigh muscles tense and expectant, every nerve ending sizzling, her whole being was, 'switched on': this was Karen at her quintessence. I could feel her strong heart hammering in her chest, distending her veins and arteries; the big vein in her neck stood proud - fit to burst. I was caught up in the madness by now, descending with her, deeper and deeper into her wanton madness. "Take me, take me Julian..." she cried. I didn't need to be asked again.

As for Garcia, perhaps he was just a 'silly old fool!' At least that's what I had hoped, but I knew that in reality he was anything but a fool. He held both men and women in his power. He was a Svengali type character. A manipulator of minds. I looked over at Karen as she lay in momentary repose. I knew it had ended too soon for her. Now, a man like Garcia, *he* would have satisfied her. He had what it took to please a girl like Karen. He was one of those, 'big' men, one of those men women cannot resist.

"What do you think of Garcia?" I said, in as casual a manner, as I could muster.

Karen groaned. "Oh I don't know." She absently felt out my hand. "Darling I told you, you have nothing to worry about on that score."

"I know. I'm just curious what you think of him - as a man?"

"Well now, let me see, as a man he is a *wise* man, a *good* man, a *sincere* man. A man of passion. He believes strongly in things."

"He's good looking, don't you think? I mean for a man of his age. He must be in his seventies at least?"

"Yes I suppose he is." Karen turned on her side and propped up her beautiful head with her hand and stared at me. "What is this Julian? What is going on in there?" she said, tapping my skull. "You want to know if I find him sexually attractive?"

"Well do you?"

"I suppose there is a certain something that a woman would find attractive about him." Karen slithered along side me. "But he is nothing compared with you."

I had to laugh at that.

"I'm serious Julian. How many times do I have to...."

"You mean it?" I said.

"Darn toot'n!"

She lowered her head to perform exsuflation. "Marvellous," were her words when she had finished.

Karen looked on listlessly, as I persisted in my exsusitated state. "You see - not that bad...." she said languidly.

How vain we men are when a woman compliments us on our sexual prowess. It It is as though we have a selective memory when it comes to such matters. If Karen had said I was the best lover in the world, I would have denied all that my instincts told me.

I thought of Garcia again, and pushed her hand away. She looked up at me like a scolded child, that didn't quite understand what it had done wrong.

"So, have you slept with him?" I said.

"Of course. Look at your face! You wanted to know. Would you rather I lied to you?"

"No!"

"And you think I'm vain! Worrying all the time about how you compare with other men.

"Its not that."

Then what?"

I looked at her. Suddenly an impulse filled me that made me want to kill her. She was too good.

"I love you, goddamn it. The thought of you with another man...."

Karen sighed, and pulled the covers round herself.

"Julian...for god's sake!..." Tentatively she reached out her arm and let it fall. I picked up her slender hand a pressed to my lips.

"Oh Julian!..." she touched my face. "Please don't."

A look of annoyance, of frustration, momentarily passed over her face. She looked away and sighed: "yes I've been with him. It wasn't while we were here on the island. I would never do that."

"Why not?" I said, assuming that it was because she did not want to hurt my feelings."

"It would be wrong. I would be going against his plans. No - he wouldn't like that at all. You see, Garcia has it all worked out. So long as I am with you, I will be safe - for the time being at least... No, he was most adamant: 'I must not be seduced by men like him.' You see, before I met up with Garcia I was going out of control. I was spiralling away from all that was good. I was spiralling away from you. Away from what was safe. I have the potential to turn my life around. To get away from the kind of life I was living."

Karen sat up in bed. She looked at me in a rather forlorn way. "You don't understand, do you? You will. Be patient with me Julian - please try to have faith in me - and in him."

Her words sounded good, but still left me perplexed. "What do you mean, when you say, 'men such as him?' "

"You know Julian. Do I have to spell it out?"

I would have been happy to leave the matter there, but the truth was the damage had already been done.

"Don't think about it any more darling...I am with you now, isn't that all that matters? We are together again, isn't that great?" said Karen, hugging my arm. Live for the now, - this very moment."

Karen threw back the covers exposing her nakedness. "Forget Garcia, forget everything, it's you that I want. Don't you want *this!"*

She kicked out with her strong limbs, luxuriating once more in her sexual prowess. "Doesn't my body drive you wild Julian? Oh - do what you want to me. Ravish me. I'm yours for the taking."

If only it could have been that simple. If only I could have given Karen what she wanted. She began to slither and writhe around in contorted voluptuousness, luxuriating in her own voluptuousness, caressing herself, pleasuring herself with her long hands and bony fingers. She breathed in deeply exposing her muscular diaphragm, and finally Karen stretched her long body and threw her arms above her head. "Aghhh - I'm just too much, too much..," she moaned.

I looked at her in amazement; partly enthralled by the spectacle, partly repulsed. I kind of felt superfluous: a voyeur. She was a purely wanton creature, completely absorbed in her own licentiousness. I became vaguely aware of the fact that there was something about her which disgusted me. What was more, I felt disgusted with myself for allowing her to dominate my life with her sex. I looked again at her greasy glistening skin, her bony frame always visible just below the surface, there was something unnatural about her, something putrid - corpselike even.

"Well," she said, "what are you waiting for. Enter me, enter the goddess." She opened her legs and raised her knees, expectant of the coming *potency.*

I did my best to fill the emptiness she said she felt inside, but I knew that *my* potency would never be enough for a girl like Karen. She clung to me, pressing her hard bony frame against me, holding me with all her great internal energy, but it was all to no avail. I looked at her face. Her eyes were tightly shut, in concentration and excogitation. I almost felt sorry for her, knowing that no matter how hard she strained, she would never find me enough. She opened her eyes, and caught me observing her, for I felt myself more and more spectator rather than participator. And the look she gave me, I think indicated that she knew it too. It was the look of mild surprise mixed with incredulity, that seemed to say: 'what the hell is wrong with you?' or, 'what the hell do you think you are doing?'

At that moment we both knew the game was up, and I felt the great power of her loins relax a little. I felt relieved. I no longer had to try to play the part.

What she needed was a man, not a guardian, or a nursemaid. What she needed was a proper lover, someone from her own league.

I continued to struggle to satisfy the cravings she had, much as a motor response than from any conscious effort; put it down to the twitching nerves of some poor dying creature. Millions of years of evolution, geared to the survival of the species is a hard thing to deny, even for someone like myself. And as I carried on in my reluctance to give up my share in the human race, and continue to challenge what all my senses told me, was a futile effort, I suddenly became aware that it was now Karen that had become the spectator. I no longer moved her at all.

Free of her body, as I lay next to her, I realised with such perfect clarity that sexually we were incompatible. What she needed was someone like Garcia. Then it occurred, 'no she didn't need someone *like* Garcia, what she needed was the man himself. He was everything that I was not. Wise in judgement, strong in character, and of course, with little doubt, the perfect lover.'

I remember seeing him come out of the sea naked one morning, after preying to the sun god. 'There was a real man' I thought, 'just like one of those Greek gods that he worshipped.' He was completely unashamed - unashamed of his *manliness.* 'Now a man like that...' I thought. Karen of course already knew the delights such a being could bestow, upon a young girl such as herself. He was getting on in years it was true, but he still had good muscle tone, broad shoulders and colossal limbs - a colossi in every regard. 'What must it be like', I mused, 'to posses such potency? Why, one must feel almost like a god, that one could do anything - then again it was all just flesh and blood - in the end, and he had more of it than me, a lot more come to think of it.' One had to respect Karen in this regard, to look to me for satisfaction after knowing a man like Garcia.

Karen sighed and relaxed by my side. I stared up at the ceiling, aware of her eyes on me. She did her best, we both did our best, to appear content with one another, the image of Garcia's manly form though, would linger on for some time to come. Henceforth, relations of this kind between Karen and myself would remain a tentative affair, and not the explosive coming together that a girl like Karen took for granted.

'You know the kind of man, do I have to spell it out?' She had spelt it out, or rather I had written it for her. Life it seems is comprised of two types of creature. Those that eat cake, and those that are the meat eaters. Garcia was like her. She was like that beautiful cat of the plains; that perfect hunter, the cheetah. She even resembled one in her rackish form. Her abdomen curved inward towards her hips. Garcia was like a big old male lion, and his pride were the women on *his* island. When the fancy took him he would service them at will. He, like the lion, was lord and master of all he surveyed.

We were awoken early by the sound of a horn.

*

"What the hell is that!" I said.

Karen yawned and stretched like a big cat. "Oh! I forgot to tell you. That would be to announce the day of the festival. Perhaps our last chance to get in touch with the old gods, before we leave."

Karen got out of bed and stretched again, totally unselfconscious of her nakedness. She went to the window and looked out, and waved at somebody below.

"Hi there, hi there, lovely day for the festival." Turning to me: "What do you know

Rachine up and about already! It's all to do with Garcia's idea to re-establish the religion of Core and Persephone. Should be fun - what do you think?" she said, jumping on the bed like a playful kitten.

"Sounds interesting." I replied, taking hold of her hand. I puled her towards me and kissed her, but when I tried to hold her round the waist I sensed a certain resistance in her body.

"I need a shower," she said.

"Everything is OK, isn't it? I mean last night!..."

Karen looked at me as if in surprise. "Yes, I thought so! Didn't you?"

"I just wondered - I mean so long as you still don't think Garcia could give you more? keep you satisfied I mean."

"Please don't go on about it any more," she said, and turning on me with a fierce look : "its you that I want. How many times do I have to say it?"

In one swift movement she whipped round and straddled me with her thighs, thrusting her abdomen forward ostentatiously. She took hold of my hand and put it to her lips and kissed it, then looked at it for some time - as though it were some sort of strange animal.

"Are you all right?" I said. She seemed to be in a daze.

"There are more important things than being a good lover Julian."

"Such as?"

"To have a good soul. You keep me safe Julian. You keep me alive and that is more important than anything else - and when this is all over, " she said, getting off the bed and trailing me with her into the shower, "you and I can forget all about Garcia, and have a happy life together."

The invigorating and cooling sensation of the shower, brought us back to life. I watched in a kind of rapture, as the thousands of tiny water droplets bounced and ran like beads, off of her smooth brown skin.

"Massage me, will you," she said, handing me a bottle of heavily scented oil.

As always, Karen took the opportunity to luxuriate in the adoration of her flesh.

"You know Julian," she said, getting out of the shower and wrapping herself in a dressing-gown, "you really must try to relax more, I'm just a girl you know."

"You're not *just* a girl," I said, looking at her sleek golden form. "You are very special. To think that anybody would want to mar such beauty as yours!" I said, shaking my head: "No - there is something very unique and special about you."

I often wondered who it was I was exactly referring to, when I said such things: Karen? Natasha? Chloe? or, perhaps that poor witch, that was so horribly tortured and then burned.

"Do you have any memories of those terrible things that were done to you in your past life - lives?"

"Of course. Do you remember when you first met me? I said I was evil. That I was a witch. I used to have such terrible nightmares. My folks thought I was going mad, they even sent me to a shrink for a while," said Karen, as she got dressed.

"Tell me about her. What was she like?" I asked.

I sat on the bed with a towel around me watching her attentively.

"You love looking at me don't you? I sometimes think all you're good for is looking. It can be very perplexing you know!"

"I'm sorry," I said.

Karen smiled at me strangely. "That's all right my dear."

"You were going to tell me about one of your lives - as a witch."

"Are you sure you want to know? I'm not sure I want to remember!"

"Tell me. I want to understand - what it's like to be you. To have all those memories."

"Well, let me see. She was a *shy* girl, a *quiet* girl, a *wild* girl. Independent of nature. She liked to live life on her terms, the witch that is. Sounds a bit like me doesn't it! *That's because she was me...*"yelled Karen. "Now where was I? Oh yes, the witch. Yes - well she lived all alone in a wood, in a tiny house. She was really quite innocent, but just because she kept herself to herself, the village people thought there was something wrong about her - something strange." Karen let out a sardonic laugh. "They couldn't accept her. Oh no, not them, with their *small dirty little minds.*" Karen picked up her hair brush and began running it through her hair aggressively, and then banged it down. "And just because men would sometimes be seen to visit her..."

"So she was a prostitute?" I interrupted.

"That's just like you to think that! It couldn't be, that she just enjoyed the company of men? No, it has to be something else with you. You have to sully it, don't you!"

"I'm sorry," I replied, "I don't know why I said that."

"She was an innocent Julian. I should know I was her - am her, as you well know. The bastards," shouted Karen, wheeling round on me. "They tortured me. That old hag from the village. She put her stinking fingers over me. That filthy hag! How dare she touch me! how dare they!...."

"What! - what is it you want?" said Karen, in a strange child like voice, putting her hands to her head and moving them through her thick hair. " *No...no...I said no..no get off of me.. get off.... how dare you touch me like that! how dare you!"* Karen yelled, frantically waving her arms around. *"Get off I say, touching like that...!"* then for a moment she seemed to return to herself with a shock; her eyes grew even larger as she focused on me.

"There you are, leering at me again! What it is you want? Is it this?" she said, touching herself. "Is it that you want to have me? Is that all you want? But you don't even want that. All you can do is look and dissect my body and my mind with your eyes and you endless questioning."

She came at me with her fists. Her body all akimbo, brown limbs flaying madly like windmills. I managed to push her away,

"Karen, calm down." I said.

Her reply "Hi'eee'yah!.." as she came somersaulting through the air. Her feet caught me on the chine sending me to the whirling marble floor. When I came too, I was alone in my room, with a lump on the back of my head the size of a golf ball. I sloshed my face with cold water and went down to look for Karen. I found Garcia directing building work that was going on in the new Forum. I asked him if he had seen her? He immediately picked up on the fact something was wrong, and I told him what had happened.

"It's all right me boy," he said, "I'm sure it's not your fault."

He examined the bump on my head and lead me to a marble slab that was used as a seating-area, under a big spreading larch. One of his men came over and gave me some water; then Rachine rushed over, asking excitedly what was wrong? Garcia raised his arms to indicate the need for calm.

"It seems the Miss Karen has need of some time alone," he explained.

"I saw her about ten minutes ago," uttered Rachine, "I called to her but she ran off like something wild was after her."

"Which way did she go?" I said, getting to my feet.
"That way," said Rachine, pointing to a track that led away from the villa complex, and starting off in that direction herself.
"It's all right," said Garcia, putting his hand on my arm, when I was about to follow her. "It's all right! she will be all right. Leave her a moment, I think I know where she has gone."
"Don't you think we should go after her?" I said.
"Yes, she might need help," put in Rachine.
"Let us try to be calm," said Garcia, motioning downwards with the palms of his hands. "Now, let us all sit a while. Let me explain. It is important that you understand - you as well Miss Rachine, as you are her friend," then aside: "Despite what your opinions of me, or for that matter Karen, may be." Continuing to address us both: "It is important for you to understand that, all I have said concerning the Miss Karen is true. That in the course of exploring her past lives it has awakened some very powerful emotional memories. Her soul, is a soul that is in torment. It is very difficult therefore, for her - the entity we all know and love as *Karen*, to deal with all these feelings. It is as though she were living countless lives in one life - at least, that is, when the memories come flooding back to her of who she has been. It is as though a great tidal force has been set free, as in a damn breaking if you will," said Garcia. Turning to me and patting my shoulder: "Now Mr Julian, you must not blame yourself." Chuckling to himself, he went on, "I...I can only imagine the two of you..and what..and what you must have got up to. My word me boy. What with Karen's highly sensual nature and your own insecurities! it must have thrown up all kinds of stuff...!"

I was about to intercede when he raised his arm. "No - no, don't think I don't know how it is with you two. When it comes to people, if there is one thing I pride myself on, is a juge of human character. When it comes to human nature I am as astute as an old buzzard. I can tell the measure of a man in an instant," continued Garcia, and possibly detecting my discomfort: "But we won't go into your insecurities here - not in front of the Miss Rachine, anyway."

I glanced over at her and saw that she was desperately trying to keep the grin off her face.
"The thing is not to blame yourself. If anyone is to blame it is I, for reawakening these memories in the first place."

"Why did you? Why not let sleeping dogs lie?" said Rachine.

"Sleeping dogs indeed," reiterated Garcia, hitting his thigh in irritation. "But I had to, don't you see! I had to in order for Karen to face her true nature, and come to terms with the person she is. When one can understand the nature of ones own soul, one can begin to take control of ones life, instead of reeling from one disaster after another, not having a clue why things keep on happening the way they do. To know ones own soul, is to take control of ones destiny. 'know thyself,' as Socrates said. The corner stone in effect of all philosophy. Anyway, that was the purpose of taking Karen through past life regression. The down side is that for a soul such as hers, it brings out a lot of unruly emotions, which you yourself Mr Julian have been unfortunate in witnessing."

"This is not the first time she has behaved like this, is it?" I said.

"No - sad to say it is not. She has been unpredictable a couple of times running off, since she has been on the island; but nothing compared with how she was when I first met her in Italy, and brought her to my villa in Tuscany. In those early stages it was mighty traumatic." Garcia shook his head. "Yes, mighty traumatic indeed. There were times when I wondered if I was doing the right thing by attempting to integrate her present self with her past selves. You see, it is not a question of skipping the bad lives and focusing only on the good memories."

"You mean she *had* good lives?" put in Rachine.

"Oh yes, quite so. It's not all bad - even for a soul such as Karen's. In fact where she has run off to, for I have a good notion as to where we will find her, she has put herself in surroundings that give her a sense of security and fond memories. The thing to remember is that past life regression, of the type I use, is a process of confronting our bad memories which are like blocks, barriers that have to be got through, otherwise we remain stuck. But the soul usually knows where to go, and so, in a way - *it* decides when it is ready to take a deeper look at a particular past life experience."

"The witch" I said.

"Indeed so. Probably the worst experience she has had to endure. Imagine - if you can, to be tortured, raped and then slowly roasted alive."

"She was yelling something about an old hag, she kept saying 'how dare you,' and, 'get off me, get off me you old hag...."

"Ah, yes indeed, that would be the woman who denounced her. A bitter old woman, bitter and twisted through jealousy; in her day probably quite plane or ugly looking, someone no man would want. She would have singled out Karen, or, as she was then, Mirium, because of her great beauty. She would have come with the priest, and perhaps other men and women of the village, descended on her humble dwelling in the wood. There they striped her naked much to the delight of the men and the old hag, then red hot needles would be poked into Mirium's flesh. If a place was found where she felt no pain, then it was deemed the site where the devil had entered in. After much pain and humiliation, you can probably guess that sooner or later, either naturally or by some insidious contrivance, such a place was eventually found. Indeed they must have covered her body with thousands of scalding pricks, after a while you wouldn't know where the pain was coming from."

"They did this to her?" said Rachine incredulously.

"Indeed they did, and much worse, and all in the compassionate name of Jesus Christ the Lord. Christian liars, all of them," spat Garcia.

"Yes but they were simpletons. They didn't really know what they were doing," observed Rachine.

"No, indeed that is very much the case," conceded Garcia, "and I doubt very much Jesus would have approved. So much suffering has been perpetrated under his name. Its about time we let that poor soul rest in peace and forget his name for ever, at least in associating it with war and suffering. It's Christianity I hate, not the man behind it. The suffering of millions in the name of faith, any faith cannot be justified - not ever!" regaining some of his former composure Garcia continued:

"This fate did not just befall Mirium alone, but countless young girls and older women were held up as witches and sadistically tortured before being executed, and very often their only crime had been their quiet aloof nature, combined with a special innocence and beauty. Their souls were sensitive souls, their only crime an empathy with nature, and a suspicion of the works of mankind and his places."

"I suppose if one were deranged with pain and fear one would confess to anything," I said.
"What is more, it would have been an ordeal that would seem to have never come to an end. After the humiliation of being stabbed with needles, by being groped by men and ugly women, and then probably raped and tortured with hot pokers, you would then be taken out and shackled to a post and dampened rags bound around your chest and head, in order to keep you alive and maintain some level of consciousness, as your body is consumed by fire. In effect - to be slowly roasted alive. Can you imagine what it must be like?" said Garcia, with a certain level of misappropriate relish, "the searing pain, the agonies of hell: wishing for it to stop, to come to an end, to die, bound helpless - I wonder if you can?" continued Garcia, in the same blood lust tone.
"Do you mind Garcia, not putting it quite so graphically," complained Rachine. "People aren't that despicable!" she added.
"Are they not? It never ceases to amaze me the things people are capable of! But its quite simple if you think about it; all one has to do is imagine what constitutes ones greatest fear. We are all human beings, and therefore are fully aware of just how fragile a thing the human body really is, how vulnerable we are. We therefore have the capacity to inflict the worst kinds of tortures, because we know how vulnerable we are to pain. Therefore those that inflict it upon others are the worst kinds of cowards and hypocrites, for it only takes one or two others to point the finger at them. Therefore nobody is beyond suffering, therefore, one should not perpetrate it in the first place. Our capacity for love, and kindness is unfortunately matched by out capacity to inflict pain and suffering, what is even more tragic, is that more often than not in this world, it is love and kindness that is the hardest thing to find.
I looked at Garcia. When he spoke like this he wasn't the mad man, or eccentric at all, but a very wise and deep thinking man, with almost the air of a prophet, or great and wise leader.
"At least though, you see now why this memory above all others is so painful, and one of the hardest for Karen to assimilate."
"Put like that - the poor creature!" I said, " How stupid of me, I should never have asked her about it."

"Don't blame yourself, you were not to know the effect it would have on her."
"Probably Karen didn't know herself!" said Rachine, "speaking of which, don't you think we should go and look for her?" she added.
"Yes, perhaps *now* we should find her. I have a good idea where she will be," said Garcia, getting to his feet.

Rachine and I followed him down the path that Karen had been seen to take, leading to open country. The broad flag-stone path became just a narrow track after about twenty yards. To our right was a small hill populated with olive groves. We left the track we were on and followed another that lead towards the hill. As we pushed on further, one track became two, then three, soon countless deep little furrows in the hill sprang up everywhere. Somehow, Garcia knew which path to take. In the distance could be heard the clanking of bells, and then the scampering of hoofed feet. Out of the corner of my eye I caught a glimpse of the creature that was responsible for the many interlaced tracks. First one goat and then two and then suddenly dozens appeared all around us, the sound of their clanking bells filling the air. I looked up ahead to Garcia, he was like a goat himself, undaunted by the climb, he tackled the rocky outcrops seemingly effortlessly. I looked round to check on Rachine, she was following a little distance behind. I took a brief rest bite and looked on ahead toward the disappearing figure of Garcia. It was then that I first heard it. My skin suddenly ran cold, a strange uncanny feeling came over me, as the sound of Panpipes came floating through the tranquil air. It was as if I had heard those notes thousands of years before in exactly this spot. I seemed to know this place in association with the goats and the sound of the pipes. The melody and the sound was as if distilled from another more pure, more innocent age.

Rachine was nearly level with me now. I gave her a hand up a particularly steep outcrop.
"Thanks. Its quite a climb. Where is the old man?"
"Up ahead somewhere, not far I don't think," I replied.
"I wish he had told me that I would have to climb a mountain," complained Rachine.

For a fit looking creature, Rachine was breathing quite hard. "Can you hear that?" she said.

"Yes I know - Panpipes." I said.

I got goose-bumps at the sound of them. If the truth was to be told, I had waited for Rachine because I was glad of her company. We tackled the last few metres of the climb together, all the time the sound of the Panpipes grew louder and the goats more bold.

"Ooow - goddamn," cried Rachine.

"What is it?"

"I just stubbed my damn toe on a rock," Rachine sat down to inspect her foot.

"Are you OK?"

"Yeah, I guess. Its bleeding a bit, and what are you looking at?" she said, addressing a particularly bold goat that had wandered up to have a look.

"They are such lovely creatures," I said.

"They're ugly. Go away," she said, waving her arms about. The creature just looked at her before galloping up the rocky incline, sending down a mini avalanche in its wake.

"They're quite harmless things," I said, offering Rachine my hand.

We tracked our way slowly along an increasingly tortuous and rock strewn path, and behind the branches of an Olive tree I caught a glimpse of Garcia sitting on a rocky bluff.

"There they are," I called to Rachine. I went on ahead where there was a kind of clearing and the Olive trees grew less dense. I waved at Garcia and he waved back.

"What took you so long?" he said.

I sat down next to him on a spur of flat stone, and caught my breath. Garcia produced a beaker of water from somewhere and I drank greedily.

"Rachine hurt her foot."

"Not serious I hope?"

"No, here she is now."

Rachine almost collapsed next to me on the natural seat of stone.

"Give me some of that." she said, taking the beaker from me. "If I knew it was a mountain that I had to climb I would have brought some sensible shoes."

"Well these goats seem to manage without shoes." I said. Rachine just looked at me, and then poured the remainder of water on her foot. "So where is she? we've come all this way."

"Yes Garcia," I said, "where is Karen?"

Suddenly the sound of the Panpipes piped up again, this time very close by. Out of the olive grove came a young boy playing the pipes, with about a dozen goats following in a train behind him. The moment he saw us he stopped playing and hurried over to where we sat. He bowed rather stiffly to all of us. "Kalymera - kalymera." spoke the youth, before tuning to address Garcia.

"Ni," replied Garcia, then turning to me he said," he knows where Karen is, you will find her with her flock..."

"Her flock!" I replied.

"Just go with the boy, he will show you the way," said Garcia, in a slightly irritated tone of voice.

I rose and followed the nimble youth with his ever present charge, along a rock strewn ledge. Fortunately we were already virtually at the top of the small mountain so there was no more major climbing to be done.

"Feelenada - feelenada," repeated the youth smiling broadly.

I smiled at him bemused not having a clue what he was saying. Fortunately he struck up some notes on the Pipes of Pan and my spirits lifted. After only a short time he stopped and put his hand to his ear, and smiled at me. "To ganika - feelinada."

"Yes I hear it." I said, detecting the reedy notes of a flute, carrying on the air. Their sound gave me the same chilled feeling I had had, when I first heard the Panpipes. It was as if the further I came with the boy, the further back in time I went. I felt myself to be completely remote from all that I had known. I put myself in the charge of the boy, I was no more than one of his goats. I followed him faithfully on toward the sound of the flute.

The boy did not play the Pipes again. "Ganika, to ganika, poly kalos boskee, poly kalos boskas." he said, excitedly.

"Hey you there!"

I looked up to locate where the voice had come from, standing above me, on a ledge was Karen, her strong legs apart, a double stemmed flute-like instrument in her hand. I followed the boy up some steps that had been cut into the rock face, soon I was standing on flat level ground with Karen.

"He says I am a good shepherd girl, and this is good land for shepherds.

A large number of goats and sheep busied around Karen, their infernal bleating and the clanking of their bells came from all around.

"So this is your flock is it?" I said.

She wore a white loosely fitting cotton blouse and a simple white cotton skirt. I thought she looked every inch the shepherdess.

Karen laughed, "you don't have to talk as if I am mad you know. Of course they're not mine."

In this guise there seemed to be an air of reserve about her, as if she were beyond Earthly cares, and therefore in some sense inviolate. She seemed a different girl, pure and self-contained; by comparison I felt grubby and full of troubles, but Karen, here in this setting, was a thousand times more free and light of being. A light breeze blew up and lifted the hem of her skirt, momentarily revealing the strong tanned thighs beneath the light material. She moved to avoid it happening again and I thought of the Karen of old, the licentious being. In her modesty this Karen was quite a new phenomena.

"Come with me," she said, holding out her hand for me to take. I went with her to some ruins of a Greek Temple. We sat down together upon a two and a half thousand year old column, that had at some point in history been upturned and vandalised, along with the rest of the ancient sacred site.

The boy waved at us and smiled, before disappearing down the path we had come. Nearly all the goats followed him, only a few sheep remained behind, seemingly loyal to Karen.

It was in that tranquil place, suspended in time, that Karen told me the story of one of her more happier lives, spent in the land of Arcadia on the mainland of the Peloponnesse, where she had been a shepherdess. A life that was so far remote in time, neither she nor Garcia, knew exactly when it took place, only that it had been a long, long time ago.

"Never had I known such a warm feeling as that, when Garcia took me back to Arcadia, and my life there as a shepherdess. I felt so warm there, so safe with that memory, and I have always had an affinity with the innocence of such creatures as sheep and goats and remote hill top places such as this." Karen paused a moment, looking uncomfortable as she played with the hem of her skirt. "I'm sorry if a I frightened you Julian, or said anything to upset you. You know I didn't mean it. It is just that those terrible memories of the witch trials are hard to live down. All I wanted to do was escape - escape back to another life, a much happier and safer existence."

"And so you came here?"

"Yes - I ran away once before when Garcia made me remember again my suffering's at the hands of those terrible people. I just ran, until I was in the country, and then I heard the sound of the goats, and immediately I knew where I belonged. Acastos, the boy who lead you here, was very kind to me. I stayed up here for two days. Nothing happened between us. I slept here in this ruined temple. Acastos has a small hut he stays in on the other side of the hill."

"I never knew you could play the flute?"

"Oh - this thing. I never was musical, until Garcia took me back to one of my past lives where I entertained at the palace of Caligula. In fact, most of my more memorable lives were spent in the Rome and Greece of old; although being murdered by Caligula's mad sister Julia, wasn't very nice. One day Garcia gave me this instrument, and suddenly I just seemed to know how to play it. I found out other things about myself too, in that I seem to be able to understand most of what someone says in Greek or Italian. I say most, because the language has changed a lot since the time I spoke it as my native tongue. I'm also darn good with these here critters."

"I'm sure you are." I said, and we both laughed.

I still felt as though this were another Karen, not the fresh Karen I was use to. It was disconcerting to see her not make some sort of display of sexual power.

"Weren't you frightened staying here all alone and at night?" I said, looking around at the jumble of fallen masonry, that had once been a perfection of symmetrical design.

"Not in the least. I felt at home here. I felt close to all the people I had been. This was once a sacred site. Garcia would say that I was in the best place, protected by the goddess Hestia, who it is thought, this temple was in honour of. Even though it is in ruins now, don't you feel her presence here? Don't you feel her calming influence all around?"

Karen got to her feet and looked about in wonderment, as if she could see the goddess herself approaching. Suddenly a warm rush of air embraced us.

"Can't you feel her still! She *is* here, I *know it*. Oh blessed goddess, blessed art thou."

Suddenly an even stronger gust descended, stirring the dust of thousands of years. I felt not a little spooked, if not only by the uncanny feeling one got from the ancient site, but also from Karen's abandoned sense of new found faith in the goddess.

She sank to her knees, "Oh blessed One, protect me from myself, oh gracious and divine goddess," Karen chanted.

I got up and went over to her and put my hand on her shoulder and asked her if she was well. She nodded before slowly getting to her feet. A little unsteadily she made it back to where we had been sitting, but not before another smaller gust of warm air eddied and swirled around us, and then departed as quickly as it had come.

"*She was here*. I know she was. I felt her presence. Didn't you?"

"I felt something," I said.

"Did you! Did you really? You're not just saying that?"

"Well, it was rather strange I thought, how that wind suddenly got up."

Karen looked at me wide eyed, her face flushed and animated. She put her hand on my arm, "Yes - yes wasn't it!" she said, excitedly. "It was her. It had to be!" she added, with firm conviction. "And look at all my sheep, so startled they, ran away," said Karen going over to the skittish creatures. "Come - come," she called. Karen made a soft sound with her shepherdess' voice. "eoo - eoo," she sighed, which seemed to give them confidence enough to approach her.

"Perhaps they were afraid they might be sacrificed." I said.

"Ah - don't be cruel, we wouldn't do that to you, now would we," said Karen, making a fuss of the boldest in the flock, but it too became nervous when I joined her.

"But isn't that what they use to do?"

"May be so, but don't let them here." she said, taking a side long glance at the sheep.

Turning to take another look at the ruined temple, "who was the goddess that was worshipped here?" I said.

Karen came and stood by my side. "Hestia. She was the most demure and sweetest of all the gods. She was renowned for her purity." Karen said, and looking at me severely: "she was renowned for her chastity. Unlike some goddesses I could mention - she was never seduced."

One could almost see the clouds of confusion role in over Karen's face, as the memory of who she was in this life began once again to assert its dominance. One can only live a dream for so long, and Karen's Arcadia was beginning to evaporate before her eyes.

She turned away from the temple. "Come on, lets find Acastos. We should be getting back," said Karen.

"Yes the others will be wondering where we are."

"Others!"

"I came with Garcia and Rachine."

"Oh it will be good to see them. It's the day of the festival too. Oh I do hope Garcia is not angry with me, he must have so much to do?" said Karen, clinging to my arm as we went along the ridge.

"I 'm sure he will understand."

"I am *very* sorry Julian for *everything,*" said Karen, in a child like voice.

"Please, don't think any more about it," I replied.

"Did I hurt you? But I must have!" she said, touching my head.

"Let's just say, you don't know your own strength."

When we got to the flat rock, only Garcia was there. As soon as Karen saw him she rushed over to him. "I am so sorry Garcia." she said, tearfully, as they hugged one another.

"It is all right my child, you know what I told you, that these things will happen. The pull of Arcadia and Hestia will always come to your rescue."

"But it's the day of the festival - and everything! Where is Rachine?"

"It is all in hand - do not fret my dear, come let us go," said the great man, putting his arm about us both. "I sent the boy on ahead in order to escort Rachine, she was complaining so much about her bloody foot, and the state of her shoes, that I thought it best she go back."

We had to go single file down the more precipitous parts of the hill, then I held Karen's hand in mine. Often she clung to me, and all the time I could feel transmitted through her skin, the Karen of the modern age, her sure-footed shepherdess' skills, together with her innocence, was diminishing the further we went down the hill. Finally when we were at the bottom she hugged me to her violently. I looked up towards the summit and prayed in vain to Hestia, that Karen's innocence be restored.

VIII

It was the day of the festival of Demeter and Persephone, known in ancient times as the Eleusinian Mysteries, and was for many a year the most popular religious cult of it's day, even more popular than Christianity - as Garcia was only too ready to remind everybody. Basically, a pastoral celebration, where certain individuals are initiated into the sacred rites of the goddess. Not that Karen and I would be, as we had decided to leave the island for the outside world. No, the initiates were the devotees of Garcia's new faith.

As we had been up on the mountain for most of the morning, by the time we returned to Garcia's villa complex, a transformation had taken place. The villa and temple, as well as the nearly completed Forum, were all decked with garlands of flowers and bundles of wheat. Sweet smelling incense thronged the air, and pretty girls were everywhere, dressed in brightly coloured robes, as too were the men. It seemed that on this *special* day they were aloud to dispense with their more mundane white robes. Garcia himself was dressed most regally in a fine purple robe with a crimson sash about his waist and a purple and gold veil over his head and shoulders. Brightly coloured flags fluted in the soothing breeze: reds, yellows, orange, green, and purple flags, not the colours of any nation, but those of natures own beauty and special independence.

Karen seemed to have made a full recovery. She was dressed most stunningly all in orange, in a wonderful iridescent satin gown that fluttered and shimmered in the breeze. She clung to me, she skipped and laughed and danced to the music. Later, Rachine and I got her to play the flute, and for a time, in the forum she was the centre of attraction; the most divine beautiful creature that had ever been set upon the earth, or so it seemed. It was as though my shepherdess had come among the people at last; and I felt sure that Hestia too was smiling, even though the festival was not in her honour. And amongst the thrall of people that were there crowding to see her dance and play, was the young shepherd boy, who had somehow found the time to steal himself away from his flocks. He too was dressed in fine yellow robes, and to everybody's amazement he struck up in accompaniment on the Panpipes, and a great roar went up among the crowd of honest pagans there. For him and for me, and certainly Garcia, we had for a while our shepherdess back. He played the pipes of Pan, and I heard again that sound which haunted my soul and made me quiver inside. He did not join in with the dancing, he remained aloof, his presence felt by the sound of the Panpipes alone. Gradually, we felt their vibrations recede into the distance, we did not see Acastos leave.

Karen danced and swayed her broad hips; she wove and undulated her snake-like body to the ancient sound of pipe and reed. When she spotted me among the crowd, who had gradually pushed me to the fore, she cast her flute aside for someone else to play, and puled me after her centre stage, where she did a special dance of her own - just for me. I was soon drawn into the ferment and I swayed with her, my hands on her hips, and touching her about her slender waist. She was mortal again, flesh and blood, such hot and passionate blood, the cooling influence of Hestia had gone, given over to merrymaking and lust, and bawdy freshness - which I was told, was all part of the tradition and all meant in good humour. If there was one thing that was precluded on this day of days was sadness and tears, for to exhibit such emotions openly was to be disrespectful, by challenging the grief of Demeter herself, who sorrowed for the loss of her daughter Core; who had been abducted by Hades and taken to his abode in the underworld. This was not to say that the celebrations did not have a serious side. The initiation into the sacred rites themselves was a very solemn and life changing affair; not something that one entered into lightly or, that one took for granted. The initiate had to be *ready*, and prepared in their soul, before their name could be offered up to the Pontiff Maximus for initiation. This of course, ruled out Karen being nominated any time in the near future, although according to Garcia, Karen had once been a high priestess herself, but not to this particular goddess. It was something he had promised to talk to us about: the crucial moment that set Karen's soul upon its weary way of death and rebirth.

The Eleusinian Mysteries centred around the worship of Demeter and Core - Persephone. It was to be the focal point of Garcia's attempt to reintroduce paganism back to the Greeks, and eventually the world at large. Originally the

Mysteries went on for nine consecutive days held in September and October, but Garcia wanted to introduce them as soon as possible, so the festival took place in August, rather than wait for the autumn equinox; on that day he had something even bigger planned.

Much of what exists in terms of ritual in the Christian church came directly from the Eleusinian mysteries, such as baptism - the washing away of sin and the putting on of new robes, 'the new robes of righteousness.' The Christians took other motifs, such as wine and cakes, yet other symbolism was solely the domain of the worship of the goddess: pomegranates, baskets of corn, carded wool, sesame seeds and poppies, fig branches, and fennel stalks, ivy leaves, salt, cakes and wine; such was the bounteous tribute that was laid at her feet in the portico of the Temple. Two iconic figures of Demeter and Core were carved out of wood and painted by craftsmen on the island. As each person came up to the goddess to place their tribute, be it more cakes or wine, or just bunches of brightly coloured flowers to garland her hair, the crowd sang out, 'hail Ceres, cheers to Demeter Core and Persephone, long live the Mysteries.'

There was much drinking of wine, and song and dance, eventually though, towards late afternoon a change of expectation and a certain amount of tension began to fill the air, and the singing and dancing died down. Honest pagans began to move towards the temple and the carved statues became their focal point. Karen Rachine and myself hung back from the proceedings, we felt it was not our place to be among Garcia's true followers of the faith at this time. We saw the torch lite procession leave from the forum: Garcia's top men, about a dozen of them walking two abreast carrying torches, in the middle of them, somewhere was Garcia, the Pontiff Maximus, occasionally one caught a glimpse of his purple head gear. We heard a cheer go up as the crowd parted to let their leader through.

We all looked at each other, we knew we wouldn't be able to resist going in for a closer look.

"Come on," said Rachine, "we can't miss it! lets see what the old man is up to, it will be exciting."

"Yes I know, but its all very sacred." I said.

"Come on Julian, it will be fun, don't you want to hear what he has to say?" said Karen.

The truth was I was as excited to see the event as as either Karen or Rachine , so it didn't take much for me to be persuaded.

"Behold our sacred lady." boomed Garcia's voice, "behold the gifts of the *kistophoroi*, our tribute to you our supernal goddess of pomegranates and the ripe ear, products of our toil and the fruits of the earth, that without you could not come forth. We honour you this day, the inauguration and return of the sacred rites begun so long ago at Eleusis."
"We honour you." spoke the voice of the crowd. "Hail Demeter and Persephone."
Two older women then brought forth a large earthenware pot which was placed in front of the Pontiff on a tripod.
"Behold, I have feasted I have drunk the *kykeon*. I have reached into the big basket, I have consumed the tambourine, I have drunk in the the cymbal. I have penetrated beyond the veil."
He placed his hands into the pot, and the crowd let out a strange sigh.
"What was it? Did you see?" asked Rachine.
Non of us saw what he brought out of the large pot, but it evidently impressed those that witnessed the event.
The two older women returned to take away the large amphora, there then followed a great cheer from the crowd and we could just make out his favourite girl, Alisiya, the elfin featured one, climb the steps of the Temple escorted by the Magna Marta. The girl was dressed in a long white satin robe, her only adornment a single orchid placed in her raven hair. Her companion was dressed in a purple kimono, her dark hair bedecked by garlands of coloured flowers. Garcia stood aside for the two women when they stood upon the stage of the portico. The Magna Marta and the young girl stood face to face.
Garcia raised both arms out to the women. "Behold, behold Baubo and Demeter, so as it was then, distraught and weary from her search, so as it is now, Demeter, Core and Baubo, the Goddess in triad."
The older woman then untied Alisiya's robe so that she was exposed to her. "Demeter is most pleased by the sight. She shall receive the draught most gratified is she by what she sees."

The woman then presented the young girls nakedness to the crowd.
"Behold this body, and the three in the one. Although Demeter was saddened still from the loss of her daughter Core, what was revealed made her smile."

We did not see what she did as the older woman stood in such a way as to block everyone's view, but I was sure I saw the glint of a blade in her hand, and sinking to her knees before the girl, "and from the glancing cup she did drink."

The old Magna Marta then stood up and showed her blood stained hands to the crowd. I couldn't see the young girl at first, then I noticed that she was on her knees her head bent over. Garcia, went over to her and helped her to her feet. I was shocked to see that the lower half of her white robe was heavily stained with blood, and she seemed to be grimacing with pain. If the girl made any sound at all it was lost in another loud cry from the crowd, and people nodded to one another seemingly impressed by the pantomime.

"Epopteia." cried Garcia.

"Epopteia..epopteia," echoed the crowd, and I looked at Karen, who mouthed the words too, '*epopteia*.'

"What does that mean?" I said.

"Look!" said Karen.

We watched as the young girl, wrapped in a white robe, was lead into the Temple supported by Garcia on one side and the Marta on the other. Another cheer went up from the crowd as they finally disappeared inside.

"The girl is going to be initiated into the sacred rites," said Karen. "I think if I recall correctly, *epopteia* means 'sacred vision.'

"But did you see?" I said in, horror, " the girls robe was covered in blood!"

"No I didn't notice," replied Karen.

"How could you not? the older woman's hands were covered in it!" I persisted.

Rachine gave a long knowing look towards Karen.

"Were they! Well, it was probably just fake," said Karen, dismissive. "You know what Garcia is like, its all just a show - a pantomime." Karen laughed, and looked at Rachine, "I think Julian thinks we actually sacrifice people here," she said.

"Yes, to think such a thing!" Rachine replied dryly.

"I guarantee you, you will meet that girl later and she will be quite all right," said Karen.

Whatever the case, it seemed that one would have to wait to discover the fate of the girl. Garcia's top men lined up in front of the steps to the temple, their torches flaming still. One got the distinct impression one was not permitted to go beyond them. Gradually the crowd began to disperse and make their way back to the Forum, where more merry making in the form of music and dance, and wine, even love making, would take place.

"I didn't know there were so many folks on the island," I said.

"Apparently followers have been arriving by boat all day," replied Rachine.

"Friends of Garcia's. In honour of the Mysteries," added Karen

And someone in the crowd said:, "In honour of the Mysteries."

"In honour of the Mysteries," said another passer-by."

"In honour of the Mysteries," replied Karen, bowing her head slightly to the person with the greeting.

"In honour of Demeter and Persephone," said another person.

Then two girls and a boy, the older girl very beautiful, went past waving red handkerchiefs, and said in unison, "send our love to Father."

"Who were *they*?" I said

Karen shrugged her shoulders, "don't know, never seen them before, probably some part of the celebrations."

"I think they belong in another story," observed Rachine. Then she stopped and put her hand on Karen's arm. "Do you remember him?" she said, pointing.

"Who?"

"That boy over there. He was in Italy. Hey, I wonder if Anastasia and Analisa are here."

"Oh - how exciting if they were to be!"

Rachine looked at me in that mischievous way of hers: "Better keep an eye on Julian if they are here. You know what Analisa is like," said Rachine, laughing.

"Why?" I said, dumbly.

Karen gave me a side-long glance, and put her hand round my arm.

"They would eat you alive." said Rachine, still laughing.

She waved her arm at seeing someone else she knew and called out to them:

"I'll see you guys later," she said, before hurrying over to a long youth with flowers in his hair, 'another Antinious.'

As the evening wore on, more and more people arrived; the island quadrupling in its population. Couples were openly cavorting with one another, and occasionally a cry of rapture and delight could be heard coming out of the darkness - all in honour of Demeter and the 'Mysteries' - we were constantly being reminded. Although it had its solemn ritualistic aspect, the outward manifestation of the 'Mysteries,' was that of a celebration of life. An expression of the joy of life, as has been pointed out: any display of sorrow was strictly taboo.

As Karen had promised, at one point in the evening we saw Garcia's favourite, Alisiya, that gorgeous elfin creature that had been 'initiated.' She seemed changed somehow, more beautiful than ever, although there was something about her bearing and her look that was more mature. There was a kind of 'spaced out look' in her eyes, as if she had seen something she could not forget. I looked at her gown, there were no traces of blood on it now, and apart from the distracted look on her face, she seemed well enough.

Karen asked, in her Greek, how she was. The girl looked at Karen and then at me. "I have seen the goddess," she said, and she looked up at the darkening gentian heaven, "I saw the sun rise at night. I saw much beauty."

The Magna Marta who accompanied her, addressed Karen in Greek and smiled faintly, before leading the girl away in the direction of the main building.

"What did the woman say?"

"I'm not sure, I'm not that good with modern Greek. I think she said the girl was tired," replied Karen.

"I wonder what they did to her?" I said, looking at them as they made their way through the crowd.

"D'know," said Karen, "but she's *epopteia* now, that's for sure!"

Karen grabbed my arm and puled me away from the torch light. "Come," she said, "I want you."

"What here! - Now!"

"Why not? look around you, everyone is doing it. Its what pagans do. They celebrate life, and what better way is there than to make love to you favourite."

I looked around and saw that she was right, there were no miserable faces to be seen anywhere. People laughed and drank and kissed one another, others undressed one another and made love in the open, completely unselfconscious. Karen, who was only too well aware of my own self-consciousness, lead me into the cover of some strategically placed bushes. She took hold of my hand and guided it beneath her gown. "Think how lucky you are to be with the best," she whispered.

And it wasn't an idle claim either Put quite simply: a statement of truth! On down through the ages there had never been another that felt so good as Karen, except perhaps another incarnation of herself. It felt strange to be with her in the darkness; in the darkness I could only feel her body, and the thrills that it sent through me; in the darkness I could not see her face only feel her lips on me; there in the darkness I wasn't just with Karen, but Natasha, Mirium, Clytemnestra, Chloe, Nachash. All those that she had been before, were right there beneath my finger tips; it was only the face and the time that had changed.

"You know Julian," said Karen, as we came out of the darkness, "if it is to get any better with you and me like *that*, you really must try to think of me as an ordinary girl. After all, that is all I am - a girl, just like any other *girl."*

"You are anything but ordinary. You said it yourself. '*You are the best!'*"

Karen smoothed her beautiful orange gown over her breasts, and tightened the belt around her narrow waist. She looked down and smiled, knowing the effect her actions had on others around her. " I know - but try anyway."

"Hey you two! what have you been doing?"

My heart sank, I knew Rachine's acid strident tone instantly. I couldn't bring myself to even say 'hi', but Karen was polite enough to acknowledge her.

"This is Hadrianus." said Rachine, introducing us.

For a moment I felt it incumbent upon me to say something such as: 'in honour of the mysteries,' I could see his dark eyes grow large as they lit upon Karen, and he made no pretence about looking her over.

"Greetings," he said, "Isn't it all so wonderful, the New Age. I mean the real New Age - It is here, right here!" he said, stamping the ground, "not all that silly hippie thing - you know 'love and peace man!' and drugs," he went on, giving us the hippie two finger salute. "And then you have all these folks dressed in black, thinking that they are *bruja!* What is it in English?"

"Witch..!" interjected Rachine, giving Karen a quick glance.

"Ah yes, witchcraft, and what is even more silly, the worship of the devil."

"Silly," said Rachine, shaking her head, "*esta muy tonto!*"

"*Si! - si! - si! los modernos esta tonto, con todo, todo loco!* Do you not agree Señior? This is what *La Religiòn de la. paganas* is all about. The truth - Demeter and the reunion with her daughter. It is about colour and joy, such are the Eleusinian Mysteries, Señior!"

At last I found my opportunity to say, 'in honour of the Mysteries,' and I felt quite pleased about that.

"In honour of the Mysteries," he responded, but his attention was now firmly directed towards Karen. My moment of triumph quickly dissipating when I saw the look in his eyes.

"But what of beauty! I forgot about beauty, but here it is, and such beauty. Perfectión. Such perfectión. You never told me she was - hermosura!"

Rachine shrugged her shoulders, looking slightly perplexed she said in an off hand manner: "how could I ever do her justice."

Hadrianus, totally unabashed, took hold of Karen's hand and kissed it, and then drew her to him and ravished her on the neck. Karen yielded, giving up her neck to his mouth, her body melting into his arms. To be fair, I didn't think any of us, even Rachine had expected that! When Hadrianus eventually released her out of his strong arms Karen was quite disorientated for a moment, and a little out of breath. She smiled, looking towards me rather in the manner of a naughty little school girl.

In the end it was Rachine who felt obliged to address her friends outlandish flirtations. "Hands off Hadrianus! She is Monsieur Julian's." With that, Karen put her arm in mine.

"Yes I'm afraid I am," said Karen, looking at the interloper with defiance. Or was it that I wanted to believe it was defiance, and not - daring!

"But you must be a great lover Señior," he said, still looking at Karen. "To have such a woman as this!"

Rachine laughed uproariously. "*He is the best,*" she said, "*you have no idea!*"

With this Rachine took Hadrianus' hand and began to drag him off.

"Hasta luego Señor Julian," he called.

"Hasta Mañana Monsieur," said Rachine, her fiendish laughter pealing through the air.

"Don't let her get to you. Any way you are the best - for me."

"It's all right Karen you don't have to patronise me. You can go with him if you want to. I saw the way you were looking at each other. You enjoyed him kissing your neck."

Karen looked down and scraped the ground with her foot. "I didn't want to go with him," she said, in a sullen voice. "I didn't know he was going to do that!"

"It was disgusting."

"I told you I couldn't help it."

"He is very god looking though, don't you think? Long limbed, and did you see his hands."

"You're obsessed Julian. You think all men are better than you. It's not even about size, or machismo, there are other things too, that a girl finds attractive in a man."

"Such as?"

"I don't know - intelligence, sensitivity..."

"That may be true to a certain extent but in the end what impresses women is manliness, a mans strength, physical and mental." I said.

Karen looked off into the distance in the direction Rachine and Hadrianus had gone. She scuffed the ground again with her foot, her behaviour reminded me still, of a naughty school girl, one that had been caught kissing behind the bike sheds.

"I said I didn't want to go with him," she reiterated.

"But you could if you wanted."

"If I wanted! Besides Rachine likes him well enough."

"But you could take him off her - if you wanted?"

"I should guess so."

"I bet you could lure any man away from his woman?" I said, knowing that my words sounded provocative, and that Karen was easily turned on by such language, for she really believed that *she* was the best, and in this respect she was the same as most attractive women. The thing is they couldn't *all* be the best!

"Of course."

"Even if they were happily married and deeply in love with one another?"

"Well I don't know about that. Besides which, how many people do you know who are happily married?"

"Well, now you mention it....back home folks are getting divorced all the time."

"That's because modern people get bored easily. They always want more; they come together out of lust, mistaking it for love. Then they see someone else, someone prettier, someone with more dough, a bigger car, a bigger house - and they're off. There is very little genuine love to found in the world today," added Karen.

"But I love you." I said.

Karen looked at me quizzically for a moment, before replying: "I wonder if you do?"

"But I do." I protested.

"I wonder if anybody really knows what love is!" she mussed. "And in the end is it really all that important? All those love songs and poetry written about love, but where has it ever got anyone? Where has it got the human race?

"Put like that I guess it doesn't sound too good. Do you believe in love Karen?"

She gazed at me for several moments before answering. "I don't know to be honest. I guess it exists for some. I don't think people of today know what it is though! It is too demanding for them. It requires commitment. Then there are those that come together out of laziness, it looks like love, but they are really scared of the big bad world; they can't face it alone, so they seek shelter in each other, that's not love either. I guess believing in love is like believing in Santa Claus, I don't know whether he's real or not, but I've seen this guy in red, down the shopping-mall, he's real - isn't he?"

I looked at her, the little girl was nowhere to be seen when she talked like this. She seemed so superior and out of reach. I suddenly felt a great need to prove she was real, that she was mine. A feeling of frustration grew in me, something overtook me, something like anger, and I suddenly grabbed hold of her round the waist and pushed her up against a nearby tree. She didn't resist. She let me kiss her, she was completely acquiescent, allowing me to take full possession of her strong body.

"My word Julian!" said Karen, all flustered and flushed.

"I'm sorry." I said, feeling shocked and embarrassed.

Karen took my hand in hers. "Don't be. It was *quite* a surprise...it was most... exhilarating - you just caught me off my guard that was all," she said, laughing. She pulled me after her. "Come on..."

For an anxious moment I thought Karen was about to drag me into the undergrowth again, instead we headed into the throng of people who were gathering more and more towards the centre of the Forum. We asked someone why there were so many people.

"Señior Garcia and some other followers are about to offer prayers to the deity, and recite poetry and sing songs in her honour," he said.

Although most of it was in Greek, Karen was able to translate, so that the proceedings went something like this:

'The Prayer to the Magna Marta Kybele,'

'Oh Mother of the Gods and men - Oh life giving Goddess that art the council and the providence and the creator of our souls - thou that giveth all good things - do thou grant to all men happiness and the chief happiness of all, the knowledge of the Gods!,'

'Pray ye now to Demeter and the Divine Maiden, the Holy Trine. Pray ye to Pluto and to the mother of all beauty, the fruitful nourishing Earth! Prey ye to Hermes and the Graces.'

The gathering, including Karen and myself, all spoke out in unison, 'Hail Demeter, Hail Persephone.' It was a very moving and solemn moment, and then the voice of the young initiate, the *epopteia*, sang out:

"Hear me, hear me, I who have beheld the face of the Goddess, I who approached the confines of death, and having trodden on the threshold of Persephone, returned having been carried through the elements. In the shadow of the evening and the coming of the night I saw the sun glittering with stupendous light, and with the light I beheld the infernal and the supernal gods, and to the divinities, approached and paid tribute of devout adoration. Blessed be the Gods."

Again everyone joined in: 'Blessed be,' and clapped and cheered the young initiate. There then followed some poetry, finally another loud cheer went up, gradually the crowd settled and we heard the familiar strident voice of Garcia.
"For those who have the ears to hear let them hear," he said.

There followed a silence among the gathering, in preparedness for the receiving of some great wisdom - it seemed.
"Of the Old and the New. We are the born and the unborn, we are the eternal truth, we are that which is and that which is yet to be, we are for all time, we are the future and the past."
"We are the Now," he called out forcibly, "We are the New Age, and the age that has past, unborn and never ending and everlasting, and always fleeting, coming forth and receding, always and forever, changing, and never changing - The New Age. I give you - The Mysteries."
"The Mysteries," responded the crowd.

I found myself almost moved to tears by the coming together of so many followers, and their expression of devout faith in an idea that seemed so pure and innocent. I was grateful when the tone of the evening lifted and the sound of flutes and lyres began to ring out again against the general hubbub of conversation and laughter.
"Well what should we do now?" I said.
"Let's find somewhere quiet to sit down. I like sitting down. Do you like sitting down?"
"Yes it's all right," I said, looking at Karen.

Before we had got very far I felt a hand on my shoulder. Straight away, by the very weight of it I guessed who it belonged to.
"My children," said the great man, putting his arm about the both of us. "Well what did you think of our little show?"
"I enjoyed the poetry readings," said Karen. "We were about to find somewhere to sit down."
"Karen likes to sit down, don't you?"
"Yes," she said, nodding and smiling gaily, "I like sitting down."
"Well that is about the last of my official duties for tonight, and let me tell you I'm looking forward to nothing better than having a good sit down myself."

We all smiled, happy at the prospect of being able to sit down together, just the three of us.

"Come on, let's all go back to the villa and sit on the terrace in private. I haven't been able to spend much time with you. There is still much that I want to say to you, before you leave my little island world."

People looked at us as we went our way with Garcia. We felt quite privileged and important, now that we were in his company.

The boy came with wine, and we sat down at the marble table as we had the night before.

"It is good to get away from the crowds," he said.

We looked at Garcia. I thought he suddenly looked all of his seventy years, his face was pale and drawn.

"Are you all right Garcia? You look tired. We can go if you want?"

"No - no I will be all right in a moment. Let's have some wine. To the Goddess, " he said, when our glasses were full.

"To the goddess," we said, raising our silver goblets.

"Oh - my word! My, my, my, my, my but that is good, and I tell you what, and I will - I will tell you! it is so good - so good at last, to have a good *sit down,* and what is more! to sit in such delightful company."

Garcia drained his wine and the boy filled his cup again, and replenished our own.

"And how do you feel Miss Karen - now that you are at last sitting down?"

"Wonderful," said Karen, beaming, "It's so wonderful to be sitting down."

"Where did all these people come from? and where will they stay?" I said.

"From here and from there. Some from the neighbouring islands. The majority are from further afield, some as far away as Italy and Spain. As for where they stay, they have the island and the sky for a canopy, what more could one ask!"

"And they all follow you?" I enquired.

"Not me - so much as we share the same ideas. A coming together of like minded individuals. That is the thing you see. Ours is not a church, There are no guide books, no rule books, no bibles, no propaganda, no hierarchy as such. We recognise that what is important is the *individual,* there is no need to moralise when one has the single basic code of how to live decently already in ones heart. I don't need to tell you for example Mr Julian, that it is wrong to steal or, to be malicious - is it not so? Treat people with respect, give them the courage to choose the right path for themselves and you will be surprised what man is capable of. Closet him, keep him away from truth, treat him like a child - well, look at what happens, it is self-evident! Sometimes I feel that this," he said, raising his hands and looking about, "is the only sanity left in the world."

Garcia sighed as if the weight of the world rested upon his shoulders alone.

"But there are more pressing issues that are pertinent to our present situation, than the follies of mankind in general," he said.

Karen and I looked at one another wondering what he had in mind.

"I'm speaking of course of the Miss Karen here. I trust you are feeling better since this morning and your little trip up the hill?"

Karen looked down somewhat as a child again, embarrassed perhaps at the thought of her behaviour.

"Yes, much better," she said.

"If only the sheepherder in you, was more prominent," said Garcia, "but alas it is not, so therefore we must address the remaining issues at hand."

"What remaining issues?" I said.

Garcia through open his hands. "Well who she is? Where did she begin? and where did it all go wrong? We have to take you back Karen to the seat of your beginning. To *draw* you back to that most distant and most significant of lives - that of the High Priestess herself."

"I thought you said it couldn't be done? That we would never know for sure?" protested Karen.

"I said, that I strongly suspected that I knew who you were, but now, *now* we know. *Now,* now we know - we never knew for sure before, but now we know or, at least I strongly suspect. You see I have this day acquired through an associate some poetry written about a certain - 'High Priestess' of the Phoenician Goddess Tanit. That priestess, I strongly suspect, is non other than yourself."

"Is it this 'Taanach,' that I have been hearing so much about?" I said.

"Taanach, Nachash, Ówlam - she has many names. As you know the phoenicians are an ancient trading people dating back to before the rise of the

Greeks; therefore they had many cultural influences, even the desert dwelling tribes of North Africa, the Bedouin, it is said, can trace their lineage back to the Phoenicians. Amongst the desert people she was known as Shaula, the scorpions sting, and Unuk al hay, relating to her serpent qualities. In Greek texts she appears as Ofisiodeis and Savra...."

"It seems that this Phoenician priestess certainly put it about a bit!" I remarked.

"According to these writings, she was notorious. What you have to bear in mind Mr Julian is that every priestess of Tanit was a kind of holy whore, and that sex was a part of a sacred rite. A practice that is not uncommon among pagan peoples. Mary Magdalene was I believe one. Except that with Nachash, it seems she took things a bit too far, believing herself to be, not just a high priestess of Tanit, but an incarnation of the goddess herself. It is most probable that it was this Priestess of Tanit, who was the first incarnation to skew your existence into the direction it has since taken. If we could speak to *her* directly, we would have a better idea what we are up against. To dig down to the core, the very quick of your soul Karen, and expose the poison - *draw it out...!*"

"*Yess, yesss....letss draw it out!*" hissed Karen, getting carried away by the madness.

Garcia shouted for the boy. Moments later he appeared, carrying a small bulbous vessel with a spout - a teapot, for want of a better name, and a small silver cup, which he set down on the table.

"Now drink this," said Garcia, pouring out a greenish colour liquid from the pot and placing it before Karen.

"Just a minute, what is this stuff?" I said.

"You remember," said Karen, "it's the herb tea! You had it before - right Garcia?"

"Quite so, but this time it is a much stronger concoction, and it has a few added ingredients." Garcia looked at me, observing my scepticism. "It's the only way you know, if Karen is to discover who she really is, and what happened so long ago to spin her lives into such a turmoil! To this end - drink the tea."

Karen looked up at the old man and put her hands around the cup. She then turned to look at me, then back to Garcia.

"Do you want to do this?" I said.

Karen nodded. "Yes - yes I will be all right. Garcia is right, it *is* the only way you know!"

"So long as you're sure?"

"Drink it my girl. All will be well I assure you," Garcia prompted.

Karen raised the cup to her lips, paused a moment and then in one swift movement threw her head back, draining the contents in one draught. She put the cup down on the table and stared at Garcia.

"Hmmm - that was nice. Can I have some more?"

Garcia looked at the boy, who was still hovering by the table. He nodded to him, and the boy came forward to replenish the vessel.

"That's enough for now. It is a strong mixture."

Karen didn't pause before drinking, but took the cup and drained it in one greedy gulp. Again Karen stared fixedly at Garcia, her eyes growing wide, her pupils dilated into large black discs, which made her look seem piercing and mad.

"More!" she said, frowning, "*please!*"

"Only a very little then." This time Garcia filled the cup himself, only half way. Karen stared at the cup and when she saw that he wasn't going to pour any more of the tea, she picked it up with feverish hands, as if it contained liquid gold and drained the cup, tipping it back as far as she could to get at every last drop.

The cup went down on the table with a 'bang.' Karen slumped forward after it. I touched her back, and she looked round at me, her eyes glassy, like they belonged to a china-doll.

"I feel all woo - oozy," she said, in a dreamy kind of voice.

I looked at Garcia.

"It's natural," he said, unconvincingly. "help her up."

Garcia totted to his feet. The day had obviously taken it's toll on the old boy. "Bring her though here - this way...this way..."

I must say, he struck me as a rather pathetic figure, not one that instilled confidence. If he was about to take Karen on a mind journey through time, then it was rather like putting ones confidence in a pilot who was drunk.

"Where are you? come along - come along." he said, and seeing that I was having some difficulty with Karen he returned to give me a hand. Together we brought her into a kind of antechamber, a semicircular room about twelve feet

feet across, decorated with in marble from the floor to it's domed roof, upon which were painted zodiacal symbols. Extending along the circumference of the wall was a seating area in the form of a marble bench, which was almost continuous except for a more elaborate seat, for want of a better word, a 'throne,' situated in an alcove facing north. In the centre of the room was an iron tripod and a brazier which contained burning white embers. Garcia reached into a pot and threw incense into the brazier. Instantly sparks and smoke shot forth and drifted upwards through a small circular aperture in the centre of the roof. A sickly sweet cloying kind of smell lingered on, reminding me of a Catholic church I once entered by accident.

Garcia mumbled some words I could not discern, and then threw on more incense. He then picked up a silver chalice and drank from it himself, before handing it to Karen.

"Don't you think she's had enough of that stuff," I remonstrated.

"Silence - it is part of the ritual she will come to no harm, *I promise you.*"

Still requiring my support, Karen stood in front of Garcia and took the chalice in both hands.

"Blessed Be the Holy Trinity. Blessed Be Persephone, Demeter and Hecate."

"Blessed be the Trinity," Karen repeated, in a faraway kind of voice. She put the cup to her lips and then handed it back to Garcia.

"Now that you have drunk from the cup of memory we will begin."

"I have drunk from the cup of memory, my mind sees all I have been, and am yet to be." Karen said, in the same somnambulistic tones.

I realised as Karen handed Garcia back the cup, that this was a ritual she had participated in before.

"You are now standing upon the threshold of time past."

"I stand upon the threshold."

"Are you ready to take the step across the threshold?" said Garcia, holding out his hand.

"Yes - yes," sighed Karen, "I am ready."

I suddenly sensed Karen's body transform itself from one of languid torpor, into remote hardness. This new stronger Karen, no longer required my support. She took a couple of faltering steps towards Garcia."

"I cross the threshold into the other realm of what once was, and still is," said Karen, taking Garcia's hand.

"Who are you?"

"I am she - she of the night - night black as ravens wing. I am she of the silvery light. I am she, she who is known among many and is unheard of. I am she who is envied and despised. I am the one whose name is spoken among the Greeks. I am the one who is worshipped in Lebanon, and she who is honoured in Egypt. I am the whore and the holy one."

"I say again - who is it that comes to us from the furthest tracks of time?"

"Why, I am she who reflects the light and wisdom of the Goddess. I am High Priestess of the Moon Goddess - *Tanit!*"

Garcia looked at me a moment, before leading the haughty presence of the priestess around the brazier towards the throne.

"Behold, " he said, "Tanit - your seat awaits."

The person Garcia and I knew as Karen was no longer in the room, of this I am certain. Her whole bearing, every aspect of her demeanour had changed. She was now full of disdain, a person who was used to being obeyed; her look was one of spectacular haughtiness (all right, so perhaps she wasn't a whole lot different), a haughtiness that was beyond mere pride, this girl saw herself truly as something akin to a Goddess.

"I shall take my seat and receive the offerings that are for the Goddess."

For the first time I felt a little reassured, I couldn't help smiling, thinking, 'how little things change.' To my surprise Garcia got down on his knees before the presence of the seated girl. He looked over towards me again and signalled for me to do the same. Some what reluctantly I obeyed. The seated figure then began to mumble and chatter in a strange tongue, the likes of which I had never heard before.

"What is it? What is it you say?" said Garcia, sounding alarmed.

The priestess began to groan, her hands became agitated; she began to pull at her robe.

"Remember who you are? Do not loose yourself to her. You are Karen."

"No, I am she, I *am* - Tanit!" said the would-be goddess, getting to her feet, "I command you all to honour me as *Tanit!*"

"No," persisted Garcia, bravely in the face of such a powerful personality." You are not Tanit, you are her high priestess, you are Taannach el Nachash. You are a mere interloper, who has stolen the name of the goddess. Repent and your soul shall be saved Taanach...!"

She now took off her robe, and bore her naked body, as if by way of some sort of proof of her divinity. She raised her hands above her head and looked up towards the painted heavenly symbols.

"I am the splendour of the heavens. I am she - Goddess of the sky; the Moon is my symbol, and all in heaven and earth honour me, the resplendent one. I am the everlasting love. I satiate all desire. I quell all thirst in man's mortal desire. I am she whose name is great in the east. I am she that is great in Palestine and Syria, and whose name is spoken among the people of the northern isles. Many different races of man speak my name, by some I am known as Juno, yet others call me Diana of the hunt, still others call me Astarte. The home of my worship is Carthage, where I am known as Tanit, the glorious and Almighty! No one is above me, I command *you all,*"

The arms of the goddess were open wide, her eyes ranged about the room, beautiful, alarming, in their demonic madness.

Finally she sank down again on her throne. Garcia was still kneeling before her. After all that she had said, he *dared* to look her in the face. It was then that she screeched something in that strange language. As if in slow motion she raised her hand, and seemingly without effort swat Garcia about the face, sending him sprawling across the floor like a rag-doll. When I started to come to his aid, she screamed something again, and was on her feet ready to strike *me.*

"I'm all right me boy. Leave me alone, and keep kneeling or she'll have us all!"

I had to admire the tenacity of the man. Undiminished he picked himself up and went straight back for more. He faced up to the goddess again, whom he knew was masquerading as a 'mere slip of a girl,' and again, 'the mere slip of a girl' gave him another hard whack that sent him flying. He put his hand up to signal for me to stay put. Garcia shook his head like a prize fighter who did not know when to quit.

"I've had enough of this nonsense!" he said, marching straight up to her.

Nachash or, whoever the hell she was, straightened her stupendous body and pointed to the floor. "Kneel before the goddess," she screeched.

"I shall not kneel before an interloper."

The priestess looked slightly taken aback by Garcia's boldness. Clearly nobody had ever dared defy her before.

"You are Taanach el Nachash," he said, as he smashed her hard across the face. "You are an interloper, an impostor, a transgressor - Nachash!.." Garcia hit her again on the other cheek. "Get down from your high place Taanach, you are a whore and a thief who has stolen the mantle of a goddess....." hitting her again with all his force, hard enough to break any girls face, but this girl just took each blow, first one side of her beautiful face and then the other. She just looked straight ahead hardly batting an eyelid.

"That's enough," Garcia, I said, when he was about to hit her again.

He lowered his hand.

"Karen, come back to us...." I beseeched.

"Karen - you are Karen, do you hear?" enjoined Garcia. "You must come back. Step back from the other side, step back across the threshold. I command you."

Karen spoke in her normal voice: "I can't, she is too powerful, too powerful...the priestess....she's...." and then in the strident tones of Taanach: "*She is all powerful...*"

"She is you! She cannot be more powerful, she is you! Before all else you are Karen - you live in the here and now," said Garcia, shaking Karen by the shoulders.

"Get away from me, how dare you!" she yelled. "I shall smite thee..."

In one swift movement, exhibiting almost superhuman strength she struck out at Garcia again, this time lifting him into the air and sending him crashing into the brazier, splattering the white hot coals of 'Hestia' across the floor. I had to be quick on my toes, to avoid getting burnt. How Garcia survived without receiving serious injury I don't know?

Karen, or should I say, the priestess of Tanit, or whoever she happened to be at that particular moment; suddenly looked startled, and I deduced that it wasn't the commotion she had caused, that was responsible for the look of horror on her face. She began to touch her body, her face, and finally stared at her hands: her grey eyes wide with fear or, perhaps incredulity!

Letting out a loud piercing scream: "My hands, my hands, my beautiful body," she yelled, clutching at herself. Then I saw her eyes light upon me. Karen lifted her hand and pointed towards me, then let out a groan, took one step and fell - a dead unconscious weight. I ran forward and caught her in the nick of time to break her fall, before she hit her head on the marble floor. Karen lay inert for some moments, her head cradled in my arms. Garcia came over with her kimono and put it over her naked body.

"Stay with her, I'll go and get a physician," said Garcia.

I heard voices from behind me as he opened the door. The noise from the screams and the overturned brazier must have attracted some attention. Garcia returned with a glass of water, and the news that he had sent the boy for help. He pushed the glass in my hand and I tried to get Karen to drink, which had the desired effect of bringing her round. She gasped for breath and coughed and then began to thrash out, but her *divine* strength had departed her, she was just an ordinary mortal, but being Karen, she was still very strong.

"It's all right," I said, "it's all over now."

She looked at me and then to Garcia, and it seemed to dawn on her where she was, and what had happened.

"You are back with us at last, then Karen?" said Garcia, looking intently into her eyes, not about to take any more chances.

Karen smiled and then laughed. "Yes - it's all right, I am me again," she said, becoming suddenly fretful and beginning to cry.

I drew her to me and kissed her face. "It's all right, everything will be all right." I intoned, not believing a word of it.

"Come, let's get you up on to your seat," said Garcia.

"Yes," I said, trying to inject a bit of levity, "you know how you like to sit."

We soon had her planted on her throne again and dressed in her kimono, but this time she was just like a frightened little girl, not a powerful goddess.

Although I tried to make light of things for Karen's sake, inside I was raging at Garcia, for doing what he had done, for risking her sanity, for what seemed just a crazy idea: 'Meddling fool, meddling old man, meddling in things he doesn't quite understand! Trying to look big.' So ran my train of thought, and I planned to let him know how I felt at the earliest opportunity I got.

The fact that he had narrowly missed serious injury or, worse was not lost on me.

"Are you all right Garcia?" I asked.

"Just a few bruises, don't worry about me, my boy."

Karen looked from me to Garcia, "Did I do that!" she said, noticing the overturned brazier.

"You pack quite a kick me girl," Laughed Garcia. Karen put her hand to her mouth, and touched the old man's arm.

"Yes, I can vouch for that," I added.

Karen's lavender eyes rolled in her head, "Oh...I'm so horrible to you - both of you."

"We're just happy we have you back with us," I said.

"Yes, my child..." said Garcia, patting her arm, looking not a little relieved.

Karen's tears subsided but she remained in an agitated state, ringing her hands together, as if she didn't know what to do with them. She seemed not to want to notice anything about herself - her physical being.

"How do I look to you?" she asked me.

"You look fine, just a bit upset."

"I don't look old - do I?"

And again her hands went to her face.

"No, you are as beautiful as ever."

"Am I - *really!*"

She continued to ring her hands, and press her thighs, never still for a moment, finally she seemed to find the courage to look at them. She laughed, as someone realising their misapprehension.

"My hands, my hands, they're - they're mine, *my* hands again!"

Karen hugged me tightly, and then looked at her hands again, she was smiling. "They are normal again."

"Of course they are yours, silly," I said, taking hold of a long sleek hand.

"I saw her! I saw her!" she said, looking at Garcia, " I saw who I was, and it was horrible, just *horrible!*"

"It's OK, you don't have to go over it Karen."

"Yes she does," said Garcia, forcefully, "it is the only way if she is to have complete recall."

"You just don't care do you what you may have done to her? All you care about is proving your crazy theory!"
"She has to remember *now*, otherwise it would all have been for nothing."
I looked back at Karen, aware my temper was close to breaking point with the old man, fortunately just at that moment the physician arrived to check on her.
I hadn't seen him on the island before, and he wasn't wearing any of the usual regalior, so I figured he was an 'off-islander': about thirty years old dressed in shorts and a T-shirt. He smelt and looked of the modern world, incongruous somehow in the pagan surroundings to which he had been summoned. I was thankful in a way; I half expected one of those priestly types who consulted the oracle before deciding that the best course of action was to *trepan* a hole in the poor suffers head. Modern or not, this guy still came with his bag of tricks. It still smelt of a sort of *hocus-pocus*, but it's funny how reassuring it is to see the magical devices at the aid of the modern physician. Lo and behold, he produced out of his magic bag a stethoscope, which he then preceded to place against Karen's lovely chest; he even opened up her Kimono to place it against her skin. He listened carefully for a moment, then produced another piece of magic kit, a kind of bandage which he wrapped around Karen's arm and then proceeded to pump air into...very strange! He even had a magic torch which he shined in Karen's lovely grey eyes. Held up two fingers and asked her how many she could see? 'Two,' she duly replied, and the physician laughed, she had passed with flying colours.
The man of science and the modern world, having done his magic bit, stepped back from his bemused patient.
"There is nothing really wrong with you as far as I can see," he said, looking to Garcia and then me. "A good strong heart, should live to be ninety," he chuckled, "she has a slightly elevated pulse rate," he continued, in a more serious tone, and now ignoring the patient altogether, "make sure she takes two of these before bed," he said, reaching into his bag and handing me a little brown bottle. "They are just a mild sedative, nothing more. You will be fine after a good nights rest," he said, taking a long lingering look at Karen.
"You see, you are fine, you just need to get some rest," I said, after the doctor had gone.

"I will. But Garcia is right, I need to tell him what I saw. I need to get it out."

Garcia returned after going with the doctor to the door, the ever gracious host. "I hope you are satisfied now Mr Julian that no serious harm has befallen the Miss Karen, now my dear," said Garcia, taking her hands in his, "do you feel up to telling us what you saw?"

Karen looked up at Garcia with wide expectant eyes, like the dutiful prodigy. I knew for the time being she was lost to me, held now in the sway of the great man, with the big personality and the big ideas.

"I was the high priestess to a goddess known as Tanit - you know, the Carthaginian that you suspected all along. The one known as Taanach. She was very beautiful and very very powerful, and very very lustful, proud of her sexual exploits - but she was frightening!" said Karen, looking at me for a moment. "She was so caught up in her self, her absolute conviction in her superiority - she was a monster, a tyrant, who cared nothing for others. It was quite terrible this power, it consumed her, she thought of herself as immortal - she was quite convinced of it." Karen shivered and put her arms about herself. "I feel her presence still. She feels very alone! But once this belief in her divinity had begun, there was no way back. It was like a drug! I felt it - Garcia, I felt what it was like to be *her*, to command such complete and utter power. It was terrible and yet addictive - exhilarating!"

"But why were you concerned so much about your hands?" I said.

"In the end this power or, whatever it was, became too much, even for *her*," said Karen, shaking her head. "she, or rather I, as I keep forgetting - it was me that it happened to, and it explains now, so much about my own character, any way it literally ate her alive; it was terrible - gross!" Karen stared at her hands. "She was so beautiful and so proud of her looks, but by the time she was thirty she was transformed into a bent and twisted old hag. Some terrible disfiguring disease took hold, and bent my once straight body, twisted my limbs. My unblemished skin came up in boils and pustules. It was my hands I remember most vividly; they were such fine long and slender hands, but towards the end they were gnarled and bent like an old woman's, as bent and twisted as one of those ancient olive trees, and the veins stood up in them, heavily veined arms and hands, and yet I was no ore than thirty and in my prime. I looked so ugly

Julian! I keep thinking I still look like her - I know I don't...." said Karen, touching her face.
"That is it then!" Garcia pronounced. "You incurred the wrath of the goddess, and you have been doing so ever since! You have been living under the shadow of Taanach, just as I had suspected. I tried to talk to her myself, bring her down to earth a bit - but you saw what happened."
"You could never do that Garcia," said Karen, shaking her head, "she is too arrogant, to wrapped up in herself to ever listen to anybody. If you had persisted she would have killed you - and me probably...."
"What can we do then?" I said.
"It is clear what must be done, we must pay tribute to Tanit and ask her to lift the curse."
"What curse?" I asked.
"Well isn't obvious! When she was Nachash she abused the powers that the goddess had given her; so as punishment she took away that which she valued most - her great beauty - leaving her a bent old hag."
"You really believe that?"
"Why yes of course, you saw yourself an example of her strength, her power." Garcia chuckled to himself...."I tell you - huh! that was no Earthly power."
"Even if that is the case, look at Karen's skin, she is perfect, and so was Natasha by all accounts, so why should it be a curse of the goddess?"
"Yes that's right, why should it be a curse?" chimed Karen, "may be it was for the high priestess, may be for her it was a curse for trying to live as a goddess, but why should Tanit make me suffer? didn't Taanach suffer enough for all of us!"
Señor Garcia smiled wryly like the wise old man he was, or the man who held all the cards.
"You have made an interesting observation Mr Julian, and thereby still exhibit a certain scepticism concerning my ideas, but in your haste to attack my beliefs you overlook the *obvious*, namely that, Taanach, Chloe Mirium, and all the others on down to Natasha, and of course Karen, are all the same person, they just happen to live in different periods. Think back Mr Julian, to the life that was Mirium's, wasn't her body mutilated, what can be worse than being burnt alive

and didn't Natasha also end up badly scared, her looks spoiled forever!

I had to concede that the old man was right, there was a pattern after all to all of Karen's past lives.

"No - no Garcia," piped up Karen excitedly, "no we were *not* all the same person! We may have shared the same soul but our bodies were different and we lived in completely different times. Taanach's experiences were completely different to that of Natsha's or mine - *she* was separated from us by more than three thousand years. Taanach was a completely different kind of person, she was totally absorbed in herself, her power, her grandeur...."

"And you are not?" said Garcia.

For a moment Karen was silenced. "No - no I'm *not* like her, I'm *not* like her! I...I'm...more like Chloe the shepherdess...."

Even *I* had to smile at that. Less than eight hours earlier she had been commanding me to, 'enter the goddess.'

"I *am,* I am more like Chloe." persisted Karen, whose mannerisms had begun to resemble those of a petulant child.

She looked at me but I stayed silent. I wasn't interested in helping Garcia's argument any.

"I think you ought to be honest with yourself Karen," said Garcia, "remember I have made you my life's work. I know *you* - my girl, better than you know yourself. But you have hit upon a good point. The salvation for your soul could rest with the one known as Chloe. She was pure and innocent - herself a priestess of Hestia.

"Yes! - Yes Hestia! She's lovely Hestia, so pure, blessed is Hestia..." said Karen smiling.

"She is in you, she *is* there! You must try to cultivate her." ministered Garcia. "Draw her out!"

"I will! I shall prey to Hestia every day, I promise."

I shook my head, depressed by all this talk of goddess worship. Karen had gone into some sort of trance and found hidden reserves of strength, we all have them. There still was no concrete proof that Karen was a reincarnation of anybody. At least one could argue that point...

"Why do you shake your head Mr Julian? You still doubt!.."

Karen turned her head and looked at me quizzically, and I felt forced to reluctantly articulate my thoughts.

"My word what upstarts are being bread these days, these godless day's! The problem with moderns is that they have forgotten how to dream, they no longer see the magic in the world. Their world is black and white, the black and white of cold logic. Huh! Mankind, the rationalising animal. It will be his downfall.... Soon and it is coming *mark my words*," said Garcia, waving his finger at me, "it is coming, the day when the gods will unleash their fury upon mankind for his reckless and selfish actions, and he will be smote from the surface of the Earth."

"The day of judgement hey!"

Garcia shrugged his shoulders: "Perhaps - why not!"

I realised it was ridiculous to ague any further with Garcia. If one took the premise of the argument that Karen was a reincarnation of the high priestess of Tanit, or a reincarnation of Natasha, one had to take the rest of the argument as a given. There really wasn't a lot else to say, even Garcia could see that, so the conversation dried up.

"I will make an offering to Tanit rest assured." he said, by way of a conclusion to the evenings events. "But in any event," he went on, "we have already honoured her in our celebrations as expressed through the worship of Demeter and Persephone. It doesn't hurt though to mention her name. I will prey for you and make supplication," said Garcia, as if to underscore the point.

Garcia accompanied us as far as the library, where he asked us to wait a moment. He came back with a small neatly bound leather volume which he handed to Karen. It was a book of Greek poetry, but we were also informed that it contained *a history* by one*: Diomenes of Elaea,* which he impressed upon us to read.

"Will you be leaving tomorrow?" he asked, anxiously.

"I don't know," I replied, looking at Karen.

"We will see!" *I* am *very* tired now. Perhaps the day after."

Garcia smiled. "Yes well do get some rest both of you. Come see me tomorrow, after you have had a chance to read the history, I am sure you will find it interesting in light of what has transpired this evening!"

We promised him we would and bid him goodnight. Karen clung to my arm in a sleepy reverie; occasionally she would glance down at her hands. She didn't want to be left on her own, so I went with her back to her rooms. No sooner had we got in, than she flopped down on the bed. Before she slept I made her take two of the tablets that the doctor had prescribed. Almost immediately afterward she fell into a deep sleep. It was the most peaceful night I had ever spent with her, even though for myself I found it impossible to sleep.

I looked at her for a long while, wondering what dreams she dreamed? What lives she was reliving? If it were true that Karen's soul had been reincarnated many times before, then I wondered about the many people she had known and the things she had done, the places she had been, the things she had seen, over the many thousands of years.

'If ever a person needed to rest and sleep soundly,' I thought, 'it is you Karen', and I was pleased that she seemed to have found a moments peace, even if it were no more than an interlude of a few hours.

After a while I remembered the book of poetry and I opened it at the place Garcia had marked. Before reading the history by the obscure author Diomenes, there was an introduction dealing with the the nature of Tanit the Phoenician goddess of the moon, and her relationship to other goddesses, such as Astarte, and the pastoral Goddess in triad, such as Demeter Persephone and Hecate, as well as the triadic system Tanit herself was a part of, as worshipped in Carthage, as Baal-Hammon Tanit and Eshmun.

The history was a Greek copy of an earlier, possibly even Phoenician text. The great antiquity of the work, itself copied many times since Diomenes' day was fragmentary at best, but what remained extant, was enough to chill me to the marrow; not least because, the source of those very words, over three thousand years old, lay peacefully asleep on a bed, not more than a few feet away.

Note on the Text

'The following codex is from an early Greek papyrus. It relates a time when the High Priestess was at her most powerful, and charts her inevitable decline. It is my belief that the hand behind most of the following text is non other than the priestess herself, or else one of her scribes, or else someone writing shortly after her demise.'

From: 'Offerings to Tanit.'

The sentences of Diomenes recording the life of the high priestess Taanach

Tanit - your seat awaits *(......) ' (......) ' most precious, most divine ' (......) The priestess of Tanit was pure in spirit and body. No blemish lay upon her silvery white skin. Those who looked upon her, looked, (......) greatest of beauty. Yet (......) ' (......) 'hips (.....) ankles, neck (......) of her body. Her love was for the goddess alone. (......) ' (......) 'Her duty was to Tanit alone, whom she worshipped (.....) ' (.....) ' and was but a mouth piece. She who is all (......) great is your name ' (......) glories. Her hair - as black as the raven's wing. Her eyes - piercing bright, like the moon. as blue as deepest lapis Her skin- iridescent like (the) silver Moon. (.....) honour many gifts were bestowed. (......) ' glorious light, silver crescent (....) In the moonlight the worshipers came ' (......) ' (.....) the worshipers (......) looked to the high priestess ' (......) ' (......) ' Her hair as dark as the deepest night. Her body, shone silver in the moonlight, (.....) ' (......) like the snow capped mountain peak. The goddess Tanit of the waxing moon. (.....) 'Shaula '(......) ' (......) no other, (......) the desire of many (.....) Many she received to her bed. (.....) many challenged her claims. Of herself she remained ' (......) ' unto herself ' (.....)

* Indicates a missing part of the original text.

proud. (......) of her broad hips, ' (......) when the moon was new, frenzied ' (....) 'all eyes fell upon her ' (.....) ' Many envied her ' (.....) of all the high priestesses before her non equalled her beauty or strength. (.....) her straight limbs, her breasts, her (....)' (......) ' (......) had to prove her supremacy.(......) With lust in their eyes. (.....) ' she met their gaze. Frenzied (......) ' exultation's ' (......) ' still she was victorious. earning her the name *endoxos* (glorious one). Many from afar knew of the high priestess. Many came to look upon her beauty, (.....) no other that could equal her, (.....) great and powerful. (.....) 'And that even the gods were jealous of her, (.....) driven mad by desire. In these matters she had no equal. (.....) Tanit. And yet so it is said ' (......) ' She moved among mortals all hungry after her flesh, driven mad by her presence. (......) 'The high priestess (.....)non compared in such (things). She could not meet every challenge. (....) such was the power of the goddess. Such was her growing lack of humility that, (......) ' goddess.(......) ' (......) ' the passions of the flesh ' (......) ' (.....) the pallor of death upon her skin. ' (......) Egypt, to the west and north, (......) as she was once. '(......) ' (......) Tanit ' (......) they came (......) ' (......) She once moved with great pride in her appearance. (.....) to her loins ' (......) Her lost supremacy. Now look upon her. The eyes (are not so) keen. The once strong stem. (......) Her once proud body became bowed ' (......) the high priestess. ' (......) ' (......) Nachash, had lost her bite. ' (......) degenerated (......) filth, (......) whore ' (.....) Nachash (.....) she would not heed, (.....) ' (......) shameless lust ' (.....) swollen with lust ' (......) hung low, and bent over. Her once silver skin, see now (how it has become) tarnished. sunken and dulled were her eyes. (....) blood. (......) that they dare not look.' (.....) ' shunned the light of truth, only despair and darkness,' (.....) ' befell her, (.....) corruption of the flesh, (.....) a sin, (.....) Behold she who has fallen, (.....) ' blood and entrails, (.....) putrid flesh. (......) endless nights and frustration. She shunned the light of day. Those others now point the finger and ridicule ' (......) ' (......) Those that once longed to touch her flesh see now how they (recoil) She walks alone and spends her (nights) alone. (.....) such misery (has come) to her that was so proud and haughty. (......) the works of the goddess ' (......) ' (.....) ' an injury (......) to the goddess brought pain ' (......) sordes ' (.......) detested ' (.....) corruptible flesh, mortal flesh (......) defiled ' (......) ' such bitter fruit.

IX

And there she slept - Taanach in another life! And it had all been just as she had described it. A fall from grace, brought down by some disfiguring disease, whether through the will of the goddess or not, one may never know, although Garcia would say that Karen and all the others that she had been, were still tainted by the actions of Taanach, the greatest of all the priestesses of Tanit. "Sleep on my priestess," I said softly, as I closed the book. "After such a life you most surely need all the peace you can get."

And then I did a most strange and profound thing for one such as I, not given as I am to strong religious fervour, indeed quite the contrary. I suddenly sank down on to my knees, bowed my head and began to prey, at first not to any god in particular; I preyed for Karen's salvation, the salvation of her soul, and then I preyed to *her* - to Tanit herself, I said aloud: "Tanit, oh great and powerful goddess of the moon, forgive this child of yours, forgive her strong will, forgive her lascivious nature, forgive her jealousy, and her lust for power, for she is only a naïve child, forgive her and let her tortured soul rest at last. Surely now after so many centuries she has atoned for her misdeed. I humbly beseech thee oh great and powerful Tanit, return her purity and her innocence again, and make her like the shepherdess Chloe who she longs to be. So let it be."

I mean, I was as shocked as you my reader, speaking in such colourful language, honouring a *goddess*. Well, I suppose Garcia would say that somewhere along the line I too had been a priest - a man of god! Although, in this life I felt that there were too many different gods, too many *one god's*, and when you only have *one* god, he obviously has to be the *only* god, the one *true* god, and that, as far as I can see, is the problem with monotheism, it is too narrow, too bigoted! I made a mental note to take this argument up with Garcia in the morning, that is after I too had got some rest.

I fell into a deep sleep and had a wonderful dream, you know, the kind you don't want to wake up from. A dreamt of a girl with fantastic black hair and pure white skin that glowed like phosphorous. I never had a clear image of her face, she wore a sort of veil, but I remember her eyes, they shone brightly like a cat's silver-grey. At first I was afraid of her, then she reached out to me with outstretched hands and I went towards her. She laid her hand on my head and suddenly I felt the most wonderful sense of calm. The sense of peace is hard to convey. I just had the most perfect feeling of calm and security. I knew that so long as she was there everything would be all right. She lead me into a garden and I walked with her for what seemed like a long time, she was leading me somewhere I felt, but we never seemed to get to the end of our journey. I can't quite work out whether it was night or day either, everything seemed to have an effulgence around it, the trees, the girl, the sky, and I had the distinct impression that I was not on Earth, but on some far off alien world, yet the girl, apart from her eyes, looked perfectly perfectly human. I know what you are thinking, 'that it was Tanit who had visited me in my dreams to tell me that my prayer's had been answered?' Yes that is a lovely thought, so let us say that it *was* so! Either way, it was I that was the sleepyhead; Karen had woken first and had gone to see Garcia, according to the note she left on the bedside table; I noted also that she had taken the small volume with her.

Indeed I was the sleepyhead and Karen the bright and bushy tailed one. I was reluctant to begin the day surrounded as I was with the wonderful reverie of my dream. Eventually though, like Lazarus, I was able to get my sleepy old head up off the pillow. I showered and made myself some coffee in the small kitchen. I thought it prudent to let Karen have a few hours alone with Garcia, now that we were coming to the end of our stay on the island. He surely would have much to discuss with her, then of course there was Diomenes' history to go through. After an hour though, I decided to go in search for her. On my way to the library I had the misfortune to run into Rachine and Hadrianus.

"So what do you think of this new book of his?" said Rachine.

'Who, Felix's? - let me tell you, I *know* him and it's like everything he does, it will come to nothing - ashes, just ashes."

"I am not sure this time..."

Ah! - but here is Señor Julian," said Hadrianus.

"Hi." I said, not trying hard to hide my disappointment on stumbling into the pair.

"If you are looking for Karen," said Rachine, "I think she is still with Garcia, we saw her earlier."

"Ah yes, the beautiful Karen! You are a very lucky man senior."

"Here she comes now," said Rachine.

"Julian was just on his way to find you," she said.

"Yes I was just on my way to find you."

"I told you in my note where I was!" replied Karen, somewhat petulantly.

Hadrianus went up to her and took both her hands in his and kissed her on each cheek. "The beautiful Karen, I was just saying how lucky your young man is."

Karen looked at me askance: "Yes well...."

Rachine then kissed her, and put her arm about her, Hadrianus the other side of her, the three of them facing me.

"Did you read the history..." I said, feeling self-conscious.

"Yes I read it. I was talking to Garcia about it - you know that anyway!"

Karen looked up at Hadrianus, who had now got his arm around her waist. I looked at him and he stared back at me unabashed. I felt that *I* was the intruder!

"Well I'll go then, I wanted a word with Garcia in any case." I said.

"I think he's still in the library."

"Right then - see'ya..." I said, turning to go.

"Julian!" called Karen. Suddenly she ran up to me and hugged me tightly, "see you soon my love."

I felt my heart contract. I drew back, still holding her hands. "You are all right aren't you?"

"Of course," said Karen looking down.

I kissed her on the side of her face. Her lavender eyes met mine for a moment, they conveyed neither joy nor passion.

Rachine came over and put her arm about Karen. Immediately I let her hands fall from mine; like a sword she cut us in twain. I found myself then slipping further and further away from her, and moving off in the direction of Garcia's.

"Don't worry," called Rachine, "*We'll* look after her for you."

I waved limply, and watched as they moved off, Karen between the two of them. It's funny how things work out. I was completely powerless to prevent what had just occurred. I knew instinctively what would happen to Karen with *them*, I accepted it as an inevitability, while another part of me fort to reason:

'what harm can come to her, after all it is broad daylight?' I was left with a sick sinking feeling in my stomach; I would go to Garcia with a heavy heart, and not the light one I had begun the day with, not more than twenty minutes ago.

The libidinous young thing Urania showed me into Garcia's private rooms. The sight of her young lithe body did nothing for my mood, except accentuate my sense of failure and inadequacy. When she stood near me she leaned her tight firm body against mine. I considered that any normal red blooded male would be unable to resist such an opportunity, and put an end to the tension, but again I let it go. Her coal-black eyes lingered over me and I wondered what she thought of me: ' a cold passionless soul', I imagine.

Garcia was on the balcony drinking tea. He entreated me to join him in a cup.

"Is it the....?"

"Oh, no - no - no..." He chuckled to himself, "No - just tea, well lapsang souchong in fact."

"I met Karen just now." I said, sitting down opposite him.

"Yes - yes me boy, she was here. We had a good long talk, so much to discuss, well you can imagine," he said, as he poured the tea. "She has many concerns of course, but I told her all would be well, and not to worry. After all she has you, so why should she worry - hey! You know, she worries about you, I laughed, I said that boy is as sound as they come, stick with him and all will be well. But you know what she is like! She does doubt herself - even after all that I showed her. Of course you read the little book I gave you about a certain *priestess....*"

"Yes I read it last night. It did seem remarkably similar to the way Karen described her experience."

"Well there we are then! Now do you still doubt me boy?"

"No, I have to say it was quite disturbing to read. No, I have more doubts concerning myself."

Garcia looked at me quizzically.

"How is that! You know I can't help Karen any more than in showing her who she is, or rather was."

"You know what Karen's nature is better than anyone." I said, "I'm not sure - I'm not sure," I said, suddenly being overcome.

"I say me boy, what is all this!"

Garcia got up and patted me on the back. I could tell he was a man averse to emotional displays, especially by members of his own gender.

"I'm sorry Garcia," I said, recovering my composure.

"So I should think. You have to be strong Mr Julian. Now what is all this nonsense about?"

"I'm not sure you've picked the right man for the job."

Garcia still looked puzzled so I went on tremulously. "I'm not sure I have what it takes."

Garcia looked me up and down. "Not got what it takes! I thought we had cleared all this nonsense up? You're a man aren't you!"

"Yes, but am I enough of a man for a woman like Karen? Just now I saw her go off with Rachine and Hadrianus. I could tell she likes him. That is the kind of man she should be with."

"Hadrianus! You let her go off with him? That rapscallion! What were you thinking of? He'll have her knickers off faster than...." Garcia scratched his head, realising what he had just said. "Rachine will look after her." He said, registering the look of horror on my face.

"Rachine!" I said, suddenly getting to my feet.

"Please Mr Julian sit down. I mean, what is the worst that can happen? They have intercourse! What does it matter? You're leaving soon in any case."

"So it doesn't bother you? You don't think I should mind ? Are you mad! I must go to her. I have to stop them."

"I said sit down Mr Julian." said Garcia, putting a big hand on my arm. "Control yourself man. Going off half-cocked! What good will that do!"

I found myself sitting again staring across the table at the old man, trying to understand what he was saying. Trying to work out what was going on behind that inscrutable look that came over his face so often.

He shook his big head and sighed. "When oh when, will you understand that you can't control a girl like that? It's no good trying to prevent her from going off with - whoever. You will never be able to change her nature, and I am afraid that it *is* in her nature to do these things. There is nothing you nor I can do to change that. *All* you can do is try to guide her away from the wrong sort. Those that would take advantage of her Priapean disposition - her weakness for men of the type who would exploit her. In short, you don't want her running off with every Tom Dick or Harry." Garcia seemed to consider a moment: "But - I shouldn't worry - Hah! - hah, hah...Hadrianus! *He's not so bad....*Reminds me of myself when I was his age. Not a girl was safe....."

"But! - But...I....I just can't..." I spluttered.

I knew what Garcia was saying made sense. I knew well enough her nature but it was accepting it that I found so hard to do.

"No there are no 'buts,' Mr Julian, it would do no good at all trying to prevent what is. What could you hope to achieve? Above all else one must *leave* things to destiny."

"*Destiny!* That's your answer to everything isn't it?"

Garcia shrugged his shoulders. "Pretty much! I mean, what else is there already. One day mankind may realise that resisting destiny is a waste of time, it gets you know where; if anything it just makes matter worse - and believe me, me boy," he went on, wagging his fat finger at me, "things will only get worse as time wears on. That is the result of resisting nature, resisting ones fate. There really is nothing one can do in the end! A man should not fret just because he can't keep his woman. In the end a girl like Karen has to be kept on a short rein, or perhaps - even a very, very long one. Now, I *know* you have had your difficulties in the past, but you were both younger then. Don't worry she has immense skill in matters - well you know well enough what I mean!"

"When it comes to sex you mean?"

"I know you don't feel adequate in the face of things....How shall I put it - so much woman."

I shifted uncomfortably and felt a rush of blood to my face.

"It's all right, Karen has told me. She tells me everything."

"What - exactly has she told you?"

"She told me you have some deep concerns in that area."

The great man leant across the table in that conspiratorial way of his: "Size isn't everything," he whispered, and then leaning back expansively, "I suppose it's all verywell for me to say that though."

I looked around for signs of Urania, I felt naked. I just looked at Garcia, as I sat, struck dumb.

"Don't worry me boy, we'll keep it to ouselves - hey! What she wants you to know is that she is not ashamed of you in any way. She just wants you to be more...more....spontaneous."

I laughed nervously. "Spontaneous!"

"Yes spontaneous. You'll find it all comes together much quicker that way. You know the trouble with you, you think too much."

Garcia suddenly banged his hands flat on the table. "Put your hands out like that," he said.

I did as he directed. "Now let's have a look...."

"What can you tell from looking at my hands?"

"Why everything! Everything is in a man's hands - his temperament, his likes and dislikes, what he is like as a lover. His talents or lack of. His past and his future, all of it is there written for those who have the eyes to see. Some men are of a strong Priapean persuasion, others are Apollonian, while others are Dionysian. We must all accept what is our ruling principle."

"And what is mine?"

"You! You are Apollonian, now doubt about it."

"And Karen?"

"Karen!" Garcia, put his hand to his jaw. "Karen reminds me a lot of Anastasia. Now there's a girl! My word what a girl! She would have sorted you out. Thank your lucky stars she is not here at the moment. Pure Dionysian, and a worshiper of Priapus. Never satisfied that one. I often wonder," mused Garcia, "Which one of them has the edge over the other, and what it would be like to find out? Then of course there is Rachine. Quite a different Dionysian creature altogether. Perhaps....perhaps it might not be a bad idea at that!"

"What may not be a bad idea?" I said, hiding my hands under the table.

"No forget it....I was thinking, if you were to perhaps experience another woman, Rachine perhaps. You don't have much experience do you - with woman I mean?"

Again I looked at him, dumb struck.

"It's all right me boy. I understand. My word that Rachine! She has a very different approach than the Miss Karen. She would show you a thing or two. Karen is very good of course, but she is rather wrapped up in herself, you need to see a woman for what she is. Don't put her on a pedestal."

"But...I...I....It's just that I...I...I..."

"What? - What? Spit it out man..."

"Nothing....it's nothing."

My god I hope I haven't misjudged you, you do like women?"

"Of course! I told you. It's just that...."

"Just nothing!" yelled Garcia, banging his big fist hard down on the table so that the cups jumped out of their saucers, splashing tea everywhere. "You must be a man goddamn it! A man has to take control - especially with a girl like Karen. My god, you are not completely inept! You will just have to make do, we all have to make do one way or another, make do with the way the gods made us, and if one man is bigger in one way than another, he just - well he just has to *make do.* You get my meaning?"

I nodded without adding anything. I felt foolish and at a loss to explain to Garcia how I really felt. For a man versed in metaphysics and the study of reincarnation, he was surprisingly black and white. Men were men and women were women. I guess that was his secret of success with the opposite sex. They knew what they were getting with a man like that. With someone such as myself there were too many shades and subtleties. I guess I gave out mixed signals, a woman, especially one like Karen needed to know where she stood from the word go.

'You look at me in a certain way? OK then lets do it. You want me, I want you.' That was the reasoning behind men like Garcia and Hadrianus. That was why she was so turned on by him. He let it be known to her that he wanted her, and Karen in return, needed to be wanted more than anything else. What was more, they never let anything, but anything get in their way, once their minds had been made up.

Garcia looked at me for some moments without speaking. "I must confess," he said, "you are a strange one. In Karen you have probably one of the most desirable females of the species Sapiens that the gods have ever put among us. She is yours for the taking at any time, and yet you dither and speculate upon all kinds of silly nonsense. She is pure quality *coño!* You will never find better me boy, she is ripe *all of the time.* Take her. Make her yours, a girl like

that needs to be possessed by her man."
I shook my head. "That's just it Garcia, I don't think that way. I don't want her *that* way."
"By the gods you *are* homosexual!"
I laughed and shook my head. "No you don't understand, I don't want to own or possess anybody. There is something about that kind of thinking that puts me off. I'm not interested in playing games. There is just something about me - I don't know what it is, 'by the gods' as you would say, I wish I did!"
"You are a strange young man indeed Mr Julian, which is probably why you must play the role you do in Karen's life, but it will be a circuitous path that you will follow have no doubt. Sometimes the gods smile upon souls such as yours, sometimes though - they damn them to hell!"
"Well let them damn me then," I replied. "I am what I am."
Garcia in a sudden flurry of excitement leapt across the table and gave me a big hug.
"Me boy! - me boy! I knew I'd picked a good'n. Spoken like a man. What a game one you are me boy! to square up to the gods like that. Karen will be safe in your hands I can rest easy on that, even if you are not much good in the sack! Perhaps the answer lies not in seeing yourself so much as a lover to Karen as a shepherd? A shepherd shepherding the shepherdess."
Garcia laughed uproariously at this play on words.
"After all, it's not *so* bad. For every shepherd there is a shepherdess, Chloe had her Daphnis, if I remember rightly, and Callirhoe had her Chaeras, and Cleitophon had her Leucippe, I could go on...."
"But it's not that I don't want to make love to her, I do. It doesn't matter how well endowed one is if it doesn't work. It's something else about Karen. Not her looks - I mean if that was all then it wouldn't be a problem. You know sometimes all her sexy moves she makes, all her stretching, and showing off - well they make me want to laugh. I just can't take her seriously sometimes. Sometimes she acts like a common whore and other times like an innocent little girl."
"You know I had Rachine in my room the other day," I continued, feeling at last that I was getting through to Garcia. "She was acting in the same kind of way Karen does, trying to lure me into having sex with her, telling me that she was

the best, but to my eyes there is nothing to choose between the pair of them - in terms of looks I mean. I mean they can't *all* be the best can they?"

"Who can say. It is a quest I have set my whole life upon, " replied Garcia.

"But there is your girl, Alisiya, she is just as beautiful as Karen, or Rachine even or, any of a number of beautiful girls that you have on this island paradise of yours! I mean is it possible there exists one girl who is the *ne plus ultra?*"

Suddenly I felt as though I had gone too far. Garcia's face clouded.

"Once - once I thought I had found the best," he said, "but because she really *did* believe she was too, she put herself beyond the reach of any man, any man that is, who truly wanted her."

I knew now I had hit a nerve. The very crux of the big mans ego. I had found his Achilles heel. The ill-fated Bethany. The one who had rejected him. But it was too late, I decided instead to push it on, bring it on.

"Was she *very* beautiful?"

"You saw her. Her image anyway."

"The statue in the temple?"

Garcia nodded.

"What happened to her?"

"I was a selfish man then, probably still am. You need not concern yourself over her fate, let's just say that no man will have the girl, *I knew* as Bethany. She lives on in my heart, and as you saw, I have deified her. She is the goddess of this island. The central force, the underpinning to my life, my very being, my essence."

"Do you mind me asking what you had done to her?"

Garcia gave me a long hard stare. "You go too far Mr Julian. Let's just say she is no longer I contender for the crown."

I knew enough when to stop, besides the old man looked all his years again. Of course I knew the story of what happened to Bethany, but it still shook me to hear it from the great Garcia's lips. I thought: 'really, you are just a spoilt child.'

"Going on what I saw in the temple I imagine she was the best, but how could you mar something so perfect?" I said.

"I said you go too far Mr Julian. Who are you anyway, to judge me? when you can't even lay your own woman. I loved her, I loved her and she rejected me. I -

I the great Garcia! How dare she reject *me*. I am a man, a big man!" he yelled, and smashed his big fist down on the table sending everything flying.

Alisiya came over looking very concerned, she stooped to pick up some of the shattered remains of the teapot. Seeing her again, I was struck even more, by how closely her features resembled that of the statue. Bethany must have been a very amazing woman, I reasoned, to have effected Garcia so deeply, my only wish was that I had met her in the flesh.

There followed a long and uneasy silence. Neither man knew what to do, and for my part I felt reluctant to leave, perhaps because I felt a little ashamed of myself for pushing so many questions at Garcia.

"Well I've done all I can, you are on your own now," said Garcia, like the father addressing the stubborn son. "I will make an offering to Tanit today, and again on every full moon."

"Thank you Garcia, I'm sure Karen we feel comforted knowing that. I preyed to Tanit last night, not something I am normally given to do - I mean preying."

"Did you! Did you really?" replied Garcia, "how wonderful."

There were tears in the old man's eyes.

"I'm sorry Garcia for just now. I had no right to make any judgements. I am apt to be rather quick to judge."

"It's all right me boy," he said, the smile returning to his distinguished old face. "There is a lot in you that reminds me of myself when I was your age. I too was rather foolhardy. I suppose it is a characteristic of the young! You have a good soul Mr Julian, a chaste soul. Always remember that the soul is not meant to be associated with the body, it's nature is something light and free. So you shouldn't feel that there is anything wrong with you regarding your sexual feelings for Karen." Garcia laughed, "you want to know the truth, sex is overrated."

I joined in with the laughter out of relief I think. It didn't matter if Garcia was telling the truth or not, knowing him he probably only wanted me to feel better about myself.

"So you will be leaving us today?"

"Today!"

Garcia raised a defensive hand: "Don't get me wrong, I'm not trying to get rid of you. I thought Karen had spoken to you; apparently she is feeling a lot better and is in a hurry to be off."

"She never said anything to me," I replied, my heart growing heavy again when I thought of what she might be doing with Hadrianus. But as Garcia said, there was nothing I could do about that.

"She expressed a wish to see more of Europe before going back to America."

"Did she? Well if that is what she wants! I must admit the most I've seen of it, is this island," I replied.

"I take it you are all right for money?"

"Yes I think so, together we will be OK. There is the money from Karen's modelling, and if things do get bad I can always sell the odd story."

"You know money is not a problem Mr Julian. No need to worry about that. Concentrate on having a good time."

"I'm sure everything will work out for the best - won't it?"

Garcia just looked at me, prompting me to ask the question out right. "What will happen to us? To Karen?"

Garcia put his hands on the table palms upward.

"We all have our destiny to fulfil, the only thing we can do is to follow it where it takes us. The more we struggle against it the harder we make life for ourselves. Your destiny and that of Karen's is irrevocably tied together - no doubt about that! At the present she wishes to travel around Europe with you, after that - who can say?"

"But can't you look into the future for us?"

Garcia held up a hand. "It is not my place to play god."

"But you have done, you have looked into the past."

"In this instance it would not be provident for me to delve to deeply into these things. All I will say is that you will be severely tested. In part it is why I wanted a quick word before you leave."

Garcia leaned forward and continued in earnest. "Be ware of one who follows the Christian path."

"The priest?"

"Quite so. In some way his destiny is tied to Karen's through Natasha. If he still lives he will be in his fifties, so be on your guard, he will be looking for her. He has his own powers of discernment just as I. Do not underestimate him. He may well be aware that Natasha has been reborn, but he does not know she is Karen - at least as far as I am aware. That is all I can say. This is a game of much intrigue Mr Julian, and the stakes are a lot higher than you imagine. Be on your guard, be vigilant of all those who follow *that* faith, I cannot stress the importance of your role in this enough. This is all I am prepared to say, the rest must be left to destiny. Now Mr Julian can I get you some more tea?"

Alisiya arrived with a fresh pot and a plate of hors d'œvres. "Quails eggs, or would you prefer dormouse perhaps?" said Garcia.

I declined the offer of dormouse and helped myself to a few quails eggs before going off in search of Karen.

I went to Karen's room to find it in disarray. Drawers were opened and the wardrobe empty, their contents: fine brightly coloured silk kimono's, gowns and other clothes were draped all over the place. The bed sheet was thrown back and on the table stood three champagne glasses and an opened bottle of champagne, with about a quarter remaining. There was a horrible sickly odour, like stale perfume. My stomach tightened. I turned and rushed out of the room, fortunately a rush of cool air met me on the landing, before I was sick.

I rushed down to the Forum where I found Rachine with a group of girls. They were laughing in that conspiratorial way girls do when there is a gang of them, and no men are present.

"Have you seen Karen?" I asked, breathlessly.

She gave me a long lizard like look, then turned to a tall attractive girl with short blond hair. "That's him," she said.

"*That's* him? Hi - I'm Anastasia. I've heard a lot about you Julian, may be we can *hang out* together?" said the tall attractive blond, offering me her long hand.

"I'd like to stay and talk but I need to find my friend."

"He's kind of cute!" said Anastasia.

"Where is she?" I persisted.

"I have no idea, the last I saw of her she was with Hadrianus," replied Rachine.

"Where? Where were they?"

Rachine laughed demoniacally. "Oh I don't know - here there," she said, going back to her friends, who began to join in with the crazy laughter.

In a fit of fury I grabbed hold of Rachine's arm. "Where is she? Tell me?"

Rachine looked down at my hand as if it were a bug. "Get your stink'n hand off of me."

"Please just tell me where she is?" I said, letting go.

Rachine shrugged her perfect shoulders, "dn'know."

"Forget Karen," said the attractive blond. "I'll show you a much better time."

I smiled acidly at her and persisted with my questioning. Rachine glanced up toward the path that lead out of the complex, "why don't you have a look on her hill. May be she is up there!"

I immediately followed Rachine's suggestion cursing myself for not having thought of it myself.

"Don't be surprised if she is not on her own though," called Rachine, followed by another shriek of twisted laughter. I stopped in my tracks seized by a spasm of pure hatred.

"If anything has happened to her I'll kill you."

Suddenly Rachine left her friends, moving so fast she was nearly running.

"What did you say?" she said, waving her long lizard head in my face.

"You heard - I said I'd kill you."

"Hah...you? you haven't got the guts." She hung her long sinewy body on one side, her hand on her hip. "You know, you should have stuck around, my word you should have seen her with him. Karen is quite something - pure animal when she meets up with her *own* kind."

I raised my hand, my whole body shaking. Rachine didn't flinch. She tilted her lovely long lizard face up slightly and just looked at it. I let my hand fall. Rachine smirked .

"You're no *blady goud!* You haven't got it in you!"

"You're not worth it." I said, turning my back on her and resuming my quest.

"Come here Come here she yelled. I want you Mr. I know you. I know what you are."

It wasn't long before I was well out of earshot and into the countryside. I had to stop after a short time by a tree, in order to throw up the quails eggs that I I had had for breakfast. I felt a bit better for that.

I knew the path well enough having only taken it the day before with Rachine and Garcia. Then I had helped Rachine up the steeper parts, now all I thought of was, how good it would be to throw her down them.

It wasn't long before I heard the now familiar sound of the Panpipes. Their haunting sound had the effect of reassuring me, at least I knew I had one friend on the mountain, and that if Karen was here she would be safe with the goat herder. I listened out for the reedy sound of Karen's flute responding to the Panpipes, but I heard nothing but the scurry of goats and sheep amongst the juniper bushes.

It was stifling hot now. The heat reflected up off the outcrop of bear rock where Garcia and Rachine had rested. I climbed up the last face and followed the narrow path which lead to the vandalised temple of Hestia. On the plane of white flat stone, the morning heat was even more intense. I called out to Karen desperately hoping she would come out of the shadow of the ruins. I went toward them my heart pounding with trepidation, afraid of what I might find there. I small flock of white doves suddenly flew up from a thicket, followed by two sheep.

"Come on, come on out of there, you stubborn thing."

Suddenly another sheep bolted out of the thicket, bleating for all its worth, followed by Karen. She seemed to be enveloped in a blinding light. I tried to draw her attention to this fact but I must have collapsed before I was able to, for the next thing I was aware of was the boys face looking down at me, with an expression of concern, and a pair of soft hands touching me.

"Here drink this," said Karen, putting a bottle to my mouth.

"Karen! - you were all silvery." I said.

"It was the heat - you fainted."

"Where am I?"

"In the ruins. I had to get Acastos the goat herder, to help me bring you into the shade."

I grabbed Karen and hugged her tightly. "I was so afraid...."

"Don't be silly, it's you *who* fainted. Silly - coming up here without water!"

Karen put the bottle to my mouth again and I drank greedily, until the boy said something to Karen. "You mustn't drink too much at one go." she said, taking the bottle from my lips.

I sat up, resting my head against the cool surface of a marble column, my senses quickly returning.

"You are looking a bit better now. You gave me a real fright."

I tried to smile but my head was full of questions, questions I now found I was too afraid to ask. I looked up at the boy who was smiling. Karen spoke to him in Greek and he gave a swift bow, before disappearing to the sound of the Panpipes.

I hugged Karen again in a kind of desperation, which she picked up on. "What is it! - You silly thing."

"Nothing! Just the heat." I said, feebly, but it was no good, I couldn't prevent the tears from coming.

"Yes there is! What is it? What's wrong?"

"Nothing," I said, shaking my head.

Karen held my face up to hers, "tell me."

"No."

"I think I can guess. You thought you would find me with Hadrianus, that's it! isn't it?"

Defenceless, I just looked at her beautiful face, hating myself for doubting her, yet unable to forget what Rachine had said.

"Were you?"

"Yes I was with him, but not in the way you think."

I took the bottle from Karen and tipped it back.

"I hate her. I hate Rachine. She said you *had* been with him."

"Rachine is a mischief maker. She is jealous of me and you, that's all. She doesn't understand you the way I do."

"So you didn't" I suddenly knew what it was like to want to laugh and cry at the same time.

"No we didn't - do it! We went back to mine with Rachine and opened a bottle of champagne. We all got a bit merry and then some of Rachine's friends came over, who had just arrived from Italy."

"Yes I went to your room," I said, before sinking my head between my knees in shame.

"I know, it's all a bit of a mess. Rachine and her friends tried on some of my stuff;

we dressed up Hadrianus too. That's all that happened."

Karen gave me a sidelong glance. "I know what you think of me, and how it must have seemed."

I laughed, this time out of embarrassment as much as share relief.

"And that was all!" I said.

"Yes *it is*," replied Karen, with a distinct edge to her voice. "If you are going to continually doubt me what hope do we have?"

"I know, but what *was* I to think when Rachine said that you..."

"Rachine, Rachine, fuck Rachine! Who would you rather believe, me or her?"

Karen turned her face away. I could tell by her voice that she was upset. I held her to me and kissed her face, tasting its saltiness. My hand travelled along her arm, a pulse of desire transmitted itself from the surface of her smooth flesh through my finger tips, as fierce as an electrical discharge. We began to kiss one another, my lips falling over her full vulnerable throat. I felt the strength in her body as she pressed herself against me. Her body was a ceaseless wonder to me, an endless source of excitement. I loved every part of it, every tiny detail, such as the way her veins stood out on her strong neck, or the minute creases in her skin, over her throat. Every tiny detail, or minor imperfection in her body held its own fascination for me, and each one alone was enough to send me over the edge; in the end though, the transmission of energy through our bodies was interrupted, when Karen puled away as I began to undo her silk bodice.

"No - not here," said Karen. "She looked around. "it wouldn't be right. Not here."

"You mean the goddess wouldn't like it?"

Karen shook her head. "*No* - she wouldn't. It wouldn't be right, not after all she has done for me."

It didn't take a lot to understand Karen's reasoning. We were in the place of goats and sheep, in the domain of Chloe, the domain of innocence and the one place where the memory of Chloe dominated; and it was Karen's only respite from the madness that gnawed away at her soul, the rest of the time. This was the one place where she could find peace. In the precincts of the sacred temple of the most sweetest and innocent of deities, making love to Karen here of all places would have been especially wrong. Here, as I had seen with mine own two eyes, the goddess Hestia had crowned Karen with a divine effulgence. To have exploited Karen's sensual nature here, would have been to defile the virgin goddess herself. Instead I hugged her, not wanting to ever let her go, not wanting to ever leave this place, knowing that out there beyond the remains of the temple, beyond the confines of Garcia's island, a whole world of horrors and temptations of the flesh existed. In the end though, like all embraces, ours too, at exactly the right moment, came to an end.

Karen helped me up. To my surprise I still felt distinctly light headed and after only a couple of steps I had to rest again against another marble pillar.

"Will you be all right?"

"I think so. It was just getting up."

"Drink some more water. Do you want me to get Acastos?"

"No I think I will be all right."

"You seemed fine a minute ago," said Karen, with a cheeky grin on her face.

Karen put her arm around me and we began to walk slowly away from the temple refuge. She stopped and looked back.

"I don't know if I will ever come back here? I just want to say a private good-by, a sort of prayer to the goddess," said Karen, propping me up in the shade of an olive tree.

At that moment, just as it had the other day, a beautiful cooling breeze suddenly swirled up from nowhere. Karen and I looked at one another both cognoscente of its significance.

"She is already with you." I said.

Karen looked at me slightly perplexed.

"Remember I told you, you were all 'silvery!' Before I past-out I saw you come out of the bushes and you were full of a bright blinding light."

"You had too much sun."

"Maybe. But I know what I saw."

Karen kissed me on the mouth. "Will you be all right? I won't be long."

Suddenly another gust of wonderful refreshing air gathered up as I watched Karen's marvellous form, disappear into the temple remains.

I sat down under the tree and closed my eyes and immediately went into a dream. A sequence of images chased one another through my minding going back to the day when I first set foot on the island of Sapphos to the present. This time I didn't see her coming out of a mass of overgrown scrub, instead I saw the temple in all its gleaming magnificence as it must have looked before the Christian era: that is, before it had been desecrated and subsequently vandalised. I saw Karen kneel before the sacred hearth. She was dressed in a long white flowing gown. On her head she worse a mantle of white flowers. Her skin shone translucent, as lit from some inner radiance. I knew that what I beheld was a vision of the priestess Chloe! When I opened my eyes the image of Karen as the priestess lingered on for a few seconds, before it became superimposed by the present day - Earthly Karen."

"Come on sleepyhead," she said, smiling brightly.

"Did you say your good-byes to the goddess?"

"I did, I preyed to Hestia and I felt her presence. I feel all is going to be good from now on," said Karen, putting her arm around me.

"When you were gone I had a dream, and I saw you as the lovely high priestess Chloe. Well I suppose it was her."

"Did you! Did you really? How wonderful. What did I look like?"

"You looked beautiful. You looked like a goddess, you were all dressed in white and you had flowers in your hear and your skin sort of glowed white, like a pearl."

"Oh, my sweet!" she exclaimed, seeing the tears in my eyes.

"She was so beautiful Karen! She looked so at peace, not at all like that other high priestess." I said, fiercely hugging her. "I love you Karen," I suddenly blurted out.

"Oh - I know! And I love you."

"If only it was Chloe! if only it was her sweet and perfect soul that dominated your existence!"

"It can - it will in time. I promise it will. I am her in part, as much as any of the others."

Karen let go of my arm and skipped and danced ahead of me. "Come on Julian - don't look so worried, we have Hestia on our side, and may be we shouldn't be too quick to forget Tanit - after all, it wasn't her fault remember! It was when I was that horrible snake-woman Nachash!"

"Perhaps we should go back and make some sort of offering?" I said, finding to my dismay how quickly one got carried away with such pagan notions; and only after a *couple* of mystical experiences!

"We could, but may be we shouldn't? I'm not sure of the relationship between Hestia and Tanit, and after all, it is really Hestia's place of worship - I know what we could do! Lets sing a song to her."

Karen took out of her bag her flute and began to play a strange staccato kind of tune. I followed her down the twisty winding path to the sound of her flute, much like a rat to the pied piper, my lovely piper. Far away came the haunting sound of Acastos' Panpipes, as he responded to the sound of the flute, and in his own unique way said his farewell to the shepherdess, whom he knew only as 'Chloe'.

After a few bars of the unusual melody, Karen began to sing the song of Tanit: 'Tanit oh Tanit we love you we love you, Tanit Oh Tanit we worship you we worship you. Oh Ta-anit Ta-anit we honour you we honour you, Oh Tanit Ta-anit Ta-a-nit.'

"That's a strange little song you were singing just now."

"Yes, it just sort of came to me. I think I heard it last over two thousand years ago," replied Karen. "Its funny - when I was up on the hill more memories of what it was like to be the high priestess came back to me. She wasn't really that bad a person, she was quite naïve really, a bit like Chloe, and I suppose all the others. Except she got lost in the belief that she *was* Tanit herself. She was very beautiful and as the history suggests, she was the object of everyone's desire.

"That has been the bane of all your incarnations," I said.
"I know - can I help it if I am just so goddamn sexy," said Karen, flouncing her hips in a silly exaggerated way.

I grabbed her round the waist and Karen giggled. "you're too much, too much!" I said.

"I know I am," she replied.

She squealed with laughter: "heeeee - aaah - heeee," as she squirmed free of my grasp and ran ahead of me.

By the time we came off the mountain the second day of the celebrations were well under way. After the relative solitude and peace up there, it was a shock to suddenly be confronted by so many people. We were both surprised by how popular Garcia was. By now there must have been over five hundred of his followers on the island. At least a two fold increase. There were people singing and dancing and milling around. We had a difficult time getting through the crowds.

"Its getting late. We should start to pack our stuff," I shouted, trying to be heard over the noise.

Karen looked around like one who is reluctant to leave the party.

"Are you sure you feel up to it?" she called back.

"Yes are you?"

Karen nodded. "Lets do it then. Yes lets get off the island."

"How will we get off?" I said, still afraid at the back of my mind that we may never get away.

Karen laughed, "don't worry, Garcia will get someone to row us to one of the larger islands, there are lots of boats on the island. From there we can get a ferry to Piraeus."

I gave Karen a hug and arranged to meet her in an hour outside the main entrance to the villa. As I went off I could not help but feel apprehensive. I was afraid something might go wrong at the last minute. That Karen would mysteriously vanish again or, worse be put under a trance again by Garcia, or perhaps Rachine and Hadrianus, or someone would get to her!

It wasn't until faced with our imminent departure that I realised how utterly bored I had become with the island, and Garcia's pontificating as well as all the issues concerning reincarnation. It was all so intense and serious and life threatening, and it had become a burden without me ever realising it. Oh yes, on the surface of things it all sounds like an idyllic kind of lifestyle, 'an island that has renounced all the trappings of modern living, etcetera', the truth was the feeling of being a prisoner had never really left me. There was a part of me that had a hankering after the modern world, with all its associated noise and pollution and hustle and bustle.

It didn't take long to get my things together and throw them in a bag. Promptly at the prescribed time I was outside the villa at the appointed spot. An hour came and an hour went without any sign of Karen. A half hour later and I was outright anxious hoping from one foot to the next, my head in a whirl, as I tried to spy Karen amongst the swirl of faces that swayed to and fro before my vision. I was now caught in the old dilemma of staying put or going to look for her, and run the risk of missing one another. And then I saw the man himself: Garcia striding towards me through the multitude.

"Me boy - Julian, so glad I found you," he said, embracing me, "The Miss Karen was afraid you might have got lost. I have just been to see her."

Garcia shook his head and laughed, "You should see the amount of things she has to pack! Well you know what women are like. Mostly clothes. She doesn't know what to take and what to leave. I said to her, 'my dear this is as much your home as it is mine so leave anything you don't think you will be needing here."

Garcia picked up my bag and handed it to one of his acolytes. "He will take your luggage down to the boat," said Garcia, putting his arm about me. Now come let us have a drink together."

"What about Karen! perhaps I should go and help her?"

"Nonsense, you would only get in the way - relax Mr Julian," Garcia squeezed my shoulder. "I gave her instructions to come to the library when she is done."

We went into his private wing and sat on the balcony as we had done so many times before. My apprehension was replaced by a pang of regret at having to leave. Despite his arrogance Garcia was a likeable old rascal, as are so many charismatic leaders. There was something enigmatic about his character that one just couldn't get enough of.

"You will enjoy Europe Mr Julian. It is the bedrock of western culture, you Americans seem to forget that. It is a fascinating world in its own right! Where will you go first?" asked Garcia as he poured me a beaker of wine.
"I don't know, I think Karen wanted to show me the Parthenon."
"Oh indeed, indeed yes you must see it. A pure marvel of ancient architectural genius."
"After that I don't really know. Rome I suppose."
Garcia nodded, "indeed - indeed you must visit the capitol of the western empire. As I said to Karen, me casa su casa, so if you are in Italy you may stay at my apartment in Rome and Tuscany."
"That's very generous of you Garcia. Thank you."
He held up his hand smiling, "it is nothing, I assure you." Garcia was silent for a moment. "I suppose you can hardly wait to get away with Karen?" he said at length,
"Well I am looking forward to getting off this island of yours. No disrespect to you Garcia, but I feel somewhat..."
"But you were never a prisoner you know," Garcia interrupted.
"I know. I know I wasn't." I replied, trying to put on a smile.
"I can understand your impatience, but be good to my Karen," he said, leaning forward and waving a critical finger at me.
"Of course," I said, noting his fatherly affection.
"I know you will. She has been through an awful lot. I am aware that you still have your reservations concerning my ideas..."
"Less than I did." I interjected.
Garcia regarded me for a moment before opening his mouth to speak. "In many ways Miss Karen is a fragile creature. Oh, robust physically, as I am sure you are well aware." He paused a moment. He was obviously finding it difficult to express what was on his mind. "In many ways she is just like a new born child."
"She is tougher than you think. One tough hombre - in every respect."
Garcia sighed heavily. "I hope you are right Mr Julian, for Karen's sake. But remember this, you will never be able to relax your vigilance. Remeber the priest is out there, and you are all that stands between Karen and him. It would

not bode well if she were to fall under his influence again, mistaking it for true love, or whatever it is she takes for love! It will only take a moments lapse in concentration on the part of yourself to loose her, but it will be worse for Karen for in loosing you she looses her soul."

"You don't sound optimistic Garcia. I know you have your doubts about me."

"Not at all me boy...." replied Garcia, "it is the modern world and the evil that exists out there that cause me the greatest concern. It is not your fault that you are a product of that world, as indeed is the Miss Karen, despite everything I've tried to show her."

He sighed heavily and we lapsed into a silence. "You may not like this world," I said at last, "but its all there is. You can't change things by going back to the past. You can pretend that the modern world doesn't exist. If you want to change things for the better, you have to tackle them here in the present, not hide away on an island, or behind fanciful notions of a paradise lost, populated by Gods!"

My frank speaking seemed to have perked the old man up. He smiled broadly and chuckled to himself.

"My word Mr Julian, but you are a card really you are! You don't care about what people think do you! You don't care if you sound disrespectful," he said, puling his face into a grimace. "After...hah, hah....after all I have done for you, and this is how you repay me. My word, you modern scaly."

"I was just trying to be honest."

"Of course you were, and I respect you for it. Now, let me give you some advice. What you need to do young man is loosen up some. *You can't* go on seeing the Miss Karen as your possession. At most you are only a custodian, a *watcher*, call it what you will. Enjoy the delights of her body as often or as little as you like, you will never be able to satisfy a girl like that, probably no man alive could, so don't be hard on yourself, on that score, but if you were to be honest with yourself - well you know as well as I that you don't have it where it counts, but good fun trying - hey! Your task is to keep her safe, safe from those bastards that would seek to exploit her sexual nature, as Natasha and the others were."

"I'll do my best," I said, with a note of irritation.

"That's all one can ask. You are all that stands between reincarnation and damnation."

"But there is nothing one can do, if her soul is fated to be destroyed?"

"It is true that, that which is, is when it is, and if it is true that her soul shall be corrupt then it must take place."

Garcia smiled enigmatically; I think he enjoyed it when he said something profound and mysterious, even if in reality it was quite banal.

"You must understand Mr Julian, there exists only the present. Time itself, I mean ones common notion of it being a linear thing, is simply illusory. It is true we live from moment to moment, but the moment that just *was*, is gone, therefore all that exists, as far as we are concerned, is the *now*. At least that is our common notion of time, its true nature is something else again. All moments, those that were, and those that are yet to be, exist simultaneously. Hence my phrase, 'that which is, is when it is,' just as my words follow on one from another and my heart beats one beat after another...."

Garcia suddenly broke off as I became aware of a strong aroma of Jasmine. I felt Karen's lips on my cheek. She pressed her wondrous face hard against mine, her arms encircling my body.

"*Kalymera pateras,*" said Karen, sitting down next to me and taking my hand in hers.

I looked at her and thought I had never seen anything so exquisite; she was exotic, otherworldly, astounding. We were both liberated now from the dress code of the island, although it is important to note that there was no element of compulsion behind it. I was wearing my usual Bermuda shorts and one of my more brightly coloured Hawaiian shirts. Karen was dressed in a long blue patterned pencil skirt with a slit up one side, and red silk Japanese style blouse, that was undone at the neck in such a way that the wonderful arch of her bosom was discernible.

"Everyone is calling me 'father,'" said Garcia, smiling at Karen, "I will soon be feeling my age."

"You are father, father of the island, father of the faith, and perhaps even father to me."

The old man smiled again, and I could tell that he was moved almost to tears by Karen's sentiment.

"You certainly do know a heck of a lot of people Garcia? The celebrations are a real hit," I said.

"Yes I never imagined there would be so many followers," put in Karen.
"Followers - pfui! Most of them are freeloaders, on the look out for a party, friends of friends of friends, except each one of them would probably stab the other in the back."
"Then you should kick them off the island, its not right that they take advantage of you father!"
"What does it matter, so long as they are happy, that's all I want - people to be happy. There seems so little of it these days! Who am I to tell people to, 'bugger of this is my island?' It doesn't matter if they don't *believe* in the gods, so long as they embrace the general idea - that they get a real feel for the celebrations as being one of peace and harmony with the world. With one another. That's all I'm concerned with."
"Peace and love!" I said.
"I'm not a damn hippie Mr Julian. I'm a follower of the true path - a Dionysian! I'll have no drug snorting pretentious hippie wasters on my island, and if I find any of the suns of bitches I'll kick their buts all the way to the sea!"
"I thought you just said your main concern was that people were happy, kicking people's buts into the sea doesn't sound very nice?" said Karen, coolly.
"Yes that's exactly right *mon chéri*. I am concerned about happiness, and when have you ever seen a happy drug addict? Some of these hippie scum are the most depressed lot I have ever come across, always secretly envious of the rich, that is, those that aren't already rich, the others go around bleating about how bad the world is, how the end is *nigh,* never doing anything themselves to try and change things." Garcia put two fingers in the air. "Peace and love man!" he said mimicking the hippie talk, "screw peace and love, since when has mankind been concerned with *peace and love?* It's a load of baloney. Its the same baloney the monotheists come out with. It's unreal pie in the sky, crap! Human beings are fundamentally nasty selfish, warring creatures. If we start from that premise we can't go wrong. But that is not to say we can't still try to be happy. I say it, time and time again - 'Know thyself!' "

Karen and I looked at one another. There was a moments awkward silence. When Garcia spoke like this you genuinely felt that you were in the presence of a great mind. He saw the whole issue clearly defined, when most people only saw the shadowy outline.

Karen nodded. "You are right of course," she said, "drug addiction is a miserable thing."

It is my hope that one day people will wake up to themselves," said Garcia, dismissing Karen's response as if it were the utterance of a child. We could tell we were in for the full treatment. Karen stole another glance at me, I think she was on the verge of cracking up with laughter.

"Mankind is a funny thing you know! He can conceive of some wonderful things, create truly astonishing works of art, while at the same time have the equal capacity to bring down upon the world and himself, unspeakable horrors.

The thing is, non of it is unnatural. Nature just says: 'Here I am! I am not this or that, I simply *am.'* And mankind comes along and says: 'This is not enough! I am not content with just *being,* There must be something more!' But *why* must there be more? You see there is a schism at the heart of mankind, between himself and the universe, which..." said Garcia, pausing to wag a countenancing finger in our direction, "is at the heart of mankind's misery. But where would I be without that book of *epigrams* that Mr Felix wrote?" went on Garcia, waving his arms about. "All this would never have come about were it not for him."

"I overhead Rachine talking about a new book he is writing. At least I am pretty sure they mentioned *Felix*?" I said.

"Who knows!" said Garcia, chuckling to himself. "The man is full of ideas. What a mind - what a mind he has! Such imagination! So many ideas! Metaphysician theoretician, essayist, novelist - a born writer if ever there was one! A poet, artist sculptor - genius! What more can I say? His, is the quiet voice behind my actions. *You know,* one day they will come to me and ask for *my* advice! They will call me wise one, or perhaps *father,* I will be know as the *Shukti...*"

Garcia laughed awkwardly. I think for the first time I saw him actually embarrassed by his own words. He had perhaps given away a little bit too much of his secret ambition - to perhaps one day rule the world? 'Absurd' you say! Others far more humble than Garcia have had such notions. I can think of two straight off!

"I am sure you will have many more followers Garcia," I said, aware of his faux pas. And there I was forever the intuitive, even willing to come to the rescue of a megalomaniac. Garcia was always going on about the importance of knowing yourself, well it hit me there and then exactly what I was, or rather, was not, and one thing I could never be was an acolyte of anybody, be it of Jesus, Genghis Khan, Napoleon, Gandhi, or Adolph Hitler, or any of those other *big* names. In this sense I was my own man, and would cow-tow to no one.

We drank a bit more wine and talked of lighter things, such as all the different places we were planning to visit, gradually though the momentousness of the occasion came upon us and conversation became more difficult between the three of us. In timely fashion one of *Garcia's* acolytes arrived to say that our transport was ready to take us down to the jetty, where the boat was waiting.

Karen and I boarded the same rickety cart, puled by the same weary animal, that had first brought me to Garcia's residence all those weeks ago; while Garcia went on ahead, riding his own, more sturdy mount. Karen and I didn't say much to each other on the short journey. People stood all along the route some of them waving coloured handkerchiefs. Karen and I waved back. For my part I was bemused by the spectacle, but Karen embraced the moment for all it was worth, occasionally calling back to the gathered multitude the now familiar sentiment, which was to, 'send our love to Father.' But it was *for* father and not for us that so many came out to cheer.

Rachine and Garcia were waiting for us at the jetty, where a modern motorised launch was moored. Our luggage had gone on ahead and was already stored on board. It was, as I had expected, a very emotional moment. Tears began to stream down Karen's face as she hugged Rachine, she then fell into the arms of Garcia. She was now sobbing uncontrollably. I looked on, feeling quite inadequate to the situation. Rachine, showing a side to her that I had always suspected existed, came over to try and console Karen, only ending up becoming emotional herself. Garcia hugged Karen tightly, whispering soothing words in her ear such as, 'come - come my child, quieten now, it is not the end but a beginning. Come - come now, quieten - quieten now my child.'

I could see that he was trying to be strong, but he was as soft as any of us, and it wasn't long before tears were streaming down his weathered cheeks. He looked to me, to take a firm hand, and I felt for his sake, as well as Karen's that I had to be up to the situation, and - 'be a man.' Karen then fell on to me still sobbing her heart out. I spoke similar words of optimism and the need for stoicism, as Garcia had used, but to no avail.

"Oh no, oh no" - Karen wailed, "I will never see him again! I shall never see this place again! I shall die, I know I shall die! I'm afraid, *so afraid!*" she whimpered, "Oh please, please don't let me die."

"I shan't ever let you die," I said. "Come now, lets get on the boat."

At this point even the Captain of the vessel, who had been looking on concernedly, stepped over to take Karen's hand. His face was darkened by many a year travelling the sea-ways between the islands of the Aegean. He was the kind of man you felt you could trust your life with, but even then, Karen turned back, resisting his kind intentions.

"No! Please Garcia, help me, Garcia! My sheep! Who will look after my sheep? where is Acastos? I want Acastos! I want to go back! I want my sheep! Please, please," she screamed, now almost hysterical.

The captain looked at me,. full of surprise, even hurt in his wonderful blue eyes. I just looked back at him. Rachine was looking at Garcia, and then Garcia looked towards me. For a moment non of us knew what to do, and then quite unexpectedly an old woman stepped up from the crowd dressed all in black. She was spluttering words in Greek; and with a strong hand took hold of Karen and shook her. It was an amazing sight. I have no idea what the woman said to Karen, but she seemed to sober up almost straight away. The old woman gave her a quick hug and then lead her over to me. She spoke to me rapidly in Greek. I nodded and looked towards Garcia for help.

"She is a woman of these islands, one of the wise ones, she says just for you to take care of her now, that is all; that Karen is one of natures rarities, that you must guard her with your life, that she is one of gods chosen," related Garcia.

Karen, now in a sort of daze was rubbing her face. I took it as my opportunity to lead her by the hand onto the boat, once onboard she seemed to calm down even more, I suppose because now she was no longer physically connected with the island ? resigned now - almost, to her fate.

"Everything will be all right won't it?" she said, in a child like voice.

I held her trembling body close to me and soothed her hot brow, placing kiss upon kiss upon her face, as tenderly as a moths wing.

The captain glanced over at Karen and I, and seeing that all looked well, took the opportunity to cast off. Suddenly there came the burble of an engine spluttering into life.

"Everything will be all right, nothing will harm you." I said.

She looked up at me, her grey eyes wide, magnified by tears, displaying all her vulnerability. She was a child and no more than a child, an innocent child.

I became aware of the launch moving. Karen looked up startled still clinging to me as tight as she could.

I looked towards the jetty, and saw Garcia. He was speaking to Rachine, then Rachine began to wave, and Garcia joined in along with everyone else on the key side. I looked for the woman in black but it was impossible to distinguish her among the crowd.

"Good-bye my child," called Garcia, "be brave my child. Good-bye Mr Julian. Take good care of her."

"I will." I shouted back.

"Farewell Karen," called Rachine, "bon voyage..."

Karen wiped her eyes and even smiled vaguely, waving frantically as the launch drifted further out.

"Good-bye, good-bye I love you. Take good care of my sheep, send my love to Acastos and my sheep, good-bye Rachine."

For a second I thought I heard the haunting melody of the Panpipes, coming from some place far off - beyond the many. If Karen had called out anything else no one on the jetty would have heard, as the engines suddenly went to full throttle and the launch roared away, showing us that this was its true nature, and not to tarry by the key, when its true element beckoned. How quickly Garcia, Rachine and all the multitude diminished in size once the launch was well under way,and heading out into open water!

Soon it became silly to wave any more as the people on the jetty were hardly discernible, and yet Karen still stared at the diminishing spit of land, as if she had the eyes of a hawk, and she could still see them waving.

I realised that there wasn't anywhere for her to run, and so I let go of her, and sunk into one of the plush seats in the stern. I looked at her stiff figure, as she stood staring into the distance like one of Garcia's statues. I recalled with vivid clarity everything Garcia had said concerning Karen's nature, and it dawned on me what a tremendous burden I had taken upon myself. I looked out at the expanse of beautiful blue sea, I looked up at the Captain and his Mate at the helm, and back to Karen, and suddenly felt very alone.

I reached out and took Karen's hand and reluctantly she sat down next to me. She looked at me and smiled forlornly and then looked out at sea again, still staring in the general direction from which we had come, even though at this distance Garcia's island was no more distinguishable from any of the other smaller Greek islands that came into view.

X

It was about an hours journey by fast motor-launch from Garcia's island to the Cycladic island of Siros, which was supplied by regular ferry to the mainland, and the Athenian port of Piraeus.

Throughout the journey Karen sat frozen, staring fixedly out to sea. Even a hawk with the largest of eyes could not see the tiny island of Sapphos from such a distance, but still she stared transfixed at a point on the horizon. After a time I gave up asking her how she was, and if I stroked her arm she would turn to look at me with big, sad grey eyes that were never far away from tears. Sometimes she would give a sad forlorn smile. The job of a custodian, I was fast becoming aware, was a lonely and thankless one.

On arrival at Siros we were taken by taxi to a small hotel that had been pre-booked for us by one of Garcia's people. Karen had brought so much luggage that most of it had to be sent on ahead on the late night ferry.

Our room was neat and tidy and clean. I looked at the double bed with a measure of trepidation. Karen had hardly said two words to me the entire journey. I laid down, grateful for a moments rest to myself, while Karen showered. I thought, 'not that long ago and we would have both been in there together. She would have been commanding me to lather her body or cover it with oil. And I had taken it all for granted',' funny that! I had to smile.

She was a long time. When she did come out, she had a big bath towel tightly wound round her body.

"You can go in there now if you want?" she said.

For a second I wanted to go over to her and take away her towel, but her demeanour made it clear that her body was temporarily off limits. Besides which, I felt too tired to tarry with such notions, and decided the best thing was to take up Karen's offer of a solitary shower. When I came out she had dressed and was drying her hair.

"You look beautiful," I said.

"You always say that! Of course I'm beautiful." Giving me a hostile look:
"Aren't you going to get dressed? I'm hungry. I want to get something to eat."
The hotel had a small restaurant; the staff were all extremely courteous, embarrassingly so, whether it was because we were known as 'Garcia's people,' or that they thought we were big spenders, who can say? I suspected that they were genuinely polite; the slimy ones who are just after your money, exhibit a special kind of eagerness to please, that borders on rudeness. The food was delicious, as most Greek cuisine is. We both had Greek salad, followed by stuffed vine leaves, okras and a sea food platter. Although Karen said she was hungry she only picked at her salad.

She stared at me for several moments whilst I tried to finish my fish. Finally she took a large gulp of wine and set the glass down on the table, twirling it around by its stem. Her beautiful mouth contorted into a sort of grimace.

"Well, " she said, at length, "now that you have me all to yourself what do you propose to do with me?"

I suddenly felt a slight pang of indigestion. I set my fork down and just starred at her a moment before replying.

"Do with you!" I exclaimed.

"Well you have me now. It won't be long before you get pissed off with me. Especially when you can't get what you want. I saw you in the room earlier, you hated it because I didn't come on to you."

"You just seemed a bit distant, not yourself."

I picked up my drink, deciding that it was not a good idea to continue with my remaining platter. Karen remained silent.

"If you want we can go back?" I said.

I picked up my fork and stuffed another okra in my mouth.

"No that wouldn't be right," she said, staring at me for some moments more. "You probably hate it - this - me! I'm sorry, I must be such a terrible burden to you?" said Karen, pushing her glass away.

Tears came into her eyes despite a brave attempt to stifle them.

"Hey....Look, its all right. You're not a burden. I just thought that may be you weren't ready to leave the island. You were *very upset.*"

"I feel embarrassed now," said Karen, resting her forehead on her tightly wound fist.

"Don't be. You've been through a heck of a lot. If it's anyone's fault it's Garcia's."
"No - no don't blame him. Its me, I'm a stupid child," said Karen, wiping her eyes on a serviette and blowing her nose. At that moment she looked so pathetic and just like a child it wrenched my heart to look at her.
"I love you Karen," I said, self-consciously "I'll try my best to be what you want me to be."
Karen stretched her long slender hand across the table. "You're so sweet. I don't deserve you." she said, taking my hand in hers.
"Probably not," I replied.
Karen laughed for the first time, in what seemed like a long while. "I don't want you to be *like* anything. Who you *are* is just perfect - just perfect."
"You mean that?"
"Of course. I trust you...Oh I feel so stupid. What must everyone think," said Karen, letting go of my hand and taking another drink.
"Garcia did say it would be difficult for you. I had no idea..."
"I feel better than I was - but you must know I *do* find it hard. I miss that place so much," she said, putting her hand to her mouth again, tears coming into her eyes. "My little sheep..."
"You'll see them again."
Karen, unable to answer, just shook her head. I got up from the table and put my arm around her. Her body made tiny little jerking movements as the weight of her sadness got the upper hand.
"I shan't - I shan't ever see them a...again...." she stammered, as her body went through more tiny convulsions. "Nor...nor A..A..Acastos...or....or Garcia."
"You will, I promise," I said, trying to make my voice sound confident.
I looked over my shoulder to check who else was witnessing this little scene. There was only one other couple, who were quite polite by doing their best to ignore us. But one of the waiters came over and inquired if all was well, which had the effect of jolting Karen back into the - *now!*
I went back to my seat gingerly, keeping my eyes on Karen. I would be forever the man keeping an eye out for Karen. The waiter, in such a sweet display of humanity, came over to our table again and left a box of tissues. Karen smiled through her tears. She grabbed a couple, and blew her nose loudly.

"Its understandable you will miss the island, but I promise you, *you will* see Garcia again. He might even come and visit us!"
"Yes he did say. Oh..you will contact him?"
"Of course I will - now, have some more retsina," I said, replenishing Karen's glass.
"Promise me you won't leave me...." she said, taking the opportunity to grab hold of my hand.
I glanced at her beautiful distraught face and the look of panic in her wonderful lavender-grey eyes. "I'll never leave you!" I said.
I had to look away from that amazing face, and those eyes magnified by tears. And it was true what the ancients believed! The eyes were the windows of the soul, and I saw her soul flitting under the surface of her tears, a soul terribly lost and frightened. I had to look away, no man could behold such a sight and remain unmoved. I had to be strong for her. I had to look away. I could not bear to see that poor lost creature illuminated in the candle light, so lost and afraid, and I knew now that Garcia too must have beheld it. I had to look away.
"We will have a good time Karen," I continued, on a more upbeat note. "Think how exciting it will be, the whole of Europe before us to discover, just the two of us."
"The two of us..." said Karen. I wasn't sure by her intonation if she meant that as a question or a statement?
"Yes it will be exciting," she added, trying a little bit too hard now to sound convincing. Karen picked up her glass of retsina and looked at me wistfully over the rim, "can we contact Garcia?"
"Yes of course, just as soon as we get settled at the hotel in Athens. But Garcia knows we will be there anyway."
"Yes, but I would like him to know we arrived safely, and we can invite him to stay a while."
"If that's what you want?"
Brightening a little: "yes I think I should like that." Her face darkened again almost immediately. "I think I have a headache coming," she said, frowning, then in a childlike voice, "*I'm* feeling *very tired.* I think I would like to go to bed now!"

"Oh - all right! I thought may be we could have gone for a walk by the sea?"
"What, after today! I couldn't bear to look at the sea. I would think of Sapphos. No, I think I just want to sleep."
"You don't mind if I go out for a while?"
"No darling, of course not. You go. You'll have a far better time than having me around."
"Don't say it like that."
"Why not? It's true. I'm a burden to *you* - to everyone. But you don't have to worry, it won't be long before my fate catches up with me. I shall die quite soon, I know I will. I shall never see Sapphos or Garcia, or the sheep - all of that, gone forever."
"Please don't say that," I said, becoming angry and upset.
"Ah, poor sweet Julian. I'm sorry."
Karen got up, lent forward, and kissed me. "See you later, have a good walk." With that she went off to our room leaving me alone at the table. I looked around me self-consciously. The people who ran the hotel would think we had had a lovers tiff. They could *never* know the true nature of our relationship. I quickly left them to their speculations. Outside I took a large gulp of air, and the horrible fact dawned on me, 'yes I *was* glad to be on my own at last!'
I went to the key-side. There was no distinction between the sky and the sea, everything was pitch black. I turned away towards the lights that came from the small town and went in search of a bar, somewhere where not a *soul* would know me. Somewhere where I could think plenty and drink plenty. I was off-duty at last, free of my charge. I could begin to relax a little. I was glad of a few moments to myself, with no responsibility but to myself. I lit a cigarette and ordered a beer. It was just a small local bar, but no one was going to bother me. Fortunately there were no tourists here either; I didn't even want to hear my own language spoken. I suppose what I was in search of, was - *oblivion!*
I had no idea what time I got back. Karen appeared to be asleep, but almost as soon as I got into bed I felt her hand reach out for mine beneath the covers. The next morning we were onboard the ferry to Piraeus. Karen spent virtually the entire three hour voyage on deck towards the stern of the vessel, staring out to sea. She was sullen and uncommunicative. She even spurned my advances,

for example, if I touched her arm she would look at my hand and tell me to, 'get off that', or 'stop pawing me.' In the end I took the hint and spent most of my time at the bar, occasionally coming out to check on Karen, as was my duty as a 'watcher'. But I could only tolerate Karen's petulance so far. I asked myself, 'what would Garcia do? What would he expect of me?' He would expect me to take her in hand, that's what, I reasoned. To that end I went out on deck again and gave her a good talking to, which merely had the effect of reducing her to tears. She ran off yelling that, 'I didn't love her', and that she was, 'going to die'. I was now afraid that she would throw herself overboard; eventually I found her at the bow of the ship, staring down into the foaming water. I ran up behind her fearing the worst, and grabbed hold of her by the waste. I felt that hidden reserve of power again as she pushed me away.

"Please Julian get off me!"

"I thought you were about to throw yourself overboard."

Karen looked at me, pushing the hair from her face. "Idiot! If I wanted to do that I had plenty of opportunity earlier."

She turned to look out to sea again. There was a strong cool wind that tussled her hair. The sky was very dark in the direction in which we were sailing.

"It looks stormy," I said.

"Yes. I don't like it."

We could feel the motion of the ship as it began to encounter large waves. Occasionally a gust of wind would carry sea spray into the air and on to our faces. Karen looked towards me, just then there was a long arc of lightning that reached down from the firmament to the abyss.

"Did you see that?"

Suddenly there was a deafening thunder clap, sounding like an explosion, then another silver splinter of light zigzagged its way across the sky.

Karen put her hand out for me to take. She gripped the handrail tightly with her other hand. A few seconds and there was another loud rumble of thunder. She looked round at me again, her pretty face transported into a look of share terror. I put my arm about her and held her close. She had on a tiny blouse made of a light gauzelike material, beneath it her body felt hard and stiff by comparison. She tensed every time there was lightening, her body became tense in my arms, tense and as hard as taut steel. Every muscle became tensed, coiled like a hard steel spring. Again the lightning stretched between the dark clouds, arching down to the darkening, wine-dark sea. Silvery light danced momentarily, flickering across the water. Again and again the lightning shuddered from the sky, momentarily illuminating the darkening day, while thunder constantly reverberated around the sky, bouncing off of distant islands.

"I don't like it," she said, in a terrified, small childlike voice.

"Its only a summer storm," I relied.

One or two hard droplets of rain splattered onto the metal decking.

"I don't like it. It's a bad omen."

Again and again the lightning splintered across the heavens, like so many *sparks* from Thor's hammer, their reflection dancing across the waters.

Karen caught her breath and reeled away from the sight of the lightning.

"Lets go inside."

"No!" screamed Karen. She looked back towards the sea and pointed to where the lightning came, from across a distant shore.

"What is that! Out there towards the lightning, over that distant shore?"

"Well I don't know. I guess, it must be the mainland. I looked at my watch. "We must be nearly there by now. Yes I'm sure that must be Greece," I said.

"Then it's Europe too," said Karen, in a cold emotionless voice. All her energy seemed to be suddenly spent, although her body still twitched every time she saw the lightning flickering over a now, not so distant shore.

By the time we arrived in port the rain had turned into a torrential downpour. Occasionally there was still the odd flash of lightning but for the most part the electrical storm seemed to have abated.

We had booked rooms at an hotel that had wonderful views of the Acropolis. A small place, but very select, that was one of a number of places Garcia recommended, it seemed that he was known all over Europe.

"Will you send the telex to Garcia?" This was my first command as soon as we arrived.

"Yes of course." I replied.

"He said he would get to one of the islands and telephone. Darn it! his dum religion, why can't he at least have a phone on Sapphos?"

Karen ran her hands through her hair and then went over to the desk.
"Damn it! I can't even remember my Greek," said Karen, extremely agitated.
"I speak very good English Madam," replied the manager.
"Don't worry, I'll sort it out." I said.

Karen frowned and touched her stomach. Tentatively I put my hand on her shoulder. "Are you all right?"
"No, I don't feel well."

The manager smartly clicked his fingers and almost at once a bellhop appeared at the desk. Straight away he began to take our luggage over to the elevator.
"Perhaps Madam would like to go straight to her room? I have sent the boy up with your luggage."
"Yes I think I will," said Karen, turning to me. "Don't forget *Garcia*, tell him to come if he can," she said, leaning forward to kiss me. "And don't be long."
"No," I replied.

The hotel manager looked on as Karen went to the elevator. No one failed to notice her.
"It is perhaps the air? It is very heavy. Sometimes a storm can be good for clearing the air," he said.
"Yes," I said, "It's perhaps the storm!" I replied, half listening to him.

The rest of Karen's luggage was on its way from the boat by a separate car. In all there were two large trunks and four large, very heavy suitcases. Garcia had done well to get her down to this number, by all accounts. All my stuff fitted in one medium sized hold-all.

Dutifully the message for Garcia was sent off. I figured we would get a reply some time in the next couple of days, I imagined it would be sooner rather than later, judging by Karen's dramatic departure at the jetty.

The manager was right; the storm *had* cleared the air. Karen's heaviness of mood, her agitation seemed less. We went for a meal that evening at a small restaurant on the Acropolis. The setting was magical, with the Parthenon all lit up. Strangely though, when we went to the temple, I did not feel close to the ancient world as I had done on Sapphos. The Parthenon was part of the city of Athens - modern day noisy polluted Athens, the Athens of the modern world. It was difficult to separate the two. The sacred site of the goddess Palas Athena was just *another* ancient monument, another tourist stop - a pile of marble blocks. One had to try very hard indeed to recapture the aura of the ancient world. It would be the same in most of the cities we were to visit, a few places held on to the magic, and even then it was not a good sensation. One felt that the ghosts of the old world were restless unhappy spirits, trapped between times.

At the top of the Acropolis we sat down and looked out across the city. We were just one among many couples who, if anything found the place romantic. What was it about ruins that so attracted loving couples? Find a pile of stones, and romance will always flourish. In this sense the Parthenon was no different. I put my arm around Karen and looked down at the temple of Aires. It should have worked, Karen should have melted into my body, instead her muscular frame stiffened as it had when I tried to touch her during the voyage. Taction contact seemed to make her tense, so we sat not touching, and in silence for several minutes.

"Julian," she said, staring out into the darkness.

"Yes."

There followed another uncomfortable pause. "Julian....will....you...will you, you know....!"

If there had been more light I am sure I would have seen Karen blush.

"Will I what?"

"Oh dear...." Karen put her hand to her head, "How do I say this? Will you want me tonight - or any night? Its just that I'm not sure about things."

"Oh - I see!"

"Now I have upset you," said Karen, feebly touching my hand.

"No - really."

"It's just I don't know how I feel about doing *that* with you! I'm not sure it would be right somehow?"

"I see!"

"I mean," she said, putting on a smile, "it's not like you seem that interested in doing *it* - with me. I sometimes wonder if you like me at all?"

"What do you mean?"

"At first I thought may be you prefer men, then I thought, 'no, no he doesn't,' because I've seen the way you look at other women, so I can only think that you find me disgusting in some way."
"You're beautiful. How many times have I told you. I love you."
"love!" jeered Karen, "perhaps you think you do, perhaps you even think I am beautiful, but really you find my body disgusting! You find what I am, and have been, what I have *done* with my body - disgusting."
Karen turned and looked at me intently. I had no reply.
"It's true isn't it?"
"No - no it's not." I said, touching her arm.
"Don't deny it. We both know it's true. I can tell. I can tell when you have been with me, you are secretly repulsed by me. Don't deny it," she said, mockingly waging a long finger in my face. "You can't lie to me, to the high priestess of Tanit. She sees all," said Karen, touching my chest, "in here," she added, "it is the heart that always speaks the truth, what comes out of the mouth is another thing altogether."
Of course she was right. It was pointless to deny it. I mean how can one lie to a priestess? how can one lie to a soul that has lived so many lives as she?
I just looked back at her sexy face, with tears in my eyes.
"Please don't get upset. It's not the end of the world," she said, taking hold of my hand. "perhaps you do love me, in your way."
"I do love you," I said.
"Perhaps what you love isn't me. What you love is Chloe, the innocent girl on the hill. Chloe the shepherdess. But I am not her, she is just a memory of a girl who once lived long long ago. I wish with all my heart that I could be like her in *this* life, but I can't. I tried to be. I tried so desperately to be like her, but I can't! I can't *deny* what I truly am here and now. Look into my eyes. You know it's true. I am Karen, and Karen is more like Natasha. In a way, Karen *is* Natasha."
Karen, or whoever the hell she was paused and put her hand beneath her bodice.
"I have a terrible demon in me," she said, rubbing her firm stomach. She looked down at herself. "It is in here," she said, continuing to touch herself lower down. "It eats away at me all the time. It never stops."

Karen's eyes grew wide. What she was doing aroused me, but I knew she was trying to present to me the reality of her demon. She took my hand and guided it to her thigh so that I could feel what she was doing with her other hand.

"A lot of the time I have a physical ache! Sometimes it gets bad, really bad, and there is only one way to stop it," she said, continuing to touch herself intimately. She looked at me. "I know it turns you on, but it also disgusts you. I am trying to tell you how it is with me. I expect Garcia has told you, no one man could ever satisfy me, so don't feel inadequate like that. Not one man, not a hundred nor a thousand could ever help. I would always want more. That is why I have done the things I have done, and it's partly those things that you think of when you touch me, or look at me. In many ways I am worse than Natasha. I am the perfection of Natasha. What she only did half-heartedly, I embrace fully as my true nature. I would probably have died by now of some sort of *excess* were it not for Garcia. He made me aware of what I was doing to myself. He made me aware of so many things about myself."

Karen withdrew her hand and rested it over mine. Unable to resist I drew her towards me and tried to kiss her.

"No, let me finish. I know you want me. But it would be wrong. In your mind you would see me with other men. You will always be comparing yourself with them, even though it is foolish to do so; and then there is this aspect of me, that you *do* find truly repulses you. But you are a man and you still find me attractive, but that is just your animal instincts coming out, your higher self, which is much higher than it is in me; it is that, which you can never deny. Julian, sweet Julian we are all composite," Karen laughed, "I sound like Garcia, but it's true, we all have a lower and a higher aspect to ourselves, except where your soul is light, mine is heavy and weighed down, sunk deep into the flesh, sunk deep into the animal in me."

Karen and I remained quite still and silent for several moments.

"I'm all right now you know."

"You are?" I replied.

"Before - I mean when we left the island I was afraid. Afraid of what would become of me. There I felt safe. I felt close to those that had gone, those *lighter* souls like Chloe's, seemed always to be close by, somehow? Having to leave was like a rebirth, and all birth is a traumatic experience. Garcia knew it would be a hard birth," she continued, in a detached kind of way.

"Do you think so?" I said, wondering if he really *did* expect the scene at the jetty.

"Yes, didn't you? He knew it wouldn't be easy, but now - now I am out of the womb, it's all a bit strange. But I had a good midwife, and what is more," she said, gripping my hand tightly, "I am not alone, I have you. Garcia chose well."

Ashamed I tried to conceal my tears by burying my head against her, but the dam of emotion broke, and I wept openly.

"Hey!" said Karen, after a while, "That's enough! I need you to be strong."

"I know - I'm sorry." I said, fighting to gain control over my feelings.

I didn't care what others must have thought. I vaguely wondered how many displays of emotional outpourings, the sacred way to the Parthenon must have seen, and then for a moment, *that other* world, the time of innocence flickered back into memory and became real for a second.

Karen and I wandered back to the hotel arm in arm, for all it seemed, as lovers. Except we were *more*, so much more than mere lovers.

Back at our room Karen went to the window and looked out into the darkness, and I wondered what it was she saw out there? After several minutes she turned round and stared long and hard at me. Her lavender eyes intense, her pupils madly, widely dilated.

"I wonder if you can ever know - if any man can ever know, what it is like to be me? To live like this: afraid of your own body, afraid of what it can bring - the power it can wield."

Slowly Karen began to undo her silk bodice. She then unfastened the red bra, she had on, finally unwinding her blue sarong: "Here I am Julian," she said, "Do like what you see?" she stretched her long svelte body. "Or do I disgust you?"

I got up off the bed and moved towards her but she puled back.

"No Julian!"

She turned and went into the bathroom, locking the door.

"Karen, it's all right," I called through the door, "I won't do anything you don't want me to."

I listened intently. I could hear the sound of her weeping. Several minutes passed and I heard her at the door.

"I'm all right Julian. I'm going to have a shower. Just leave me alone a while. Go to the bar and get a drink or something."
"If you are sure?"
"Yes," she said, in a strange slightly raised tone. "I'll be fine. Just go!"
Reluctantly I left. I left her in there, in there with the razors and the scissors, and god knows what else that could cut, and dispatch. I left her there, knowing full well what she intended to do! And still I left her in there?
I ordered a beer and smoked a cigarette feeling, and perhaps looking like an accomplice to a murder. I only managed to smoke half the cigarette. I was not the murdering kind, and perhaps neither was Karen the pure suicidal type? For when I went got back to the room the bathroom door was unlocked. The white basin was red with blood. The shower was running and Karen was sitting beneath it, naked, holding her wounded wrist. She looked up at me, giving me that naughty childlike look of hers.
"I'm sorry Julian."
"It's all right," I said, helping her up. "Let me see."
Reluctantly she presented me her wrist, while she looked away - ashamed.
"'I'm sorry, I'm so sorry," she repeated. I sat her down on the bed and switched on the bedside lamp.
"I don't think it's bad," I said, after a close inspection of the wound. "it's not *that* deep."
"Don't tell any one. I don' want any one to know."
I ran into the bathroom and got out the medical bag which contained bandages and antiseptic cream.
"Hold your wrist up - up like that," I said, and began to tightly wind the bandage over the cut. "I'm not a medical expert, but I think it should be stitched."
"No," she winced. Brave enough it seemed to cut her wrist open but not to have it stitched up again.
"It will be all right, just bind it tight."
I helped Karen on with her bathrobe. She sat up in bed looking at me forlornly.
"I know you think I'm crazy." she said.
"No," I replied.
"What are doing?" she said, seeing me pick up the phone.

"I need a drink."

"Give me a cigarette," Karen demanded.

We both sat tensely waiting for the drinks to arrive, smoking nervously and feeling like conspirators, not welcoming any intrusion.

"Did you clean up in the bathroom?" said Karen, coolly.

"I'll do it now."

While I was in there the drinks arrived. Karen ushered the waiter out as fast as she could, like the guilty partner.

"Why?" I said, when we were alone.

"I don't know. I guess I wanted it to end. To end for me *and* for you. You don't *deserve* this," Karen said, drawing out the word 'deserve.' No one should have to carry on living like *this!"*

"We'll get through some how," I said, trying to sound optimistic.

"Will we?" replied Karen, doubtfully.

"I thought everything was fine?"

"So did I." She shook her head, and laughed. "it's that damn demon."

I laughed with her. You had to laugh, it was madness. All madness! I was tired and exhausted and fed up with her god damn demon. We both were. All there was left to do, was get drunk, which is what we did. The irony was that even then the demon didn't go away. At some point in the evening Karen opened her dressing gown. Rapidly becoming prehensile, her tubular shaped body became fixed upon its inevitable trajectory. Perfunctorily, and somewhat inexpertly, I made love to her. The nights experiences however, together with the alcohol, had taken there toll on her, and it wasn't long before her long snake like body became stilled by sleep.

I woke a little before dawn. I lay awake listening to the sound of Karen as she slept. She made a noise that was rather like a cat purring. Non of the conflict of her soul showed in her flawless features. She was a sleeping beauty, an angel pure. But it was not true, she was no angel. When her daemon shifted in her sleep so did the body; when her daemon woke, so did the body.

I watched her for a long time. I loved looking at her face, while she was *vulnerable.* I came to the conclusion that something had to be done to supply Karen's *needs.* As the great man himself had said: '*no one man would ever be enough for her!*'

In the small hours I devised a course of action. I had to realise my true role as: '*watcher*', and what it really entailed. It meant, apart from keeping Karen safe, she had to be kept happy, amused if you will, or rather her daemon had to be kept amused, and the only thing that kept *it* happy was the engagement of its licentious nature - Karen's licentious nature! We both knew by now that I was not up to the job - no one man, as Garcia had said, ever could be; but the world was full of men, and since Karen could not be trusted to pick the right ones herself, that duty as her 'watcher' must fall to me. I would be shepherd to her unruly soul, and like any good shepherd I would make sure that all the hungry wolves were kept well away. It seemed exquisitely justified that it should be I that shepherded the shepherdess!

XI

I was eventually woken again by the sensation of a dead weight bearing down on me. I opened my eyes to see Karen straddling me. She had on a nightgown made from a material as light and as fine as gossamer, which revealed her dark body beneath like a brides veil.

"Wake up sleepy," she said.

Karen bent forward and shook her head showering me with tiny water droplets from her wet hair. She laughed at its effect.

"How dare you." I said, grabbing her and pushing her off balance. I suddenly found myself over her. I puled back the veil that shrouded her, and felt her hard damp body.

"You're perfect." I said. Then I looked at her arm, and saw the blood stained bandage.

"What's wrong?"

"Your wrist!"

"Oh that. Yes I had a shower and it bled some. I put another bandage on and tied it tight, but the blood has come through."

I lifted her arm and inspected the bandage and the red blood stain.

"It's still bleeding!" I said.

"It will stop," replied Karen, nonchalantly.

"I don't know? It's perhaps deeper than we thought!"

Karen looked at me seriously. She moved her body and I let her get free of me.

"You worry to much. It's just a little cut. The shower washed the scab away that's all."

"Well at least it's a clean wound."

"I used the last of the bandages." Karen confessed, like a naughty girl who had just taken the last piece of candy."

"We'll have to go to the drugstore and get a stock of them in by the looks of things,"

Every morning the first thing Karen did was check at the desk if there were any messages. Surprisingly there were non for three days, and then a telegram arrived sent from Mikinos, it was from Garcia.

"I don't believe it!" said Karen, looking at the small piece of paper.

"What does it say?"

"He's not coming! Just a lot of stuff about trusting, and growing. Here read it."

Basically it was just as Karen said, along the lines of: 'I can do nothing more. STOP. You must face you fate. STOP. Trust in yourself and Mr Julian. STOP. Be brave. STOP. Will meet sometime in Italy. STOP. Bon voyage. STOP.'

"How dare he!"

"Well, you seem a lot more confident than you did! He must know you really well."

"Yes but....but how dare he!" Karen seemed to reflect a moment and reread the short message. "I suppose I am OK now, but I feel kind of let down. It's like he doesn't care!"

"He does care, he cares a lot, but he knows - as he said, 'there is nothing more he can do.' The best way of helping you is to kind of, let you stand alone."

"Yes I know. He must trust you an awful lot too."

"I guess he must," I said, feeling the burden of responsibility again.

I noticed, as one does when one is a *watcher*, the way Karen looked at men, like the bellhop for example, and the way he surreptitiously eyed Karen when ever he thought I was not looking. There was even a slight tension between them if they were in the lobby together. I felt it opportune to put my stratagem into operation.

"What do you think of the bellboy?" I said, after breakfast one morning.

"Who?" replied Karen, nonchalantly.

"The bellboy?"

"I haven't noticed him," said Karen, playing with her coffee cup.

"He noticed you."

Karen laughed, "please Julian, all men who are not dead or gay notice me; besides, " she said, looking over her shoulder, "he's just a *boy*."

"How old do you think he is?"

"I don't know! eighteen, nineteen?"

"So you have noticed him?" I said.

Karen laughed, and even blushed a little. "Stop it Julian. What are you driving at? I know you can't be jealous?"

"I was thinking," I began coyly, "of you know - a kind of party."

Karen stood her cup down and stared at me open mouthed. "Are you seriously suggesting that - that boy," she said, pointing in the general direction of the lobby, "and me!" she said, pointing at her self.

"Why not?" I replied coolly.

Karen laughed and shook her head.

"Are you mad?"

"No I'm serious. I think it could be arrange for you and him..."

"Please stop it. You're killing me," she said, laughing still.

"Why? I think it would be a good thing."

Karen stopped laughing and dried her eyes on a napkin.

"You are serious, aren't you?"

"I've given it a lot of thought these last couple of days."

Suddenly Karen became more serious. "Well I don't know!" she began, "I suppose it would be....interesting."

I knew Karen well enough now, that she was trying her best to suppress her excitement at the prospect. It clearly turned her on.

"But you are supposed to protect me against men! You're my guardian angel remember, not my pimp!"

"I was only trying to think of you. What would be best for you."

"You shouldn't play games like this with your Karen."

"I'm not playing games."

"But you shouldn't be trying to indulge me in these ideas Julian!" she said. feigning shock." You have to think of me as if I were an alcoholic. You wouldn't give an alcoholic a Vodka-Martini, now would you?"

"But your addiction is nothing like alcoholism. I know I am not enough for you. Garcia said I shouldn't see you as my property. If I must care for you, I have to accept you for who you are. Look at your wrist! Denying who you are is driving you crazy."

"It's getting better."

"I don't believe you. Just because you keep it hidden with that red silk bandanna!"
"It is!" remonstrated Karen.
"The point is..I mean after all, it's only your body. It's not the real you."
"What is the real me Julian? My corrupt soul. I'm rotten ,rotten to the core."
"No you're not, " I said, taking her hand.
"Oh Julian!" she said, looking at me, her lavender eyes shining brightly.
"Remember what Garcia said, 'only a part of your soul is lower...Its lower....' "
"Faculty," interposed Karen.
"Yes, faculty. Only it's lower faculty is associated with matter, with the physical element."
"You forget how unruly my soul is."
"We'll tame it - gradually, bit by bit."
Karen laughed again, but she was excited by the thought. "But you can't; it would be mad to try. You can never tame it."
"How do you know! If I selected who you go with in terms of their character."
"I trust you completely."
"OK then," I said, getting up.
Karen looked up at me startled, and put her hand on mine. "What now?"
"Oh - unless you don't feel like it? You do like him?"
"You really are serious, aren't you?"
"Of course," I replied, sitting back down again. "I mean we don't have to do this if you don't want to?"
"No," began Karen, slowly, "not so long as you don't mind? I guess he is kind of cute and he is *young*."
"Think of the experience you'll be imparting."
"And you really don't mind me - you know, doing *it?*"
"I'm not saying I find the idea of you sleeping with someone else easy, but I can accept it if it is what you need, and we are both only too well aware of my own limitations in *that* department!"
Karen looked over her shoulder anxiously and bit her lip. "Oh Julian, I don't know what to say."
"Don't say anything. Go up to the room, I'll find the boy and get him to bring up a

bottle of champagne. The rest my dear, I leave to your own charms."

We got up, Karen hugged me tightly pressing her face hard against mine.

"I don't deserve you. Will you come up?"

"No. I don't think that would be a good idea. In the mean time I'll have a scout around the docks for some fresh blood."

"Why the docks?"

"Full of strong virile young men, and *not* the type to cause any trouble. We are looking for young innocent souls for you to corrupt. Unlike Natasha, who was *corrupted.*"

"Yes poor Natasha, what chance did she have without a guardian angel like you to watch over her? But how will you do it?"

"I don't know yet, but leave it to *Washington,* he'll do most of the talking."

I found the bellhop, slipped him twenty bucks and told him to bring a bottle of the best champagne in the house, to our room. I looked at the youth, he had a lean wiry frame, she would like that, more importantly he looked innocent. Perhaps even too innocent. He was a sacrificial lamb. Did I have the right?

My task complete I hoped a taxi for the big bustling port of Piraeus. I figured it would help take my mind off of events unfolding back at the hotel.

I was right about there being plenty of strong young prey for my Karen, but they were nothing like the bellhop. The young lads I saw all had a mischievous look in their eye, some of them looked downright mean. It would be impossible, with my poor command of the language to approach them without Karen, so I went to a bar and ordered a beer. I was on my third bottle and I wasn't finding it at all easy to get the scene of the bellhop and Karen, out of my mind. Twice I had been on the verge of going back and breaking up the party, but I realised that by the time I got back it would have been way too late. So you can imagine my shock, followed by relief, when I looked up and saw Karen standing a few metres away, looking up and down the key-side. I stood up and called to her. She reeled around, a look of relief immediately coming to her face. She came over, and I hugged and kissed her madly, so relieved she had not gone through with it; to think that she must have really cared *that* much for my feelings. 'Perhaps there was hope for her after all,' I thought.

Karen sat down, she was a little out of breath. She looked at my beer and took a large gulp out of the bottle.

"You'll never believe what happened?" began Karen, pausing between draughts. "your bellhop was a was a real disappointment. He rejected me, can you believe it, *me!* He rejected *me!*"

"How come?"

"I d'know?" Karen looked up, instead of her usual Greek persuasion she went on, addressing the waiter, "hey you bring us two more beers will you."

"So what happened?"

"Well I went up and put on my sexy long skirt, you know the black one with the slit all the way up one side, and a red lace blouse, I left most of the top buttons undone." Karen put her hand to her mouth. "Do you think may be I went too far?"

"Possibly. He looked very innocent."

"Any way, he came with the champagne as dully arranged. I sat on the edge of the bed, crossed my legs so that he got a good view of my thigh, and I asked him to open the bottle." Karen paused to take a swig of beer. "At this point he looked a bit concerned. I guess he was wondering when you would make an appearance. Any way, I got up and held out a glass, I then took the bottle off of him and put the glass in his hand. 'It's for you,' I said. At this point he looked really nervous. I poured myself some champagne and we clinked glasses." Karen paused a moment, and chuckled to herself, "I guess it's funny, when I picture the look on his face. I then sat down on the bed. Told him it was OK, and indicated for him to sit next to me. At this point he stood the glass down and backed away towards the door. 'It's all right,' I told him, 'my boyfriend knows, he won't be angry. Don't you like me?' I started to come over to him, he just turned and bolted like a scalded cat."

Karen broke down in fits of laughter. She put her hand on my arm. "Do you think I was too direct?"

"I'll have to have a word with the management," I said, joining in Karen's hilarity, while all the time feeling a huge sense of relief. "It's just not good enough, we pay good money for hotel services."

"What will they think of me at the hotel?"

"Don't know what you're talking about; it's probably quite normal practice among modern western couples."

"Yes, but not when they are put up to it by their boyfriend or husband. I wonder if he'll say anything?" said Karen, touching her lip.
"I shouldn't worry about it. It'll just be a bit of gossip. Stuff like that happens all the time. They'll think we're just another crazy American couple, that's all."
"I suppose," she replied, distracted.
Karen looked over at the two young fisherman at the bar. She was obviously very intent upon putting into practice my idea once the green light had been shown, and more determined than ever now that she had suffered a kind of rejection, something that was completely alien to her. Now that her juices were flowing she was like a dog with a bone.
"So have you had any luck then, or have you just been sitting at the bar all the time?"
"They all look a bit frightening. I figured we would have more luck together."
"Yes they are a burley lot aren't they."
"Not your type?"
"Ooh...." Karen looked towards the bar again. "I wouldn't say that. What about those two?"
I glanced over at the two Karen had spied. "I guess." I said.
Karen drained the last of her beer and banged the empty glass down on the table. "Hmmm - Let's do it," she said, getting to her feet, and falling a little bit against the table.
Before she got to her target, both men turned and started to walk out. Karen nearly went straight into the taller of the two. Whether it was planned or not, who can say? He was a big fellow, so he could have quite easily knocked her over. He put his hand out in reflex, and Karen took hold of it and looked up into the Greek's eyes; it was just like a scene out of a cheap novel. He took off his cap and smiled at her. Karen allowed them to guide her to the bar in the manner of an invalid. Karen was giving them her little girl lost look, talking to them in their language, smiling and occasionally pointing towards me. Predictably a round of *ouzo* appeared on the bar. At this point Karen winked at me, and signalled for me to join them.
"This is Aristachus and...."
"Sebas..." said the other.

He put out his hand for me to shake. Although on the surface they looked a rough cut-throat lot, these two at least, appeared very polite and upright characters.

"They are both fishermen," said Karen, I told them we were new here and loved the boats. Sadly they have to go soon but they said they would be here later this evening. They have invited us both to a meal."

The taller and more handsome of the two was Aristachus. He was a very charismatic man that held Karen's gaze with his deep blue eyes. He was clearly not the kind to be intimidated by beauty or, let an opportunity pass him by.

"Aristachus is very impressed by my odd sounding Greek," said Karen, smiling like a Cheshire cat.

He put his big hand on her shoulder, and Karen swooned, looking up into his eyes and taking in his dark ruddy features. He spoke in a deep voice that came from the chest.

"He says you are a very lucky man to have such a young and beautiful wife. He's quite the charmer don't you think?"

"Why don't you tell him you're not my wife."

Karen looked at me doubtfully, and then turned on her smile again when she looked at Aristachus.

"They say it is a very good place to come for sea food."

Like so many establishments of its type the bar was very spacious inside and mostly empty of people during the day, with most of the activity happening under the verandas out-front.

We all downed our *ouzo*, the young fishermen put on their caps and before departing each took their tun to kiss Karen's long outstretched hand; Karen trying her utmost to look abashed and not giggle.

"Looks like you are in business then?" I said, when we were alone.

"You don't like them do you?"

"They seem all right"

"It was your idea......unless you rather we didn't meet them later?" said Karen sipping her beer and looking at me coyly."

"No, you're right; it was my idea."

Karen touched my hand. "You are just too good, too good!"

We arrived back at the key-side bar at eight, as had been arranged. It was one of those places that came to life at night. Instead of the single barman there were now five or six waiters dashing about with huge trays of dishes. The air was filled with the noise of animated Greek conversation and the aroma of Greek cuisine. Our two friends waved at us from a table where there were seated about a dozen men. Sebas came over and greeted us warmly while his companion brought up two more chairs for us, at the already quite crowded table. Most of the men there were of a similar age, early to mid twenties. The youngest was about seventeen and there were a few older ones in their sixties, but being brought up on healthy food and in a healthy climate, they were probably a lot older than that. There were platters of fish dishes on the table consisting of all varieties from: red mullet, octopus, sardines, sea bass swordfish, there was also bottles of wine, beer and spirits, and we, Karen and I, appeared to be the guests of honour.

Needless to say Karen quickly became everyone's favourite; they were all impressed by her ability to communicate with them so freely in their language, even if at times her diction failed her. But her slightly quirky way of speaking and her general cuteness in this respect, enthralled them even more. As the evening wore on it became obvious that it was Aristachus, the taller and more dominant of the two, that had won Karen's favour. He was even bold enough to brush his hand against hers at times, and then she would quickly gather it up for a moment and then let it go, both pretending that no one could see. If he saw me looking at him he would smile and offer me some more *ouzo* - which I have to say is as good a ploy as any!

"What was he saying to you?" I asked Karen, when I noticed him speaking to her in earnest.

"He asked what the situation was between you and me."

"What did you say?"

"I said we had a relaxed kind of relationship." Karen paused a moment, and then looked at me, with slightly bloodshot lavender eyes. "Well we do, don't we? I mean, how else would you describe it?"

I held up my glass of ouzo and saluted Aristachus before knocking it back.

"If you are going to do it, make it soon," I said, still smiling at him.

Karen squeezed my hand tightly and kissed the side of my face. "I know it can't be easy."

I lit a cigarette and looked over at her chosen one. "Do you really want him?"

"*Yeah...*" replied Karen enthusiastically.

"Then you have my blessings."

Karen whispered in Aristachus' ear. A few seconds later they got up and headed towards a wide staircase at the rear of the bar. A subdued cheer went up from the gathering. I lifted my glass: "to the happy couple.' I said, giving everyone licence to cheer more loudly. Now that Karen had left, I felt distinctly out of my depth. But a lovely old soul with grey hair and a heavily weathered face got up and sat down in the vacant seat next to me, and put his arm about me. I have no idea what he said but I felt intuitively they were words of comfort. He filled up my empty glass with more of that *dangerous* spirit, and saluted me. I smiled vaguely, understanding the old mans message, that the only thing I *could* do was to get very drunk.

Strangely enough, I didn't feel that phased by the realisation that only a few metres from where I sat, Karen was having sex with another man. After all, nothing really had changed. Each man stood up at the table and saluted me. They must have seen in me as some sort of mad philanthropist, or perhaps, what the English call, 'a jolly good sport.' But inside I was quaking!

From somewhere, Sebas had found a an attractive woman, of which I gathered he was making a present of to me. He ushered the old man out of Karen's seat and sat her down, introducing her as: 'Pandora.'

"You are American no? I have a cousin in New York and another in Cleveland, I have visited many times America," said the girl.

"Your America is very god," I replied. "What did you think of the good old U S of A?"

"The country is great but the people, " she said, waving her hand, "I think they are a little mad."

"I'll drink to that - and the maddest of them all is me!"

"I think not. You are strange, but not mad."

I felt Pandora's hand on my thigh. For the first time I became properly aware of her. She was dressed in a tiny black skirt and a low tight fitting top that seemed barely adequate to restrain the two perfect hemispheres of her buoyant bosom. She had a sexy pouting face. Her lips were painted a bright red and her dark eyes were lost in a wide halo of black eye-shadow. Her skin was wan and greasy, her pallor, indicative of a creature that seldom saw the light of day.

I looked up at the drunken laughing faces opposite me, and then at the round lustful figure of Pandora. A feeling of nausea swept over me.

"I need to get some air," I said, getting to my feet.

"Shall I go with you?"

"No, I want to be alone."

I took a deep breath of air. I felt better now; now that I was in darkness and I had escaped the smell of dead fish and ouzo. I sat on the key-side and watched the fishing boats with their black sails and little lamps, thinking they were all part of the *entrapment*. I looked into the inky black water beneath my feet and saw reflected, the distorted image of my face. The more I looked the more I felt myself gravitate towards the black abyss. I edged further and further to the side. Only my hands behind me prevented me from loosing my balance. All I need do was to bring them forward and then my own weight would do the rest. Suddenly I heard a noise and felt a girls arms around me. "Karen!" I called without looking, almost straightaway I knew it was not her.

"No - no - no - what are you doing!"

"Oh...it's you! I thought you were my friend."

I allowed Pandora to guide me a way from the waters edge.

"What are you doing out here on your own?" she said, sitting me down.

"I don't know...."

I felt Pandora's arm go about me. I looked at her - her head had the appearance of a semi-luminous skull; her eyes were like the empty sockets - just large black circles in her pallid face.

"Yes your friend! Sebas told me she has gone with Aristachus and that you do not mind this?"

"No I don't mind."

"I do not think this is true! No woman is worth drowning yourself for."

"Is that what you thought I was going to do?" I said, looking into the darkness and trying to laugh it off.

"Come..." she murmured..."come, there is no need to be alone."

Pandora pressed her body against mine. I could smell the faint odour of aniseed and cheap perfume. She took my hand and put it against her thigh. Her flesh was cold and smooth. She wanted me to do more with it but I moved it away.

"Do you not like me?"

"You are very lovely to touch," I said, in a detached sort of way, as if she were some sort of inanimate object that was either pleasant or unpleasant to touch.

Pandora shook her head. If I could have seen her face she would have worn the look of incredulity on it, but it was just a skull in the dark.

"You love her! You love her and you let her do this thing?"

"Call me a philanthropist." I replied, dryly.

"Ah - *philanthopia!* I think not. Why you let her do this thing when clearly you are not happy?"

"I love her."

From out of the darkness I felt the warmth of her lips on my face. Her strange spectral luminosity ceased for a moment to have any deathly associations.

"I think not many men would do this? You are very *psyche areòs, is spaneos...*"

I think the fact that I was a *rare soul*, in her eyes turned her on. She pushed her delightful thigh against me and lent towards me thrusting her well larded bosom in front of my face.

"Is this girl you love as beautiful as I am told? Sebas behaves like she is Aphrodite. But then men often like north European women. *Aghh..yinéka xsanthus!*" Pandora expostulated. I just looked at her. "Blond women," she explained: "Greek men go weak as soon as they see one."

"I don't see why? Dark women are just as good, if not better," I said.

"Do you like me? I am dark - no!"

"Yes," I said. Suddenly catching sight of her profile in the semi-darkness. The white vulnerability of her strong neck reminded me of Karen.

"I'm as good as her," she whispered in my ear. "Just let me show you." She began to touch me, becoming prehensile. There was a noise in the darkness which broke her concentration, quick like a startled cat Pandora looked round. She spoke sharply in Greek. Coming towards us was the old man who had befriended me in the bar.

Pandora looked to me. "It is your friend! She has done Aristachus, and has now gone with Sebas..."

I got up quickly. Pandora grabbed my hand. The old man began waving his hands and remonstrating, pointing towards the bar.

"No - it is too late," said Pandora. "She has already gone with him. It is too late, do not go after her now. It is to late. Wait here."

Pandora went off to talk with the old man. I looked down again into the inky abyss and my distorted image. Seconds later Pandora was by my side clutching me tightly.

"Let me get you away from here. I know a quiet place where we can go."

Pandora helped me to my feet and we began to walk briskly. "I do not think she is good for you!" she said, as we walked. Shaking her head sprinkling me with her long black hair like a web, "No, no she is not good, she is a bad one!"

"She can't help it. It's her daemon, or as most call it, her *demon!* Karen used to say it was her darkness."

"Yes, I think so. It is a very bad, very dark *psyche*"

"No, she is just a child, just a child."

"*Tératos!* To do this. It is bad. A creature...*tératos!* monster! - you say - no? *Plàsmatos,* a thing, a creature!"

"She doesn't mean it. Where are we going?"

"Not far. It is just a small bar, my friend runs it. I told Mantias, the old man, where we have gone, so your friend will know, but why you want to be with such a creature as this, I do not understand!"

We turned down a narrow side-street, not long after we were standing outside a small bar with wide smoked windows. Written in English in large red letters were the words: 'Pandora's Box.'

"Is this your bar?"

"No," she said, "it belongs to a friend, he named it after me. Come, let us go inside."

The first thing that hit me on entering was how wonderfully cool it was, the air-conditioning was so effective it was almost cold, at least until one became acclimatised. The bar was quite small, there were five low tables and the seating was in the form of plush leather armchairs, the subdued lighting came from a candle which burned in a little lantern on each table. A girl dressed in a short black skirt and fishnet tights, with a similar full figure to Pandora's, sat alone at table near the window. After a few seconds a tall man with long black hair appeared from behind a red curtain at the far end of the bar. Both Pandora and he must have known each other well judging by the warmth of their greeting. The man, who was in his forties smiled affably as he shook my hand while Pandora made our introduction.

"Very pleased to meet you. Any friend of Pandora is friend of mine also," said Stephanos, in a strong Greek accent, "please be seated. Now what is it you drink? I know, ouzo!" he said, going behind the bar.

"No, he won't. Just a beer for Julian," interceded Pandora.

"Very good idea. What you want Pandora? I know - your usual!"

She lead me over to a seat at the far corner of the bar, near where it had been curtained-off.

Stephanos brought over our drinks on a tray. Pandora had a green coloured drink in a long chilled glass, which she sipped periodically through a straw. Stephanos went back behind the bar, but at some point disappeared again behind the curtain. I felt secure and comfortable in my surroundings. I had all but forgotten about Karen's exploits, but Pandora was intrigued by the nights events. She wanted to understand the kind of relationship we had, which allowed Karen to go off with other men and, yet still cause me so much pain. I ended up telling Pandora everything, from the time I first met Karen at high school up to our stay on Garcia's crazy island. When she had finally been brought up to date she just shook her head, and put her hand in mine.

"But this...this Karen, you really believe her *psyche*, her soul to be accursed!"

"I do, after what I saw. Her soul is either cursed or else, like Garcia she is insane. After tonight, I'm not sure who is more insane, me or her?"

"I do not know about her soul, or if she is insane as you say, but I know that you are a good man. You are not insane, but a girl like that, she could drive any man insane. And these things she has done; in Greek the word *porn*, means prostitute, that is what she is. It is worse than being a prostitute, to sell your body like *that*, it is some how a cheat. At least what I do is honest. But this *pornography*, is not right, it cheapens women and sex." Pandora sighed, and sucked her straw. "And you, such a good person. What are you doing with a woman like this, this *pòrní?* I do not think there is anything wrong with you! It is just that you have not met the right kind of woman yet. This Karen is *zo-òdis..*."

I nodded, and allowed myself to melt into her wonderful body. "Come..."she, said, disengaging from me and leading me behind the curtain. Here, the lighting was even more subdued, so much so I could barely see in front of me. I put my trust in Pandora. She lead me to a booth with a single wide bench seat covered in a kind of velvet material, it was very comfortable, with cushions everywhere. In front of the seating area was a low table, the whole thing was curtained all around, so providing absolute seclusion. Stephanos, as if by magic appeared briefly, set down a beer and another green drink for Pandora, and was gone in a flash.

Pandora instructed me to relax, and began to massage my head. "You have much stress in you," she said.

I nodded allowing her to do whatever she wanted. Her hands were smooth and dextrous, her movements slow and assured. I reached out in the red haze and felt Pandora. Her edges were soft and round not hard curves like Karen, her big breasts hung naturally under their own weight and were not gravity defying. Her body was voluptuous and giving, not muscular and sordid. She was a female as god intended and not what Hollywood imagined. It was so natural to make love to Pandora. Her body seemed to flow over one like water. It was wonderful to be lost in her. To drown oneself in her touch. She was, without doubt a revelation. Eventually though Pandora brook free, and took a sip of her fluorescent green drink.

"You are very lovely," I said, putting my arm about her and kissing her wonderful creamy white neck.

"But you love this Karen, even though she is a *tératos?* - a monster!"

"I don't know any more?" I said. "What I didn't tell you was Karen is really the only girl I have ever been with. Only one other, and that was a disaster, but *you*, you are different," I said.

"I did not know, but I can guess." Pandora paused, as if weighing something in her mind. "If you want, we can go somewhere where we are properly alone?"

I began kissing her again. There was the faint taste of mint in her mouth, her long tongue was as cool as a glacier. I was hungry after her. I wanted her desperately, in a way I had never wanted Karen. At last it seemed I had found a *real* woman, one who had a healthy attitude towards sex. She fought me off to admonish me: "There is just one thing, you must not want to possess me. I can be your lover, even your close friend, but you will not be the only one to take pleasure in my body. So long as you understand this?" Pandora held me with her deep black eyes, when she spoke again her voice quavered a little: "So long as you know what I do! What I am!"

"I can guess," I said.

"And it doesn't *matter? she* said, unable to conceal her relief.

"No - how could it?" I said, puling her to me once more, and laying kiss upon kiss on the broad white expanse of her throat.

Pandora was soft and smooth and round to the touch. Karen was hard and lean. As far as I was concerned this was the only difference between the two women, what it came down to was a question of physiological preference. Karen explained her licentious nature through a plea to metaphysical phenomena. Pandora on the other hand had no recourse to the paranormal in order to explain away *her* nature. There was no inner conflict betwixt her body and her mind, therefore there was no sense of urgency or turmoil transmitted through to her actions. Every movement she made was cool and collected. She moved completely within herself, she never overreached herself, she was a lady in complete command of herself. Pandora was on good terms with her *daemon*. She was not ashamed of what she was. She described what she did as: 'providing a service,' she relieved men and sometimes women too, of their tensions while delivering immense pleasure; her wonderful body just happened to be the source of that pleasure, and as such she expected remuneration for what she did. The only difference between Pandora and Karen, was that Karen regarded herself as something a bit special, when in fact she was something a lot worse than a whore, at least according to Pandora.

As I was considering all of this, and how it kills the mood, Stephanos appeared round the curtain to our booth.

"Sorry, most sorry Julian, I heard you talking, otherwise:....You are wanted on the telephone Pandora."

Pandora got up, but before leaving bent over and kissed me, unable to resist her wonderful shape I drew her close and tasted once more her glacial freshness, reluctantly to let her go. "Think about what I said," she concluded.

Pandora was gone a few minutes, when she came back she was looking a bit flustered. She ran her fingers through her long black hair and just stood staring at me a moment.

"What is? What's wrong?"

She held out her hand and I got up and took it in mine.

"There's been some kind of trouble at the bar. A fight or something. We'd better get back."

"And Karen?"

"I don't know. The barman was very angry. He insisted that someone come and get the *American girl* who had caused the trouble. Well, he called her something more than that!"

"I must go." I said, hurrying out.

"Wait," called Pandora, "I'll come with you."

About fifteen minutes later we were outside the key-side bar. All the lights were on. The big doors that opened on to the street were flung wide. A man was mopping the floor and parked outside the bar was a police car.

"Don't say anything let me deal with it," said Pandora.

She walked briskly up to one of the police-officers. They talked for a few minutes, he pointed towards the bar. There was much gesticulation, eventually the police-officer gave a brief salute, got back in his transport and drove away.

"It's all right," said Pandora, "Karen is inside. There was some trouble. One of the men who went with Karen was married and his wife came to the bar and found them together."

I started to go forward, Pandora put her arm in front of me. "You are lucky," she said, "the man who runs this bar wanted to have her arrested. I told the police she was one of my girls, and that she was drunk. Most of the police know me. Some of them very well."

I pushed on ahead up to the bar, the man in charge was busy cleaning glasses: "The American girl?"

He scowled, grunted something making a gesture with his head.

We found Karen in a dark corner of the bar at the very rare, she sat alone at a table with a cup of coffee in front of her. Her head was slumped forward, her hair was tangled and in disarray. Pandora hung back while I went and sat down opposite her. When she looked up I saw that it was more than her hair that had been messed up. Her bottom lip was split and heavily swollen, there was blood all over her mouth and chin, she had a nasty gash across her left cheek and both eyes were swollen and bruised.

"Don't look at me," she said, shielding her face.

"Let's get you out of here," I said, taking hold of a blood stained hand.

Pandora came over to help me get her to her feet. The scowling man behind the bar shouted in Greek, and then in English: "get her out, get out of my bar get out and don'ts comes back. Hey!" he said, "Hey you! You here me? I give her the big one! You know?" he taunted making a gesture with his fist, then both he and his colleague laughed uproariously, while continuing to make obscene gestures.

"Ignore them," said Pandora, shouting back at them in their language.

We limped Karen over to a bench and sat her down. Karen covered her eyes from the glare of the early morning sun. She rubbed her nose and looked at the blood on her hand.

"Darn it, my nose is still bleeding! I think that bitch must have broke it?"

"That cut on you face looks bad."

Karen tentatively touched the wound to her beautiful face.

"We should get it seen to. It could leave a scar."

"I said *no!* leave it Julian, stop...stop fussing will you."

"It looks bad," observed Pandora.

Karen wrinkled her bruised and bloodied face. "Who the hell are you?"

"This is Pandora," I said.

"That's right," said Karen, in dismay. "You're the bitch that started it!"

"She didn't! she was with me the whole time," I intervened.

"No - she was the one who told everyone that I was a prostitute. That's how that mad woman came to attack me," said Karen, struggling to her feet in order to face Pandora.

Pandora shook her head. To my surprise she looked genuinely intimidated by

Karen, but then again her battered face did look pretty frightening.
"Don't fucking lie to me, you Greek slut," yelled Karen, screwing her hand into a bony fist.
Pandora backed away.
"I didn't say anything. It was Mantias, the old man," she protested.
Karen looked at me. "Yes, the old man, he said you'd gone off with her. I was looking for you and you'd gone! I couldn't believe it!"
"I was told that after you had been with Aristachus you then went with Sebas," I explained.
"You weren't there! What did you expect me to do? You were with *her*" said Karen, giving Pandora a filthy look.
Pandora looked back at Karen, and seemed to rally her confidence.
"If you want men I know of plenty?"
"I imagine so," replied Karen, dryly.
Pandora came nearer. "As I look at you, I do not see any thing special....I doubt very much you have what it takes, for what I have in mind."
Karen sniffed and roughly wiped away the blood that was still trickling from her nose. She looked at Pandora slowly up and down with such complete disdain, any one would think that it was Pandora that had been messed up.
"Huh!...you are nothing, you fat old whore! I'm not afraid of you, or anyone. Don't let this deceive you," she said, holding out her bloodstained fist. "I assure you, the one that did this is in a much worse state."
Pandora did not seem to be at all impressed with these theatrics, and audaciously put her hand out and nipped Karen's biceps. So ostentatious was the act, Karen looked at Pandora completely aghast. It took her a few seconds of open mouthed incredulity before Karen could respond by grabbing hold Pandora's long hair and dragging her to the ground.
"Stop it! Both of you," I yelled.
I managed to seize hold of Karen, and with less effort than I imagined would be necessary, I was able to separate the two girls, although not without Karen coming away with two large handfuls of Pandora's black hair.
"Have you gone mad!" I said, continuing to restrain her.
Pandora got up and dusted herself down, while muttering Greek obscenities by

the score. Karen eventually shook herself free, and both girls eyed one another like two wild cats sizing each other up, one waiting for the other to look away. In the end it was Pandora who acquiesced.

"I will not fight you," she said.

"Then I'll show you how weak I am by out doing you at your own game."

"If you think you can?"

"When and where?""

Pandora went on to explain how every so often, what she described as a 'fest', was held at her apartment. Sometimes as many as three hundred to four hundred guests would come, mostly male and both she and another girl would make themselves available to everyone there. These occasions would always lend themselves to rivalry between the two girls, their sexual exploits often becoming the focal point of the whole evening. Pandora proudly announced that she was undefeated, boasting that she had had over four hundred men in a single night.

Karen of course was undeterred by such claims, indeed she listened with mounting excitement at the prospect of pitting herself against another woman in this way. It was something I think she had long dreamt of doing, except that the circumstance had never presented itself, at least in her current life time, but if one new anything about the worship of Tanit, then they will realise that as a goddess of *fecundity,* it was incumbent upon every high priestess to avail themselves of as many vigorous males as possible.

"It will take a few days to arrange," concluded Pandora. " I will leave word at your hotel."

"I look forward to it," said Karen, shouldering Pandora out of the way. After limping a metre or so she stopped and looked back.

"Well are you coming with me Julian or, are you going to stay with your whore?"

I looked at Karen and then at Pandora.

"Go with her, at the moment she needs you more, any way you are her *watcher,* are you not?

XII

After having showered, unabashed she came out of the bathroom naked and began showing me the extent of her injuries. She had suffered a lot of bruising to her ribs and there were long red wales on her arms, neck and breasts and on the top half of her inner thigh was an ugly bruise that had been made, according to Karen, by a bite. I took in all of these contusions with an air of detachment, but I had to admit she looked as if she had been partially savaged by a wild animal.

"Don't you think you should go to the hospital?" I said, when she had finished pointing out each blemish on her once flawless skin.

"Why should I want to do that for goodness sakes?"

"Well," I said, noticing the blood on the floor, "your wrist seems to be bleeding again for one thing."

Karen glanced down at the trail of blood she had left behind.

"Oh that," she said, tritely, "well what did you expect I've just been in a fight with a mad woman."

"That deep scratch on your face doesn't look too good either."

She went over to the mirror. "I heal quickly. I doubt it will leave a scar." She turned side-on to the long mirror and ran her hands down her thin body. "My beautiful body...."she said with a note of melancholy.

"I know," I said, peering over her shoulder and handing her a fresh bandage. "Not as perfect as it was!"

She took the bandage from me without reply, and began the usual ritual of winding it tightly around her lacerated wrist.

"My nose!" she said, going up close to the mirror, "I think it's broken."

"Won't it effect your modelling - I mean should you want to go back to it some day?"

"I will have to get it fixed-up state side, it will be just like new."

I sat down and admired as usual her fantastic snake like form. But that was as far as my interest went.

"Why not take the opportunity of having it altered!"
"Why? What's wrong with my nose?"
"You mean apart from the fact it might be broken?"
I began to laugh. Karen looked round at me menacingly. "I'm serious Julian, stop kidding, or I'll give *you* a broken nose." Coming closer and clenching her bony little fist. "I mean it."
"There's nothing wrong with your nose," I said.
Karen turned back to the mirror and began once again to appreciate her body. "Of course not! There's nothing about myself I would want to change. In actual fact I am quite perfect, apart from what that bitch did to me, but I'll heal, and soon too - you know why?" she continued, without waiting for a reply: "because I'm *fit* and I'm *strong* - stronger than *her* any way!"
"You've got a hard head Karen, you'll be fine."
Some sadistic quality in me enjoyed the fact that Karen's perfect face had been given a good bashing, but it frustrated me that, even then, her utter confidence and arrogance was still in tact. Perhaps that's why I went on: "I guess you nose can be put right, but how many models do you know who have scared faces?"
I registered with satisfaction a look of alarm on Karen's face. She looked back into the mirror and examined the ugly blemish.
"Don't say that!" she said, tilting her head into the light. She ran her finger over the growing scab on the side of her cheek. "It will heal I tell you."
"What if it doesn't?"
"If it doesn't! No - don't say such things. It must...You just think it will mean I have to sop modelling! Analisa was badly scared in a car accident, she carried on modelling - well for a bit anyway. There is a lot that can be done with make-up these days, and then there's retouching. Don't be so negative Julian. I think you would actually like it if I was scared for life!"
Karen turned away from the mirror and began to rub embrocation over her ribs and sour limbs. I sat and watched her as she sprawled her long body across the bed. There was something animal, something slightly disgusting in her actions, her total lack of regard for anyone else, her complete lack of self-consciousness. She was like a cat licking itself.

"So you did it with Aristachus and Sebas?"

Karen looked up all bright eyed, if not slightly bloodshot.

"*Course!* - Why? Perhaps you'd like to watch next time? They were all animal. No hang-ups, just pure brute *instinct*" she said, pronouncing the word 'instinct' slowly and in a sexy deep voice.

"I'm glad you enjoyed yourself Karen."

"I did, until I was attacked by a mad woman. How was I too know his wife was downstairs. Such a young good-looking boy and virile....phoo'ey. Far too good to be married to an old harpy like that. And then there was that other boy...must have been...oh I guess seventeen...?"

"You didn't!"

"Sure thing. I had a feeling I was not his first."

"So how many in all?"

"I don't know, six...I think, I don't know."

"You'd have had them all if that woman hadn't come along! Even the old man."

Karen spread her legs apart and began massaging her inner thigh with the liniment. I looked away. "You disgust me Karen."

"Why? It was your idea remember. Anyway, I wouldn't have gone with so many had you come back when you should, instead you went off with that fat old whore."

"Lets face it Karen, you couldn't help yourself."

"You know me!" Karen said nonchalantly.

The biting smell of the liniment that Karen was assiduously applying to her body filled the room.

"Must you do that?"

"It's the only way to bring out the bruising. You want me to heal properly don't you? You do want me to look good?" Karen laughed.

"What's funny?" I said, regretting my words instantly.

"You are. I do believe you really would love to watch."

"I've already seen you in action, remember!"

"I know - but it's nothing like the real thing. Anyway, I wasn't the only one having fun by all accounts!"

"For your information I never slept with Pandora."

Karen looked at me, narrowing her eyes, and it wasn't due to the camphor in the liniment either. .

"No, no I don't suppose you did. I guess you just admired her from afar. That would be your idea of making love. That is so you Julian."

Karen began to splutter and cough as she tried to laugh but ended up inhaling the embrocation.

"That's enough of that," she said, screwing the lid back on the jar. "Anyway," she continued turning back to her perfect image. "I don't get what you see in her?....Owww! That bitch really has broken it."

"If you keep touching it, you'll make it worse."

"it hurts so... Besides, " she went on absently, "I just can't see why you would want to go with a fat old slut like that! I mean she's *fat - fat*, Julian. You know, *fat*...A fat old thing!"

"Yes I heard you."

"Well! Why would you?" said Karen, running her hands down her serpentine body, and enjoying no doubt the warm sensation of the liniment. She stuck out her belly, so that she took on even more, the look of a serpent, all the time stroking the swell of her golden belly.

"You must be the most vain creature that ever lived," I said, staring at her.

Karen looked at me askew, "perhaps," she said, in a childlike cute voice: "Certainly the sexiest."

She stuck her long tongue out at me in the mirror. "Darn it!"

"What now?"

"I think one of my teeth have come loose too."

"Are you sure you won this fight?"

"Of course! Didn't I tell you, they took her away in an ambulance!"

Karen's clash with the enraged wife of one of the men she went with, is reputed to have been one of the most viscous fights between two women to have taken place on the waterfront in a number of years. Rather than break the fight up, the combatants were actively encouraged by the men present at the bar, even bets were taken on the outcome of the affray. By all accounts, towards the end it was Karen who was getting the worst of it, until she managed to grab a piece of bar furniture and administer the knock out blow which necessitated the arrival of the ambulance. Argument still rages in bars along the dockside, about who actually was the victor, but since there are no rules about using whatever weapons come to hand in a barroom brawl, I guess Karen won on a technical knockout.

"You wait," she said, continuing to admire herself. "I'll finish her."

"Who?" "

"Pandora, your fat little whore."

"Why do you have to do this thing?"

"Because it must be done," Karen replied, shaking her head and looking at me as if I were stupid.

"I do wish you wouldn't?"

"What do you care? It's between me and her."

"Are you serious! Look at you! Your body is black and blue and for some reason you're going around with a limp, and you have a cut wrist that won't stop bleeding. How do you honestly hope to have enough strength to take on a professional? The whole thing is bizarre in itself."

"It demands a different kind of strength. A deeper inner strength, a kind that I have in abundance.. It's what I am born for. I tell you...hah! she has no idea what she is up against."

"The only thing you have in abundance as far as I can see, apart from a massive ego, are cuts and bruises."

Karen ignored me and carried on obsessing with her figure. "Don't I have a wonderful profile?" she said. "What woman do you know that can come close to me? All those supermodels...Pamela Lloyd and Lucia Marsh! not even Vanessa Drake is really as sexy as me! I met her once in the flesh, she had so many moles and freckles, she reminded me of one of those dot puzzles, its amazing what can be done with photographs these days, and she's starting to look her age too...you see its all a question of inner strength I'm far better than her. *Aren't* I?"

I sighed and put the book down I was trying to read. "You are very lovely Karen, but there is just no such thing as the best."

"But there is, there has to be - I am it!" said Karen, with a look of dismay.

One had to laugh. At times she was so horribly arrogant and stupid and self obsessed, it was ridiculous.

"Stop it. Stop laughing at me," she said, swiping me. It was meant in play I think but it still stung. I pushed her away and catching her off-balance she rolled onto the bed. She lay on her back her hands wondering over her breasts, she couldn't leave herself alone at times. Perhaps the fight had made her horny.

"If you really want to know, Pandora is more like a woman should be...."

"*What.....!* screeched Karen, jumping up. "what that slut!.....How can you say that? Look at me! look at my body!"

I looked at her. "Yes, you're very good, but...."

"But what?" she said, trying to control her temper, all the time her lavender eyes growing wider and darker like a cats.

"All I was about to say was that Pandora has a more feminine figure."

"What that fat old thing! Come on Julian, really, comparing me, one of the best glamour models in the world, to that old thing!...please Julian! - I bet if she took off her bra her breasts would sag to her knees...." Karen laughed demoniacally.

"You forget my girl, I've followed your career closely, right up to the time you left the states for Europe. I never told you this but I kept virtually every calendar, every filthy magazine, every video and news article that you ever appeared in."

"No I didn't know. I figured you saw me in a magazine, I mean I was doing a hell of a lot of shoots then, but I never knew you followed me that closely...Don't you think it is a bit obsessive of you Julian?"

"Perhaps - some might say so. I guess it was a way of being close to you."

"Ahhh...Julian that's really sweet."

"I use to look at your photograph in one of the more raunchier poses you would adopt and I use to sit and wonder about the person you were, or rather, had become. I wondered about the life you lead, the kind of people you knew."

Karen looked away. "Id rather not think about that..."

"No and neither do I really. I guess what I'm trying to say is that, gradually I became fascinated by you, I mean your life. I thought I'd lost the Karen I knew forever, and perhaps I have. You never rally hit the big time did you?"

"I could have."

"But you didn't. Everyone has heard of Pamela Lloyd and Liza Redcliffe but how many people know of Natasha?"

"I will have you know, that I have quite a following. I receive fan mail all the time and from all over the world."

"Who from - dirty old men who buy those magazines and porn videos? You're a porn star Karen, that's not being famous. The only way you got attention was by kicking up a media storm by slagging off other models. Models that were arguably better looking and more famous. Lets face it Karen, you were jealous of them."

"That's not true. I was putting the record straight. *Oh yeah...every one loves Pamela Lloyd and Liza Redcliffe and the Marsh woman!..*" snarled Karen. "They are nothing, *nothing...nothing!*" she screamed. "You hear me - *nothing!* I..I am the best...Why...why Pamela Lloyd - hah! She is finsihed! My breasts are far better than hers, she is nothing, all of them, I was better than all of them, but oh no they couldn't see it, so I had to tell them. Fucking Liza Redcliffe! I could out do them all...."

I had hit the nerve! Karen was prancing up and down the room sticking her chest out, It was an awesome disturbing sight to witness first hand, the fury of thousands of years of *failure*. The failure of her Demon to accept it's Earthly limitations.

Karen was breathing hard and holding her chest. "Fucking Redcliffe!" she muttered, then twisting round at me again. "Let me tell you this *buster* - every man who has ever seen me naked have commented that I had the sexiest body they had ever seen. I use to get paid thousands of dollars a week, just to strip off in front of a camera. I was the best at what I did. Most men would pay hundreds of dollars just to be near me, *just* to look at me! And then there's you - who apparently prefers some common old tart, to the likes of me - *me!*" she reiterated, whilst thrusting a bony finger into her bosom. "I suppose everyone else is wrong, apart from Mr Julian?"

"At least Pandora's breasts are real and not pumped-up full of silicon, or whatever it is!"

Karen picked up an magazine and hurled it at me at as hard as she could. "How dare you, you fucking bastard! I'll have you know these," she said squeezing her big tits, "are real!"

"Oh come on, be serious Karen! I know *you* remember. I know all there is to know about you. I've made your career my life's work. If they are real, how is it your bust size has increased since I knew you at high school?"
"I hadn't fully developed."
"All right, how is it then, that your bust size went from a 34D - I think it was, to a 36E?"
Karen sat down on the end of the bed and just scowled at me.
"It's all right Karen, I can understand the pressure you models must be under, there is a lot of competition out there. I know that Pamela Lloyd's breasts are not genuine, but at least she's honest about it."
"Pamela Lloyd...aghhh! Will you stop using that old cows name! God, I hate her!"
"I'm not interested in her or any of them. I think they are ridiculous. The whole thing is ridiculous. All I'm saying is that Pandora is different that's all, that she has a fuller more feminine figure."
"Hah! - fat more like."
I was growing annoyed at the constant slating of Pandora, calling her: 'fat'.
"The truth is," I began coolly, "there are times when your body reminds me of a flayed rabbit."
Karen looked stunned for a second. I raised my hands to protect my face half expecting some sort of physical retaliation, but nothing came.
"I see," she said, getting off the bed and putting her top on. "Thanks for telling me."
"Karen..." I began.
"No!" she said, holding up a hand: "It's OK, I understand now! *It* explains everything - why you don't fancy me. You prefer fat women, that's it isn't it? You think I'm skinny. You hate my breasts, you think I'm artificial - a fake!"
She hit her bruised head with her hand. "Aghh...how stupid of me! I feel such a fool. Throwing myself at you like I have, and all the time you hating me. Hating my body and the way I look. You must have been laughing at me all this time?"
"No, it's not true," I said.
"No, it's perfectly true and I thank you Julian, I *really* do, I thank you for your honesty." Karen laughed: "Now, now I can see why you like Pandora. Of course

how stupid of me!" She shook her head. "Well you listen to me buster, when I've finished with your goddamn Pandora...."

Karen sprang up and went into the bathroom slamming the door behind her.

I left it for a few seconds, but the old fear came back. I went over and knocked, calling her name several times.

"Go away Julian, leave me alone."

I listened carefully and thought I detected the sound of her crying. After about five minutes she unlocked the door and came out. She pushed me out of the way and tumbled on to the bed face down. I watched her for a second or two as her body made tiny little jerking movents.

Tentatively I lay my hand on her shoulder.

"Go away."

"I'm sorry," I said. "I didn't mean what I said. It's just you do go on a lot about how good-looking you are...."

"Yes and why do you think that is? Because I'm vain and empty headed?" she said, turning round sharply. The sight of her face wet with tears together with its battered appearance would have touched the heart of the hardest of men.

"No..." I replied.

She slumped down again. "And to think, I thought you really cared about me!"

"I do care. To me it's obvious you're beautiful so why....?"

Karen made a cynical laughing sound. "*Why!..huhh!* why do you think? Because deep down I don't have that much confidence. You of all people must know how hard it is for me, just to survive from one day to the next? Deep down Julian, I hate myself." She swung round and thrust her wrist in front of me, "look, look at this, remember this? What do you think this says? You're suppose to be so damned clever?"

I began to apologise profusely.

"I sometimes wonder where you're coming from Julian? You say you think I am self absorbed, I have an excuse Julian, what is yours?" Karen shook her head. "You really don't seem to understand me at all. I thought by now you would begin to at least. And if you want to believe in all this stuff about reincarnation, which incidentally I do, then Natasha and all the others, were only looking for some sort of appreciation, some sort of validity in a world that is sick and full of degradation, but we were so low in self-esteem we gravitated to the lowest depths. Now do you get it? do you huh!" she said, punching my head

"Yes, *Ow!"* I called out, in genuine pain. She had long bony hands that when made into a fist were a formidable weapon.

"I'm so damned sick of you Julian."

"I know...." I said, lamely.

"Know! - what do you know?"

"I say stupid things. Of course you're beautiful, and I do love you."

"Oh please Julian! save it. I think you care more about this damned Pandora than you do me! That was why you were asking all those questions. But if you asked her: 'why' then she would probably tell you the same thing."

There was an awkward silence for some minutes. Karen lit a cigarette and looked at me contemplatively.

"Do you really think I'm skinny?"

"No." I replied, guardedly, "skinny is the wrong word." I looked at her trying to sum up in one word what best described her in terms of her physique. "You are definitely not fat, you're lean - *athletic."*

"Athletic." Karen replied, smiling vaguely. "Does that mean I'm strong?"

"Of course it does."

Karen was evidently very pleased by my choice of word, and it was no exaggeration on my part either. Her whole body was really no more than one long muscle. She flexed her arm and looked at her well defined biceps. Her musculature was not great but unlike other women it was very well defined.

"Come here feel it," she said.

I touched her muscle, it felt hard. "You're amazing."

"Do you really like me?"

"You know I do."

"More than Pandora?"

"Who?"

Karen suddenly leapt on top of me, pinning me down playfully. I tried to kiss her but she puled her head away. I felt the power in her thighs and her arms, immobilising me. She had me (again) completely at her mercy.

"Am I sexiest thing you've ever seen....say it.."

"Yes...yes your are the sexiest."

"More than Pamela Lloyd?"

"Much more. She's nothing compared with you..."

"That's right, she isn't. Am I better than Liza Redcliffe?"

"Well I don't know...Liza Redcliffe!"

Karen squeezed me with her thighs until it hurt.."yes..yes..you are better, better than her..."

"Than who? Say it..."

"You're better than Liza Redcliffe."

Karen relaxed her grip a little. "That's better Julian. Now make love to me. Prove you want me more than anyone. More than that old whore."

"What, now?"

Karen frowned, relinquished her hold and moved off in a sulk."

"It's just you injuries....?"

"If you loved me, if you really wanted me they wouldn't matter. What's a bit of pain. In a way it's better, it's more intense."

"Come here then," I said, grabbing her shoulder. Karen turned to face me, a big smile on her bruised face.

She bent forward and took off her top. "Just think," she said, throwing it aside, "how lucky you are to get to sleep with a girl with the body of a super-model, the best in the world, and any time you want."

"Any time?"

"Ah ha, any time you want."

Karen was right about her powers of recovery, after only a few days the swelling from her contusions had markedly gone down, what gave her most concern was the deep cut on her left cheek, which looked very much as though it would leave a lasting impression, apart from that, she was almost at her peak of condition again; certainly her libido had suffered no ill effects from the pummelling she had received.

Everyday, dressed in leotards, she would work out with weights for two hours. She loved for me to attend these physical displays, when I would keep tally of the number of sit-ups she had done, of which she was capable of at least one hundred and fifty, and on a good day exceed over two hundred. Afterwards, all hot and sweaty, she would strip off her leotard and pull me into the shower after her - where the workout would continue.

"I want to get this thing with Pandora over with. I'm getting bored with Athens," said Karen, coming out of the shower and wrapping a towel around her gorgeous body.

"Why don't we just leave? We could go to one of the islands? We don't have to stay?"

"We will when this thing is done. When Pandora is ground into dust."

"You don't have to go through with it? Let's just pack our bags and go?"

"No...you know I can't," said Karen adamantly. "I know you care, but I must do it."

"May be she won't be able to organise enough......clients?"

"If she is worth her salt she will. She did say it would take time. A girl like *that* - she will." Karen took my hand. "Don't worry, we'll have a great time, we'll travel lots of places, see all the islands."

I felt Karen's hand tighten. She frowned, as if in pain and held herself.

"Is it......that?"

"Yes it grows, like a huge darkness inside of me."

"What can I do?"

"It's all right, there is nothing you or anybody can do. It's so frustrating. I know you do your best, it's me, I'm so damn demanding I know. I'm going to do some more workouts - if you know what I mean." she touched my arm, "It's the only way. You understand!"

I nodded. "Don't worry I shan't disturb you," I said.

Karen leaned forward and kissed me on the cheek. "You're a sweet." She picked up her towel and headed back into the bathroom.

Karen was peculiarly prudish when it came to admitting that there was only one sure way of finding relief from the dark urges that plagued her mind and body. I heard the shower go on to mask any sound she may happen to utter. Perhaps no one will ever know just how hard she fought against this dark god. Giving in to her animal instincts in *this* way, was like admitting defeat. As time went on I got to know that the phrase 'I need to take a shower,' had more than one meaning for Karen. It could be an invitation, other times a wish to be left to her own *devices.*

So when she came out of the shower just over an hour later, her face slightly flushed, I didn't ask any more than: "Did you have a good shower my dear?"
"Yes, it was all right thanks. I needed it - you know, there's nothing like a *shower* to set you up for the day."
"Good, I'm glad you're feeling better."
"Yes much, thanks," she said, as she slipped into her favourite green silk kimono. Sitting in front of her looking-glass she began to brush her hair. It was wonderful thick fair hair, that when it grew long was very difficult to manage. She often spoke of going back to wearing it in dreadlocks, and I remembered seeing images in one of the magazines she use to appear regularly in, with her hair arranged in such a style. It suited her, it was unusual. At the time she was the only white model to wear her hair like that.
"Do you think?" she began, after staring at herself as if she were in a trance.
"Do I think what - you're beautiful?" I said, pre-empting her normal line of thinking, when she stood for too long in front of a mirror.
"No, I was wondering," she looked round at me for a second and went back in to her contemplative mood again.
"What! - what were you wondering?"
"Do you think I *can* better Pandora?" she said, biting her finger nervously.
I looked up from my copy of the Herald Tribune. This was far more interesting news: 'stop press, Karen Veronica Stockwell finally admits to human weakness of self-doubt.'
"Who knows," I said, in the most pessimistic tones I could muster.
"I can, can't I?" she said, and began to slowly brush her hair again,. "I *can*, of course I can."
"Well I don't know. She is a big girl, and she's probably had lots of experience. I mean a girl like that, a *professional* - she's probably has hundreds of callers every night."
Karen looked at me and frowned. "No! Don't say that."
"Well you wanted to know." I said, before going on in my most gravest voice: "You can never tell, sooner or later one confronts ones Nemesis. May be Pandora is your Nemesis."
Karen ran her fingers through her hair and looked quite perplexed until she

spied me in her looking-glass and quickly saw through my earnest approach. Looking round at me sharply: "I Know your game silly, you're trying to do a numbered on me *a la Garcia* - Nemesis indeed!"

"I'm serious! She may do this thing all the time. Anyway, I've never heard you express any doubts...over your abilities before."

"Well I've never done it with *that* many, not consecutively."

"I thought you said that at times you felt like you could take on the whole world?"

"Oh, please Julian! There is a limit to what a girl can take, even for *me.*" Karen traced the outline of her mouth with her finger tip and then bit her lip.

The topic of our discussion was beginning to have an uncomfortable effect on me; together with the pose she struck, which made her look so vulnerable, I went over and put my arms around her.

"There is no one like you," I said, despite my wish to dissuade her from the madness.

"No, you're right - there isn't, is there?"

"No - no one. You feel so good, so powerful."

"Athletic."

"Yes athletic. If they made sex into an Olympic event you would get gold every time."

Karen grinned, her long body squirming under my touch. "World champion." she mused. "It's highly underrated as a physically demanding activity, requiring much stamina, not to mention skill - that is if you are going to take it seriously."

She undid her kimono, and demonstrated why she would reign supreme if such an event were to exist.

"I thought I might have another crack at the bellhop," said Karen, as she lay next to me.

"Yes," I replied, coming quickly back from a light sleep. It was obvious that I barely ever scratched the surface of her passion, for she never showed the slightest signs of exultation, or even fatigue. The equally disturbing fact was that she seldom exhibited any sense of empathy. It was always *her* needs, *her* rampant and insatiable desires that must be met on demand.

"Yes well," continued Karen, trying to sound casual, " I asked him if he would come and see me. I said there were things I needed to explain to him." Karen looked at me quizzically. "Did you hear me?" she said.

"Yes I heard you, I just can't believe it, that's all."

Karen wound her Kimono tightly round her tubular shaped body, so that she took on an appearance of a long green slender stem.

"Well you must believe it."

"For goodness sakes! What *things* do you want to talk to him about?"

Karen lite a cigarette and stared, "I don't know, just things," she said, awkwardly. "So I was thinking may be you could go out for a while. You don't mind do you?"

I just looked at her astounded.

"Oh, you do!" she said, in a flat tone of voice. "I might have known. I'm sorry, so soon after an' all, but it's not like you really want it with me, is it? You only did it just now because of our discussion, but the last couple of days I can tell you don't really want me - like *that*."

"Aren't you forgetting something! - It's me who gets to say who you debase yourself with."

"But you already said it was OK," said Karen, in her petulant teenager voice.

"It's true I did. I would have thought you'd had enough after the way it turned out last time?"

"This is different. It's here, and he's just a boy really."

"All the more reason not to do it."

"Oh come on! It was you, you who lit the flame."

"No," I interjected, "*that* was done long ago."

Karen remained without speaking for some time, in her petulant juvenile mood.

"Well, I can't stop you, so if you must...."

Karen smiled. "I knew you'd understand."

"No I don't understand, but I know there is nothing I can do or say that will stop you. Anyway how did you arrange it, especially after last time?"

"He asked how I was, what with the way I was looking, an' all."

"And what did you say?"

Karen put her finger in her mouth, and gave me that vulnerable cute look.
"Tell me?" I persisted.

Karen looked down. " I said you loose your temper sometimes," she said, in a tiny voice.

"You did what?" I shouted.

Karen shushed me, "Be quiet, otherwise they'll think you've started hitting in on me again."

"I just don't believe you! After all I've done for you!"

"Well, I had to say something, and the sympathy line always arouses those manly feelings of protection."

"Well thanks a lot. You've made me out to be a wife beater. No wonder I got some odd looks from the staff!"

"Well I could hardly tell them what really happened, now could I?" said Karen, "Anyway I want you out of here later this afternoon."

"Don't worry, I won't interrupt you carnal exploits."

"Why don't you find your fat old whore and get up to some carnal exploits of you own? It's a good release for all that pent-up anger you carry around."

"Well yes, we wouldn't want me to vent it on your pretty face again, now would we!"

"I know you'd like to stay and watch, but under the circumstances..." said Karen, coolly. "I know you'd love to watch."

For a second I seriously contemplate renewing some of her bruises. I began to get dressed quickly. "Don't worry I shan't ruin your little party."

"You don't have to go *now*."

"I do! I can't stand the sight of you. All this, it's just madness, share madness."

"Well it was your idea."

"Don't I know it! But you didn't have to take it up so damned enthusiastically."

Karen watched me in a bemused kind of way as I began to gather together the few clothes I had unpacked.

"What are you doing?"

"What does it look like?" I said, making a cynical laughing sound, "you don't honestly expect me to stay here any more? You've already told every one I beat you, and now to top it all you are going to have sex with the bellhop!"

I shook my head and began to laugh in a genuine way. "You amaze me Karen you really do. I do believe you are completely mad! You live in your own little world and expect everyone to do your bidding! Well you know what? I have had enough. That's it, *I've had enough,!*"

Karen looked at me nervously. She had never seen me act this way before, and I think it frightened her a little.

"You don't have to go! Please don't go!"

I went over to the long green stem of a girl and shook it. "Didn't you hear anything I just said?"

"Don't leave me."

"What choice do you give me?"

Karen had no reply to this, she just sat down and watched me pack the rest of my things. If she had recanted on her decision to sleep with the bellhop it might have helped the situation but no attempt at conciliation was forthcoming.

"Well that's that then," I said, when everything was packed.

Karen lit a cigarette. "I don't know what all the fuss is about!" she said. She shook her head. "You'll never understand me. It's you who never listens, it's you who is self-indulgent. You're a goddamn hypocrite. You don't love me, if you did it wouldn't matter what people thought." Karen looked away, and mumbled: "Just wait until Garcia finds out."

"What was that?" I said, ranging round at her.

"Garcia! When he finds out how you ran out on me!" said Karen, flicking her ash nonchalantly into a bowl. She shook her head, "boy will he be pissed with you buster! He'll kick your ass boy! Make no mistake, he'll hunt you down like a dog and kick your ass all the way back to California!"

"Yeah, that figures! He's no more than a goddamn thug. When I think of that poor girl who he had done over, simply because he couldn't get his way. People like that are pathetic! They're the real hypocrites, and you my dear, are not that much different."

Karen nodded slowly smoking her cigarette, occasionally looking towards me malevolently.

"We'll see," she said, trying to sound enigmatic. "He'll be so disappointed in you, but I tried to tell him you were never man enough for someone such as I."

"No, I guess not, hopefully your bellhop might be." The irony of it all made me laugh again. "What does it matter? God knows how many you would have been through by the end of the week? I think I will go and find Pandora, try and talk some sense in to her!"

"Yes go on. Go to her, and tell her everything, Go and cry on her shoulder. Oh, and while you're there you might ask her when she will be ready? Tell her I can't wait to grind her into the dirt where she belongs."

I went to the door, "I will be sure to, my dear," I said, in a feigned English accent. "Toodle-pip old thing."

"Good-bye you insidious little man," called Karen. Just as I closed the door I heard the impact of a breakable object upon it.

I went straight to Pandora's pub where I found her behind the bar. She explained how she had to cover sometimes when Stephanos went out on business. She was so excited to see me I guess she didn't notice the hold-all I had with me. It didn't take her long though for her to see that there was something wrong.

"You're in trouble! What is it?" she said, taking my hand.

I felt like crying. I had to look away from her beautiful face for a second.

"Oh, Julian! It's her isn't it? What has she done now?" Pandora got me a beer. "You can tell Pandora, tell her everything."

And so over the course of several more beers I told her all that had transpired between Karen and myself.

For Pandora it simply reaffirmed what she already believed, that Karen was bad for me. She was pleased when I told her that I had packed my bags and left, but when I expressed my continued concern for Karen's well being she became even more adamant that I had done the right thing by leaving.

"You are good person" said Pandora, "it is only natural for you to worry, but please do not say again you are in love with her! This....this monster! She is very bad woman. very *bad*."

"She is?" I nodded, in a kind of haze. "Where is the right woman though? and where will I find any one like Karen?"

"Perhaps you need not look very far?" said Pandora, gripping my hand tightly, and bringing the full force of her jet black eyes to bear upon me.

"Really, do I not need to?"

Pandora leaned over the bar and I felt her kiss, and the cool peppermint taste of her mouth. Suddenly all my pain and fears melted away. I kissed her again, this time with more passion, kissing her hard on the mouth. She smiled with pleasure. "All will be well. You need not look any further. Have no fear," she said, with such confidence, as though she held the secrets of life's mysteries herself.

I looked at my watch. "It's getting late. She will be with him now. I can't go back there," I looked at Pandora. "I'd better go, try and find somewhere to stay."

"Stephanos will be here in a short time, you can leave with me, he has a villa a short drive away, sometimes I stay there, he will let *you* stay there."

I thought about Karen again, and felt bad for running out on her. Pandora must have seen the look of confusion on my face. She stopped what she was doing and took hold of my hand again: the long fingers and the long dark red painted nails, enclosing tightly about my hand. "I want you to go there with *me*, you understand?"

"Yes I understand," I said, "but you and he, aren't you....?"

Pandora smiled faintly, "no, once but not now, not for a long while now. It is a long story, I tell you some time. Don't worry everything will be all right, from now on all will be good for you, so long as you trust me."

Just as Pandora had indicated, Stephanos was only too happy to let us stay at his villa. I detected however the faintest trace of reservation and sadness on seeing us leave together, something that is always present in an old love, but there was genuine happiness for us too.

We left 'Pub Pandora' and the claustrophobic port area behind. Piraeus, like most ports, like all places of passage, lacked any sense of permanence and lent itself to the seedy side of life, which comes from catering to the needs of the, 'passer by,' so the fairly new Mercedes that Pandora drove and the villa on the coast that belonged to Stephanos was not indicative of the location of 'Pub Pandora,' but then again, the existence of the establishment only went to prove that the 'passer by' represented a lucrative trade. As any one with worldly knowledge will tell you, trade in the exotic and the rare, as well as the illegal, flourishes in a large port like Piraeus.

The villa was set on top of a kind of rocky promontory that jutted out over the sea. A long winding driveway lead up to the rear of the property, the other route was from the road, via a series of steps that had been cut into the surrounding rock. A large veranda stretched nearly the entire length of the building on the sea facing side. Bedecked with table and chairs, sun-beds, exotic plants and vines, I sat there and drank the drink Pandora had made for me and waited for her while she showered and got changed. Apart from excitement there was a growing trepidation; I recalled that first night with Karen, when we had driven down to the beach. It seemed so long ago now, it was as though it had happened to another person. My reverie was immediately swept away when I felt Pandora's fingers on my neck. She brought with her the aroma of some sort of exotic oil that spoke to the mind of mysteries, of mists at twilight, of dew in long grass, of silvery cool moonlight, and pale nocturnal flowers. I turned and saw her dark eyes intent on me. She was wearing a long black see-through negligee, and sexy black underwear. We kissed briefly and then she lead me by the hand to the bedroom. Reed blinds closed out most of the evening sunlight, bathing the room in a sort of muted yellow. Half the room was filled by a large king-size bed, with a closet and side tables. Pandora, sensing my nervousness came over to me and began to kiss me, very gently, very soothingly, in a way that did not initiate the immediate descent into the Dionysian worship of the flesh.

"Try to relax Julian. Nothing bad will ever happen to you hear."

"Nothing bad?"

Pandora shook her head. "Nothing, because I won't let it."

I hugged her luscious body not wanting to let her go. "look, why don't you take a shower, it's just across the hall. I'll be here waiting when you return. There are some scented oils. Use tea-tree or rose oil, they will help you relax."

I showered and used the oils she said. Afterwards my body felt new; I felt the stress burn away leaving me naked and exposed, and yet unafraid. Pandora was waiting on the bed where I had left her. I began to tell her how good the shower was, how happy I felt to be with her. Pandora gently silenced my lips with her finger.

"Let us just be still for a moment," she said.

We lay next to one another, our bodies nestling up close. I held her gently and kissed her lips, her eyes, her strong marble white, marble smooth neck and the broad expanse of her white prone throat. I found in the closeness of her body such peace, such tranquillity as I had never known before. In her arms there was sublime bliss, perfect peace and stillness, not to have to struggle, to clamour with another body, but to be still with it, and yet to know that in this stillness one already possessed it; but this possession was a cool still possession, not a wanting or a striving to cancel out the other, this was a union as much about mind as it was body, in this still togetherness the Dionysian madness had no place, here cool Apollo ruled.

And so we stayed in this gentle magical union for - I don't know how long. It seemed like a long time, but when the pulse moves slowly time itself seems to become extended, so perhaps it was not that long in real time. I kissed Pandora's mouth: the broad arc of her waxen throat, I kissed her long black hair and her deep black eyes. At some point, the Dionysian flame was lit in her, as it would surely be lit in me, existing as I did, in such close proximity to a creature as desirous as Pandora. Our kisses grew more forceful and urgent, our bodies cleaved to one another more forcibly. "Touch me," she murmured, puling back her negligée and leading my hand to her breast. Her flesh was as cool and refreshing to the touch as rain on a spring day, And even as the Dionysian passions began to rage, in her loving she moved cool and still, glacial cool and smooth, but inside the fire raged fierce. She moved on top of me and made herself naked. In the gloom of the room her wonderful full body took on a kind of yellowish waxy effulgence, her form: that of a sallow Aphrodite.

For a while the Apollonian stillness returned. Pandora tried to re-establish a sense of peace and calm in the middle of the tumult that we had created. It was easy to see she was a proud woman, proud of her body and happy for me to just look at it for a moment. To simply share the pleasure of knowing that one could look, or one could touch, but sometimes the touching clouds the vision, and we become lost again in the blizzards of raging passions. So Pandora through her powerful will, brought back for a moment that special union that went beyond the physical, and calmed the storm that besieged our senses.

She lay back allowing me to touch and sense the resilience and heaviness of her breasts. I spoke and told her how much she was beautiful, and it seemed to shatter her stillness, which inevitably lead towards the old striving for oblivion in one anothers body. The way of dissolution, the way of Dionysus, which cancelled out the spiritual, and for a moment at the climax, even the physical.

And when that moment passed the urgency passed, and we clung to one another, but in a different sort of stillness. The stillness of rest, of satiation, of trust. Then of course, this was loving, and this was the path of loving, which is really the repetition of all that has so far been put down. The stillness the stirring of the passion and the stillness again, and so it went on throughout the night and on into the dawn.

"Now do you see," she said, in the light of the morning, "how it can be, and how it is meant to be? And you thought you were no good! It was never you that was at fault, it is simply you had the bad experience of knowing only the wrong kind of woman."

I laughed through a joyous sense of relief. A wonderful liberating feeling of release. It had never been *my* deficiency which I had striven to explain through a constant critical examination of my own perceived physical shortcomings. Pandora got out of bed and opened the shutters, immediately dispelling the yellow lustre of her body into that of bright clear marble. That she was not inviolate as a statue, but had moved through life and therefore had been subject to violation, was undeniable. The most striking *visual* evidence for this came from the way in which the pearl white lustre of her upper thigh had been used as a canvas for a striking finely chiselled tattoo of a dragon holding a dagger, it's long serpentine tail coiled around the blade. Only now, as the light struck her, had it's existence become irrefutable.

"Don't look at me like that," said Pandora.

"How was I looking at you?"

"As if you did not know me. It shocks you, doesn't it?" she said, glancing down at the design, while indicating neither shame nor pride in the markings.

"I suppose it's a bit of a shock. I never saw it until now."

"You don't like it? Does Karen have any tattoos?"

"No. She would never have anything like that done to her. She believes her body is sacrosanct."

"It was done many years ago." said Pandora, putting on her negligée and returning to the bed.
"It doesn't mater. You're still beautiful - it's very erotic!"
"Ah - yes, I suppose you might think that, but it is not the main reason why I had it done."
"Why did you?"
Pandora's bright face clouded a little. "It comes from my early days on the streets of Athens."
I listened intently as she told me about her life. She had run away from home when she was very young. She fell under the influence of disreputable people who turned her on to drugs, and then prostitution in order to finance her addiction. Eventually she became co-opted into a gang, there she gained a shaky kind of security, so long as she played by their rules. In short she had learned how to survive outside the law. She puled back her gown, and explained the meaning of the dragon as a symbol of inner strength.
"And the dagger?" I enquired.
"My brother came to Athens to find me, when he tried to take me out of the gang they killed him. I said I would revenge his death one day." Pandora paused, seemingly reluctant to go on.
"And did you?" I prompted.
"No, not yet. When I do, the dagger will be sheathed." Pandora covered herself and looked at me beseechingly. "But I am not like that now," she said. "I am not sure I even believe in revenge any more. The one that took my brothers life will pay for his actions to God Almighty."
"You sound very wise."
"Not wise, I just grew tired of hating. If it were not for Stephanos I would have died a long time ago, either through drugs or by trying to revenge my brothers death."
Pandora went on to explain how Stephanos had found her and saved her from herself, for she was bent on a trajectory of self-destruction, consumed by a single desire for revenge, and bitter hatred. He had the power and the respect of the gang leaders, so that he was able to free her from their tyranny, where her brother had failed. Stephanos went on to help her quit drugs, and gave her

a home, and a sense of self worth; he educated her, sent her to study English, even financing her trip to America. Yes they had been lovers, but the love changed into something deeper, something like the love she once had for her deceased brother. But of course, all this came at a price, there is a word for people like Stephanos, in the final analysis he was an astute business man, he saw in Pandora great potential, he recognised her beauty and intelligence and used it to build up the business. He did not run a bordello, all the girls who worked for him were respectable, some of them he had saved, as he had Pandora. Only occasionally did Pandora ever have to allow herself to be used the way she had in the past, but this became more and more seldom, as the business became more profitable and younger sexier girls were taken on. I forcibly deny that there could be anyone more desirable than Pandora.

"Look at my face Julian. The lines. The time I spent on the streets and the drugs have taken their toll on me. Unlike your Karen I am not so vain as to know that my body and my looks are failing me." Pandora looked at me frankly, but was unable to keep out the note of resentment in her voice: "I cannot blame Stephanos for going with other younger more beautiful women, he has many to choose from, I dare say he would even like to enrol the services of your Karen."

"She is not *my* Karen."

Pandora did not bother to reply. We both knew she had conjured up a demon by mentioning her name and comparing herself with *her*.

"I don't understand," I said, "it seems you have come a long way since you met Stephanos, you no longer have to go with men, so why put yourself through it all again by paying attention to Karen."

Pandora was some time in replying: "Perhaps I do it to prove something to myself?"

"What! That you are better than her?"

Pandora shrugged her shoulders. "May be I am not so smart after all."

"Don't do it Pandora. She's not worth it. You'll just be playing into her hands."

Pandora tried to appease me with a kiss, she even tried to make me forget with the solicitous use of her body. "Oh, *come on....*" she moaned.

"I'm serious! You have no idea what she is like."

"Oh I think I do - some things must be done. It will hurt no one."

"It will hurt me. It will hurt Stephanos. He would not want to see you return to the way you were."

Pandora seemed to consider a moment. "I would not do it then, but Karen will not have it. Anyway it is all arranged for this Friday. Over two hundred are invited."

"And what about Stephanos?"

Pandora looked past me towards the window. "He will allow it. He was not happy that I should have to work hard like that again but I said I must. It is a matter of honour. He will allow it. It will happen here at his villa."

"You don't know what she is like!" I said. I took Pandora's head between my hands and forcing her to look at me: "Karen is not like other women."

"Please Julian!" cried Pandora, "what is she?....."

"You haven't seen her the way I have. Garcia took her through a thing called past life regression, she went wild - she had incredible strength."

"Oh please," repeated Pandora, laughing: "Not this story about her being the priestess of Tiamat?"

"The priestess of Tanit - yes!"

"She is nothing, this *Tellus* and her *priestess!*" said Pandora, making an animated sine with her hands.

"It's bad to say such things!"

"I believe in God the Almighty, he has made me strong. He will protect me against such *tèras* as Karen and her Tailte or, whatever she is called!..." continued Pandora taking up a strident position. She bent her head down to kiss me, her long hair covering me like a back veil. She pulled her head up and flicked the hair from her face. I looked up at her; for a second the early morning sun caught her features, highlighting their wan appearance. There were deep creases dividing her cheeks running down to the corner of her mouth, and there were lines by her eyes. Her skin had a sallow pallid appearance. She offered me her body to touch as she had in the night. Tremulously I puled back her negligée. Her breasts hung heavy but without any real resilience: almost flaccid. I looked at her white hips and the tattoo on her inner thigh, it no longer seemed erotic on such flabby flesh scared by hundreds of lines of cellulite. I looked over her shoulder towards the window and cursed the sun for it's brutal honesty.

She was definitely no statue, the signs of repeated violation were all to evident. Looking at her in the bright light of morning I was left in little doubt what she had been. Her skin no longer reminded me of cold marble, and her kiss was no longer glacial fresh, and instead of the aroma of magical vernal evenings, there came from her the odour of decay and death.

"What is it?" she said.

I looked up at her, still cursing the light. I felt my body inwardly recoil from her touch.

"Nothing," I said, guiltily.

"I know you are thinking of her. A certain kind of look comes into your face, and your body grows rigid when you think of her."

I was thankful she had come to *this* conclusion. She moved off of me; I turned my head away so that I didn't have to see her naked. She threw the phone on the bed and told me to use it to call Karen.

"You don't mind?"

"Do it so I can have you back again."

The reedy voice of the manger came on the line. Karen had booked out of the hotel having left no forwarding address, but her luggage was till there: 'when was I coming to get it?' he wanted to know. I told him within the hour.

"What is wrong?" said Pandora, her long fingers searching out my hand and taking the receiver from me.

"She's gone," I said, staring at her blankly. "She's gone!" I repeated. "God knows where?"

"It does not seem I will get you back so soon!"

"Where could she have gone?"

"She will make her presence felt. Do not worry about her, like me she is a survivor." Pandora took my hand. "You need to relax. Come - first I need to shower, then we will go to the hotel. Come, don't be shy, " she said.

I hesitated, reluctantly I went with her. It was better than I imagined. She covered our bodies in scented oils. The steamy water and the fragrance of the oils seemed to rejuvenate her, enliven her flesh. How strange it seemed, that moments before she had repelled me, but now I found myself wanting her with a keenness and urgency that took Pandora by surprise. When the madness passed Pandora looked at me, her jet eyes wide with a mad and unfathomable mixture of emotions. For a moment she seemed breathless and I had to support her. She leaned her back against the tiles, her big chest heaving as the water cascaded over breasts.

"Ah! - Julian. How could you have ever doubted yourself?" she sighed. I held her to me, allowing the water to envelop us.

"When I'm with you it's different," I said. May be it was the nature of the environment: hot and steamy, but I felt a kind of intoxication. My senses were saturated with the pungent fragrance of the aromatic oils, and with the sight and feel of Pandora's pale slithery flesh. We leaned against one another in a kind of torpor, yet all the time I was aware of my own keenness, to which Pandora, to my surprise, had no reply.

"No more - no more!" she said, pushing me aside and stepping out of the shower.

"What is it?" I asked, following her.

Ignoring me, she sat down with the towel around her, her right hand inside covering her breast. Her face streamed with perspiration. She looked defeated, her complexion, ashen, her cheeks sunken, her features gaunt, lantern jawed.

Occasionally she would disappear in a big cloud of vapour. I went to turn off the shower.

"Leave it!" called Pandora, from somewhere amidst the steam. "I just want to be here on my own a moment. Why don't you go and make some coffee!" she said, in laboured tones.

"Are you sure you're OK?"

"Yes, just go will you! I'll be out in minute."

I saw her come out of the bathroom and go straight to her room. She was a long time in there. When she came out she didn't speak. I noticed she had made her face up. The usual heavy black eyeliner, painted lips, and she had put a touch of rouge on her cheeks. She seemed distracted. Now and again she would look over at me furtively, not wanting to catch my eye.

"We had best get Karen's things from the hotel," she said.

"Is anything wrong?"

"No, it is just that I am a little surprised at you," she paused. "But pleasantly so.

I see now there is nothing unusual about *you.* You are just like any other man."

"I don't understand?"

"I was not prepared for what happened in the shower."

"Neither was I, it just happened. Can I help it if I find you attractive like that?"

"I just wanted...." Pandora broke off. "It does not matter."

"I'm not like all the others."

Pandora regarded me coolly, her composure had returned. Her face was an enigma, in a certain light she could appear astoundingly beautiful in another her features looked warn and haggard.

"You want of me what all men want. You are no different. It is just that with you I thought I could just *be*, without this constant wanting. I know my face has a certain look, they look at my body and all they see is sex. It has always been like that, why should it be any different with you? It is naïve of me to think it should."

"No!" I protested, and suddenly found myself saying: "it is different, I love you."

"Don't say it if you do not mean it?" She fixed her jet eyes intently upon me. "I think you do?"

"I do."

Pandora was unable to restrain the sudden welling of feeling. Her black eyes filled with tears magnifying their intensity. Forgetting herself she began to speak rapidly in Greek, laughing and crying at the same time. She rushed over to me, and covered my face with kisses.

"It is true, it is true," she repeated.

"It's true." I said, hugging Pandora tightly.

Our excitement in this new found understanding was broken by the telephone. It was Stephanos, and the news that he brought dispelled our brief moment of happiness. The news was that Karen had arrived at the pub asking for me. Without giving me the opportunity to speak to her, Pandora told Stephanos we were on our way, and put the receiver down.

She turned to to me, there was a strange twist on her mouth, almost a smirk. "Well, I am right am I not? I said she would make her presence felt. It seems Stephanos and she are getting along very well. No need to worry, she is *very* well."

XIII

When we arrived at the pub we found Karen at the bar, apparently having a great time, speaking in Greek and laughing and drinking with Stephanos. So enthralled in their own company they demonstrated a certain reluctance to even acknowledge Pandora and myself.

"Mr Julian, so good to see you again, so good," he said, shaking my hand vigorously.

"I see you have found Karen!" said Pandora.

Both girls eyed one another with hostility; Pandora's black eyes seemed to bore into the heart of Karen's rancid soul, forcing her, in the end, to look away.

"She is such a fun girl," said Stephanos blindly.

"Well I'm glad you're safe Karen;" I said, taking the chair next to her.

Slowly she looked me up and down with her bright lavender eyes. "No thanks to you!" she said.

Stephanos put a beer in front of me and went to the other end of the bar where Pandora stood. They began to speak in raised voices, Pandora wagging her finger at Stephanos and occasionally in the direction of Karen and myself.

"So how was she?" said Karen, glancing in their direction.

I lit a cigarette, and then took a long drink of my beer.

"I think we should talk," she said. Karen swung round on her chair and spoke rapidly to Stephanos, who pointed to the curtained area. "Come on," she said, getting up and taking my arm, "we can go in there, where we won't be disturbed."

Karen stood uncomfortable, looking about the room and the vacant cubicles.

"So this is where she plies her trade!"

"Listen Karen, I don't want to hear that kind of thing."

"Why? This is where she brings her clients, isn't it? Has she entertained you here?"

"Yes, she has."

Karen looked distracted, and sat down at the nearest table and flung her head back and rested it on a cushion. "I'm sorry," she said, looking up.

I sat down next to her. "So what happened?" I asked.

"You were right." There was a pause. "I couldn't stay at the hotel, not after...."

"So you slept with him?"

Karen looked at me, giving me one of her best pouting adolescent looks. She tried to take my hand. When she saw that I wasn't about to be tempted by it she took a different stance. Her body stiffened and her face became firm and hard.

"You left me no choice! What did you expect me to do?"

"I left *you* no choice! And you call *her* a whore?"

Karen made no reply. She drew hard on her cigarette, and just gave me a long lingering look.

"Are you going to tell me you haven't slept with *her?* What was she like? I imagine she can be quite fun in bed!"

"What was the bellhop like?"

Karen smirked, "Hah!..He was like a *bull*." she said, with great relish, pronouncing the word slowly pouting her lips as she pronounced the letter b, so that the word had hardly any middle: *'b'll* "

I looked down and shook my head. She could see she had got the better of me now, so she went in for the kill.

"You should have been there, you would have witnessed a truly great performance. I know you love it! He was amazing - once he got over the shyness. All afternoon. Such energy! Such *Potency!*"

"So why not stay with him?"

"Oh - I don't know. He started to get possessive, even wanted me to come back to his folks place....so I remembered what you said about Pandora's pub, so here I am."

"Here you are!"

"Stephanos is kind of sexy don't you think?"

"Haven't you had enough?"

"You've started something - you know, like they say, once the jinni is out of his bottle!.."she replied, her eyes wide, the candle light glimmering a shade too much in those lavender pools of hers. I tried to look her in the eye but Karen purposively turned her head. Despite everything I found myself reaching for her hand.

"It's still not too late. We could just leave. Go some place. Anywhere!"
"No - impossible," said Karen, "not now. It's gone too far, besides you slept with her - that.. that whore! How could you Julian - how could you?" She got up and walked towards the curtain. "This thing with Pandora - I must have it!"
"Would it be enough?"
"Oh - I don't know."

She had on one of her sarongs, a vivid purple thing which fitted her low across her hips, her Japanese style bodice was cut short like a waist coat, the lower catches she left unfastened. She stretched, showing off several inches of flat hard abdomen. She seemed to grow leaner and stronger with every encounter. Karen shrugged and looked down at her naked belly as if the answer was there. In some sense it was; if she could stick her hand inside herself and rip out the demon that lie within, and it wasn't for the want of trying - god Knows! (even if she didn't admit it to herself,) but it lay too deep and imbedded for that. Instead all she could do was rub the effected area. She loved to touch herself, it wasn't always meant as a display of vanity. The demon grew restless, that was all, it somersaulted and jumped about, wriggling and squirming inside her.
"Does it grow again.?"
"All the time. Worse than ever," she said, in a strange voice that seemed to catch in her throat. She put her hand to her neck and swallowed. She looked towards me almost pleading. "Pandora, is it all prepared?"

I looked back at her. I could keep nothing from her, not even in a darkened room. She smiled and walked towards me. "I shall tell her I am ready. Is it to be here?"
"No they have a villa."
"Cheer up! Don't be so glum! I'll finish her, and then you and I will leave. That is what you want isn't it?"
"I don't know!"
"What do you mean, you don't know?" said Karen, with a look of incredulity. "Just now you said...." she smiled wryly: "Ah! - I see, you are still thinking of your whore."

Karen came up close, and stood before me in a proud and defiant stance. Her look was determined, her eyes ranged over me and then she looked down at herself, running her hands down the length of her body, "You'll come," she said, "you'll come for this." She thrust her hips forward pressing her hard bony groin against my leg. Her eyes challenged me for a second, and then I gave way. There was something in her look, in her whole *being* that was out of the ordinary, that at times was transcendent of the ordinary mundanity of every day life. With her, one felt that anything was possible. When she oriented all of her stark sexual power towards a desired goal one was powerless, and one found oneself being drawn up into her own demonic madness. Oh yes! there will be those who will say I was fickle, that I had professed to be in love with Pandora, and it is true, I was, but what Karen offered was something very different to love, what she offered was worship - after all she was the *high priestess of Tanit!"*

When Karen and I came back from behind the curtain Pandora was sitting at the far end of the bar. Her mood appeared sullen, Stephanos was talking with another girl who, judging by what she was wearing, was also on the payroll. Karen ignored the other girl and marched straight up to Pandora. She stood before her taking up a slinky kind of stance, with one hip thrust forward of the other. Pandora nonchalantly flicked some ash from her cigarette into an ashtray and indolently turned her head towards Karen: her long painted lashes flickering as she lifted her eyelids to expose the black radiance of her eyes: An awesome spectacle. Karen, with renewed confidence, steeled herself and matched her challenge, glaring back at her maniacally.

"So it is all arranged?" said Karen.

"Yes it is," replied Pandora.

Stephanos stopped talking to the the other girl and came over. "The party will take place at the villa tomorrow," he said.

"I look forward to it," replied Karen. She looked over Stephanos' shoulder at me. "Come Julian," she said, holding out her hand to me. Obediently I took it.

"Julian, the ever sensitive and caring is not happy with our little arrangement," continued Karen, addressing Stephanos.

"I too have had my concerns, but for other reasons," he replied, looking at Pandora.

She exhaled clouds of blue smoke and waved a dismissive hand. He put his hand on hers and spoke earnestly in their language. Her reply was sharp and - no doubt, to the point. Stephanos held up his hands.

"What can be done with a head strong woman Mr Julian?"

I looked at Karen. "I know exactly what you mean. They are as bad as each other."

"I agree with you, but what beauty we have." As he said this he was looking at Karen. "We are both lucky men - no!"

I looked over at Pandora, who tried her best to put across an air of bord indifference. She picked up her car keys sighing heavily: "If you want we can get Karen's things from the hotel," said Pandora, desperate to escape.

"Yes, go with her darling," said Karen, "there won't be room for us all, I will stay here and keep Stephanos company."

Karen glanced furtively towards the other man, then looking back at me: She oriented her power once more towards me and moved my hand to her bare waist, so that it rested on the wide swell of muscle above her hip, which in large part, attributed to the hourglass shape of her figure; her other hand went round my neck and puled my head towards hers. The kiss she gave me was long, using her long tongue to its full advantage. It was obvious what she was doing, she was like a cat marking her territory, and her territory included any man in the world she found worthy. Pandora looked on; her face turning ashen, her soul almost visibly contracting until the light of pride vanished from her distinct black eyes. They now appeared as they had done when I first met her, the look of a skull with two black empty orbs. Stephanos on the other hand was amused by the whole spectacle. As for my part, when a man is damned there is no point in making excuses. I had no more free thought, or power of decision making than a slave or an automaton. I flowed like flotsam to whatever tide was the strongest.

I heard the door of the pub slam shut. Karen brought the kiss to an end. She had achieved her desired goal.

"Oh - was that Pandora?" said Karen. "You'd better go with her - but be good!"

"What about you?"

"I can't come, there won't be room for all of us."

Karen let go of my hand and went over to Stephanos and lay her hand against

his chest. "Don't worry, I have Stephanos to keep me company."
"Yes Mr Julian, I will look after her," he said grinning, "we will meet you back at the villa later this evening."
I looked at the pair of them, hesitating, now that I was caught between two tides. To my surprise Karen came over to me and kissed me once more.
"Don't worry Julian everything will be just fine," she said, opening the door for me and giving me a gentle shove in the right direction.
Pandora was sitting in the car waiting for me. Her face looked cadaverous and distorted with simmering rage. When I got in next to her she beat the steering wheel hard several times with her fist, cursing in her tongue.
"Why! - Why!" she screamed. "Why you let her? Why?"
She went back to speaking in her language, which made no difference to me since I had no answers for her either way. I remained still and dumb like seaweed on a some distant shore, waiting - waiting for the new tied to carry me off again.
"Stupid! - So stupid!" She said, changing the target of her blows to her own head. This, the sensitive soul could not stand, and so I tried to stop her, which only made matters worse. She puled her hands from me violently, her long fingernails making weals on the back of my hand.
"Don't touch me," she spat.
I sat quite still, afraid that at any minute she would attack me with her talons again. Gradually though she seemed to calm down, but I noticed her heavy chest still laboured hard. She fumbled in her bag for a cigarette, found one and put it to her mouth and lit it, her hands trembling. She exhaled, breathing deeply and turned the black void of her eyes on me.
"You have betrayed me!" she said.
"You don' know what she is like," I replied.
"No! Tell me - what is she like?"
I sighed. I could feel the tide moving me.
"Ah, well!" Pandora gave a cynical little laugh. "I should have guessed. You are a man! You are like all men! They speak of love, but all they want is the flesh."
"I know you don't believe me, but it's true - she's not...." I paused, looking for the right word: "She's not *normal.*"

"Oh, please Julian! Not all this nonsense about her being a goddess, and reincarnation of whoever - Tefnut or some such person?"

I shook my head. "I don't know, but I think she is some sort of witch. She has some sort of power - superhuman power!"

"She is a woman, she has what all men want. Wait and see, I will prove to you that she can suffer, that she is just mortal flesh. She will bleed yet!" Pandora started the engine of the Mercedes, let off the brake and wheel spun away from the curb.

"Did you have to kiss her like that?"

"I was trying to explain. She did it to annoy you."

"What did you do in there all that time? Did you do *it* with her?"

I looked out of the window exasperated. "Of course not," I replied, knowing full well that we both knew I would do *anything* that she wanted.

Pandora didn't say much more until we got to the hotel and had collected up most of Karen's luggage, the rest would have to be brought later. I felt a bit more at ease now, now that a new tide was under me, and Pandora's storm had begun to quell.

"Why does she need all this stuff?"

"D'know." I said. "It's just how she is."

"She must have a lot of money to afford such things?"

"She's a model, apart from other things! With the kind of figure she has - 'the body of a super-model', she could have become world famous - a 'supermodel!'

"Why didn't she stick to that?"

"She can't help herself," I said, feeling bored with the whole thing. I felt nothing now, as we drove towards the villa; I just wanted to flow with the tide and not to have to think or analyse anybody's behaviour.

"She wants to destroy," said Pandora. "She destroys what she comes into contact with. She is *Kakos*, how you say, wicked, very bad?"

"You mean evil!" I said.

"Ah yes, evil. You believe this also?"

"I don't know - I don't know if I believe in evil. People just *are*. Karen is what Karen is! We are what we are, nothing more!"

Pandora just glanced towards me without speaking. She lay her hand briefly on mine. "I suppose I shouldn't blame you," she said, at length, "you are just a child really. What can you do with a woman that has the devil in her?" She looked at me a second and smiled sadly, her hand tightening on mine. It felt good. It felt strong. One needed strength to fight demons. "Just a child," repeated Pandora to herself. "Don't worry Julian, I will finish her one way or another!" Pandora smiled ruefully to herself: "You will see, I will show you, she is just an ordinary woman."

"What do you mean?" I said, concerned.

Pandora patted my hand. "Fear not, we have seen how she can bleed. She has been beaten before, this time she will not be able to walk away so easily. You think she can do this to me! Take away my business! Come between Stephanos and me! Just because she gives her sex so freely," Pandora sneered. I looked at the speedometer we were doing over a hundred. "She will not be so eager to give of herself in the future. It will pain her to even think of it. She does not even have looks to fall back on when everything else is used up!" She shook her head, her long black hair flowed around her face, flying about madly in the warm air. "What is it you see in her? Do you think she is beautiful?"

"I don't know. She has a kind of beauty, or did have until she was in that fight. I suppose it's her body?"

Pandora nodded, "Ah yes! her body - her filthy body!" she spate out words of venom in her language. The look of mania in Pandora's dead black eyes made me fear for Karen's well-being, as well as that of my own, as the car swerved momentarily into the middle of the road.

"Ughhh!...How I would like to....Arggg!" She uttered, as she curled her hand into a fist and banged it hard against the steering-wheel.

"You won't hurt her?"

"Poor Julian, so innocent." Pandora tutted and shook her head: "And to think you still care about her! She does not deserve such loyalty."

"She has been through a lot. Garcia entrusted me to look after her."

Pandora spoke in a weird spooky kind of way, deepening her voice: "Don't worry my dear, I won't hurt her....Quite the opposite. I will show you she is only a woman - only a woman with a woman's feelings a woman's desires."

She coughed and looked out of the window and then carried on speaking in her usual voice: "So you are her keeper! You have only the responsibility to yourself - no!"

I looked at her. "Is it not so?" Pandora laughed in her throat. "You are like all men. They see a woman with a good body and run after it. How silly all men are. So like children really. Influenced by such things; what men forget is that the body is a changing thing....It is how you say - not permanent?"

"Transient." I said.

"Yes it is this. A girl like that will age fast. I have seen them before. They come they go. Her face is already marred, pretty soon her body will follow. You will see her for what she is: *teratos* - a monster! Not very pretty hey!"

"She is stronger than you think," I said, almost as a warning.

Pandora looked at me. She did not speak again for some moments.

"You think she can outdo me - hah! is that it?"

"Don't underestimate her."

"She has an impressive body I admit this, but she will need more than just a strong body." Pandora tapped her head. "In here here is where she must be strong. As cold as ice. She burns hot though. She is in love with herself."

"She can't help what she is," I offered.

Pandora smiled wickedly to herself. "Girls like her are easy." she said.

"Easy!"

She smiled and pattered my hand again. "So innocent - you will see."

I was relieved when out journey came to an end. At the villa we unloaded all of Karen's things and stored them in the room allocated to her. All the time Pandora went on about how much stuff Karen had. How rich she must be. She stood in front of a mirror and held up one of Karen's favourite kimonos, the green one with the floral pattern. I thought how well the colour suited Pandora, her lovely long black hair cascaded down her front, she looked quite the part of the Japanese Geisha, far more than Karen ever did in such styles.

"Such a beautiful thing," she said, "she does not deserve such things."

"It is beautiful but so are you. If you want I can buy you the same beautiful things," I said.

Pandora looked unimpressed, which made me wonder whether it was not a case of: 'to the victor the spoils.' She continued to admire the silk garment. There was so much envy in her dark eyes, so much loathing too, for the one who owned such beautiful things.

"Can I try it on?"

"I don't know. Karen is very possessive about her clothes."

"She will never know!" said Pandora, running off to her room to change. A few minutes later she called me in and stood before me in the green kimono. "Tell me what you think. Is it right on me?" She ran her hands over the fine material.

"You look better in it than her. It's meant for you," I said going, to her and holding her around the waist, sensing the smooth silk and the curve of Pandora's broad hips.

Pandora took my hand and put it inside the dress and held it against her bosom. "You feel wonderful," I said. "You have lovely breasts, they are so big."

"Karen has good breasts - no?"

"Yes, but yours are bigger and real. Karen's are fake. Karen is a fake."

Pandora looked at me askance. "They are?"

"Of course, can't you tell."

"I did not think of it. I should like breasts like that - firm and round."

"If you want. Then they would be far better than Karen's."

"They would?"

"They already are. You are better than her."

"Am I?"

I pulled her close to me taking her off balance and we fell on to the bed kissing madly. Much much better," I whispered, as I began to peel back the layers of silk robe to reveal the soft white flesh of Pandora.

"I am better than her and I will prove it to you."

"Don't be like her, you don't need to prove a thing to me."

I made love to Pandora with the vestiges of Karen's green kimono still about her shoulders. We lay still and close to one another.

"I forgive you for earlier," she sighed.

"You don't know what she is like! You must protect me from her."

"You are like a child. Don't worry I will protect you, so long as you still love me?"

"Of course I do."
"She is such evil! All Stephanos could do was talk about how great she would be at the pub. The pub he named after me. *My pub!*"
"You mean he wants her to work there?"
"Of course! He is very taken by her. Right now they will be with each other."
"She won't want to do that, not stay with him."
Pandora lifted her eyes, her large black lashes revealing the deeper dark depths of her injured soul. "Who can say what she will do?" she sighed heavily, "all I know is that nowadays Stephanos has the pick of any woman he wants. He can throw me away - I am finished. Throw me a way and get a new one!"
"You are not that old! Only a few years older than Karen?"
"Look at me Julian. My face looks older than it should. Once I was very beautiful. Once I had a truly great body, my breasts did not sag they way they do now. How I envy Karen her firm breasts."
"I want you as you are. You are beautiful," I persisted.
"Oh, Julian, I know that in part you are repelled by me, but in some way you like it that...I am worn-out!" Pandora rested her hand on her chest. A pained expression came into her face. She suddenly looked old: twice her years, her face looking particularly gaunt and haggard. The years of drug abuse and physical excess - of all kinds, had taken a heavy toll on her looks. In spite of, or because of the way she looked, I felt myself wanting her body again. I began to kiss her. The look of anguish went from her face, distracted by my renewed interest in her body.
Pandora at first let me kiss her and touch her, at the last moment though she turned her heavy body away. The pained expression came back on her face. She clutched at the silk garment.
"What is it? What's wrong?"
"You are very amorous Julian - very demanding." She lay on her back and puled the kimono tight round her, covering her bare flesh with the silk garment. She turned to face me and smiled, but in her eyes there was confusion, pain, sorrow even.
"Why won't you let me? What is it?"
"Nothing, it is nothing I tell you! Can't we just hug one another, must it always be sex."

She hugged me tightly, I could feel her heart pounding madly; she hugged me desperately. I reasoned that she had had enough of the penetration, what she wanted was to be loved and appreciated for what she was, and not for what men could get from her. And so I contented myself by simply holding her close.

It was late evening by the time Stephanos arrived with Karen. The 'party,' was to take place the following day. An elaborate system of ticket allocation had been devised by Stephanos which would keep a tally of the number guests that visited each girls room: Green for Pandora and red for Karen. The total for each girl would then be added up at the end of the proceedings. There were estimated to be over two hundred and fifty guests expected, and there were over a thousand of each type of ticket, and just to be on the safe side Stephanos had had a spare set printed to cater for greater demand. An initial fee was charged for the 'invite,' thereafter all amenities were free. Stephanos' usual practice, since he had held a number of these 'fests', was to split the proceeds three ways, each girl receiving twenty five percent of the takings, and he the remainder, except in this case, Karen, in her usual superior manner insisted that: 'she *never* did it for money,' that for *her* it was a - 'personal thing!' Stephanos had enlisted the help of a few of his other girls, some to act as adjudicators and others to assist in the more mundane aspects of the event, such as the dispensing of food and drinks and others to act as chaperons - for those who wanted one. He was meticulous in his planning of such events. He had to protect his investment, he knew that where there were men and women, there was the potential for trouble. Leaving nothing to chance, the presence of several burley doormen would hopefully send the appropriate message.

"Well I hope you don't expect me to take part in it?" I said, after Stephanos had gone through the details.

"It's OK Julian," said Karen, "no one is expecting you to."

"No," said Pandora, keeping a firm grip on me. "I would not want you to be here to witness it in any case."

"Why not?" said Karen, flashing her lovely clear lavender eyes, "why shouldn't he see you as you really are?"

Stephanos who was sitting at the bar situated near the terrace got up. "Girls! Please let us not go back to the arguing and the insults. Julian has every right to stay or go as he please. Now let us all have a good time. Let us drink Julian, to two of the sexiest women in the world."

We raised our glasses, Pandora clinked mine. "May the best girl win," she said.

Karen slunk over to Stephanos and put her arm about him and raised her glass high. "To the best girl!" she echoed.

Pandora looked at the other girl and then kissed me on the mouth and Karen started to do the same with Stephanos. It was ridiculous really, both girls trying to out manoeuvre the other. I couldn't stand it any more. I got up and went on to the terrace for some air. Pandora followed me, putting her arm about mine.

"What is wrong?"

I laughed sardonically. "Wrong - wrong! This - this whole thing is wrong."

"It upsets you to see Karen kissing Stephanos?"

"It annoys you as well! I don't like to be used like some pawn in a game."

"Come back in side, it is nothing. Do not be upset."

Pandora took my hand and I reluctantly followed her. Stephanos and Karen were well at it by then, his hand down her front. I looked away disgusted.

Karen lifted her head and looked over at me and grinned. She held out her hand to me. "Come - come here..." she intoned.

I kept hold of Pandora's hand. The truth was I was afraid to let go of it.

"You're disgusting!" I said.

"Come on Julian, it turns you on."

"Pay no attention to her," said Pandora trying to kiss me.

Stephanos had now removed his hand from Karen's bosom. "What is wrong Julian? It angers you to see me with your Karen?"

"Stay out of it Stephanos! You don't know her the way I do! She is rotten to the core. Her soul is damned!"

"It was you who first suggested that I find men to go with," said Karen.

"But to do this - and with so many!"

"That was all Pandora's idea. Nothing to do with me - *nothing!*"

"Didn't what Garcia have to say, mean *anything* to you?"

"Hah! You're a fine one to talk! He expected you to lead me along the correct path, instead you introduce me to debauchery!"

"He also said I had to accept your nature," I replied, reluctant to go further.

Karen looked me up and down. "If you were more of a man..." she looked at Stephanos and put her hand in his, as much to say: 'here is a real man!'

"No man could meet your needs; Garcia told me that himself. You're not normal Karen!"

"You see how horrible he is to me."

"Yes Mr Julian, let's not be insulting!"

"I said stay out of it Stephanos, this is between me and Karen." Realising I had gone too far: "Look honey, let's just go. We can leave now! Try and start again! - I'll admit I went about it the wrong way."

Stephanos stood up. "You can't do that! It's all arranged! I have guests, important guests coming. They expect to be entertained."

"Entertained!" I sneered.

"Yes, I told them on the invite that a super-model...." he looked over at Karen, "a super-model will be...be providing the services - as well as Pandora of course."

"Get real Julian," said Karen.

"Yes relax," offered Pandora.

"You're no better! Haven't you had enough of it by now? Haven't you had enough of men using your body as though it were just a piece of meat? You don't have to go with men any more in order to make a living - I can only assume you are like Karen!"

"I am nothing like *her*" snarled Karen.

"I think you are exactly alike. You are both hung up on your own ego's! You both think you are the hottest stuff around, and you will go to any lengths to prove it. You love to cast spells over men with your bodies."

Pandora looked at me without replying. She looked ashen, yet beautiful in the evening light. Then I looked at Karen who had the air about her, of one bored by my usual line of condemnation.

There was an uneasy silence. "All I am saying is reconsider," I proffered.

"You will simply never understand the true nature of sacrifice," said Pandora.

"Mr Julian, you do not have to stay. You are free to leave if...if you are so displeased," put in Stephanos.

"Yes, since you think so bad of me why stick around?" Eyeing me maliciously: "Oh, I *forgot* - you love to watch so!"

Pandora tightened her grip on my hand. She cocked her head to one side.
"Don't go! - stay - stay the night. Go tomorrow, but stay now."
"Enjoy yourself Julian. Don't think about tomorrow. Look, enjoy yourself now."
He gave Karen a little push. "You might as well stay. Don't be so stuffy Julian."
"Yes relax," said Pandora, running her hand through my hair.
"Here drink this." Stephanos came over with a large glass of ouzo. "we have the apartment to ourselves, we have wine and beautiful women, I'm sure Karen and Pandora can put away their differences.

Stephanos guided Karen over to Pandora and put their hands in each other. Both girls looked at one another but not with hostility, but with a kind of mutual respect. Pandora was the first to make a move. She lowered her lips on to Karen's neck and Karen responded by taking her head in her hands and pressing it against her breasts. Pandora looked up at the other girl, her big dark eyes full of a strange and incomprehensible yearning, and then suddenly both girls crushed their lips upon the other in a violent kiss, when they stopped they looked at one another their breasts heaving, their eyes expanded their mouths open. Stephanos, in a manner that indicated that he had dealt with such situations before, gently took both girls hands and lead them into the bedroom. He looked back at me, and indicated for me to go with him. I downed my ouzo and followed.

Ironically, or perhaps not quite, if one thought about it, but it was the only way we could be with one another: all four of us together, that didn't involve having to talk, and it was what the girls did best. The Greek and I looked on agog as the two Titanic forces came together. Like two immovable objects, two powerful gargantuan wills came thundering together, smashing together like some awesome storm, crashing together like a terrible tide, their bodies chafing like granite on steel, both seemingly as unyielding! Such was their tumult that I think the gods themselves must have been stilled. Violent passion suffused their bodies searing their skin and welding them together, a violence of passion that seemed to be unending - but in the end it did have its end!

"I doubt you have ever seen your Karen like this?"
"No, never. I never knew, I never knew...."

"There is nothing like it," he said, lighting a cigarette and offering me one. "When two women of such power come together. Nothing like it. I bet you are glad you stayed now!"

Gradually one girl became more dominant over the other. It was a slow natural process not a fighting and a yielding, but a gradual slow giving of ground. Pandora though, was relentless.

"But Karen!..." I said in dismay.

Stephanos laughed. "You would think it..."

She was fighting back an onslaught she had not been prepared for.

"Look at her! look at Pandora!...." Stephanos shook his head. "look at her, if only Arabella could be here to see this!" And then more to himself: "And they said she was finished."

Pandora was watching Karen's face intently, her eyes as keen and wide as an Eagle Owl's; watching for effect as she touched Karen. Listening to her sighs, both girls though were respiring vigorously, noisily, but Karen more so, as she sought to fight off the onslaught, but Pandora's hands were all over Karen. She squeezed her breasts, and played her where she was most vulnerable, Karen making herself more and more accessible to the other girls advances.

"Oh yeah! Oh! Oh yeah! Oh yeah! yeah-yeah-yeah-oh-oh-oh! Yeah! Oh yeah!" Karen called. She threw her head back, gritting her teeth, every muscle straining. "Ahh! Ah! Ah! Oh! Oh yeah!-yeah-yeah-yeah! Oh yeah!" Karen called out.

'My poor Karen,' I thought, what a thing to witness! Succumbing to Pandora like this and so quickly. Her cries of rapture were an embarrassment. I looked to Stephanos in the hope he would do something, I didn't know what, stop it perhaps! He looked at me and licked his lips.

"What a girl your Karen is! - such fire!

It was obvious from Karen's increased vocalisations that she was beginning to acquiesce. Occasionally Karen might reach out and touch Pandora's thigh, her breasts, perhaps becoming more adventurous; Pandora allowed her these forays knowing that they would come to nothing, that she, Pandora, held sway over the the other girl. Karen flung her hands back over her head and allowed Pandora full reign to do as was her wont, surrendering completely to the imagination of the other woman. Most of the time Karen touched herself, pleasuring herself while she drifted further and further under the spell of Pandora's touch. Almost with pity, Pandora looked at Karen as she continued to wreak havoc on her body, exploiting her innate narcissism and licentiousness.

Pandora put her hand around the small of Karen's back, and Karen flexed her body, raising her buttocks off the bed. Pandora squeezed each cheek, sensing their ripeness, their firmness. Karen began to flex and writhe in the other girls arms like some crazy eel. I think even Pandora was a little surprised by the robustness of Karen's response, causing her to speak the first cogent words:

"You like it then, what I do?"

"Oh yes!...Oh yes!" sighed Karen.

Pandora smiled to herself as she watched the other girl squirm and writhe under her spell. Karen kicked out with her powerful limbs, raising her long muscular trunk and arching her back, making of herself a bridge, falling and rising, falling and rising. Pandora stroked Karen's wet skin, feeling her hard erect nipples and her big firm tits. If she lost her concentration it was then, excited with envy at Karen's superb breasts. Karen put her hand around Pandora's head thrusting her face into them rocking her head from side to side, Pandora though was not to be lulled asleep between these two stupendous orbs. She pulled herself free and played with them at arms length, squeezing and pulling them roughly about, sending Karen *ecstatic.*

By the time she had ridden this fresh wave of sybaritism, Karen's chest was labouring harder than ever, her hands flopping loosely over her head, as one gone over to complete abandon. She arched her strong neck, where rivulets of sweat followed the course of the big vein in her neck, that was so gorged with blood that it looked fit to burst.

Pandora breathed in deeply and seemed to asses the situation. She held herself up, her hands either side of Karen, so that her heavy breasts swayed in front of her face. Karen looked up at Pandora, her lavender eyes wide and expectant. Pandora relished the moment, pursing her lips and smiling:

"Hmmm... you want I do more?"

"Yes..." hissed Karen, rasing her hips into the air.

Stephanos looked at me raising his eyebrows. I don't think even he had expected such a show.

Pandora put her hand over Karen's proud mount of Venus and pushed her hips down firmly in the manner one must take when taming wild beasts.

"Be patient," ordered Pandora, and smacked Karen hard on her thigh.

Karen moaned and simpered like a little girl.

"Hmmm..." mused Pandora, as she roughly parted Karen's powerful thighs, the red mark of her hand still present on one of them. "You like it - hey! So you want that I do more!"

"Yes...yes...." hissed Karen, her long serpentine body squirming.

Pandora slid her hand along Karen's thigh sending her into paroxysms. Pandora smiled ruefully to herself, relishing the way she could so easily play the other girl, teasing her in such a way that it was almost cruel to watch.

She put her hand over the soft skin of Karen's ravaged *Venus Mons,* playing and teasing her so expertly, that after a short time Karen was actually sobbing.

"All right my lovely...I think you cannot take any more. Admit it, I have broken you, I have bettered you, admit you cannot take it!"

"Never!" hissed Karen, with a look of intransigence, or perhaps asinine folly on her face.

"All right then if you think you can take more!"

"Hmmm!" Karen nodded, unable or unwilling to articulate further.

Pandora roughly parted Karen's powerful thighs, Karen eager that Pandora should witness the true extent of her glory! Despite her resentment for the other girl, Pandora could not help but show surprise, if not admiration. Both girls stared darkly into the quick of each others soul. They were in many respects very similar souls and perhaps because of this there was little tolerance for the other. Pandora having minimum regard for Karen's glory, a glory that was undeniable, a glory that had made Taanach great. Pandora though was there to plunder and not to worship at her sacred site! Karen felt the pain and flexed her body forward as far as she could, only to slump back on the bed like a dying woman. Pandora was enjoying herself smiling fiendishly. The other girl, now totally at her mercy intoxicated by having so much coiled energy on the end of her hand. How she despised the other girls tenacity. She could feel her powerful muscles working, contracting around her wrist. How she would love to denigrate her temple, break her down, quell her fury, her impudence, when she must know she was done. Her wrist was hurting such was the grip Karen had on it. She moved again pushing apart, tearing asunder the walls of the temple.

Unable to hold it back, Karen cried out again in pain. For the first time since their colossal struggle had begun, there was a genuine look of annoyance on Karen's face.

Pandora looked at her, putting her head on one side, regarding her with an air of disappointment, or was it - frustration. She sighed. "Can't you take it?"

Karen in even greater frustration tossed her head from side to side, biting her lip, unable or unwilling to converse with the other girl

How Pandora hated her, hated Karen's intransigence, hated her arrogance, her conceitedness for her body, how she would love to break her, mar her glory, render her impotent.

"Admit it, I am too much for you, my pretty girl."

She licked her finger and traced the crescent shape scar on her cheek. "Although...you are not quite so pretty are you! - silly girl!"

She traced her fingernails down the side of Karen's face, down along the line of her powerful neck, finally resting her hands across it.

Pandora smacked Karen's face. "silly girl - think that you can come here and challenge Pandora! - silly girl." She pressed her fingers into the thick veins in her neck making them bulge hideously, Pandora's face only inches away.

"Have you had enough yet? Does it turn you on?"

"Hmmm! Hmmm!" Breathed Karen.

"And how does the priestess of *Tanit* like it?" Gripping her bulging throat and squeezing, Pandora's long fingernails cutting in to her skin.

Pandora suddenly became aware of a standing figure. She looked over and saw Stephanos. He spoke to her sternly. A man's command. Pandora immediately desisted in her action.

Karen gulped air and coughed, rubbing her neck, her lovely clear lavender eyes now clouded, as the tiny capillaries in them haemorrhaged blood.

"Priestess of *Tanit!*" Jeered Pandora. "A priestess who bleeds!"

Karen worked what little saliva she could make in her mouth and spat in Pandora's face, spitting out the word: "*Nachash!...*"

Pandora wiped her face and sat back, straddling Karen with her own formidable thighs.

"Stupid girl! Do you not see it is I that am master. "She dug her fist deep into Karen's insides.

Karen stifled her *cries*, but nothing could stop the tears from springing up, magnifying her lovely eyes. I know I should have done something, ran over and stopped the madness, but I remained rooted to the spot, aware of a big sadistic streak in me that enjoyed watching Karen suffer like this, not just the physical damage, but the humiliation she must have felt.

She brushed her tears away roughly, breathing hard through her nose, her nostrils flaring, her wonderful eyes wide, challenging the other girl to do her worst, and to that end Pandora was good - good enough in the end to break Karen's proud will. She realised she was undone, feeling something give inside her. The walls of her temple had been smashed, Pandora had seized hold of the sacred fire that burned deep inside there, hungry after her power, hunting down her demon. The look of proud defiance had gone from Karen's eyes. She had only one desire now, that the release should come. She strained hard for it and Pandora felt the bite of her demon as it coiled and writhed around her hand. She looked at Karen, stunned that she still had so much zest left in her for the fight.

And out of the sacred blood red flame rose Nachash writhing in the flames that licked through her insides, revelling in her new found servitude to Pandora, her cruel master.

At some point Karen caught my eye and looked at me guiltily, like the naughty school girl found doing something inappropriate. But she recovered herself and it was replaced by one of insouciance and a sardonic smile that seemed to say: 'are you enjoying the show Julian?' and then to put it beyond all doubt, and god knows how she did it, amidst such havoc that was being wreaked about her person, but she slowly shut one eye. What tenacity of spirit! what audaciousness is hers! But though she tried to make light of it, and carry it off as best she could, she must have felt deep down a sense of humiliation. To allow herself the ignominy of being abused in the way she was, and so brutally and without regard or sensitivity, and by a common whore who was on the wane. For it was Pandora a great victory to break down a girl like Karen, a girl so full of spunk and arrogance, a girl she despised and hated. For Pandora it was a great victory; but what did Karen get out of it apart from revelling perhaps in her own debasement? No doubt she wondered to herself as she began to accept the inevitable, how on earth she ever found herself in the submissive role; after all, she was Karen, the heiress of a Phoenician dynasty, a high Priestess!

Regardless of her birth, that of a sacred whore, she could not deny the irrefutable proof that she had in the end succumbed, not to an Adonis or beautiful woman, who matched her own beauty but to a common whore, not even a young one with the bloom of youth still in tact, but an older one, one that had seen much abuse, and whose powers were on the wane, but it was irrefutable! It had happened, somehow Karen acquiesced. She had found her true level in the order of things, to be beneath a whore. It was irrefutable! It must have smarted, it must have perplexed her big ego, as it must have perplexed Taanach over three millennia ago when she discovered that she was not immortal! as she started to watch all her great power and beauty leave her, as she saw her once fine limbs and body becoming distorted and ugly. It was irrefutable. It had happened; it was in the natural order of things. Running through Karen was that same fundamental flaw, her blind spot, her Achilles heel, essentially her own unflagging arrogance and deep love - no worship, of *herself!* - which bordered on insanity. She didn't really need people to make love to her, she could do that herself, what she *needed* was to constantly show to others just how perfect she thought she was. She didn't need people, she was one of those breed that are self-sufficient, the only trouble was she ran the danger of taking self-love too far!

At some point Stephanos, who by now was visibly excited, went over and sat on the end of the bed to get a better view. Pandora looked over at him and they exchanged a conspiratorial smile. She looked back at Karen bemused as she continued to squirm under the last convulsions of what was a gargantuan orgasm, one that had shaken her to the very essence, the very quick of her being.

Karen looked up at Pandora, her whole face in a crisis, her eyes full of delirium, her body shivering uncontrollably with aftershocks.

"You want I do more?" said Pandora, gloating

Still being swept along by the crisis, she was unable to speak coherently: "Hmmm! - hmm- Mmmm!"
"I think you are done!" said Pandora

Karen shook her head from side to side and raised her hips and looked down at the site of the quake, the place where she had been rent asunder. The presence of the other was still there, irrefutable.

"This time you are finished I say!"

"Yes it is enough now!" said Stephanos, no doubt thinking of the forthcoming event, than simply Karen's well-being! He looked to me but I said nothing. Pandora could finish her off once and for all, for all I cared! It was obvious that this last orgasm had done her in. She was *orgasmic!* having once boasted of having reached a climax eighteen times in succession, after another girl had claimed to have been able to bring herself off nine times: that it had nearly killed this girl, such was the strain it put on her heart, didn't deter Karen one bit, out doing the other girl twice over, although Karen did say she felt a bit sore the day after! How one can verify such claims, is beyond me? I believed her! But then I knew her, knew what she was capable of. How many times she had come this time, only Karen knew, since to those that witnessed this orgy, Karen seemed in a perpetual state of orgasm, her body writhing and twisting around nearly the whole time. But now her rserves of strength and will definetly seemed spent.

Karen tried to pull herself up on the bed but she seemed to lack the strength or even the will. She slumped back groaning like a dying woman, her body fevered and wet with perspiration. She touched her body, lightly stroking her bruised breasts and eventually letting one hand come to rest protectively over her batted pubis. She rolled her head to one side and our eyes met for a second and then she looked away her look: insouciant, seemingly disinterested in what I thought. And to be honest, I was bored with her already. The spectacle was all but over. Occasionally she would frown and let out an imperceptible sigh, but to a large part the show was over - it was over now and there was nothing more to see! Karen had succumbed, Karen had been shown she was a woman and not a goddess - so what! Karen would be undiminished by this little show of sexual excess. Pandora hadn't even scratched the surface!

What perplexed me most of all was that for all her boasting about grinding Pandora into dust, yet again it was Karen who had been beaten into the submissive role! What was even more perplexing was that I knew that in the long run she would turn it into a victory.

The voice of Stephanos broke my reverie: "I doubt you have ever seen such a thing?" said Stephanos, coming over and lighting a cigarette. I noticed his hands were trembling slightly.

I had to agree with him. I had seen her in a porn movie doing similar stuff but it didn't compare with what I had just seen unfold in the flesh!

"No never," I said. "I never thought it possible....."

He shook his head and laughed and spoke some words in Greek. "What a girl! He then put his arm about Pandora and kissed her, smiling and speaking words of admiration. Looking up, as if suddenly noticing me she smiled, and glancing back at the listless prone figure of Karen: "You see Julian, you see how she comes? Easy - no?"

'Not so easy,' I thought, but I had no words. I just nodded.

Karen, still faraway and listless, looked over, her face still registering neither pleasure nor pain.

"A woman with many weakness'," added Pandora, so that Karen would hear. Karen just rolled her head away as if not interested in what anyone thought. She raised her knees in a protective posture, as Stephanos went over to her. I saw him hand her her green silk robe, which she hastily put round her. He asked if she was all right. I got the impression his presence was unwelcome, so he came back quickly. He put his arms around Pandora's waist and hugged her tightly: "You really bust her up!" he said, smiling. "Boy did you bust her...My Pandora! My Pandora! - I never doubted you," he said, kissing her porcelain neck, throwing her head back, exposing her wide throat, his lips unable to resist it.

"Yes, yes I bettered her. She was easy, easy!" boasted Pandora, looking at me.

Stephanos kissed her passionately. "Yes - yes, you exploded her!"

Pandora laughed:. "she was easy! - her type always are." She glanced over again at her victim. It will not be much of a competition tomorrow," she said, with a note of disappointment.

Stephanos glanced at the supine figure on the bed. "Yes it's a pity. I expected more from her. We may have to get Arabella, if Karen is a complete flop!" said Stephanos, with a look of concern on his face.
"Hmm! - Arabella! Yes that would be interesting," replied Pandora, with relish.
"It is a pity! Karen may have good tits and a good body, but she lacks the staying power," he concluded. "But you my dear, you did well."
I looked at Karen as she lay there with her back to us, her skin still shiny with sweat, accentuating her wonderful toned musculature, but where had it got her? I would have liked to go over to her but for the moment her body remained inviolable, it was as if there existed an invisible barrier round her that precluded anyone going near her - let alone touching her!
Although I admitted to a sadistic pleasure in seeing Karen suffer at the hands of Pandora, now that it was done, and Karen lay there looking so depleted and vulnerable, my softer side: the empath came to the fore. The other girls boasting annoyed me. I turned to Pandora: "You didn't have to hurt her like that!"
Pandora laughed. "I didn't really hurt, may be a little at the start. She is a big girl." Making her hand into a fist. "I think she has had it done to her many times....Many times!"
To my horror I saw that she had blood on her knuckles. Karen's blood. The horror of it so great I said nothing, but I felt sure she must have caused Karen some lasting damage!
"Why you care anyway, what I do to her? You do not still love her? You saw - you saw what she is! You saw what I did to her! she *arriver* did she not, like a woman, just as I said she would? What immortal bleeds!" she said, holding up her big fist. I turned my head away from it, repelled by the sight of it, the sight of Pandora's haggard face and Karen's blood.
"You had no right!"
Pandora looked again at Karen with complete disdain and contempt, her look full of foul loathing for the other girl. She shook her head, looking back at me hard in the eyes. Her black eyes were like foul bottomless pits. "Why do you care so much! I tell you her type do not last. What is that I saw on her wrist? There was blood from a wound. She did this to herself? I tell you she will not

last long this one. Her type never do. She will destroy herself!"

She was right of course, but I felt she had gone too far. She had no right to this knowledge, it was sacred, between me and Karen, it was a personal thing between me and Karen, the rest of the world could stay out of it! It was our secret - the very corner stone of our trust! The spilling of her own blood by herself was like a benediction. Pandora, a heathen, had no right to this knowledge. I should have wanted to ravish her, I should have been turned on by the way she so beautifully played her and then mercilessly, brutally levelled her, in a sense I was excited by it, but again some unfathomable part of me kept my passion and rage in check. Instead I found myself despising Pandora, so I goaded her, wanting to get back at her for stealing the sacred truth!

"My poor little Karen. My poor sweet Karen, what have you done to her? You've ruined my babe - my honey!"

Even Karen looked over at me somewhat bemused, scratching her head, but at least it was a reaction! But I had succeeded in sending Pandora into a fit of rage.

"Your sweet Karen! You honey! You saw her, you saw the *tératos, terástios,* such a foul thing, she is...how you say! she is...she is..." Pandora thinking hard tapping her foot.

"Depraved?" I offered.

"Yes-yes-yes she is this, she is depraved as you say," she continued, excitedly. "Yes-yes, this is so - depraved, she is this - depraved yes yes! You saw her, her filthy body around me, you saw how she was, like she is so mighty, so proud with her fine big breasts and her thin skinny body and while in other places she is a colossus, never have I seen such a colossus, She must have been with many, and done many things to end up a colossus. My! - my - my, what a ugly *Kelos* she has! My! - my! - my! it is so ugly how can you like such a thing? I say to you she is not normal - that one! I tell you, you poor foolish man, to prefer such a thing as that, when you could have me, I am still good down there," she said, moving her hand to indicate the place she was referring to, whilst looking at Karen defiantly. "You unfortunate man, it is small wonder you could not satisfy her, no man could! - only this it seems she understands," said Pandora, holding up her fist. "I - I Pandora make her beg! She is nothing! nothing! I tell you! she is a filthy nothing!" Pandora had to catch her breath, so wound up was she, her words catching in her throat; she swallowed hard, before going on: "You saw, you saw how I took her, so easy! She has no control like a virgin! Yet it is not new for her, she take it like that many times - many times I say, to get like that! She is filth, she said spitting, filth and then ran on in her language, finally stopping, her big chest heaving hard. "I tell you, don't go far it will not last long. Her voice full of scorn: "I tell you, I did as I said I would. I - Pandora made your Karen weep like a baby, as she will tomorrow when it really begins. She will not last long, she cannot last!" she said, shaking her head emphatically. I thought that Pandora like Karen was truly a little mad. "She will weep, she will prey for mercy, if she tries to compete with me!" Pandora laughed, "she will be no good for any man. It is a pity you won't be here to witness her destruction!"

My only response to this deluge of denigration: To laugh in her face.

"Why you laugh like a crazy man?"

"You haven't bettered her," I said, and told Pandora of Karen's boasting.

Pandora looked a shade flummoxed by this declaration: "Impossible! May be nine times yes, but not eighteen?" Pandora took another quick glance over her shoulder and frowned. "No, impossible, look at her she is finished."

She looked again, and this time Karen was sitting up, she had put her green robe on, tying it loosely around her middle. She smoked her cigarette laughing and talking with Stephanos, inhaling deeply taking the smoke deep into her lungs. She did all things *totally:* no halves! Pandora looked towards Karen, we both did, as though she were some curious creature that had undergone some sort of metamorphosis, the question was, what had she become?

"You took it hard!" said Stephanos, "will you be all right for tomorrow?"

Looking at her cigarette: "Of course - why not?" she inhaled deeply again, blowing out the smoke noisily, glancing over momentarily at Pandora.

She shook her head and ran her fingers through her thick hair, her robe falling open. Stephanos looked on appreciatively. Karen looked down at her lovely breasts and then looked him straight in the eye. She pushed out her chest throwing her shoulders back, as she displayed her glistening bosom.

"You like them? You like what you see?" Karen glanced over at her other audience. She smiled audaciously.

So moved was he, that Stephanos could only utter his own tongue, finally saying something that sounded like: 'Stupendous, marvellous - marvellous!'

"You want me?"

Pandora tried her best to hide her surprise but I saw her mouth open and her eyes grow wide.

"Yes all right then," he said, trying to be casual.

Karen looked at us as she roughly started to undo Stephanos' belt buckle, throwing it away unceremoniously, and then did the same with his pants. All Pandora could do was look on stupefied. Stephanos was eager, and not surprisingly, I saw how excited he had been earlier - hardly able to contain himself. Like Garica he was a big man, a *very big man!* They began to kiss, and Karen laughed and rolled over on to her belly, presenting her lovely ass to him. Without any more ado he proceeded t take her roughly from behind

Karen craned her neck round to look at him, and caught my eye, now it was her turn to smile, and it was full of source; then she winced as Stephanos thrust hard, and she looked away, clutching her magnificent breasts and pressing them together. Magnetically Pandora was drawn to the cavorting couple eager to get in on the act.

"Come on Julian," she called to me.

I went over to the three of them. Pandora was attending to that part of Karen in the way only a woman knows best, while occasionally squeezing Karen's breasts (she so loved them.) I put my hand on her ass, not really knowing what I should do. Karen looked round at me her eyes laughing, her look cajoling. She opened her mouth wide and stretched her neck, and simpered: "Hhhmmmm!"

Stephanos didn't last long, the excitement of earlier had clearly taken its toll. When he was done Karen fell forward with a sigh, touching herself and sighing: "Hmmm! Hmmmm!...." She looked at me, her eyes cruel, mocking, her hand resting on Pandora's head, as she still worked on her - beneath her, still attending to her.

"Don't worry about Julian, he likes to watch," said Karen.

I moved away. Stephanos looked at me bemused. Pandora was already active again, fascinated by Karen's breasts and no doubt eager to confirm what I said concerning Karen's prowess in these things. After a time the three of them seemed to forget about my presence.

I was right about Pandora, she wanted to find out if what I had said was true.
"Yes it's true, said Karen, proudly.
"I do not believe you can come this many times. You are a liar!"
Karen sat up cross-legged showing off her wonderful thighs. She knew that in this stance they were imposing. Having been a model she knew all the right moves to accentuate her lovely curves! She absently stroked her legs smiling self-confidently. She looked at Pandora, who was scowling at her, ready it seemed, to smash her at any minute. Karen looked down at her naked thighs and pressed her fingers up them. Pandora following her with her eyes. Karen looked the other girl in the eye as if the sight of such powerful limbs was in itself proof enough.
"I tell you it is true," said Karen, casually. She saw the dark malevolence in the other girls eyes and put out a simpering sickly smile.
"And I say you lie! I saw you, I saw how you begged me to stop, you could not take any more. You wept like a child for me to stop." Pandora turned to Stephanos. "Did you not see her? did you not see how I bettered her? how she *arrive!"*
He was silent for a moment and then lent forward opening his hands. Reluctantly: "You seemed to take it hard. It seemed to take much out of you. You must think about tomorrow. I do not want a complete - how you say...flop!"
"You were done I tell you. I finished you good. You begged me to stop. I had you...I had you I say!" joined Pandora, yelling the last. "All this with Stephanos is nothing I say! You are a nothing!
Karen smiled acidly while watching Pandora closely, as she screwed her hand into a tight ball.
Karen's response was predictable. She stretched out her long legs still sitting up and then opened her big thighs, presenting both Pandora and Stephanos with her sacred gate, the seat of her glory. The glory that had made Taanach notorious. A glory that was undeniable. I wanted to leave them to it. To go and hide, but even I was intrigued, forcing me to linger uncomfortably. The room was charged with energy and it emanated from one site, and all eyes were upon it. Their eyes were hungry after it, as they had been for millennia! Karen was in complete control, or rather, Taanach el Nachash, high priestess of TANIT - was in control!

Slowly Karen put her hand there and opened up her glory and it was as though some ancient dark star had burst forth into the universe of light, swallowing up all light. We peered like children into the vast void of blood red darkness, the deep cavern of her void lit by her sacred raging fires and the abode of her demon.

I looked at Karen's eyes, the only one able to do so. The were paler than I had ever seen them, quite grey - almost silver, like those of a lonely wolf. So still so cold, so old, as old as time it seemed, and I knew then that it was for real. That Taanach was for real! That what I saw *was Taanach:* the high priestess of the greatest goddess of them all, the most powerful and awesome goddess of all - the Phoenician goddess of fecundity! Her power was unlimited. Pandora, as powerful as she had once been on Earth was but a spot of grease to Taanach, who was herself, 'but a mouth piece!'

Karen - or Nachash through Tanit, had silenced them. She puled her sacred flesh back so that they should see all, tight against her high golden mount of Venus, that with that goddess shielded her vulnerability.

Karen lay back and let them feats upon her, praising her glory, praising her fecundity and her mind-boggling powers of recovery, for in truth Karen had been shook cold, shaken to her quick by Pandora's unrelenting attack, but Karen's deep fire had only briefly been extinguished, the white hot embers at her core could never been put out, they lived on from one incarnation to the next, always there, waiting to ignite the fires. They did not know this, they did not know that her fire could never been completely extinguished. They did not know what they were up against, it would be Pandora and Stephanos who in the end would burn themselves out. Karen had steel in her soul, a steel that had been tempered long ago in the forge of Hephaestus himself. It was not a case of steel grinding against granite, the steel in Karen's soul would wear down the hardest stone.

I had no wish to take part, Stephanos was in for a great show, but I had seen enough of it. The two girls were so intent on each other, and Stephanos was also joining in; they were unaware I had left the room. I went into the large lounge and sat in a chair and drank more ouzo, listening to Karen's overtures, reaching crescendo after crescendo my blood running cold, as she sacrificed herself again and again on the alter of her demon; giving herself over to her demon, impaling herself on her own sacrificial sword, her own licentiousness and wanton narcissism.

At some point I found myself being lulled to sleep by Karen's rhythmic mantra, a mantra that had its peaks and troughs, but never seemed to come to an end, and as I slept I began to dream a strange and vivid dream.

The Dream of Shaula and Nachash.

It began in the reality I had left behind, the reality of Karen twisting and writhing like a snake in the paroxysms of her spine shattering climax. Strange and incomprehensible sounds issued from her mouth, sounds that even a great writer like a Lawrence or Hemingway would struggle to relate. Strange and disconcerting in timbre, her voice shaking and quivering: "Ahrananhrajal - Mamamphoramah! - Ahnahnahraannda! - Arahappuch! - Andarahandandal.." and so on - incomprehensible, coming from some place deep inside, perhaps some archaic half forgotten language of the soul? Perhaps it is what is meant by: 'speaking in tongues?' Gradually her convulsions became less strenuous and the strange sounds ceased. Pandora and I looked on as Karen began to metamorphose into a serpent, her long muscular body was just like that of a huge snake, thicker than any python's, and also having the distinction of being endowed with Karen's fine golden bosom. The serpent slithered over the bed moving towards Pandora, its long tongue constantly scenting the air. Stephanos and I backed away leaving Pandora standing alone, her large black eyes full of horror and dread at the sight of the creature.

"The serpent spoke: "I am Nachash and I have come to do battle with the one who desecrated Taanach's sacred site!"

Pandora spoke back in a strange unearthly voice: "I am ready for you snake-woman, it has been long since I did battle with your kind!"

"So you too are of old?"

"Yes.." rasped Pandora," "I - like you, come from a time before great cities were built, before the illustrious ones came to the Earth and taught man the gift of fire."

"So - you are the one who is responsible for the unhappiness of mankind?"

"I did not force his sufferings on him, I did not make him look inside my box!"

"These things are done, and man is a foolish best! Enough talking old one, I come to punish Pandora, not for her crimes against man, but for dishonouring the goddess of the Phoenician's."

"Very well Nachash, serpent-woman, but do not expect your fight to be an easy one. I too can change my form."

I saw the tattoo of the dragon on Pandora's thigh come to life, as it began to twist its way up her thigh, gradually her whole leg and then her whole body underwent transmutation into the dragon. A fearsome and ugly creature with black leathery skin. Nachash hissed and puled back, opening her mouth wide, and presenting the dragon with its long fangs, its forked tongue whipping the air.

The dragon seemed undeterred, and reared up on its hind legs and roared. It too had awesome fangs, but also formidable talons at the end of its fingers. Although it did not breath fire as such, its breath could scald like steam. With no further posturing battle was quickly joined. Nachash twisted her long golden body around the dragons neck, while the dragons tail coiled itself around the other half of Nachash, its long talons clawing and cutting deep into the serpents skin, as Nachash clamped her mouth on the dragons neck, its long fangs sinking deep. The struggle was long and bloody, Nachash withstood the searing breath of the dragon, gradually though she seemed to weaken, her long golden body streaming with blood, where it had been clawed by the fearsome beast; the blackness of the dragons skin made it hard to see how badly it had been wounded, but its skin too shone with blood, but most of it I feared belonged to Nachash!

Pandora - the dragon, seized Nachash in its mouth flinging its thick cylindrical body from side to side, scoring deep into the long muscle of the creature. Finally Nachash had to let go its bite and recoiled.

"I have beaten you again Nachash, just as I bettered you in mortal form."

Nachash came forward hissing:

"It is true you have bloodied my body, and if it were not for the fact that I am complex you would surely put an end to me, but in wounding me you have only awoken the wrath of my other self. For I am Shaula, and my sting is deadly, and your days foul creature will soon be at an end."

Nachash hissed again in fury and agony, and brought its tail up, at the end of which was a deadly scorpion's sting.

The dragon reared up about to lunge once more at the body of the serpent, but in a lightning fast move Shaula struck at the dragons chest. The creature stopped in its tracks and fell dead before Shaula. Changing back into human form, Pandora lay clutching her bosom.

"Your bite is deep old one, but my sting is more deadly, but I fear I may have left it too late."

Shaula then turned back into human form, Pandora lay inert before Karen's towering thighs, but although Shaula had struck the mortal blow, the dragon had inflicted heavy wounds upon the serpent-woman. Karen's body streamed with blood, where she had been viscerated by the dragons talons, her beautiful breasts lacerated and torn, her golden skin scalded red by the dragons breath.

Karen looked at me forlornly as I wept for her marred beauty. She put her hand to her side and looked down at a huge gash, wide enough to place her hand into. She took it out and looked at it and seemed to accept her fate. She turned and stumbled on to the bed, holding her body. I went over and took her bloodstained hand.

"You can't die! Please don't die!" I begged.

"Don not lament for your Karen. Her soul is immortal. She will come again."

Stephanos and I did what we could to stem the flow of blood from her wounds but her *élan vital* continued to ooze out of her, the dream coming to an end before I had to accept what seemed the inevitable.

When I woke it was light. I walked out on to the veranda and lit a cigarette. The morning air was cool and sobering. I reflected on the nights proceeding and wondered at what kind of man I was. I suddenly realised I wanted to get away from *them* - particularly one of *them!* I put my cigarette out and listened. The house was dead still. I crept into the bedroom There the three of them lie, their bodies naked, their limbs tangled about one another lying across the bed, in the centre was Karen, her body still glistening with sweat; her skin caught the morning sun turning her into a blood red effigy. I suddenly became aware of a pair of eyes on me, scanning me dispassionately, and then one eye closed.

I turned and fled from its gaze.

*

I took Pandora's Mercedes and drove along the coast away from the populated isthmus. I drove through *Eleusis* and along the gulf of *Corinth*, and on into *Arcadia* in the heart of the *Peloponnese*. In *Arcadia* among the myrtle bushes and the juniper I searched for *her*. For my girl, my *shepherdess*. *'Calaroe, Calaroe*, Calaroe...' I called, 'where, oh where my sweet shepherdess can you be hiding?' *Argos, Tegea, Leuctra, Phigalia, Andania,* such were the places I passed in my search for her. Then I struck north to *Azania, symphalus, Pheneus,* until I finally came to the river *Styx*. I came back along the coast via *Corinth* and on into *Boeotia;* I had no recollection of how long I had been away, but when I returned Pandora was no more.

Stephanos was it his villa with Arabella. He told me that Karen had gone to an hotel in Athens. I sensed a lot of hostility from the girl, especially when Karen's name was mentioned. He blamed himself for what had happened. He knew Pandora had a problem with her heart, what amounted to some sort of congenital defect: 'a hole in the heart.' She could have gone any time, but the stress of the ordeal proved too much for her in the end. When he finished telling me, his eyes were red. Occasionally he shook his head, repeating: 'my poor Pandora! - my poor Pandora!'

He levelled his gaze at me from puffy bloodshot eyes. His face was pale and unshaven, a cigarette drooped from his mouth.

I said: 'sorry!' I felt nothing - nothing I tell you! I was numb! He took the cigarette out of his mouth and knocked back the drink he had in his hand. I asked him if there was anything I could do.

"Just do one thing for me," he said.

"Anything," I replied.

Go away," he said slowly, "go away from Athens and take *her* with you!" pronouncing, 'her', in an almost inaudible sigh, as if the mere thought of Karen, was too much for him. "I never want to see or hear of that *magíssa* again, in all the years I live."

Of course he was right in calling her a witch, after all it was what I had been trying to tell them all along. But the man was destroyed, there was no point in getting into the: 'I told you so,' routine. He got up and went to the bar, Arabella followed him. "No offence Mr Julian, you of all of us are least to blame," he continued, "but that one - she, she is as you say - bad luck!"

The frosty faced girl continued to glare at me finally seizing her opportunity. I didn't understand half of what she said, but the odd phrase of English she threw in, was enough to convince me that Karen's life was in jeopardy, if I didn't take Stephanos' advice. I thought it best, under the circumstances to decline the drink he offered me, and leave them to their grief.

I found Karen at the address he gave, a plush hotel on the outskirts of the city. She answered the door with a towel around her, her wet hair cascading down over her shoulders putting me in mind of a mermaid.

"Julian! - Where the goddamn hell have you been?" she said, looking shocked to see me. "I guess you know what happened?"

"Yes I know."

I followed her into the room. "Wait there honey, fix yourself a drink," she called, wandering back into the bathroom. She came back a few minutes later wearing her green silk kimono, the one with the floral pattern, the one Pandora so much admired. I was right about one thing, Pandora looked better in it than she did!

XIV

Karen was understandably anxious to get out of Athens, but it had less to do ~~with the threats on her life, and more to do with wanting to put behind her~~ the whole unpleasant experience associated with Pandora.

I harboured the misconception that we would leave Greece altogether and fly to another part of Europe or, may be travel through Greece and take a ferry from one of the ports along the west coast, such as *Corfu* to *Brindisi*, but no, Karen displayed a distinct reluctance to head into mainland Europe. Instead she came up with the idea of hiring some sort of vessel and explore more of the Aegean islands. I was happy to go along with this idea so long as we were out of Athens.

We found a yacht skippered by a young boy called Androgeos. Our first island stop was *Aegina*, from there we sailed to *Poros*, and by the time we got to the island of *Hydra* tension on board ship was becoming unbearable. Karen spent the whole voyage sunning herself on deck in the skimpiest bikini imaginable. It certainly got everyone's attention, in particular our young skipper. I eventually lost my cool and was seriously thinking of jumping ship.

"Why don't you go with Androgeos!" I said "Explore the rest of the islands with him - as well as each other - I'm sure!"

Karen furrowed her brow as if she hadn't got a clue what I was alluding to.

Somewhat exasperated: "*Now* what has got into you?"

"Oh please!" I said, looking at the way she flaunted herself, "the whole time you have done nothing but flirt with him. Going around half naked like that. I don't know why you bother wearing anything at all!"

"Well I don't have to! I'm not ashamed of my body. Do you know what you are Julian? - you're a prude."

I had to laugh, it was impossible to stay mad at her for long, after all she was no more than a spoilt child.

"Don't laugh at me," she said, in a feigned hurt voice.

"I've seen the way he looks at you!" I said, recovering myself.
"So what if he does! If I want to screw him I will. I can do anything I want."
"Go right ahead. You've been with so many, what does one more *boy* mater?"
"I'm not like your Pandora, I get to choose who I want to sleep with!"

We both realised that by mentioning her name for the first time since leaving Athens, Karen had gone back on an unspoken oath to never make any allusions to Pandora and the whole sordid ordeal surrounding her death.

"There's no need to talk about her like that! She's dead for god's sake - we killed her!"
"She was weak and I am strong, that is all there is to it."
"You have no remorse?"

Karen moved her long glistening snake-like body, and made a noise in her full cobra-like throat. "For what? She was just a whore!"

"And you're not I suppose? Just how many men did you go with at the party?"

Karen looked at me, her eyes mocking. "Wouldn't you love to know!" She drew her legs up towards her torso and moved her hands down to her hips so that they lingered over the strap of her bikini-thong.

"She was right," I said, observing her, "you are an animal!"

Karen laughed, slithering around on the deck leaving a trail of greasy sweat and suntan oil.

"But you want me! You want this!" she said, puling her bikini further down. "They all want it! I am the best, and you know it!" she stretched the meagre garment across her thighs exposing herself.

"For god's sake Karen," I said, turning away in a mixture of shock and disgust.

Karen laughed derisively. "You are such a prude Julian - really you are!"

I turned back to her and stood over her prone figure. She hoisted up her bikini and raised her tubular-like form, her abdomen becoming ribbed: her body was really like one long muscle, a long serpentine shape, far too reminiscent of the serpent in my dream. She sat up supporting her upper body with her arms behind her, her body twitching, alive with muscle and sinew. She didn't look human to me, it was as if her body had a presence all of its own. It was as if her body, this long serpentine thing dominated, so that one could say that Karen had about as much control over it as a sufferer of St Vitus's dance.

"What are you looking at?" she asked, contemptuously.

A mad impulse ran through me to kick Karen in the face. The corners of her mouth curled in a smirk, as if she dared me to. I moved nearer to her. It would have been so easy. She glanced down and imperceptibly flinched, as if anticipating the blow. Perhaps for the first time in her life she was actually a little afraid of me - of what I might do!

"Get rid of him," I said, "or I'll go - and leave you to be swallowed up by whatever it is that drives you."

Karen reached over and began to wind her orange silk kimono around her greasy body, hugging the soft material against her skin. She looked up and stared at me for several seconds without speaking. "All right," she said at last, "If that is what you want!"

"That is what I want!"

"Fine - fine, but where are you going to find someone else to take over the ship? Some old salty sea-dog perhaps, with a grey old beard?"

"No, I've been watching our young skipper, it's not that hard to captain a small vessel."

Karen laughed. "You mean you?"

"Why not! I've sailed before."

"When?"

"When I was at college, a whole bunch of us sailed up to Tijuana."

Karen looked impressed. "I never knew that." Suddenly she seemed excited. "Just you and me on the high seas?" she mused.

"Why not! we need some time alone!"

"Yes - why not! It could be really good fun - how exciting!" she said, biting her lip. "We can go anywhere we want." Karen began pacing up and down. "I know what we'll do! We'll buy a yacht - a big one, we'll live on it!" Holding my arms and jumping up and down: "yes, it will be great! We can sail all over the world!"

"Well hang on a minute, I never meant the ocean, I only ever crewed before."

"Don't be silly, it will be great. Oh, come on, you can do it! We can do it together!"

Of course - it was impossible to resist that face and her enthusiasm. 'How hard could it be?' I reasoned. 'All one needed was a sturdy ship, a good set of charts, global positioning did the rest, and then of course I had the sexiest first mate ever - what could go wrong?

"But do we have the kind of money for a big ocean-going yacht?" I said.

"Money is no problem!" replied Karen, with confidence.

As I've already said, Karen never did things by halves. If we were going to sail the high seas then she meant to do it in style. I had to point out that a luxury sea-going motor-cruiser of the type she was looking at (on average nothing under two hundred feet,) would require a small crew to run it, as well as taking into account other practicalities, such as finding a harbour or marina big enough to moor the thing! I had conceived of something that was both navigable by one person and yet big enough for our needs. In the end we found the *Idhra*, a 75 foot streamline ocean-going luxury motor-cruiser, boasting: five berths, two cabins one forward and aft, with a bar forward, a spacious galley, a dinning room, and a smaller 'chart room', a large cockpit aft, fitted out in teak and all the latest navigational equipment. Two eight cylinder Packard motors delivered a lusty eight hundred and fifty horse power between them. I tell you there was nothing like it! knowing that you had all that power at your finger tips, and when you opened up those engines and felt that immediate surge of power and then the reassuring throb from the eight cylinders beneath your feet - my god! it was intoxicating! I guess it was as close as I was going to get, to knowing how Karen must have felt most of the time! We purchased her from an Italian couple who owned one of the large mansions for which the island was famous, and which, ironically our vessel was named after.

We spent several idyllic days on the peaceful island of *Hydra*. In the evening we would moor up at some isolated inlet and during the day make short excursions to some of the nearby islands. It wasn't long before I could declare to Karen that I felt I had gained enough experience at the helm to begin our voyage of the Aegean. One evening we consulted the charts.

"Why don't we go there?" said Karen, pointing to one of the islands in the Cycladic group, her finger covering Sapphos.

I pushed her hand out of the way. "Oh yes, and look may be we could drop by and see Garcia, I suppose?"

"Oh, I didn't see that," she replied, trying to sound all innocent

I laughed: "No, I think we will head further south towards Crete." Which we did, the very next day - using the island of *Milos* as a stopping-off point. We stayed a couple of days: whilst there we visited the site where one of the most famous statues from antiquity was discovered, which spurred a long debate about beauty.

"I just don't know what people see in her!" said Karen, looking at a life-size replica.

"Ideas on beauty change over time," I pointed out.

"She's fat!" declared Karen.

If modern beauty was defined by the svelte athletic type, then Karen was the new *Venus de Milo*. We promised in the end to make a visit to the *Lourvre* one day and make a more direct comparison. The truth was I wouldn't want to be another *Paris*, even with Karen's scarred face and broken nose. To my eyes she was still magnificent - a work of art!

One of the first places Karen wanted to visit on our arrival at Crete was the Minoan palace at Knossos. Karen was most happy in the throne room. She immediately took up her place on the throne of the high priestess. An inauspicious seat in itself, carved out of a solid piece of stone. In most respects very similar to the one in Garcia's rotunda.

"I wonder if they realise," I said, "that a priestess is sitting once more on her throne!"

Karen looked at me mischievously. "Yes I wonder! Suddenly she stood up and raised her hands above her head and spoke: "Oh blessed Tanit, we thank thee. We honour thee. We love thee - Oh Tanit! - Oh Tanit!"

"Tanit!" I said, holding out my hands to Karen, "You seat awaits!"

Karen elegantly lowered her gorgeous butt on the throne, holding her body erect - regal - divine!

The tourists that were milling around looked at us with curiosity, and then a little busybody of an official in a peaked hat came over and curtly indicated for her to get up. Karen just turned her head slowly in his direction.

"Don't know who she is?" I said, "She is the high priestess of Tanit!"

"Get up! Get up!" he yelled. "Out! - Out!"

Karen looked at the busybody with total disdain, as if he were some sort of insect.

"How dare you address the high priestess of Tanit in such a way! Get down on your knees before the goddess!"

He looked at Karen and then at me, the little official was most perplexed. Quite a crowd had begun to gather, clearly nothing like this had happened before. Then again, it isn't everyday one confronts a high priestess actually sitting on her throne! He gestured some more and finally gave up with threats of 'reinforcements!'

The crowd still milled around waiting to see what would happen next. Karen was well in her role now, and addressed the gathering: "You may honour Tanit by leaving your offerings at my feet, then you may go."

The crowd clapped and laughed, someone cheered: 'Hail Tanit!' This was followed by more 'Hails' from the crowd, and pretty soon everyone was shouting and applauding the high priestess of Tanit. Such was the gathering and the general flow of good will, that the security when they arrived, were quite disarmed - in the end smiling and applauding too! Gracefully, and in her own time, Karen rose to her feet and with her palms inverted she stretched out her hands in front of her. The mood then seemed to change, the gathering became still and quite sombre, reverential even, as she slowly, and with perfect elegance, walked towards the multitude. They quietly parted for her, as she in her own time, took her leave of the throne room. I came along side her and she looked over to me and winked. From behind us went up a tremendous roar and everyone clapped. Someone in the crowd must have gone to the media, because there was a short piece in the local newspaper the very next day, which roughly translated read: 'High priestess visits Minoan palace and takes up her throne for the first time in three thousand years. Better late than never!'

Below the article was a photograph of Karen and I being escorted off the premises by two bemused looking security guards. I sent a copy to Garcia with a short note: 'As you can see Karen has already made a big impression on the locals. Tanit rules again in Knossos!"

We spent about two months on Crete exploring other ancient Minoan, Greek and Roman sites. I was always a little anxious that Karen might completely loose herself in some past life memory. Either that, or be swept off her feet by some rich playboy! So, I was always relieved when we returned to the boat towards evening. Often we visited the bays, especially the more isolated ones along the south coast. Karen was an excellent swimmer. She had tremendous lung capacity and would often dive for more than ten minutes at a time. I was afraid that she would drown herself; and got mad at her when she had gone down for a long time, which she found highly amusing. It didn't matter though that she scared the hell out of me at times, it was good to see her happy.

These were idyllic days that we spent on Crete. Often, if we were in a secluded spot Karen would bathe naked! usually going around in just the lower half of her bikini, other times she wore just a pair of old cut down denims and a skimpy T-shirt, or blouse, with sandals or deck-shoes: in this casual style she became quite the salty sea-lass. It was as if this indolent and carefree lifestyle, lived so close to nature, brought out a previously unknown Karen. Perhaps this image of her was the real and unclouded Karen? Gone were the stuffy sexy kimono's and tight high necked bodices. They never really seemed to suit her, they reflected Garcia's taste, and his somewhat peculiar fascination with the orient.

The salty sea-lass - beach bum girl, was a much happier person, and it made me happy to see her like this. This was the real Karen as far as I was concerned, not Natasha or Chloe even! There were so many aspects to her character one could fall in love with Karen again and again, but this latest carefree Karen was the one I most wanted to be around. I really began to feel that we had her demon on the back foot for the first time, so long as we remained on the high-seas, and separated ourselves from the modern world and all its crazy selfish and self deluding ways: the nature loving carefree Karen would be safe, I felt sure, so long as there were several hundred square miles of water between us and *it!* When we were on the open sea and there was no land in sight, Karen became even more relaxed and settled in herself. The sea and the warm air seemed to quite literally wash away the perturbations of her soul. She would lay up on the foredeck and sun-bathe naked for most of the day, her skin becoming tanned a deep bronze, almost as dark as Rachine's. The shock of thick fair hair and her lavender eyes against her dark nut brown complexion, gave to her look that of some exotic new race of being. A creature of the sea and sun: the creature that was not a whole lot different from the girl I had first known and fell in love with at high school.

During some of our longer spells at sea, in order to preserve her athletic look, as well as to engage her mind, she would workout on deck using twenty kilogram weights, it was also not unusual for her to do as many as a hundred sit-ups followed by callisthenics and various other exercises such as Tai Chi. Karen would show me the different positions she could put her flexible cobriform into. It was quite astonishing to see her transform a simple handstand into a position where she would arch her whole body forward until she was touching the soles of her feet with her nose - equally, she could do this position in reverse, then she would raise herself up with her hands, before returning to a handstand. Karen would try to get me to do a simple exercise like a handstand, but I would always collapse in a heap and more than once fell overboard, much to Karen's merriment.

"You know," I said to her one morning, as she sat in front of me with one leg diametrically opposed to the other, "you could have done so much more with your talents. I mean - you really do have a great body, not just in the sexual sense!..."

"Don't you think I know that! I could have been a gymnast or a great dancer."

"Then why didn't you?"

Karen stretched her body to one side and grabbed her toes with her hands. "Because...." she began, pausing to bring her torso forward and then upright, "It would demand discipline - a thing I never had until now!"

As well adjusted as this new Karen seemed to be, she was still the exhibitionist, watching me closely to observe the effect she had on me. She still needed to be appreciated, but no longer through a physical consummation through the body. She was becoming whole in herself, discovering an inner contentment through this simple life. We came together in mutual accordance with one anothers more base instincts, but I no longer felt as though I had to run to catch her up - in fact there were times when Karen seemed quite blasé about sex.

One evening we sat out on deck with a bottle of wine as we had done a hundred times or more; Karen was devout as ever in her worship of the sun, was intent as ever upon gathering the last of the dying rays on her bare flesh. We watched the sun set: the ruins of some ancient city were silhouetted against an orange and magenta sky.

"Isn't it beautiful," I commented.

"Another beautiful sunset!" She looked at me. "Hold me Julian."

I took her in my arms like a golden statue. The biblical phrase: 'thy belly is as golden as a sheath of corn,' for some reason ran through my mind.

"I must have seen millions of them," she said.

"What is it!" I said, sensing her body grow tense.

She shivered and put her arms about herself. She bit her lip and looked up at me as she lay resting in my arms.

"I'm afraid!"

She moved my hand over her smooth skin. "You do like me don't you?"

"Of course!"

"Will you always like me?"

I laughed. "What is this?"

"You'll think I'm stupid." she paused a moment. "It's just that I've never grown old before!"

I looked out at the wine dark sea, the sun was now an orange ball near to the horizon.

"We all grow old," I said

"Not all of us Julian - at least not for me."

She had moved away from me a little, I drew her close again.

"I look at old people sometimes and wonder what it must be like. I don't know if I want to be old like that."

I laughed. "It's what happens. No one wants to get old. It's just part of life."

Karen punched me playfully. "I mean it! It's all your fault! If you are the one to save me I shall grow old and then I shall look ugly."

"It's only the body that grows old."

"I've never thought like this before. I've never considered the possibility of growing old. I've always been caught up in the moment, too preoccupied with living. I've never reflected on things as deeply as this until now!" She turned to me. "I'm sacred Julian!"

"Don't be," I said, hugging her tight.

"But what if you die before me? What if I am left all alone, old and ugly?"

"By then you would have grown so much more."

"Do you think so? But who would want me? May be we should take our lives at a certain time - I mean before we get really old?" Karen sat up and looked at the red orb that was sinking into the wine dark Aegean, turning her from a golden statue into a blood red effigy. "Yes, that's what we'll do! We will make some sort of pledge!"

"What age do you suggest?" I said, indulging her.

"I don't know. I'm twenty three now, so we've got a few years before us, and some women can look quite good at forty, after that they quickly go down hill."

"You'll still have a great figure if you lived to be seventy."

"Oh! Don't say that. I don't think I could live that long! Anyway I think these would look a bit odd on a seventy year old," she said, pushing her breasts together. No matter what one does, they will sag in the end. I will look disgusting at that age."

"It's silly of you to worrying about what you will look like when you're old!"

"Silly! - how dare you! You are my soul mate! You are supposed to understand me - sympathise with my plight!"

"And I do, only too well!" I said. "Don't you see it's not just about the body, it's your soul I was sent to save. Your soul is who you are, not your body, no matter how fantastic it looks and feels, it won't last, it's only an outer covering. You may have once thought you were immortal - I mean in that very first life as Taanach, but you are not immortal, don't you see - that is what you have to learn!"

Karen looked at me wide eyed, in the manner of an innocent child.

"Garcia said that the soul goes on forever," I continued, "but there comes a time when even the soul can grow weary of rebirth."

Karen nodded, "I'm weary all right!" she sucked on her finger.

"I know you are. Weary of having undergone so many rebirths, so any tragic existence's, weary of so much pain!"

"I am - I am," nodded Karen, still sucking like a little girl.

I took her finger out of her mouth and kissed her hand. "You poor little thing! You're lost to life really!"

"You know me so well Julian. I am weary so very weary." She lay back and sighed. "Will you always love me and protect me - even if I get old?"

"Of course I will, but you will never be ugly, it is your soul, as much as it is it's outer covering that I love; and in any case you are strong - I think you will always look good, no matter how old you get!"

~~I could tell Karen liked being praised for her strength. I felt her breath deeply~~ with self-satisfaction, and stretched like a cat. "Yes, strong..." she sighed.

"What ever comes, I prey to Tanit and Astarte, and all the other gods that we will be together."

"Oh yes," she said, "clutching at my arm, "yes let us prey that!" Karen got to her knees and I followed her example and clasping my hand in hers she lifted it aloft: "Oh sweet Tanit forgive me my sin. I am so full of pride. Please safeguard my guardian angel Julian here, may our bond grow stronger with each passing day. Blessed be Astarte, blessed be the divine and pure Tanit." And in unison: "Blessed be."

And so we made our prayer to the dying sun. Karen was proud by nature and it had been her pride that had set her soul on its destructive trajectory. For a girl like her it would be hard for her to forget the presence of her body and the vital force it contained. Her animus was strong, exuding its vital presence the whole time, so powerful was it that it radiated out to the farthest shore.

She looked at me as if for an answer to some unspoken question. All I saw were wide childlike eyes, and it struck me that I was looking directly into her soul.

"There," I said, "right there is your true beauty."

Her pupils dilated wide and black and I saw into the mote of her eye, her quivering restless soul. I came forward and kissed her lavender eyes. Karen giggled and turned her head away.

"I don't want to grow old though! My lovely body will be all bent and twisted like Taanach's was."

She ran her hand down the long serpentine shape of her form until it rested against her broad thigh.

"When we're old do you think you could still want me?"

I answered her with a kiss and allowed her to guide my hand to wherever was her wont.

"You'll always want me, won't you? Tell me you can never get enough of me. Not ever enough!"

"I can never get enough of you - you know that."

It was true that I, as much as the next man found her body to be infinitely desirable. but I wondered if this, almost desperate appeal to the sensual, meant that she still didn't fully appreciate the jeopardy such displays put her soul in? I resisted with all my will her growing ardent need for confirmation. It was as if she wanted to blot out the future with the use of her immediate physical presence? Was this not what she had always done?

"You must not be afraid," I said, taking both her hands in mine

"Kiss me!" she demanded. "Touch me!"

"No! - You must face the truth."

Karen violently shook her head. "No, I can't, I'm afraid of growing old - afraid to die even!"

"Welcome to the human race."

Karen sobbed and laughed at the same time.

"Listen to me..." I said, lifting her head.

"What!"

"Your whole existence has always been spent on the physical level. Your soul has only ever known itself, it is dreadfully alone."

Karen looked at me quizzically.

"You have never known what it is like to be truly yourself. To be at peace with yourself - until now, that is! It's the same for your soul, it very rarely knows what it is like to be without a body, which in point of fact is its true nature. If you are afraid it is because your soul is afraid. It leaves one young body after another, returning again and again. What you say about your body and your fear of growing old, is what your soul is afraid of! But your soul has no business here in the material world.

"No - it hasn't?"

"No," I said.

"Where did it go when Natasha died, before it came into me."

"I don't know where the soul goes exactly but you know as well as me that each period of rebirth is growing closer to the next." I paused a moment. "You know that after you there may not be another....reincarnation of your soul!"

Karen turned away and peered over the gunwales into the inky blackness. "You mean it will be the end of me? My extinction!" she laughed sardonically, "Hah! I'm the last of my kind, like the Mohicans. I will become extinct like the Thylacine! You see me moving but I'm not really here."

I put my hand on her arm and she fell against me. "Well I don't care," she said, bravely, "Oblivion! - well why not!"

"It may not be oblivion - nothingness! It could still be something. There must be something!"

Karen laughed. "Something in between you mean! Not life not rebirth, but no place among the dead either!"

She met my empty gaze, and turned her head on one side and pulled a strange face. "Say it Julian! - A ghost, a whill-o-the-wisp!" She made a funny ghostly noise raising her hands in the air, and then looked away again, resting her arms on the bulwark. There were tears in her eyes. "My silly self - my silly soul always in such a hurry. In a hurry to live, a hurry to die and then in a hurry to live again! It's funny you know - I always use to feel in such a hurry, always wanting to get the most out of everything - afraid there wouldn't be any time, you know, like I haven't got long; that I have to *cram it all in!*"

"Until now!" I said.

"Even now I kind of feel in a bit of a hurry."

"But I've never seen you so happy - so relaxed."

"It's true, I have felt - better!" She roughly rubbed her tears way in her no nonsense manner. "Look at me, getting all upset over nothing, after all that is what I'll become."

I took her arm. "No you won't," I said, shaking her.

"I will - I will, you said, its the end of me!" In a somnambulistic tone: "I'm the last of my kind."

"It's only what Garcia said might happen. It doesn't have to be like that!"

"It doesn't? Oh, Julian I'm all confused."

"At least this life is different. We are in control. For the first time - *you are* in control!"

"I guess so. It's true these last few months I have felt so much more...you know

at ease. Not wanting to - be physical *that* way! But still enjoying being me, you know, in the physical sense!"
"I sure do! You would have been so good as a gymnast."
"Perhaps, but I'm too old now - in any case I'm the wrong shape." Becoming serious: "You mustn't leave me - no mater what!"
"I won't, but if anything does happen you must find Garcia."
"Yes, but even he's old!"
"You have to trust to the future. Most of all, have faith in yourself. In the end it has to come from you - you can in the end only be yourself! and you are not a bad person, otherwise Garcia and myself would not want to help you."
Karen pressed her lithesome body against me. Her face was wet. "You are a good man Julian."
I felt her body shiver. The sky had grown darker, changing from crimson to a deep mauve. She lay her head back, her broad cobra throat exposed and vulnerable. I lifted her up and took her below, where she would be safe from the ghosts that dwelt in the old city. I lay her down on the bed, her wide mouth fell upon me delivering her own sweet venom.

The ruined city that the morning sun lit upon was that other eternal city called *Ephesus*. In the early morning, the city is empty and quiet but for the Rock Nuthatches, Serins, and the yell of Jackdaws. Its impressive Arcadian Way and grand civic buildings such as the library of Celsus, mark it out as one of the major centres of trade and commerce as well as learning, that came to the fore in the ancient world. But its proud monuments, constructed by a people long since dead, was brought down, not by invading hordes, or invading armies, but by a class of people unique in their perversity of thought, a people who believed in the doctrine of meekness, but who in actual fact were anything but! The greatest defensive ramparts and walls are no defence to an idea. Like a malignant disease it crept through the population of Ephesus, as it did all the great cities of the empire! But in Ephesus one could still sense the spirit of the place, for not all of its citizens were easy converts. Their restless ghosts still plough up and down the streets, only chased away by a daily new kind of invasion, that of the modern tourist. The well preserved condition of many of its buildings contribute to its strong classical aura, an aura both Karen and I tuned into straightaway. Karen in particular felt herself transported back to their time, a time of purity and grace, a time that ran with nature, and not against her. We moored offshore from the great city for three days, and early every morning, before the masses arrived, Karen would climb to the top of Mount Pion and announce her presence to the ghosts that inhabited the dusty streets and dwellings. That last morning, we rose rather late but we went there in any case, Karen going as usual to the top of Mount, and climbing up on to a piece of ruined stonework made her usual address 'to the people of Ephesus':

"I have returned to your great city," she called out, "I, high priestess of Tanit have come to re-establish the ways of my people. The Phoenicians are here! I shall drive out the one lie that has prevailed for too long. In the name of Ball-Hamon, Tanit and Eshmun, I have returned with the truth. I have come back to you!" Karen called out, her arms open wide.

Appearing upon her rock a bit later than usual Karen had a larger more manifest audience than the normal Serins and Jackdaws. Apart from the odd strange look her presence was largely ignored just the same.

After making her address she opened her eyes and looked around and then turned to me: "Why are they ignoring me? What's wrong with them?"

"They are modern," I said, "their ears are stopped-up! They don't have time for gods and goddesses anymore, they're all to busy being tourists!"

"They see but they do not believe," said Karen.

"That's about it. They believe in the god Mammon."

"Who?"

"The god of riches - the worship of money. The one who moderns worship."

"Oh, him, another *false god!*" Karen raised her arms aloft and called out again: "Do you know who I am!" and then holding out her hand and pointing to the money grubbers and followers of Mammon: "Sinners, you who have cast your eyes away from the glory of the gods. The day will come when you shall repent. Just you wait until I am at my power base - then you will know of the wrath of the *Phoenicians!*"

Again most of the living ignored her, all except a group of uniformed men who met us just as we were about to leave the city. They wanted to know what we were doing up on Mount Pion. Karen exerted her usual authoritative air - but these guys were not so easily swayed. These were not security guards but the upholders of the law of the land.

"I am the priestess of Tanit. We are Phoenicians."

"*Phoenicians!*" said one officer, looking askance. He gestured with his hands becoming belligerent and repeated the word: 'passport,' several times. I tried to intervene seeing that these guys were no pushover.

"Look we're Americans," I said, "we just love all your history!"

"Well he's an American, but my birth right goes back over three thousand years, in truth I am a Phoenician and this is *my* city!" insisted Karen.

This finally proved too much for them and we were roughly manhandled into the back of a waiting police van. It took several hours before their captain believed my story that we were not, 'Phoenicians' but genuine American citizens, and that our vessel was moored less than a mile off the coast. Even then they insisted on coming out to the *Idhra* to inspect our passports. They were very apologetic afterwards, advising us that in the future when visiting *Asia Minor*, that we do not claim to be Phoenicians, but who we actually were.

"These modern people have no respect for royal blood," said Karen, once we were aboard our vessel and safe from further state intervention!

"I think we should keep our visits a bit more low key in the future."

"Why? I'm not ashamed of my heritage. How many people can claim to be a direct blood line to a Phoenician high priestess. I have more right in my ancient cities than any of them!"

"I understand *that* - but do they? Obviously word must have got round of your regular appearance at Mt. Pion. In this day and age some people are very sensitive about these things."

"What things?"

"Oh, you know - religion, race, that kind of thing!"

"Well that's just silly! My people and the objects of their veneration predate their culture, their idea of god by thousands of years! In any case they are not religious, they are not pious, they use their religion to reinforce their identity. Without it they would be nothing!"

As honest and clear thinking as this insight was I wondered if the world was ready to hear this kind of truth? I wondered if it would ever be ready! It was as I had feared, rather than cool her zeal, the further along the coast of Asia Minor we voyaged and the more ancient Greek and Roman - nay, even Phoenician sites we visited, the more immersed Karen became in her persona as the high priestess of Tanit. Gradually before my eyes I saw my salty sea-lass turn into the haughty Taanach el Nachash.

In all the great cities we visited along the coast of Asia Minor we were greeted by the same mixture of curiosity and indifference: at that other great city of Miletus, home of the pre-Socratic thinkers, at Didyma, the place of Apollo, at Iasus, Pergamon, Elaea, Cyme, Colophon, at Myria and Halicarnassus, it was the same. They had not the ears to hear. It was possible that Karen could have been mistaken as a part of some sort of re-enactment show, dressed in a beautiful purple Sari, woven from the finest silk and uttering ancient Greek phrases. Through her apparel and her utterances, the way she moved, as if gliding over the surface of the ground, such was her grace - a poetry of motion, every gesture conducted with the utmost refinement and subtlety; there was something unearthly about her. To see her amidst the splendour of such ancient architecture, left one in little doubt one was in the presence of a high priestess, the presence of a being that transcended the profane - and there was all about her such gross profanity and debasement of that which was sacred. I remember it was at Mytilene on the island of Lesbos that Karen and I first had our close encounter with Japanese tourists. Karen was by now speaking in fluent Ionic Greek. A group of them stood looking at Karen as she spoke some sacred rite at the site of the temple of Hestia. They began to be quite animated, laughing and gesticulating, then they began to take photographs of her. She was a splendid sight it has to be said: in her purple robe, her hair in dreadlocks and tied with purple ribbons, with a large pearl encrusted comb, that even Ceres would have envied, while about her neck hung yet more pearls and a heavy silver chain, from which was suspended a large sapphire, about her arms she wore silver amulets and around her ankles silver anklets, from which hung tiny silver bells that made a beautiful sound every time Karen moved, accompanying her in her songs, as she danced her praise to the gods!

When Karen had finished her dance she stepped out of the confines of the sacred site.

"What on Earth are these people doing? Do they have no respect for the sacred places of the gods?" said Karen, as they began to take photographs of each other with Karen standing next to them.

One had to admit it was a strange thing to behold, to see these frenetic little people posing for their photograph: Karen in her regalia towering above them, and looking slightly awkward.

One of them came over to me, I guess he thought I was part of the show, I wasn't about to be co-opted into their sick little world.

"Hail Tanit! Goddess of the Phoenicians," I called, gesturing towards Karen.

He turned with great excitement to his compatriots who were still busy *snapping* away. "Ah - so! ah - so! Tahneet! Tahneet! Hoy'ah Tahneet!"

"Hoy'ah Tahneet, Hoy'ah Tahneet!, ah so! Tahneet! Tahneet! Ah - so!..." said the Japanese in unison.

Karen looked at me and put her hand to her head. "Oh, this is ridiculous! I give up! Who are these funny little people. What on Earth are they saying - they're too much!" she said laughing.

"They are Japanese tourists I believe! They get everywhere these days!"

"What peculiar little people! To spend all ones time taking pictures of each other, using the world as a backdrop!"

Although Karen's antics had there funny side, and by and large, most of the ordinary visitors to the ancient sites we visited, looked at her with curiosity and sometimes mild amusement, the authorities however took a much dimmer view, reaching their most extreme when we were physically ejected from Myria and then Halicarnassus.

"Get you stink'n hands off me!" protested Karen to one of the guards.

"Yeah goddamn it," I joined, "if you lay one finger on her I'll fucking goddamn kill you!"

Their reply to this was a swift beating with their batons. We were pushed into another police van and whisked downtown to the local police station. We showed them our passports only to have them taken from us. We were then directed into a stuffy little room where we were told to wait - which we did for nearly an hour in diabolically hot conditions and with no water.

"I thought you were really brave," said Karen.

"Fat lot of good it did me," I said, nursing my bruises.

Karen kissed me on the side of the face. "Still, you tried to protect me, that's what matters."

"How dare they touch you like that, no one does that!"

Karen held my hand. "My darling, I know! - The truth is, it's all my fault."

"No! Why shouldn't you be able to go where you want! pray to whoever you want! and dress any way you please! It's not like you're doing any one any harm?"

"Oh honey, you're so sweet," she said, kissing me again.

"Shucks!..." I said, touching the spot where she kissed me.

Eventually we were ushered through into the sheriff's office, or their equivalent. A fat middle aged man with a moustache sat behind a desk shuffling our passports in his fat hands. He motioned for us to sit. Two chairs had been strategically placed the other side of the desk.

"So you are American's!" he began, looking at our passports. "Is it your yacht that is anchored off the coast?"

"Yes the *Idhra*," I replied.

"You fly the Greek flag! And you..." he said looking at Karen. "You speak Greek at the ancient site?"

"Yes, I speak fluent Ionic and Doric forms of Greek," replied Karen proudly, before adding: "and also a little Phoenician and Aramaic..."

"So you are a scholar of ancient languages then?"

"No - they are the languages I speak. I am the priestess of Tanit."

The sheriff leaned back and laughed uproariously. "Tanit! - what is this Tanit? and Phoenicians! I know a little of these things and these are dead languages - dead ideas!"

"Are they! I'm here am I not?"

I smiled to myself. Karen gave me the wink!

The sheriff was no longer amused and threw our passports down on the table, making a noise in his throat: "I suggest to you that you practice your dead languages and your dead religion else where in the future."

Karen's eyes grew bold. "Why should I! Halicarnassus was once a thriving Greek colony!"

"More than two thousand years ago perhaps!" He sighed heavily. "Young lady, go back to your hippie colony on the west coast of America and forget all these mad ideas."

Karen flew to her feet. "I am not one of those goddamn hippies! I am the priestess of Tanit I tell you!"

The sheriff looked at me. "You seem a reasonable man, take your crazy girlfriend away from here, out of my country before she lands herself in big trouble."

Karen leaned across the table. "How dare you! I am not crazy, you are the ones that are crazy," said Karen, pointing the finger of Tanit at him.

The sheriff pressed a buzzer under his desk and two officers rushed in.

Handing me our passports: "Get out of here before I change my mind. If I catch you again trying to stir up trouble I will not be so lenient." He spoke something to his men and they came forward. I put my hand around Karen's waist so that they wouldn't have to touch her, (I so hoped they wouldn't touch her!) and I lead her away towards the door; but Karen's blood was up, she was livid.

"Just a minute buster! You should show more respect, *I am* the priestess of Tanit! - I am, I tell you! The likes of you, who the goddamn hell are you to tell me what to do! you should get down on your knees and grovel for mercy!"

There then ensued a struggle between me - the officers and Karen, we were kind of all fighting each other, (if only they wouldn't touch her so!) In the end Karen was half in and half out of the sheriffs office, he was standing on his feet directing and yelling to his men - Karen, in the affray, managed to grab hold of a great big stack of papers off the top of a filing cabinet, and began throwing them around the room screaming:

"All this - this stuff, this modern stuff, this modern world of yours is nothing! - nothing I tell you! Greece and Rome were here, Greece and Rome are gone! - modern man is here and modern man will soon be - gone!" she cried, flinging a load of them in the sheriff's face.

Somehow we ended up on the street - papers were blowing out of the door while some of the officers were running around trying to catch them. Karen laughed and pointed at them. I put my arm around her trying to restrain her. "Modern man will be gone, gone I tell you, your days are over, your faith is false rotten to the core! - look at what it has done to the Earth! - murderers! killers!" she screeched. "You won't get away with it, not now the Phoenicians are here - the Phoenicians are coming beware...beware!" she sang, "the Phoenicians are coming, be ware!"

My arms still round her waist trying to contain her, drunk with madness, reeling from side to side, laughing and screaming she was like a wild cat! - a tempest - a fiery purple Catherine-wheel. I don't think any of the officers felt like tangling with her. In the end they just closed the door on us.

All the way back to the port in a cab, Karen was laughing hysterically shouting out the window: "The Phoenicians are here beware beware, we are the Phoenicians!" She thought it was fantastic fun. For my part I only wanted to get her to safety, get her out to the *Idhra* and weigh-anchor, and leave their shores behind.

At the port I paid the cabby, and he cocked his head to one side, towards Karen who was waiting at the key-side: "You know," he said, in a thick accent, "we have trouble with these Phoenicians before!"

We had had a close brush with the law, but it only demonstrated the narrowness of thinking of the times. If I cautioned restraint it was because Karen's safety was my prime concern. I knew what these moderns were capable of, there was no limit to how low they would stoop to silence those who speak the truth. Karen's passion galvanised my love of the ancients and their ways, and put into stark relief the sorry state of the ways of modern man! Karen had the most amazing insights, her purity her *naïveté*, her divinity almost, enabled her to see right to the heart of the matter. After all, what did these monotheists worship? An invisible entity! a ghost! a word! an idea! They did not worship the Sun, the Moon, the Sea, the Earth - well clearly not the latter two, judging by the state of things! Give me these things to worship and honour! Honour means to respect, but where is the respect for the Earth? Show me how these monotheists have honoured the world they live and depend upon? How dare they preach to the likes of me and Karen! Who are they? They would do best to shut their mouths and walk off in shame. We want not a particle of *your* world, people like *us* have no need of your ways. The way of lies and trickery.

The ways of deceit and ignominy! I am my own voice, be gone I say! we renounce you, nay - condemn you! You will bow before the old gods before the day is through. Shame upon you and your creed. You insidious ones!

We worship the rain, the open skies, the fields, the air, the sun, we do not hide ourselves away in a claustrophobic dank cellar of the mind. Be they Jew or Muslim, Sikh or Christian, Buddhist or Shinto, you have nothing to show us for your faith, but the spilling of blood and the degradation of all that is truly holy. What have you done, but to turn what was pure into a foul smelling sess pit! You blaspheme, I say, in the name of what you call God or saviour. Give me affirmation of life, and not your stinking hypocrisy!

As Karen moved further into a more spiritual zone of being, I tended to develop a sense of indignation toward the modern world, (well as you can see). Before I had met Garcia and learned the true nature of Karen's darkness, like millions of other people, I had merely accepted the world as it was: never considered that there existed an alternative. One didn't have to live life like a machine, one didn't have to conform to the modern world and its latest technological fads. We had lived outside of it for more than a year, and I had grown accustomed to thinking as a man living outside of time. I was aware though that one can go too far with these thoughts. I did not want to become completely embittered towards the world of the modern - as Garcia seemed to have become. The reality of the situation was that most people in the so called modern world already knew how to live in peace with one another, but ordinary people are not in charge of their lives, in the sense that they do not hold the destiny of their nation in their hands - by and large this is held by mad men and megalomaniacs concerned only with their place in history. Such people generally come under the heading of: priest, or minister, politician, president or prime minister. These minority who hold power over peoples lives, force ordinary sensible individuals to follow a narrow set of rules. They are not encouraged to view themselves as individuals, they are not encouraged to take the wide view - to think for themselves! And this myopia they call religion, and belief in flag and national identity. From this misconception, from these lies, the ingredients for conflict come into being. When one or more set of people (tribe) come together with conflicting *beliefs,* (which are themselves based on myth and fable), then the filth and puss of these lies and half-truths, erupt on the face of the world in the form of war. Most war then is born out of laziness and fear of other people and their ideas. The feeling of national identity is further reinforced through an awareness of understanding of historical cultural values. If one can forget a moment about *history*, and view oneself as existing outside of time, and live for the now, then there would be no validation for war or conflict of any kind. If one could see oneself as one truly is, a living entity whose existence will, by and large, go unrecorded, then one can embrace ones freedom and no longer be a slave to history - to dogma, and the words of bigots, and the preaching of hypocrites. These things would no longer have any influence in our lives if one saw oneself as one truly is, a human being, an entity, living on a planet going about a star. And just as the Earth was born from the stars, as our own star was born from the dust of even more ancient stars, so too - were you! Where was Mohammed, or Jesus, or Yahweh when the Earth was born? Who was there to utter their names? and yet life still thrived - as life thrives on other worlds too, yet these beings never heard these names either! Will you go to the stars and find others to kill there, who have never heard of your lies? So you see, it is hard when one understands the true nature of being, not to become exasperated by the ignorance that surround one!

Karen and I had voyaged around the Aegean rim, and at every city, be it Roman, Greek, Minoan, Phoenician, Babylonian or Hitite, we only saw the same thing - evidence of a superior civilisation that had passed away, whose basic moral tenets were so advanced as to have come from another world. That morality had its origins in a very different set of values. They saw nature as something that was a part of themselves. It was alive with gods and spirit beings; they saw nature imbued with mind. Their religious beliefs and practices were a reflection of this 'attitude' towards their world. It was a sacred and visible thing. One could quite literally touch the face of god. Everywhere they found a concord, a symmetry a balance, and mankind lived according to this balance. One stepped outside of it at ones peril, they called it *hubris*. And in order to give reverence to this balance, this symmetry they left us a legacy of their religious beliefs in hard stone, something very different I think, from words which in the hands of sophists and charlatans, so easily becomes dogma and lies. There was no divine artificer working in the background, one felt the gods under ones feet, in the very air one breathed. And such a religious approach to life could only lead to a lightness of spirit, a love of nature and a celebration of life. To be an Epicurean was perhaps the most profound expression of this morality.

To a very large extent Karen and I were Epicureans. In essence we were sensualists, although clearly there was no greater sensualist than Karen! She had not always been Epicurean, to live to excess, as she had done does not lead to the maximising of pleasure through the senses. Our life, whilst we explored the Aegean however, had enabled Karen to keep the modern world and its negative influence at bay. But this trick could not be kept up forever, our period of isolation would find a pause when Karen made footfall on the island of Rhodes.

"Look," said Karen, "my foot print on the Rhodian shore."

"Behold the mark of the high priestess upon the Rhodian shore!"

"We're becoming very biblical sounding," laughed Karen

"Well these moments have to be related in the right kind of language. To think, the people of Rhodes have no clue that the high priestess of Tanit is once more among them."

Karen stretched her hands above her head and faced the sun. "Yes they should get down on their knees before me."

Just as Karen said these words a massive surge came up the beach engulfing her up to her waist. When the waters receded there was no longer any trace of Karen's mark upon the shore.

"I thought for a second you were gong to be swept away!" I said, securing the dingy to a wooden pile.

"Yes I know," she replied breathlessly, "and look, there is no longer any sign of my foot print upon this Rhodian shore!"

She looked at me distracted a moment before turning abruptly and walking off up the beach alone. I caught up with her half way along the pass which lead to a Hellenistic temple that had originally been a Phoenician place of worship. Karen remained sullen and uncommunicative. When we finally reached the top of the bluff that overlooked the bay, there was little to show for our effort. The temple complex was in a sorry old state, but worse was that the weather had begun to close in. Dark clouds hampered what was supposed to be a superb view of the island. It seemed that the surge that had erased Karen's fist footfall on the island, had been but a prelude to an advancing storm.

"There's nothing - nothing left off it!" said Karen, disillusioned - kicking around pieces of marble masonry.

"It is over five thousand years old, what did you expect! The guide book just said it was the site of a Phoenician temple."

Karen half smiled but refused to go all the way for fear it would spoil her mood. "Still it's no excuse." she said, petulantly. To my surprise she sat down on an overturned Doric column and put her head in her hands and began to sob. At first I thought she was playing some sort of joke on me, but when I went over to her I saw that her tears were genuine, and that she was terribly inconsolable.

"What on Earth is the matter?" I asked, to no avail. "Is it that the temple is ruined?" The notion of rebuilding it, or one like it, ran through my head.

There was a rumble of thunder in the distance, the visibility was such that I could no longer see the *Idhra*. It now began to rain in great big drops which splashed noisily on the wrecked marble column on which Karen had planted herself. And there she remained, a hunched up ball of woe, seemingly immovable and as impervious as a statue, to the growing deluge. The sound of her sobs mixed with the splashing of rain and rumblings of distant thunder made her a rain storm within a storm. Her dark body, visible beneath her light cotton sari, made translucent by the down pour, heaved and convulsed as each fresh sob wracked her taut frame. It wasn't long before she began to resembled a soggy rag-doll of a thing, hunched over and crying for all her worth, she was the most forlorn thing I had ever seen. My concern though was torn between Karen and the *Idhra,* moored in the bay below.

"Look - we can't stay here! We have to get back to the boat! We have to find some place to put in, otherwise we could loose her if this storm gets any worse."

Karen slowly stirred, and raised her head to me. Rivulets of tears and rain water washed over her face and down her proud neck; her knotted dreadlocks, which to begin with had withstood the rain rather like the wool of one of Chloe's

blessed sheep, had suddenly become very soggy, so that it now looked something like a wet lump of cotton-candy. I helped her up. All the strength seemed to be gone from her body.
"Its bad," she mumbled, "Bad, bad, bad..." she kept repeating. But once on her feet we began to make some progress down the pass.
"What's bad?"
"Its a bad omen, a bad omen," said Karen, looking at me her eyes wild, her pupils madly dilated.

Sometimes she would crumple up and fall to the stony path. The rain was falling harder now, causing a tiny avalanche of pebbles and sand.
"You must help me Karen! - Get up!"
"No, leave me, I'm going to die here," she said, as she lay face down in the mud seemingly enjoying her last moments. Her hands scrabbled into the sandy soil as she tried to pull herself along. Eventually though she decided this wasn't the exact spot for her ascension, so she aloud me to pull her up again. After a few more of these set backs, miraculously, so it seemed to me, we came down off the pass and onto the beach. The sea now was coming up high along the shore in huge foaming surges. The dingy was some way out, the only way to get at it would be to swim. Once on the beach Karen seemed to come back to her senses. She quickly comprehended the danger the *Idhra*, and ourselves faced. The waves were now quite large and occasionally we lost sight of our vessel altogether.

Karen pushed her wet locks from her forehead and began to wade into the tumult. I shouted to her to come back but she kept on going, only looking back when the sea was up to her neck.
"I'll go, it's the only way. Don't worry," she called.

A big wave suddenly went right over her head and I lost sight of her. 'So this was to be her end,' I thought, 'a watery grave.' I was not a strong swimmer but I thought the only thing to do was go in after her. Just as I was getting out of my shoes I saw her head bob up, she turned to me and waved, and began to clamber into the dingy. After a few more anxious moments I heard the little outboard motor cough into life. Karen brought the dingy in close enough for me to wade on board, the motor struggled hard against the tide but gradually we came alongside the *Idhra*. Once on board we soon had the big engine gurgling reassuringly beneath our feet.

"We'll have to take her into the port of Rhodes," I said, "it's not far."

Even though we seemed safe enough on the *Idhra,* after all, she was a good sized ocean-going vessel, the seas were very high and it was all I could do to keep her on course. It was certainly the biggest test of my seamanship! At this point in our sojourn we had never experienced this side of the Aegean's temperament.

"Do we have to go there? why can't we head to one of the other islands?"

"In this weather! I won't risk it!"

"Oh please - plea'ease," she wined. Frustrated, she made a half-hearted attempt to grab control of the wheel.

"Are you mad? Do you want to drown us all! Why don't you go below? you look cold."

"I'm fine," she replied, obstinately. Karen turned to regard the white sea-horses, as they were swept along by the near gale force winds. What ever it was that frightened her, she found the current battle with the elements far more preferable. But even Karen looked a little relieved when the lights of the port came into view.

With our vessel safely moored in the harbour there was nothing to be done but to wait out the bad weather. According to the forecast it would be at least two days before the current conditions would moderate. We had pushed our luck with the seasons, apparently such storms were not unusual for late October. Despite Karen's protestations to me, and the harbour master, we were informed that: 'there was nothing to be done but wait for the *meltemi* to lessen, and such heavy weather as this could last *weeks*.' This did not go down at all well with Karen, who cursed the wind, but even *she,* high priestess of Tanit, could not get nature to do her beckoning.

"I don't like it! I don't like it here Julian!" she said, as she paced up and down in the lobby of the five star hotel.

"It's supposed to be the best hotel on the island," I said, being purposively obtuse.

"Not the hotel, this-this," she said, spinning round waving her hands about. "It's a bad omen!"

The manager showed us to a suite on the top floor overlooking the harbour. "This is one of our very best residences, you are lucky normally we are booked out, but it is not so busy this time of year."

Karen looked around with an air of dissatisfaction. "It will have to do I suppose," she said, finally slumping down in a plush leather armchair.

The manager looked quite perplexed. "It is the very best, I assure you."

"Yeah, yeah just dandy."

"It's great, she loves it! Really - we both love it." I said, pushing a fifty in the managers hand, which had the effect of putting an immediate smile on his face.

"What ever you want, anything, you just ring and you have, anything, anytime."

"We will," I said, edging him out of the door.

"Typical creepy manager," observed Karen.

"I guess business is tough this time of year."

Karen got up and strolled nonchalantly to the window. "Look at the goddamn weather! No wonder business is bad, and I am stuck on this hateful little island." Suddenly as if to prove a point, the gods who controlled the weather hurled with great force a mixture of sea and rain and hail at the window.

Still unimpressed, Karen turned slowly away. "Well at least there's a bar," she said, going over and mixing two large Martinis.

"Who controls the sea? I asked, sitting down opposite her.

"Poseidon - is god of the sea, and natural forces....I think" she replied, handing me a drink.

"Perhaps you offended him in some way - or else Tanit did?"

"Do you think so? Yes that could be it." she said, seizing on it as motif. "Poseidon is out to get me, I know he is. Here's to you Poseidon." .

She raised her glass. I smiled and shook my head.

"You think it's all a big joke!"

"No - honestly," I said, trying to take her hand, "it's just that the harbour master told us that this kind of weather is not unusual for this time of year. We were lucky not to run into it before now!"

"I guess - but it don't feel right, some how!"

"Well he should know, and I think you had no call to loose your temper with him, telling him he was an idiot. I think he knows the weather better than us hon.!"

"Does he? Better than me? Better than one who has lived god knows how many times in this part of the world?"

Karen knocked back her Martini and made herself another.

"How silly of me to forget, of course, you were born a high priestess, an auger, a diviner of portents."

Karen eyed me demurely, as if she were not quite sure if I was being facetious or not, after all she had been all of those things.

"Perhaps," I went on, to placate her, "you died here a long long time a go?"

Every now and again a particularly strong gust would rattle the windows. Karen gazed over my shoulder as the squall beat itself against the thin barrier, as if it were trying to get through, to smash the windows in, and get at her.

"Perhaps," she replied, looking away.

"What happened up there on the Acropolis?" I said. This time she let me take her hand, but only for a second.

"I don't know," said Karen, lighting a cigarette. She shrugged her shoulders. "My demon I guess. He's never far away."

And she was right, there was a return of that restless wild look in her lavender eyes. During our months at sea when she had been at her happiest, her eyes had a soft light glow to them, now they looked heavy and intense. I noticed too that she didn't pack any of her sari's but left them on the boat, preferring instead the high necked low cut Japanese style vests, and tight fitting satin skirts that showed off her figure, although she still had on her usual cut downs and denim jacket beneath her black sable coat, which she defensively pulled around her.

"You know, " I said, "You are very brave."

"How so?"

"Swimming out the way you did. Without you the boat could have gone down."

Karen shrugged again, drawing heavily on her cigarette. "It was no big deal."

"For a second I thought I had lost you."

"Yes - well - here I am, still!" Karen sighed, "I didn't really care if I drown or not, so It wasn't really bravery."

"Please don't say that."

"I'm sorry *honey*," she said, in a patronising tone, and patting my hand, "but it's true. It had to be done, that was all. I was the stronger swimmer. Really that is all there is to it." Karen stubbed out her cigarette aggressively. She looked at me a second. I wondered what it was that was going on in her mind. Was it a look of pity? She got up and wandered over to the window once more, and then went over to one of her bags and started to unpack, laying out, one by one, her silken garments, and erotic underwear. She picked out some black fishnet stockings and a red lace basque, and throwing off her sable began to pop the eager buttons on her jacket.

"I'm going to take a shower, I may be a while." She picked up the underwear and flounced over to the bathroom, where upon she paused a moment, her jacket now completely open, she looked back at me a second her eyes cajoling, evocative of the pleasures that would unfold therein and yet I would have no part in. Karen had made her statement, as definitive and sharp as her profile. I turned back to my Martini clear in the understanding that 'Natasha' was once more in the ascendency.

XV

The weather remained squally over the next few days tying us down to the island. Every day we would go down to the port and check on the *Idhra, and* after wander round the narrow medieval streets, usually ending up in a bar or a café, before going back to the hotel.

Karen continued in her pensive mood, often agitated, looking around her as if someone was going to leap out and grab her. The dark narrow streets freaked her out. She was happiest when we got back to the hotel. In the evening we would go up to the hotel restaurant. I don't think any of the guests, who were mostly middle aged Germans and a few Italians, had ever seen anything quite as exotic as Karen, not even if they were from Milan Her ensemble from bottom up would include: blood red stilettos, white fishnet stockings, a satin pencil skirt usually red, with a gold leaf pattern, (she had a vast array of these narrow style skirts in various colours, but red was her favourite) a satin vest, or bodice, in the same colour as the skirt, it had a high neck which she always buttoned all the way to the top. Her hair was finely woven in long thick dreadlocks, some were arranged around her shoulders, the rest she pilled up on top of her head, holding them in place with a profusion of clips. One might conclude that any feel for the orient was lost in her hair, but for the fact that two long ornately decorated wood pins, resembling chopsticks were driven into the thickest of her locks, at opposing angles. In such a get-up she resembled one of those femme fatale's of the nineteen twenties, but the look was confused by the oriental influence - she was then a mixture of western glamour and eastern exotic, Geisha. Her make up made her face look paler than it really was, the slightest hint of blusher, dark red lipstick, dark blue eye shadow and black eyeliner and mascara. She was east meets west with a bit of the west Indies thrown in.

The long slit up one side of her skirt was necessary for movement, but it also gave Karen the opportunity to display to the greatest effect the most western influence of her entire look, that of her stockings and their means of support. it was little wonder then, that there was scarcely a head, male or female, that failed to turn as she sauntered to her table.

There would be a moment of silence as we sat down, gradually people would begin to resume their meal and talk amongst themselves, but throughout the proceedings the odd head would turn in Karen's direction, and hushed conversation would follow.

After having finished our meal we would retire to the bar. Occasionally a brave German would approach us in order to lavish praise on Karen, recognising perhaps, the courage it took to wear such an ensemble. Curiously it was always the men that seemed fascinated by her dress.

One evening we were at the bar as usual, Karen was dressed all in black. I must say that on this particular evening she looked spectacular - unearthly in her beauty! It wasn't until Karen got up to go to the washroom that I noticed the two men who were sitting a little further down the bar. The fatter of the two watched Karen leave and then let out a whistle and turned to the man next to him, there followed a loud guffaw from the pair of them. I continued to sip my Martini deciding that the best thing to do was ignore them. It wasn't unusual for men to whistle at Karen, but in the bar of a five star hotel I considered it rather cheap. When Karen, returned the fat man whistled again, and in a loud voice said to his friend: "well look'ee, look'ee what I've just seen, I do declare! What do we have here!"

Both men then moved down the bar to the two vacant seats next to Karen.

"Excuse me Miss" said the first man again, in a strong Texas accent.

Karen slowly turned her head towards the fat Texan.

"I was just say'n to my friend over here that I seem to recollect see'n you some place before?"

"I don't think we've met!" Said Karen.

"Well, you see we ain't met exactly, no Mam - I'm sorry to say! It's just that - well, heck! You don't forget a gal with your kind of assets - if you get my drift!"

The Texan looked her up and down, "No sir'ee, I says to my friend, ain't that right Bert, "continued the Texan, glancing to his companion, "I says, when I watched you get up just now, 'you don't forget an ass like that,' heck no! But how rude of me, I haven't introduced myself," he continued, as he extended a fat hand towards Karen, who just looked at it like so much distasteful meat.

"Well I knows your name any how's," he went on.

Karen slowly picked up her Martini,

"Yes sir'ee I never forget a face, or a name - Natasha!"

The Texan could see by the look on Karen's face that he had hit home. He gave a little laugh and went on: "course then you hadn't had that nose job done, but the eyes - well and the rest of yah, now that a man cannot forget!"

Karen put her cocktail glass down on the bar and twisted it round and round with her fingers, staring at it intently. The fat Texan turned to his friend and whispered something in his ear that caused the other man to laugh uproariously.

"Yes sir'ee! I tell you we are in the presence of a star. Why the things this girl can do, would amaze you! Why, I seen her do two at a time! ain't that right - *Natasha!*"

"I'm afraid you've got the wrong girl," I said.

"Well I beg to differ, any way who the hell are you? What is that accent Bert, do you know? blast if I do!"

"Sounds like a goddamn cock suck'n Limy," put in Bert.

"We're from L.A." said Karen.

Both men laughed loudly. "Well that just about explains all! Now are you going to admit to me I'm right or are you call'n John Dexter the second, a liar? Heck if you wa'n hangout with fags that's your affair, but I knows you *girl!*"

"No I'm her," said Karen, turning to face the Texan.

I protested, she raised her hand. "No - it's all right!"

"Well come on - that's more like it! Let me by you and your friend a drink," said John Dexter the second, slapping Karen firmly on the thigh. "Put these drinks on my tab," he said to the bar man, "Give me and Bert here another Scotch. Now when are you go'n do another one of those saucy movies?" he went on, placing his hand on Karen's thigh.

"I don't do those kind of movies anymore," she said, seemingly ignoring the presence of the man's hand on her person.

"Well that's just a cry'n shame. This gal, I tell *you*" he laughed, "this here gal - why she'll do just about anything, ain't that right - honey, I mean *anything!*"

Karen smiled faintly. "Just about."

She took the Texan's hand and moved it between her legs, setting her jaw firmly she squeezed her monumental thighs. Moments later the Texan let out a loud yell and yanked it away from her grip fast as he could, shaking it and holding his wrist.

"Goddamn it! You crazy bitch!"

Karen then picked up the Texan's scotch and threw it in his face; before he could react she then leapt up as quick as a flash and pushed him out of his seat sending him sprawling to the floor.

Like all truly dramatic moments, this one too seemed to unfold in slow motion. I remember clearly the stunned look on John Dexter's face after Karen had thrown the Whiskey over him, and the look of horror on his friend Bert's face as he watched him end up a heap on the floor, while Karen stood menacingly over him. At some point a tall young man in a dark suit came over and guided Karen away from the supine Texan. Seeing Karen safe he returned to help Dexter to his feet.

"Signore! - signore! please let me help you," he said.

By now the manager and two other members of staff had arrived. "I think the signore has had too much to drink," the stranger explained.

"Too much to drink!" yelled the Texan, brushing himself down, and wiping his face. "That crazy bitch damn near brook my hand and then threw drink in my face before throwing me out of my goddamn chair!"

Karen and I stood at the bar looking quite bemused.

"Is this true?" said the manager, looking at Karen.

"I don't know what you mean!" She replied, lighting a cigarette.

"He said some highly offensive things to the lady," I said.

"I tell you one thing," said John Dexter, waving a finger at Karen, "if there's one thing she ain't, she's no darn lady - that's for sure!"

"You see," said Karen, looking helpless and shrinking into my arms,

"I am so very sorry Madam," said the manager,

The tall man in the suit who spoke with an Italian accent remained between the Texan and Karen, "I think you should perhaps leave señior, before you get yourself into more trouble - no?"

The barman came over with John Dexter's Stetson,

"We're leav'n," he said, snatching his hat, "but don't think this is over Missy! Nobody pushers John Dexter the second around and gets away with it, especially some two bit stripper and her fag boyfriend!"
"Oh - how dare you! " Said Karen, pointing at me, "He is ten times than man you will ever be."
The Texan just looked at the both of us, he wanted to get closer but it would have meant pushing the the Italian out of the way.
"Come signore," he said, touching his elbow. The Italian was one of those people who seem to exude goodwill, which even had the power to calm irate Texan's. As he came along side Karen though, he couldn't resist one last attempt to lunge at her, "This ain't over," he yelled, "I know you, I know what you are, I know you..." he repeated, finally being retrained by is friend Bert and the hotel staff.
"I am sorry Signorina you had to witness such an ordeal," said the suave Italian, bowing slightly and holding out his hand, "allow me to introduce myself, Antonio Alfons de Maxamilliano at your service."
Karen took his hand. "Well hi - Antonio thanks for sticking around."
"Yes thanks, " I said, shaking his hand, " I think it could have got a bit nasty."
"I could have handled him, the jerk-off, I was about to kick him in the head," said Karen.
"It was his friend I was worried about," I said.
"Even *you* could have taken him. Together we're a team!" She said, rasing her glass.
"Like the three musketeers," put in Antonio.
"All for one and one for all," the three of us said, in unison.
"Although I do not approve of violence myself," continued Antonio, "sometimes it is necessary - but please allow me to get you both another drink."
"How much did you see?" asked Karen.
"All of it."
Karen put her head in her hands. "Oh no, all of it? Did you hear what he said about me? Because it's true."
"Yes I was sitting right there the whole time, " said Antonio, pointing to a table by the entrance to the bar. "But I don't care, he was a rude pig of a man, and what you did was just magnificent."

We all burst into laughter, "wasn't it though," said Karen, "you should have seen the look on his face Julian, as I crushed his fat hand."

Antonio held Karen's gaze for a moment before allowing his eyes to travel down the length of her body.

"You must have great strength?" he said, before looking at her face once more.

There followed a moment of tension between all three of us.

"Yes I am *very* strong," she said.

On cue the barman presented the drinks and the manger came over with a flurry of apologies and instruction that the drinks for the three of us were free for the rest of the evening; which was, of course, the perfect opportunity for us all to get well acquainted

"What do you suppose he meant?" said Karen, looking first at Alfons and then to me, her lavender eyes rolling from one to the other, " 'this ain't over,' " she said, mimicking his accent.

"Don't worry," said Alfons, "it is simple you will come and stay with me, at my Chateau, both of *you,* as my gusts, and we will leave this very night."

There were the usual protestations that one makes but in the end we, that is, *Karen* accepted Alfons' invitation.

"You're not staying at the hotel then?" I asked.

"No, but the food is good. The truth is I saw the pair of you the night before and was intrigued, especially by you Karen. You seem so - unafraid - so bold, and there is a magical quality to your eyes, as though they have bore witness to a thousand life times - I know you will think I am crazy, but that is what I feel, and I only wished to make your acquaintance and see if you are really as I imagined." Turning to me, and grasping my hand firmly: "How I envy you monsieur, I should not say such a thing but it is true, "extending an open hand towards Karen, "to know such a beautiful woman as this, you are blessed by the gods!"

"And am I what you expected?" put in Karen.

"Oh yes, every bit, and so much more - much, much more!"

Before we knew what was happening we were in Antonio's chauffeur driven limousine. About thirty kilometres south of Rhodes town, in Lindhos Old Town; Antonio owned a seventeenth century, 'Captain's residence', a building with a massive facade and private courtyard. Such grand dwellings as these were indicative of the islands significance as a major trading point between east and west. Antonio explained how the cavernous mansion with its echoing galleries and inner courtyard, filled with orange and fig trees and grape vines, had been in his families possession for over five generations. His true title was in fact, *Duke Antonio Alfons do Maxamilliano*. His family had relocated to the Italian speaking part of Switzerland during the period of the Fascists, but they owned land and property all over Europe. Karen was very impressed by the fact that she had met of all things an *Italian duke*. If it had only been his title that she found impressive! But Karen was swept off her feet by everything that Antonio said or did. He had style, he was suave and sophisticated in a way an American could never be. It came from within, from years of breeding and belief in ones superiority. He was as equally fascinated by her as she with him. In Karen, he found someone fresh and naïve, yet very bold - someone whom he recognised as being distinctly not from the usual modern mould. The thing I hated mot was that there was nothing - nothing I tell, you that one could find in his character to hate. OK, he may have been rather arrogant but hell, the guy was a millionaire and a member of the Italian aristocracy. For the most part he was courteous, polite kind, affable, generous to a fault. What amazed me most about him was the subtlety of skill he employed in his seduction of Karen, for clearly that was his primary goal from the moment he set eyes on her. But final acceptance of him as a lover had to come from *her*. I feel sure, if she had displayed the slightest hesitancy in this respect, declaring her fidelity towards me, then I am sure he would have respected her. But who the hell am I trying to kid! You see what I mean, one simply can't find fault with the man, not even when he takes your girl from under your nose. You see, everything he lavished upon Karen, down to the smallest degree of attention, he also lavished upon me. Had I been inclined in a certain other way, as I am sure Antonio was capable of being, well I dare say he would have seduced me too. In the end, through the brutality of the moment, the cold hard reality of truth, that the woman you love is fornicating with another man right under your nose, whether it be a complete stranger, a bellhop, or someone with impeccable taste, good looks and manners, the fact is, that hard truth is still just as painful to bear!

Antonio though was no inexperienced bellhop; he was as proficient and expert in the act of love making as he was in every other social nicety, and judging by Karen's response, this was his forte. I'm not going to torture myself about how he did it, what he said, but she in reply might well have said: 'Oh Alfons - don't, I am a different girl now. I am a good girl. And what about Julian, *he* has been so good to me?' But in Antonios' presence, with that look in his eye, her resolve would melt away like the dew on a hot summers day. Touching him, and looking up into his dark Latin eyes: 'Oh Alfons....Please - please no!' As for the act itself, in such a place, in such a Mansion, as the 'Captain's residence', in such an echoing cavernous building, where every *footfall* echoes around the gallery walls, provided that is, one is wearing shoes - in such a place everything came to ones awareness: voice, cry, sob, whisper, reverberated from wall to wall, gallery to gallery, to take their place in the past and lonely decadence of the building; an echo, a memory of a time long since departed. And so Karen and Antonio took up their place in the walls of the Mansion. It had not taken him long! And so on the night of the fourth day of our stay at the 'residence', I woke in the early hours to find Karen's bed unoccupied. At first of course I hoped, but I knew deep down what her vacant bed said! At first I buried my head beneath the sheets: 'I'll deny you, deny you - you terrible truth!'

I shivered although I was not cold. Terrible truth cannot be denied, and so I sat up in bed - and *listened.* I heard faint murmuring almost inaudible. A woman's voice, a man's deeper soothing tones. I crept to the door and opened it - a jar. I listened again; at first the sound of my own heart pounding blocked out any other noise. Gradually my senses attuned themselves and I listened, in the dead of night I listened. In the distance, in the stillness came a murmuring a regular sound of a woman's murmur, and a deeper male groaning. I went out on to the landing. Like a cat I crept. The murmuring continued - slow, regular in short bursts. I followed the sound until I was outside Maxamillian's bedroom door. The sound now I recognised as Karen's *mantra,* and then abruptly it stopped - she cried out! It began again. I stood as if all time, my own existence had ceased. I was just a vessel into which sound was poured. My hand moved to the handle of the door, and there it rested.

"Oh god," I heard her moan. To the creator she appealed again, finally calling out a long extended cry and sobbing: "*Yeah!*" repeated time and again. And then the regular mantra, began again, continuous, rhapsodic: "Hmmm-hmmm-hmmm." I pushed down on the lever of the door, at that moment she cried out some guttural noise that came from some place deep, deep within her. A groan, a wail, that came from the quick of her. It didn't sound like her at all, and yet I knew it was her, I had heard it before; it was her demon ~~crying out~~ from the deep dark seat of its abode. It sounded old, barely formed.

I felt the pressure of the handle beneath my hand, just a tiny bit more and it would have opened, but I let it go. Clutching at my stomach I staggered back to my room, that sound, ever present in my head. I got beneath the covers, still clutching at myself, after some time I heard it again, louder now, the sobbing came, louder since my ears were attuned to her noise, in the stillness that surrounded the mating couple.

At some point towards first light I heard Karen creep back into the room and slink into her bed. I lay still a while more, and then when I felt sure she was asleep, quietly got dressed and made my way as softly as a cat down the broad marble stair case to the big echoing atrium. In the courtyard I sat at a big oak table and wrote out two letters. One to Karen, the other to the *Duke*. There was very little to say as so much had already been said before. Occasionally the sound of *her*, with him played over in my head, and I shivered and clutched at myself. I sat a moment trying to gather myself, but I was aware I had to be out of the place, and far far away from the pair of them. I stood up a little unsteady.

"Can you not sleep Julian?"

I turned round slowly, supporting myself against the solid table. "How long have you been there?" I said, resenting being observed.

"Not long. You look pale."

"I'm going," I replied.

The Duke, who was wearing a long red silk dressing-gown, seemed quite unperplexed by this news.

He sighed heavily and nodding gravely: "Ah - yes but of course!"

"I think....it...is for the best," I said, feeling rather foolish. "I've written a few words, there's a letter for Karen and one for you."

"I see," replied the Duke. He frowned and this time looked genuinely upset.

"I have wronged you Monsieur. How terribly, terribly ghastly of me!"
"Well - anyway - amm! - I thought I'd get away - you know, before..."
"Before she wakes!" Put in the Duke. "He shook his head and took a step towards me. To my astonishment there were tears in his eyes. "You will of course take you revenge?" He said.
"I'm sorry! I don't understand?"

He went over to a big mahogany bureau, unlocked a drawer and placed a gun on the table in front of me. A Smith and Wesson revolver, to be exact. I looked at it and laughed nervously.
"Pick it up. It is loaded."
"I hate guns," I said.
"Use it on me." Tears were now streaming down his sallow face.
"How very mellow dramatic." I said. I looked at the gun lying there, heavy and inert. Pregnant with death.
"I have wronged you. I never meant to hurt you - never, I swear upon my mothers grave. Never!"

Antonio came towards me, his arms outstretched. It was rather disgusting, this display of emotion. I didn't trust it. I pulled away.
"It's all right Antonio," I said, having to be strong for him, when my own soul felt as though it were dying. "You are the one who can make her happy. *You* are the better man! You understood Karen the moment you met her. You are the one who can quite clearly satisfy her Earthly needs. I never could. It's all in there," I said, glancing towards the sheets of paper folded on the desk. "You'll find her demanding though - but I think you - no I am sure you will be up to the challenge. I'm sure I am leaving her in good hands."
He shook his head. "You are so wrong. So very wrong!"
"I'm tired of it," I said.

He put his hand on my shoulder, finally I let him embrace me. "You signore - you are the better man, not I!"

I just looked at him. He seemed to have regained his superior composure, but his face did look full of remorse. "I could never have the strength of courage - to be so honest with myself; to be able to walk away from a woman such as her! I do not have that courage. I have always got what I wanted, often at the expense of my own happiness - and others. But to put someone else's feeling before my own, this I have never known."

"It's my duty. It's - what I do. To look after her. It's logical that is all to leave her with you. She'll be better off with you. I've done all I can," I said, I even found myself smiling. I patted him on the shoulder. "I'm happy to leave her with you, I love her, but *it* is not enough in the end." I touched the letters which lay on the desk. Matter-of-factly I continued: "Now I've written a letter to you both, mine to you says more or less what I've just said. Well they both do actually, I just wanted to let Karen know I'm taking the launch she bought, over to Garcia's island. You remember we spoke of him. I felt I should see him. You know let him know! I thought I'd do it that way, so I could sort things out in my head. I'll leave the *Idhra* there for Karen to collect. You'll like Garcia, he is a wise old man, and a similar kind of person as yourself."

"What then will you do?"

I sighed, aware of how exhausted I was. For more than a year I had played this game, and now it was coming to an end.

"I don't know, I guess I'll get a flight from Athens back to the states - well take care of her won't you." I said, extending my hand.

"Ourevau. and bon voyage. Rest assured I will do all that is in my power to make her happy. I assure *you - all* that is in my power!

It was all I could do now to stand. Waves of nausea swept along my insides. My one need now was to be gone, gone from that place, gone from their presence. Especially hers, for I knew if I saw her I would be unable to leave.

There was nothing left for either of us to say. He asked if I wanted to wait while he woke his chauffeur but I told him I'd hitch a ride to Rhodes Town; the last thing I did was to tell him to get rid of the gun.

"yes - of course. Here you take it, and throw it in the sea."

The morning was blustery but the weather had improved over the last few days. The storm had passed, but Karen had been happy to dick around with the Duke. I knew it was inevitable that she would end up with him. The irony was she had been impatient to leave the island, in some way I guess she knew what was to come. I guess she was afraid, as we all are, of meeting our perfect match

I thought it was I who was her soul mate. It had taken me several weeks to grapple with the concept of Karen being reincarnated, Antonio seemed to have known it from the first! So, as I navigated out of the marina, I felt I had done the right thing. I had left Karen with a man of integrity, a man with means, a man who understood her needs, and what is more, was capable of supplying those needs. I had only met her spiritually, Antonio, it was my belief, met her on the Earthly plane as well as the spiritual one.

I had got less than a mile out of port when the Greek coastguard came alongside. Apparently they had been following in my wake since I had left Rhodes. I was instructed to turn back or face being boarded. They looked in no mode to be crossed, brandishing as they were, automatic weapons, so reluctantly I was forced to see the logic in returning to port. I followed them towards a designated area along the key-side. Upon securing the *Idhra* the moment I stepped on shore I was accosted by two police officers. They searched me and quickly found the gun that the Duke had given me to dispose of; the police officers looked at each other conspiratorially, as if they had just solved the crime of the century. Handcuffed, I was then lead along the key to a waiting police car. Despite my appeals I was not told anything, except I had to come with them, whereupon I was bundled into the car, and with sirens blaring driven down to police headquarters.

Still handcuffed I was lead into a smoky office. A thin moustachioed, sallow faced man sat behind a desk which was covered in a mass of paperwork. He leaned back in his chair and regarded me, smiling smugly whilst blowing out clouds of blue tobacco smoke. He picked up a cane lying on his desk and leaned forward flexing it between his hands.

In very bad English he informed me that I had been apprehended for the theft of the motor cruiser: *The Idhra,* as well as the theft and possession of an unlicensed firearm. Of course as soon as he said this I breathed I sigh of relief. It was obvious Karen and Antonio were behind the whole thing. However, the police inspector then went on to explain that I was also being held under a separate charge of the theft of what was the equivalent of several thousand dollars from the hotel Athena, which totally mystified me. Of course, I protested that I knew nothing about the theft of the money, but that Antonio Maxamilliano would testify to my innocence of the initial charge. Surprisingly the inspector looked unimpressed. He asked me about my accomplice: 'the girl,' I said, 'I knew nothing about any money or any accomplice'. I then had my handcuffs taken off by another officer and escorted down to the cells. To my horror, less than half an hour later Karen was apprehended and thrown into an adjacent cell. When I called to her a guard smashed on the bars with his truncheon.

"Julian," she called, "I'm sorry. It's all my fault! It was supposed to be a joke."

"They said something about the theft of some money from the hotel!"

"I don't know anything about it either," she said

"It must be the Texans."

"Don't worry Max will get us out."

At that point two officers came down the steps followed by the inspector, they went straight to Karen's cell; there was some sort of scuffle - I heard her cry out. The inspector stood outside the cell twiddling his moustache, in his other hand he held the cane behind his back, twitching it against his thigh. He looked towards me with a disgusting smirk on his face.

"Please don't hurt her," I begged.

He grinned and went into Karen's cell. She called out, something like: 'No! - No!' and then a stifled cry, after that I heard no more, except some strange sounds of what sounded like heavy breathing.

He and his men remained in the cell for some considerable time, when he came out he appeared agitated, his face was flushed and he mopped his brow with a handkerchief - all the time twitching his cane nervously. His men followed him out, sallow faced and grim! He anxiously glanced towards me before ascending the steps ignoring my implores to see her.

I called to Karen but there was no sound from her cell. It was several hours before any one came back, when they did they brought Karen out dragging her up the steps. It was Karen, but it didn't look like her, she didn't heed my calls, she didn't even look in my direction. It was about another hour before I was finally let out. I was marched into the inspectors office; he was sitting behind his desk, his small head poking above a pile of papers, on the top of which was an American passport. He was looking a little less smug. I demanded again to see Karen, wanting to know what they had done to her, in response he lit another

cigarette and threw my passport at me, telling me I was free to go, that the girl had been freed too. I was shown the door, and bundled out onto the street. It was dark now and I had the feeling of having been away for a very long time, although in reality it had only been a few hours. I looked about me somewhat dazed, to my relief I saw Antonio's limousine a few yards down the street. He pulled up and opened the rear door and I got in next to him. I asked again where Karen was, he was solemn faced, he gave the order to his driver to go.
"It's Karen, isn't it! What did that bastard do to her?"
Antonio laid his hand on my arm. "She is safe - now!"
"What happened? Where is she?"
Antonio's silence was enough. I wondered why I hadn't guessed it earlier, why I hadn't done anything when I was at the station!
"She is at the chateau. She is going to be all right Julian. I called a doctor, the very best on the island. She is very stubborn, she wouldn't hear of going to a hospital."
"A hospital, how bad is she?"
"It is best you see, we will soon be there. I feel very bad! what started off as a joke...It is all my fault, I should have been stronger, we should have let you go."
"It was those Texans. They would have got her any way."
"Don't worry I will fix them and the police."
Antonio touched his pocket, which contained the dead weight of the revolver.

"She is up there," said Antonio when we arrived at the residence. He looked up to her room but remained at the base of the stairs. I ran up and went straight in. It still didn't look like Karen, not the Karen I knew! She was laying in bed, a white sheet covering her and a blanket. She looked pale and gaunt, she seemed to be asleep, she turned her head and opened her eyes and smiled faintly, I noticed that there was a bruise on her jaw.
"Hello," she said, in a small voice.
'Strange,' I thought, 'It didn't even sound like her.'
Karen groaned. "The doctor gave me something to sleep - I'm sorry."
"Don't be."
"I should be asleep." She lay her head to one side. Her neck was bathed in sweat.
"I'll go. You need to rest."

"No - don't go," she said reaching out. I took her hand, it felt cold and damp."

I sat down on the edge of the bed. Karen sighed heavily and put her other hand over her stomach and grimaced.

"They sure did some *bad* stuff - *bad stuff* to your Karen. I'm sorry."

"It's OK."

Karen shifted as if uncomfortable or in pain. "It's not though, I'll never be OK.."

Karen closed her eyes and seemed to go into a deep sleep. Moments later a nurse came in and ushered me out of the room. I watched as she held up Karen's wrist to take her pulse.

When I went down Antonio was talking to the doctor.

"How did you find her Julian?"

"I left her sleeping."

"So you are the young ladies companion," said the doctor.

I looked at Antonio. "I guess so. I know her."

The doctor coughed and looked uncomfortable.

"Well," I said.

"She has lost a lot of blood. I have give her a sedative." he fidgeted nervously on his seat looking from me to Antonio. "I have done all I can - you understand, the young lady - she did not want to go to a hospital - really there is nothing more I can do! She is suffering from shock - mostly. You say you know her?"

"They are like husband and wife," put in Antonio.

"Well there may be some questions the nurse may wish to ask you. As I say there is nothing more I can do, nothing you understand!" he said, lifting his sweaty hands. "The nurse, she will see to her. Time," he said, looking at his watch and getting to his feet, "time is the best healer. Plenty of rest! - rest! To be left alone! To rest. You understand," he went on, addressing us both.

"Si - si comprende," said Antonio."

The doctor got to his feet. He looked relieved to being going, to have discharged his duty. Antonio put his arm round his shoulder and escorted him to the main entrance. When he came back he went straight to the drinks cabinet and poured me and himself two large cognacs.

"You need it Julian. You too have had a bad shock I think!"

"Yes," I replied, taking the glass in both hands.

"I'm sorry it took so long for me to get you out."

"It's all right."

"You know of course it was the Americans?"

"Yes."

"They must have bribed the hotel manager to make the false statement that the money had been stolen, they must have scared him, it took longer than I expected for him to drop the charges, but in the end he was more scared of me."

"And the Texans?"

"He said they had gone, but the man who did this, he will pay with his life. I will get them all Julian! Karen will be avenged, I Antonio Alfons de Maxamilliano swear upon my family, they will pay for what they have done to her."

"I hope so. If she dies I'll kill them myself!"

"No - if she dies you can kill me, it is I who am to blame.

"It's no good blaming each other, its fate. Karen knew this island was bad luck. She begged me not to come, but I had to put in somewhere - the storm you see, it was the storm, it was all destined!"

I suppose I should have felt more, but I was kind of numb, I guess I was in shock after all, but I should have felt something! - anger, remorse.. I tried to feel grief but it didn't work: "My poor sweet Karen," I said, "what did they do to you?"

Antonio looked away. "Why didn't I do anything? I should have done something!"

"What could be done signore! - And you, did they?.. "

"Did they beat me? - no, but I wish they had!"

"Come Julian, all this blaming - as you say it was her destiny." He chuckled. You know - she had no intention of letting you go. Oh no not *her!* When I told her you had gone she became extremely angry. What a temper!"

"Yes she has." I said, smiling.

"Most formidable....and then she became upset." Antonio swirled his cognac and regarded me shrewdly from the top of his glass. "You know signore, you are a lucky man."

"Am I? How so?"

"She loves you. si...si, she loves you very much," he said, raising his glass to his lips. There was a moments pause. "Yes Julian. I see now. She would never have stayed with me. She is a very complex person. Such depths of passion. It would take a very patient man to understand a woman like Karen. I am not that person. Sadly no - not I."

Antonio tipped his glass back again and drained its contents. He went over to the cabinet and poured himself another.

"In many ways," he continued, "Karen is a strong and proud woman...*while*, at the same time she is very much like a child. How you say, a child who loves the *candy*, always wanting, what she can't have. That is how she views sex. It is just like candy for her."

I found myself laughing at the analogy, not necessarily because I thought it was accurate. "You see, " I commented, "you do understand her."

"Perhaps because I am like her, that is all. If it were not me, it would have been some other man. There will always be some other man - you know that, don't you!"

I nodded in reply and took a gulp of my drink.

"This sex thing, it is nothing! Just so much stimulation of nerve endings - No more."

"You make it sound simple. Its more than that!"

Antonio looked into his glass and swirled the contents. "Primitive animals do it."

"Yes but we're not *primitive* - are we? Those nerve ending you mention are connected to quite a sophisticated mind - And from what I heard the other night....well!"

"What you heard!" He laughed. If I had known Antonio better I might have thought he was embarrassed.

"Are you sure *you* are not the one for her?" I said.

"Why because I can make her have the orgasm?" He laughed again. "Some men are good at Poker, some good with horses - others good with women. Those signore are my repertoire. Women are just part of my enjoyment." He took a sip of his cognac and stood the glass down. "You know," he said, waging a finger at me, "we spoke a great deal about you - yes a great deal. I hope you will not be offended by what I have to say."

"Please - go on."
"Well it is this, Karen told me.." Antonio picked up his drink, took a sip and cleared his throat. "she told me," he went on, "how you feel inferior sometimes to other men. It is so, is it not?" He raised his hand, "no Julian - it does not matter, you focus too much on the physical element." He smiled rather fiendishly, "from what she says," he said, glancing in the direction of her room, You have nothing to feel inferior over - Nothing!"
"She told you that?"
"Yes and more. The love, the devotion," he went on expansively; "the patience you have for her ways - No nothing can compare with that! How I envy you. For you it is simple. You love her, that is all that is important for you. *Her* nothing more! You don't gamble or drink or go after other women. I, unfortunately I am not perfect, I *do* gamble and drink and womanise. I am use to getting what I want. I too like the *candy.*"

I took another large gulp; some how I began to resent Antonio a little. But still *darn-it,* I couldn't bring myself to dislike the man entirely. In a way his weakness' made him even more likeable. He was fallible, like everybody else.
"You see I am use to getting what I want," he continued, "But believe me Julian if I had any understanding of the depth of feeling she has for you, the love you share, then I would not have dreamed of intervening."

His looked up at the room in which Karen lay fighting for her life, (for all we knew). His expression was one of sadness.
"And look now what my selfishness, my greed and stupid pride has done, to you, and to the fairest flower of all the field."
"Don't be so hard on yourself," I said. "Karen is a very attractive, a very desirable girl, most men can't help themselves when they are near her. I knew her well enough. I knew from the first moment you set eyes on one another that sooner or later you would be with one another like *that.* I thought I'd leave the field to the better man."

Antonio stood his drink down with a thud. "I tell you no! It was *our* actions, Karen's and mine that were selfish. You are not a *thing*....some....some object to be picked up and put down, to be ignored, to be there at some whim - as if you were devoid of all feelings. I spoke to Karen most strongly about this. 'It is most terrible what we have done,' I said. 'The gods will punish us.' I said.

Before I could make any reply, sick of gods as I was, the nurse came out of Karen's room. She and Antonio spoke a moment before showing her to one of the guest rooms.

The following day the nurse allowed me some moments alone with Karen. ~~When I went in she was sitting up in bed leafing through a fashion magazine.~~ As soon as she saw me she dropped it and hugged me with all of her old vigour.

"Oh Julian. It seems so long since I've seen you. Can you ever forgive me?"

"Of course. You are all that matters."

She looked less pale but there were dark circles around her eyes, and the bruise on her lower jaw was starting to come out. The truth wa she looked near death but her spirits were up.

"How are you?" I asked rather solemnly, as one might talk to a dying woman.

"I'll never be the same again. They've ruined me," she said, rather matter-of-factly, even though her eyes glistened with pregnant tears.

"You are strong..."

"Its no good saying I will heal. We both know I'm not going to be the same any more. Not there."

I sat in stunned silence for a moment.

"I want you to get rid of that nurse. She's very nice but I just want to be alone with you. I'm feeling better anyhow."

Her hand went beneath the sheet. I could see it moving over her stomach.

"Are you in pain?"

"It's nothing, the doctor gave me some pills. Get rid of her Julian. I want to get off this island." She said, almost in the same pleading voice, she used after her breakdown at the acropolis. "I don't like it here," she continued, in a quiet in a quiet circumspect way.

"We will leave just as soon as the doctor says its OK."

She grabbed my wrist and I was reminded of her astonishing vigour and her remarkable powers of recovery.

"I don't want to wait!" she said, through clenched teeth.

"All right, we'll go, in a couple of days."

Karen lay back, and looked towards the window, her body listless. And in tones as if the world were far away: "What is the weather like?"
"Windy - as usual, but the forecast is good. No storms."
"That's good! I wanted to get up but the nurse wouldn't let me. My bleeding has stopped. How's Antonio? Tell him he can come in and see me, he hasn't been in once to see me. We are leaving aren't we?" she said, grabbing my hand again.

I promised her we would leave, even though it seemed to me that she was in no condition to get out of bed let alone embark upon a sea voyage. It wasn't just that she looked tired, her mind seemed unfocused. Her voice sounded dreamy, as if her real essence was some other place, far, far away. It was as though the very marrow of her soul had been struck, so that she was not wholly in her body any more. Her *elan vital* had been scotched.

That temple which was her body, that divine portal which had been a seat of reverence had been smashed and the temple desecrated beyond all hope of repair.

The following day Karen dismissed the nurse in a violent tirade of Greek. The doctor advised caution, less the bleeding begin again. She was a little more tolerant of him, but only because she regarded him an imbecile.
"look you idiot, I can walk, I'm fine." she said.

He looked to me and Antonio. We just shrugged. Tutting and shaking his head he followed in the wake of the nurse. Later that same day Karen was ambling about marvellously, we were all astonished by her amazing powers of recoperation, which gave hope that perhaps the rest of her would heel one day. The follwing evening we had a kind of farewell meal. The formality of it was eased by Antonio's well stocked wine cellar. But it seemed, regardless of how much champagne Karen drank she never got any happier or sadder. She remained in a world of her own, wearing a kind of dazed expression on her face. Now that her *elan vital* had been burnt out of her marrow, there was nothing *special* about her anymore, she was just this *dizzy broad*. During the course of the evening Antonio tried to engage her in conversation several times. In response she would just smile vaguely before going back to staring at the tablecloth again, although when the Champagne was offered her glass was always there. If she did care to make some remark it seldom had any relevance to the conversation in hand. To my great amusement this *zany* Karen proved very irksome to Antonio.

"Well it was very nice meeting you Mr Max, and allowing Julian and I to stay in your wonderful big house.," she said, shaking his hand.

"You are leaving - so soon?" Antonio looked from Karen to me and back again. "But are you well enough? Tell her Julian, she must stay and get better."

"I tried," I replied, nonchalantly, "she has amazing powers of recovery. Just amazing!"

Karen put her arm around me. "Yes, I'm as tough as old boots! Julian knows what I'm like. You know don't you?"

Antonio looked visibly shaken by the news of our imminent departure.

"But you must stay. Please - a little longer!"

"Tell him Julian - Oh..." she groaned. "Tell him how this island is bad for me. My goddess is calling me. 'leave, leave this place she says!' " said Karen, wobbling on her feet. I put my arm around her to support her. "Now take me to bed, Goodnight, *arrive derci, kaliníh-ta* - or whatever Mr Max!"

She waved to him as I helped her up the stairs to her room. Alcohol always affected her in the legs and we must have each drunk at least a bottle of champagne as well as other wine.

Poor Antonio just stood there dumbfounded. I felt for him. I told him I'd join him for a night cap just as soon as I got Karen into her her bed.

As we made our way along the landing Karen whispered in my ear: "He's very proud isn't he. But don't worry Julian, I shan't marry him."

"You won't?"

"Oh no - it would be too boring. Say - aren't you going to sleep with me?" she said, as she got into bed.

"You need to rest."

"But I want you here with me, but not like that. Not the way *he* wants me. I can't I just can't be that way any more."

"You don't have to be."

Karen pulled me towards her. "You won't let them will you. He only wants my body. Did you see how he looked at me? Those eyes of his boring into me!"

I reassured her that I would never let any harm come to her. She fell back on to the pillow and in moments was in a deep sleep.

Antonio was petulant and taciturn when I told him I was unable to change her mind. He excused himself early and went to his room with a bottle of cognac. My estimations of him as a man fell quite dramatically after that. Karen was right, he was just like any other modern, who was only after what he could get.

The following morning Karen woke early, and the two of us left Rhodes.

XVI

We set out for Sapphos without Antonio. Karen had wanted him to come with us but his pride I think prevented him. In his way he was as headstrong as Karen. He said he was planning to spend Christmas at the family home on the shores of lake Lugano, while Karen and I would spend Saturnalia with Garcia.

The constant *meltemi* at the onset of the winter months meant that we were in for a lot of *chop* during our voyage from the Dodecanes to the Cyclades. And with no sign of the coastguard, I was as relieved as Karen to put *that* island finally behind us.

The *Idhra* had acquired a figurehead at her bow: seemingly impervious to the elements, motionless for most of the time, Karen sat on the foredeck staring blankly out at the frothy sea, whilst allowing the waves to splash her from head to toe. Sometimes she would spot a pod of dolphins, then she would look over to me and point at them and laugh, such moments were the only indication that she was not some sort of lifeless effigy carved out of oak. At the end of the day, or when she had had enough for a while, and she joined me at the helm, her face and hair would be encrusted with salt, where she had allowed the sea water to evaporated on her skin.

Her demon had taken a heavy physical battering, so that it had gone off yelping to lick its wounds in some crevice of her being. The result was to leave Karen's persona flat. It was curious, but I mist that *pep* in her spirit which made her so dangerous and exciting to be around.

Although Karen was lost to me for most part, occasionally she would leave her station and come over to me and put her arm about me before wandering back to her favourite spot. This simple display of affection meant more to me than anything, because it meant she cared, it meant that she wasn't so rapped up in herself not to appreciate how hard it must be for me. She was tantalising and remote as a stiff figurehead, so that when she came to me her presence was unbearable. She pressed her face against mine and I tasted her salt encrusted flesh.

"You taste all salty," I said, after kissing her.

"Like Lot's wife?"

"I doubt Lot's wife wore cut down jeans and a skimpy cashmere top."

She thrust her belly forward pressing herself against me. I grabbed her round the waist, I could feel the salt crumbling beneath my hands.

"I doubt Lot's wife was any where near as sexy as you?"

Against, her dark skin and salty complexion, her lavender eyes, were striking. She opened them wide and looked at me intently. "Are you proposing to me Julian?"

I guess I must have appeared surprised. Karen laughed.

"What if I was?"

Karen shrugged. "Say it - just say it!"

"Be my wife!"

Karen suddenly became more serious. One could almost see the clouds, like great banks of fog rolling in over her soul. She looked over my shoulder out at the cresting waves.

"I'm afraid Julian!"

"Of what?"

"I'm not meant to be happy. My days are numbered, I'd only bring you sadness."

Karen put her hand on my chest and looked up at me and smiled forlornly.

"I see you more as a brother. If we got married we would be normal. I mean, could it ever work?" she said, shaking her head.

"You would be my salty sea-lass and we would sail over the oceans together."

"Like Anthony and Cleopatra?"

"Why not!"

"Yes, and look what happened to them!"

"Yes, but they had the world at their feet."

"*They did...*" said Karen, wistfully. "Would you really want a salty sea-lass like me? After a time my skin would go all hard and horrible."

"Salt preserves things too."

"Like Lot's wife!" Karen mused. "I suppose we could get Garcia to do the ceremony - you know, as it use to be done?"

"So it's yes then?"

Karen put her finger to her mouth and turned to face the cresting white horses, she turned round and jumped in the air like an excited school girl screaming:
"Yes - yes - yes, why not!"

We hugged and kissed for a few seconds. It was like a bottle of pop that had been all shook up, there was loads of fizz for a few seconds and then it all went flat. It had been decided, it was done. She walked back to her place at the bow, her head down, her finger stuck back in her mouth. Any reservations she may have harboured soon soon faded and Karen came to look at me with renewed light in her eyes. The idea intrigued her, made her sparkle again and brought us closer to one another, but I could detect an increasing pensive air about her the closer we came to Sapphos.

Our vessel, which had taken us all around the Aegean, stood up well to the constant battering from the *meltemi;*. Karen loved the rough sea, but it was a great relief to me to finally put in at the jetty on Sapphos. The old man who had first brought me to Garcia's villa on the cart pulled by his tired old Ass, was curiously there to greet us. This time though, he shook my hand warmly. Karen informed me that he felt it would be safer if I moored the vessel on the south side of the island, where there was a sheltered cove. The long spindly jetty not being designed as a permanent mooring, especially in bad weather, offered little protection.

Karen clung to me desperately. "Oh no, I'm going to loose you before we get married, I know something dreadful will happen!"
"I'm only going a little way round the coast. I expect I'll see you in an hour or so."
"I know, but the sea! - it's so rough, and there are jagged rocks and you know what a useless swimmer you are!"
"I have my life-preserver," I called, as I began to reverse the *Idhra* out from the jetty.
"Remember Lot..," she yelled back, whilst waving frantically, "just go quickly and don't look back."

When I looked back I saw her on the cart disappearing along the dusty, windy road I had first travelled along so many months ago. I understood though, how she felt, after all we had been through one could never take things for granted. Her experiences had left her already beleaguered soul in tatters. As I watched her disappear from view I wondered to myself, 'it was a miracle she had survived as long as she had without loosing her mind, or worse even! All that was needed was another major blow and it could quite easily send her over the edge.'

It wasn't far to go, just around the other side of the island. 'I'll see you in an hour or so,' I had said. What was it, but one tiny part of a voyage that had already covered a thousand miles or more! A simple matter of navigating the rocky eastern tip to the cove which lay beyond, and shelter from the relentless wind. There is many a slip betwixt the cup and the lip! On the face of it, it seemed a simple enough matter, but the *meltemi* on the extreme eastern tip was ferocious, and I could see the jagged rocks of Sapphos' ancient coastline jutting out against the waves only a few yards from the boat. With the engines at maximum and the helm all the way over, the *Idhra* still seemed to be getting closer to the rocks. It didn't make sense - I knew where they were on the chart, and I had allowed for the strength and direction of the wind! There must have been some unfathomable mad current running beneath the waves. For what seemed like hours the *Idhra* barely made any headway at all. My heart pounded frantically, knowing that if I allowed the *Idhra* to founder in these rocky shoals, it wouldn't just be my life and that of the *Idhra* that was in jeopardy. I tied the wheel hard-over, and stepped out on to the deck, looking over the side I could see only feet away the rocky pinnacles of Sapphos' most easterly point. I could hear the murmur of Poseidon, the sucking and gurgling of the waves, as the sea bubbled around them. Through the haze of sea spray, in the distance I could see the cove, and two figures standing on the shore; I wondered if they had any notion of the battle I was engaged in with the sea, and I preyed that Karen was not there to witness the spectacle.

I went back inside and put on my life-preserver, resigned to the inevitable. When I looked again I saw that we were clear of the shoals. Having past the peninsula I brought the vessel around and headed for the cove; as if by magic the wind suddenly ceased, and the sea grew less torrid, just as the old man had said. The *Idhra* and I had come through, and only we knew just how close we came to defeat at the hands of Poseidon! We had escaped his clutches, we would never speak of it. It would remain *our secret*.

"We did it girl, my other salty sea-lass. Only the Gods will Know what a close run thing it was," I said, as I lowered the dinghy.

Garcia was at the cove to greet me with one of his male followers. And I was right, by his tone he seemed quite unaware of the tragedy that so nearly came to pass before his eyes.

"Me boy! me boy!" he said, embracing me, "you have returned. Blessed are the gods for bringing yourself and the Miss Karen safely to my island once again."

"Glad to *be* back." I said, knowing he could have no idea of just how glad I was.

He saw me looking towards the launch. "Yes, it was a close run thing was it not! Come lets us go."

As soon as Karen saw me she rushed over and hugged me, smothering me in kisses, as though I had been away at sea for many months.

"I can't believe it's you! You are safe! Oh thank the Gods, thank you *Tanit!* Oh thank you! thank you! thank you!" she said, looking skyward.

"What on Earth's wrong?"

She held her heart. "I was so afraid something would happen. I had this terrible feeling that you would be shipwrecked and that I would never see you again. I wanted to come with Garcia, but he wouldn't let me."

"I told you he would be safe," said the old man. He looked at me shrewdly. "Quite a seaman is Mr Julian! It takes a lot of guts and not a little skill to cross the eastern cape this time of year when the *meltemi* is at her full strength, but it is the only way to safe waters. Sometimes one must take a risk to get to something more worthy on the other side!"

I looked about me with some surprise. Garcia's villa complex had grown considerably in the months that Karen and I had been away - so that now one was quite justified in describing it as a town in its own right.

"You've been busy Garcia."

Garcia stretched out his arms expansively. "Yes - it grows does it not!"

Karen hung on my arm. "Come on," she said, "there's some people I want you to meet."

Karen introduced me to some girls that she use to model with in the States. Anastasia, I had already met briefly, but Casey, Tricia and Eustacia were fresh faces to me. All of them exotic - unearthly in their beauty. Together they made five Graces, and it was hard to say which one had the edge over the other. Rachine was conspicuous by her absence. I can't say I was disappointed not to see her. We learnt that she had left in order to pursue a modelling contract, but I couldn't help feeling that there was some other reason for her departure.

That evening a great feast was laid on for us. All of Karen's friends were there as was Garcia of course, and his favourite, Alisiya, who seemed to have grown even more wonderful in the nine months we had been away. She still possessed that air of absolute confidence, that air of superiority without being pretentious. The slight swell of her belly indicated that she was at least two months pregnant. The way he looked at her, and then at me and Karen, made it obvious he was very proud of the young mother to be.

Normally, I mean a normal man, with his mind full of happy thoughts of fatherhood, would not have picked up on the subtle changes that had occurred in Karen. But with Garcia there was little that was *normal*. Karen laughed a little too loud, was a little too enthusiastic, dressed a shade too provocatively. Karen was capable of being like Alisiya, that is: full of haughty pride. Not the kind of pride that issued from the other *Graces*: a pride that came instead, not from the body but from the soul. The kind of pride that comes when one know one is, 'of the elect.' He was a clever old buzzard! He sat Karen and I apart, Karen of course wanted to be with her friends; for the most part she seemed to be having a great time, but every now and again she would glance over to me, and I could tell that she was putting on a show for them all, and of course, Garcia was sure to have spotted it too.

The Graces loved Garcia's wardrobe, each one wore a different colour kimono, except for Alisiya and Karen. Alisiya had on a shimmering silver gown cut in the Classical style of Greece and Rome. Karen wore an ensemble of her own creation. Garcia loved to dress his women in wonderful bright garments, consequently there was a vast array of materials available on the island. Karen had decided upon gold. She had wrapped long lengths of a fine chiffon material around the pertinent parts of her body, and secured them with brooches set with semi-precious stones such amethyst and citrine, at strategic points on the garment. The Graces were impressed by her inventiveness. For most girls it would have been a daring thing to wear, the material being as fine and translucent as gossamer, and in certain parts barely adequate to cover the intended area, but for Karen, and for that matter her friends, who were use to the demands of modelling, it was seen as just another way-out look. But it was the kind of thing Karen did when she was least settled in herself, now she was on dry land that salty girl of the sea, who was so carefree and at one with herself and the elements, was no where to be seen. She was trying hard to be what her friends, what Garcia even, expected her to be. Provocative, ostentatious and licentious, but she didn't have me or Garcia fooled for a moment!

"Anastasia says I should get a tattoo. What do you think Julian?"

I looked disapprovingly at the girl next to her and imagined that her body was covered with them.

"I didn't think you believed in them?"

"She would be even more sexy don't you think. How about a snake along your inner thigh!" said the big sexy blond, as she put her hand on Karen's leg.

"The ancient Amazon's were renowned for their tattoos," said Garcia soberly.

"But Karen is not an Amazon," I replied.

"No, but she is as brave as one," replied Garcia, touching his cheek, in the same place where Karen's sickle shape scar lay.

"And strong too," said Anastasia, looking intently into Karen's eyes.

Karen laid her hand on Anastasia's. Both girls stared at one another, for a second I even thought they were going to kiss! "You came through all right?" she added.

Karen looked at me. "Darn toot'n - tough as old boots *that's me!*"

"You wear the mark of Tanit - no! my child," he said, brushing his cheek again with his finger.

Karen looked at Garcia full in the eyes without flinching, no one else could have! She touched the Sickle mark of Tanit that lay high up on her left cheek.

"Yes Garcia, I wear it - and with pride!" She picked up her wine glass adjusting the ever present red bandanna on her wrist. Garcia noticed *that* too, and looked ever so slightly saddened.

"Well I think Julian is right," said Casey, breaking the tension. "I think you are perfect the way you are. Having a tattoo won't make you any sexier, you are the sexiest thing imaginable already!"

Casey stroked Karen's face with her finger tips. "You are so beautiful my honey child. Such a rare beauty as yours can never be dimmed!"

Karen took Casey's hand in hers and kissed it, both girls hugging one another. "You are so sweet Casey. May be you're right, but I do feel I should do something! I'm bored with the way I am."

"Have you had your tongue pierced?" said Tricia, demonstrating the fact she had had hers done.

"The only thing I have pierced are my ears."

"Well Tricia will do anything you want," said Anastasia.

"Yeah sure man, its easy, so long as you're not afraid of a little pain."

"Yes I think I should like that. Yes do everything."

Garcia and I looked at one another. Alisiya put her hand in his and he smiled sadly.

I looked at Karen who was now on her second bottle of champagne, talking earnestly to Tricia about the various parts of her body she would like to have done.

I stood up. "Well I think I shall be going. If you can show me where I'll be staying Garcia."

"You're not running out on me again, are you Julian?" put in Karen.

"I'm tired aren't you?"

"No - you forget my powers of endurance. They come from on high."

Alisiya bent her head to Garcia's ear. He nodded and stood up. "Come, both of you, I have a surprise for you, follow me."

Garcia went over to Karen and took her hand. "The rest of you, please do stay. There is food and drink and the night is still young for those who wish it be."

"Where are you taking me Garcia?" said Karen, after he had lead us some distance from the main villa complex. I remembered the large Cypress trees on the edge of town and the track which lead up to the hill. It had been paved since since Karen and I had last been there on the first day of the *Mysteries*.

"Just follow me," said Garcia, pushing on ahead. In the distance could be heard the scampering of cloven hooves and the clanging of bells.

"My sheep - my goats!" exclaimed Karen. "Can you hear them?"

We continued to follow Garcia until we came to a clearing about half way from the summit, where there stood a small stone built house. A lantern hung over the door and a long wooden table stood beneath the portico.

"This wasn't here before!" I said, turning to the old man.

"It is for you - for you both. My gift to you," said Garcia.

Several goats came up to the house and bleated. Karen pointed to them and laughed, and then suddenly broke down in floods of tears. Garcia put his big arms around her and she began to sob inconsolably. Eventually we sat her down beneath the portico.

"My child, my child do not be despondent. We must not offend the Gods. It is a time to be happy."

Karen wiped her eyes. "I know Garcia, its just I don't deserve it. I'm horrible."

"You're not horrible," I said, sitting down next to her and putting my hand on her shoulder.

"Trust *you* to say that! I am especially horrible to you. I'm not worthy of you - of either of you."

"Come let us go inside," said Garcia.

The small stone construction was very sparsely appointed, yet every essential amenity was present for day to day living: a large table, chairs, a cabinet, a sink, and a wood burning range, on which to cook; and a small bedroom, where there was a double sized futon.

"It's wonderful Garcia," she said.

"I want you to feel safe Karen. I want you to have something that is your own, somewhere for you both to call home. If you go away it will always be here. No one else will be allowed to live here - and of course you have your friends."

"My friends? Oh yes, look Julian," said Karen, indicating a pair of goats that had wandered across the threshold.

"I think its perfect," said Karen giving Garcia a hug, "just perfect!"

"I took the liberty of having some of your things brought over," he said, indicating one of Karen's huge trunks full of her apparel.

Garcia had left the small larder stocked with food and wine. A small fire already smouldered in the hearth which Garcia pointed out should never be left to go out as it was in honour of Hestia.

"You are so kind Garcia," tears began to well up in her lovely eyes again.

Gently, he took her hand in his and lifted her chin and looked hard into her eyes. "You have been through some terrible ordeal."

Karen looked away. "I don't just mean this and this," he said, indicating her more obvious battle scars. Tears were streaming down Karen's face now.

"*Niño!* My baby-child! *niño, pobreta!* - my sweet baby-child!" Tears were streaming down the old mans face too, as he crushed Karen against his heaving bosom. I left them to it and wandered outside and talked to the goats. He came out a minute or two later, and put his big arm about my shoulder.

"Ay! - ay! - ay! It could not be easy for you either!" he said, his voice sounding hoarse.

"Did she tell you?"

"Not really - she didn't need to. I can see in her eyes she has suffered deeply. A deep wound that may never heal. A terrible thing!"

"I did all I could - honest I did!" I said.

"I believe you me boy!" he looked back at the lodge, at the flitting shadow of Karen as she began to unpack her things. "Let us pray that she has been tested all she is going to be, by her goddess!"

"There may be more to come?"

He slapped my back. "You need to be with her now. Make her as happy as you can, as happy as you can. I am going back down now. My blessings me boy!" He briefly hugged me and set off down the hill.

"I don't think at first they knew who I was, then I realised it was my sable," said Karen, coming up behind me trying to catch one of her disobedient sheep.

"They know it's you. Are you all right my sweet?"

She looked at me bemused. "Oh that!" Karen straightened up and put her brave face on, "Of course! - I was just being silly. Now go in and open a bottle of wine," she said, pushing me playfully." Turning back to her flock: "I've so missed them. I forgot all about this part of me. The Chloe half, I want to be like this all the time."

Karen sipped her wine and looked down. She smoothed the sable about her, so that her naked flesh was protected from the chill of the night air.

"Look at me!" she went on, "This thing I have on. What must you think of me? I have no business dressing like this anymore, it's all a farce!"

"I thought it was alluring."

"Its not me. Its not how I really am. How can it be!"

"I know."

Karen looked about her. "Here among the sheep and goats, among the Juniper and olives of this hillside, here I can be me."

"It's just Chloe the shepherdess speaking."

"Is it? Do you think so? Who would you rather me be, that horrible Natasha girl down there, or your sweet Chloe?"

"You know who I prefer, but I'd rather you were that happy girl in cut down jeans and a T-shirt and sneakers when we were on the boat before Rhodes - then you were happy!"

Karen's face darkened. "Yes before Rhodes. Don't you see I am fated never to be that girl again."

"I don't believe that to be so. You pushed through, you were someone other than Natasha, or Chloe, or any of the others. You were free of the demon. And if you were her once then you can be again."

"Do you really think so Julian? Do think I can be me, whatever me is?"

"Why not?"

"What should I do then, sail around the world forever as your salty sea-lass?" Karen laughed. "It wouldn't last! But living up here with my sheep and goats, it will be such good fun." Karen looked distracted and touched my hand. "I know I have been horrible to you. The thing with Antonio, and the sleeping around!"

"You think I'd be use to it by now! I thought that with Antonio you would be happier."

Karen moved close to me and looked at me squarely. "I was never going to let you go, you know that. I want you with me. Stay close to me Julian no matter what."

She took my hand and guided it beneath her fur. I felt her cool flesh and inevitably I became excited at the mere touch of her - so that I had to kiss her, to know her *that* way. Breaking off suddenly: "*You know* - I can't be like *that* with you!"

"Because of Rhodes?"

"Yes because of that."

"Is there pain?"

Karen nodded, "yes there is some. You know, I don't think I will ever be the same again - not after..." Karen looked at me sympathetically. "Do you mind so very much?"

My eyes filled with tears. "They've destroyed you haven't they?"

"Pretty much." Karen touched my face. "Come on Julian, its not like we ever came together *that* way."

"I was thinking of you."

"Oh Julian! - you're always thinking of me. Always - always so understanding. I don't deserve you and that's a fact!"

I looked into her grey eyes and I too could see the pain, could see her scotched demon reeling in its agonies, yowling and tearing at the battered walls of her temple. I thought of what she had been through, even before her recent trauma, at the hands of Pandora. In a curious dichotomy, so proud and boasting of her power, her sexual superiority over other women, and yet seemingly not valuing her own self, her dignity even, by allowing others less worthy than herself to so callously and brutally debase her, those that should have gone down on their knees and honoured her! How was it possible one such as Karen, with such strength of body and will, came to submit so easily to one so lowly? It was perplexing to witness such humiliation, it was almost as if Karen had wanted to debase herself at the hands of such a lowly wretch.

I touched her face gently in the manner Casey had, and remembering her words: "You are a honey child," I said, feeling the groove of her crescent scar.

"Please don't!" said Karen, pushing my hand away.

"Do you ever think about Pandora?" I asked tentatively.

"Oh her," Karen turned away. "She was nothing."

"Why did you let her get the upper hand?"

Karen shrugged. "Who said I let her."

"I was there remember. You were so submissive, and she was so - punishing!"

Karen looked at me demurely. "She was."

"It was horrible to see."

"Come on! you loved it really. There is no great a turn on than see two sexy girls getting it on with one another. I know you Julian, and there is a lot of the voyeur about you."

She knew me! I had to look away in shame.

"When did it happen?"

"Pandora you mean?"

"Yes, were there...many. Was it an ordeal?"

"*Enough!*" Karen laughed. "Look at you! You want to know everything - it excites you doesn't it! I'm sorry to disappoint you Julian, the truth is she died quite soon into the proceedings. I guess she fatigued herself too much the night before trying to outdo me - the stupid rabbit! To tell the truth I was glad she died when she did, because I was feeling pretty jaded myself."

I looked at her with some surprise.

"It's true! - I doubt I could have lasted - that long! She was punishing - as you say!"

"Why did you let her? - or was she stronger than you after all?"

"How dare you! Pandora was a big old thing, a dead weight over me!"

"I had a dream that night," I confessed.

"A dream! What kind of dream?"

"I saw you lying on the bed after having been with Pandora. You turned into a snake."

"Nachash!"

"Yes, and Pandora became a dragon and you both started to fight one another."

"Did I win, did Nachash win?" said Karen eagerly.

I paused a moment before replying cautiously: "Ye-s..."

"Well did she or not?"

"You - or Nachash, whatever, was badly wounded, but yes her sting killed Pandora."

Karen raised her arms up triumphantly. "*Endoxos! - endoxos!*" she called, meaning glorious in victory. (another name attributed to Taanach).

I guessed by Karen's impromptu celebrations in the face of so much pain, that she guessed there was more to my dream than I was letting on, and that she was equally happy to let sleeping serpents lie!

"They didn't know what they were dealing with," Karen sneered. "Tough as old boots that's me."

She tipped the bottle for more wine and found it empty.

"Let's have another bottle. Open another bottle of wine Julian - the goddess commands it!"
"Don't you think you've had enough!"
"I am a goddess, I can drink any amount I like." She stood up and staggered against the bench. "Woops!" I put my hand out to steady her.
Sitting back down: "I'm not drunk Julian, just a bit unsteady." ~~She looked at me,~~ and commanded: "the wine, the wine, bring more wine."
I humbly did her bidding. The wine brought out the audaciousness of Natasha, perhaps it was good for her to forget her suffering for a time. When she was like this she was exciting, mad crazy-unpredictable, and it was infectious.
"I am Better than all of them, all that crowd that damn Pamela Lloyd and those others! And Pandora, that great big old thing, thought she could better me! - me! a high priestess! I know I gave you concern at first my dear, but in the end I proved myself to be the stronger. Now she is dead the fat old whore, and I live!"
"You are the best." I said, finding myself kissing her neck and feeling her strong body. I suddenly wanted her desperately, becoming lost in my own greedy desire for her, that raged all the more because I knew deep down it was taboo.
"No Julian! No more I say! no more!" She put her hand to her brow and frowned while clutching at her self with her other hand.
"I'm so sorry," I said, touching her gently.
"Get off me Julian! It's all right, it's my fault. I forgot who I was for a second that was all! We can never be like that, it's too late Julian - too late for *that* now. Pandora has got her last laugh. Nachash has been bloodied *and* bowed!"
She sighed and knocked back the rest of her wine and poured herself some more.
"Look at you, all sad. Cheer up, have some wine, there's loads left. You can kiss me if you want," offering me her cheek.
"No; it's all right," I said, pouring myself some wine.
"I'm sorry I have hurt you Julian. All I ever do is hurt you, your poor soul must be cut to shreds too by now, how much longer do you want to impale yourself on my horrible barbs."
I picked up her hand and kissed it. "Until there is no more of me."
"My poor sweet Julian," ~~she said,~~ touching my face. ~~You suffer~~ so silently for me

and yet I am not worth a thousand of you." She held up her hand to stifle any protest. "No! - it's true." She took my hand and put it to her own lips. "I have hurt you terribly, especially over Antonio. Can you ever forgive me."

"It's how you are, there's nothing to forgive."

"Still - it was wrong, we were wrong - very wrong! under your nose like that!"

"You know I heard you with him!"

"So I understand."

"I realised then I could never make you feel like *that.* I know that Antonio and men like him have much more to give in that respect."

"No! - you're right of course, you're not like him at all!" Karen gently cuffed me round the head. "you dumb ass, you have a heck of a lot more to give!"

"I do?"

Karen nodded. "Aha! - darn toot'n!"

"In what way?" I said, out to push my luck.

Karen gave me a shrew sidelong glance. "I think you know perfectly well what I mean - Mr Julian!"

Karen got up and puled her fur tight round her and shivered. "Come on let's go on inside, it's getting cold."

"I hugged her tightly. She would never know how grateful I was for that small morsel of comfort - then again may be she did, may be she was aware that this was all she could ever give!

"Come on *buster!* let's go inside now."

Karen closed the door on the night and I stoked the fire and put some more wood on the burner. We were snug and safe in our new home. Karen stood before the fire and unwound the golden filament from her body. Ever the exhibitionist, she stretched her long body revelling in the feel of the heat of the fire on her naked skin. In the light of the burning embers, and the lamplight her torso took on a golden-red waxy effulgence. Lower down was the dark shadow of her thighs and the place of the trauma.

"Pleas don't look at me like that. Pass me my white cotton gown, the one I wore in the summer."

She slipped it over her head, picked up the folds of golden silk and threw then into the flames.

"Huh! - to think I could ever have thought of being *her* again!" She turned to me, "What do you think, now you have your shepherdess back?"

"She's beautiful."

"I saw the way you looked at me just now. I know it looks ugly!" she said, covering the damage.

"No!" I replied pointedly.

"I heard what Pandora said. How she thought I was ugly there."

"She was just jealous, why care what she said!" I moved her hand. "I think you're wondrous, like no other, wondrous."

"You do? you mean it? - the swelling and the bruising will go down in time, then I will look less ugly."

"Even so - wondrous! - marvellous! like a world within a world."

"Don't get carried away. Poor Julian, now you want me and it's too late - you're stuck with a virgin goddess from now on!"

"I can't believe it. Is it so very bad?"

"The wound lies within - very deep!"

Karen frowned as if the mere thought of it caused her pain. She put her hand beneath her gown and stroked her solar plexus.

"You'll heal. You're as tough as old boots remember!"

"Hah!..May be not so tough as you hoped I'd be!"

"Your pain is my pain,"

We held each other tight, "I do believe it is..." she whispered.

*

Every morning at breakfast the sheep and goats would join us on the veranda where we ate most of our meals, often Acastos would come along too and Karen would play the flute in accompaniment to his Panpipes. Dressed in the simple white cotton robe of a shepherdess she was gone for most of the day. She had a wonderful time with Acastos and the sheep and goats. Never had I seen her so happy as when I came upon her with her flock high up on the hill. Then there were the other times, when she was forlorn and full of sorrow. After a long day she would come back at dusk and a heaviness of heart would descend upon her. At the onset of night she would languish beneath the portico, sometimes she would pick up her flute and play a few melancholy notes, mostly she just sat without speaking, almost in a catatonic trance. For some, happiness is a hard thing to accept, perhaps her rediscovered happiness as a shepherdess was the source of her sadness? Whatever the cause, I knew that there was nothing I could do, except be there for her.

We didn't take part much in the celebrations of Saturnalia, it was a special rite that had to be marked with joy and laughter, so we made a concession in order not to offend mighty *Jove* - to this end Karen and I held our own small occasion. The goats and sheep of course were instantly invited, as was Acastos, Garcia, Alisiya and the four Graces. Garcia couldn't be there all the time as he had to officiate at the celebrations taking place in the town, but he managed to get away and spend some time with us. We all had a great time, there was lots of food and drink, and Karen seemed really happy. She had a great time pointing and laughing at the goats as they scampered and ran around one another larking about as goats do. The four Graces seemed to have a jolly time too, making fun of poor Acastos, who really didn't know what to make of them at all, but it was all in good humour. It was easy to see that they were all taken by his special beauty, and by the end of the night he had engaged in not a few amorous moments with each of them.

"He's so beautiful," I heard Eustacia say to Karen, who seemed the most taken by Acastos. "How do you manage to keep your hands off of him - or do you?"

Karen just gave her a hostile look.

"What a waste," Eustacia went on, choosing to ignore Karen's obvious displeasure, "to spend all his time with a bunch of old goats and smelly sheep."

"How dare you!" interjected Karen, "my goats and sheep are lovely!"

Eustacia put her arm around Acastos' waste. "So strong, so athletic! Karen, let me take him back with me."

"Do you think Eustacia is beautiful?" said Karen, addressing Acastos. It was easy to tell that his answer was in the affirmative: "Would you like to go with her or stay with your goats?"

Acastos' preference was as equally obvious: backing away from the delectable

Eustacia and throwing his arms around his favourite sheep. We all laughed, except Eustacia, who had never been out done by a four legged creature before.

If there was one thing Karen was passionate about, that was her flock of cloven footed ones. She would not hear a word spoken against them, even if it was rather trying for others, especially as she used to smell quite strongly of their aroma by the end of a long day on the hill. She would grab her flute and be off at first light. She loved it there among the magnolia, and mimosa, among the fig trees and olive groves, the juniper, myrtle and Jasmine; she would laugh and play there all day long - although it wasn't always play by any means, sometimes the pesky varmints would get themselves into all kinds of trouble. Once Karen ran back to the house, her arms all cut and bleeding.

"You must come, you must come, please quickly."

For a second I thought something had happened to Acastos but Karen explained that one of her favourite sheep had got itself stuck down a ravine. It was in a real fix, and difficult to get to, shrouded in thick spiky gorse, which is how Karen came to be so lacerated. In the end we had to get help from the town and winch the poor critter to safety! Normally, if they got themselves into a predicament Karen could lure them out with some of her ghostly flute playing.

For the most part, our time spent on the hill was a kind of Shangri-La existence. We were not only isolated from the outside world but also the day to day life of the town below. They were precious days, and we seemed to know that they were passing rapidly away. The innocence of those days was being lived moment by moment, we were in them, living them; we wanted to make them last forever, there was nothing to be done to stop them going - going, and they were passing - passing. It was an important time for Karen, a healing time, both physically and mentally, as well as a time of spiritual growth. She took to spending long hours in meditative prayer at the site of the temple at the summit of the mountain. Alisiya and Garcia went with her one day, and in a very private ceremony Karen was initiated into the rites of Hestia, 'the most sweet and pure'. When she came back down she was transformed. Gone were her fuzzy dreadlocks. Her long golden hair had been woven into platted chords of gold, interspersed with pieces of lavender coloured ribbon. Her face was suffused with the light of the goddess. Never had I seen her so serene, so inscrutable. She took her vows to Hestia very seriously, although during the day she was still the shepherdess Chloe, or even Callirhoe, running and playing with her flock, or playing the flute with Acastos, but when she attened to Hestia 'the sweet and pure', she put on a silk gown as light and as fine as gossamer. Her body had become a living shrine to the goddess. It had become sacrosanct, and you have no idea how tantalising such beauty is when one sees it up close and yet to know that it is out of bounds to the touch of human hand. There would be the thinnest most fragile wall of gossamer silk between me and her dark body beneath, it was asking too much of any man to resist. As a result I began to spend more and more time in the town. To be honest, I felt rather ashamed of myself. My weakness for her flesh was such that I had to put her out of sight. It is a strange thing, the more spiritual and devout Karen became, the more my own thoughts ran only to corrupting, and defiling that which she had made sacred. A weird transmutation of roles was taking place, so that I began to get an inkling into what it was like to live with a demon inside one. With such wanton feelings I felt unworthy of her; perplexed, I would look up towards the hill where I could see the light still burning in the portico. I would roam around at the foot of the mountain like a mountain-cat who could smell its mate, waiting patiently for her to come on heat. It was sickening but there we are!

Eventually Garcia had had enough of me loitering around on the fringes of the village half the night, and moved me back into a wing in his villa. During my stay there he became fully cognoscente of the trials that we had been through since leaving the island. He didn't seem at all surprised. I got the impression that he was just happy to see her in one peace.

"When I first saw her I thought to myself, 'you have had some escapades, the pair of you', her face said it all." The old man laughed, " To be honest I'm surprised she's lasted as long as she has. A nature such as hers, attracts trouble wherever she goes - she is, to put it bluntly a walking tragedy."

"A little Miss tragedy - hey!"

"Quite so. I fear that the worst is yet to come."

"Perhaps you should have let her be - let nature take its course?" I said.

"And have her waste another life. At least this way she stands a chance."

"But what if you are wrong! What if she is just a mixed up girl with a personality disorder, did you ever consider at any time you may have this whole thing wrong?"
"Never! I know I am right. But I admire your thinking Mr Julian. It is your place to keep an open mind, but you are not one of the *elect*, not yet any way. You see, I have no option - I either act or I let her soul become corrupt - become one of the indistinct ones, flitting around like a will-o'-the-wisp!"
"Like a ghost you mean?"
"Yes, a trapped soul, caught between the this world and the next. We - are subsatnce Mr Julian, we occupy space and time. If you don't believe me - you see my hand, you see my finger - you see my fist!"
Suddenly Garcia's fist was less than an inch away from my nose. He laughed uproariously at the look of shock on my face. "You get my point Mr Julian," he said, gaining control of himself, "it may not be great, but being alive is better than being one of the indistinct."

During my stay in the town I became acquainted with Eustacia. She was one of these modern girls whose face resembled a pin cushion: so many studs and rings had been driven into her flesh, which was a pity really because it was quite a lovely face. Her features were very pointed, she had a long straight nose, the bridge of which followed in one straight line from her brow. Her eyes were almond shape and as black as coals. Her mouth was wide, her lips, full, like a negress, but her skin tone, although very dark was that of a European. She was born in Algeria, her father being French and her mother a native. She had lived in several different countries: Syria, Egypt, Lebanon, finally leaving there because of the troubles and settling in France. It was there she was 'discovered' - so that now she was quite a famous model.
I found a deep solace in her companionship. Yes all right, we did sometimes do more than just talk - she was after all the most gorgeous creature I had ever come across, apart from Karen, and may be Anastasia, and Rachine, and then there was Casey - she had that special beauty too, as did Tricia, and come to think of it so did Alisiya, then there was Urania (et al).
"You know, I worry about her," said Eustacia, "she has changed so very much since I first met her in Paris."

"What was she like then?"
"A wild thing! - I worried about her then too. There were men, not nice men she hung with. There was drugs too! I did not think she would last long. I don't think she cared either, if she did or not!"
"Do you think she is mad?"
"No - she has a jinn - how you say, a bad spirit."
"A demon!"
"Ah - yes it is this that she has I think."
"You believe in what Garcia says? In all of this?"
"Yes, *av cause*. She would be dead by now if she had not met Garcia. As most probably would I."
"You?"
"Why *av'cause!* I am no saint you know! He also said I have been reincarnated. He said I was once someone very famous."
"Who were you?"
"Can't you guess."
I touched her long hand and she moved it to her body, our lips met. "Now! - now! Mr Julian." said Garcia coming upon us as we sat on the terrace. Normally we were more discrete but it's not often one discovers that one is in the presence of one of the most beautiful and famous women in history.
Garcia sat down opposite us. "I wondered how long it would take you to get your talons stuck into Mr Julian."
"It's not like that Garcia." I said, in Eustacia's defence.
Garcia laughed. "Its all right me boy, we all have desires that need to be fulfilled."
"I was telling Julian of my heritage."
Garcia nodded. "Ah - it is understandable in that case, that one might forget oneself, in the presence of such distinguished and noble descent."
Garcia threw a newspaper on to the table. "I thought you might be interested in this."
"A newspaper Garcia? Isn't that cheating," said Eustacia.
"Someone picked it up on the mainland, there is an article in you might find of interest."

Translated it ran something like this: 'A spate of firebomb attacks has hit Rhodes Town. The hotel Athena and the police station were both targeted in what is thought to be a co-ordinated attack. The hotel manager escaped with burns to his hands, no one else was seriously injured at the hotel, a police inspector was less fortunate, having been trapped in his office during the fire. He was taken to the local hospital and died later of his injuries. Local police are interested in talking to two Americans, both male, who were staying at the hotel shortly before the blaze!'

Garcia threw up his hands: "Oh - Don't look at me! I assure you I had nothing to do with it."

"It must have been Maxamillian!" I concluded.

"Well these Italians can be very resourceful when it comes to these sort of things," replied Garcia. He regarded Eustacia and myself. Eustacia took the hint and made some excuse about having to get up early.

We both turned out heads and watched her as she sautered away.

"Ah! Ay! Ay! *Qué chica! - qué guapa!*" Garcia whistled and shook his head. "Ay! Ay! Ay! *Qué trasera!* - or as you would say say - 'what a woman, what an ass' - hey, me boy!" said Garcia, slapping me on the back. "What do you think! Even better than Karen's - no!"

I looked at Garcia quizzically. "Well I certainly would not deny Eustacia has a wonderful figure - that's for sure, but I don't know if its better than Karen's!"

He chuckled to himself. "Well certainly a fascinating point of conjecture," said Garcia. Leaning across the table and continuing in more earnest tones: "I know its difficult me boy; Eustacia is a very beautiful woman, I can see that, very beautiful! one might say notoriously so, but you don't want to complicate things - not now - you get what I'm saying! - not now!" he said, shaking his head. "It wouldn't be good for any of us, including *her*, she is just as vulnerable as Karen. Don't worry me boy, if I know Karen she won't last long up there on her own. She needs this time to be alone you will know when she is ready."

The following evening I went up to the house with the excuse of collecting a few things.

"And just what do you think you're doing?"

"Oh - hi! Just packing a few things to take with me back to Garcia's," I said.

"Oh no your not," she said, picking up the hold-all and shaking it empty.

I looked at her slightly perturbed. I didn't know whether to get angry with her or just laugh.

"Don't you think you're taking this high priestess thing a bit far? You can't order me about like I'm one of your slaves."

"Can't I! I can do any damn thing I want! I'm not having you go back down there with that girl!"

"Which girl?" I said, laughing.

"You know very well who I mean. I here things up here, and a little bird told me that you have been seeing a lot of Eustacia lately. Do you have any idea who *she* is?"

"She never got round to telling me."

"She's worse than Anastasia that one."

"I got the feeling she cares about you. She has been at a loose end since the others went. She is just good company, which is more than I can say for you of late. Ever since you were initiated into the rites of Hestia..."

"Most divine and pure," interrupted Karen.

"Most divine and pure," I echoed, "ever since then you have been unbearable to live with"

"Have I!" said Karen, looking quite surprised.

"Do you have any idea what it's like to...to..."

"To what? said Karen, giving me a perfectly innocent look.

"Well look at you!"

"What's wrong with me?"

"That's the point, there is nothing wrong with you. That gown you wear!"

"I have to wear what is appropriate to the goddess. I can't go about in my old shepherdess' smock when I go to *her* - 'the most sweet and pure' ".

"But..but you you might as well be naked girl!"

"I never really thought...." said Karen, putting her finger to her mouth.

"You have no idea what it is like to see you like *that* - and knowing that I can't touch you!"

Karen took hold of my hand. "You mean like this," she said, pressing it hard to her bosom. She smiled as she put my other hand to the small of her back.

"Yes...yes," I stammered, "Like...like that."

In the morning we both woke with a sense of guilt and foreboding but when the heavens did not descend upon us we saw no reason to leave the bed at all that day. Karen's flock would have to go without their mistress, and Hestia without her priestess. Karen had returned to me just as Garcia said she would. She was physically strong again and the burdensome melancholy of her spirit had receeded too. Yet after only a few days the bad dreams began. One night Karen sat bolt upright in bed, her silken night-gown sticking to her perspiring body.

"What is it Karen? Another bad dream?

"It was her!"

"Who?"

"Her!" she repeated, opening her eyes wide, which in the dark made her resemble an owl. "*Her!*" Karen said, tilting her head, "She's calling me back. I saw this beautiful light and this voice in my head was saying: 'go forth and redeem yourself, go forth into the land of our ancestors and spread my name so that they might know the truth.' And then I saw myself as a kind of golden statue, adorned in precious jewels, and before me were thousands of people *thousands* there were! and they were all chanting the name of the goddess."

"Who? - Hestia!"

"No - not her, Tanit of course!" Karen's face looked ghostly pale in the dim light, like a phantom. She laid her hand on my arm, it felt cold and damp.

"We have to leave Julian. We have to go to Africa."

XVII

Before we began our sojourn to the northern coast of that great continent Karen came to me with words of caution and gratitude.

"I don't think I have ever really told you how much you mean to me. No, don't say anything. You've put up with me when others would have left. I know I'll never find anyone else like you. In the months ahead it's not going to get any easier."

Karen gave me the full effect of her lavender eyes. "You realise that don't you! I'll need you to stay close to me."

"I will - of course I will."

She reached out and held my hand lightly. "I know you will, that's why I thought we might as well get married."

Karen smiled at the look of elation and disbelief on my face. "That is if you still want to?" she added coyly. "I know you thought I had forgot. I had been thinking about it all along. We can get Garcia to perform the ritual in the time honoured way."

For the date of our wedding she chose that most sacred of days, that day which is said to be in honour of the Carthaginian triad, and the gift of fire from Tanit: the first day of May, the Celtic ritual feast of Beltane, which heralds the onset of spring, and is symbolic of rebirth, and generation.

For our marriage there was an entirely new look for Karen. She clearly intended it to be a 'launching point' towards another horizon of her lost being. Gone was Chloe of the flock, and the pure simple dress of a devotee of Hestia. I had never seen her so regal, so majestic. Atop of her head she wore a gold comb in the shape of an inverted crescent moon. Her hair was tightly platted over her entire head so that it resembled hundreds of lengths of golden chord. Her naked breasts were concealed under beads of amber which hung in profusion around the tower of her neck. Slung low across her hips was a girdle of solid gold from which was suspended a cascade of fine gold chain-mail, the length of which came just above her ankles. About half an inch above the coil of her navel was inserted a small gold pin which held in place a blood red ruby. For many years she had considered her body sacrosanct, but now she had allowed it to be defiled by having it skewered and pierced in every conceivable spot. In her ears she wore large golden rings, from which a length of fine gold chain ran to the corner of her mouth, where it was secured by a small gold stud. Another diamond stud was located below her lower lip, and another through her nose. Other more intimate regions of herself had also been pierced by rings or studs, such as her tongue.

A fine golden thread of chain ran from beneath her girdle towards her solar plexus, where it was linked with another gold thread that encircled her waist a few inches bellow her jewel adorned umbilicus. This meretricious ensemble was further enhanced by a bewildering array of gold bracelets and chains that adorned both her arms. Of particular note was a gift from Garcia that was of great antiquity - in the form of a thick gold band studded with rubies, which Karen wore around her left arm.

Around her ankles were golden anklets with petit golden bells which jangled every time she moved. As well as this, each of her beautifully formed toes were adorned with a golden ring. In such apparel as this she had the look of a gypsy queen or perhaps even the bride of Pharaoh!

Karen's handmaidens were Alisiya and Eustacia. They were not so ostentatiously dressed, but they were apparelled in long orange robes, their hair bedecked with garlands of the first spring flowers. On such an auspicious occasion as this I was permitted to wear the purple robe of 'king for a day', Garcia as 'Pontiff' wore a white robe with a purple sash. Flower girls lined the avenue to the old temple where the ceremony would take place, scattering petals as we proceeded along the route. Acastos, our 'ring bearer', followed at the rear, dancing and playing the Panpipes, accompanied by a number of Karen's very best friends: her favourite goats and sheep were not left out, they too were bedecked in garlands of fresh spring blooms!

And so Garcia, in the time honoured way bound our wrists, and taking a knife, opened our veins so that Karen's blood mingled with that of my own. We were now the 'two in the one', our energies or *elan vital* now joined as one. She in me and I in her; her essence ran through *my* veins and mine through *her* veins.

Our destines were now spliced into the same weave. The knot of our lives entwined, spun upon *Clotho's* spindle, our fate measured by *Lachesis,* only the action of *Atropos,* who is the epitome of the fates, for it is said that neither man nor god can avoid her, only she would part us - the Great Goddess *Necessity!*

Garcia already knew that Karen and I were as one: that is that we were 'soul mates', and I am sure Karen believed this also. It didn't matter whether we were married or not, we were tethered to one another by fate. I think Karen asked Garcia to make our bond official because she knew deep down that it was what I wanted. For me it manifested in a physical way a bond between us that I often found hard to accept. Looking at this jewel encrusted apparition standing by my side, I still found it hard to believe that it should be my fortune to know such a meracious thing as she. But now it was done, witnessed before man and God, there was no getting away from it - no going back in a pagan wedding! Only death could tear us asunder, but even then we would still be connected by some divine thread. A true bond as this, a distinctly unmodern bond as this, a true and old fashioned love as this, goes beyond the grave. Love can outlast a single life time, I truly believe this to be so! I found the whole ritual very emotional. I mean normally - *normally* it is the bride that cries, but ours after all, was a pagan wedding.

Acastos, his beautiful raven locks bedecked with lilies, handed Garcia the rings, which we then placed on our fingers. Garcia then shouted out the last of the blessings: 'in the name of Flora, Zeus and on this eve of Beltane we honour Baal-Hammon, Tanit and, Eshmun, let no man or false God put asunder these children!' After proclaiming us man and wife a great cheer went up from the gathering and the flower girls threw rose petals into the air.

At the conclusion of the ceremony the congregation went back down the hill to our little stone built house, where much revelry was to be had. At an appropriate time during the festivities Karen and I took our leave. It was a very discreet departure, there were non of the tears and hysterics as last time, this was a more mature, more composed Karen, a very meracious and focused Karen - one that was seemingly unafraid of her destiny.

Garcia and a few of the others went with us to the cove to bid us farewell. Somebody had gone to the trouble of going out to the *Idhra* and scattering her deck with flowers. Such was the immense feeling of love and outpouring of goodwill yet more joyous tears sprung from my eyes. It was Karen who had to *tell me* to 'pull myself together!'

"look aren't they beautiful," she said, thrusting a massive bouquet of white lilies and orchids in my face, "there's a note, it says 'from Garcia and Alisiya with love, may the gods protect you!' Aren't they wonderful!"

"Its wonderful Karen, I don't think I have ever been so happy," I replied, with tears streaming down my face.

Karen just laughed and gave me a playful cuff around the head. "you are silly!" she said. "Come on - hurry up," pushing me towards the cabin: "Let's be going, going, I I want to be going," she said excitedly, "I want to be out there, with just you and me and the deep sea, alone just you and me, I promise I will make you even more happy, I will show you such a time, you will never forget this night, I promise you that. I want to show you what it can be like when time converges upon a twin soul."

The demands of the *Idhra* soon focused my mind. Soon we were underway on a southerly heading. The wine dark Aegean was quickly swallowing us up, Sapphos and the other islands were now distant shores. That night, would be a special one, shared alone by Karen and I. What took place I have vowed never to divulge, but she was right, it was a time that I will never forget. For a while it was as if we stood outside of time itself. I suppose the Python spoke through our being and showed us the full potential of what it can be to be fully open to ones senses, to be fully human. To say more would be inappropriate, and perhaps unintelligible in any case, to modern ears!

It was early morning and sill dark when the lights of Alexandria came into view. The coast of Africa stretched out before us, we could go no further south than this. It was a calm and perfectly tranquil night. The stars were so crystalline bright, one felt the heavens were simply a canopy that held back the face of God. No wonder the ancient people of Egypt had tried to replicate heaven on Earth, and why their pantheon was filled with sky gods!

I poured out the wine while Karen prepared a simple super of goats cheese, olives and figs, and we sat up on deck, and watched the shimmering lights of that great city. For all the world we could have been Anthony and Cleopartra the gulf between their time and our own, I realised, was not that far apart at all. Karen lay back and looked up at the starry sky and the bright river of stars that flowed from one horizon to the other. She too I thought, must have seen those same stars when she was the high priestess of Tanit.

"I wonder if she was as beautiful as they say?" I said.

"Who?"

"Cleopatra."

"Oh yes - and more."

"More than you."

"That I leave for you to decide my dear."

Karen picked up a bunch of grapes and plucked one off the stem with her mouth. She looked at me askance waiting for the import of her words to hit me, then she threw her head back and laughed, taking another grape between her lips.

"I had no idea it was *her*," I replied.

"Don't let it worry you. Come here - by my side."

I lay next to her and viewed the heavens, content with her nearness. We lay counting meteorites until the sky began to brighten. Languidly Karen rose to her feet and surveyed the shimmering lights of the city. There was a coolness in her eye. She bid me come near her and hold her. She was shivering slightly, although the air was not cold.

"You know I trust you with my life," she said, with her eyes still fixed on the city.

"I know."

"Things may never be the same again! You know that? I don't want you to worry - that's all. There may be times when you will think you have lost me altogether, but no matter what, that part of me you know as your Karen will still be with you. Stay close!" she said, gripping my hand tightly, "I'll need you!"

I listened to the gentle lapping of the water against the hull. I had no response, but I too felt the forbodding, it lay out there in that dark continent.

"It will soon be dawn." said Karen, with a little trepidation. "Is there anything you want to ask?"

"Will it be the end?"

"Of my life you mean - this life? I don't know."

"You died somewhere out there - didn't you?"

"Yes - many times."

"Have we - you know...ever met before?"

"In another life you mean?" Karen suddenly laughed somewhat hysterically, her laughter echoing over the empty waters and on into the beyond.

"Didn't Garcia ever tell you," she said, recovering herself, " why silly - you have been with me all along, through it all - right from the very start!"

"I have!" I said, in complete dismay.

Karen hugged me tightly, "yes but I never saw you for what you were!"

"And now you have?"

"Yes at last," Karen looked up at me, "my husband, my soul mate - at last I've found you."

We berthed the *Idhra* in Alexandria's extensive Marina. Alongside some of the other streamliners moored there she looked quite humble, but we still loved her. She had brought us through many a challenge set by mighty Poseidon. Neither of us knew what lie ahead, but we both sensed that for the time being at least, the sea half of our voyage was at an end. We both said our private good-bye to her and Karen gave the blessing of Tanit. As captain (at least that's how I saw myself - even if Karen, and for that the *Idhra* herself at times thought otherwise) I insisted that I should be the last to step ashore, but Karen cheekily jumped on board again just as I had stepped off the gangplank.

"Now you have to help me down," said Karen, extending her arm. "You have to be the gentleman - you insist you are the master of this *eer* vessel," she said, putting on a silly nautical accent.

Even though Karen was as agile as a cat and could leap the few feet from the deck with ease, I laughed and took her hand.

"Come ashore then my salty sea-lass." As I said this we both realised that she had stopped being my salt sea-lass several months ago. Her whole bearing, her dress, was that of a daughter of Pharaoh. She exuded an aura of gravity of power, of one who is obeyed! Instantly I fell under this sequacious spell, from now on Karen, and Karen alone plotted our course.

The moment we set foot in that ancient country we knew we were under the sway of different gods. The land and the people exuded a different kind of energy. It was more vital, more immediate; the forces of life and death mingled that much more closely with one another. One could see in the eyes of the people an open acknowledgement that destiny ruled supreme. That the 'lot' of a mans life was already written. One could see the ghosts of past lives filtering everywhere behind their dark eyes.

We travelled first to the Pyramids of Giza, there we were befriended by a boy of about fourteen called Almoud, who was of Bedouin origin, and who offered to be our guide into the Sahara and the site of the oracle of Apollo. There we met more of these pure blooded tribes people, who immediately recognised Karen for who she was. They saw that she was unlike other western women. I could see a strange mingle of fear and respect in the way they behaved around her. More and more tribes people began to appear on camels and horseback, rendezvousing at the site of the oracle. It then became clear that word had spread among these people of our presence at the ancient site. They had all come to see the one they called *Ra - a Kull,* or the one who sees all, she was also less flatteringly know as *Unuk al hay,* meaning serpent neck, still others called her Shaula, as she was known in ancient times.

We were being transported swiftly on destinies wing. Within a matter of weeks of arriving in Egypt, Karen had already built up a following among the tribes people of the desert, numbering in the hundreds. The site of the oracle became a busy encampment for Bedouins

"Why are they coming here?" I asked our guide, Almoud.

"To see her, to se Unuk!"

"Yes but why?"

"They are waiting for her to guide them."

"Guide them where?"

"Only she who sees all, can know this."

"They won't do anything to harm her, will they?" I asked, remembering some of Karen's more unfortunate incarnations: equally disturbing was the fact that most of the desert people I saw carried a gun or a knife.

"Harm her!" He laughed, "it is not permitted to even touch her. The elders of the tribes people prophesied her coming: 'A priestess from the north with the eyes of a thousand dead in them will come among us', so it is said, 'and she will wear the mark of the crescent moon upon her face, and she shall be revered as a queen!' I tell you - no monsieur! - she could not be more safe. Why some fear even to look into her eye, those that dare, say they have never met a person who is so strongly fated, that in her eyes, are more than a thousand different people."

"Like the old man we first met here, who told her her fortune."

"Yes, he is one - but now," said Almoud, looking around at the massing tents, now there are many such as he. Soon word will spread further and then there will be such joy among my people. We have been waiting for thousands of years for her return - 'she that was great will be great again', now that she is here..." Almoud opened his hands.

"Now that she is here?"

"That is all we ask. We are here to do her biding."

And her biding was that we go east into Syria and then Lebanon, we avoided Is'ra'el, there was nothing for us there. And it was just as Almoud had said, wherever we went the tribes people were there to greet her. We lived by their hospitality, they treated Karen as though she were of royal blood. In the heart of the Syrian desert, and the home of many of the Bedouin of Syria, Karen gave her first address to the desert dwelling nomads. Hundreds came from all around, from Lebanon, and Egypt, to the ancient Assyrian city of Palmyra, to hear her speak.

The air was still and a silence passed among the gathering as she walked out in front of the temple of Baal Shamin. The only noise apart from the occasional bay of a donkey or the snorting of a camel, was the jangle of bells that came from Karen's anklets. Mahkmoud, a young Bedouin man of great stature and myself, as well as seven elders of the desert people, processed behind her to the temple. As dawn broke, the first rays of light caught her golden mantle that she wore around her neck and which covered her breasts, its rays reflected all around her face so that she was bathed in a golden halo of light. Around her hips she wore her golden girdle, and her skirt of golden mail. Her arms too were adorned with gold bracelets, from which hung numerous trinkets symbolising the Phoenician triad. The crowning glory of which was the golden comb of an inverted crescent moon, which sat atop her head, symbol of Caelestis.

It took a few moments for the momentousness of the occasion and the spectacle of her glorious presence to effect the people, but as she stood there amongst the ruins, which themselves took on a golden appearance, an almost imperceptible sigh went through the multitude. When she raised her arms out before the rising sun, this sigh became and audible gasp.

"Behold the sun, blessed is the sun."

Mahkmoud repeated her words in Arabic, and they returned the phrase *en masse.*

The sun was now fully above the limb of the Earth and shining directly into Karen's face. I could see her squinting at the light.

"Blessed is the sun, praise to her, for she has returned."

Again Mahkmoud boomed out the words in Arabic, and again they were repeated *en masse.* Karen turned to me and smiled nervously, briefly taking my hand. "What do I say?" she whispered, whilst looking blindly into the crowd.

"I don't know you're the priestess."

"But am I? I'm just a model from L.A."

"They seem fairly certain who you are. Just go with the moment," I replied.

"is anything wrong?" asked Mahkmoud of me.

"Stage fright," I answered.

There was an uneasiness among the gathering. Someone shouted something that was incomprehensible to my western ears.

"They ask oh great one, 'how shall they prey? What must they do?' "

These calls from the crowd seemed to galvanise Karen into action. She raised her hands aloft, "Pay homage to the sun when she is rising, and the moon when she is at her thinnest and she is full, and pay tribute to Tanit."

At the word Tanit there was a great raw went up from the crowd.

"Blessed be Tanit, Baal - Hammon and Eshmun,"

Mahkmoud had no need to translate, the crowd instantly fell to their knees and shouted out the names of the Carthaginian Gods! Mahkmoud then kneeled, as did the elders, feeling duty bound I I followed suit, and finally Karen herself.

There followed about five minutes of silence as the sun gathered pace and began to shine down on the gathering: the first in the name of the old gods for nearly four thousand years.

There was a wonderful sense of magic, of awe, that went around those ruins, such that the hair was standing on the back of my neck the whole time.

Eventually Karen got up, revealed by a jangling of her bells and charms, and the people raised their heads to her, but remained sitting cross-legged.

"Speak to them, divinity," prompted Mahkmoud.

"Yes, amm! - well thank you for coming, I'm sure Tanit and the others will be most gratified." Karen paused as a murmur of Tanit went through the crowd, "Blessed art Tanit!" she said. Karen coughed nervously, "I am sure you have all come a long way, as have I, or rather us, this is my husband."

I waved nervously, unsure of how my introduction would be received, but every single face was beaming with joy and good will. "I will try to be a good priestess to the Phoenician triad, and always honour her come sun up and sun down."

This part Mahkmoud translated, which seemed to gratify the people even more, for they cheered loudly. Then Karen seemed to remember something, her mood became quite serious and the crowd seemed to sense it too, it was as if we were all connected to her - all one mind!

Karen coughed, this time clearing her throat, "*I was sent forth from the power.... and I have come to those who reflect upon me, and I have been found among those who seek after me. Look after me, look upon me, you who reflect upon me, and you hearers hear me....*" Karen paused a moment in order to let Mahkmoud catch up, but it was as if the crowd already understood the import of her words, "*You who are waiting for me, take me to yourselves. Do not banish me from your sight, and do not make your voice hate me, do not be ignorant of me anywhere, be on your guard lest those who would forsake me come to thee.....*

I am the one who comes to you from the north. I am she who comes to you from out of Egypt, I am the one whose image is great in Egypt and the one who has no image among the barbarians, I am the one who has been hated everywhere and the one who is loved. For I am the wisdom of the Greeks why then have you hated me! I am the one they call life and also your death.....Blessed be Tanit, blessed be Baal - Hammon and Eshmun...."

Karen turned to Mahkmoud to indicate she had finished speaking. He was smiling broadly. He had liked her words.

Karen looked to me, rather helplessly. "It was all I could remember from that book you took from Garcia."

"Don't worry they loved it."

The elder came forward applauding and then spoke to the gathering indicating that it was time to disperse, and so they did reluctantly yet not without a final salute to Karen, the 'one who sees all,' and a final salute to the old ones.

Afterwards we returned the few miles to the west, to the Bedouin encampment and sat down with some of the elders. Mahkmoud and Almoud were there too.

"I don't know about you but I need a drink," she said, "and its no good looking at me like that Mahkmoud, if the Bedouin people are truly children of Tanit and are to embrace her ways, then you'll have to loosen up a bit when it comes to alcohol. These are new times, wine is a libation, tell the old man that. Tanit will not frown on a bottle or two of good Greek wine: cheers everybody," she said raising her glass

"Salute," said Almoud, breaking ranks with his people and joining Karen and I.

"But tell me, honestly what did you think? I know I was terrible!"

"Arkhmed says your words were poetry."

"Yes," persisted Karen, but they were taken from a Gnostic text."

"He says it does not matter, Gnostic ancient Egyptian, all speak the same, all speak the truth - the greater *g-nosis,"* said Arkhmed, using the Greek word for knowledge.

"I know it was a Gnostic text, but that particular one is very old and unusual, probably Egyptian. In the end it's all the same - the same idea." I said.

The elder nodded and pointed. "The wise one speaks, he understands." Karen smirked. "The wise one - *is he?"*

"So says Arkhmed...It is Arkhmed, isn't it." I said.

The old grey bearded man nodded and smiled.

"It's you they come to hear, you they come to see," I continued.

"She is very magnificent," said Almoud,

"Glorious like the sun....Like Tanyt herself," reiterated Mahkmoud.

For nearly a month we stayed with the Bedouin in the encampment, travelling to the ancient city of Palmyra each morning at the coming up of the sun and at its going down, and at every new moon and when the moon was at its fattest! During this period the numbers of followers of this new *tradition* swelled from a few hundred to many thousands. Karen and I seemed the only ones amazed by the share numbers, although I detected a certain uneasiness among the elders. They knew only too well what could happen if word got out to the wrong people of the Bedouins new found faith in a moon goddess. One evening just before the New Moon Karen and I were still in camp with Mahkmoud and some of the older ones when word reached us that the 'authorities' were on their way to Palmyra to break up the gathering. To begin with Karen was adamant that she would not leave 'her people', but this time she was clearly out numbered, and when Mahkmoud pointed out that he was charged with her safety, and that if any harm came to her he would have to pay with *his* life, it seemed to put an end to any further argument. In the dead of night we slopped off into the desert, about a dozen or so on camels. After we had been travelling for nearly an hour we heard the sound of gun fire in the direction from whence we had come. It was a very sombre night and no one spoke of what they heard. Just before dawn we made camp about twenty miles from the border with Lebanon. A few hours later we were joined by others from Palmyra, including Almoud. We learned what everybody was dreading, that at least twelve Bedouin had lost their lives in the night resisting the authorities.

"They would not leave," he said, "they were waiting for the return of the moon goddess, then the shooting began."

Karen looked visibly shaken. "But why? why didn't they leave?" stammered Karen. "They were doing as you bid them do, to reverence the new Moon."

"I....I did?" said Karen pressing her finger to her chest.

"Don't you think its gone on far enough? Now we have blood on our hands," I said. "Innocent people, these lovely people have died because of us!"

"Because of us! Because of me. It was me that told them to prey," raged Karen.

Almoud stood back, looking somewhat slightly dazed.

"Don't you see! - we have to go back to Alexandria."

"No! - never, not now. I've come this far, I'm not going back - Not now!"

"You can not be serious about continuing with this charade?"

"Charade! Is that what you think this is? A charade? How could you Julian!"

said Karen, screwing up her face, "if that's how you feel then go," she yelled, pointing towards the desert.

"No - not without you."

"Huh! - do you honestly think they would let you take me away from them? You wouldn't get fifty yards, why they would slit your throat, ear to ear," said Karen.

I looked at Mahkmoud, he smiled fingering his dagger and thought, 'yeah, and you would too, if not you, then one of the others!'

"These people are *my* people, where I go they follow. By the gods Julian do not stand against *me!*"

"Then have you no will of your own?"

"My will is Tanit's will, and Tanit is with them now," she said, looking over her shoulder towards the caravan. "I can't believe you Julian! You still don't really see it do you! You still think this is all some sort of game! You heard the old man, and the others, they foretold my coming."

"I didn't mean to say it was a sham."

Karen shook her head and pursed her lips. Sighing: "How could you Julian? Don't you know that I need you - especially now?"

"I guess I'm just shocked and upset - the thought of having blood on my hands...Blood being spilt in your name," I said.

"No, not in my name." Karen turned to Almoud who was still standing listening. and told him to leave along with the others, so that we were relatively alone in one corner of the camp.

"I'm as shocked and upset as you Julian, but don't you see it's out of our hands - out of my hands now!"

"Tanit - you mean?"

Karen nodded with an air of inscrutability.

"You're like all the rest," I said.

"What do you mean by that?"

"Religions! They're all the same. My god is better than your god... And then before you know it people are dying. And for what, some stupid idea?"

"What is happening here is not about religion. It is about a way of life. The Bedouin are peaceful people. We are not the aggressors here and we never were. You know as well as me that it was the Christians that persecuted us.

I should know," laughed Karen, "I died enough times at their filthy hands. We do not draw our sword, not even to defend ourselves, but the Christian priest - *he* comes with a sword hidden beneath his robe, he seeks powers and riches and Earthly glory, and if you believe anything else, then you are deluding yourself; and people have been deluding themselves over the truth concerning Christianity for far too long." Karen looked despondent, shaking her head: "no Julian, you do me a grave disservice by talking about the worship of Tanit and Christianity in the same breath."

"I never mentioned anything about Christianity!"

"When you speak of *religion* I assumed you meant established religion."

"I did, but those that attacked the camp were not Christians!"

"What difference is there between one dogmatic religion and the next!"

There followed an awkward silence. Karen stared at the desert horizon. "I feel her hair, strong in my heart," she said, clutching at her breast. When Karen turned to me there were tears streaming down her dusty face. But these were strange tears, tears I did not understand.

"Your gods have had their day. To live in this world along side Muslims - well it would be like bringing back dinosaurs and introducing them to mankind, and all the rest that goes with modern society!"

"Who are you to say we have had our day?" Karen wiped her bitter tears away. "We have had to live with new ideas before," she continued.

"Exactly," I replied, feeling slightly sorry for her. "And look what happened! The many gods were swept away by the one. Monotheism is what rules today. In truth not even that. Mammon - Mammon rules - the dollar and the yen."

Now it was her turn to look at me pityingly. "The old ways never disappeared you fool! Why else do you think we are called - *pagans!*"

"I know. *Paganus*, meaning country folk."

"When they drove us from the cities, when they smashed up our temples we simply went back to what we understood best. We knew that the Earth, the air, fire, and water, were where the spirit of man lie. We *are* for all time as eternal as the mountains and the springs which we worship, as eternal as the air we breath and the sun that warms us. This *other* god is just an invention. It will fade away. It is already nearly did in any case. It is just a *chimera*, followed by cardboard-cut-out people!"

"There is nothing of the *authentic* in any of it." Karen laughed sardonically. "If you want proof of what a charade it is, and where believing in lies takes one, then look around you Julian - at the world, and what a right muff up they've made of things! That's what happens when their is lack of reverence, lack of respect, lack of dignity, lack of cohesion, lack of trust...lack of love. Don't dare mention my gods, my ancestors in the same breath as these *heathens*, these *monotheists."* she said, pronouncing the last word as though she were a snake. We are pagan, we *love* the Earth - all of creation, *we* reverence her in a thousand different forms - Tanit, Baal-Shamin, Eshmun, or do you prefer Caelestis, or Juno, or perhaps the Greek Gods of Demeter Persephone, Hecate, or Kore, Prosepina, Ceres, of the Roman, or the Mesopotamian equivalents of Inanna, Beltis, Ishtar, or we could go to the Egyptian pantheon and site Hathor, Isis and Osiris.....and I could go on, the point is Julian, all these are but different names for the same idea, the same belief in the One Divine Life giving principle, or Divine Mind - Protennoia - The One, call it what you will!"

"Oh - so you do believe there is one over-aching principle? Shall we call it what it is.....God!"

"Oh yes - but I'm not so arrogant as to think that *I* could know of its nature. It is so far removed from ones understanding. Even the greatest philosophers, the Neoplatonist's said that the first principle was unknowable and referred to it as the 'The One'. Personally though, I think the Gnostics came closest to revealing her nature when they spoke of 'the Voice speaking softly and dwelling in the Silence', or something like that. To believe in nothingness, that is what it means to be a monotheist and how many people can do that? What paganism does is enable the fragile mind of human beings to grab hold of the idea of the awesome power and magnitude of the universe, but without leaving himself out of it. To that end paganism is about worshipping *real* things - the Sun, the Moon, the Earth - trees, flowers, insects, animals, all is imbued with mind, with God. Why make things difficult? Why make God invisible when she is everywhere?"

Karen paused a moment in reflection. When she spoke like this I loved her. She was so passionate and yet still kept her feet on the ground. She knew what she was about. One didn't get the impression, as one so often did from religious types, that they are feeding you a line. It all came down to common sense in the end, and she knew it.

"Monotheism makes it hard for the imagination; relying as it does on words, it lacks colour and depth. Words are dangerous things; they can speak the truth, but if you have power, then you can edit out the truth, just as the early Church Fathers did with the Gnostic gospel. Words themselves, which the established churches of the world conveniently rely upon, open the way for corruption, for lies, for dogma. Religion based upon 'word' alone, upon *scriptures*, leave the way open for manipulation, misinterpretation, and rearrangement, yes there is much power in words it is true, but the Sun and the Moon, Water, the Earth," said Karen, pushing her sandalled feet in the sand, "refute them if you will!" She stared at me, giving the full effect of her startling lavender eyes. "They never lie!"

She was right of course, paganism the way Karen described it, was as consistent as the Sun. It didn't require a leap of 'blind faith'! It was irrefutable - the Sun and the Moon, trees and plants, etcetera, were all there to be seen just as she said, but what it did require of one, was to see again with the eyes of a child. This is perhaps where the leap of faith was required. It is difficult not to see the Sun as a vast sphere of boiling gas, undergoing thermonuclear reaction. And perhaps that is *our* problem, for who is to say that the Sun is not a God, or at the very least, an ensouled entity. The fact of the matter is, there are more things in heaven and Earth than can be accounted for by science, and science is only another way of understanding the universe, therefore who is to say that *it* has any more validity than some other system?

Perhaps science has killed off our imagination? It forces on to us a rigid view of the universe, we therefore run the risk of missing an awful lot! And if we look at the account of where this rigid view has got mankind, then perhaps we should re-evaluate our values?

Karen looked up at the sky and put her arms about herself. She looked at me as if she were terrified.

"What is it?" I asked.

"I don't know, I feel strange - No don't I'll be all right." she said, when I went to touch her. "It's such a weird feeling. I feel as though I could fill this vast desert; that I am some how a part of it, every grain of sand every rock, every lizard and snake is part of me."

She wandered a little further away still holding herself, her arms wound tightly around herself as if she were cold, even though it was over a hundred degrees. "I think I need to be on my own for a while, tell the others not to follow," said Karen, as she walked off towards the limitless horizon. Mahkmoud came over to me and asked after her. I told him that 'as far as I knew she just wanted to be alone.'

"Ah yes! Indeed it is understandable. Do not blame yourselves for what happened."

I sat down and waited for Karen to return. She had wandered off about a hundred yards or so, a small dark shape against the white sand. She stood seemingly motionless for nearly a whole hour, then she raised her hands and faced the sun before kneeling down, and bowing her head as in deep prayer. When she returned all doubt concerning her mission had been erased, her confidence and clarity of thought comunicated itself to me, so that I no longer doubted her sanity or sense of divine purpose. Saquacouly I fell in line. I would be as the Bedouin were to her, I would follow her wherever was her wont, and her wont was that we cross over into Lebanon, the ancient heartland of the Phoenicians.

*

We travelled throughout that land, from Mount Lebanon in the north to the famous port of Tyre in the south. Wherever we went Karen was received among the local populace with a mixture of curiosity and complete indifference. A country like the Lebanon sensed a threat when it saw one, it had existed next to one for long enough, and it did not see Karen or her band of followers in this light. We were allowed to move about the country and it's ancient sites unhindered. On the whole it was a very indifferent nation, a country that wanted to get on but was held back by world politics and outright belligerence.

Karen was in raptures over this land of Lebanon. She loved the country: it's rugged mountains and the wilderness of the *Al Shouf* with its mighty cedar forests, where the air is pungent with their fragrance. Sometimes when she addressed her people she recited the Song of Solomon: 'Thy plants *are* an orchard of pomegranates, with pleasant fruits; camphire, with spikenard and saffron, calmus and cinnamon, with all trees of frankincense; myrrh and aloes, with all the chief spices:

A fountain of gardens, a well of living waters, and streams from Lebanon.' (Chapter four, Song of Solomon verses 13-15)

Yes, Karen loved the spices, and the lilies, the ripe grapes of the vineyards. She loved this land as it were her own, for it was the heartland of the Phoenicians.

Our time in Lebanon was reaching it's climax when we came to *''The Akkar'* region in the extreme north of the country. Karen addressed her growing clan at *Tell Arqa*. Standing amongst the pink granite ruins of thousands of years of civilisation, with the mountains to the north and the fertile plains to the south, it was a magical setting:

"Behold my land of the Phoenicians. The land of Baal-Hammon, Tanit and Eshmun. Behold great ones, that you are not forgotten. Behold your high Priestess. You will reverence *her* my people, and in so doing reverence the gods of our ancestors. Reverence her with ointments and unguents, spices of spikenard and sweet myrrh. Adorn her body that is without blemish, with chains of gold and precious stones, and set all about her bright lilies, and succulent fruits - the fig and the grape." Karen put out her arms in front of her. "Do these things and Tanit will smile upon you."

"We reverence thee," came the reply some speaking in English, others in Arabic and Turkoman, still others in French, Greek and other languages.

Then, quoting from the *scriptures* again, she began: "Come with me from Lebanon ...from the top of Arqa, from Shenir and Hermon, from the Lion's den, from the mountains of the Leopard,"

Looking about her from the top of the *Tell,* towards the mountains to the north and then to the fertile coastal plain to the south: "Oh Lebanon, thy beauty has ravished my heart. My memory of her high cedars and their pungent air, I will keep with me for always until I return. Blessed be this land of Lebanon, land of proud standing cedar and home of Tanit."

"Blessed be Lebanon, land of cedar," rang the reply. "Blessed be Tanit."

"Come," said Karen, addressing a small number of her intimates, "let us go down to the sea."

Attired in her regal gold mail, with amulets of gold about her wrists and neck, a gold comb of the crescent moon set in her tightly platted hair, the bells about her ankles jangling, we went with her onto the beach. Almoud watched in awe as she went down to the water. One got use to knowing when she needed space about her; it was a special sense one developed over time, she also needed her audience.

Karen faced towards the sea and stretched so that she showed off the long svelte line of her middle. "Here is good," she said, looking about the deserted beach, and she began to remove her finery, her gold comb, her gold mantle her amulets and bracelets until she was naked apart from her anklets and the ruby that adorned the shallow bowl of her umbilicus. Her body was dark from the many months we had spent under the searing flames of the Sahara sun, and the words of *The Song*, came to mind: 'I am dark but comely, for the sun hath looked upon me.'

"Take my things," she said, beckoning to Almoud, who went towards her, and on seeing her naked fell to his knees and kissed the rings on her toes.

The priestess touched his head. "Look to me," she said.

"Oh - my priestess, never have I beheld such beauty as thine!"

"You like what you see young man?"

"My eyes are not worthy of such a sight. Thy beauty confounds my mind."

"Speak of what thou see'est." (It was a recent innovation of Karen to encourage such a biblical way of speech.)

"I see thy body that is straight as the palm, thy legs, that are like two sturdy trunks of the cedar, set in sockets of gold. Thou art like a statue, wrought by some cunning craftsman, thy breasts I liken to the fruit of the ripe grape, thy neck is like a tower of ivory, and thine face is golden like the sun, thine hair like chords of gold, thine eyes shine brightly like jewels in a golden crown." Almoud paused in his recital. Words that had almost taken on the form of a prayer. 'The Song of Karen, the High Priestess'

Karen moved her hands over her body, visibly stirred by his words. "Speak of my breats again."

"Thou knowest - they are full like the ripe grape that hangeth on the vine. They are the most bounteous of all!"

Karen looked around her, as if for a moment she had forgotten her audience, so taken was she by Almoud's words. She then looked down again at the attentive youth.

"What else pleases you *habeebee?"* said Karen, thrusting her pelvis forward ostentatiously.

"Thine thighs, thine hips," murmured Almoud, in cofusion. "Thine calves, thine, feet and toes," looking up at her: "Thy whole body is like a golden temple."

Karen took the youths quivering hands and placed them on her broad hips. "Now speak of them so that all might here and know how to reverence me."

"Thine thighs are long and curved like the broad trunk of the sturdiest cedar, thy joints of thy hips are set in sockets of gold and well parted." Almoud put his lips to the ruby set in the goblet of her navel. "Thy belly is like an heap of wheat, thou art ripe, and fertile as the Earth of Lebanon!"

Karen lifted the boys face and smiled somewhat languishingly. "Alas," she said, shaking her head, "but this tree of Lebanon can bear no fruit."

"No - I do not believe it! No! - not so. It cannot be! One such as you must surely bring forth many sons?"

"Perhaps - we must see what Tanit brings." She looked at Almoud almost pityingly, for it had effected him deeply, that his priestess was as barren as the Gobi desert. She touched his face, and boldly he reached up and kissed her belly. "You are the goddess!" he said.

Karen smiled and looked up pressing his dark head against her golden loins.

"My blessings on you child of Tanit, thou knowest how to reverence a *goddess!"*

She looked at the small number that had gathered, and turned abruptly and went down to the sea.

I had witnessed the setting of a precedent that day, for previously no man had been aloud to touch her, they even frowned upon me, her husband, if I held her hand or touched her arm in front of them. But all these references to the words of Solomon and their sensuous, even erotic overtones, together with her antiquated for of speech was all part of a new, more overtly sexual priestess, and as I think back, it all began around the time she came back from her prayers alone in the desert.

Almoud watched transfixed as his high priestess walked out into the sea, her hands aloft, allowing the waves to break over her head, reciting all the time, no doubt, some song or other of Tanit. But I felt sure that it wasn't to wash off the grime of the desert, or pay homage to Tanit, or some god of the sea, that she had so thoroughly immersed herself for! All the oceans of the world could not extinguish the flames that licked between those cedar thighs, and from what I had witnessed, it was beyond any doubt now that the fire had begun to rage again, perhaps more fiercely than it ever had before!

"She is divine is she not," said Almoud, as he stood next to me watching Karen cavorting in the waves.

"Thou becomest most bold, young Almoud." I looked at him. "You know it was my wife that you were speaking to and touching like that!"

"A thousand apologies Monsieur Julian, I would never offend another man by being so familiar with his wife, but she:.." he said, putting out his arm towards the Mediterranean, "she is just a wife to you, to us she *is* the goddess! - for how can there be any greater beauty than hers?"

"True, she is special, yet I know her well enough now to be aware of her weakness."

"In my eyes I see non. How can there be any weakness in one that is divine?"

"She is like no other," I conceded. "She is supra-nature."

Almoud looked at me without speaking, a puzzled expression on his face. "She is beyond what is normal, whether one believes in her divinity or not, she is, *not natural!"* I added.

As I spoke I was thinking about the shape of her body. Her rakish form put one in the mind of a lithe animal, a cheetah perhaps, or panther. Her physique was extreme, especially in profile.

'No, she is definitely not normal', I mused.

Karen disappeared from view occasionally when she divided into a wave, only to re-emerge and look back to the shore. She waved and disappeared again. Eventually Almoud and I got undressed and went into the sea with her. She swam over to me and I tasted her salty lips. We came together beneath the surging waves. It had been a long time since we had been this way together. After having witnessed what had taken place between her and Almoud on the beach earlier, I guess she felt the need to reinforce her commitment to me as her husband and consort. To this end she was as keen as ever! Beneath the raging current that swelled and heaved around our bodies was an even stronger tow. Almoud could only look on with envy, but I knew that his manhood, which was all too evident, would not have to wait long before it too would be given as tribute to the goddess.

XVIII

From the Lebanon we crossed the border back into Syria. The intention being to follow the old caravan rout across the Egyptian Sahara on into Libya and thence to Tunisia, effectively retracing the footsteps of the Phoenicians in north Africa, whom Karen believed, the Bedouin and desert people to be direct descendent of; but for some reason Karen, swollen with pride and confidence insisted we journey into the Old City of Damascus, to pay homage to the goddess there. Arkhmed, the most outspoken of the elder tribes people pointed out that his people were not of the city. That it would be unwise to enter the old city of Damascus.

"I shall go there," said Karen, haughtily.

Arkhmed rolled his eyes, "speak to her *Hakim'a,*" he said. (Hakim'a means wise one. I don't know why he called me that, but there you are!), speak to her, tell Shaula it is unwise to go there - she will listen to you!"

I told him I would do my best, but warned that there was little hope of changing her mind once it was set. I felt pleased with myself I suppose because I was perceived as having some sort of influence over her, but Karen, now more than ever, was a law unto herself! And so the high priestess, and a small number of her people entered the Old City at the site of the Citadel. Dressed in her full golden regalia she made an offering to Tanit amongst the throngs of tourists and merchants. At some point as we were leaving the Citadel via one of the numerous narrow streets, a group of city people, including women dressed in black from head to toe, began screaming and shouting, and pointing at Karen. At some point a scuffle broke out which separated me from the rest of our number. I saw Karen looking round helplessly and then the women, about seven or eight of them, descended upon her like a great big menacing dark cloud. I remember there being a lot of shouting and people running in every direction, my only concern was to get to Karen, then somebody ran straight into me and knocked me over; eventually Almoud found me wandering the streets of the Old City, lost and dazed.

The Rape of a Goddess

When the dark cloud lifted from Karen's inert body they left it naked and torn. But for her golden mail skirts, her golden crescent comb had gone from her head, the golden chains that adorned her proud breasts had gone, as had her bracelets of gold and jewel encrusted amulets. The fine gold chain which ran from the corner of her mouth to her nose, secured by diamond studs had been ripped asunder, splitting her nose and lip. The delicate lotus of her umbilicus had been torn apart when they ripped out its ruby centre. The gold chain around her middle and other gold chains, had been torn away from their points of anchorage, doing much harm; even her anklets and golden bells had been ripped from her feet.

*

Almoud took me to a make shift camp about two miles out of the city situated near the river. He explained how his people had got her away before any of the authorities arrived on the scene. I could tell from his grave countenance that it was bad. He would only tell me that she had been cut and that her gold had been stolen. I prepared myself for the worst.

When I pulled back the flap of the tent there was an overwhelming smell of incense, never had my senses met such a cloying stink - it was sickly and overwhelming. Two women in black robes were busying themselves around Karen who lay on a straw mattress, her body covered by a piece of light muslin cloth. Every now and then the women would lift back the muslin to bathe the various wounds about her body; they also had unguents and ointments which they smeared all over her skin. I looked at one of the women who returned my gaze with a strange menace, but I do not think it was directed at me, more towards whoever it was that had committed this vile act of sacrilege.

Karen's face was hot and greasy, perhaps because she had been smeared with some kind of unguent.

I sat down on a stool next to her bed. Karen tried to push away one of the women who was dabbing her face with a moist cloth, she turned and saw me, suddenly becoming calm:

"Oh its you," she said, in a dry voice. "Come here," She reached out her hand for me to take. It seemed like an effort for her to move. Her hand was bandaged and there was blood under her fingernails.

"What happened?" I said, lamely.

"Didn't Almoud tell you?"

"Only that you were attacked by some women and that your gold had been stolen."

"Karen coughed and spat out some blood on to the floor. "The bastards - the cowards," she croaked, "They did for me good - the bastards!"

When she turned her head I could see a long deep cut on the left hand side of her cheek. She saw me looking at it and put her hand to her face.

"Is it that bad?"

One of the women admonished her harshly for touching it and quickly put more ointment over it.

"Look what they did," she said, puling back the muslin. This time it seemed her beauty had been put paid to for good by a pernicious act intent upon despoiling that which she was most proud of - but it wasn't just her breasts, her whole body had been scored by their knives; the worst injury though was a stab wound in her side, just above her hip, as well as more deep lacerations to her thighs.

"We have to get you to a hospital, and quick!"

"No Julian, I won't have that..." Karen broke off coughing, "My people will look after me."

"But you are in a bad way Karen!"

Karen tried to laugh but she was obviously in a lot of pain. "Idiot! Don't you think I already know that - look at me, I'm cut to ribbon's!"

I looked on gravely as a dark red stain began to grow on the light muslin cloth around her lower body.

"She will not die," said one of the women, as if reading my mind.

"You see! - my people know what they are doing." Karen replied, trying to smile at the woman.

They took off the bandage around her thigh, it was saturated in blood. The fresh one they applied was made from the same muslin type cloth that covered her body.

"And tie it tighter this time!" insisted Karen.

"My god you're bleeding badly!"

"Don't fret Julian they know what they are doing."

I looked at her astonished at the faith she had in these people. "But you could bleed to death! Please let me take you to a hospital!"

Karen tried to lean forward but fell back. "I said no Julian! They know what they are doing I tell you! They weave herbs into the linen that prevent infection, and put on an ointment that helps clot the blood."

I stayed with her for as long as I was allowed, the smell of the place though, together with the site of so much blood made me feel nauseous. The incense: spikenard and myrrh, frankincense, aloes, saffron, camphor, the spices of Lebanon must have had some sort of combined narcotic effect. Most of the time Karen slept, but when she came round her speech was slurred, her eyes barely opened.

"You're still here?" she said.

"Of course I am."

"Where were you? You said you'd never leave me."

"I'm sorry. I got separated from the rest, there was so much confusion that I lost site of you. The Bedouin whisked you away so fast..."

"Don't leave me again."

Despite her trauma I could still feel Karen's strength travel through her hand and into my own. I lifted it and kissed it, my tears falling on her bloodstained bandage. "I'll never leave you!" I said.

One of the women mopped Karen's feverish brow. She glanced at me, looking away quickly lest I saw the fear in her eyes.

"She should rest, come back in the morning," said the woman.

When I turned to Karen she was already unconscious again.

Further appeals to the elders of the tribes to have Karen moved to a proper hospital went unheeded. A litter was prepared for her, their intention being to transport her to an oasis further south, deep in the desert. The fact that Karen might easily die on this journey did not seem to unduly perturb these people. It was only testimony to Karen's great reserves of strength that she did not! But by the time we arrived at the safety of the oasis, Karen was deep in fever and delirious. The women who tended to her, who had previously appeared confident and in control, now busied themselves around her with a hastened air of concern, their brows deeply furrowed.

"She's going to die isn't she?" I said, as I watched them change her bandages and anoint her body with more foul smelling potions. They ignored me and carried on with their work, muttering under their breath.

Mahkmoud the old man came into the tent and put his arm on my shoulder. I turned to him and asked him the same question.

"Her life hangs in the balance. It is gods will. If the fever breaks..."

"And if it doesn't?"

The old man looked skywards and raised his hands. He put his hand gently on my shoulder before leaving me alone with my concern.

Karen's people, the Bedouin, were an extremely fatalistic lot: 'What would be would be.' Often their blasé attitude was only an acknowledgement of the limitations of mankind. There was nothing that could be done to save Karen's life, apart from doing ones utmost, other than that the fate of her life was already decided, as indeed all our lives were.

'It is written', the elders would say; even Karen's coming to them was 'written', so much for the fickle hand of fate, she provided little comfort!

Doing ones utmost also meant trying to appease the gods. To this end a cockerel was sacrificed to *Asclepius,* god of healing, each morning at the break of dawn. Also goats and sheep were sacrificed on a regular basis to *Tanit*. We all preyed hard to *Tanit*. Even I preyed, invoking the name of the goddess. The truth was that it was Karen's own haughty pride, and *Tanit* herself, which had brought her to the very threshold of death. Every time Karen had tried to become the goddess something dreadful befell her, it was what is know to the ancients as *hubris*.

On the fifth day after arriving at the oasis Karen's fever broke. There followed much rejoicing and those that had been closest to her and nursed her, those that said, 'she would not die,' now breathed a huge sigh of relief and went about with a bit more of a spring in their step.

Although Karen was out of Hades grasp, at least for the moment, her tussle with the underworld had left her very weak; the truth was she would never be the same again. I knew it, Almoud knew it, they all did, even Karen herself, but no one would admit it openly by voicing concern. She found it hard to walk very far before her limbs gave way. The wound in her side had still not fully healed it was as if her vitality, her life essence, was steadily leaking away through this deep ugly gash, the presence of which brought to mind the disconcerting dream of Nachas, and the deep gash in *her* side - wide enough to insert a hand!

Far from being crestfallen though, or perhaps because she wished to mask her real fears, Karen's attitude was boastful and uncompromising, as I found out when I challenged her on her judgement.

"As high priestess of Tanit I have every right to worship the goddess wherever it pleases me, in her land. I have my own duty to perform as high priestess, just as they have a duty to serve me, as you have your duty as my husband to protect me, and Karen expects everybody to perform their duty as according to the gods."

"So you seriously intend to go on, even after what has happened?" I said, incredulous.

"A'v course, just as soon as I am well enough. There *is* no going back, you must understand that. Nothing must get in the way of my mission."

"And just what is that?"

"Apart from re-establishing the name of the goddess in her homeland, I do not know - she will let me know what else she requires of me."

"But look what your *mission* - your *Tanit* has done to you!" I said, looking at the new scar on her face which was much longer and deeper, than the somewhat aesthetic crescent mark of Tanit.

Karen put her hand to her cheek self-consciously. "It is nothing, it will heal in time."

But it was a deep cut, right to the very quick. We both knew it would never go away.

"And the rest of your beautiful body..?" I shook my head, too assailed by grief to go on. Karen lingered in front of me looking uncomfortable. I knew deep down that she too was grieving for the loss of her perfection, especially her breasts that had been so grievously assailed. Unlike those once splendid orbs, her spirit seemed less crest fallen.

"Either way - so what if they have destroyed my beauty! I hated it anyway, it was such a burden. Now I am completely immersed in my destiny; there can be no going back. I am like Analisa, no one wanted her after her accident, just as they will not want me either, looking as I do. Don't look so worried Julian, my body is nothing, it is just a vessel for the worship of the goddess. You really must try to embrace the true spirit of sacrifice!"

"I don't believe you Karen! I know what your figure - your looks mean to you. I don't believe you can accept it so easily! You were so proud of your lovely breasts - my god I thought you would never sacrifice them?"

Karen looked at me venomously before limping off with another wound to her already viscerated self.

A few days after this confrontation Karen insisted the caravan pushed on into the desert. Before we left, to honour the return of their priestess, a fine new shining gold mantle was wrought, to be worn around her shoulders and over her chest. (No priestess of Tanit should cover her upper body by a woven garment, the function though of this solid gold collar was also to hide the horror of her injuries). The elders also presented her with a beautiful large pink sapphire, to be worn in her navel.

In order to conceal the truth from her followers of the extent of her injuries, Karen was presented with the golden mantle in a private ceremony attended by a small number of her closest acolytes. Layer upon layer of tightly wound muslin cloth further disguised the havoc that had been wreaked upon those once perfect orbs. Another bandage was wound around her hips and waist at the site of her other major wound, so that the overall effect was rather that of a partly clad Egyptian mummy, although to a large extent the bandaging to her lower body was covered by her long golden chain-linked tresses.

Coming out of the tent, the glory of the sun burst upon the solid gold breastplate, dazzling her audience.

Mahkmoud, and some of her other close followers were waiting outside. I looked at Mahkmoud, his eyes were wide and full of lust after her. I could see how desperate he was to touch her jewels - to mount her gold.

"See how high the gold sits upon her glorious breasts. Ah! - but surely she is still perfect. Tell me Julian, are her breasts still like the bursting ripe fruit of the vine?"

"Yes bursting," I said, and then mumbled: "bursting all right! - like overripe fruit gone bad!"

I turned to Karen who was looking a little dazed, perhaps from coming out suddenly into the light, but it was also her first big audience since the attack. I took her hand and gripped it tightly.

"How do I look?" she asked, shielding her scarred face with her raised hand.

I took hold of it gently and brought it down by her side.

"You look magnificent my love! Don't worry you can hardly see it."

Karen smiled vaguely, "You still think I am...magnificent?" I noticed she was trembling slightly.

I lifted her arm. "Behold, " I said, to the gathering that had come to witness her new inauguration, "the priestess of Tanit. The most beautiful of all! - Hail Tanit!"

"Hail Tanit! - Hail Tanit! - Hail Tanit, echoed the reply from her followers.

Their priestess was back among them, or so it seemed, the excitement of the event quickly exhausted her, forcing her to retire early to her tent.

Although Karen tried hard, it became obvious that she was finding the desert conditions arduous. Increasingly she had to rely on being carried on her litter which had been fitted with a canopy, offering some respite from the onslaught of the sun. The women of the desert administered to Karen's needs solicitously, plying her with fresh unguents and potions, constantly weary that she may undergo a relapse. After only a few days into the journey it became evident that their fears were well founded, as Karen fell back more and more into fever and delirium.

Because of Karen's deterioration we made slow progress through the Libyan Sahara. At night I would stay with her; even though the smell of the incense, as well as the ointments that were plastered over her wounds was stifling, but they only masked another more effluvial smell that came from the body of Karen itself. The air of death was all about her. To remain in her presence for any length of time made me feel ill. The smell of her, the look of her, resembled more an embalmed cadaver than a living person. Her skin gradually took on a permanent waxy appearance. Her bright eyes became dull and yellow, and would dart about in their sockets, in a crazy erratic manner, as she chased down winged delusory beasts.

It was eventually decided that a final push to the coast, where the air would be fresher, was Karen's only hope. We arrived at *Leptis Magna* towards dusk and set up camp close by the ruins of the ancient city. Later that night sacrifice was made to the gods *Asclepius* and *Apollo*. Whether it was the act of the gods, or the sea air, or the fates themselves, by morning Karen was sitting up and asking for water. We remained camped along the shore near the ancient city until Karen had regained her strength, but the months in the desert, and the ravages of the attack, had taken their toll. But even the most caustic ravages of illness cannot undermine a truly robust physique, to this end her towers of cedar retained most of their former glory, as for the rest of her though, as skeletal as she already was, her upper body had become cadaverous and vulnerable looking; to the extent that the extreme narrowness of her waist prompted one to imagine one could, without too much effort, snap her in half. Even her strong neck gave way to a somewhat lantern-jaw appearance; but for all of that, her jaundiced pallor had gone and her verve for life, for nature had returned. Everyday she went to bathe in the warm waters of the Mediterranean. It was as if, by each immersion into the salty environment, her body was slowly being healed. It was the sea that proved to be her protector. It was on or near the sea that she felt most at ease. Little by little Karen began to approach something like her former level of fitness - before the attack. Even so, she was reluctant to go naked again in public, the bandages remained in place! Even when we were alone together and she would undo them before retiring at the end of the day, she wrapped herself in a fine translucent crepe material, and always sought the shadows. The truth though was only realised when my hand would light upon her in the darkness, and I would confront all too readily the hardness of her ribs, where once there had been buoyant resilience! But we did not speak of it. She was still magnificent, the memory of her in a thousand different poses, and at that last occasion in Lebanon, when Karen went naked down to the sea, would remain mine and their ever lasting memory of her.

Our nomadic way of life also ended at *Leptis Magna*, or rather at the town of Al-Khoms, situated about two miles east. Karen and I moved into a small villa on the coast not far from the town. Almoud, as well as Mahkmoud and Arkhmed, were our most regular visitors, the rest of the caravan had dispersed into the desert, but many of her more devout followers remained encamped not far from the ancient ruins. Karen would travel there at least two or three time a week, where she would ask her people to supplicate themselves before the goddess. The biggest celebration held was at the villa itself, where a shrine was set up to Tanit; and on the eve of Beltane, which coincided with the eve of our first wedding anniversary, a great feast was held. Fires were lit in honour of the goddess around which much revelry, much cavorting with the high priestess took place: Karen dancing and swaying her body licentiously, her oiled skin shimmering in the yellow light, like gold. For three days the celebrations lasted. It demonstrated that she still had stamina, it also showed that Karen still had every intention of living up to her duties as high priestess, in the style of the Sumerians and Phoenicians.

We had been travelling in North Africa for a whole year. Despite Karen's renewed vigour, the events of the past had left their mark in other ways too, such as the natural scars that come from having had to endure more than perhaps the soul can bear. As a result, deep lines ran from the corners of her mouth to her nose, there was also a certain hardness to her features, not helped by the deep scar on her cheek. The overall impression was that she had aged not one year but five! After being humiliated in the manner that she had been, having to endure long physical suffering, it is perhaps asking too much, even of a person of Karen's stamina, not to come through such an ordeal unscathed in spirit as well as body.

Part of this suffering manifested itself in a lack of tolerance of others. She had never been an impolite girl, she had always been considerate, even though she was inwardly self-centred - what model isn't, but now it seemed she had no time for the sensibilities of others, in any way whatsoever! She would become impatient and fly into rages, she would kick her Bedouin servants around, treating them as mere slaves. What *Karen* wanted was all that mattered to *Karen*, and of course when this came to being lascivious, she did what she liked, with whom she liked, regardless of how I felt about it! I had long suspected that she had had Almoud in her sites, and would have bedded him long ago had she not been struck down in her path in Damascus. We hadn't been at the villa more than a month before she had him on her litter, after him it was Mahkmoud, after that the list becomes too long. When she went to the temple in the old city, she would find some young thing to take into the desert, only returning home at first light, like an alley cat with the musky smell of her nocturnal activities on her. But I was married to a high priestess of a fertility goddess, therefore it was her duty to select good looking fit young men in order to share the *mysteries* of the goddess - and in this regard Karen took her duties very seriously. Eventually another larger more ostentatious villa was purchased further along the coast very near the ancient Phoenician city of *Sabratha* - in order that her 'supplicatory activities' could be conducted in greater privacy and comfort. To this end a special *shrine room* was set aside in one wing of the villa. It was a common site to see boys as young as fifteen or sixteen, waiting nervously in the huge marble reception room, eventually the doors would open to the sanctum and they would be received inside, where the delights of the goddess would be revealed.

Despite our more sedentary way of life the people of the *caravan* continued to form the core of her following. They would come out of the desert to go among the ruins in order to hear her words. They would send their sons to pay honour to the goddess. They heaped jewels and spices and slaves upon her in the hope that the goddess would protect them and make them fruitful. There were others who also wanted *favour* from the goddess. A shadowy group of individuals with money and power, who enabled us to live in the opulence that we had become use to. This select band of people were as different from the simple down to Earth people of the desert, as it was possible to be. Their concerns were with the Earth too, but not how they could live with it, rather what they could get out of it. Their interests were in oil and diamonds, and other subterranean activities. It is perhaps not surprising then, that their interests should include the unconventional and the exotic.

Karen's previous notoriety in the realm of modelling, together with her new associations with the rich and powerful, meant that the 'big eye' of the media fell upon her once again. Offers from international periodicals as well newspapers and television came flooding in. At this stage Karen was still quite devout in her following of Tanit, and saw in such media attention a certain level of betrayal of the true spirit of paganism. These hungry eyes were firmly embedded in the modern world, therefore they were not of her belief, therefore they were incapable of understanding the spirit in which Karen came to these beliefs. They would, in short, attempt to appropriate the goddess - down grade her, sully her in their sick narrow confining, conforming way, the way of the *modern!*

Given Karen's love of the 'eye', it must have been very tough for her not to accept these lucrative and rewarding offers. Eventually these magazines and newspapers did articles on her any way, based on heresy and what they could rake together, and they found plenty of juicy stuff! Her previous life as a topless model, her appearances in numerous pornographic films, right up to her associations with Garcia, and her introduction to paganism, were all grist for their mill.

The old adage that time is a great healer must be true, because, as fate would have it, as Karen was put more and more under the media spotlight she also began to grow more bold! The old women who had attended to her wounds when they were young, and had continued to embalm them over the months that followed must have mixed their potions well, for much of Karen's damaged flesh began to heal without leaving a lasting blemish - although the deep furrow on her face persisted, as did the ugly wound in her side, which continued to be a cause for concern - apart from these detractions, Karen became more confident of her beauty and began to bathe naked, and sunbathe topless on her private beech. She didn't mind showing off her body to me and her lovers but still held back from parading it around in front of the masses. If she went before them she would always put on her golden mantle, or else drape long strings of amber or pearls around her neck. To this end the paparazzi found her found her an extremely easy target to photograph: Karen was anything but shy and retiring when it came to the camera - so artistic and sharp were these images it is hard to imagine they were made without her being aware of the photographers presence the whole time - not least because, not one image was from her bad side. Even so she was discrete, not because of bashfulness, she knew she could not afford her public to see that her crowning glory, her wonderful breasts were now passé, therefore, even when she was topless she would cover them with her long golden braids or else a self-conscious arm which also had the effect of bunching them together, making them appear fuller than they were. In the end though the paparazzi got the shot they were after, showing her topless on the beech in front of the villa with the caption: 'The true Karen Stockwell, better known as 'Natasha', former glamour model and star of porn!' It was uncompromising and unflattering in that it depicted the indisputable physical lassitude that her body had undergone. This of course was only damaging to Karen's ego, myself and her close circle knew for a long time that naked, her look was - *effete!* What was more damaging was the claims made in the accompanying long winded piece which talked about her sexual promiscuity, her inexhaustible appetite for young boys, and claims of drug induced orgies, of blood sacrifices, bestiality, and black magic.

Although she had refrained from dealing with the press directly, Karen felt that these latest allegations needed to be addressed. The claims of sexual orgies, of promiscuity and the like, were of course well founded, what outraged her more than anything, was that most of the article was devoted to running-down her modelling career, terming her as: 'a 'failure, who had tried to punch outside her weight,' and who, 'lacked the necessary temperament as well as the look to become one of the greats!': ridiculing her for comparing herself with the likes of top model Pamela Lloyd and the classy Liza Redcliffe - describing her as an 'overreacher,' brandishing her as, 'arrogant and naive!'

Yes, her arch nemesis Pamela LLoyd and the string of names associated with the top line glamour models of the world, had once more been paraded before her, and once more 'Natasha' had been compared in negative terms.

"How dare they print this goddamn rubbish about me, I'll show them!" raged Karen. To this end Karen agreed to an exclusive interview and film shoot with the internationally acclaimed editorial: 'Scenes of Life Magazine'. Although Karen wanted to set the record straight over who was the best model in the world, she also wanted to genuinely educate her readers about the true nature of the pagan tradition she followed. However, it proved to be too late, these latest allegations, as well as more photo releases of Karen in compromising poses, came to the attention of the Libyan authorities, giving them no alternative but to insist that Karen and her entourage leave the country at their earliest opportunity.

Before leaving, Karen went ahead with the film shoot which took place in the perfect setting, among the ruins of *Sabratha*. It was the first time I had seen her at her 'work', she had a natural love of the lens, she saw it as a great big eye - the eye of the world! - the exhibitionist that she was meant she loved every second of it. She wore her gold mantle and other adornments, a gold sari slung low across her hips, and her master embalmers doubled as make-up artists. Her eyes were blacked with eye shadow in the style of an Egyptian queen - a la *Karenhappuch,* her skin was greased with a bronze pigment, so that her scar was almost invisible. Her mark of Tanit - rather than disguise *that,* was highlighted with silver paint. She looked as if she had just come from three hundred BCE! Amongst the ancient architecture she looked every inch the priestess of Tanit. The shoot went extremely well; the photographer obviously knew his way around a pro like Karen. It was inevitable, I suppose, that eventually Karen would dispense with her formal attire. Not that it mattered since she was being thrown out of the country for indecency in any case. A concession to art, as she claimed it, if not decency, were the layers of amber necklaces which she draped around her neck, which partially obscured her naked bosom.

I'm sure that Karen would have dispensed with the beads and the see-through sari, if she thought she could get away with it. The thing is, I thought the shoot was far more erotic for what was not revealed. The fact that Karen played down the whole thing, indicated I think, that she was secretly impressed, and that given the right props she still had what it took to cut it as a top model. The kid had class, if she did but realise it - so frustrating but there we are, we wouldn't be where we were now, if she could have kept a lid on it!

The fact that we were being forced to leave Libya, was not in itself a great inconvenience, since Tunisia was Karen's ultimate objective. A property on the *Cap Bon* peninsula had in any case, already been secured for us. Karen's wealth at this stage was such that she could afford to live anywhere she wanted, but Tunisia represented something more than just a convenient - hop skip, it was something far more than just another country, it was the climax of our sojourn in North Africa, for it was, as the preamble to her interview with 'Scenes of Life Magazine', described: 'the heartland of the Phoenicians and the home of Tanit worship!'

The Phoenicians were a sea fearing people who rose out of Mesopotamia some time around two thousand BCE, (before the common era) and settled along the fertile coastal strip by the Mediterranean, from the Euphrates in the north to Egypt and the Sinai in the south. The heartland of the Phoenicians was in the Lebanon, although as a people they were not territorial by nature, rather it was a shared world view, as well as blood ties which bound them together. By the first millennium BCE a number of city states had been established along the North coast of Africa from the Sinai in the east, to what is modern day Morocco in the west. Their reach however went much further than this, with trading networks with Spain and as far north as Britain.

Eventually their homelands in the east were systematically overrun by Egyptians and eventually the Greeks, under Alexander. But it was in the west, principally modern day Tunisia that the Phoenicians flourished, the crowning glory of which was Carthage, which was established in 814 BCE. This prosperity and expansion brought by trade meant that Carthage was on a collision course with another fast developing people to the north. The three punic wars with Rome finally saw Carthage sacked in 146 BCE. and effectively marked the end of the Phoenicians. That is, until Karen's re-establishment of Tanit worship. Her entry into the lands of Carthage would be the first footfall of a priestess of Tanit for nearly three thousand years.

*

A larger and even more opulent residence was made available to Karen and her growing entourage at *kerkouane* on the *Cap Bon.* A truly remarkable and dramatic setting. A series of whitewashed buildings perched high up on the rugged cliff top of the cape, with the remains of the ancient Phoenician city on one side and the sparkling aquamarine of the Mediterranean on the other. In this almost fortified location Karen made *Kerkouane* her new Carthage, only about forty miles from the real Carthage, situated across the gulf of Tunis.

When 'Scenes of Life Magazine' released their edition with Karen on the front cover it sparked a new media frenzy, the like of which even Karen had never experienced, but our position on the *Cap Bon* made her almost inaccessible to their prying eyes. The only visitors to the retreat arrived in Limousines, who deposited their gaily dressed occupants, surrounded by dark suited body guards. These were the shadowy people I spoke of before. Who they were, what their connections were, it is not my place to say, but they had power and they had wealth, and for some reason they wished to pour some of this wealth our way, or principally Karen's way, since it was her they came to see. They also brought women with them, all of them exotic looking: Japanese, and other Orientals, some as audaciously dressed as Karen herself. They were all magnificent looking creatures. I was even more surprised to find that any of them were available to me, at any time day or night, to do with as was my wont. They insisted that I bathe, so they made up the hottest bathtub! I imagine it was how a lobster must feel! Afterwards they would give me the most wonderful massage imaginable. They were all highly trained, highly expert Geishas, who were expected to fulfil my every whim. I will go no further than to say that this they did with mind-blowing conviction! It would be unfair to compare Karen with them, obviously, outwardly she was stronger, being a lusty Celt or Anglo-Saxon, or whatever her genetic origins may have been, but for all her notorious sexual exploits and superlative expertise, I think in any one of those lithe little creatures she would have met her match! They were so distracting that whilst in their presence I completely forgot about Karen altogether. I can tell you, they were a welcome distraction from the haughtiness and overbearing temperament of Karen. Of course, while I availed myself of the delights that these nymphs from Nipon, so assiduously showered upon me, Karen was herself entertaining their shadowy masters in her own special - Anglo-Saxon / Phoenician way!

We had first set foot in Egypt a little more than a year and a half ago, and it hardly seemed credible that so much dramatic change could undergo one person and in such a relatively short space of time. Karen's followers numbered in their thousands, perhaps hundreds of thousands, if one included all the people from different parts of the world who had heard of her, and who wanted to know more about her and the goddess she worshipped. To those that were devout, to those first people of the desert, the Bedouin and later the Berbers and Tuareg, who embraced Karen as one of their own, she was treated - nay, not just as if she were of royal blood, but as the living breathing presence of the divinity - Tanit herself! Then of course there were the others who represented a growing voice of dissension that eventually manifested itself in the form of abuse: threats of physical harm, even death. Karen responded by giving them scant credence, even deriding them as, 'worthless fools', and 'jealous idiots'. It was as though her attack had never happened - so brazen was she! I think she even encouraged it by making outlandish and provocative statements, such as: 'the way of Tanit will sweep away all falsehood in the world and then there will be no more war and no more suffering!' Where had I heard that before? When the question was put to her by journalists: 'do you regard yourself as the goddess?' Karen was more circumspect: 'I am she who is the personification of the Phoenician triad, I am the mouth piece of the goddess, my loins, my breasts, my blood, my bones are her temple, through worshipping me you worship her. Through me you will find the godhead, through me and me alone you will know TANIT!'

In more predictable ways Karen continued to court infamy. She would not be Karen if she did not persist in going down to the beach and bathe naked in the sea, offering the paparazzi the opportunity of a cheap shot or two. She no longer seemed to care whether they cast her in a bad light by focusing on her effete breasts, and the wound in her side that had healed up like some ugly burn. She knew now that she was powerful in her own right. She no longer saw herself exclusively through the prism of her looks - her body. She knew, that she still possessed an unquantifiable beauty, a sexual presence that was like an aura burst! Yes, her body was scarred, but if anything it added rather than detracted to her lure. The Bedouin women's healing ointments had not been a complete success, yet her physique was still an imposing one, of which Karen was aware more than anybody. It was as though she were making some sort of statement by parading her naked body: 'look at me! You can cut me with your long knives but I am still strong and unashamed of my look! It is you, you who wrap yourself in robes, it is you that are ashamed - and for that you marred my body! - though you have not broken my pride - my will!'

In this vain she defied the sensibilities of the majority of the population who regarded her presence as an outrage. And so Karen continued to flaunt her presence, continued to flaunt her destiny.

I suppose she was like all those great and powerful figures of history, who believed themselves to be invincible, and for a time they are, until their weave too is severed by Atropos's shears.

Although a divinity in many eyes, Karen was also known as queen of the *maghreb*, and every queen has her throne, in this Karen was no different. Set about fifty yards from the main dwelling area, close to the cliff edge, was a semicircle of tiered seating, as in an amphitheatre, six deep, twenty five feet across, and constructed of solid black granite. At the centre, facing towards the sea and the semicircle, was a dais which towered some twelve feet above the rest of the arena. On top of this construction was a throne carved from a solid block of red granite. The Tanit motif was inscribed on the back in such a way that the crescent moon appeared above the sitters head, the horns pointing skyward. Two leopard heads were carved at the end of each arm. A set of marble steps ran up to the top of the dais. Beyond the western aspect of the arena, was situated an imposing *stele*, about twelve feet high, composed of the same red granite as the throne. Carved on it were the familiar Tanit markings of the moon, the square, the triangle and the sun disc. To the east was a bronze brazier heaped with coal, which was kept constantly burning; it also was decorated with Phoenician motifs. On either side of the red granite throne was space for two smaller seats, usually wooden chairs of ebony. These high places were set aside for her closest initiate, (that would be me), and an advisor or augur, usually one of the tribal elders. In front of the throne, set into the stone was a bronze disc about two feet across, inscribed with the name of the goddess and her symbols. Upon this disc various offerings to the goddess were placed. Other decorative and symbolic items were also positioned on the dais to either side of the throne, these usually included two tall vases in which were placed white lilies and a single white orchid. Also two wrought iron torches positioned a little further back were lit towards dusk to provide illumination. Other torches at the back of the arena also provided further lighting, but were also symbolic of Tanit, whose very name means fire! At set times, such as dusk about an hour before the sunset, or when the moon is at its thinnest crescent, and when the moon is at its fattest, the devotees would take their places in the arena and supplicate themselves before the goddess.

At the epicentre of all of this pomp and paraphernalia was the golden statue of Karen herself. Her appearance was befitting her station, as supreme priestess, draped in gold ornamentation from her toes to her head: even her body anointed in oil and mixed with gold dust, glittered and glistened in the dying red rays of the sun. She was an unparalleled sight, something not of these times; uncanny, unsettling, for how many people witness the sight of a living statue of gold?

A large pink sapphire decorated the ravaged flower of her navel, upon her hips rested a broad girdle of gold, studded with precious stones, such as emeralds, rubies and blue sapphires. Below this hung a curtain of finely linked gold chain, the ends of which came just above her ankles. Around her neck was a wide collar of gold, plainly decorated with the symbol of Tanit: the triangle, inverted crescent moon and the sun. Her long limbs too were adorned with gold bracelets from which hung different pagan talesmen. On her fingers and toes she wore gold rings set with diamonds and other precious stones. Her platted hair resembled lengths of golden twine, embalmed with a kind of resin. Set on the top her head was the golden crown of Tanit in the form of the horned crescent moon. Around each ankle she wore a wide gold clasp, between which ran a fine golden chain, rather like a convict might wear to restrict his movement, in the same manner Karen's step was also hampered, there being only just enough length of chain to allow her to climb the marble steps to her throne. The symbolism of this being: like the convict, Karen too was in bondage, but her bondage was not an Earthly one, but symbolic of her sublimation to the goddess! She was the manifestation of the will of the goddess on Earth. At such times as the new moon, Karen had no will of her own, she would sit upon her throne staring deep in trance, the old augur by her side mumbling preys and incantations under his breath, while the smouldering brazier filled the air with the aroma of incense. Her devotees sat before her contemplating the perplexing inscrutability of the effigy before them. She was but a statue of gold until she stood and raised her arms above her head, and the awsome beauty and splendour of the high priestess would send an audible sigh therough the gathering. Prayers to the goddess would begin, followed by presentations of gifts, from certain individuals wishing special favour from the goddess.

The high priestess was the recipient of a great number of gifts, not just of gold and precious stones, but of rare and expensive spices and perfumes, silks and furs, although she did not usually look favourably upon the latter. Her favourite and most treasured gift was that of a cheetah which usually sat half asleep by her feet. She loved that cat, it followed he everywhere. I'm not too sure her servants found it as much fun to be around. It usually kept a weary eye out for men, so you can tell both the cat and I got on quite well.

At the foot of the dais, standing one either side of the marble steps were two Negro men, spartanly clad in plain red cloth. Their sombre countenance and immense musculature left one in little doubt as to their function. These were colossi of men, perfect physical examples. Anybody wishing to approach the high priestess had to be escorted up the steps by these two gargantuan.

Karen rose from her throne so that she could get a better view of the little Berber who kneeled at the base of the marble steps. She thrust out her golden belly in that conceited manner of hers, and motioned lazily with her hand to one of her giant Negroids. The little man ascended the marble stairs, with his dark escorts either side. Karen sat herself down, arranging her skirts of gold chain-mail, whilst taking up her most haughty and regal look.

"Do you see how they kneel before me, my chosen one!" said Karen, as the Berber kneeled before her.

"Yes I see it," I replied. "Aren't you a little afraid?"

"Afraid! Why should I be afraid? They love me, they worship me."

"That's what I mean. To have so much power!"

The Berber mumbled something in Arabic. All I understood was: 'Eshmun Baal-Hammon, Baal-Shamin, Tanith Ba'alim.' The Negroid Marbo explained to the high priestess the nature of the gift that the little man had brought, and was careful to take it from him. He placed in her hand a dagger in a gold scabbed, encrusted with emeralds. Karen unsheathed it and inspected the blade.

"Look husband - look what he brought, he said it once belonged to a maharaja."

Karen held up the dagger and twisted it so that the sun glinted on the blade. She trailed her finger along its edge until a tiny trickle of blood stained its mirror like surface. "What a fine edge it has," she said, with a mad look of fascination in her eyes, as she continued to watch the progress of her blood as it flowed over the surface of the cold metal. Detecting the scent of blood in the air, her cheetah, 'Pharaoh', which had been asleep at her side stretched and yawned. Lazily he looked up to his mistress, sniffed the air a couple of times, and on seeing that all looked well enough, lay his head down again on his big paws, sighing heavily of boredom, before closing its jewel-like eyes.

The Berber looked up to his queen as she played with her gift, rather in the manner of a father, full of pride that he has made his daughter happy. Karen suddenly became aware of the little Berber and held up the knife a few inches in front of his face. His looked suddenly changed.

"Ask him if he is prepared to die for his goddess."

I leaned forward in my ebony chair. "Karen! - No, you can't!" I said.

"Shut up! - or I'll have you removed," spat Karen, slowly turning her head towards me. She looked at me a moment, the pupils of her eyes wildly dilated like a cat that was about to pounce. I sat back in my seat resigned to let the drama unfold before me, taking Pharaoh's example, who seemed unimpressed by all things human.

Staring at the knife in front of him, the little man quivered in his fine silk robe. It was all too much for him in the end, and letting out a sob he threw himself face down against the bronze seal of Tanit at the feet of his priestess.

The Berber groaned and murmured something. Karen looked at Marbo. "What is it? What does he say?"

"He says his life is already yours to take. All is yours to give or take as you please - great one."

"Tell him the goddess is pleased - That she will not be requiring his life today. "Tell him I am pleased by his gift. May Tanit protect his family and make him fruitful."

Karen indicated to Marbo and the other Negro, that the Berber may leave her presence. They stood and watched a while as he bowed and scrapped, allowing him to kiss the seal of Tanit, before finally hauling him off.

Karen sat a moment, looking pleased with herself. She stroked the head of her cheetah. "Now do you see the extent of my powers!" she said.

I remained silent, what I had witnessed needed no reply from me. A great cheer went up from the assembly as the Berber went back to his seat.

"Hail Tanit! - Hail Tanit!, hail queen of the maghreb!" they roared.

Karen got to her feet and moved forward until she was standing upon the bronze seal, she looked down a moment, before raising her hands above her head. "Blessed be the goddess!" she called.

She brandished the blade again, whilst taking up her proud defiant stance, thrusting forward her hips in that jaunty fashion.

"Praise Tanith - the greatest power that has ever been!"

The masses leaned forward bowing their heads: Praise thee! praise thee! Tanith! - Tanith! - Tanith!" came the response, (or something like that!)

Karen looked over at me. I was hoping for the wink, instead there was a strange look in her eye. I raised an eyebrow, and prepared myself for something special.

"There are those out there," she said, pointing the glinting blade to the assembled, "out there, beyond this sanctuary that would wish to destroy your goddess."

"No - never, never," came the reply *en masse*...(or some such words of disbelief.)

"Yes my people! - yes," she said, nodding, "it is true, you have seen how they have wounded your beloved priestess - how they have tarnished her beauty, but they shall feel yet the steel of Tanit! - They shall feel her revenge! for they will be smote from the land, burned clean by the holy fire of Tanit! Yes - yes they shall brethren, - oh yes - yes they shall!.." called Karen, over the noise of the crowd.

The place was in uproar screams of: 'burn the infidels, and kill and smite, and other such madness rang out from the frenzied mob. Karen all the time nodding and smiling demonically. She came forward to the very edge of the dais, both Marbo and Oudoso looked up at her with concerned expressions on their faces. She spread her legs apart in a defiant stance, like the rock of Tanit, and ran her hands over her body, bringing them up from her loins to her neck, where her hand lingered, and I saw her tighten her grip and swallow hard. She then lay the white steel flat against the gold of her soft belly, and the phrase, 'like a knife through hot butter,' ran through my head. I thought how easy it would be to sink the point of the blade into her solar plexus, so keen was its edge, that it *would* be like a knife going through butter. 'You were brought down once by your haughty pride, and you can be brought down again,' I said to myself, 'all it would take was an interloper to break through your cordon, even that old man could have easily destroyed you, and where would your goddess be then?'

To my releif karen moved the knife away from that ulnerable place and raising her hands aloft - the multitude gradualy stilled itself.

"Behold your godess," said Karen, her voice on the point of breaking, "Would you see the blood of a goddess shed again!" she said, in a strange half sobbing voice.

Suddenly to my absolute horror I heard the steady pitter-patter of blood, as it splashed onto the bronze disc that had been set into the white stone of the dais. I rushed forward and grabbed hold of her hand. The dagger fell to the ground, its bright blade soaked in the blood of the priestess. Karen was reeling around, laughing hystericaly. "Behold - behold the blood of a goddess," she screached.

"Somebody help, she's cut her wrist!" I yelled.

Pharaoh got up to inspect the scene and began sniffing and licking up the blood. Togther the old augur and I managed to seat Karen back in her throne. She had cut deep to the quick this time; blood was simply gushing from her wrist. Karen began to look pale, the smile going off her face. She looked down at her arm which was completely red from her elbow to her fingertips. A slow look of realisation at what she had done began to dawn on her face. She sat helpless, as Marbo and the others rushed to the scene. Somebody eventually came with lengths of cloth, which was hastily turned into a tourniquet and makeshift bandage. Gradually the flow of blood was contained to a steady trickle. The two Negro's lifted her up and carried her quickly down the steps and towards the residence. Pharaoh padded off after his mistress, following the spatterings of blood on the white marble steps. I stared at the congealing blood on the bronze disc, then turned back to her throne, its red granite darkened; her blood lay all about, as in a scene of carnage. I looked towards the crowds that were milling around; on everyone's face there was a look of horror and dismay. Eventually one of the elders climbed the steps, pushing me aside, he put his hands in Karen's blood and raised them before the multitude. "Behold," he called, "behold the blood of the goddess."

Suddenly the gathering turned towards the dais, and began to surge forward as one like mind, with one sole intent, to be anointed with Karen's blood. I looked on, stupefied as each man came up to wallow in her spent life force. With a mounting sense of horror and disgust I pushed my way through the multitude, the only person it seemed to be heading away.

The blood that was not taken away on the hands and forehead of her followers, was left where it lay, to slowly tarnish the bronze seal of Tanit. It had become sanctified now. I had witnessed the birth of a place of pilgrimage, a focal point for perhaps millions of Tanit worshipers in the future. But I was not in awe of this, instead I sped away from the scene in disgust, looking back only briefly, at the clambering horde each vying for space, like a pack of dogs around a rotting carcass.

The Berber women, accomplished as they are in needle point, were able to complete a neat job of sewing up the three inches or so gash in Karen's wrist, but it was obvious from the shear force of entry of the blade, that the wound would require excpert medical attention. Fortunately a young Algerian doctor happened to be not far away, and was summoned by one of her concerned followers, probably after witnessing the share volume of spilt blood.

"Let me see, give me space," said the young doctor, gently pushing aside the Berber women, with their needles. It was obvious they resented the impudent young Algerian, 'what did he know, he was a mere boy, and a European to boot! - you impudent young rascal, with you bag of tricks and your needles that squirt!'

"What were you trying to do?" he said, gently lifting Karen's arm, "cut your damned hand off?"

"She is brave, she is the priestess of Tanith. She gives her blood for her people," said one of the Berber women.

"Does she now! " said Mersell, glancing up at the woman, "well - I don't doubt she is a priestess, what I do know is that she is a silly young girl!"

This silenced the old woman who only tutted and pursed her lips. "Well, let's have a look. A neat job, but you've probably severed the artery. You're lucky you haven't bled to death by now!"

And sure enough, when Mersell made Karen lay he arm flat, blood began to ooze out of the stitched flesh. Karen just looked at the boy insouciantly.

"I'm going to give you an injection, it will hurt, but I don't suppose you'll care about that!"

He began to take off the broad leather strap that Karen always wore on that part of her wrist.

"What are you doing?" she said.

"I need to get at the wound more easily, it has to be properly cleaned and then bandaged properly."

Karen was in no real state to argue. The thick black leather binding came away to reveal a red silk bandanna beneath.

"What do we have here?"

"Don't," said Karen, covering it with her hand.

Mersell untied the silk bandage to reveal the site of her first wound.

"Do you do this often?" he said, grabbing her other wrist. "What is this one?"

"That was when I was married."

"I see. It is this one - this other one that concerns me."

"It hurts me sometimes."

"I am not surprised! Covering it up like this won't make it go away. It is infected, you should have gone to a hospital straight away."

"I know - I know," replied Karen, as one who was bored of hearing about it. "I bathe it regularly. I keep it clean, I go in the sea a lot - the great mother will heal me."

"It is perhaps this that has prevented it from becoming gangrenous by now. It won't heal because the infection is deep inside. It will have to be operated on, to get to the source of the infection.

"No!" said the Berber woman, "no operation! No hospital!"

Karen lay her good hand on his. "You must do it here," said Karen.

Mersell looked around as one who was out of his depth, but he also knew there was no way of getting around the situation.

He sighed heavily: "All right. But I am no surgeon!"

"Do what you can," said Karen, lethargically.

As it was, Mersell had underestimated his own skills as a surgeon, attending to both her wounds with an air of great expertise and professional satisfaction. Finally he closed up the old wound, the one that still *wept,* having dug down into its bowels and cleaned away the festering poison that he had found there.

"You have been very brave," he said, after it was done.

"She is the priestess, a goddess incarnate," said the old woman, who had watched the actions of the doctor like a hawk.

"Yes, I have heard much of you!" he said.

"What things have you heard?"

"Many things," he said, looking into her eyes, which were unfathomable and as old as her expression - that of the sphinx!

"Such as?"

"Oh - many things! Your great pride for instance."

"What else...?"

"Your great beauty - of course!"

"Av'course!"

They smiled furtively at one another! Karen wound her red silk bandanna over the clean bandage that he had put in place there.

"Why do you do that?"

"I don't want my husband to know that after all this time it has not healed."

"I see." Mersell shook his head. He lifted her long hand. "Such a lovely wrist, a shame to spoil it so."

Karen eyed him coldly like a snake, biding her time. "If you say so."

"This one is not so deep," said Mersell, looking at the mark left from her marriage binding ceremony.

"No, not so deep," replied Karen. "Normally I like it taken to the quick!"

Being of French extraction I suppose he could not help himself, so he gently lifted her hand to within a centimetre of his lips.

"Adieu Mademoiselle! or should I say - *Madame!* You need to rest you have lost much blood."

Karen eyed the young doctor circumspectly. "*Hasta Mañana Monsieur!*"

It was very unlikely Karen had known the young doctor before, but all the signs were there to be read: those animal signs which indicate that consent for copulation has been accepted. The flared nostrils, the widely dilated pupils, the long lingering looks, the subtle touches and movements of the body. How sickeningly predictable they all were, especially to someone who had seen them a thousand times or more.

The young doctor made visits to his patient on a regular basis, two or three times a week, for the next three weeks. Karen made her usual fast recovery, and then, surprisingly we didn't see him again. 'Surely,' I thought, 'you must be able to find some reason to see her again?' And although Karen was quickly back to her former health, her mood was rattier than ever. When I asked her of the whereabouts of our young doctor, after not having seen him for several days, I was curtly told that he had: 'gone away,' but it was obvious something seminal to their relationship had forced him to leave.

Then one day as I was passing the main gate I happened to spy our young doctor, pacing up and down nervously. He had obviously been let through the first cordon by the guards. At that time just after the: 'letting of the blood!' there was a constant vigil of devotees and press outside the villa the whole time.

"Do you wish to check on your patient?" I said, nodding to Zaraxes, the gate keeper, who pushed across the heavy steel bars which secured the gate.

The young doctor came forward nervously. "Well I expect you'll find Karen around somewhere. You might try down on the beech."

Mersell put his hand on my arm and expressed his earnest wish to speak with me; so I took him somewhere quiet. After many faltering attempts he finally unburdened himself. It turned out that I had had the guy all wrong. I mean normally - *normally,* I can read the signs, as it was, he was at pains to stress that he had not laid an unprofessional finger on her. The signs *were* there, at least from Karen's side, but not acted on by Mersell, by all accounts. It was not usually my practice to associate with men that Karen wished to fornicate with, so of course, I had stared well clear of the doctor. What a great loss it would have been never to have known him. I found him one of the most open and down to earth people I had met in a long while. Truly, he was a breath of fresh air, in the incense ridden claustrophobia of *priestess worship*, which I had had to endure for so many months.

It turned out that Karen had summoned him. I had to put his mind at ease by informing him that, as far as I was aware, Karen was as healthy as a roach; having entertained a number of young men over the last couple of days.

"How do you put up with it Julian, this constant flow of men - some of them no more than boys I understand?"

"So long as I don't know them - you know have to have anything to do with them, I can put it to one side of my mind. That way she remains my sweet Karen - and not the holly whore that she really is. You can accuse me of being in denial if you like, but it works for me. And for my sake she is usually discrete..."

Mersell shook his head and a hurt look came into his eyes. "And you thought that all this time I...."

"I'm sorry," I said, not wishing to cause him distress.

"No, Monsieur! - it is I who should apologise. I must have given you reason to think...but I swear to you, on my mothers grave I have never been with her - 'like that.' "

I laughed. "Its all right Mersell," I said, finding myself liking the man even more for his conscience. "I believe you."

He looked about nervously. "Don't worry," I said, "she doesn't normally come to this side of the villa, this is *my* terrace, where I sit and think - although I dare say she will get to find out!"

I snapped my fingers and my Geisha came promptly to my side. I called her Tricksy, although I didn't normally call her that, she kind of fell in love with me and refused to go when the shadowy masters left, I struck a deal with one of them and bought her for a few grand, I can't remember how much - in fact Karen sealed the deal! - I guess she thought it only fair I should have a little fun of my own! Ironically Karen was usually very possessive over me, but I think because Tricksy was so tiny, so different from Karen, she didn't regard her as real female with a sexuality of her own. I guess she only thought there was one type of woman I could be attracted to and that was the Celt and the Anglo-Saxon. If only Karen had any inkling into Tricksy's capabilities...! Whatever Tricksy cost, I can tell you she was worth every darn scent!

Tricksy gave the doctor a quick shrewd look, she was very intelligent. I gave her instructions to bring us wine, and not to breath a word to the *mistress* - that I was *entertaining!* She smiled and touched her cute little nose and bowed dutifully before scurrying off on her errand.

He was quite probably the only man not to be swayed by Karen's sexual powers. I personally liked Mersell, there was something in his nature that appealed to me, he was not of these modern times - there was about him a certain rare quality of 'uprightness'!

But for my rule, of not befriending Karen's conquests, I would have liked to have known Mersell a lot better. Even though I knew she had sex with young men by the cart load, as long as I did not know them, then in some small part of my head, she remained my sweet Karen, and not the holy whore that she was. It was in this vain that I further elaborated my position, when Tricksy returned with two bottles of Tunisian wine, which she opened and poured for us.

"Is the coast clear?" I asked.

"No sign of the great lady," smiled Tricksy.

She hovered before us a moment. "You can join us if you want?"

Tricksy smiled sweetly and glanced from me to the doctor. "No, Tricksy go, leave men talk - man talk." she laughed and turned her head coyly.

We all laughed , and Tricksy bowed and scurried away in that cute little way of her kind.

We toasted one anothers health. "It is good wine," said Mersell, "and from what I see you live very well!"

"Oh - you mean Tricksy - yes it has its moments!" I said, before going on to elaborate how I came by her, and how it was that Karen managed to tolerate her.

There was a moments awkward silence.

"Your wife is very beautiful," he said at last.

"She is - but she was once a lot more beautiful."

"Ah yes - the scars! I did not wish to be rude and ask abut the one on her face, or the others I saw on her body. It was this that I was concerned about."

I told Mersell the story of how she came by them. He opened his eyes wide, his air of professional judgement returning. "It is a wonder she did not die - out there in the desert. She must be very strong indeed."

"Yes, she is, but of late she has begun to look old, she has lines on her face she never had before."

"We all get old Monsieur, it is life - No?"

"Its not that she is getting old, it's what she does that makes her look that way!"

"There is only so much a body can take, even one such as hers," put in Mersell.

"Yes - I knew someone once, who said Karen would come to look like a monster."

"A monster! - No, a girl like that will always keep her beauty. She is just a little too caught up in herself, that is all."

"Yes that's always been her weakness - she is too in love with herself. I think at times she really believes she is this goddess." I looked at Mersell across my glass. "What do you think of all this Tanit business? I mean you're not a follower are you?"

Mersell laughed. "Me! No Monsieur. The first I knew was when someone ran up to me and told me to hurry, that a girl was bleeding to death."

"She could have died?"

"Oh - quite possibly!"

"To die though! For what? A silly idea?"

"Is that what you think it is?"

I sighed... "I don't know," I said at length. "I don't know about a lot of things anymore."

Mersell shook his head. "Why does she cut herself like this?"

"I shrugged, "I don't know, I guess she has a death wish. I believe she finds being herself, whatever that is - too much of a burden at times."

"Yes, I have seen this before in some young people."

"What happens to them in the end?" I asked.

"Some of them succeed Monsieur."

I finished off the wine in my glass and replenished it, before going on to tell Mersell the rest of Karen's story.

"So you are saying Karen is a reincarnation of all these different people? It is incredible!"

"It does sound like it is, doesn't it. And yet I have witnessed things that tell me it could be true....But I don't know what to think. She has changed so very much. I sit up here now, on my terrace trying to figure a way out of it, slowly getting drunk on Tunisian wine."

"It must get very lonely for you - but for your friend, I mean?"

I looked at him as he spread his long hands on the table, his fine tapering fingers pointed towards me. For a moment I thought I was reading an animal sign, one directed at me.

I opened the other bottle Tricksy had brought, and I thought, 'how well she knows me!'

"Yes Tricksy is sweet, but..but..."

"But you do not love her!"

I just looked at him. 'And you too know me well,' I thought.

"I can't help it," I said, having to fight back the tears. "I love her so much and yet..."

Mersell leaned forward and touched my hand, we both suddenly understood one another, far more than words alone can relate.

Mersell began to look restless. I suddenly felt afraid he would leave. "You'll stay for another glass? I know its Tunisian but its the best they have."

"It is good wine." Mersell relaxed a little. We sat in silence for some moments. I regarded the perfect blue of the sea and the sky, and my mind wandered to metaphysics.

"Do you believe in god Monsieur Mersell?"

"I was brought up as Catholic, but I am not sure there is a god. I am a man of science. Man, is the measure of all things."

"I don't know about that," I replied. "I believe there has to be some divine power some unmoved mover. I have seen too much evidence for it to be otherwise. Things seem connected some how. We each have a destiny."

"Destiny! Quite possible. We can never know, either way."

"I fear for her," I said. "Where her destiny will lead her. I had hoped this Tanit business would run its course. You know - get it of her system, get all the screwing around out of her system."

"Then she would come back to you - your Karen?"

"Yes. Once, on our launch, when we cruised the Aegean, she was happy. The real Karen - just a good fun loving kid. Not this arrogant priestess - come *holy whore!"*

Mersell shook his head. "I fear she will not come back. The name of Tanit is synonymous with Karen: she is famous now, known the world over. She will never be the same again."

I looked out at the perfect blue horizon; his words were bitter truth. Mersell suddenly moved closer to me and I felt the presence of his hand on my shoulder. "You do not have to be alone any more Julian. I will be with you."

I looked at him - eventually! It was difficult because I did not want to show my emotion. The prospect that someone might share my burden was too much to take in at once.

"She is all right, isn't she?" I asked, childlike.

Mersell moved away a little and drank some of his wine. "Of course. The wound has nearly healed."

"I mean, there's nothing else?"

"What can there be? You said yourself she is as strong as the ox. One only has to look at her to see that physically she is *superb* - No?"

"Its just...well you see she's been through a lot..." I said, before going on to speak of more of her ordeals, starting with my dream of the wounded snake woman and the relentless pugilism of Pandora, and finally our foundering on the island of Rhodes, how Antonio and I had feared for her life after she was attacked in the police cell. At each new revelation, yet more grim than the last, Mersell shook his head and made some exclamation in French.

When I finished recounting her liturgy of abuse at the hands of lesser mortals than herself, Mersell sat back in silence a moment, silently digesting all that I had told him. I could see that even he, a surgeon, used to seeing and hearing of the consequences of pain and suffering was surprised that one such as she could still be so sprightly and full of verve!

"Well! - what are you thinking?" I asked.

He scratched his head. "It is incredible, that a body can take such - such punishment. And still to carry on the way she does! It is incredible! But it must have been bad for you - No! To see one you love abused, at the hands of others, to witness such things at the hands of this...this Pandora! it is an abomination!

"Indeed! - so you see I am concerned for her."

"Understandably. Does she - you know, complain of having pain?"

I laughed sardonically and shook my head. "No Monsieur, she would never tell me or anyone else for that matter, but I know her, I know that she is till hurting, I can see it etched on her face and in the way she holds her body some times - I know she suffers still, probably more than any of us will ever know."

"Well I will try to get her to come to my clinic, although I must add it would not be I that would do the examination - it would not be fitting, her wrist is quite another thing."

"Yes of course, I understand, but you will try?"

Mersell lay his hand on mine a second, and his dark eyes were moist with compassion. "But of course Julian - I tell you, you do not have to carry the burden alone anymore. I will do all in my power to help both Karen - and you!"

A few seconds later and one of Karen's servants, a Berber woman, came on to the terrace closely followed by a fraught Tricksy, who pushed past her. She clasped her hands and bowed.

"A thousand apologies master Julian, but I could not stop her," said Tricksy.

The Berber woman scowled at my beautiful Geisha.

"The Priestess demands the doctors attendance - and you Monsieur Julian."

I smiled wryly. "It's all right Tricksy..." turning to the Berber woman: "tell the great one we are coming." To the doctor: "I guess we'd better see what she wants."

"Yes perhaps," he said, and again I saw the signs. He lingered in his seat, there seemed to be something more that he wanted to unburden himself of, but the words did not come out in English.

"Its all right Mersell," I replied, "I think I understand."

We found Karen on the large ground floor terrace. She was dressed scantily in beech attire, a bottle of wine in front of her. As we arrived she got up and pretended to be embarrassed at Mersell's presence, but made sure he saw her in all her glory, before winding a blue silk sarong around her hips.

"Julian! Where the hell have you been? I've been looking for you everywhere. Then I heard you were on your terrace with Mersell and your Japanese floozy."

I turned to Mersell and smiled.

"Is there anything wrong Karen?" he said, in his professional tone.

Karen in her helpless little girl voice put out her wrist for him to inspect. "Its been aching a lot and it feels like its bleeding."

The doctor guided Karen back to her seat and carefully removed the bandage. "Yes it has opened. Have you been in the sea?"

Karen looked guilty.

"I told you not to. The sea water will dissolve the sutures."

"But it's so hot, and the sea is so beautiful. Why don't you come swimming with me? And you Julian."

"You heard what the doctor said."

"Oh, you're so boring - both of you."

"It will have to be stitched again," said Mersell, officciouly. "Come to the clinic tomorrow and one of my nurses will see to it, in the meantime I will bind it tightly, but please do not go in the sea again."

"But it feels all throby!"

Mersell looked over at me, and then to his patient. "I can't do it here I didn't bring anything with me. I am sure you can put up with a bit of discomfort. You are the high priestess are you not?" said the doctor.

Karen, as if suddenly remembering who she was straightened her body and flung her head back, whilst stroking her cobraform throat.

"Yes - yes I am, and in future when I ask you to come to me you will. I could have been bleeding to death for all you knew, whilst drinking wine with Julian! And you - you are no better encouraging him like that! If I want to go in the sea I shall. As it is I will refrain from doing so if you think it best, but do not expect me to go to your horrible little clinic."

"If you want me to look after it properly you must."

"Oh - very well, but I want you to do it."

"Very well."

"Now you will stay and drink wine with me. You too if you like Julian? - unless you are going to play with your little Japanese whore! Yes Julian I know..."

"Leave Tricksy out of it!" I said.

"Please - Julian, stay!" implored Mersell, putting his hand on my arm.

I saw Karen's eyes grow wide, as she looked from me to Mersell and back to me again.

"*I see!*" she said. No one wanted to know what she saw.

The next day Karen attended Mersell's clinic, pulling up outside in her limousine and escorted to the entrance by both her big Negroes: Marbo and Oudoso. When she returned to the villa an hour or so later she was in one heck of a vile temper. Later that same evening I received a message from Mersell requesting my immediate presence at his office, whereupon I learnt all that had transpired earlier that day.

She had seen Mersell as arranged, and he had duly tended to her wrist, he then persuaded her to undergo a further examination, and surprisingly she was only too willing to accept. Mersell told Karen to go behind the screen and loosen her clothing and lie down on the couch. Karen, never to do things by halves, took off all her clothes and lay back, closing her eyes expectant of the doctors immediate attendance.

"What soft hands you have Mersell," she said, suddenly upon opening her eyes she saw his female associate.

"What the hell is this!" yelled Karen, leaping up and smacking her hard in the face. As shocked and dismayed as Karen, no doubt, the young doctor ran out of the examining room crying, and screaming, she had been attacked!

When I saw Mersell he appeared anxious and guilty looking. Solemnly he greeted me and showed me into his office, giving me a seat at his desk. Unfortunately I was rather off with him, judging from his nervous manner I assumed that Karen had finally got the better of him.

"She forced me you understand, I had to..."

I lit a cigarette and looked at the man, I could perfectly well see why she would go to such lengths.

"Of course you did old man!" I said.

" I swear I did no more than examine her!"

"You expect me to believe you Mersell? Karen, stark naked on you couch," I laughed, "remember - I Know her, I know the ways of men and women!"

"It is not like that," he said, banging his fist down on the desk. "She forced me to....to look at her, or else she would claim that I was the one to take advantage of *her!*"

"That doesn't sound like Karen, she's not malicious like that!"

"I swear it."

I regarded him coolly. I could see how desperate he was that I believe him. If it had been anyone else I would have doubted them, but Mersell was different.
"All right," I conceded, after a moment or two: "I guess she would do anything to get her way - at that!"
"You understand Monsieur, if it were anyone else I would not discuss it, but this is different. I felt I must make a clean breast of it, tell you all, so you knew - I have my reputation..."
"Of course," I said, my estimation of him dropping slightly. "You saw her then - what she is like?"
His face darkened. "I did Monsieur. I did not want to see, but yes - yes I did."
He took out a bottle of brandy from a drawer and poured out two small measures. Mersell knocked his back in one and poured himself another.
"The things she said Monsieur Julian! She was without shame - forcing me to look at her....Oh! - oh Monsieur! Now I understand what you have had to endure! Without shame - without shame!" he went on, then mumbled something in French.
"I can well imagine." I knocked back my own drink and helped myself to another. " So, she played her ace and it didn't come off." I laughed sardonically. "Karen the gambler, playing her highest card! But what an ace - nay?"
"Hm..." Scratching his chin: *"Formidable!"*
"Well - now she's played it, what more can she do?" I continued. "I'm sorry she inflicted herself on you, in the way that she did."
"It is nothing. One sees many things, many kinds of people in a career such as mine," he said. But I could detect from the tone of his voice that she had made more of an impact on him, than he was prepared to admit. He laughed nervously. "She was not pleased when I told her to cover herself, that I had seen all I needed to."
"That would explain her mood when she got back. I imagine you made her as mad as wildcat."
Mersell looked away, I guess there was stuff that happened after all, but he was too proud to admit it. "She is a silly girl, a bit too infatuated with herself for her own good!"
"Indeed, you did right, the last thing you want to do is in courage her," I said, giving him a shrewd look.

"This is so." He poured himself another and put the bottle away.

I drew heavily on my cigarette, knowing I would never know the entire truth of what happened.

"And what did your 'examination' of her reveal Doctor Mersell?"

He sighed deeply, the man visibly shaken. The Hippocratic oath I guessed.

"You understand Monsieur that this is a special case, normally I would never reveal any of my patients details."

"Of course," I said.

"I found indications of extensive trauma, just as you said I would. She spoke of having some pain and other related problems - you have to understand I run a small clinic, there was nothing I could do for her here - even if the situation I found myself in had been more congenial. I said I was happy to refer her to a specialist where tests and a more detailed examination could be done, but she wouldn't hear of it."

"Is it bad?"

"I think that there could be something wrong! - look, I'm not going to say anymore, the whole thing was highly inappropriate to say the least! I have only told you what I have because I did not want you to think badly of me. My reputation is one thing, but I also value your opinion of me. My words Julian, are not empty ones!"

"Of course," I said, wanting to reach out to him.

"She did ask one revealing thing which I feel you ought to know."

I sat forward. "She was... concerned about whether she would ever be able to bear a child."

"And what was your prognosis Doctor?"

"I told her I was unable to form an opinion, but I advised her that by the kind of lifestyle she lived she was not improving her chances."

"But you didn't rule it out?"

"With a girl like that! - certainly, externally I could see no reason why she should not have a hundred children, but without a proper examination it is difficult to be sure - as I have said Julian, I am not expert in this area - certainly her behaviour in my clinic, and the way she trated my coleague! - she was very badly shaken!"

"I can only apaologise for Karen, I am so sorry for what happened, and I Know you've gone out on a limb, but I appreciate your confiding in me."

I looked at my half empty glass. I suddenly felt a warmth grow in my stomach that did not originate solely from the brandy. 'So she wants to have a child!' I thought, repeating in my mind: 'she wants to have a child - a child, my child! May be that is what she needs, what she really really wants. A daughter would be good, a daughter, as beautiful as Karen...'

"Come let's drink up," I said. "We'll speak no more of it - nay!"

"Yes Monsieur Julian, I would appreciate that."

"Is there a bar, somewhere where we can get a drink?"

"That sounds like a good idea, there is a bistro at the end of the road."

I got up, and taking me by surprise, Mersell came up to me and embraced me, declaring passionately: "*Mon ami! Mon ami!*"

Clearly the man was relieved, and I let myself believe that, being French this was how he expressed his gratitude. He held my hand briefly and there followed a moments silent repose before we left for the bistro.

We became close friends after that, an 'understanding' had been reached between us, that required no words of explanation. I knew from then on that no matter what, I could ask of Mersell anything, never to be disapointed. I say to you, is this not what friendship is?

Mersell continued to be a regular visitor to the villa, but for other reasons than before. To begin with, Karen met his presence with a cold hostility, gradually though she became more amenable, until she began to throw herself at him once more. It must have driven her nuts, that despite all her best efforts she was unable, at least as far as I am aware, to seduce him. I won't bore you with the untold ploys and little devices she would use to entrap him, he would come to me, his hands trembling, and I would laugh, imagining all kinds of things.

"That girl," he said, after reaching the safety of my terrace and the calming influence of Tricksy. Running his fingers through his dark hair: "forgive me Julian, but she is shameless!"

I would laugh smacking his thigh teasingly. "Come on Mersell, what has she done this time..?"

And so he would recount some incident or other, where she contrived to get him ~~alone, and expose herself, making~~ up some story or other of a lump here, a

pain there - well you can imagine how she played-up!
"Please Julian," he would say, if I appeared to be on the point of leaving the room, grabbing hold of my lapel he would whisper: "please don't leave me alone with her!"

I laughed, "don't worry, I'll only be in the next room," knowing full well Karen couldn't care less where I was - the closer I was the more of a frisson it gave her. And I would walk back again two or three minutes later humming, or whistling my little tune, and Karen would be in the middle of the room smoothing her kimono over her bosom, Mersell cowering in his seat, whilst with a shaking hand, putting a cigarette to his mouth.

Her campaign was ceaseless, believing as she did, that all men - *all men,* in the end succumb to her irresistible sexuality. To that end, she was as remorseless as the sea, which eventually breaks down the hardest of rocky headlands. Karen, far from being discouraged by Mersell's resoluteness, saw in him a challenge - proof that her sexual powers were not on the wane, and that he, like all rocky headlands would eventually be worn down. Although it infuriated Karen at times, it was Mersell who easily had the worst of it. It played havoc with his nerves. I guess the sadist in me encouraged it, by leaving them alone just along enough for her to make some proposition, but not long enough for either of them to carry it through. I know its terrible, but it was one of the few pleasures I had left; in any case I knew I'd push things too far, and I guessed that in the end Mersell, only being mortal flesh, at some time or other gave way to temptation. I could see it in his eyes, or rather they way he averted them whenever I talked about Karen. With Karen, knowing she never gave up once she was on the scent of her man, the fact she pursued him with less intent indicated she had run her quarry to the ground. I dare say she would have taken him up again if so inclined, his reluctance was the only thing that saved our friendship. I didn't blame him tripping up on her once - twice even!
"We don't see Mersell as often as we did," Karen remarked.
"Now I wonder why that could be?"
"I tell you - I have n idea."

I gave Karen a shrewd look.
"You're very much a like," said Karen, coming closer. "You and he - very much!"

"Are we?" I replied, in as neutral a voice as I could muster.

She put her hand on my thigh. "Oh yes, very much - in temperament, stature - *size!"*

I felt the excitement mount in me. Karen moistened her lips and began to unbuckle my belt. She looked at me coolly as her hand moved over me.

Unable to contain it any longer, our mouths came together in an iridescent explosion of mad unassuaged passion, of a kind that had not erupted between us with such furry in many many months. She drew away smiling faintly, her hand still tight on me, feeling - comparing in her mind.

"Not that different at all," she said.

"Really! Not that different?"

Did she think she was complementing me, or was she just an adroit tease? If there was one guy I could feel jealous over it was Mersell, for exactly the reasons Karen gave. If he had been a Garcia, or an Antonio, then I wouldn't have cared, they were out of my league and I knew it, but Mersell! He was most definitely not, and it drove me crazy just thinking about it - I guess in this respect I was not much different from Karen, and so unwittingly I played her game, she had me!

"Not a whole lot - no! but I know which I prefer," she said, insouciantly.

We kissed again spiralling into a voluptuous vortex of sensation, orbiting around each others conceited desire, like two cold suns in an empty cold universe, lit only by our love of ourselves.

"I have the edge over him, tell me I do?"

"You know you do, you have me."

"But really, tell me I do!" I persisted insanely.

"You do, you do, its you I want"

"Tell me!"

"I don't know, it's close, oh so close - you have me, isn't that enough? That should be enough for any man..!!"

In the end it always came back to her, I would never get the resounding endorsement I wanted from her; it always came back to her, my sun was always thrown back into orbit about her, and so it would go on in our lonely universe, one bent in upon the other, forever circling until all the stars burned out!

AVANT!

XIX

The bloody scene that had occurred over a month earlier had put increased pressure on security. The gates to the property were besieged night and day by a growing number of Tanit worshippers, intent on getting a glimpse of their priestess, or at the very least being allowed in, so that they may pay homage at the shrine of Karen. In order to avoid their clamouring, the fox left its lair while the hounds still clambered at the door. Late one night Karen, along with her closest acolytes, boarded a vessel to sail the short distance across the gulf to another villa on the *Cap Gammarth,* only a mile or so from the ancient capitol of the Phoenician empire, *Carthage.*

At this new and much smaller residence, Karen made plans for an extensive exploration of the ancient Phoenician homeland. When she wasn't looking at maps and guidebooks, or making up lists of places to visit, she was sunbathing topless on the beech adjacent to the villa, whilst at night dancing with her friends around bonfires to the accompaniment of panpipes, flutes and lyres. Such activities of course ensured that it was not long before her whereabouts became known once more, and not just to those who adored her, also to those who abhorred her.

"I will not hide away like some frightened creature. It is about time we got out among the people!" Declared Karen one morning. An uneasy look passed between those that were responsible for her safety.

"Before we leave here it is my intention to visit *Carthage,* as well as other Phoenician sites close by, such as *Utica* and *Megara."*

"But your magnificence," said Serapis, one of her chief advisors, " the people! Do you not think of them? It is not safe!"

"Oh! - will you stop whining! In the name of Eshmun! All will be well. By the name of the hidden symbols - Elissa and Tiratha! I know what I am doing!"

Serapis presented his hands, palms facing up. "As is your wish. Oh high priestess." Karen flicked her hand, and Serapis sloped off muttering and shaking his head.

Her visit to these cities passed without incident. The other part of her *grand tour* began a fortnight letter. Early one morning a small fleet of vehicles left the main gate, Karen and I travelling in a long black limousine accompanied by Almoud and Arkhmed, the rest of her people, as well as her copious wardrobe travelled in separate vehicles, including Pharaoh, Karen's cheetah, who brought up the rear of the cavalcade in a jeep. It must have been a spectacle for the locals, as we roared into one ancient city after another: 'the Tanit show had come to town.' A far cry from those early days, when we had travelled with the Bedouin through the desert, silent and unseen. Perhaps this, more than any other feature revealed the extent to which Karen had changed.

Travelling east we first came upon the Roman remains at *Bulla Regia,* then their were the Punic cities of *Sbeitla,* impressive *Dougga, Thurbo Majus,* with its majestic Corinthian columns, *Makthar,* and her wonderful mosaics, then there was *Ziqua, Thysdrus, Nabeul, El Jem,* and I don't know how many others! After a while each of these once proud cities drifted into a kind of vapour of pastel buff and grey, an endless stream of shattered buildings, half recked columns, broken arches and desecrated temples. At each place though, regardless of what was left, if it was of Punic origin, Karen would perform a sacred rite to Tanit, usually at the temple of Juno, her Roman equivalent: 'Juno Caelestis', since all of these Punic cities were later Romanised after the sacking of Carthage in 143 BCE

Wherever we went there was always an open door for us, and it was all too evident that many of these people, mostly Berbers, had far more generosity than they had material wealth. But they were always well rewarded for their hospitality, and very often Karen would leave them a gift in the form of a little trinket of gold from her bracelet, or else one of her gold bangles or some other item of hers, knowing full well that it would never be parted with by the family to which she gave it, regarding it as a sacred object to be passed down through the generations.

Karen loved the *Sahel,* situated along the eastern fringe of the country. We had all travelled many miles and seen many wondrous sites, the *Sahel* was the perfect place to pause and reflect. A beautiful villa was found for us, hugging the beech situated ten miles north of the modern city of *Sfax.* One of the things

Karen loved most of all about the Sahel were the wonderful white beeches which stretched from *Nabeul* in the north, to the Libyan frontier in the south. Idyllic: the scent of Jasmine ever present in the air, and the crashing of waves upon the beach at night. It is not surprising, that given such a setting, during those long nights Karen came close to me once more; discovering that her love for me had not been completely vanquished by her fame. Perhaps it was because, here she was not constantly besieged by those who wished only to venerate her as the body and mouthpiece of a goddess. Here, I was able to worship her as flesh and blood, as Karen, that mixed up kid. Karen my wife, my friend, and soul mate! But as always with precious moments, we were only too well aware of their transience. And I wondered if we would ever be this happy again? One could sense an aura of change in the air, the tide was turning fast. Was it really true that the Jasmine no longer smelt so sweet? It wasn't long before Karen's presence at even this remote location became known, but this time for reasons other than adulation. Karen insisted on sun bathing, or just lounging around the villa on its open terraces, completely naked or in the skimpiest bikini imaginable. Was it a last ditch attempt to seduce Mersell who had come to stay with us? The truth was she could not help herself. It was part of her provocative nature that she should be noticed. It was as if she was constantly straining towards the frontier of her own being, the adulation of the world would not leave her content - she always wanted more, even though she had long since surpassed any of her former rivals; it was almost as if she wanted to be more than she was! - when in fact it was her arch nemesis Pamela Lloyd who was now feeling Karen's sting, commenting in a magazine interview: ' Natasha, or Karen as she calls herself now, is first: a phoney - the head of a freak show! Second: ugly, disfigured! Third: a megalomaniac who never knew when to quite the stage!' In other parlance, it was probably the superb Liza Redcliffe who came closest of all to the last word on Karen's rise to fame, speaking in a top US journal: 'Of late Natasha has attained a precarious notoriety we should not be surprised at this, for she is so obsessed with the idea of fame she would go to any lengths, even to the extent of believing she is a goddess, and inventing a religion around herself. The real sex goddess needs no such devices, but comes to fame through her own innate beauty and sexuality: it is endorsed by those that believe in her. The spectacle of Karen is an invention of Natasha and because she was always passé in my eyes, and those of my colleagues in glamour and entertainment, it cannot last. True beauty and fame speaks for itself and is further endorsed in perpetuity!'

But whatever they said it no longer mattered, Karen was now truly world famous, regardless of how it had happened; whether it was long lasting - well the name of Tanit with which Karen was synonymous, had already lasted several thousand years, so I guess Karen's, 'precarious notoriety,' as Liza Redcliffe called it, would probably stick around a lot longer than the name of Liza Redcliffe - even so, a lot of what she had said was true! Liza Redcliffe possessed an indefatigable quality that did not rest in a simply amazing figure and incredible good looks. She was also a talented actress, singer and performer. She had entranced the world with this magic of hers and she was not about to relinquish quickly, her crown, as the worlds foremost sex symbol, especially to a lowly star of porn of the likes of 'Natasha!' Where once Natasha was always slamming her opponents, now these famous names were making noises of their own. When Liza Redcliffe and Pamela Lloyd, and others felt the need to speak out, then it was obvious they were smarting from Karen's fame, for it was *her* image, *her* name that was appearing in all the papers and magazines, and through her very elusiveness engendered even greater demand.

So, you may be wondering, I *d'know* - but if she had all this fame and notoriety, why wasn't she happy? I guess if I could answer that question we wouldn't be where we are now in this veil of tears. We are all woven from the same mortal fabric, and contained within the pattern is our own 'Moroccan flaw', and in human terms it gives rise to that strange emotion called jealously: so powerful an emotion that even the gods do not escape its effect; I guess it was jealously that made Karen so goddamn peevish at times:

"I don't know what you see in that little Japanese I got you!"

"She soothes my nerves," I said.

"She gives me the creeps, she's so quiet, and those funny little eyes of hers, always watching but she never says anything! - still waters! She's like a little rat that gets under my feet."

"Please don't speak about her like that, she is a lovely creature, a gentle soul."
"To hear you talk anybody would think you care more about her than you do me! It's me they all hate. Me they can't wait to stick with their knives again, not your little piece of Jap ass!"
'This was bad,' I thought, my little Tricksy had finally come under Karen's Eagle Owl gaze, and to continue the analogy, my little Tricksy stood about as much chance of survival under her roof as a mouse in an Eagle Owls nest. At *Kerkouane* the place was big enough to keep Tricksy out of Karen's way, but our new location on the *Sahel* was a lot smaller. I tired to watch out for her as best I could, but in the end Karen would get her pound of flesh regardless. I suppose then, it was inevitable that the final humiliating showdown should occur.
"Come here," demanded Karen, when she spied her one day scurry away, much like a little mouse, or in Karen's eyes: 'a rat!' Tricksy pulled up and padded over to Karen, her head hung. She was a smart kid, intuitive too, so I guess she had a fair inclining into what was coming.
"Look at you," said Karen, "come closer! come here!" Karen stretched out her hand and felt Tricksy's arm. "God! - you're so skinny, just skin and bone. Doesn't Julian feed you - hey little rat?" Tricksy remained silent. Sullen even.
"Did you hear me rat? I asked you a question!"
"Julian good to Tricksy," came the reply.
"Yes I'm sure he is...Ah! - there you are Julian. I was just saying to...to," Karen gestured with her hand, "I was remarking how thin your little Japanese thing is!"
Karen still had hold of Tricksy's arm, her dark eyes filtered over me, a pained expression in them already. My stomach turned over, it was too late she was already as good as done for.
Karen began to feel the rest of her: her shoulders, her body. "There's - there's nothing to you - is there!"
Ironically Karen was wearing one of her high neck tight fitting Japanese bodices, a red silk affair with gold embroidered lotus pattern. She began to undo the snacks: they eagerly gave up their burden. Karen looked down at the swell of her bosom, which was only achieved these days with ample support from a fortified brassier.

"This - this is what a woman is supposed to look like," said Karen, and putting her hand beneath her chest she lifted her breasts, so that they bunched together like two plump pumpkins in a basket. Karen looked down at herself admiringly. The truth was, without support they tended to loll like wilted fruit on a dead vine. Not surprising I suppose, since they had been skewed more times than the head of Moby Dick!

"A woman should have curves, where are your curves?"

Tricksy momentarily flashed her dark eyes at Karen and then threw them to the floor again.

"I don't know what Julian sees in you! And look at your skin, look at you! So pale, and ill looking. Like snow. Snow white - that's what I shall call you. What do you think Julian - snow white?"

Tricksy looked over to me. I looked away guilty. "Yes if you like, now come on Tricks lets get going."

"Ah! - ah - ah!...Not so hasty," said Karen, griping Tricksy's thin wrist, I haven't finished with snow white yet. I'm curious as to what you look like under all this," indicating Tricksy's somewhat lavish Kimono.

"Strip!" Demanded Karen.

I took a step forward. "Karen, don't please! Don't make her," I protested.

Tricksy now stared at me, her eyes pleading, I looked away again.

"Strip, I said! Take off your robe, I want to look at your body." Glancing at me, "I want to see what you have hidden there, that so fascinates Julian."

Tricksy remained immobile. "Karen stood up, her big chest inches from Tricksy's nose. "Insolent little rat!"

The flat of Karen's hand came down hard and fast on Tricksy's face, leaving a red imprint of Karen's hand on her white flesh. Karen grabbed the wide black binding around her middle and shook it free. Defeated, Tricksy looked up, trying desperately to fight back her tears. Karen watched and waited, as Tricksy slowly began to remove the various fastenings, and unwind the yards of silk that went up to make her magnificent kimono, until there was a bundle of glorious shimmering silk at her feet. Tricksy stood partially naked in just a tiny vest and knickers.

"And *this,*" said Karen, grabbing hold of the thin cotton undergarment.

Tricksy challenged Karen's grey eyes a second but knew what she would get if she didn't comply, quickly she pulled it off from over her head.

Karen could not help reveal through imperceptible movements of the muscles around her eyes and mouth, a perverse enjoyment at what she saw, she also could not hide the fact that she was also taken slightly aback by Tricksy's physique. I don't think she expected it to be so finely toned. Karen slowly looked her up and down,"

"Look at you," said Karen, "you're so thin and scrawny, and so small! What are these?" she said, pinching her stiff little breasts. Oh Julian!" exclaimed Karen, expelling an ugly forced laugh. "She's just like a boy - a boy I tell you! But then that's may be what you see in her? - I d'know!"

"Leave her alone Karen - stop it now."

"I will, you can have her back in a second, I just want to look."

I could see Tricksy had begun to tremble, trying hard not to let her knees knock.

"Please Karen let her alone - don't!"

"Don't get hysterical Julian, I'm curious that's all, I want to see what she's got."

Karen moved her attention lower down and was forced to recognise the fact that Tricksy had fine well developed thighs, a quality that was expected in a top class Geisha. She put her hand between them and Tricksy bit her lip as Karen started to investigate her, all the time watching Tricksy's face. Finally the tears began to run down her flushed cheeks.

"How do you manage Julian, when she's so small!" said Karen, removing her hand. She rubbed her fingers togther and like an expert in animal smells put them to her nose. "Hmmm!" she remarked, raising her eyebrows.

She observed again, Tricksy's strong thighs and well toned abdominals. "There's more to you than meets the eye snow white."

Sighing heavily, as one who is bored: "It's all right," she said, turning away and waving her hand nonchalantly, "put your things back on, you can go now."

I rushed over to Tricksy who was on the point of collapse and helped her on with her vest, and gathering up he shimmering silks bundled them around her; suddenly she turned and ran sobbing from the room, yards of silk trailing behind her. I turned to Karen who was sitting down fanning herself. I stood in front of her.

"I've seen you do some horrible things Karen, but I never knew you could be as cruel as that!"

Karen sneered. "Do what? I wanted to see what she looked like that's all...She is my property after all - bought and paid for. I only gave her to you to keep you company, I didn't expect you to fuck it all the time - which," she said, rubbing her fingers and smelling them again, "if I am not mistaken, you have been doing a lot just recently!"

Karen was right of course, whenever she could, Tricksy would scamper into my bed and then it would be inevitable, I could never reject her.

"Admit it Julian."

"Yes - she's a Geisha for goodness sakes what did you expect!"

"Well I don't know! I thought she just gave you baths and stuff, a sort of masseuse, as well as some company for you!"

I laughed. Could Karen be so naive! Yes - yes she could actually, especially about things like that. "Oh, really Karen!"

"What is she like? Is she good? I imagine she could be a lot of fun in bed."

"Yes - yes she is actually. I told you, she's a Geisha, her whole function in life is to please men."

Karen rolled her eyes. "I see, are you saying you prefer her over me? - is that it! Are you saying she is better in bed than me?"

"If you want the truth Karen..."

"Yes go on..."

"You don't care about pleasing men, you only think about yourself, you are the most selfish lover I have ever known." Aside: "admittedly I haven't known that many." Renewing my attack: "but Tricksy knows how to make a man happy, she is generous and sweet and giving, and expert at what she does. You wouldn't have the first idea how to truly please a man. With these people sex is an art form." I paused, feeling I had gone too far. My intention was not to wound Karen, there had already been too much wounding, but I felt some redress was in order. "You are conceited Karen! OK so Tricksy hasn't got big tits like you but she is still every inch a woman, I can vouch for that, one hundred and ten percent!"

"Have you finished."

"I'm sorry Karen. Although I like being with Tricksy, I don't love her. Its you I love. I always have," I said, starting to feel the desperation creeping in.
"No, its all right Julian, you've made it abundantly clear what you think of me. I'm a crap lover in your eyes! All the time we've known each other, and you hated the way we made love! - well thanks! Why don't you go with your Geisha, go and fuck each other senseless for all I care!"

Karen got up and started to pace. A very bad sign. "Hah! - you - you have the audacity to tell me - *me!* that I'm a crap lover! *Me!* - of all people! A high priestess of Tanit! Men, young boys just queue up for me, they can't get enough of me, and you compare me with that little slip of a girl. You think she is better than me, that she could outdo me! - *yeah right!"*

I could see the way it was going: Pandora all over again. I had to do something - think fast to stare her off that inevitable conclusion. The truth was, I wasn't trying to protect Tricksy, it was Karen that I feared for. Like Pandora, she had underestimated her. She was a little dynamo, a small hard bundle of muscle and nerve that could go forever. I never even got close to scratching the surface. I could never get her to climax through normal intercourse, but such was her consummate control over mind and body, together with a powerful set of internal muscles, she was able to climax on demand, and in such a way as to leave one in no doubt that she had!
"Do you want that we find out who is the best?" Karen called to one of her servants to: 'bring the Jap girl!'

I cast my eyes to the floor, "Oh Karen, do we have to do this?
"Well you started it. You said she was better than me, and you know how I am, I get curious about these things, so lets see shall we! I'll get Marbo and Almoud to round up some of the local men - and boys; shouldn't be too difficult! Ah, here she is, your expert whore! Julian has been telling me of your great skill as a lover. Is he right?"

Tricksy I noticed was still crying, her lovely white face was streaked with tears and her beautiful clear complexion blotchy: her gorgeous eyes reddened and swollen.
"I make him happy that is all." A fresh set of emotion came bursting through like a Niagara. "Julian, he so unhappy - so unhappy."

I ran over to her. "No I'm not! - No I'm not Tricksy! - I'm not unhappy!"
"You unhappy because of her," persisted Tricksy, pointing to Karen, who was looking a little bemused.
"How so?" asked Karen, putting her head on one side. All her verve and gusto seemed to be evaporating before my eyes.
"Tricksy know because he tell." she looked over at me, her dark eyes like topazes that cut me to the core of my being.
"Please!" I begged.
"He is very unhappy man."
"Why? Why Tricksy, why is he unhappy..?"
She closed her narrow beautiful lids over those jewels and then looked away: a subtle move of the head that *only* a consummate artist - a high class Geisha, could perform!
"Because he loves you. His heart brakes for you. He would give his life for you, he would rather die in fact."
"Please, please *Trickatoisha'yamah!"*
"I must! Great lady demand truth. Tricksy tell - Tricksy always tell truth!"
She turned to me, in some control now, almost proud: "You do not love me, I try to make you love me but you do not. I know I can never make you love me, that you will never look at me the way you do her. I know that when I am in your arms it is she that you are thinking of - all time, all time it is she!"
Suddenly it got too much for her and she broke down again in floods of tears, "Tricksy try to make happy, she try but no - no!"
I went to her and she fell into my arms, her tight little body vibrating, convulsing with emotion.
"I'm sorry Tricksy." I said.
Karen noticed the servants and ushered them away. I felt Karen's hand on my shoulder.
"I had no idea. Take her back to her room Julian."
When I came back Karen was sitting on the terrace, a cold wind had got up. It was getting late in the afternoon, the sea had white horses on it, and I thought of the time we had chased them into the port of Rhodes, and I got a yearning for the sea, and the *Idhra.* I sat down next to her, her face looked strained. Neither

of us spoke, we had gone beyond words. She sniffed and wiped her eyes in that proud way of hers and took my hand in hers. It felt good, it felt warm and strong.

The following morning I looked in on Tricksy, to my concern she was still crying. She had been crying all day and all night apparently. When she saw me she stopped - momentarily.

"I'm sorry for what happened."

"She disgraced me!" said Tricksy, raising herself and sitting on the edge of the bed. She put her head in her hands and fresh deluge sprung from her eyes. I put my arm about her and for the first time ever I felt her body tense at my touch. I moved it away.

"It is no good - Tricksy must go away," she said, between her sobs.

"Don't go Tricksy. Don' let her win, she is the one with the disgrace, not you."

"*Ahey...!* Julian you stupid sometimes! It is not just the disgrace."

"Oh, I see!" I said, slightly taken aback. She had never been this familiar before.

"How can I stay? You do not love me; if you did you would never let her do those things to me. I thought may be you could in time, but no!"

I remained silent. She looked at me closely. "Ah! - but I think you are happy a little? You and the great one get it together - get funky no!"

Tricksy actually laughed, and then cried again.

"It is good, you are meant for each other. May be Tricksy do good thing, bring you together both before it too late."

"Too late,"

"It is nothing."

"You know, you mustn't hate her. She has had a hard time of it, her life - lives, if you believe in that, have made her self-centred, but deep down she is a very wonderful person - really she is! She told me to tell you that she is sorry for what she did. She didn't say you should leave either."

"I think may be best Tricksy go."

"Look, stay a while. Think about it. May be, who knows you and the great lady could become friends?"

"Julian please!"

"Well stay any way, at least for a while. You know what she is like, she'll be off

again soon, and then you'll have the place to yourself more or less, I'll see to it."
"May be I stay, may be go," was Tricksy's response.

I kissed the side of her face, which only caused a fresh burgeoning of tears. I got up to leave and she reached out for my hand. I took it, and she held it tight - deathly tight. "Tricksy always love you, stay - go, Tricksy love."
"I know."

What I also knew, and tried to put at the back of my mind, was that Tricksy had a distinct bent towards certain sexual pecadillos - that I personally found difficult to take serious. But she claimed: 'all men like to tie their women up and beat them.' "Beat Tricksy," she would intone, offering me her cute little butt, and handing me a switch: "she's been very bad girl!" So I guess, out of such a masochistic streak, I should not have been surprised when she decided to stay on at the villa.

Often, in the dead of night, after one had filtered out the continual battering of the surf upon the not so distant shore, one could detect emanating from Tricksy's room, the muffled sound of her sobs - which meant I guess, she was enjoying herself! And if she needed reason, one needed little guile nor cunning, to spy Karen and I in the throws of sexual union. It was as if Karen had never heard of the word: discretion!

Tricksy's confession of her love for me, and just how rotten Karen's treatment of me had been in the face of the love I had for her, had the effect of bringing Karen up sharp as to just how self-indulgent she could be at times. Karen's response was to direct a flow of libidinous affection towards me, the likes I had never experienced before. I guess she also wanted to stamp her claim on me while Tricksy was still around. The result was, Karen was even hotter stuff than usual, she wanted to make love all the time - I mean all the time! - and anywhere, especially on the beach towards dusk. Returning, after we had taken her cheetah for a walk, Karen would strip off and run into the sea. I of course would follow, soon we were close together as one, with the cloak of Poseidon's fertile waters around us, just as we had at *Tel Arqa*, and a hundred other shores.
"I'm sorry I treated you bad," she said, as we lay on the beach, the surf washing around our bodies.

"It's all right," I said, kissing her neck.

"It's not. I never realised just how unhappy I was making you. I'm such a selfish bitch!"

"You are, but it's OK."

She hit me playfully around the head. "You're not supposed to agree with me all the time you know! Still - I have said and done some rotten things."

Her hand moved down my body in an investigative move.

"Hmm!" she moaned, with satisfaction. "You are good Julian, really you are. I shouldn't have teased you before about Mersell." She moved her mouth to my ear and whispered: "You're much bigger!"

"Am I?" At that moment a wave crashed over us. We rolled around in the surf and in the sea spray I made love as I never had before. Afterwards we walked up the beach together and slumped down to let our bodies dry out in the dying rays of the evening sun.

Karen felt out my hand, and it wasn't long before she was being prehensile again. She took out a bottle of after-sun oil and encouraged me to cover her in it; it was always glorious to massage her supple body, which always had the effect of turning her on towards self-adoration. Luxuriating in the touch of my hand over her skin, she stretch her long body.

"Hmm! Julian, you do that so good. You still like my body, it still sends you mad doesn't it?"

"It has never failed yet."

"I know I shouldn't ask, but you do like me better than Trickatoishah, don't you?"

"You know I do. You know it's you that I love."

"I know that, but did you - you know, like it better with her? I have to say, she may not be very big but she does have a good body - I could see that!"

Here was my opportunity to get my own back, but I was too tired of the games, there had been to much hurt, to many tears and misunderstandings. There is a time for teasing and I time for honesty.

"She was very nice to be with, but the truth is, when I was with her I always thought of you..."

"You did? you really did, every time?"

"All the time," I said, although it was not entirely true.

My words had the desired effect - sending her kind of crazy! She slid her hands down her torso to her thighs and arched her back: massaging her thighs, moving towards a self-induced climax. "Ah! -ah ah ahh! - oh! oh yeah! Yeah! Oh, hold me Julian!" And her body writhed in my arms as she came. She looked up at me, breathing hard, her mouth open incredibly wide: cavernous - lascivious. "Ah! - oh yes, yes!" she groaned, "Tell me Julian, tell me again, I am better than her aren't I? - I am aren't I?"

I lay on my side, propping myself up on an elbow observing her as she twisted and contorted like a serpent in some mad delirium of self love.

"There's no comparison."

"No comparison! - no no comparison, no comparison!" she chanted, as she felt her big breasts that lolled across her chest. After a while the madness abated and her body became less animated.

"Poor thing, to have such little breasts, she really is like a boy in that respect," she said, still absently fondling herself.

"She is," I had to agree, reluctantly.

"I could have taken her couldn't I, I mean if it came to it - don't you think?"

"It would have been no contest," I said.

"You're right, what was I thinking of! Poor girl, to let a slip of a thing like that get to me."

"It was my fault,"

"No, she was right about that, I deserved it, I treat you rotten. To think I nearly let you get away." She suddenly straddled me, pinning me down, "You are mine buster, and don't you forget it!" Grabbing me, feeling me out, her wonderful head bent over me, her long braids covering me like a golden curtain, the cave of her mouth surrounding me, taking me into her. And so it would go on, lost in each other, sometimes till dawn.

I was glad Mersell had come to stay when he had, as Karen continued to indulge her licentious nature with increasing abandon. I found his presence a sobering influence since I was now complicit in her sexual outrage. It would have been so easy to do as Karen did, and throw all caution to the four winds.

"What are you doing Mr Julian, going with her dressed like that?" observed Mersell.

Karen had painted my face with Tyrian dye and shaven my body and bedecked me in the robes of a priest of Tanit. I guess I had started to turn native - well Phoenician homeland of three thousand years ago native!

"You must be more prudent in your activities," he said, eyeing me with a degree of alarm.

"Yes I know, but I am her consort, and she has made me her *pontiff maximus.* She is the goddess! - I see that now. She is fantastic, you have no idea what she is like to be with. She wants me, wants me - *all the time!"*

"I have an idea what she is like."

"Yes, I'm sure you do Mersell! She is still my wife, don't forget that!"

"She is a woman, and like all good-looking women they can beguile a man with their sexual charms; but only for a time. You are drunk with passion Mr Julian, she has gone to your head. She is a wanton temptress..."

He continued on in this vain speaking to me earnestly of all the dangers that Karen had blinked my eyes to, and reminded me of my duty, which was to protect her, that: 'how could I when I was so immersed in her?'

He made me see the danger we were putting ourselves under. What he feared most of all, and had every reason to, was a backlash from the indigenous people of the area, who did not share Karen's love of all things 'natural'.

The devout Muslims were obviously offended, seeing her naked displays and sexual cavortings as a direct effrontery to their religious sensibilities. They were not quiet either, when it came to voicing their descent. They would hurl abuse at her followers in the street, they openly called her *putain:* scrawling graffiti on the walls of the villa, and other places in the surrounding villages. Hate male arrived declaring all manner of malicious intent. Even an article appeared in one of the local newspapers calling for her expulsion from the *Sahel,* siting her as: 'the whore of the Maghreb.'

"I will not be pushed around by these people," said Karen, when Arkhmed tried to caution prudence.

"It's not my fault they are *stuffed up!"* replied Karen, indignantly.

"Yes but it is their religion, oh magnificence."

"Our ways predate their *ideas* by more than five thousand years."

"Yes, oh sublime one, but it is their country, it is their way which dominate now," persisted Arkhmed, somewhat bravely.

Karen's usual response to any form of censure, was to wave her hand and tell her advisors to: 'be gone!' Both Mersell and I were the the last appeal for common sense. Normally we were able to get through to her, but for some reason, almost as if she wanted to bring things to a head, she persisted in doing things that upset the natives. Apart from flaunting her lovely body, she would indulge Pharaoh's love of the beech, taking him for long walks, and when it was quiet, just before dusk, she would let him off the lead to let him have a - 'good run.' He may not have been the fastest cheetah, what with all the snacks Karen gave him, but he was good for at least 70 Kph. He was very well behaved for a top predator, and as far as we knew, he had only ever eaten two dogs during our stay. OK, so Pharaoh may have got on the wrong side of the canine community, and put a few backs up among local dog owners, but they had no call in doing what they did. We heard Karen scream one morning: rushing out we saw her bent over Pharaohs lovely svelte body. He had been poisoned and left stretched out on the beach at the foot of the veranda.

"I'll get them for this," said Karen, through her teeth, They'll pay for this.... Why? - Why? What had he ever done to anybody? The only truly sweet thing I've ever known," she said, gently running her fingers through Pharaoh's soft fur.

Of course, what can one say! - this was nasty. Only a nasty brutish people could do a thing like that. Only cowards and brutes could do such a thing to a creature such as Pharaoh. But it was a clear message that these people were not prepared to put up with any more of Karen's - *sassy* ways.

We laid Pharaoh to rest in a beautiful wooded glade scented with Jasmine and pine.

Karen gave him the blessing of the goddess and offered up a prayer to the gods of the underworld for ease of passage to his happy hunting ground.

After his *murder*, the atmosphere at the villa became even more oppressive.

"You should go away, perhaps. Leave here," suggested Mersell, when it became clear that Karen was taking the loss of her friend deeply.

"Yes, I don't think I want to stay here any longer. Everything reminds me of him, and the people here are so nasty. I'm afraid of what I might do if I ever found those that did it," said Karen, curling her fist up into a tight little ball.

A few days after this tragic episode a letter arrived from Garcia, inviting us to his island to celebrate the Eleusinian Mysteries: always guaranteed to be a good bash! It could not have come at a better time. 'At last,' I thought, 'an opportunity to get her away from North Africa and the the frenzy of Tanit worshipers, and the growing threat from the locals.' Karen's response however, was not as enthusiastic as my own.

"Shall I write and tell him we are coming?"

"I don't know," Karen replied.

"But why not?"

"There is still much to do among the Tunisian's - then of course there is Algeria, and Morocco, may be even Western Sarah, and I haven't finished with Libya yet."

"You can't be serious?"

"I like it here."

"But the people don't like you being here. In actual fact they hate you. Only a tiny proportion of tribal people have any affinity with your ideas, and even that is on the wane."

"My people are loyal. They love me....Look - if you want to go, then you have my blessings. Why don't you take Mersell with you? I'm sure he would love to witness the rites and meet Garcia."

"Perhaps I will," I replied, nonchalantly.

"It is your life Julian. You must do as you please. But don't worry I am leaving here. I can't stand it any more, if I stay any longer I kill one of those bastards, Just for the hell of it."

I can sometimes tell when Karen is joking, but I knew the fixed glare in her eye told me she was deadly serious. It was pointless in discussing anything with her when she was being crazy like this. The following day, as if to underline the point, news came from *Kerkouane* that two Berbers had been shot dead near to the villa on the Cape *Gammarth,* after disturbances broke out between a small group of Tanit worshipers and Muslims.

"Isn't that enough now? You have to leave!" I said.

"What it means is that, more than ever I am needed here." Karen turned to one of her servants. "Tell the messenger that I shall return to *Kerkouane* at my earliest opportunity. I shall be going south to visit the *Tuareg* people, then I shall return to Cape *Bon.*"

"Share madness! Don't you see its madness to stay?" I said, waving my hands around.

Karen was at her most superior and composed. "Calm yourself Julian. The goddess will protect me."

"The goddess! Hah...!"

"Do not speak ill of her," said Karen, sternly.

"In desperation I turned to her *augur* who was hovering in the background. "Tell her," I said, "tell her she *cannot* stay!"

Slowly, reluctantly, he moved closer. Karen craned her neck round as she sat on her makeshift thrown. "Where the hell is he? Come here man. What is it you have to say now. *Aghh..!* What do the livers say today then?"

"It..it..is..." faltered the grey faced man, drowning in his voluminous purple robe.

"Well - out with. In the name of the gods!" Karen turned to me: "You know I don't like augurs, they're always so gloomy." She mimicked an old persons croaky voice: "*ooh it doesn't bode well...*"

"The signs are not...*good,* oh most regal one."

"Not good! What does that mean?"

"Hmm...crows - gathering in the west. Strange birds seen...flying...west. Eight. I council caution in any new venture in that..quadrant."

"You see Julian, nothing to worry about. I'm not going west I'm going south." Karen yawned...and raised a languid arm towards her augur. "Oh,you may go. And it won't hurt to smile sometimes," she called after him.

The following day found Karen in her closet sorting through her vast array of clothes.

"Oh! - it's you. What do you think of this?" said Karen holding up a long shimmering gold chiffon skirt. She had on just a tiny black garment and a kind of vest made of gold webbing. "one must try I suppose to dress for these people - these *criminals.*"

"So your mind is made up then, you're definitely going?"

"Yes, you know I am."

"Who are these people anyway?"
"The *Tuareg* are desert dwellers. They go back *thousands* of years. They were here even before the Phoenicians came. Anyway they have asked if I will visit them."
"Well, can't they come here, or to *Kerkouane?"*
"Oh Julian! - they are a very secretive people. They, like me are not part of this modern world." Karen swished round in her skirt: "Now what do you think?"
"Lovely," I said, barely taking any notice. She began to get out of it and look for another to try on. "Anyhows," she continued, in a matter-of-fact way, "they want to meet me, it's only natural I suppose," she said, admiring her figure. "If they are as ancient as they say they are, they may perhaps have some knowledge of who I once was."
"So where is this place?"
"I don't know, some place in the south. They are semi-nomadic, but they tend to herd their goats in some of these old abandoned Berber villages at this time of the year. Somewhere on the edge of the Sahara. Sounds like fun doesn't it! Are you in or not? Oh! - but I forgot, you're going to see Garcia with Mersell." Karen gave me a fiendish look.
"I'm not going anywhere without you. You're still my wife goddamn it..." I broke off when Karen bent over and began rummaging through a large basket of her clothes. The view she presented of herself made me lose my concentration.
"Ah! Here it is. I haven't worn this in ages," she said, straightening up. She fastened around her hips a beautiful gold shimmering silk sarong. Standing in front of a full length mirror she adjusted it so that it covered part of the ugly scar just above her left hip, but puled it down lower over the other side.
"What do you think?"
"Don't you think its a bit low? I can see your underwear...whatever that thing is?
"Oh, not you as well! Don't be such a prude Julian!"
"I was thinking of you. You can't keep going around half naked. Not here."
"I'm not half naked." Karen puled her sarong further down keeping it all akimbo, and turned back to the mirror: thrusting out her hip in that jaunty provocative stance of hers. She seemed satisfied by what she saw until she focused on the site of her wound. She ran her hand over it and frowned. She quickly swung round. "Don't look Julian."

"You're gorgeous," I responded.

"Av'course I am," she said, in that silly way of hers.

Then it struck me: she was really just a child, and like a child unable to comprehend the narrowness and fixity of adult ideas. And suddenly to my great surprise there were tears in my eyes, and despite my efforts they began to stream copiously down my face. "I'll *never* leave you...*Never.*" I said in a strained kind of voice.

"What on Earth is the matter?" said Karen, turning round. She dropped the green Kimono she had picked out and took a couple of steps towards me, her lavender eyes wide with surprise. I fell into her arms and began to sob like a child.

"I'm so afraid. Afraid for you. I love you so much Karen...If anything should happen to you..."

Karen tried to comfort me, but I could tell from her stiffening stance she felt that this unequivocal outburst of emotion had gone on long enough. She put her hands to my face and made me look at her. The site of her ravaged beauty made me want to cry even more.

I touched the deep cleft in her cheek left by the Syrian knife. "Your poor sweet face. What have they done to you," I said, mawkishly wallowing.

"Stop it! Stop it now!" she said, shaking me."

She looked serious so I did my best to hold back the deluge. "Now look, there's nothing going to happen to me. I have Marbo and there is Oudoso, and there's..." she paused, on the tip of her tongue was the name of her cheetah. She even cast her eyes about for him - "And there are others, so there really is no need to get upset - nay?"

I nodded, and hid my face against her shoulder, feeling suddenly ashamed of my outburst. She soothed my head with her long fingers.

"I know how much you love me," she whispered in my ear. "I don't know why you do, but I do know..."

"You're my soul mate," I responded.

"That's right," she said, breathlessly - "soul mates."

If I had to guess I would have said that there were tears in her eyes too.

"Now come on," she said, sniffing loudly and wiping her face, "help me to pick out something practical to wear for the desert. How about this?" she said, retrieving her beautiful emerald colour Kimono.

It was arranged that Marbo and the majority of Karen's other servants and followers would remain behind at the villa. She was most adamant that not one inch of ground would be lost. That she would not be pushed out by bigotry. Her presence would remain in some form on the *Sahel.* Marbo was most indignant about being left behind, but Karen assured him that it would be safer for her in the desert among the more friendly tribes, but that she would take her other Negro bodyguard, the gargantuan Oudoso, as well as Mahkmoud who had an imposing figure also.

All of her people were completely distraught on the morning we left, the colossi, Marbo, in particular was in floods of tears and seemingly inconsolable.

"Honestly Marbo! pull yourself together," said Karen, brushing her lips against his cheek.

"Please mistress do not leave us. Do not go," he pleaded.

These sentiments were echoed by Tricksy, who not to be outdone by such displays of emotion, rushed forward and threw her arms around me.

"Please don't go - please! Tricksy go, you stay. Oh, my brave Julian! - I will never see you again - never! - never! - I know it."

I tried to reassure her, but she was set in her grief. She held her puffy face up to mine, her eyes like two boiled eggs: so swollen were they, from weeks of continual crying.

I noticed Karen at my side, tapping her sandalled feet impatiently, as Tricksy still held on to me - limpet fashion, while lamenting my imminent loss to her - 'forever!'

"Come on Julian," snapped Karen. In the end Marbo and some of the Berber women had to prize her off of me before I could get away: screaming and crying, it reminded me of Karen's first departure from Sapphos.

"Poor girl," I said, as I got in the jeep next to Karen.

"Quite mad," she replied dryly.

If the truth was to be told, everyone's heart was heavy on that day of departure. But it was too late for regrets, we all fell, one way or another, in the long shadow of Karen's fate: the die had been cast!

A four wheel drive vehicle, had been hastily acquired for us, along with a driver and guide. Non of us knew who these people were, only that the driver was supposed to be of the Berber clan. The guide, who it was said was knowledgeable of the *Grand Erg*, and had special knowledge of the *Tuareg* people, and their movements, was of unknown Arab extraction. Along with Oudoso who rode up-front, in all there were eight of us, Mahkmoud, Karen, myself, Mersell, and a Berber woman, who watched over Karen like a tawny eagle.

The *Tuareg*, as I pointed out earlier, are renowned for their fierce independence. A semi-nomadic people, they range across southern Libya, Algeria, Niger, Mali and southern Tunisia. Another name for these people which fairly sums them up is the *imashaghen*, meaning: 'the noble and the free'. What fascinated Karen more than anything was their other handle, 'the blue people,' famed as they are for their indigo dyed cloth which stains their hands blue. Her own Phoenicians were known as the 'purple people,' the word 'Phoenician' being a corruption of the Greek for purple: 'porphyry'. This, judging by Karen's enthusiasm, was enough to cement a firm relationship between these two ancient peoples.

"You see," said Karen excitedly, "the true origins of the Tuareg are unknown. It says right here," she said, handing me her book on ancient African culture.

"Perhaps they were always here, even before the Phoenicians?"

"Perhaps," said Karen, pensively, her eyes seemed to gaze beyond the present, one could only surmise what kind of world, full of gayly decorated peoples, she was inhabiting.

Suddenly our Jeep went over a large boulder which threw Karen against me, jolting her out of her reverie. I looked out of the window, all I could see were clouds of red dust.

"Looks as if we are getting closer to the desert."

"Yes," replied Karen, screwing up her face as a swirl of sand engulfed our vehicle. My sari is getting all dusty."

"Where is it exactly we are going?" I asked.

"According to the guide, the group of Tuareg that offered to meet me, herd their goats at a place called *Ksar-Rhilane.*"

I looked on my map and found it marked: a tiny little dot in a remote location about twenty miles inside the *Grand Erg Oriental.*
"That's strange," said Karen, "we should be going south, but we seem to be skirting the salt lake for some reason."
I consulted the map again, "The *Chott el-Jerid,* That takes us *west!"*
Karen leaned forward and got Oudoso's attention, "Ask him where we are going, this isn't the way," said Karen.
Oudoso conversed with the guide in Arabic. The guide shook his head and spoke rapidly, in that off hand manner that seems normal behaviour for Arabs.
"He says we go west. Tuareg people move. We go to mountain oasis - *Mides."*
Karen and I looked at one another. A tiny movement of the muscles around her mouth, was the only indication of inner stress, otherwise she remained her usual inscrutable self. "Oh well.." She said, lightly.
"*That's* on the border with Algeria," I observed. "Do you have folks in Algeria?" I asked Mersell. "You could pay them a surprise visit."
"In the north Monsieur Julian, a long way from here."
"We are heading west Karen," I remarked.
"Are we," she replied, nonchalantly. Distracted: "Look at the lake, isn't it incredible! - so many colours! Look Julian, isn't it amazing? Lets stop!"
She communicated her wish to Oudoso. We came to a halt a few miles further along the causeway, which ran from the south shore to the north. "I'm sure I can see people out there," said Karen, once we were out of the jeep. "Isn't that a Camel? Look can you see it?"
"Mahkmoud laughed."
"What is it?"
"Mirage! This time of day you see many," he said, laughing.
"Spooky!" exclaimed Karen as she walked a little way towards the spectre, her eyes wide with childlike fascination. "I'd love just to walk out there - to the middle. You'd be surrounded then by mirages, but you wouldn't know what was real and what was false." She kicked the surface with her foot and broke through its crusty outer skin. "Its all so dead. Nothing could live here."
"Its dangerous to go too far," I said.
Karen thrust her hand into the thin crust of salt at the edge of the lake, bringing

it out shimmering: "look," she said, holding up her hand. I picked up some of the fine crystals and smeared them on her face.
"Now you look like Lots wife," I said, and we both laughed. She ran towards meher hands full of crystals, intent on reprisal. Finally I grabbed hold of her and she let me push her over, rolling her in the salt, Karen laughing hysterically all the time. The others looked on baffled, but amused. She stood up, covered from head to foot in the strange sparkling substance.
"Now you really do look like Lot's wife," I said.
Karen would have loved to stay and play longer on the shimmering petrified lake of salt, but our guide was anxious we reach the oasis before nightfall.
We camped just outside a deserted Berber village, close to a deep ravine. Our guide informed us that the *Tuareg* sometimes used the village as shelter for their goats. If we did not find them there by morning, then they might be further to the west, at another oasis a few miles across the border. In any case, by the time we had made camp and eaten it was dark and therefore too late to go looking for these elusive 'indigo people'.

Karen and I shared a black canvas tent, of the kind used by Bedouin. Although the others were nearby, Oudoso probably still awake sitting by the fire keeping a watchful eye on our tent, and the Berber woman concealed in her own tent, but her ears as receptive as a Genet's, to the smallest of sound: for all of that Karen and I felt snug and alone.
"I had a great day today, didn't you? I loved the lake."
"Yes and you still taste salty," I said, kissing her shoulder.
Karen stretched luxuriously and sighed with satisfaction at her own being. She looked across at me intently.
"Come here," she said, "join your sleeping-bag with mine."
"What a good idea."
"How do you like your Lot's wife?"
"She's superb," I said.
"Be careful you don't dissolve her with your kisses."
"That would be a terrible loss."
"You know I said the lake was dead, well I'm not a pillar of salt. I'm not barren like that lake."
"You're not?"

"I don't think so. If you plant a seed deep enough it will grow - even now, and there's nothing I want more. Do you feel the same?"
"I do, and I have for a long time," I replied, my heart filling with excitement and joy.
"You would really like a child?"
"Yes, if it came from us."
"What would you want, a girl or a boy."
"I always thought it would be good to have a daughter. She would be every bit as beautiful as her mother."
"Only the body comes from the union of a man and a woman," said Karen, after a moments pause.
"Then because of you it is sure to be beautiful," I said.
"But what of its soul?" mused Karen. "Still you have a good soul Julian, don't you?"
"It would be a completely different person, a different being from us," I replied.
"When do you think the soul enters the body?"
"I don't know, just before birth some say."
"Why did I enter this body?" said Karen, perplexed.
"I'm glad it did," I said, kissing her neck.
She turned round to look at me. "I'm serious, *why* this body and not some other body?"
"Because, doubtless as Garcia would say in his assiduous way, it was the destiny of your soul to choose the body it inhabits on this material plane. And I must say it could not have chosen a better one."
"You would say that," she said, digging me playfully in the side. "But it doesn't figure. I have a rotten nature Julian. I should be in some horrible bent body."
"That's the point. Where would the challenge be?"
"You're quite clever aren't you! Yes, I see what you mean. If I was ugly and my soul was wanton, then no one would want me any way. Then it would just be retribution."
"Indeed - and only Christians could come up with an idea like that, since what would be the point in it? How would a soul ever get to learn and grow?"
"So you think there is still hope for me?" said Karen, plaintively.

I kissed her fantastic face again. "There is every hope for you." I said, touching her body. It felt so vital, so stark: the darkness was filled by her essence. Nothing else existed to me except Karen's body, her resplendent form filled my senses, as I drifted with her through our empty dark universe.

Karen pressed her face against mine and whispered from the darkness: "Come to me Julian, I want your child."

I felt her great strength surround me, holding me fast, in that other world into which the spark of life enters. We felt so at ease with oneanother now, there was no longer the desperate straining for some peak that was always just out of reach, instead, a wonderful flow of one body into another. When it was done she thrust her hips upward; gradually relaxing them and stretching, luxuriating in the sense of her own resplendence.

"I felt you Julian, I felt you there. I'm sure a child will come," she said, a little breathlessly. She sighed deeply, and languidly reached out for my hand. "I hope it happens, I hope I am fertile enough."

"Of course," I said, kissing her neck, her face. "You have to be."

"I don't know."

"Because of Pandora?" I said, still haunted by the dream of the wounded Nachash.

Karen shook her head. "Hah! she was a bitch. You thought that was bad?"

"I was there, I saw how - how brutal she was. I could see it was hurting. I should have done something.

Karen smiled forlornly. "It wasn't the pain, it was knowing I had left it too late - that in the end I allowed her to - get the upper had. But I finished the pair of them in the end."

"I know, I saw - remember!"

"That's right you did," said Karen, giving me the wink again. It always drove me crazy, that wink, and it lead to us fooling around for a time. Then Karen became more serious, and sensing what was on her mind I uttered the name of the island.

"Yes, I thought after what happened on Rhodes it might have fucked me up for good!" said Karen. "To be honest,I never thought about it much - until now. You see, I've always taken my precautions. You know I always use a coil - I have for years; I always supposed that the reason I've never got pregnant was because of that. I guess we'll find out though, because recently I got Mersell to remove it."

"He never told me."

"I told him not to."

"He told me how you tried to seduce him once at his clinic."

"He told you that?"

"I guess he felt he had to."

"Oh Julian, how dreadful of me! How have you ever managed to put up with me? When I think of the things I've done - allowed to be done to me!"

"It's not you, it's your demon."

"Yes my demon." Karen looked pensive. "Perhaps having a child will quieten it some."

"Perhaps," I said, giving in to a forlorn hope. I didn't articulate the thought that came to mind, that it might get passed on from mother to daughter: another hell raiser!"

"It was silly of me to do what I did with Mersell - but you and he are so much alike, I wondered how far the similarity went."

"Now you know."

"Yes we do, don't we," she said, playfully, "it stops here," her hands getting busy. And as she began to move me, that old persistent knowledge that she had known so many this way, came back to frustrate me.

"What's wrong Julian?"

"Nothing."

"Come on Julian, I can tell - it's obvious," she said, laughing, trying to make light of it. "If its Mersell, how many times..."

"It's not him..."

"Oh! - I see! "she said, releasing me. "You know what I am - what I've been! - oh, Julian, for heavens sakes!" she said, fretfully. Karen put her hand to her brow and frowned perplexed.

"Its not that I'm jealous."

"I should hope not!"

"I was just wondering how many?"

"How many men I've been with? - not that many actually. It's mostly symbolic, my body is symbolic of the goddess in fecundity."

"You don't expect me to believe that!"

Karen looked sheepish. "It's true!"

"Come on Karen, tell me the truth. I'm not jealous, just curious - really I am"

"Really you are!" said Karen, her eyes narrowing. "I wonder about you at times."

"Me!"

"Yes, don't get all innocent with *me!* - you get off on this don't you? You're a sly one Julian."

Her hand went down to her favourite place again. "Hmmm! - I see!"

"Julian you're a dark horse." Karen stretched her hands over her head, her muscular body stiffening like a cat after it has woken after a long sleep. Relaxing again: "I don't know Julian, I've lost count. It sounds dreadful but its true. I don't know how many there have been."

"Well how many - at a guess. A thousand?"

Karen began to laugh, "You're too much, I don't know." Then becoming serious, I guess because she was reminded of who she was. "More than a thousand easily," she boasted proudly. "There have been so many - so many," mused the high priestess of Tanit, "so many it's hard to remember them all - but for a few."

I gave her a questioning glance. She returned it with coquettishness. "You know I have my weakness for a certain type of man."

Karen burst into laughter and mussed with my hair. "Don't be so glum looking - you wanted to know."

I had to laugh at myself, my stupid vanity.

"Don't worry," she continued, in a playful tone of voice, "from now on you are all I want. From now on things will be different." She kissed me deep and long. "You have your Karen back; isn't that what you want?"

"All I've ever wanted," I replied.

We came together again, spontaneously joining as one, and afterwards lay content in each others arms, lost for a while in our own reverie, staring up at the blackness of the canopy above our heads, our own starless universe.

"I do miss Garcia," said Karen, after a time. "Perhaps when this is all over with, we should go see him."

"You mean it?" I said, squeezing her tight.

"Only if you make love to me again. You know that if we want this child we have to do it a lot to be sure."

Karen's gargantuan libido would ensure that she would never have it enough times, but knowing that it was for a reason made it easier for me.

I lay back exhausted. Karen soothed my brow. "Poor Julian, am I being too much for you?"

"No - no, "I said, turning on my side to face her, eager to get started again.

"Oh, Julian, are you sure? You look all in."

"No - no," I insisted, "it's for a reason, I have to get you pregnant."

Karen laughed: "Goddess in fecundity hey!"

"You are the goddess, my goddess, all right!"

"I wonder if I am?"

"What?"

"Fecund."

"You were made to be fecund."

"I was!"

I traced the contours of her rakish form: "Look how broad your hips are, we'll probably have dozens of offspring," I said. "Garcia will be a godfather - rather, godsfather a dozen times over."

"Yes they are broad, aren't they," she said, feeling the swell of her hips as they rose from the curve of her slender waist. "Fecundate me, my chosen one!" she said, in the language of her goddess.

I was able to fecundate her one more time, even though I knew I was pushing the flesh to it's limit, but with the language of the goddess, one was able to go beyond oneself at times, in the end, the mind was willing, but the flesh lagged behind.

"I think you should rest Julian, we have a long way to go tomorrow and we have plenty of nights to come." Barely able to see her in our dark universe I knew Karen's eyes were intent on me. "The rest of our lives," she mused.

These were the last words I heard, before sleep came down on me with the finality of a hammer blow!

In the morning Karen and I rose late, in fact we had to be woken by her Berber woman. "Mistress - mistress," we heard her call. Finally coming awake, for me it was like coming back from the dead, so deep and sound was my sleep. We sat around the campfire and drank mint tea, becoming gradually revived - Karen and I were acting like a couple of love struck teenagers, we couldn't stop grinning like overindulged Cheshire cats, the moody countenance of our guide, and driver, made everything even more strained and funny at the same time.

Mahkmoud said that the guide was anxious to find the *Tuareg*, so reluctantly we made the fifteen or so minute walk into the ruined Berber stronghold. Apart from a gathering of Red-Necked crows, the village was completely deserted. Below in the ravine, vultures circled over the remains of some unfortunate animal that had lost its footing, and tumbled to its lonely resting place. Karen kicked a stone and watched it fall, clattering on the steep walls of the canyon.

I came up behind her and put my arms around her narrow waist, which scared her. "careful, don't fall, " I said.

She swung round and fell into my arms. Karen still holding my hand peered over the edge at the broken body below. "What do you suppose it is?"

"Don't know, a goat perhaps?"

"Poor thing!...I wonder how my goats are? It will be good to see them again."

When we looked round the others had moved on ahead, except for the Berber woman, who, torn between her duty and the need for discretion, lingered uncomfortably a yard or so away. When I kissed Karen, I turned and saw the woman smile to herself. By the time we got back to camp Karen's mood had changed.

"Well! - where are they then? - these people!" She said, glaring at the guide, who was leaning against the jeep nonchalantly smoking a cigarette.

He looked at Karen and took the cigarette out of his mouth and spat. He then spoke some fast words in his tongue, and got in the jeep. Oudoso, who was looking a bit confused, pointed to beyond the canyon and said something like: 'the next oasis.'

I felt uneasy about the whole idea of it. One got the impression that our guide did not seem to care whether we found the *Tuareg*, or not. The whole thing looked like a farce, and neither did I like the way they looked at Karen, there was no respect for the goddess in their eyes, I only saw disdain, so I advised Karen accordingly: 'that we should turn back, that I didn't trust them.'

"Tell him we'll go to the next oasis and then if they are not there I want to go home," said Karen.

Not long into the journey, just across the border, our jeep broke down. After a brief look under the hood the driver declared the problem not fixable, and that he and the guide would go into a village which was just over the hill and get help, advising us, in most profuse body language, that it would be best if we remain with the vehicle.

We were on the limit of the ravine, where the rocky terraces gradually petered out to form a kind of rise or plateau, where the rock strewn *serir,* began to give way to the more sandy *erg,* giving rise to a desolate, featureless landscape.

"I'm *bored,*" said Karen. "How long have they been gone?"

"Not long. About ten or fifteen minutes."

Karen got out of the jeep and wandered off a few yards, her perfect form was silhouetted beneath the light yellow sari that she had on.

Mersell laughed. "You cannot keep your eyes off her Julian?"

"No I guess not."

"It seems what you want most of all has come to you at last?"

"You mean Karen? Yes it does seem I have her back again."

"I am happy for you."

I got out of the vehicle and went over to Karen. "Look Julian." She held in her palm a translucent greenish crystal.

"Lets see if there are any more," I said.

The Berber woman made a shushing noise and we both looked up. "*Priestess, priestess,*" she called, "where you go? Be careful."

"Just looking for some rocks - not far."

"It is not safe," called the woman.

Karen looked around her and sighed. "There's nothing here - nothing!" She made a gesture with her hand, "don't worry, come on Julian lets walk a bit, that woman is starting to get on my nerves." We walked on a few metres: our heads down searching for more crystals. Karen stopped and looked about her. "look at this place! Have you ever seen anywhere so barren?" she said, kicking the pebbles that lay strewn about everywhere.

"It's like the surface of Mars," I replied.

"*Id'iss* - look! here's another one!" cried Karen, picking up an even larger rock with beautiful red crystals embedded in it.
"Oh look, and here's another," I said.
"Karen and I began to find more and more rock crystals, the best ones we put to one side. Suddenly Karen looked up as a large rock landed close to her foot. She looked at me: "How dare you! Did *you* just throw that?"
"It wasn't me, I swear."

Another rock landed close by, followed by another that hit me on the shoulder. As Karen ran over to me an even larger stone caught her hard in the side, almost knocking her off balance. "*Owww.....!*" she cried out.

We heard the echoing sound of rocks being pelted against metal. Our jeep was the target, as well as us it seemed. About twenty or thirty men, and women were a few feet from the vehicle. The men wore the Burnous of the local Arab people, the women wore black burkhas. It is strange how it all happened, because Karen and I seemed to watch the events at the jeep unfold, independent of our perspective, as if we ourselves were not a target. It was simply that we were further away, and most of the hale of rocks were at that point landing short of us; therefore we saw events unfold in a strange detached way. I guess we just couldn't believe what we were witnessing! We watched the giant Oudoso get out of the jeep. For a moment they must have been intimidated by his share bulk because the hail of rocks ceased for a moment. Then we saw the crowd of Arabs engulf his massive form. His strong black arms descended and rose, descended again, until he finally disappeared from view. Then it was the turn of Mahkmoud, who was dragged from the vehicle. We heard the sound of two gun shots, and then he too was submerged by the frenzied swarm. While all this was happening the Berber woman was running straight towards us, all the time screaming for us to: "run! hide!" A smaller group of Arabs had split off from the main herd and were pelting her with rocks. They struck her in every part of her body as she ran for all she was worth, eventually she was cut down by a welter of shattering blows to her head. To the very end her eyes were fixed on her charge. I will never forget that look. Such surprise mixed with shame: 'you need not feel ashamed brave woman, you did your best to the end, you served your priestess well!'

Karen and I gradually backed off, I could feel the fear in Karen causing her to shrink against my body. She made a funny whimpering sound and was holding her side. After the Berber fell the smaller band of stone throwers began to close on us; the others were still venting their frenzied attack on the jeep. We heard the explosion of the windscreen, and windows as one by one they were smashed in. I remember wondering about Mersell, we had not seen him dragged out. He must have still be in there, god help him. 'God help us.' I thought.

With the brave Berber woman felled in her tracks, Karen and I now bore the brunt of the onslaught. The storm fell down on us, rocks and smaller stones splattering all around us. More and more began to hit their mark. Karen began to make a terrible winning sound. I covered her head with my arms, momentarily she raised her face to me, it was covered with a fine film of sand, grime and dried blood. Channels had been cut through the dust on her face by the course of her salty tears, as through some beautiful remote wilderness. On it was written terror and a silent farewell; it was I suppose, an acquiesce to fate, an acknowledgement that our fates were intertwined to the very end, and I felt as she, and spoke it in my eyes, that no matter what, I would not have wanted it any other way. Several smaller sharper projectiles were mixed with the larger ones, some as big as a man's fist, the smaller ones I saw spin stingingly through the air, slicing into Karen's bare flesh. Her face contorted with pain and out of her mouth issued a terrible yowl, like the cry of some poor wild beast caught in a snare...'*Ahhrrrww..! Ahhhrrrughh! - oh! - please - no! oh please no - aghhhhh! - nahwwwwwr.....!*' On and on her caterwauling shrieks of pain went, all the time twisting the fibres of my heart. For my own part, fear left me dumb. My hands, arms were covered with blood, as I tried to deflect the worst of the storm from Karen's head and face. I remember saying something like: 'it's all right sweetheart, I'll protect you...' something stupid like that, because there was no wear to run, no place to hide, and I could no more protect myself than I could Karen. Finally I was felled by a rock or small boulder that struck me in the thigh. Karen screamed out: *"No..."* and did her best to break my fall. She knelt down next to me, shielding my body with hers. She grimaced through a fresh hail of viscous shards that pelted her back. She took my hand and I felt encouraged by

her strong grasp. The realisation that I was now incapacitated: my hip smashed, seemed to numb her to the pain and fear she had felt before.
"Stay now," she said, softly. It didn't sound like Karen; it was like the voice of an angel or perhaps a being that saw *all things* for what they were! But still this angel did feel pain because she grimaced again through yet another downpour of hard rain. "I...*ahhh,*" she groaned - "I will..." She broke off as the rocks continued to fall pell-mell all around. "I must go. Know I love you," she said. The meaning of her words struck me as incomprehensible. Where was she going to go to? "Know I love you, and I will find a way back to you." Slowly, fighting against the thrall of ballistics, Karen started to rise. I reached out to her, afraid I guess, of being left alone.

Her hands, her nails, were coated in grime and dried blood, her beautiful face stained with the passage of blood and tears.
"We're finished," I said. "Die with me - here."
"Ssssh." she placed a blood stained finger against my lips. "*You* are not going to die. I'll find a way back....*I shall never leave - YOU!*" She smiled sweetly, as though we had all the time in the world to share; then she closed her eyes and fixed her jaw in grim determination towards some *unfathomable* end.

She let go of my hand and finished getting to her feet. I shouted for her to run, but to my dismay she remained standing in front of me: her broad thighs planted well apart, her fists curled into a tight ball, her lavender eyes bright and wide with pain and fear. The barrage of stones gradually diminished. I think they held back the torrent for a while out of respect for her bravery, or perhaps it was because, like me, they were dismayed by her audacity. The moment or so of reprieve offered an opportunity for my mind to begin to comprehend the scene my eyes had so far reluctantly bore witness to.

The smaller troupe had joined up with the larger pack. The women had gathered up their burkhas which they used as a kind of basket to store their supply of projectiles: stones and other sharp shards of rock and small boulders. They made a terrible din, a kind of high pitched squealing sound, like a pig that had been stuck. The men leered and made rude gestures towards us.

How proud and silent Karen was. How strong and proud Karen stood. How invincible and right she seemed. Even when her legs and arms were caked in blood and sordes, how much more alive she seemed. Her beautiful gold sari hung in tatters on her body, stained black with her blood, yet how much cleaner and wholesome was she! Her body was covered in a patchwork of whitish dust, which gave to her appearance that of some terrible statue of salt from which miraculously, issued forth blood. And even then she seemed more human than those that taunted her and pelted her with stones. She fingered the thick silver chain which hung about her strong neck, from which was suspended a large heavy amulet, the symbol of her deity: similar in shape to an Egyptian *Ankh*. She lifted it to her parched lips and preyed to the goddess for deliverance. She lowered her eyes and raised her arms above her head. Her enemies chanting ceased. After a moment she opened her lavender eyes and cast her scornful countenance over the malicious pack. She began to take large purposeful strides towards them, "It is I you want, not him," she called, beating her fist against the silver amulet that lay over her chest. "It is I that you have come for. Crush *my* bones, flay open *my* flesh, but spare his! For he is an innocent. It is I that suffer - *look to me!"* She showed them her red palms. "Do what thou wilt with thy body. Smash it to pieces, my soul you will set free from bondage, and for this I thank you. She raised the symbol of Tanit to the mass. "So be it," she shouted. *"here is my body!"* And looking up at the *symbol*, *"This body, these poor bones, this blood, this heart, this mind, this soul I offer to thee, pure and all mighty Tanit! Take pity on my soul, I, your priestess who has long loved thee and worshipped thee, take me to thine light and set mine soul free."*

"You are a filthy whore," shouted a man from the crowd. "Go to your heathen god. Whore of the *Maghreb"*

"You are infidel..die as one, die as a filthy dog," shouted another.

"Your soul is damned," shouted a woman. Another yelled, "go to the devil - whore of whores..."

"Putain," called another, and whose sentiments were echoed by countless many.

Karen gave them a simpering look. She picked up a rock. Held it in her fist, and then threw it to the ground with great force, splitting open a boulder in front of her, from which issued forth wondrous green and pink shimmering crystals: similar to the ones we had collected earlier. Karen smiled and picked up one of the largest to hand, and held it tight. Then a large rock was hurled from the mob and splintered into pieces not far from her, undaunted she continued to march towards the ruck, the troop - though they soon found their aim, and projectiles fell on her as in a blizzard, yet *still* she marched towards them. The rocks seemed to bounce off her body as though it were made of rubber, but gradually her progress grew slower as the avalanche continued to fall on her alone. Her body now was bent, her hands over her head, still she moved on. I saw several large stones strike her on the hip, which momentarily stopped her progress. Yet she managed to straighten herself and carry on. Eventually there was only a few feet that separated her from her enemies. They, and not she, began to back off, splitting into smaller groups. They continued to taunt her, chiding her. The males spat and snarled, the females screamed 'putain', and howled like mad dogs. She stopped, her body swayed, bent over to one side. She pointed at the mob: "You- you do not see..." she called to them.

To my relief and amazement the hail of stones slackened and the pack began to disperse. 'The power of the goddess is truly strong in her,' I thought. Then, in the distance I heard the roar of vehicles. The mass had all but melted away. A few younger men, most of them no more than teenagers, lingered on in a small group, more I think out of youthful bravado and ghoulish curiosity, than from any genuine feelings of maleficence. They laughed and jeered her still, but only half-heartedly, then I saw one of them bend down and pick up a stone and toss it with great force, at that moment the others ran off laughing and shouting. The vehicles were very close now, I could see their dust trails rising above the plateau. The boy that had thrown the last stone lingered though, it was as if both he and Karen were caught in some strange incomprehensible loop of destiny, the boy waiting as he must to witness the results of his actions. He had found his mark, the stone struck Karen full on the side of the head close to the temple. She remained still for a moment, then fell to her knees, before slumping forward heavily, like a pillar of salt, face down in the sand; only then did the boy, shame faced, run for all he was worth, after his compatriots.

XX

What of the others? Powerful Oudoso lay not far from the jeep with his throat cut, as did Mahkmoud. He at least had got a couple of shots off. We never knew if he had killed any of them. The brave Berber woman, Karen's personal aid, lay where she had been struck down, her eyes still fixed on the point she last saw Karen. And like her mistresss, she had been felled by a blow to the head, and not just one, but several, such was her concern for her charge, she gave little regard for her own safety. 'What a brave woman,' I thought, 'or was she just plain dumb?'

And then there was the mystery of Mersell, which was no mystery at all. He was found unconscious on the floor of the jeep. A rock or something had struck him, and laid him out - cold. And then there was me. Well I was less fortunate. I had to bare witness to the whole ugly event, how I would have loved a rock to have landed on *my* cranium. As it was, I had a fair list of injuries. A smashed up shoulder, a broken collar bone, a broken wrist, numerous small bones in my hand, and several cracked and broken ribs. The biggest injury was that which floored me. My hip had been smashed and I also had a fractured femur. The medics who first treated me at the scene, were amazed I had not suffered more internal injuries. The best I could manage was to cough up a good deal of blood over the next few days. But the injuries, especially the one to my hip, which had to be rebuilt, ensured a lengthy stay in hospital.

And now, for what you are all dying to know. Did Karen survive? Well of course she did, she's Karen, the heroin of this story and a born survivor. I must admit, when I crawled my way over to her inert body, I was pretty darn sure she was dead. Her face was covered in a fine film of sand, and just bellow her nose was a small smudge of blood. A tiny wound near her temple was the only evidence that she had been hit in the head, that and a small trickle of blood from her ear, just below the wound. I remember gently, very gently brushing the dust off her honey coloured braids, and asking her to wake up, but she went on sleeping like a statue raised from the sand. It wasn't until the medics arrived on the scene, that they could confirm she was indeed still on this Earth, that is, her living body was; where her mind was, her soul even, that is another matter? But once life of a sort had been found, then their urgency around her supine form was redoubled. Karen would have taken much comfort in knowing that the men who saved her life came to her aid in a white vehicle, with the red symbol of Tanit marked on it's side.

Karen's injuries will take somewhat longer to list than those of my own. In fact it would be quicker to list the bones in her body that were not either broken or fractured. Like me, her hip had been well and truly smashed, in her case resulting in a fractured pelvis, her hands and arms too were pretty smashed up, where she had used them to fend off the habitual downpour of rocks and stones, but it was that last rock which got her, the one thrown with such mindless force, by a mindless person - *that one*, struck home. That alone did more damage than all her other injuries put together; and they were bad enough: made worse by the corresponding internal injuries. Her left lung had been punctured, her spleen had been ruptured, she had suffered damage to her kidneys and liver, and possibly she would never be able to carry a child through full term, but all of these injuries could and were put right, and once put right, stabilised her condition. The blow to the head, however, was not so straightforward. The internal injury in this case, could not so easily be put right. The stone had fractured her skull in three places, causing: *'trauma'*, as it was described to me; resulting in the rupture of a number of small blood vessels that pattern the surface of the brain. These blood vessels bleed and then clot, it is the clotting of the blood, which causes pressure to build in certain areas of the head, resulting in a shut down - of sorts, of certain basic functions, such as, 'consciousness'. Excuse me: my elaborate way of saying Karen was in a coma.

And like any aspect of the conscious mind, or the unconscious, in Karen's case, science has little understanding of its dynamic, that is - it's true nature. In other words, no one had a clue how long she would be in a coma for, or if she would ever wake up at all. The good sign was that her heart and lungs were strong, although the longer she remained in limbo, the more pressure it put on her damaged internal organs.

In short it was not like a scene from one of those romantic movies where the heroin can remain in a comatose state indefinitely. At best, without dialysis and other medical intervention, Karen might last, according to one prognosis, twelve to sixteen months. The only hope was for a highly risky operation to remove the blood clot. Then it would simply be, if I dare say such a thing, since there is nothing simple or straightforward about this organ, then it would be a case of the brain healing itself. The only place that this could be done, the nearest place, would be France. By the time I was hobbling around on crutches, with my new artificial hip, that is to say about a month, Karen was registered with a specialist clinic in Paris in order to undergo a series of preliminary tests. Although the surgeons did not look impressed by my Karen as she lay there like a wax effigy, the various tests and x-rays were favourable. The brain surgeon of course did not know this at the time, but he would have gone through with the operation regardless of the outcome of the tests, because I and several other people would have made him - at gun point if necessary.

And who were the other people? What others? Those I suppose, apart from myself, who loved her most: Garcia, Anastasia, Eustacia, Rachine, Antonio, Almoud, Arkhmend, certain Berber women, and then of course the many Tanit worshipers who knew her from *Kerkouane*, and the villa at *Cap Gammarth,* and those who knew her from The *Sahel,* such as Marbo and Mersell. In the end the list grows too long. If one read the newspapers and all the magazines, one got the impression that the whole world was holding its breath for news of Karen's well being. At first the rumour was that she was dead; that she had died in an ambush in the desert at the hands of the *Tuareg,* who she had come to find. But this was not the case. The attack, as far as it possible to ascertain, was perpetrated by ordinary Arabs from a village just across the border in Algeria, not far from an oasis called *Mides.* Then, it was reported that she was not dead at all but very close to death, dying slowly from her injuries, at an unknown location in Algeria.

Any one of these stories could so easily have been the truth, even for those who knew her, and saw her each day.

Garcia came out straight away I contacted him. I was still in hospital at the time in Constantine, having just undergone my hip operation. He was the only person I really wanted around, but he also came with Rachine and Eustacia.

Mersell, I was happy to have near, apart from that, Almoud and Arkhmed and all the others from our early days in Egypt and Syria, were just a morbid reminder of the dark path Karen had been encouraged to follow, which ultimately lead to her plight. I felt that they were culpable, and that they weren't really interested in Karen's well-being for her own sake, they just wanted their high priestess back, they wanted their goddess incarnate to go on, they wanted the 'Tanit show' on the road again! They hung about the hospital, either Almoud or someone else from *Kerkouane*, just waiting for news, like so many vultures that I had seen that day, that hung about in the desert as Karen lay bleeding in the hot sticky sun. It is true that their compatriot Mahkmoud had died as had the Berber woman, but they didn't have to witness the scene of Karen being smashed to pieces: Karen my wife, the love and core of my being. Each one of those stones that fell on her perfect body cut my soul to the quick. They had lost a figure head, I, potentially had lost the love of my life. As it was, the Tanit show would go on, with or without Karen at it's head. She had already become immortalised. Some even believed she was already dead and had been resurrected. People will believe anything! Thousands flocked to *Kerkouane* to touch the bronze seal of Tanit which was still stained by Karen's blood, believing it to have special healing powers. Every site she had been to on her travels through Tunisia, became the: 'sacred way of Karen'. People took the same route, starting from *Kerkouane*, the epicentre of her worship, then to the villa on *The Cap Gammath,* then on to *Carthage, Utica* and all places in between, until they got to The *Sahel,* then, if you were really devout you would go on into the desert, the small oasis of *Mides* becoming just as important a site of pilgrimage as any of the others - as it lie not far from the barren location where Karen offered up her mortal body as a sacrifice to the goddess, and, according to ones version of the *Faith*, her life came to an end, or where she was mortally wounded, and carried back to *Mides,* and was resurrected after drinking the life giving waters there, such are the hack sentimentalities of the *devout!* Whatever version one beleived, they overlooked the reasons she was matryred in the first place.

The events which came to pass at the villa on The *Sahel,* spoke volumes for the animosity that other more, *traditionalists*, felt for Karen and the Tanit show. Shortly after we left the villa near *El Amra,* and she was right about that much, it was attacked and besieged by aggrieved locals. They did not know it at the time, but Karen had departed for the desert a few days earlier, but one should make no mistake, that they were intent upon fulfilling in *The Sahel* what eventually came to pass among the sands of Algeria. The villa was eventually set on fire, at least three Berber men suffered the same fate as Oudoso and Mahkmoud, in fact the whole thing was a much bloodier scene. Marbo escaped barely with his life, no one came away from that place unscathed, not least sweet Tricksy, who, despite the brave efforts of Marbo and others to reach her, lost her life in the blaze. Given these facts, it is perhaps not difficult to see why I was eager to get out of Africa. I was sick of the place. At the earliest opportunity, that is, when the doctors were happy with Karen's condition, we flew out to Paris; accompanied by Garcia and some of the others, her inner core of followers: the 'hangers on', the king vultures, those who believed still, she was the goddess incarnate, and claimed her for themselves.

The truth is, there would have been no Karen were it not for the professionalism and solicitous actions of all the hospital staff who attended to both Karen and myself. The various operations she underwent essentially saved her life. From the moment the army trucks arrived on the scene with the red symbol of Tanit on the side, everything conceivable was done to bring her back from the brink of death. To witness that cedar tower of strength felled by a single blow, after surviving such a storm, to see that body, supine and motionless in the dust, and to know that there was nothing I could do - nothing I could have done to help: this will be the suffering I will always have to bare. Yes all that could be done had now been done by those at the hospital in Constantine. They had held back Hades from the door, but they had not vanquished his shadow. Slowly her condition would worsen unless she underwent one more life saving operation, and this could only be done by a specialist team in Paris.

There are so many individuals that I am indebted to, or rather Karen and I are indebted to, for their help and support. Those that *genuinely* loved her. One in particular was Antonio. Once I had feared him as my most significant rival for Karen's love. Now I call him my friend. He wasted no time and spared no expense in getting Karen the very best surgeons and specialists in their field.

She was booked into one of the most prestigious clinics in the whole of France. For myself he found an exquisite apartment in a sheikh suburb of Paris; he was prepared to find accommodation for all of Karen's closest friends. It was great to know that there were people like Antonio fighting for her, people like Garcia and Mersell. One of the more surprising though was Rachine. That I had not figured on. I knew of course that they had first met in Italy during Karen's modelling days but I never got the impression they were the closest of friends. In fact they seemed more like rivals than friends, but I guess when you get two girls who are closely matched in looks and in Karen and Rachine's case, libido, then one will always find a healthy rivalry between the two.

Mersell stayed for a time at the apartment. Rachine was immediately intrigued by this suave good-looking young doctor, just as Karen had been. I was glad he was around, it kept Rachine off my back. There was also Antonio who, although not living in Paris, jetted over to see Karen whenever he could, then he too would stay at the apartment, offering yet more distraction for Rachine, who was always coming over to offer *her* support.

"She looked so restful today when I saw her," said Rachine.

"She deserves to have some peace," I replied.

"Yes but she's not. Not really," put in Mersell.

"What do you mean?" I said.

"She is engaged in a struggle. A struggle to come back to us. It may not seem so but this what it is."

Rachine sighed, and sipped her wine. "Poor kid, she never had much luck. If she knew what was good for her she would give it up. It's not worth all the effort!"

"Then if I know Karen she will come back for more," I said, "she has unfinished business here."

Rachine stretched her legs making sure we all saw how good they were. She parted her lips and looked at Mersell, and then looked to me, moistening them with wine.

"Yes well - I'm sure she does, that's all the more reason. She would be better off dead. I know it sounds bad but she was the most mixed up kid I ever met - now she looks at peace..."

I just stared back at Rachine who, recognising the look of hostility, had to bow her head. Staing at her wine:

"*I'm sorry* Julian, I guess that came out wrong. I don't know what to think! It's just seeing her there like that. She used to be such a dynamic person. It's frustrating!"

"Yes it is hard on all of us," said Antonio. "she was - I mean *is* the most wonderful and vibrant person I have ever known."

"She must come through this," I said,

They could all see I was close to tears. Rachine came over and put her arm around me. "I'm sorry for what I said. She'll come through, don't worry, you are not alone."

"Yes, do not worry Julian, we all love her. We all want her back," said Antonio. When I looked up I could see that there were tears in his eyes too, and Mersell had to get up and quickly and go to the bathroom.

"Come Julian. Drink your wine," said Rachine, "she wouldn't want you to be sad - now would she!"

Karen had a large room all to herself, which was festooned with flowers and bright cards that arrived daily from well-wishers from all over the world. There were too many bouquet's for one person, so we distributed the excess to patients on other wards. I made sure she always had fresh Jasmine next to her bed. Jasmine always reminded her of Pharaoh and the good times she spent on the beaches of the *Sahel* with him. She also liked Mimosa and Marigolds, Lilies and of course - Lotus blossom and white Orchids.

I read somewhere once, that the olfactory sense is the sense which most strongly evokes memories of the past. Perhaps on some deep primitive level Karen could smell the scent of the Jasmine and Mimosa, and she would feel safe in the knowledge that she was surrounded by those that loved her.

Her Tanit followers prayed to the *Great Mother* every day for her return to the living, and in *Kerkouane*, and other centres of her worship, sacrifice to the gods *Apollo*, *Asclepius* and *Eshmun*, were made each day. Of course, Garcia too, offered up his prayers and sacrifices to the gods *he* followed: all powerful and magnificent Persephone, who has knowledge of the world of darkness and light.

In Karen's room he cast a pentacle of protection, invoking her *other* deity, the resplendent Hestia, goddess of the hearth and home, and the inner hearth of the soul: "Oh blessed goddess," Spake the Pontifex, "most pure and full of light, keep this child Karen, safe from eternal darkness, keep the hearth fire of her soul alight, goddess of wonder, goddess of splendour, guide her to your eternal light. *So Mote it be!"* Garcia completed the ceremony by hanging some Ivy on the door, to protect against maleficent spirits. Everyone prayed in their own way that she might be given back to us. *Her* people, insisted that she wear a small silver Tanit motif around her neck, as well as her gold talisman charm bracelet. They wanted to put incense in her room too, but I wouldn't have any of that: it would mask the scent of the Jasmine - as it was, I could always tell when one of them had been round to see her, because of the odour of frankincense and myrrh, and various other scents of Lebanon, that they saturated themselves with, and then swished around in front of her. I suppose if there was the slightest chance that these scents as well as those of the flowers, could have some beneficial help, then one had to accept them.

"She doesn't look well," said Rachine, as we sat by Karen's bed one morning.
"What do you expect, she's in a coma!" I replied.
"I mean, over the last day or so since she's been here - she looks worse. Sort of more waxy and yellow than usual."
"She's all right," I said, taking Karen's clammy hand. "She's a fighter, she'll never give up, 'will you my sweet.' " I kissed her dead looking hand, aware of a tiny wave of revulsion pass through me as my lips contacted with her damp flesh.
Rachine looked away. "Well if you say so."
I knew what Rachine was thinking, that she hadn't got long. And I knew it too, that she was looking worse by the day. Her face was like a mask: a death mask, set in a permanent blank look, that related nothing. One could smack her round the face, give her the biggest fuck imaginable, and still she would retain that same vacant look: the look of the dead.
Her flesh was drawn tightly over her cheeks, her eyes were sunk into their sockets, leaving dark shadows, making it hard not to see a skull rather than the head of a living person!

Karen had been at the clinic for four days and still they had not operated. Eventually the surgeon who was going to conduct the operation requested he speak with me in his office as a matter of urgency. I brought Antonio with me, ideally I would have liked to have had Mersell there too, his medical knowledge would be invaluable, but unfortunately pressing matters at his own clinic had forced his temporary return to Algeria. Essentially the surgeon outlined what we already feared. He told us that her liver function was deteriorating and one of her kidneys was failing. He wanted to know about the scar on her side, and had she ever had problems with her kidneys. I told him it was a result of a stab wound, and that she had never been hospitalised for it. He seemed to consider this a moment before indicating that this was the cause of the current problem. It dawned on me then, that all this time she had been living with a damaged kidney, all because the Bedouin had refused her hospitalisation. No one had guessed just how severe that knife attack had been, and I wondered how Mersell even, had not spotted it, but then he wasn't looking for problems *there;* to everyone she appeared as healthy as a roach! I guess without a suntan her skin tone was quite wan: yellow more than brown! - so she had hid the truth, the only person to know how severe that knife attack had been was perhaps Karen herself. Given this knowledge it was a miracle she had survived at all.

'It's destiny,' I thought to myself, 'in effect she died by that Syrian knife more than two years ago. What had happened *then*, had already sealed her fate!'

"You see my position," the surgeon went on to say. "Normally if it were not for the complications I would go ahead straight away and operate, as it is...She is quite remarkable. She never complained of pains in her side?"

"No, never."

The surgeon got up and indicated to an x-ray: "you see here, a quite clear lesion on her left kidney. You see it?"

He then looked at another x-ray of her head, and then switched off the back-illumination, as if that particular x-ray was, 'old news.'

"Of course she can be made comfortable. Put her on dialysis, but ideally that should be at some other hospital."

He leaned back in his leather seat like a man who had just been let off the hook.

"You mean a hospice?" I said, dryly.

Antonio suddenly lent across the desk and spoke strongly in French. Pointing at the surgeon he looked at me. "I will not listen to this Julian," he said, banging the desk. "This man wants to give up on her."

I admired Antonio his Italian spirit, and smiled wryly. For me there was no question of *anybody* giving up on Karen.

"You don't seem to understand," I said, calmly to the surgeon. "You will do the operation," and then feeling my anger: "you have been wasting time doing tests while all the time she's been getting worse."

"But Monsieur it is no good performing the operation if she dies on the table."

"What are her chances if you don't do it?" I asked.

He got up and switched on the light panel which illuminated the x-ray of her skull. He pointed to a small dark patch just above her temple about the size of a pea.

"It is extremely unlikely she will ever regain consciousness. The surgery alone is not without its own risks. Even then it is fifty fifty that she would come out of her coma."

The surgeon sat down again. The image of Karen's skull shone menacingly behind him. He took up a conciliatory stance putting his hands on the table.

"Monsieur, I can understand how you must feel, I only present to you the facts - the reality of the situation. Karen is a very ill young lady, make no mistake. Quite frankly, when I heard of her injuries I was amazed she had survived as long as she had. She must have a tenacious will to live?"

Antonio burst forth with some phrase or other in Italian and then French. I steadied him.

"Its all right," I said. "I think *Monsieur,* you are afraid of failure? But you won't be failing Karen, or us, if you try your best. You must do what you can for her."

He sank back in his plush lather seat and stroked his chin. He looked perplexed, a bit like the man who had found himself back on the hook again.

"Very well, I will have her prepped immediately."

"She is very strong you know....Her heart I mean," I added.

"All things considered. You take full responsibility?"

"Yes I do."

"We do," put in Antonio.

"My secretary will have some forms for you." He got up and I shook his hand, Antonio was more reluctant to do so. "You know I don't perform miracles." He said.
"No," I replied, "leave them to Karen."

The operation to remove the blood clot on Karen's brain was a success, a success in that she did not die in the process. I had never met a man who looked more relieved than the head surgeon, who had been in charge of the five hour operation.

He had seen a part of her I had never seen. He had looked inside her head. He had seen the white folds of her brain. I wonder if he realised he was looking at the brain of a goddess, or did he just see just another whitish mass of flesh? 'Was it the same,' I wondered, 'as everybody else's brain?' I wanted to ask him if he saw her soul, if so what was it like? When they trepanned the hole in her skull, I wonder if her soul hung about to see who was tearing down the walls of its home? or did it perhaps have more than one home? Did it wriggle down some tiny crevice, watching but not seen from her *Medulla Oblongata?* May be it was lodged in her *pineal gland?'* or was it buried deep in the labyrinth of her *cerebellum?* or was it in the limbic's *hippocampus*, that old emotional brain we had when we were fury creatures running through the trees with the cats.

I wanted to ask him these things but I knew he was a man of science, and would not have understood. As it was I was thankful enough that he had got rid of that thick congealed blob of blood that had made her head hurt so. I was there when they wheeled her out of surgery. The white bandage on her head was the only indication that they been inside there. Apart from that, the expression on her face was exactly the same as it had been before, but I contented myself with the idea that she looked more at ease.

They took her back to her room and plugged her in again, they also added another set of tubing for her dialysis. The surgeon came in the following day. He found me asleep on the reclining chair next to her bed.

"I'm sorry if I woke you," he said, as he consulted Karen's chart.

I stood up and thanked him profusely for his efforts. He seemed a little embarrassed and cast a weary eye over his patient.

"How is she?"

I could see he was pleased but didn't want to let on.
"Stable. It is good - at the moment. It's up to her now."
"I understand," I said.
He then scrutinised me with his surgeons eye, "You should get some proper rest," he said.
"I will," I replied, sitting back down again.
He smiled at me vaguely before he left. I think we had discovered some sort of mutual respect for one another. My faith in his skill, and in Karen's strength, had made him face up to something in himself, he would not otherwise have done. Sometimes meeting extraordinary people who refuse to give up no matter what, can impart a form of wisdom that would not ordinarily be accepted by those who call themselves *empiricists,* and call truth by another name.
Of course the surgeon was right. I needed some proper rest but I was afraid that if I left Karen's side something horrible would happen when I was away. In the end Antonio and Garcia, as well as Rachine, made me see how silly I was being; they promised me that she would never be left on her own: one of them would always be there to keep an eye on her. That was the only way they could get me away from her side. Even then I took the trip to the hospital to see her every day. My friends were not the only ones to keep a watch on Karen. There was always a Berber dressed in a burnous sitting on a chair outside her room, or else loitering around the lobby. I loathed the sight of these people. Rightly or wrongly, I blamed them for Karen's condition. Without them she could have got the treatment she needed as a result of her stabbing, instead they let her nearly die, and this was due in part, as much from their mistrust of the authorities as it was their fatalistic attitude to every aspect of life. To be honest they were not Berbers who had let this happen, but they were just as devout in their belief in 'Tanit power', and in any case I had to blame someone.
On one occasion, about a week after her operation I was on my way up to see Karen, when I spied a particularly evil looking character standing uncomfortably by the main entrance to the clinic, dressed in their usual conspicuous way. There was something about his look that had the air of derision and insolence. He even spat on the ground as Rachine and I approached. I stopped and looked at him. He glanced at me and then Rachine and looked away as if we were beneath him.

"Who are you?" I asked.

He looked at me blankly, either unwilling or unable to speak English. I turned to Rachine, and asked her to translate. She complied only too willing to help if a fight was in the offing. The Berber who had a dark sun worn craggy face looked Rachine up and down as if inspecting so much unclean meat. He spat out some words in French. I saw Rachine's eyes narrow slightly.

"He asks who are we?" related Rachine.

"How dare he!" I laughed at his audacity. he gave me an inscrutable look that was guaranteed to piss me off. "That girl up there," I said, pointing to the window on the second floor, "is my wife, and it's you and your kind that put her there." He seemed to get the gist of what I said. "Now *who* are you?" I asked again.

Rachine rattled off some words in French that made him look a bit more humble. "The magic name spilled out from between his thick lips: 'T'nyt' and then more expansively: "I am of the Tanith!" He glared at both me and Rachine.

"Then get out of my way, and leave Karen alone. You understand! - *Fuck off* to where you come from you goddamn vulture," I said, pushing him aside.

The Berber bowed and motioned: "Please, a thousand apologies. May the blessing of *T'nyt* be with you. Blessed is the priestess."

I was sick of hearing her referred to as 'the priestess'. Rachine watched me carefully to see what I was going to do. I think she was hoping I would stick one on him. I walked over to him. The Berber held his ground.

"She's not your priestess, she's just a girl. Her name is Karen, and I love her."

He spoke something in French. "He says she belongs to those of Tanit, That she is the living goddess," explained Rachine.

I realised it was pointless to argue with these types. "Stay away from her," I said, giving him a shove.

The Berber just smiled and bowed again, in that ingratiating manner, all to common among certain southern races. Sick of the sight of him and their ways I turned and strode away; Rachine lingered behind to give him a bit more of her mind. She caught up with me at the elevator.

"I fixed him," she said.

"What did you say?"

"I called him a cocking sucking parasite. And few other things that are untranslatable." Rachine laughed. "I said, 'if I saw him here again I'd personally cut his balls off."

We both had a good laugh at that. As we exited the elevator on Karen's floor, the weight of expectation, as I got closer to her room came crushing down on me again. I realised that it had been the first time I had laughed properly since I had been with Karen in the desert, only hours before the attack. Her condition since the operation had remained the same. Antonio was sitting by her bed, his features looked pale and drawn.

"How is she?" I asked, in a hushed voice. We always spoke quietly, not that it would have mattered to Karen.

"They came in during the night. Several nurses and a doctor that I had not seen before."

"Why, is she all right,"

"Something about blood pressure dropping!" exclaimed Antonio, giving up his seat nearest the bed.

I expected her to look worse, but she was more or less the same pale jaundice colour, may be her skin was a bit more greasy. Antonio hovered uncomfortably at the foot of the bed. "I would have called if it was bad. They gave her an injection, and hooked her up to something," he said, pointing to a new tube that ran into a vein in her arm.

"You look tired," she Rachine. "You should go back to the apartment and get some rest."

"I think I will," replied Antonio

"We'll call if there is any change," I said. He seemed relieved to get out of the room, I understood how he felt.

Rachine puled up a chair and sat the other side of the bed. She stared at Karen and sighed heavily. "Poor bitch....Look at you! What have they done to you!"

I looked at Rachine. She was so physically vibrant - between us there might have laid a corpse. I looked back at Karen. I could no longer deny what I saw, what I felt. It was obvious to me now that she was dying. If it were not for the scent of Jasmine, one might have have detected the odour of chrysanthemums.

"She doesn't look good Julian."

"No - she doesn't."

Rachine let out a nervous little laugh.. "I never knew a girl who loved to fuck as much as her. Christ she lived for it."

I smiled despite how her words fell. "Yes - she was a physical being."

I looked over at Rachine. She seemed triumphant - invincible as once thought Karen to be.

"She liked you Julian - I mean being with you. Despite what you may think."

I shook my head. "I wasn't right for her. Not in that way."

"She loved you Julian. You were all she ever talked about. She just wished you could let yourself go more. Other than that you didn't disappoint."

"I don't doubt she loved me. Still does - wherever she is!"

"It is not here!" said Rachine. She took a long look at the inert body that lay before her. I had never seen Rachine touch Karen whilst in her comatose state, but now she plucked up courage and lifted Karen's hand.

Errghh...! she's all clammy!" she let go of it, as though it were something alien. Karen's hand dropped like a dead thing. She gave Karen a sidelong glance and turned her nose up, making a noise of dissatisfaction in her throat. "I think if it was me laying there in that state, I'd want them to pull the plug."

"No you wouldn't. You'd fight to stay alive, just as Karen is doing." I said, incredulous.

"Fight! Is she I wonder?"

"When it comes right down to it, isn't that what we would all do?"

Rachine looked at me steadily. "Not always....Given the choice."

"Don't you want to live?"

"Did she? I knew her when she first came to Italy, before she met Garcia. She was messed up. Drugs! Men! She said she had a demon in her, and that one day it would destroy her. She acted like she had no time to live. Put it this way, she didn't act like somebody who valued their *own* life very highly."

"You mean she had a death wish!"

Rachine lifted Karen's inert rubbery hand again. "What do you call this?" she said, indicating the ugly jagged scar on Karen's wrist, the one she went to such lengths to conceal. Grimacing, she let go of Karen's hand and it slumped back down like a lump of dead meat. She cast a weary eye over the still figure of the girl that had once been her rival; for a second I thought Rachine looked sorry for her.

"You loved her, didn't you?"

"love - hate. Who can say?"

"There are those who would say you were jealous of her."

Rachine looked from me to Karen. "Does it really matter now?" She stood up. "I'll get us some coffee." Rachine leaned over Karen and kissed the air a few centimetres above her parched lips. "*Dormez bien dorment longtmemps mon enfant de miel!*"

Later that afternoon a doctor came round to check on Karen. The one good bit of news was that her blood pressure had stabilised. Not long after, Garcia arrived to relieve Rachine and I. I gave him the good news and then related the incident that had taken place in the morning.

"It is not wise to anger these people. For them, Karen is more than just a girl, she is their religion They sincerely believe in her as the incarnation of the goddess Tanit."

"They don't scare me. I won't have them around. She is *my* wife. She's mine not theirs!"

"At the moment she isn't anybody's. That is if she ever was?" he said.

Garcia's words stilled my indignation. It was at times like this that I found his wisdom frustrating.

"You should be more conciliatory. If you know who their leaders are I will speak with them, on your behalf."

"Well if you can get them out of my face - anything would be good."

We never saw that particular Berber again, and after that incident they kept an altogether more low profile - although it is more likely that this was due to Garcia's influence rather than anything Rachine or I might have said.

Whether wearing a Burnous or, as they had taken to wearing: black suits and sunglasses, it was still possible to pick out the Tanit crew (obviously lacking in discretion), one of Karen's enemies could easily slip by in such a get up. Therefore, Garcia brought in some of his own men from Tuscany, to keep an eye on those, who kept an eye on Karen. The result was that she was probably more heavily guarded than the president of France.

Over the next few months Karen's condition remained stable. Which is to say she hovered at deaths door. The Dialysis was enough to maintain an equilibrium, but medical intervention of this kind would only delay the inevitable. But I refused to listen to what the experts predicted. It was becoming obvious that the pressure was beginning to tell on me. Eventually Garcia and the others persuaded me to take a couple of days off from the hospital to celebrate my birthday, which had completely slipped my mind.

Anastasia and Eustacia, who were in France on a shoot, promised to fill in for me and Rachine at Karen's side. Somehow or other Rachine always managed to be with me when keeping vigil over Karen, she said she got spooked if she was in the room with her on her own.

Antonio hired a suite at an expensive hotel. A lot of Garcia's people came, Rachine was there along with some other models, who had worked with Karen. Although the occasion had ostensibly been arranged to celebrate my birthday, for me it was a celebration of nearly three months of Karen's postoperative life. Garcia was busy with friends from Italy, that he hadn't seen in years: when one spends the majority of one's life on an island, it is apt to make one hungry for news of the broader world. The truth was I had no desire to be in a large gathering of people, trying their hardest to look upbeat around me, especially when the conversation got round to Karen. In the end I made my excuses and left early into the proceedings. My intention was to go back to the hospital before heading home. I was counting on Antonio coming back to the apartment after the party, but he said he had to fly back to Zurich on business. Garcia however, had been keeping a surreptitious eye on me, and was determined that I should not be left alone. Rachine was always proffering her services, either directly or through others in a supportive role to me. I suppose it was only natural that she do so, after all she was one of Karen's closest associates, being one of the first she met and worked with on her arrival in Europe. And now that we had seemingly put aside any animosity that had previously existed between us, ideally it placed Rachine firmly in the role of big sister. Other qualities, such as her exuberant character: Rachine was the very epitome of life and optimism, prevented my natural inclination to depression and general thoughts of a more maudlin kind.

Standing on the sidewalk I took a couple of deep breaths of the autumnal air. I was glad to be out of the stuffy hotel environment. I hailed a cab and Rachine jumped in after me. She quickly gave some instructions to the driver.
"Where are you taking me?" I said, stifling my anoyance at having my transport usurped.
"You'll see," she replied, brightly.

The cabby took us on a tour of all the major landmarks of the city. It was the first time I had seen anything of the sites of Paris which was every bit as glamorous I had been lead to believe, the only thing that was missing was Karen at my side. Rachine though, who was equally as beautiful and glamorous as Karen, was not going to let circumstance deter her from trying to make the occasion every bit as memorable as if Karen had been there herself.

Rachine had a great time playing guide, pointing out the different places and telling me a little bit about their history. Her sexy face beamed with excitement and pride, at showing me the city that had played such an important part in her life.
"This is all new to you isn't it?" said Rachine, as we sat at some posh restaurant on the Champs-Elysées It was hard not to be caught up in her natural enthusiasm, even though Paris was one of the places Karen had been looking forward to showing me herself.
"I'm happy that you shared it with me," I said.

I looked at the window pain. It had begun to rain, and I thought that Karen had not seen the rain since the storm which had driven us to find shelter on the island of Rhodes.

Rachine smiled bravely through my depression. "Let's order some more wine, or better yet champagne?"
"I really should be getting back," I said.
"Not yet. There are still a lot of places left to see. We haven't been up to the *Sacré-Coeur* yet, and you must see the *Dome des Invalides* where Napoleon is buried, it is very...*atmosphérique*. He is a hero, someone I much admire!"
"Is he really," I said, finding this fact not surprising. I looked at her, she was so engaging, and it was touching to think she was doing all of this for me.
"I don' know Rachine..." I said, feeling guilty at not being at Karen's side.

"At least stay and have some champagne with me, let me celebrate your birthday with you Julian. I thought we could also have some traditional French cuisine. They do very good escargot here."

Before I could make any protest Rachine reached over and touched my hand affectionately. "Come on Julian. Look I will phone the hospital - even tell Garcia where he can reach us."

Rachine bounced over to the phone booth, she was talking with one of the waiters and pointing over to our table. I watched her closely making sure she made the call.

The afternoon was growing darker. It began to rain heavier.

Bouncing back: "I arranged for a little treat for you, since it is your birthday," said Rachine.

"Just the champagne or wine will do. Did you get through to the hospital? How is she? Did you tell Garcia where we are?"

"Oh - yes, just the same, no change," replied Rachine, aside: "Oh look the champagne."

A waiter brought over a magnum bottle of vintage Bollinger served on ice, then her face lit up as the surprise arrived: two soufflés on a silver salver. The waiter then flambéed them by adding *Grand Marnier liqueur.* Rachine's face lit up at the sight of the vivid red flames

"I love it when they do that," she said.

She reminded me of a little girl fascinated by fire. She looked so serious and proud, and naïve at the same time. I couldn't help but have a good laugh, there was something very childlike about her and yet dangerous too. Yes, they were alike in so many ways.

Another waiter uncorked the champagne and poured some of the fizzing liquid into our glasses. "*La Madame Monsieur apréciez s' il plaît*

"*Bonheur* Julian - *en votre anniversaire....*"

"What?" I said, leaning forward.

"Happy birthday - *Bon anniversaire...*"

We clinked glasses. "*A la futur,*" toasted Rachine. "May it bring you all the happiness you deserve."

"To the future - and Karen! may she soon be with us again."

"Oh well - yes, av'course." She looked at me over her glass and screwed up her nose in response to the bubbles. "Don't forget the soufflé, they do the best soufflés in Paris."

It didn't take long for her to polish hers off. The orange brandy was excellent and it went well with the champagne, as far as I was concerned it was the best I'd ever had. Rachine sure did have a sweet tooth, afterwards she had chocolate filled crêpes, with brandy and cinnamon sauce, and to follow that we shared a plate of truffles.

"What else shall we have? " said Rachine, picking up the menu.

"Nothing for me," I said. "The champagne and truffles is just fine."

"It is the best. You deserve the best Julian." Rachine played with her glass, twisting the stem round and round, watching the excited bubbles explode on the surface. "What shall we drink to now?"

"We can't drink to anything else, we have already toasted the future."

"I know," Rachine looked serious. "To us, to our friendship."

"To us."

"Long may it last and grow ever deeper."

Rachine filled her glass again and drank greedily. She touched my fingers with hers. I puled my hand away defensively.

"Are you afraid of me Julian? Yon Know you don't have to be. I am not a monster. I loved Karen too you know."

"Yes," I said, suddenly distracted by the rain as it lashed against the large window behind me.

Rachine made a little laughing noise in her throat. "You know I *was* jealous."

"Of Karen?"

"No you. I hated it because she and you were like that," she said, twisting her fingers. "You were so lucky to be so close to her - you know! The way lover's are....You know, I used to think I knew her, but I didn't. No one really got close to Karen. She was like this wild thing - you know! No one could ever tame her. Except may be you. You of all people! You had her exclusively to yourself. And now who has her? No one, not me, not you." Rachine shook her head, "what a waste - that girl deserved better."

"Nobody could tame Karen," I said, "certainly not me." I laughed. "Its funny, just before the end we were growing close again. She even spoke of having a child with me."

"And you think you didn't tame her?"

I sighed. "Well you don't have to be jealous any more."

"No?"

"Well what can she do, as you say, she is no longer anybody's."

Rachine put her glass firmly down on the table and lent towards me. "Really! Is that so? Julian look at us. All we have been talking about is Karen. She is here now. She always will be. What chance do I have? Does anybody have against a memory?"

"I don't know what to say? I'm not sure I understand you?"

Karen poured out some more champagne and lit a cigarette. "Don't be naïve Julian. Do you think she would want you to put your life on hold on the small hope that one day she might - just might regain consciousness. What do you think she would do if the situation was reversed? She would seize what was in front of her. She would go on living her life regardless."

"That slender hope is all I have."

"You don't want to take what is being offered?" Her large dark eyes grew wide. She leaned slightly forward her glass in her hand, poised elegantly near her lips.

"You mean you?" I laughed. "Oh Rachine don't you ever give up?"

"In that regard I am like her; I never give up on something I want."

"I can't believe you want *me*?

"Why not?"

"I'm not the kind of person *you* would want. I don't even know why Karen wanted me. I'd be a great disappointment to you. You *must* know? You girls talk about *that* kind of stuff all the time?"

Rachine looked bemused. She shook her head. "Karen never spoke much about you like that - but I got the impression you were more than the average kind of guy? Why else would she have been so crazy about you?"

"Huh - I don't know! It doesn't ring true! A girl like you! No - I think you would do anything to put one over on Karen?"

Rachine came across with a hurt look. "How can you think such a thing?"

"It's always been a game with you. Both of you, to see who could seduce who. And you hated it because I preferred her. The truth is she always could outdo you, you must have hated that? In the end you seduced her! That was the only way you could win! You couldn't have me, so you had Karen instead! I saw that look of triumph on your face!"

"We loved each other. That wasn't the first time. But you're right, it did give me satisfaction to see the look of shock on your face, at seeing her in *bed with me!"*

Rachine threw back her head and downed the contents of her glass. "You mist something that day. I doubt you ever saw her as she really is? Only I could get the best out of her!"

"I wouldn't be so sure about that," I said.

Rachine laughed, "come on Julian, you're not seriously suggesting that you..."

"Not me, it doesn't matter who. All you did was to exploit her biggest weakness."

"Weakness!"

"Her unmitigating love for herself. Her massive narcissistic ego."

"Yes you're right, I did - her narcissism as you say, is what made her easy. I never knew a girl to get off on herself the way Karen did. She didn't really need anyone else - except for the fact she was an awful exhibitionist."

"And you're not I suppose?"

Rachine levelled her obsidian gaze at me. "Not in the way she was, she would do it with anyone."

"The truth is, you were jealous of her. People were fascinated by her. She had something you didn't."

"What! - what did she have that I didn't? Look at me Julian - are you blind!" said Rachine, puffing her big chest out like a pigeon, whilst sticking her big bill in the air.

"She had a certain magic, I don't know - an aura about her that fascinated men - and *women!* Apart from that, she had warmth. The warmth of a good soul."

Rachine made a dismissive noise: "*Pahh!* - And what about your soul? I think you are not so innocent! You are no better than me - or Karen for that matter! I've seen the way you look at me!" Rachine leaned forward so that her big breasts rested on the table. It was impossible for me not to see down the front of her top. The swell of her orbs moved me - confused my train of thought.

"Do you like what you see Monsieur?" she leaned further forward bearing down on the table which had the effect of pushing them together, like two massive swollen balloons that looked fit to burst. "I think you do! I think you are dying to know what it is like to be with me! To touch me, to feel my breasts, You won't regret it, I promise."

"Ah - but I would. You have a lovely body, I'm not denying that, perhaps even better than Karen's - who's to say?"

"Pah!..of that there is no doubt," she said, tossing her lovely dark head. "Can't you see." She threw her shoulders back, puling herself erect, tensing her jaw, causing the thick veins in her neck to stand out. "Come on Julian, I can make you forget about her!"

"And you say you loved her! - that isn't love. All it's ever been is a competition - everything is a competition with you."

"Yes, we are alike in many ways, but if you go with me you will see that Karen is really not that special. I can show you such a time as you have never dreamt..."

"No, I couldn't."

"Why not? She is going to die any way!" said Rachine, finally exasperated.

"Why do you say such things?"

"I'm being honest. She is only kept alive by a machine. Turn it off and she would be dead in less than a day."

I lit up a cigarette and looked at the creature sitting opposite me. Trying to figure out what it was, or what made such a gorgeous creature so bitter, so self-orientated.

"Why do you look at me like that? *Voyeur!* - that is what Karen called you. All you are good for is looking. Well have a good look Monsieur."

Rachine tried to restrain herself from getting up and storming out. She sat on the edge of her seat looking about her. She was furious. Her eyes ranged over the cutlery. I think for a moment she wanted to stab me. She ran her hands through her long hair.

"Aghhh'" she groaned. She picked up a fork and threw it on the table; her face twisting into a snarl. Finally she launched into a tirade of French and Italian. Some people at a nearby table looked over, as she was finishing, spluttering:

"You *sot, idiota, impuissant, lâche...*"

"Look have some more champagne," I said, in an attempt to pacify her.

I replenished her glass. She looked at it a moment, for a second I thought she was going to throw it in my face. She picked it up and took a gulp. Gradually she began to calm down.

Rachine gave me a candid look. "You are stupid Julian. So was she."

We sat in silence for several minutes. A waiter came over. I looked at Rachine.

"We should go," I said.

"No. Karen can wait. Let's have some more champagne." She also ordered another side dish.

At the word the waiter disappeared, coming back with a fresh bottle of champagne, another waiter with a silver salver of apricots, to which he then added Grand Marnier. Rachine gave it a special name, but basically the dish consisted of apricots and some kind of syrup which was then set light to with the aid of the liqueur.

"Do you want some," she said, insouciantly.

I declined her offer. As the dish flared up vivid purple and blue flames Rachine's face lit up with it.

"You can go if you want," she said, as she prepared to tuck in to her flamed apricots. There was something touchingly childlike in the way she ate, seemingly oblivious to where she was, all that mattered was her own enjoyment. The wine waiter uncorked the champagne and poured a little of the champagne into two fresh glasses. She ate and drank with gusto. Against my intentions I found myself lingering, captivated by her childlike enthusiasm.

"Well!" said Rachine, fingering her glass.

"Well what?"

"It is customary with a fresh bottle of champagne to make some sort of toast."

"What do you want to drink to this time?"

"To us."

"There is no us."

"To life then."

I lifted my glass. That I could accept. I asked her why she thought Karen and I were stupid.

"We won't go into why *you* are stupid Julian," she said looking up from her dish

"That is all too obvious. With regards Karen, she was stupid because she thought she was something she wasn't; just like that stupid old man who put her on to that kind of thinking in the first place. He is the one who is to blame for her lying there in a coma."

"You mean Garcia?"

"*Oui - exactement.* She was stupid because she believed in his silly ideas. She believed that she was something she wasn't."

"You don't think she was reincarnated?"

Rachine shrugged her shoulders. "Who knows? I was talking about his idea of there being different gods and goddesses. There is only one true god, everyone knows that?"

I lent back in my seat and pointed at her and laughed. "My god - you're a Christian! A Christian! - Who would have thought it? You of all people?" I had a good old laugh at that, until the tears were streaming down my face.

Rachine looked perplexed. "You can laugh all you want; at least I'm not the one who was fooled into believing I was a goddess and ending up in a coma!"

I took a large gulp of champagne and lit a cigarette. 'How truth soon sobers one.' I thought.

"It's just, I never had you figured as the religious type?"

"I wouldn't say I was religious exactly. I was born a Catholic. I use to take my vows very seriously."

Despite the ugly truth about Karen, the serious look on Rachine's face as she talked about 'her vows', set me off again.

"Laugh - go on! I am glad I amuse you so?"

"I'm sorry Rachine," I said, chuckling away.

"There are a lot of things you don't know about me. You think I am just how you say - a *slut!* - a cheap thing that anybody can have? Well for a start I am not as easy as your precious Karen. She would do it with anyone, anytime, anywhere. Yes - now you do not laugh! I didn't sell my body the way *she* did. I posed naked with her for a magazine - because she wanted me to! The editor thought we looked good together. I had plenty of offers to be a nude model, instead I choose to keep some sense of decency about me. Karen was a porn star was she not?"

I admitted reluctantly that it was so.

"And you thought I...."

"I'm sorry. I just assumed....That day by the pool you were both naked. I figured...."

Rachine smirked. "Well you figured wrong. There's a difference to going around naked on an island in the Aegean and selling your body the way Karen did. On Sapphos everyone was naked. It was Garcia's thing. The dirty old man! Didn't you ever see him ogling Karen's breasts, not that she cared."

"So why did you go there?"

"To keep an eye on Karen you fool."

It began to dawn on me that just may be, I had got Rachine all wrong. She lit a cigarette. It was her turn to consider what faced her across the table.

She shook her head. "That girl deserved better! I tried my best to warn her about him and his mad ideas. Then you turn up and I thought to myself, 'he looks sensible. He will see through Garcia. See that he is only a silly old fool, a dirty old man.' But no, you fell for his superstitious nonsense as well."

Was it possible I had got it all wrong? Everything the wrong way round? I took a sip of my drink, my glass seemed like a huge weight, like drinking out of lead chalice.

"I had no idea," I said, feeling a sense of panic. "How did Garcia meet Karen? I never knew for sure."

"I don't know exactly when. He knows a lot of people. A lot of people with money. He likes the good things in life, especially women - good-looking women. He hung about the fashion shows in Milan and Rome. That's how *I* met him anyway. He invited me up to his villa in Tuscany, that's where he takes all his best looking girls."

"Oh! - and what went on there?"

"What do you think? He is a rich old man who loves to surround himself with sexy young girls." Rachine looked at me severely. "I didn't sleep with him, if that's what you think. Fortunately, at the time, he was preoccupied with this English girl, Bethany, whatever her name was. I told you about her. She drove him crazy. Karen didn't arrive on the scene until several months after. She was this crazy American girl, who was in the same fashion show as me. There was something about her which struck me as being incredibly vulnerable. I knew what Italian men were like, so I thought I'd watch out for her. I liked American's anyway, and as we all know, there was something strangely alluring about her. She told me about this person who wanted to take some nude shots of her to go in a magazine, and would I be interested. It was a good magazine. I didn't know it at the time, but Karen was considered quite a star in that line of glamour modelling. Most of the shoot took place at Garcia's villa up in Tuscany. He invited her out to Sapphos, and since we were a kind of item I got invited too, but I could tell it was Karen he was mostly interested in. I figured Garcia was fairly safe, as rich old men go. Yes it is true he had some funny ideas, I just went along with them - why not? I was having a good time, if only I knew how things would turn out in the end."

"It wasn't your fault. You did all you could. It was all my fault. It's my fault Karen is in a coma. I felt the same as you abut Garcia at one point. I didn't trust him, but he was very convincing. In fact, up until now, I still believed in him; even though it was his idea about Tanit and the whole pagan business, that has landed Karen at deaths door. God! - what an idiot I've been. You're right, I am stupid."

"Don't be hard on yourself. You weren't to know. As you said, he *is* very convincing."

Rachine paused to take a sip of her drink and lit another cigarette. She looked at me, I suddenly felt a jolt of sexual energy stream off of her; her whole being radiated sexual energy, as keen and as vivid as a stripped nerve.

"I know I said Garcia was a silly old fool," she resumed, "but don't under estimate him. He can be very dangerous. If you remember what he had done to Bethany. I didn't take part in that by the way. I was just there. It was a horrible thing to witness. For Garcia it is simple, you are either with him or against him. He shows no mercy, especially when it comes to getting his own way. What happened to that girl he would do to me, or to anybody who defied him."

Rachine played with her glass spinning it round by the stem. She turned away slightly presenting me with her profile. She smiled and turned back to me. She could see with her peripheral vision that I was loving her with my eyes.

"I would hate anything to happen to you," I said, touching her hand.

Rachine looked at me askance and glanced down at my hand. "I thought you hated me?"
"I never hated you. I just didn't understand you," I replied.
"I suppose I can be hard to take. And you are right, I was jealous of Karen. I suppose I can be a bit foolish sometimes," she said, receiving my hand in hers.
Another, even more vivid flash of sexual energy erupted off of her like a solar flare, and travelled down my arm through the whole of my body. She focused her dark eyes on me and the rush of energy was redoubled. 'My god,' I thought, 'this girl is like a volcano.' I had to disengage my hand from hers. I drew hard on my cigarette, it was all I could do to keep command of myself!
She eyed me with a strange look, I guess it was akin to curiosity, as though she just hadn't quite got the measure of me. She licked her lips and took her time, speaking slowly moving like a cat in measured steps towards her quarry.
"You know," she began, "you spoke earlier of not being the right kind of man for me."
"I did?- yes I did..." I said, suddenly hating myself for my honesty.
"Look, let me speak openly Julian, Karen - well she did talk of certain reservations she had..."
"Yes - yes I know, I'm no good..."
"No!" Rachine put her hand on mine again opening her black eyes wide. "Don't be so hard on yourself, I can show you what you must do to get the best out of a girl - *like me!* Although I imagine since I last spoke with Karen she has already completed most of your training! Look upon me as a finishing school."
I laughed nervously. Rachine's hand stroked my fingers.
"I can't promise to make you a Marquis de Sade, or a Rasputin, but I can certainly make you capable of giving a good virtuoso performance."
"You could!" I said, dumbfounded.
"Julian! - I am offering myself as your instrument - play me!"
She was just too much! I took a drink, suddenly I felt her foot on my groin. The champagne bubbles went up my nose and I began coughing and spluttering. I put my hand on her foot unsure whether to push it away or accept it. Rachine's eyes were intent on me as she manoeuvred it sliding it along my thigh.
"What if I'm tone deaf?.." I said, keeping up her melodious metaphors.

"Nonsense, you've played Karen good with your bow!" I felt her foot search me out again. "And - by all accounts it is quite a bow."

I found myself blushing. "Are you musical by any chance?" I said.

"I am an accomplished cellist and also good with the violin."

"I thought you might be," I said, chuckling nervously.

"I'm serious Julian." she engaged me with a forthright look, her black eyes scolding. "You like to be self-effacing I think, for fear of others who are better than you, when in fact you are better than most. It is fear of being found wanting, when you need not fear this at all - certainly not from where I am sitting, and where my foot is now - is it not so?"

"That's quite an observation you've made."

She batted her eyes. "Not at all. I know people, I know you Julian."

"And you are quite the poet! I know people back in the States who could put you on the radio with stuff like that."

She lent across the table and gripped my hand. "I'm serious Julian! I may be a poet of sorts, but I assure you my forte is not with words. Under my tutelage I will raise you to dizzying heights - of that I assure you. I will make of you a god, you will see stars, you will experience a new kind of being. I know...*Karen - Karen!* You love her, but you must put her to one side, she would understand; with me you will be carrying on where she left off - with me..." she rolled her big eyes "*Ooooh la la!*"

I am sure she was as she said: 'Oooooh la la!' I was tempted to laugh in her face, but as I looked at that stupendous body there was some element of the truth in what she spoke, she was on another level from Karen, and if she never recovered I knew the world would remain forever a bland place without her, only someone like Rachine could offer a way forward. She was literally out of this world! I looked up into those pitch-black eyes: another firmament! - no not a sky, but a place where whole galaxies were spiralling and colliding into one another. Her massive G cup orbs were like twin super-giant planets in close orbit around their primary. Her wonderful face shone forth like a bronze iridescent star. Her body was like a solar system unto itself, at the centre of which was a massive black hole that could devour the universe whole.

When that solar system moved, her perturbations were felt all around the room men's lusts were pulled after her, toward her dark core where they were devoured whole: as she devoured other women's scorn. Her gargantuan ego, on a par with Karen's, consumed the attentions of men like the sun devours hydrogen, except she was hotter than than any ordinary star. Her tongue was like a long leaping pink prominence bursting from the filament of her mouth, set in the iridescent photosphere of her face, the beauty of which was incandescent. Like a tiny world I felt myself falling falling falling. She licked her lips, her cascading prominence of a tongue leapt burning into my mouth.

She drew the iridescent torch of her face away, bathing me in her leaping corona. She giggled and sipped some of her champagne. She looked at me in a strange way, her mood seemed to change, but it's hard to be sure, when you have experienced an altered state of being: for it was as though I had begun to move outside of ordinary space and time - or so it seemed.

"What do you know about the priest?" asked Rachine.

I found her words incongruous in light of everything that had just occurred.

"The priest!"

"Yes the priest," she said, leaning across the table.

"I don't know what you mean. I don't know any *priest*," I said, retreating further back in my seat. Her words, despite her allure had jolted me out of my orbit about her dazzling sun.

Rachine sighed heavily and sat back stiffly. It was like experiencing an eclipse. The power had suddenly been turned down, the light dimmed. "I see! You disappoint me Julian, you still do not trust me," she said.

I remained silent, remembering Garcia's warning about anybody who asked about a priest.

"That's OK you will find out in the end who you can trust, but by then it may be too late. You know, I thought you were more intelligent Julian."

She shifted in her seat and presented me again with her beautiful profile. I had to look away. It was too much, I wanted to be the conduit for her sparkling energy, but right now the supply had been shut-off. She darted her head round and fixed me with her smouldering obsidian eyes.

"There was talk of a priest," I confided.

Rachine held her pose, frozen like a statue of lava, waiting on my words.

"Apparently," I went on, "Karen had been in love with this priest who, according to Garcia, she had known in another life. That's really all I know. And that for some reason he presented a threat. I don't know why. Garcia just warned me to be on my guard."

"Oh - well you know about as much as me then - although why would he think that this priest was a threat? It seems to me logical to assume he might want to help Karen or, Natasha as she was then." Rachine mused: "I find it very romantic. The idea that love can outlast a life time - to carry on into another life!"

"There you go again..."

"What do you mean?"

"I never took you for the romantic type."

"It is terrible Julian that you think so bad of me. I am not without feelings."

"I'm learning all the time," I said. I tried to take her hand but she moved it away and looked at me askance. "Did Garcia ever say who you might have been in another life?"

Rachine looked perplexed. "I would rather not say. I don't know if I should trust you. There is much to you I think, that does not not meet the eye. You are I think what they call the black horse."

I laughed, not jus at her faux pas but at her assessment of me.

"What is wrong? You laugh at me...stop!"

"I'm sorry Rachine, it's just you couldn't be more wrong about me. What you see is what you get - I'm afraid."

Rachine seemed to consider for a moment. "Hmmm - well...And did Garcia tell you who you were in another life?"

"I didn't want to know. But I imagine I was then as I am now, nobody particularly special - although Karen did say I had always been there with her, she just never recognised me. You see that's me, always on the periphery of things."

"It is a shame, when you deserve so much more."

"I don't know - may be I like it there."

"With me, I would make you centre stage. You would be worshipped, not as you were with Karen, treated like some sort of - eunuch!"

I had to laugh at that, she was so right. "Perhaps *that* is what I have always been to her. Why I was reluctant for Garcia to tell me who I was."

"He certainly convinced Karen. He tried to convince me, but I did not trust him. It is wrong to meddle in such things."
"It's a notion Garcia believes strongly in."
The light dawned again as she levelled me with her obsidian black eyes. "With me Julian you would get the recognition you deserve, if there is one thing I would show you above all others is how you are most definitely not a eunuch - not in this life with me!" Her words moved me uncomfortably, almost painfully so. I shifted in my seat, expectant of her foot, but it didn't arrive.
"The thing is Julian, now I have spoken openly what will you do with me now?"
"I think you are a safe bet," I replied.
"I was speaking literally. Never mind! It was stupid of me to bring up the priest. I can see you are thinking about *her* again. I can see it in your eyes. I suppose you'll be wanting to get back to her bedside."
She looked at me demurely. "I know when I'm beat. What was I thinking, that I could compete with the love you have for her! I guess I'll see you at the hospital tomorrow? Forgive me if I don't go with you now."
She was about to get up when I put my hand on hers. "No, don't go."
Rachine looked down at my hand, and then raised her jet-black eyes to mine.
"No! Karen can wait for once. If there's any change they'll call."
Rachine pushed her belly against the table edge, thrusting her chest forward across the piece of furniture as she had before, nearly taking up half the surface, plates and glasses spilling everywhere. Suddenly her sexual current was turned on - full-blast. It exploded over me like a volcano erupting, suddenly she was no longer the solid stiff statue of lava, instead she was molten and fluid. I leaned across the table and put my arms around her and drew her towards me and kissed her. Our mouths coming together in a fusion blast of passional meltdown. We both stood up in unison, nearly turning the table over: such was her powerful gravitational field, my hands, as well as my mouth seemed stuck to her. Somehow Rachine got a hand free and threw some money at a waiter. Thence from restaurant to taxi, from taxi to apartment, we tumbled as a kind of monad, a single conjoined entity - and thence forth, if not in body, all of the time, so it was for my will, my sense of person: submerged - it seemed, forever under Rachine's strange and all dominating nature.

XXI

Where Rachine originated remained a mystery. I never knew for sure if she was Italian or French; she was like Antonio: a citizen of Europe. She spoke at least six different languages all of them fluently. In the public eye she maintained an enigmatic quality, and when it came to being adept at concealment this applied as much to her body as it did her personality. She was not renowned as a nude model in the way Karen was, and yet she had far more to put on display. She only worked with photographers who understood the artistic dimensions of the human form, in other words, she was never gratuitous. Her skill was in concealment, the result: tantalising, frustrating. What bounced back from the back of her eyes through the camera lens, was a promise of unfathomable delights. Her look was always mysterious, disconcerting even: the possessor of a secret that could never be shared. Her golden body was the gift that no mortal man was worthy of. She was the equivalent of Pandora's curse on the male sex.

I have indicated on numerous occasions the extent of Karen's audaciousness, her conceitedness, her unashamed vanity, well compared with Rachine, Karen was the shy retiring type. Once she was firmly established in my admiration, she let it be known that she considered her physical essence as existing in a state that was beyond perfection. For all her boastful display, she let it be known that she did not come cheap. She was enigmatic by nature, even her body remained obscure when she was completely naked. One felt there was always more that could be known.

I said she was adept at concealment - when she needed to be discrete; such as a posh restaurant for instance. When she lent across the table it became obvious that she was offering me more than the *hors d'œuvres*, and at that precise moment she gave me more of an appetite than Karen. Rachine's basket was brimming with succulent fruit, which was enough to make any man's mouth water. Karen's basket by comparison was half empty, and what fruit there was,

was bruised and putrefying. Karen, my wife was lying on the threshold of Hades looking more dead than alive. Her pallid greasy complexion was like a grinning ghoul. The truth was I hated having to enter that room where she lay, with tubes and wires attached to her like some Frankinstein monster. I hated having to go to that place every day and pick up that clammy hand, and then look at her insipid parched lips, which had once been so hot with life and passion, and then have to steal myself to plant my lips on them, when I kissed her good-bye. It was asking too much of me, too much of a man of *my* will keep up the act. I was ground down. Mentally exhausted by nearly three years of madcap thinking, of Tanit ecstasy, of ecstatic sex, gods and goddesses. I was mythologically and deistically burnt out. I longed for the simple life. And so when Rachine reached across the table and I touched her hand and felt warm flesh, when I looked at her body that seethed with life, her undulating form, her robust fecund hips and full breasts, it was all I could do to stop myself instantly falling upon those lips which pulsated so vividly with life.

Condemn me if you will, perhaps I deserved to be lying there instead of Karen, but I wasn't! I was alive. I was human. I was weak. In my favour I will say that there had only ever been one girl for me, from the very start, and I used to think, if I can't have Karen then there will be no one else for me! As it happened I got what I wanted, and yet I never truly had her. Garcia was right about that, when he said that no one man could ever be enough for her! While she slept with countless men, some of them mere boys, I had remained faithful to the dream I had of Karen when I first saw her at high school. There had been very few other women in my life since that day. A rushed and ill-conceived encounter with a girl I met in the States, a few months after Karen had left for her new life in Europe, I had known a few Jap girls in Tripolitania, and then of course there was my ill-fated Tricksy: similar to Karen in some respects: a raging nymphomaniac and a sadomasochist to boot, but apart from that her temperament and her physicality was nothing like Karen's. I know that in these pages Karen comes across as the hottest piece of ass ever created, I know, I wrote them, but in truth I had very little to go on by way of comparison. That was until Rachine. If Karen was hot stuff then Rachine was molten like the surface of the sun. She had a healthy attitude towards sex and not an excessive addiction, and neither did she exhibit any propensity to self harm, the temptation of which was never far away for Karen. Her lovely body was in large part covered in scars that were, strictly speaking, not all of her making; I think she secretly derived some perverse kind of pleasure from their existence. The deep scar on her face, and the way her once perfect breasts were essentially mutilated, were all taken without the corresponding alarm or, horror, that one might have normally expect from a girl as proud as Karen, even discounting any personal pride, the fact that her looks, her body were an asset in terms of her modelling career: the fact that this had been compromised did not seem to unduly effect Karen. Such are some of the idiosyncrasies of the human mind. What really blew my mind, the thing that made Rachine so darn good, was the way her physique was linked in with her brain. Her mind was like quick silver, when it came to giving expression to her sexual imagination. In this regard her mind was as agile as her body. What she expressed in the physical dimension came from an imagination that was as convoluted as the insides of a snail's shell. Her passion was like a phosphorescent bomb exploding in the mind. When you touched her body it was like connecting with a bare electrical wire that sent shudders through every nerve ending. I marvelled at the endless expanse of her passion, that ran deep like the liquid core of the earth, and rose up to the surface of her flesh, invisible yet hotter than the infernal vapours of a volcano. Kiss her, and you instantly felt the intensity of the seething inferno that rose up from deep in her throat like a pyroplastic flow before her tongue, that was like unto a long river of lava, that set ones mouth and loins on fire. Touch her and her passion would flare like a solar prominence, erupting from her body, as from the molten surface of a star. Around her was an aura of torrid energy and fierce heat, you only had to get near her to feel it coming off of her in waves, like the corona of a star. She was no ordinary girl, no ordinary star, she was a supernova explosion, as endless and timeless as the universe itself. Her passion shot out through time and space and exploded over your senses: Rachine was mind blowing, mind glowing, vapourescent, incandescent.

Garcia once said Rachine was possessed of a demon of a highly malevolent and wanton nature. In the cab, on the way to my apartment she looked at me in a peculiar kind of way, a look that should have made me feel afraid, but at the time all I could feel was the wonderful pressure of her body against mine, and the sensation of her mouth that was aflame with a tongue like lava, longer than any I'd known, as long and prehensile as a snake, the effect of which was to send shivers through my brain.

"I'm not going to tell you who Garcia said I was in another life," she said to me, "You're not ready for that! - but I will tell you that I have a demon in me too and it is bigger and more dangerous than the thing Karen has in her."

Rachine's demon didn't skulk in some dark crevice of the mind. Her demon had swollen to the size of a star. It had completely taken over her body and her mind, and when I looked into those fantastic dark eyes, at their obsidian core, I felt myself falling, as into a dark star. Her demon was the power-house of her passion, that sent forth an aura, much like the corona of a star. Rachine's aura didn't just fill a room, it dominated entire cities, encapsulated an entire planet, entire universes even. When you looked into the dark mote of her eye, you felt your mind and your body being stretched out of one time continuum into another. It was discombobulating, phantasmagorical, it sent you whirling and twizzling through a whole whirlpool of feelings and experiences, that it would take a thousand lifetimes to encompass, but one felt it all, in just nanoseconds!

Rachine was literally *out of this world*, and when you looked into those cobalt eyes, when you contacted with her dark fevered exterior, she took you with her to another world - another way of being. One that was incommensurate with any other human experience.

'Yes, yes, yes,' I hear you say, 'but what was she really like? forget about the cosmic scale, what was she like on the humble human scale? Well physically she was more flowing, more naturally female and fecund than Karen, whose body often put me in mind of a lithe wild animal, than that of a human being. Rachine's curves were soft, rounder, more full, and it made all the difference. Karen's body was altogether more unyielding, harder, bonier, even her breasts possessed an unnatural resilience until they had been hacked about by the Syria knife. Rachine's figure was in every way more abundant, more feminine, more yielding. Although Rachine was cosmogonically mind blowing to make love to, it was at least a natural expression of her being. It wasn't like an Olympic event, as it sometimes seemed with Karen. There were no contestants, there were no rules, it just happened, it was - perfectly, perfectly natural. Once having entered into the wonderfully bizarre world of Rachine, you never wanted to leave it. You would never be the same again. In her world, which was so much larger than the one you left behind, you grew exponentially in mind and body in order to become a part of it. When you came back to the pallid mundane world of ordinary people, everything seemed so much smaller and insignificant. This was the afterglow of Rachine's corona flare, which swamped your senses, this is what it was like *to be* Rachine. This is how she felt all the time. Her ego was gargantuan. She saw the world from the perspective of a giant, of a super-being, like Superman on steroids. When she looked down from her colossal perspective, all she saw were lots of little people. Tiny insignificant insect people, scurrying around. Once, having shared in this *other* world, you never wanted to go back to being one of the little people - ever again. I was afraid that after the first time with her, when we had gone back to my apartment from the restaurant, that she would not want to be with me again. And I knew that if that happened, I would have to throw myself in the river Seine. That girl had a responsibility now for my sanity! To her credit, she took that responsibility deadly serious. If you were with her you were a part of her world. You were no longer a separate person with your own identity. I was no longer Julian the clumsy lover, the hapless fool, the naïve...well that's enough. I was *Rachinite*, I was *Juliorachine*, *Rachinian*, sometimes I *was* Rachine. I saw the world as she saw it. I was in her body, her skin. I saw light enter her mind through cobalt eyes. I thought her thoughts. I was submerged - in her. I know for a fact that she longed to eat the universe: to swallow it, quite literally consume it whole. She burned with a fierce resentment of humanity and it's weakness'. She wanted to cancel everything out: negate existence, destroy it all. She wanted to command, to rule like a god, as they did in ancient times. I even discovered who she had been in those times. She considered her own body to be the most perfect creation in the universe, but hated the vulnerability of flesh and blood, and the limits it put on her, which is why she lived in other universes, other times, other creatures, even! The mass of people meant nothing to her, she was disgusted by them. She regarded them as so many lice. The human race was an embarrassment to her, people were just things that she used, or else they were things that got in her way. She was a colossi that in better times would have swept the whole of humanity into oblivion. So if you were going to be one with her, one took on the proportions of a colossi. She did not suffer tiny people, let alone fools - at all. When I was with her I felt I could command the sky. I felt that when we were together, the world stopped turning. We commanded time itself! That first time with her, was the first time of all times, it was as though before her I had not really existed. There could be no other time. She was time! And - like all first times, one never forgot.

She smiled and stretched and luxuriated in the feel of being within her own skin. "Well Julian," she said, as I lay there quivering as one who had been cast up on a distant shore, "There is much more to you than meets the eye." She lowered her head over me like a planet crossing the sun. I looked up into those jet eyes and saw whole universes merging and separating. "no wonder," she said, inside my head, "that Karen kept you all to herself. Now you are mine."
"Now I am yours," I repeated, meaning I belonged to her, just as one might own a pair of boots or a straw hat.

Rachine knew exactly how to exploit a man's vanity, and - oh, how eager we are to hear our praises sung, especially when they come from the lips of a woman such as she. As I said, if you partook of her, you became, for a while at least, reflected back as something similar to Rachine herself: that is, a colossi, a giant among men. You became more potent, more virile, more masculine. You surveyed the world in the manner of Alexander or Napoleon; one commanded, dominated all that one surveyed. And all that from a fuck.

It was obvious now to Antonio, Mersell, to Garcia, Eustacia and Anastasia, may be even Karen herself, wherever she was, that what Rachine displayed towards me, was more than just sisterly affection. She openly kissed me in front of the others, and made me perform other tricks in public for her perverse enjoyment. At such times, when she had her audience, she could not keep the look of power, of fiendish satisfaction off her face. She proudly flaunted me before the others who could do no more than grudgingly and silently accept the situation - seeing it, no doubt, an inevitable outcome of all the stress I had had to endure. Rachine reserved her best performance for the guest of honour, that silent witness! Rachine would have to pull me into Karen's room, once inside she would shut the door and look over her shoulder towards her captured audience, and then her hands would be all over me. I would feel her long red, live tongue, dart in my mouth, and in a frenetic embrace she would pull me on to the edge of Karen's bed. I make no excuses, I needed little encouragement from Rachine; she would place my hand on her bosom, on her thighs - Christ she would have gone all the way! The only thing that stopped her, was fear of being caught out by one of the staff, and then not to be allowed back again to gloat. The whole time we were engaged in one another, Rachine would be staring over my shoulder at Karen. For Rachine it was the greatest aphrodisiac, it drove her wild to make love to me in front of Karen, as she lay dying. It made her wetter than March. Sometimes she would have to break off, clutching at herself and panting, 'No - no more. Oh god you drive me crazy,' she would say, whilst unable to pull her eyes away from Karen's pallid drawn features.

I could not be alone now with Karen. I was even afraid to look at her face. It was as though she were watching me beneath her shut lids. I would wake in the early hours from night terrors. I would see Karen sit bolt-upright in her bed, with the leads and tubes hanging off of her emaciated body, covered in bed sores, with bits of rotting flesh hanging off of her. She would turn her head slowly and hold out an accusing finger toward me. Other times I would be in the apartment making love to Rachine, when Karen would suddenly walk in the room as if she had just got off her death bed, and touch me on the shoulder. I would scream out loud in my dream and wake up bathed in sweat. Afraid I still might see her, I would turn on the light, which sometimes woke Rachine, who always managed to sleep soundly.

"What is it Julian? Not another bad dream? Come here." And I would hold her tightly, "there's nothing to be afraid of, Rachine is here." The touch of her lovely warm body was usually enough to dispel the terrors, sometimes we would go back to sleep, other times I would have aroused something else in Rachine, other than what I took for tenderness.

Were all these night apparitions just the manifestation of a bad conscience, or the sign of something more? Was it in fact Karen's spectre that was haunting me from the threshold of the grave? Was it her *elan vital*, reaching out to me, caught between life and death, pleading with me to stop - to not give up hope in her resurrection? Was this the final outcome for Karen and her tortured existence's? Was this what it was to be an apparition, a mere phantasm? More to the point, was this what I would have to endure for the rest of my days on Earth, because I had betrayed her?

Rachine was puling me into the hospital one day when I began to shout and scream: "No!..no! I'm not going in there. She can see us, I know she can. She's everywhere."

Rachine stopped, turned round and thwacked me hard in the face. "For god's sake Julian, pull yourself together!" I went reeling back, holding my face. "I'm sorry swee'dy," she said, rushing up to me. "We'll just stay for a little while."

"But why! Why do we have to?"

Rachine looked at me intently and grabbed hold of my hand. "My word, you really are strung out, aren't you?"

She almost had to drag me the rest of the way. Somehow I found myself standing outside the door to Karen's room. Rachine mussed with my hair and kissed me, and then giggling began to touch me in the way she liked to do.

"No Rachine. Don't do that," I said pulling back - "not in front of her. It's not right."

Suddenly a nurse went past and smiled. "*Je vous en prie! - mon Dieu! Tais-toi! Tranquille...*" Rachine implored. "We're going in and that is an end to it. We'll just have a look." Karen so loved to gloat. She put the chairs together when Anastasia and Eustacia had left, which they did with the minimm of fuss. By now they had cottoned-on to what our game was, I got the feeling neither of them liked Rachine very much, althugh they gave me a look of sympathy - I had so much *sympathy!*

We sat down, Rachine took my hand and laid it in her lap. I bowed my head unable to bring myself to look at Karen. I felt the strength in Rachine's legs, and she moved my hand so that it contacted with her hot bare thigh. Rachine smiled, and breathed a sigh of satisfaction.

"She looks bad Julian."

"Does she?"

"She has a greenish tinge to her, today."

I followed the length of wires that ran from Karen's body to the heart monitor at the side of her bed and concentrated on the passage of the transient green blip as it ran across the screen: the only indicator that Karen was - in some sense still alive.

Rachine's eye ranged about the room. "All this stink'n Jasmine and other stuff, who keeps bringing it? Not you?"

"No - Antonio, I think. He spends every hour he can with her now."

Rachine made a dismissive noise at the back of her throat. "Well, if it is true that smell is associated with the memory of people and places, then the aroma of something with a bit more class such as *L' Air du Tempes,* and *Moschino,* will certainly let her know that I have been here with you - and to you my darling it will certainly be a constant reminder of me, and the times we have shared. What is Jasmine compared with *parfum* such as *Guérlain* or, *Jean Patou?* or the *odorant* of *Vera Wang* or *Gaultier...*"

"*Issey Miyake...*" I contributed, rembering Tricksy."

Rachine put her nose in the air, as if destecting a slghtly unaccespatble *odeur.* "Hmm...*L'eua d'Issey!* I supose it is all right."

Indeed! - this *was* Rachine. One detected her scent on the air, long before one saw her. She used expensive perfumes the way other animals use musk, to mark out their territories. She put her hand on mine and moved it further along her thigh. "Look at her Julian."

"No I can't." I glanced up, and then quickly down again at Rachine's legs. The only way I could stay in the room was by concentrating on the hot palpable flesh of the living.

Rachine let out a deep sigh. The location of my hand was exciting her. "Then look at me,"she said.

I looked at Rachine's face. Her painted lips were of deep scarlet. She parted them slowly, opening her mouth, until it resembled a deep gaping cut, a blood red laceration, a deep vivid red - full of life, full of blood. I put my lips against hers and bit hard into their soft flesh. Rachine winced slightly, otherwise, almost without a flicker, she continued to kiss, as if relishing the taste of her salty blood. Suddenly there was a heart stopping knock at the door. We looked at each other like a couple of guilty vampires. A nurse came in to check on Karen. We both immediately got up and walked out, choosing to ignore the nurses entreaty to: 'stay!'

"You've got blood all around your mouth," said Rachine, when we were in the corridor. She looked in her bag and took out a small white handkerchief. Licking a corner, she attempted to wipe it off.

"So have you," I said, taking the handkerchief from her.

"I'm going to the washrooms. I suggest you do the same," she said.

"When I returned the nurse had gone, so I decided to wait outside Karen's room until Rachine returned. After about a couple of minutes the same nurse came back. She spoke to me in French, and gestured to Karen's room. I got the gist of what she was saying. I nodded and smiled in a guilty way and explained in my poor French, that I was perfectly happy where I was. The young nurse looked at me somewhat askance, before going off about her duties. A few moments later another nurse came past and gave me a similar quizzical look. I looked at the door to Karen's room. I knew she was in there lying all alone, and that I should be there with her, but that door remained an impenetrable barrier to me. A nest of vipers at my feet could not hasten me in there. At last I saw Rachine coming down the corridor towards me, and I gave a huge inward sigh of relief.

"Where the hell have you been? It's not good I can't take this anymore!" I said pacing up and down.

Rachine looked at the cause of my agitation. "Is anyone in there with her now?"

"No," I replied.

Rachine sighed, "But, don't worry it will soon be over, she can't possibly last much longer. I spoke with one of the nurses, her blood pressure is all over the place."

"I don't care. I need a rest from all of this. I need to get away for a few days, it's driving me crazy!" I looked at Rachine beseechingly. "Isn't there some way of getting away for a little while - just you and me?"

"I suppose we could? It's not like the others would not understand. After all, you *have* been through a lot lately. May be your're right honey. It might be good for both of us."

"You don't think Garcia might have something to say about us going away?"

Rachine gave a short cynical laugh. "Oh honey! I think by now they all know what is going on between us. In any case, who cares what that old fool thinks!"

Rachine mussed with my hair, and gave me a Kiss on the cheek. "Poor swee'dy, you're cracking up aren't you? You just need a little rest honey. Don't worry Rachine will take care of you - the way *Rachine* knows best." Rachine surreptitiously slid her hand down to my groin, and grinned wickedly. "Anyway," she said, glancing over her shoulder at the closed door, "it's not like the bitch is going to miss us - is it?"

Rachine wasted little time in organising our short break. A modelling friend of hers, who was on an engagement in the States, was happy to let us have the use of her Swiss apartment: A beautiful sprawling affair, overlooking Lake Constance.

I was relieved to get out of Paris. To put some distance between me and that dying woman. Of course I also brought along with me my guilt. Rachine though, catered for my every need, just as she said she would. She brought barbiturates to help me sleep, and used her fantastic imagination, in conjunction with her equally fantastic body, the rest of the time.

Her friends place was in the mountains overlooking the lake. Rachine, like all true Europeans loved to ski, and scale mountain peaks. She also loved to bathe her body in the invigorating waters of lake Constance, and then bathe her body in the warm stream of the sun. Rachine loved the sun: she glistened like a bronze statue of a goddess: anointing her body with that same pungent red oil, I had first seen her using by the pool, on Garcia's island. I was struck then by how dark her skin was. Heavily tanned, she was almost like a light skinned Negress. Among these southern Europeans I soon discovered many more dark skinned beauties like Rachine. In the thin pure air, high up on the *piste,* their faces were burned ruddy-dark from the glare of the sun, reflected back from the snow.

I was not anywhere near the accomplished skier, that Rachine was. I left her to tackle the higher slopes with people with names like *Hans,* and *Hoit,* while I contented myself with fooling around on the nursery slopes. I would quickly get bored with this and wind up drinking beer in one of the bars in the village, or else I would wait for Rachine at the ski-lodge. She would come over to me and hug and kiss me, to show *Hans* and *Hoit* that they didn't stand a chance. I would order her favourite drink: an Ameretto or a Cognac, and she would tell me all about her adventures on the *piste*; the condition of the snow: whether it was powdery or hard or what not, and how good Hans was and how she had gone faster than *Helgah*, and so on and so forth!

She carried the coolness of the snow slopes with her on her face, but only as we kissed did one become aware of the seething, torrid heat that existed beneath her cool exterior. *Hans* and *Hoit* were out of luck with this particular Fräulein, but in places like this there were plenty of girls like Rachine to go round. All of them fit and strong, and like so many German, Austrian and Swiss girls of the mountains, they all had amazing physiques, their thighs in particular were incredibly well developed, I guess from all that hiking and skiing up and down mountains all day, to the extent that Karen's pillars of cedar would have looked quite average by comparison. Like Rachine, these flaxen haired Teutons glowed with a vitality and vigour that was almost indecent, never having doubted themselves for a second in their entire life, and all of them possessing a healthy attitude towards sex, as accomplished on the high slopes of the Alps as they were in bed.

One lazy afternoon we were sunning ourselves on the terrace of the apartment, when I was filled with an Earth shattering panic. Well it would have been Earth shattering had I truly been the colossi that Rachine made me feel. Instead the chais longue just shook a bit. I looked over to Rachine who was oblivious to all things human, staring up at the blue vaulted heaven.

"Rachine," I called out.

"*Quoi!*"- what is it *chéri?*" she said, in a sleepy voice.

"What if she wakes up?"

"What if who wakes up?"

"Her - you know...." I hated even speaking her name now.

Rachine was still far off in her world, dominating some planet or other, thankfully not the Earth - (it was too small for her to bother with)

There was a pause and then Rachine looked over at me, "Oh darling, if you mean Karen say Karen."

"Well what if she wakes up? What do I say to her?"

"Oh darling," said Rachine, in a lazy voice, "come here." She took my hand and drew it across her dark glistening, slightly rotund belly. The feel of her hot slippery flesh reassured me, in other words stirred me.

"Darling, she's not going to wake up."

"She won't?" I glanced over to her. Rachine was still staring upward, her hand rested on mine.

She made a little noise in her throat. "I should hardly think so. I've never seen anyone look so dead, who was supposed to be alive. It's only a matter of time....before she's dead I mean."

"But what if she doesn't die?" I persisted. This time the feel of her glorious warm belly was not enough to still my concerns. Every time I closed my eyes I had images of Karen's emaciated body rising up from her hospital bed in order pursue me. It was an image I took from a dream I had had recently. The doctors had pronounced Karen dead. Rachine was dancing with joy around her bed. I felt slightly embarrassed by this, but I could not help feel a huge sense of relief. Then Karen suddenly sat bolt up-right and pulled off all the wire's and tubes that were connected to her body. She opened her eyes, they were a brilliant green colour. She started toward me pointing and uttering a horrible groaning sound. It was all I could take! I woke at that point bathed in sweat.

"She's very tough you know," I continued, "she was attacked and stabbed in Syria. She should have died then, but she didn't. And then to have all those rocks land on her, break nearly every bone in her body...! Even the surgeon who operated on her said it was a miracle she was still alive."

"Oh - darling...."

"And I read an article in a magazine the other day about this woman who had been in a coma for five years, and then for no apparent reason suddenly came out of it."

This last bit of news somewhat stupefied Rachine. She took off her sunglasses and looked at me, blinking like an owl. "Did she?" said Rachine, leaning forward a little.

"I've still got the article if you want to read it."

"No - no need." Rachine put her sunglasses back on and rested her lovely form again, presenting it to our humble little star. After about ten minutes she spoke again - slowly, her words perfectly measured: "Well, we shall just have to make

sure she doesn't wake up - won't we!" She looked over at me, and smiled.
"Yes we shall," I said, suddenly excited, like a little child being told he doesn't have to go to school ever again. "When, when can we do it?"
"There's plenty of time. Just relax swee'dy. Just as soon as we get back to Paris."

Rachine stretched her long body. I looked at her. She was fantastic I thought. Suddenly I wanted her; she was the most erotic thing I had ever seen. Or was it what she said that made me feel that way? I never felt so desperate for a woman as I did for Rachine at that moment. It was my first real experience of the true extent of her power - in this world. There was nothing we could not do. Together we were invincible. I think she felt the same way. It was intoxicating. She pushed my hand beneath the tiny thing she had on. I sensed the wide curvature of her *Venus Mons*, that guarded the entrance to that other world. She moaned, luxuriating in my intimate touch. Absently she felt around for me. She found what she was looking for. "hmm," she moaned again, "so *big*, so *potent*...I think I need to be oiled again Julian." She handed me the bottle of red coloured oil, and I massaged it into her skin. Her lovely body yielded beneath my oiled hand. It felt good. It felt strong and powerful; every part of her body was the *loci* of pleasure, she was the loci of a gargantuan ego. I sighed heavily. I felt safe again, deep within her world, under the shelter of that enormous ego.

Sometime in the early hours of the following morning, just as Rachine and I were returning from a higher plane of existence: we had voyaged far that night, having visited the outer spiral arm of our galaxy, I heard in some small portion of my brain, the sound of a telephone ringing. It struck me as being incongruous at the time; so rather than the usual soft descent into ordinary life, I came back to Earth with a bit of a bump.

Rachine mumbled something incomprehensible and got out of bed. I heard her talking in the next room. "*Oui! Oh!..oh..ah ha..! ah - oui! Merci au revoir!*"

Rachine padded back into the bedroom. "Heh! - you awake?" said Rachine, shaking my arm.
"Sort of."
"Ah....well swee'dy, you know you were wondering what you might say to Karen

if she woke - well you'd better think of something soon, because she came out of her coma about an hour ago; Garcia just gave me the *good news!"*

I stared at Rachine dumbfounded. I thought for a second I was having one of my nightmares. 'Very vivid,' I thought, 'for a dream'. I rolled away from her dark eyes and puled the covers over my head, and hoped that I'd wake up soon. When Rachine prodded me in the back and started shaking me again, I knew it was no dream.

"Heh! - did you hear what I said? She's awake!"

Rachine got up and went into the bathroom. She came back with a barbiturate and a glass of water. "Here swee'dy, I think you might be needing one of these."

It had been three months ago that I celebrated my birthday. Three months of living in *Rachine-world.* Three months of escaping from reality, and now the news came that brought me permanently back down to Earth. And what a jolt it was! It sent shock waves reverberating through my world. It shattered my fragile grip on reality, such as it was. The result: I underwent some sort of breakdown. Rachine could do nothing with me. *Nothing* - her powers were useless. She tried everything, from sex to violence. When she hit me round the face I just laughed back in *her* face.

"Come on Julian, pull yourself together," said Rachine, as she shook me. I just blinked at her like a rabbit caught in a car's headlights. "Come out of it! - *Mon Dieu!" - Whack!* went her hand across my face, (yet again). I think she secretly enjoyed smashing me about the face!

"I damned! - we're damned," I said, in somnabulistic tones.

"Well, you'll have to see her eventually."

"Never! I'll never go back - *never*! I'll *never* see her, you can't make me. I *won't* do it. I won't! She can see everything. She's a witch. I've been cursed. I'm evil - we're evil, *evil don't you see!"*

Rachine's response? Yes you guessed it: *thwack!* went her hand on my face.

Rachine contacted Garcia to say that we were delayed because I was suffering from some kind of illness. About three days later, more news arrived from Paris. Karen was wide awake and quickly gaining strength. No longer solely dependent on dialysis to keep her alive. The only thing was, she hadn't got a clue who or where she was. According to Garcia she was suffering from complete amnesia. My presence was urgently required at her bedside, in the hope it may jolt her memory.

"Did you here what I said? She's lost her memory Julian."

When the news finally sunk in, it perked me up a bit. "You mean she doesn't remember *anything?"*

Rachine grinned. "Not a *darn thing* - as you would say. As far as I know she remembers the name 'Natasha'...That's all. I guess that bump on the head loosened a few screws."

I walked out onto the terrace that overlooked the lake. Rachine followed me, and touched my arm tentatively. "Julian - you've got to pull yourself together. Stop acting so guilty. She doesn't know who she is, let alone who we are, or what we are to one another."

"Doesn't she? That girl is not normal. She can see into your soul. She will know I am guilty. I'm a lousy rotter. I was even willing to see her die."

Rachine grabbed my arm. "You've got to go there. You can't hide away from her forever. When you see her, you'll see that she is just a girl. Have faith Julian."

I turned round to face Rachine. She took my hands in hers, I felt her power course through me again for the first time since - *the news.* "You can do this Julian!"

"Will you be with me?"

"Of course *mon petit chou,* every step of the way."

Don't imagine though for a second that I was over my breakdown. With Karen awake again, even minus her memory, her mere presence in the world meant that my orbit about Rachine was decaying. I was imploding like a fragment of a star into my own shell-like universe. Rachine could peep in now and then, and I would catch a glimmer of her light, but it was like looking down the wrong end of a telescope. I had become the reverse of what I had been when under the total sway of Rachine's power. Now I realised I was one of the little people all along. Not just a regular little person, but something even smaller. I felt myself to be a worthless piece of crap. A nothing! A spineless no body, afraid of my own shadow.

I was lost now, alone, as on a great landscape - that landscape was Rachine's outstretched palm, and I knew that she could squash me into oblivion anytime she chose, like the louse I was. I was naked and vulnerable before her presence. A squirming, distorted wretch. A snivelling coward - which is to say, I was typically human, and we all know how much Rachine detested the weakness of humankind.

I was well aware what my malady was. I was suffering from the *tropisms*. The light I grew under was cast by the dark star of Rachine. Now though, that other star, which I thought I would never see again, was moving towards a new ascendency. Now my world had two stars in its sky, when there could only be one. I realised that under Rachine's dark light, my growth had become accelerated. The result: I resembled one of the those hot house plants that grow tall at the expense of internal vigour. The slightest breeze and I would snap in two.

Apart from porn star, super-model and the notorious priestess of Tanit, Karen's further claim to fame was that of appearing in various medical journals around the world, documenting her miraculous road to recovery. It was a long and circuitous road that she would have to tread. Even after she had regained consciousness, after having spent nearly twenty eight weeks in a coma, there was still much healing and mending that had to be done; such as building up musculature, educating neural pathways, and almost having to learn to walk all over again - on legs that had been broken and hips that had been smashed and rebuilt! Therefore, most of Karen's time was spent on daily intensive physiotherapy. It came natural to her, to want to become fit and strong again: she didn't need encouragement, in fact the nursing staff were always advising her: 'not to over do things', but non of them fully appreciated just how robust her constitution, and powers of healing were.

There were neurologists, psychologists, pathologists, endocrinologists and even scientologists, that came to conduct their various tests and then leave to write up their respective theses; all of them wishing to further mankind's understanding of the miracle that is the human body, and its ability to heal itself. But even now, her body depended on medical technology to keep her alive. Although much of her liver function had returned to normal, there was still the matter of her damaged kidney which necessitated regular dialytic intervention. Also there were all manner of drugs that she had to take, the most important ones being those that compensated for the loss of her spleen. Other drugs were used to help stabilise her endocrine system, still others guarded against any further blood clots developing on the site of her gangial lesion. All this without taking into consideration the psychological trauma of waking up and not knowing who or where she was. Indeed her road to full recovery was beset with many obstacles still. It was up hill. It was winding, but Karen had proven time and again she was more than equal to the demands it placed on her body and soul. She was unafraid of following the road, no matter how tortuous it got, she would follow it to its end. Yes of course the popular view is to call the end 'death', but to those who understand the true nature of being, know that death is not the end of the journey. The road stretches on ahead. The body can only take us so far, then it must be cast off like an an old husk, to lay by the way side. The journey though, will go on, it is only the country through which we travel, and the mode of transport, which changes. The road we find, has no end. Some walk it alone, some run, some zoom along at the speed of light, while others hardly seem to move an inch in a million million years. For those that walk alone, that part of the journey that is called life, is the hardest part of all, but even they will meet other like souls along the way. And before long we find ourselves travelling through familiar countryside again. The important thing is to confront the obstacles that lay in ones path. There are those that choose not to do so. Some stray from the way and become lost in an eternal night. They take the left hand, into darkness. They straddle the path and even try to turn back: 'fools' - the traffic only goes one way! Karen had picked herself up from the road, and had taken the first faltering steps, once more, shunning the left hand side, staying on the light side. Coming back to the light.

The only name that meant anything to her, apart from her own, was 'Natasha'. Of people and places she had no recollection at all. The nearest thing to a memory of what happened, was in the form of a recurring dream where Karen felt she had to protect herself from something falling on her, and crushing her. At first, due to the nature of her injuries, she assumed she had been involved in a bad car accident, or perhaps had fallen from a tall building. Only gradually was Karen introduced to the reality of what had befallen her.

I eventually saw her on her fourth day of re-emergence into the world of light. She still looked very ill, there were big dark circles round her eyes and her skin was grizzled, but at least there was no longer the impression of being around a corpse. Her lovely eyes were open and alert, all be it, displaying a certain amount of fear and trepidation.

"Now are you sure you don't want me to go in with you?" said Rachine

"No, I'm sure. Now that I am here - faced with it, I feel I can do it," I replied.

Rachine kissed me on the cheek. "That is so brave of you swee'dy." Turning to a nurse who was waiting to go in: "Don't you think he's brave? Now you go in swee'dy, I'll be waiting *right* here for you - *oh!* - and give Karen my love."

When I entered the room she barely took any notice of me. I looked over to Antonio, who immediately got up, and grabbing my arm, took me to one side, while the nurse busied herself about her patient. He spoke in that hushed confidential voice that one assumes around the sick, and began by telling me, in a heart-felt way, how good it was that I could come, indicating that he had been aware of my own problems, (the true nature of which was kept vague) and that it must have been serious, to have kept me away from Karen's side for as long as it had. I felt the biggest heel in the world. He left with the usual display of one who was: 'handing over the reins to the owner of the horse' - including a lovely exhibition of magnanimity, with phrases like: 'you two have a lot of catching up to do.' I just stared after him, wondering how it was possible such selfless people could exist in a world populated by so many self-centred, self-aggrandising, self-conceited, self-important, self-righteous bastards! How it was they weren't eaten up by people like, for example, Rachine?

I stood over Karen as the nurse took her blood pressure. Karen looked at me without any sense of acknowledgement. I reached down to take her hand but she puled it away. She looked at the nurse.

"No - not more tests?" said Karen, rubbing her arm, where it had been bandaged. I noticed that her skin was mottled and bruised. "If you take any more blood out of this arm there'll be non left for me - you goddamn *vampire*."

The nurse smiled and explained in her best English that I was not a doctor. That I had only come to visit her. On hearing this Karen let her arm sink by her side. The nurse completed her task, and before leaving the room gave me the sweetest of smiles.

"I'm Julian," I said to Karen.

There was a sudden look of relief on her face. "Oh - *you're* Julian."

"Do you remember me?"

"No. I only know your name, because that's all I've heard people talk about. 'Julian will be here soon. Julian is coming to see you.' "

"Well here I am."

"Here you *are*."

"I'm sorry I wasn't here for when you....woke up."

"Doesn't matter," Karen replied, some what offhandedly, "since I don't have a clue who you are - or for that matter anybody else who comes here to see me. I know the Italian guy. He's here quite a bit. Seems quite nice, but he doesn't mean anything to me." Then, looking at me severely, "Neither do you."

That cut a bit. "You're my wife. We love each other."

"Oh...Hello."

"Hi" I replied, taking Karen's hand. "I've missed you."

Karen shuffled about the bed as if suddenly uncomfortable. "Help me up a bit."

When I put my arm about her it was like touching a fragile bird. She was just skin and bone. She moaned and put her hand to her side. I was about to call for a nurse when she grabbed hold of my hand. I was surprised by the power of her grip. "No! Don't do that. It's nothing, really nothing. Just get me some water will you!"

I did as she asked. Karen took the cup from me with both hands and drank greedily.

"Thank you - Julian," she said, handing me the empty cup.

"I've missed you so very much." I said, feeling out her bony hand.

"You said. Are we very much in love?"

I couldn't reply straight off. I looked into her eyes; they were dead still, like undisturbed pools that reflected the sky like a mirror. "The last thing we spoke of was having a child together," I said, at length.

"That's not what I asked."

There was another pause before I could answer. "Yes -.yes we are. I love you,

I love you Karen, more than anything in the world." Suddenly I broke down in floods of tears

"Please...please don't," said Karen. "Do you need a nurse?"

I looked up, feeling rather foolish. "No...I'm sorry Karen," I said, wiping my face.

Karen touched my head. "It's all right. You obviously feel something. Whether it's love I have no idea - since I feel nothing back. But you would have thought I would feel something? I mean isn't love supposed to mean everything?"

There was a short pause while Karen regarded me quizzically. "I suspect that our marriage, if that is what it was, was less than ideal. Would I be right?"

I looked at Karen's face, and her frank expression. I thought: 'she looks like Karen, but the person I used to know isn't there.'

I shook my head. "Nothing was straightforward with us," I replied.

"I'm sorry Julian if I am a dissapointment to you, I don't rember anything."

"Don't say that. If there is one thing, you never disappointed me. Not even now."

Karen smiled vaguely and looked at her arms. "Look at me. What the *hell* happened to me? At first I thought I must have been in a car wreck, or else fallen off a very high building.....They say I got into some kind of scrape with some Arab's. *Arabs of all people!* Must have been one hell of a fight, that's all I can say!"

"It was," I said, "but it's over now."

"They tell me you were with me. How come you are not badly hurt?"

I looked down, shame faced. "Because you saved me."

Karen stared at me unspeaking for several moments. Then she looked towards the window. She winced and held her side again.

"I think you'd better go now. I'm feeling tired."

"Of course," I replied. "Can I get you anything?"

Karen shook her head. There was a pained expression on her face, the lines running from the corners of her mouth to her nose were deeply etched into her skin. I thought to myself, 'you are looking haggard my girl. It must have really taken it out of you. Will you ever be the same again I wonder?'

There was a moment of confusion as I got up. I didn't know anymore if I should kiss her *even*. I lent forward anyway, Karen stiffly offered her cheek.

"I'll come again....soon." I said.

Karen sighed.

"Is there anything, anything at all I can do?"

"No - No thank you." She seemed to consider a moment. "Well," she began, "may be there is something - there were these people who came to see me, they kept asking me about someone - or something called *Tanit?*..Kept calling me priestess and acting weird. I hadn't a clue what they were talking about, and they frighten me: getting down on their knees - for goodness sakes!...They frighten me. I don't want to see them anymore."

"I'll make sure they don't come again," I said, happy that I might be able to do something for her.

"Thank you," replied Karen, with a faint smile.

"There is someone else you used to know outside."

"No, no one else. Another day. You can tell Antonio he can come back a bit later if he likes."

I resigned myself to the inevitable: 'those two were always destined to be together', I thought. But I wasn't going to give up. Karen was a real person again, even though she was not the girl I knew. I couldn't carry on the deception anymore. I caught up with Rachine in the foyer chatting to a good looking young doctor. On seeing me she dismissed him immediately.

"Well - how was it? Did she know you?"

"No," I replied. "It's like everyone says, she doesn't remember a thing."

Rachine seemed eager to see her. "Well, I'll just say hello," she said, starting up the corridor.

"She doesn't want to see anyone just now - except Antonio."

"I'm *sorry* swee'dy." Rachine tried to hug me, but I gently pushed her arms away.

"No - it's all right. Seeing her again....Well I have to try. You understand?"

Rachine looked puzzled. "What are you saying?"

"Seeing her there - awake, I love her still. Even if she doesn't know me, I have to try - I love her you see. I always will I guess."

Rachine's eyes flashed as her demon raged, but she retained her composure. "Of course! I should have realised." she made a strange noise in her throat, followed by a short sardonic laugh. She looked at me up and down with eyes

burning with scorn and revenge. "What exactly are you Julian? Not a man?
"I have to try. I love her - you understand?" I repeated, bracing myself for the onslaught of her wrath.
"No, I don't understand. What I do know is, that you are a *pathetic* excuse for a man. You're like all of them," she said, her dark eyes ranging about, as if she included the whole of mankind in the statement. "You'll suffer for your *cowardly* act."
"I already do."
"Not half as much as you are going to. You, and your precious Karen!" Then her demon pierced the surface, and her wrath rent open like a storm, her face turning as black as her obsidian eyes, the veins in her columnar neck stood up, the blood turning her eyes red, like a bull's. *"Je vous ferai subir encore vous le petit homme insidieu - et quant à elle je la détruirai!...You small man you nothing,"* She laughed with derision, focusing on that part of my body that her scorn was directed. *"Vous, vous n'êtes rien, un petit homme - petit homme!"*

She spun round fast on her heels almost creating a mini whirlwind; an inexplicable compunction forced me to reach out and take hold of her arm. I hadn't a clue what I wanted to say. For a second our eyes met. I'll never forget what I saw in them: rage, contempt, scorn - for all humanity: all of it, for a second, directed straight at me. So fierce was this bitter, seething hatred that it was almost too much, *even* for her. For a second I thought I saw tears in those obsidian eyes. If I had been sure of what I saw, if 'it' meant that much too her, I would have gone with her, there and then: prepared to do her biding. I would have murdered, stole. I would have done anything she asked. I would have followed her to the ends of the universe. But I think in the end, it was just an excess of bile that I saw. Tears of emotion, would have been a symptom of weakness, something which was very alien to Rachine.

Rachine dropped her gaze and looked down at my hand as if it were a disgusting creature. She opened her mouth as if to say something more, instead she turned abruptly away, leaving me standing alone. I walked away from the scene, when I looked back I saw her talking and laughing with the young doctor. I felt a tinge of jealousy mixed with relief. 'Could it be that easy?' I thought, 'Was my escape that easy?' In a way I felt lucky, after having witnessed so much bitter contempt, to still be standing in one piece. She was wrong about one thing though, I knew only to well what her response would be if I should ever renounce her: even if I hadn't understood all that was expostulated in French, apart from the expected ridicule of me, were threats of destruction levelled at Karen. It was to be expected given the depth of resentment and viscous enmity she held for weakness, (as she saw it). In truth it took courage to do what I had done. I loved Karen, that was all there was to it. I loved her even though she hadn't a clue who I was. I loved her even if she preferred Antonio. All it took to dispel the magic of Rachine was one look at Karen's lavender eyes. All it took for me to realise the wrong I had done, was to hear my name on her lips once more. For that, I would go on loving Karen, I would go on hoping that one day she would remember me - even if, by then, she loved another.

XXII

The people that Karen said had frightened her and acted weird, were of course members of the Tanit crew. I was able to catch up with Almoud and the old man Arkhmed and explain to them that Karen was really a very different person to the one they had know as the high priestess of Tanit. Once they saw that it was true what the doctors had been saying, that she had completely lost her memory, they and others like them, melted away to whence they had come, believing that the spirit of the goddess had left Karen's body for good. The Tanit cult though would go on, but with their high priestess *in absum.* Devotees still made the pilgrimage to places such as *Kerkouane* to pay homage at the site where the priestess's blood still stained the bronze seal of Tanit. It was considered to be the most holy and sacred of Tanit sites of worship, a place where miracles can happen; such is the power of martyrdom, and sacrifice: the stuff of legend and superstition.

Antonio made the single greatest sacrifice of us all, when he donated part of his living body to Karen. When the surgeons pointed out that Karen would never regain full strength unless she underwent a kidney transplant, everybody that was associated with her offered themselves as a donor; only Antonio was found to be compatible. Following this last operation it was not long before Karen returned to something approaching full strength, although she would probably have to take some form of medication for the rest of her life. Her recovery had taken almost the same length of time she had been unconscious. At the end of it all, all she knew of herself was what others such as myself or Garcia told her, or else what she gleaned from old newspaper cuttings and magazine articles. She also had a specially prepared dossier, that documented her entire life history and psychological profile. It was the product of months of in-depth psychological analyses. These findings confirmed what we all guessed from the start, that Karen was suffering from total amnesia. The prognosis being an eighty percent chance that her memory would eventually return. What the report did not venture to say was how long this process would take. It might be anything from six months, a year, six years - no one knew. The speed of her complete recovery largely depended on Karen herself, as well as the amount of love and support she received.

When Karen left the hospital she moved into the apartment that Antonio had first acquired for myself. Now that she was well enough to sign the checks again, she insisted that she would take care of the rent.

"That man is a saint. He has given me his kidney, the very least I can do is pay for my own rent. There is only so much goodwill one can receive without payment."

"But Antonio doesn't mind, he takes care of the rents."

"That is hardly the point Julian, it is a matter of principle."

I pointed out that she owned several properties herself in Tunisia as well as a seventy five foot ocean going yacht. It had been a long time since I had seen the *Idhra,* which languished in the port of Alexandria. It wouldn't have taken long to get her over to Marseille. We could sail through the Med or tackle the high seas, just as she had once dreamed of doing, but I felt it was too good to come true, that I may have to wait a very long time before I got my *salty sea-lass* back again. Karen made it clear she had little interest in going anywhere for the present.

The Tanit worship still went on in various location in North Africa and and other parts of the world, but it frightened her to think that she had been, and still could be, the focus of so much blind devotion, not to mention all the frantic media attention. I admitted to her, that I was relieved that she had no intention of picking up from where she had left off, with regard the Tanit show. In fact, the new Karen was very much an introspective and quiet girl. Not that one could blame her, after all she had been through! She was very tentative about meeting new people, or making any kind of assessment, or comment about anything. I think she found the whole of life strange, as if she had been reborn again, and was still in many respects only a child. And yet a child who appeared to be incredibly perceptive, even intuitive, at least, about some things. Apart from Antonio and myself there was only one other person Karen wanted around, and that was Rachine. At first I thought that the reason Rachine offered Karen so much support was because she felt guilty for having the affair with me, but that was only if you believed that Rachine was capable of basic human feelings, like guilt. Given Karen's fragile state, there was little I could do but accept the situation. Rachine was, after all, the only female friend Karen had of such long standing.

Although Karen and I lived in the apartment together, she showed no inclination to share my bed with me. It was such a large place, two people could quite easily lead independent lives from one another. I did not blame her for not wanting to become intimate with me straightaway, after all, I was to all intents and purposes, still very much a stranger to her, but I had hoped after a month or so she might begin to warm to me, instead she remained distinctly cool and aloof. It seemed, sometimes, that she didn't even want to be in my company. If I came into the large sitting room, she would stay a while, reading some magazine or other, but she would become fidgety after a few minutes and eventually get up and leave without a word.

It was a perfect spring afternoon: 'spring time in Paris', what could be more romantic, one might think? I took inspiration from this old adage and asked Karen if she would care to join me for a stroll along the Champs-Elysée or some such place. I had tried to woo her before with similar suggestions. When I did she became sullen, and would soon complain of: 'having one of her heads', but on this particular occasion, much to my surprise, Karen said that: "in fact, she was rather looking forward to going for a walk." I thought to myself, 'perhaps there is something about spring and Paris that can move even Karen's intransigence, and total lack of romantic sensibility!' And that is how we ended up at the Notre Dame Cathedral.

"Don't you think it's an incredible building Julian. I love to come here."

"You've been here before?"

"Yes - often, with Rachine."

"Oh - I see."

"There's no need to pull *that* face, Julian. She is a lovely person." Karen took hold of my arm. "Come on lets go inside."

We sat down on a pew towards the rear of the Cathedral. I could see Karen was transported to another level by the splendour of the building, but I thought how unlike Karen it was to even think of entering into such a place of worship. I couldn't help but express these feelings.

Karen smiled as one who is privy to the truth. "I'm different to the Karen you knew." She looked at the palms of her hands, and the scars on her wrist's. "I don't think I would want to be *that* Karen ever again, look what she did to herself."

I tried to take her hand. For a second she let me but then puled it away again. "No Julian." She looked away a moment as two choirboys moved down the aisle. "I think we need to talk Julian."

"Do we? About what?"

"I think you know. Look, we are not even married. Not properly. This place, this is where I would want to be married. In the sight of God. The one true god. Look around you Julian. Isn't it magnificent! How can you doubt the existence of God when you are in such a place as this? Such a wondrous creation as this. Here you feel close...oh so close, that you almost feel you could reach out and touch his face." Karen raised her hand into the air, looking with rapture at the great east window and the fantastic colours that were refracted there by the April sun.

"We *are* married." I took her reluctant hand and pointed out the small scar on her left wrist "Here, this is where Garcia cut open your vein, and here, is where he did the same to me. Our blood was mingled so that we might be as one."

Karen puled away and laughed. "Oh Julian - please what nonsense."

"You didn't used to think so! It will soon be our third anniversary, it was you who chose the day, sacred to Tanit - Beltane."

"Oh Julian!" Karen sighed heavily, showing frustration. "You don't expect me to hold to something I no longer believe in, do you? What do you expect me to do?"

"I don't know. You were the one who had the strongest...commitment," I replied, wearily.

"Yes I've read about my recent past - as a priestess." Karen shook her head, "How can I explain it anymore? I have no recollections of this time. More to the point, no inclination to want to know any better, or be in any way associated with these ideas, least of all, become again the person I was. All that is done, finished, in the past - *dead!* I guess, like you, I was misdirected, swept along by the words of some silly old fool who believed in superstitious nonsense. We were just caught up in the moment. All this business with Tanit and belief in dead gods! - Julian I believe in *The One Almighty God*, who sent his only son, *Jesus Christ our Lord*, in order that we may be saved. Such is the nature of true sacrifice. It is wickedness to worship false gods; those that do will be punished. Look what happened to me in Tunisia. That was my punishment. God in his grace has seen fit to give me a second chance. To resurrect me, as he did his only son. No, it's clear to me that god saved me from committing greater sins." Karen paused a moment and looked at me steadfastly. "He has a mission for me. He has great plans in store."

"Does he now! If only you could here yourself? You're not the Karen I used to know. To here you talk one might think you were Mary Magdalen herself."

Karen seemed to ignore me, her eyes were focused on the big gold cross over the pulpit. Still staring ahead, transfixed: "You really ought to forget *that* Karen. She is dead and gone. You know what my greatest fare is?"

"No."

"That *she* should come back. I've been learning a lot about her over this last month or so. She was a *terrible* person."

"She was not terrible at all. She was a very unique person. A wonderful person, honest and unafraid of expressing herself."

"Yes and *boy* did she express herself. I was quite shocked when I came across some pictures of me in one of those filthy men's magazines."

"Which Magazine?"

"Does it matter! Rachine showed me. I was curious as to what sort of modelling I did. I never imagined I did *that kind of thing.* Apparently I was quite famous."

"You are, es|ecially for your performance in certain porn movies."

Karen made a deep intake of breath. "Disgraceful!" she uttered. "You see! God has given me a second chance. A chance to live a again, a wholesome life. A good life."

"What was so wrong with what you did?

Karen laughed. "Well Julian if you don't know!" She looked at me askance. "I have my suspicions about you."

"Oh please Karen! There is nothing sinful about the human body. What you did

gave pleasure to millions of men - and women. You indulged their fantasies, their - desires. You used to be so proud of your body."
"From what I have seen of the world so far, there is far too much *indulging* going on. Anyway - *I am* proud of my body, but just because it is pleasurable to look at, does not mean I should parade around naked at every opportunity."
Karen put her hands together and muttered something. I felt like laughing.
"I know you think I'm silly."
She closed her eyes and seemed to pray for a couple of minutes. After she finished she looked at me, her lovely lavender eyes wide, searching my face.
"I know you like me because of my body. I have prayed for you Julian, that god may show you the true path to worshipping the spirit, other than the flesh."
"I love you for who you are. It was never your body...well not just that."
"I've seen the way you look at me - and other women, especially Rachine." Karen put her hand up to silence my protest. "It's no good denying it. You are in serious jeopardy of corrupting your mortal soul by wanton thoughts. I know I have a good body Julian, I've seen the pictures of me in calendars and in magazines - *before* my injuries, but you must keep a sense of proportion. Their is a time and a place for nudity."
I couldn't help my self I had a good old laugh. A couple of priests gave me a funny look, and Karen told me to shush. "I'm sorry Karen. If only you could hear yourself. I'd call you the biggest hypocrite, if it wasn't for the fact that you've lost you memory."
Karen looked away. To my absolute horror and disgust at my own words, I had hurt the thing I loved more than my own life. I had hurt Karen again. I felt like gouging out my eyes and screaming for forgiveness at the top of my voice.
"Please Karen," I said, trying to turn her gorgeous face towards me. "I'm so sorry. Look at me. Please, please forgive me!"
Karen put her hand to her nose and sniffed. I got down on my hands and knees and kissed her legs, her feet.
"Please Julian, don't! Get up."
I grabbed both her hands in mine. "Do you forgive me?"
"Of course silly. People are looking. Get up."
"I never want to hurt you. You know that. You've been hurt far too much."

"I'm all right...really!" she said, drying her tears and even putting on a smile to reassure me.

I sat close to her and took her hand for a few moments until she moved it. "I easily get upset Julian. I often cry when I'm on my own."

"You do?"

"Sometimes when I'm out with Rachine, for no apparent reason, I'll just start to cry buckets. She is such a comfort." Karen sighed, and looked up at the wonderful stained glass window. The April sun suddenly burst through afresh, sprinkling shots of red and gold over Karen's face, and on to the grey flagstone floor. She looked radiant, possessed of peace and tranquillity again. "I'm not the strong Karen you used to know. *I get very depressed,"* she concluded, in that childlike voice of hers, that I had not heard for so long.

"I know. I'm so thoughtless," I replied.

Karen touched my hand, and I felt her take my pain away. "Don't be hard on yourself Julian. In many respects what you say is true. I must sound hypocritical. That girl was all the things I described: licentious, wanton; she was....everything I am not."

I felt entranced by her beauty. As I looked at her I almost believed in the sanctity of *Jesus Christ our Lord*, myself. For a time I thought I saw god in her face. I had to look away.

"You're beautiful," I suddenly blurted out.

Karen looked at me pityingly.

"I only meant earlier, that you could still go back to being a model again. You don't have to take your clothes off."

"I understand what you mean Julian. I suppose modelling can be respectful," said Karen, cautiously. "But I don't think it would work, not with this," she said pointing to the scar on her face, "not to mention the other wounds on my body."

"They can airbrush them out."

"I think Julian they would run out of ink or something," said Karen, frivolously, before the grave countenance of the saint returned. She looked up at the high vaulted roof of the Note Dame Cathedral. "No - God has other plans for me, more serious plans. I was not resurrected in order to pursue the trivial life of a model, all over again. You have to face facts Julian. I'm just not that girl. In fact I

might choose a whole new name. What do you think of Verity?"
"It doesn't sound right for you. Why not Natasha?"
"Yes - well, I don't know. I do feel drawn to it somehow." Karen looked perplexed for a moment, and then went on: "which is strange really, why I should like *that* name, when it was Natasha who did all those dreadful things, by selling her body." Aside: "Rachine calls me Natasha."
"Natasha was who you were, in your previous life."
"Yes - well," said Karen, dubiously, "I don't know about that! May be I will make Natasha a name associated with goodness, with purity, than one of infamy. Yes that is what I shall do, I see it now!" said Karen, excitedly, her face becoming animated, "in choosing that name for myself god is asking me to blot out the evil association with Natasha. She shall be resurrected in god's pure clean light."

We walked around the cathedral, the sun continued to sparkle through the stained glass windows, shooting forth upon the cold stone, a kaleidoscope of colours: shots of red and blue, and gold enlivened all that they touched. Our feet clicked over the big flagstones, people's voices reverberated around the colossal marble structure, and then suddenly the organ of the Notre Dame burst forth as to announce the presence of God to all our senses. Karen continued to sing the praises of the majesty and beauty of the building, and the glory of the god to which it was dedicated. She spoke in a kind of rapture of the beauty of sacrifice. She spoke of the resurrection, and of the Holy Trinity, of the lives of the saints, pointing out the different chapels set aside for their individual worship. Before leaving Karen knelt down before an effigy of The Mary Magdalen, and anointed her feet with her tears. When we came outside, a light rain had begun to fall. It was wonderful to feel Karen's body close to mine, as we sheltered under the one umbrella. We walked together - me, in a kind of trance, as I listened to Karen continue to expound on the wonders of the Christian faith. She gave gave me the whole unexpurgated version, the whole 'shooting match', from Genesis and the 'root of all evil', to Leviticus and the story of Aaron and the importance of atonement for sins committed against the Lord. She spoke of Isiah, Jeremiah and his lamentations, of Daniel and the Lions den. She spoke of the Gospels, of Matthew Mark, Luke, and John. My god! - it sounded like she had read the whole darn book, every bit of it from cover to cover a real feat of endurance, if ever there was one - as well as a sublime test of faith in its own right. By the time she had finished speaking of Jude and the dangers of false teaching and lascivious conduct, which I felt she put special emphasis on, for my own sake, and was about to start on 'Revelations', we had reached the artist's quarter of Montmartre.

It had stopped raining and the sun had come out so we decided to stop at a café. Karen paused a moment before launching into her exposition of what was probably the most enigmatic and mystical, of all of the stories of the bible. Her 'voice' was a pleasant sound, a beautiful familiar sound. It was good to hear it again, to feel a part of her again. I could have listened to her forever, as she droned on about the seven spirits, and the seven seals, and the seven stars, and the seven trumpets, and the seven last plagues, and seven vials full of the wrath of god (very nice), and some poor lamb that had been sacrificed and risen. I thought to myself, 'those old Messianic types, were sure into their numerology and necromancy: always trying to divine the end of the world, *cheerful buggers*'.

"And then the Lord god took John the Divine and showed him a woman, now you should pay special attention to this Julian, because it concerns you, she took John..."

"The Divine," I interjected.

"The Divine! - and presented him with an image of a woman dressed in scarlet and purple robes, bedecked in precious stones and she carried a poison chalice of gold. That chalice was symbolic of her *filthy dirty mind*, full of her *abominations* and *fornications*. And do you know what she had written on her forehead?"

"No - What?" I said, leaning forward, all ears.

" 'Behold Babylon! The Great Mother of Harlots and Abominations of the Earth.' You should think about that Julian! when you go lusting after women."

"I will," I said. " 'The whore of Babylon!' She sounds like hot stuff?"

"You wouldn't say that if you saw her."

"Why not?"

"She had seven heads and ten horns."

"Wow! These Semites sure know how to conjure up an image." I replied.

At that moment an artist came up to our table. He was dressed in the manner of the *undiscovered* type, which is to say: in clothes that were in a state of ill-repair. He had a dark brown head with the remains of some grey hair at the sides. His face was pockmarked and heavily lined from years of self-abuse. One might easily mistake him for a vagabond, a piece of worthless human flotsam; if it were not for the tools of his trade, which he carried with him under his arm. More than this, what marked him out as different, was his countenance. The whole essence of his being came together and was distilled in the two limpid blue pools of his eyes. They seemed to suggest that they had seen all manner of things in their long life, such that nothing could shock them any more. They had a cold disinterested aspect, the cold recording capability of that rare species nowadays: that of the artist who sees too much.

"Americans yes? I have spent many years in your country travelling."

Karen regarded the old artist cooly.

"May I?..." he said, setting up his easel. "Such beauty! - perfect, perfect beauty! Those eyes! Such eyes! Never have I beheld such beauty." he said. He studied Karen's face for a few moments, before making swift darting movements of his hand over the blank page.

Karen glared at the old artist. "There are more important things in life than mere physical beauty Monsieur! Come I want to go. I don't like it here," she said, moving to get up.

"No - let's stay. At least let him finish your portrait," I said, putting my hand on Karen's arm.

"Yes - please Mademoiselle, I beg you." He raised a gnarled shaking hand. "It will not take long and it is for free. My gift. It is my privilege to draw you. It is not often one comes across such a face. The face of innocence....and yet"

"Are you blind Monsieur," said Karen, pointing at the deep furrow on her left cheek.

"No Mademoiselle I assure you I am not. Your beauty lies much deeper than the flesh, it is in your eyes, your eyes..."

"What else is there you see?" I interjected.

Suddenly the artist seemed to become shy. He did not reply, looking to his work for refuge. Karen too, sat in silence the whole time. It was as if they both shared the same secret, the disclosure of which, was not meant for mortal ears.

When he finished drawing he showed her the results of his work. I could tell in her eyes she was secretly pleased, although Karen gave the impression of being disinterested. "Bon, ce bon," she said.

"You are very talented Monsieur," I said.

The old artist bowed, and was already looking about for his next subject, but before he could get off I thrust some cash in his hand. He looked at the amount and tried to give it back.

"No - no, no, Monsieur, you keep it," I insisted.

The old artist's keen blue eyes darted from Karen and then to me. He smiled, nodded, gave another brief bow before turning towards the throng of humanity that moved up and down Montmartre, like a never ending tide.

"Why give him so much? It must have been the equivalent of over a hundred dollars?"

"It's a good likeness," I replied.

Karen glanced at it. "Well - I suppose he was honest enough not to just show me from my good side.

"That old man has captured something of you that is unchanging. There is something about your eyes - something only an artist can see."

"Well - I don't want it."

"Then I'll have it. I'll treasure it forever."

Karen remained silent, looking on with a board expression on her face.

"He is right," I went on, "you are the most beautiful girl in the world."

I tried to take her hand again, but this time she drew it away.

"It's no good Julian. I'm sorry. I've tried, but I don't feel anything for you. I know you love me, but I'm sorry - I just don't feel anything back."

"Is it Antonio? You love him? That's it!"

Karen looked at me, slightly annoyed. "No Julian, I don't love him. I don't love anyone. I'm only just coming to terms with who I am. I'm not interested in getting involved in a relationship with anyone. Not you, not Antonio. I just want to be myself - to love god!" Karen looked at me beseechingly. She sighed, shaking her head. "How I feel now, in myself, I don't know how I could have ever done all those things - before all the bad stuff happened! But I can't really say it was bad, since I think I am better person *now,* than I ever was. I have to go on growing into this new person. I only know I have no interest in being the person I was - *ever again!"* she concluded, shaking her head vigorously.

"And yet you are friends with Rachine?"

"Why do you hate her so much?" said Karen, playing with her empty coffee cup.

"If only you knew what she is really like," I replied.

Karen gazed blankly at the table. "Yes, that's right," she laughed sardonically.

"I'm sorry Karen..."

"It's all right. I like her a lot. I admire her. She has turned her life around, through share will power. She was into Glamour too, but she never did the kind of things I did; Rachine resisted temptation, and *she* never had the opportunity of a fresh start as I did."

I shook my head in dismay as Karen praised Rachine's virtues. Did she have no inkling then, that she was nursing a viper to her bosom?

"She can't be trusted," I said.

Karen's demure behaviour pushed my indignation over the edge. "It's her isn't it?" I blurted," she's been poisoning your mind against me? She hates me! God knows what she has been saying about me?"

"Don't be silly Julian. Rachine is a good person."

"Tell me what she has been saying?..."

Karen gave me a coy little glance. "Oh Julian!"

"Please tell me."

"Look Julian - well you know anyway..." Karen became increasingly bashful tracing the pattern of the table cloth with her finger. She looked up, her eyes challenging, startlingly honest. "Things were never that good were they - I mean between us."

"Weren't they?"

"You know, in the bedroom..." Karen to my amazement blushed.

"Oh my god!" I ejaculated. "What did she say - exactly?"

"Nothing horrible. I guessed anyway. I asked her if we were - you know, close like that and she said - well that we, had out problems."

"Problems! That bitch!"

"Don't blame her. I asked Rachine and she told me. I knew anyway - a girl can sense a thing like that. Apparently I was most depraved - well as you know from my pervious career, and you, unsurprisingly found me a bit - a bit of a handful...It's not your fault, it was me. I can imagine I would have been too much for most men."

We both sat in a stunned silence for a few minutes.

"I suppose she told you as well, that we had an affair."

"She didn't have to. I know you have a thing for her."

"I do not."

Karen laughed. "It's all right, I wasn't looking particularly at my best at the time. Don't feel bad about it. I can understand. I was hardly full of the joys of spring now was I? lying there unconscious. I understand Julian, she is a very attractive girl, far better looking than me - even in my better days."

"Is that why you don't want to be with me?"

"You think that I care about a little thing like that? That sort of thing doesn't interest me I told you." Karen paused a moment, her marvellous lavender eyes swung in their orbits. "You need not feel bad. I can understand Julian, really I can. Rachine is very beautiful, very desirable."

"Will you stop saying that. You are far more beautiful."

"Oh Julian look," she said pointing to her scared face again, and then moving her hand down her front. "Do you want to see the rest of my body Julian, see what they did?.." half lifting her blouse. She looked at me askance and lowered it. "No...you'd like that wouldn't you Julian. Get a look at my body. You think far too much about that sort of thing."

"Rachine means nothing to me, she never did. I don't know - I just got caught up by her, she seduced me."

"Yes I'm sure she did. You are easily seducible. But don't feel bad about it; doesn't it just go to show how things were between us? It couldn't have been that good between us now could it?"

"It was once..." I faulted, about to speak of our time with the *Idhra* when we sailed the Aegean and she had been my salty sea-lass. But it was too painful to even think about those times, the futility of trying to convey how happy we had been - all I could tell her was how much I loved her still.

"Julian! - how can you say that? You are in love with the idea of love, that is all. I don't think you can really love me - how can you?"

"But I do," I persisted.
"Julian, it doesn't matter - not to me. Do you think I care, after all that has happened - that I care about a silly infatuation? That is all it is. I know I have a certain look, that despite how messed up I am, still attracts men. I think it's sick personally, some men are really..." she glared at a young man sitting at a café across the road from us who was obviously taken by her. Men stared at her all the time, you got use to it, and the old Karen thrived on it. "Well it's all they think about, it's disgraceful! what chance did poor Karen have in a world that exploits young good-looking girls in order to satisfy men's carnal lusts, it's disgusting."
Despite how depressed I felt I could not help laugh out loud at Karen's Victorian outburst.
"You may think it's funny but I do not!"
Her serious countenance made me laugh even more. "I'm sorry Karen," I said, not knowing if I was laughing now, or crying. "I don't find it funny, I think it's sad."
"Sad! Why?"
I made a grab for her hand, it was like holding down some cold frightened creature.
"To reject it all! All I know is how I feel right now, and it seems that without you there's no future."
"I'm sorry Julian you feel like that. What can I do, I told you! I don't feel anything; if I was going to, don't you think I would by now? I think you are a lovely person. You are warm and kind. May be you are a bit weak willed - but as a person, as a friend you are great. But no!" said Karen, shaking her head, and then resting it on one side, so that her strong neck muscles were clearly defined.
'What a perfect physical creature you are,' I thought, and a mad impulse ran through me, to lay my lips upon that perfect neck. As if reading my mind she straightened herself, looking at me square-on: "No Julian, I don't think I could ever be attracted to you - *that way*. Even if I felt inclined to start up a relationship I'm sorry Julian, I know you like me, but it would never work. Not in a physical sense at least."
I suddenly felt an overwhelming desire to join with the murky waters of the Seine, and float out of life for good.
"It's nothing personal," said Karen, touching my arm tentatively, afraid that she

might unintentionally stir-up some unwanted desire in me. "You are just - not my type I guess," she concluded, with a shrug.

"Is Antonio your type?" I said, peevishly.

"For heaven sakes Julian!" Karen shook her head, and looked away.

"Look at me Karen. Just tell me the truth," I entreated.

To my dismay Karen blushed. She became distracted and mussed with her hair. Sighing: "Yes - yes if you must know, I suppose *he is.* But I told you, I'm not interested in having a relationship with anybody right now. Now please Julian I don't want to hear any more about it."

I couldn't bring myself to look at Karen's gorgeous face. I felt close to tears.

"I'll never give up hope. You know that. Not ever. You loved me once. You can love me again."

Karen bowed her head and reached across the table for my hand. "Please Julian - don't."

I held on to it tightly. The tears started to come. I pressed her hand against my face.

"Please Julian. Don't." she repeated.

"But I love you. I was stupid. Rachine....I mean, she is nothing to me."

"Julian it has nothing to do with her. Weren't you listening?"

"Why can't you love me?"

Karen laughed, and then so did I, as I realised the stupidity of my question. "You know what I mean. What's wrong with me?"

"There's nothing wrong with you. Look Julian, I have been through a hell of a lot. It's a miracle, as every one keeps telling me, that I am alive at all. And the more I learn about what happened to me the more I understand - come to understand it, the more I think they are right. It was a miracle. But don't you see, I need time? Time to work out who I am. What god wants of me.....And I know you don't *believe,* the way I do, but it's true! God has a plan for all of us." Karen paused a moment, "You know who suffered more than anyone through all of this?"

I shook my head.

"*You...*"

I began to laugh and cry at the same time. "Me!"

"Yes you. You're suffering now. My suffering is largely over, and I don't mean the physical distress, my suffering was my life before I slept. But you! - you still suffer because you are in love with an idea. An idea of a person who, even when you knew them, was not really real. And now you go on suffering by hoping that this person will come back to you one day and love you all over again; then you think you will be happy for the rest of your days."

"Yes that's it." I replied, like the eager child.

"Well life is not a fairy tale Julian. Life is not like that." Karen leant forward across the table and took my hands in hers.

"It would be wonderful if it were that easy my darling, but it's not. Please for my sake let go of the memory. Most importantly, let go of the hope."

A fresh rush of emotion prevented me from replying straight off. Karen lent back in order to let me gain some semblance of composure.

"But...but I love you," I persisted. "You're my soul mate."

Karen lent forward and buried her face in her hands, and then looked up at the sky and put her hands together. " *'Dear god help me get through to this person. Help him to understand - dear Lord!'* "

She collapsed her arms across the table. "Julian, Julian,..What bit have you not understood? You are talking in terms of fairy tales again....Look! - I don't know if you are my *soul mate*, or if Antonio is - perhaps that old man who did my picture was, or that lady across the road? I don't know anything about *soul mates*, or if there are such things.....but let's assume for your sake that there are, I would imagine such people would have some sort of *special* connection...."

"*But we did!*" I yelled.

"*But I don't remember it,*" screamed Karen. "Don't you get it. For - *goodness sakes!*"

There was an awkward silence. Karen sighed heavily. "Look Julian..." she began, trying to control her temper. Karen looked around, distracted. "look," she began again, "*Even...even if my memory came back tomorrow*....Do you think I would still be the same person before what happened? Do you think I could ever be that person again? Do you?

"I don't know," I replied.

Think about it! After all I've been through, you really think I could just pick-up where I left off? I have a whole new set of feelings. A new way of seeing the world. Don't you think that might change things? just a little?"

"I guess so."

"You guess so?" Karen shrugged. "Well I guess that's something." She paused; she suddenly looked very tired. Running her fingers through her long golden hair: "You know you are always in my prays. Don't ever think I would forget you, or disown you. I don't want to give you false hope. I suppose somewhere deep down I do love you, but it's not how you want me to love you. That I cannot do. Not for you - not for anyone. You understand me?"

"Yes," I replied, more because I was concerned for her.

"Now I want to go back. I think I have one of my headaches coming."

Karen stood up, and then had to sit down again. I rushed to her side, she held up her hand. "I'm all right. I just feel a bit dizzy. Just give me a second."

Her features appeared draw there was almost a haggard look to her face. I got the waiter to bring a glass of water for her, while we waited for the cab to arrive.

We didn't speak anymore, at least nothing of import. We both dwelt in our own worlds. Looking at her I realised just how great a blow she had been dealt. She really was a much more fragile creature than the Karen I had known. I saw too how selfish I must appear in her eyes. She was right, life was not a fairy tale, no matter how hard I may wish: it was pointless, the Karen I knew had gone, she had died in Tunisia, giving her life for my own.

Mersell's return from Algeria was a most fortuitous event, in more than one respect. Not only did I consider him my closest friend now, but he also acted as a kind of personal physician to Karen, who, after our visit to the Notre-Dame and Montmartre, began to suffer from more frequent and intense bouts of headache - even blackouts. The severity of these seizures was such that they would confine her to bed for several days, and when she came to, what memory she did have of her 'new life' was often scrambled and confused for several days after.

Mersell became a vital pivot to our quartet. Not only was he important to Karen but when she was having one of her 'heads', without Mersell to keep me grounded, I would have allowed my own guilt and anguish to devour me, to the extent that I think I would have sort out some quiet river bank and thrown myself on the mercy of the Seine.

And what is more, Mersell had to keep a watchful eye on Antonio. Now that Karen seemed to be going through some sort of minor relapse, he spent far more time in Paris. He seemed to take her worsening condition very badly. Unfortunately his life style did not engender itself to a man with one kidney, and the response to Karen's worsening condition was for him to find solace at the end of several bottles of Chablis. I too of course sort this remedy, but I had not sacrificed one of the most important organs of the alcoholic.

Although Mersell's presence was greatly missed at his clinic in Algeria, his loyalty to his friends outweighed all other demands. He could see that the three of us were falling apart in our own different ways. He was an extremely gifted physician and councillor. As soon as Karen began to have blackouts he arranged for her to have a full set of tests. The results that the neurologists and the endocrinologists, and radiologist's all came up with were inconclusive: it was possible she was suffering from microscopic lesions in her temporal cerebral cortex - then again she may not. Mersell's prescription was for quiet and plenty of rest. Rachine of course was over joyed at having her role reinforced as confidante and now nurse, to the ailing Karen. Poor Mersell! - the burden he had to bare: not only did he look after the three of us, but he also had to deal with Rachine's lascivious nature, which she began to blatantly hurl in his direction. Being human, meant he too had his limitations; he could not watch over all of us, all of the time. Of course, by far his most important patient was Karen - somehow we *all* failed to notice the gradual deterioration of Antonio's health.

Unbeknown to us, even Mersell had no inkling, Antonio had become a day patient on a renal ward, where he received regular dialytic treatment. His condition though worsened, not helped by his refusal to quit drinking, and it wasn't long before he was admitted on a permanent basis. When I saw him, it was obvious to me that he was dying. We kept the news from Karen as long as we could, but in the final few days we felt she had a right to know. His last few hours on Earth were spent with the ones he loved most: Karen and his family.

We were all waiting in the corridor of the hospital. In the early hours Karen came out of the room where Antonio lay dead.

"Well its over," said Karen.

Rachine helped her to a seat. Mersell and I sat either side. "Poor swee'dy," said Rachine, smoothing Karen's hair, as if she were a cat. "You look tired, my honey child."

Karen smiled forlornly, "I am."

We were all expecting her to breakdown or collapse or something. Mersell looked worried, and was all set to take her pulse. "We need to get you home. You need rest," he said, with an anxious look on his face.

I looked at him and thought, 'if any one needs rest it's you old man.' I went over and got Karen a glass of water. She looked at me sweetly and smiled.

"Poor Julian," she said, come sit with me. "All of you, don't worry. I'm all right. You see in a way I still have part of him with me." She lifted her blouse and showed us the scar left from the transplant. Rubbing it: "He's here, a part of him still lives while I live. He gave his life for me. And I understand the true nature of sacrifice. It is something to be joyful over, not sad."

"Yes you're right. Of course you're right," piped up Rachine. "If anyone knows the true nature of sacrifice it is you."

Rachine put her hand on Karen's and lifted it from her side, and put it to her lips, as though she were touching the flesh of a living saint.

Karen smiled at her and touched her head. "come," she said. (She might have said, 'come my children'), let us not be sad. His soul has found its release, and still part of his body lives on inside of me," she said, putting her hand over the sight of the operation again. Rachine lifted Karen's blouse and touched it too, as though it were a sacrement.

"He would want us to enjoy life," said Rachine, as she gazed at Karen's face with what might be described as, a look of rapture.

"He certainly knew how to do that," I said.

Karen touched my face, and it really was like being touched by a saint. She lifted my heart, she lifted all our hearts. She enabled us to go forth - *unchained.*

Antonio was laid to rest in the family vault, at Lugano. Dignitaries, heads of state, famous faces from show biz, as well as the three of us, attend the service. We were concerned that Karen may find the whole occasion too much for her but she seemed to draw strength from her 'new' god, at least enough to see it through to the end, but it had clearly taken much out of her. We only just got her back to the apartment we were renting for the occasion, when she completely crumpled between Mersell and I. We all thought, I am sure, as we looked at her laid out on the bed like a corpse laying in state, that soon we would be attending another funeral service. We even thought we should stay in Switzerland - until the end, thinking it would be fitting to bury her close to Antonio, if not in the actual family vault. Her pulse remained 'fluttery' for several days as she lingered in a semiconscious state. Thinking that her time was close I sent word to Garcia. As it was our fears were unfounded, after a couple of days Karen came back to us. I prayed day and night that if she came round she would come back, her memory restored, but if anything she was more vague and spiritual-like, than ever before.

At first she seemed to possess a renewed vigour, the kind that comes from the fire and brimstone, born again variety: she felt certain god had, as she termed it, 'resurrected' her (again) for a purpose, other than saving her from a life of sin, which applied to her first resurrection. After Antonio's death, she seemed to have more certainty and confidence about her. It was as if his death finally gave some sort of shape to Karen's mission in life. It was hard to know exactly what this purpose was, I don't think even Karen knew for sure, but it definitely had something to do with sacrifice.

Garcia promised to be at Karen's side, believing her end was nigh. I sent another telegram, when it seemed certain Karen was making good recovery, but by the time word reached his island empire he was already on his way to Italy. In anticipation of his imminent arrival in that country of mountain peaks and deep sapphire lakes, Rachine indulged her hatred of the man in a way I had never witnessed before.

By now Rachine had her hooks firmly and deeply buried in Karen, and set about poisoning her mind with regard to the great man. She held nothing back. She indulged her vivid imagination, when it came to matters of a licentious nature, embellishing the facts with lurid details of drunken orgies that took place at his Tuscany villa, showing her the nudes he had done there, of Karen and Rachine. She painted a picture of a mad man, a sadist, drunk on sex and power reminding Karen of the plight of poor Bethany, who had been beaten, almost to the point of death, for daring to resist him. All the time referring to him as: 'that evil old warlock,' 'dirty old man' and 'stupid old fool.' By the time Rachine had finished, Karen's mind was quite made up about Garcia, she even had me convinced for a while.

"Why don't you tell that evil old man that we don't want his kind here. He is a pagan, a warlock. He'll put a spell on you my girl, if you are not careful. He will entice you back to his villa and perform monstrous acts of depravity and bestiality upon your body," said Rachine, getting rather a little bit too excited.

Karen just laughed in her face, to this last bit. "If he is coming to see me it is because he is concerned for me - we at least should here his side of things. I owe him that much at least - apparently we were close at one time."

"Yes you were my girl. He only seduced you - disgusting, a man of his age! I tell you, there is nothing he would not do to have his evil way with you again."

"Well, that was then, don't worry Rachine, he won't get his way with me this time."

"I hope not," I interceded.

Karen eyed me suspiciously. "That disgusting girl Karen is dead. No man will get the better of me again. Natasha is quite a different venture altogether."

To this response I just sighed and went back to my half empty bottle of Riesling.

"Well I worry about you," put in Rachine, pretending to be close to tears.

Karen went over to her and cradled her head in her arms, Rachine resting her head on her bosom. "My poor sweet Rachine. I think you are afraid of him? Afraid he might over power you?"

Rachine looked up into the light of the angels face, her big black obsidian eyes wide and expectant, glistening even, with tears. Christ knows how she did it?

Mimicking Karen's pathetic childlike voice, "*I must confess I am. I'm not as strong as you. I'm afraid he will corrupt my soul again...'*

"Hah!...Ha!..Ahhhh!"

Both Karen and Rachine looked over at me. Rachine's eyes narrowed, and for a second I saw the ~~blood course at the back of her eyes. Her~~ demon was there!

"Don't be so insensitive Julian! Poor Rachine has had to endure that old man's advances. She couldn't help it." Turning her attention back to her charge, and caressing her face, "Don't you worry my sweet love, I won't let that nasty old man get anywhere near you." Running her fingers through Rachine's thick chestnut locks: "I won't let him take advantage of you again."

Rachine looked up at *Saint Natasha* with love and all the vulnerability of the once corrupted.

"*I'll feel safe so long as you're with me.....*" Rachine glared back at me, as if daring me to say another thing. I knew my place. I remained silent.

Almost as soon as Garcia arrived his intuition told him it was a lost cause. He had no great speech to give. If he had one prepared he could see the futility in using it.

He moved about the place in his white robe, looking like a man who belonged in another time. Only on his island did his get-up look right. The vigour and health that seemed to exude from him when I knew him on Sapphos seemed to visibly bleed out of him, as he breathed in the atmosphere of enmity that was emitted by both Karen and Rachine.

For my part I was largely indifferent to him. I no longer knew what to think about anything. He looked very sad I thought. Like a man who had run out of ideas. A man who had lost all hope. But he was a clever old bird. *He knew*, it was pointless trying to get through to Karen, especially with Rachine acting as sentry. I think he also understood the predicament that I was in, and that his time and his words would be wasted in trying to rally me to his side. Rachine had done a good job on me too. He knew I was lost: Lost to him, to Karen, to myself. I didn't know who to trust anymore, least of all my own senses. But that man - he could see so much, so much more than all of us.

The only one out of the three of us he spoke at any length with, was Mersell. They seemed to have some kind of unspoken thing going on between them. It's easy to suppose that he brought Mersell into his confidence, and was depending on him to keep *me* at least, from carry through the prevalent course of action that I entertained, which was to throw myself into one of those deep icy sapphire lakes.

Garcia left after three days with the intention of returning south to his villa in Tuscany. After expressing his profound happiness at the return of Karen's health, he invited us all to go back with him, but I I think he only did this out of courtesy, he knew well enough that his goose was cooked - that if he had stayed any longer he would have succumbed to the waves of hatred and vitriol that exuded out of Rachine, and threatened to exhaust his very life force, his *:elan vital.*

I was personally glad when he went. I know the girls were, but my reasons were different. The old buzzard pricked my conscience. He reminded me of what a pathetic creature I had become. I felt weak in his presence. I couldn't stand him looking at me. Perhaps he left out of a favour to me. All I knew was, nothing had seemingly changed from his visit. All I could do was carry on with what I had always done, which was to wait - wait, wait for Karen's memory to return, wait to become a person again in her eyes, not the stupid alcoholic fool that presented itself to the present Karen, or Natasha, as she called herself now. What was becoming increasingly apparent was the hold Rachine had over her, my own role and that of Mersell, was becoming increasingly insignificant. She would take her off to the mountains for days at a time where she rented a cabin at a place not far from St Moritz. This was really Rachine's heartland, where she felt most powerful: among the cold glaciers and the hot blooded Aryans. Mersell was concerned that it would tax Karen's strength. Rachine though was adamant to point out the benefits of the pure clean Alpine air, declaring: "It is the very thing she needs." The invitation was never extended to Mersell and I, to stay at the 'Eagle's Lair' and strangely we never enquired in that direction. When Rachine said she was going to move into the cabin on a permanent basis both Mersell and I were secretly overjoyed, although we both had concerns over her intention of taking Karen with her for an extended stay. There was nothing we could do about it, and fearing that any protestation would only serve to push Karen further into Rachine's camp, all we could do was watch her pack her ski boots one morning, as she prepared to set off with Rachine bound for the *Retiche!*

God alone knows what Rachine did to her - up there, but about three weeks later she came back with a Karen whose whole demeanour had changed. She was a timid creature compared to the one that had left. Her grim determination set towards some austere righteous destination, had completely disappeared. On the day she came back she just sat in the corner mumping to herself, hugging her body, rocking backwards and forwards, her knees knocking. The only thing she expressed, through pale, almost colourless lips, was a belief in an omnipotent deity, and the desire to - 'go home'.

'Home,' both Mersell and I assumed, meant the Paris apartment.'

"Nonsense," said Rachine, she means she wants to return to the mountains."

"It doesn't look like that to me," said Mersell.

"No," I joined, "I think she wants to go home to Paris." Sitting down next to her, Karen clutched herself tightly, her body vibrating with tiny convulsions: "Is that it? You want to go to Paris? Remember Montmartre and the Notre Dame? You like the Notre Dame."

Karen nodded vigorously. "Notre Dame," she murmured, nearly smilling.

"There! - you see she wants to go back to Paris. She loves it there."

Mersell sat down next to her and felt her wrist. "Her pulse is shallow," he said. He felt the rest of her arms, "In god's name what did you do to her? She's skin and bone."

Rachine lit a cigarette. "Nothing, she wouldn't eat. She had one of her turns, so I thought it best to bring her back down the mountain.

"Mountain! In gods name, she shouldn't be up mountains - she's sick. Seriously ill."

Rachine flicked some ash nonchalantly. "Ah! - Monsieur Mersell you worry, she'll be all right - she is tough that one."

Mersell rolled back Karen's blouse and inspected her arms. "How did she get all these bruises?"

Rachine shrugged. "I d'know..."

Mersell pulled Karen's sleeve further back. The bruising extended all the way to her upper arms and shoulders. Despite her ills Karen still had a well defined set of muscles I noticed.

"I'll take her to bed when you've stopped pulling her around. She gets tired easily and starts up her wailing," said Rachine.

"No, I'll take her to bed," I said

"You want to fuck her now she's vulnerable. You disgust me Julian."
"Trust you to think like that Rachine! Your mind is a sewer. You're pathetic. I'm not letting you anywhere near her."
"Oh yeah little man! What are you going to do?" said Rachine, raising her long body into the air and coming forward.

It was the first time I really came close to hitting a woman, and it was only the desire for Karen not to witness such a thing that prevented me.

"Stop it both of you," put in Mersell. "I think Julian should take her to bed and then I will come in and do a thorough examination."

Rachine poured herself a glass of schnapps, knocked it back like one who is use to hard liquor, and sat as if waiting judgement.

I took Karen's hand, and like a somnambulist she followed me into her bedroom. She sat down on the edge of the bed, her hands clasped together as if she were doing some hard praying, but her eyes remained open. There were dark circles around them and her cheeks were hollow - her gaunt appearance made the big scar on the side of her face look *fierce!*

"Do you need any help getting undressed?" I said, feeling somewhat awkward. When there was no response I began to undo the top button on her blouse. She raised her head and looked at me with eyes that loomed like saucers in her thin face. Her look made me feel self-conscious. Despite her condition a wave of desire ran through me as I undid the top button on her blouse. She just stared at me as I undid the rest. My hands were shaking and my mouth was dry. There was something about her passivity that made me want to indulge my desire. Was that what she wanted? I took off her blouse. Underneath she was naked apart from her bra. It was the first time I had seen her body in over a year since that time in the desert. What I saw removed any thought of exploiting her vulnerability. I swallowed hard again, and undid the bra, eager to dispose of their heavy burden, immediately the catch was freed, her breasts slumped forward and down, almost to her belly. They were an awful sight, worse, if I remember rightly, than Pandora's, and her words came back to me: 'One day she will look ugly, like a monster - a *teratos!*' The curse of Pandora had come true, Karen's body was messed up good! Breasts, that were once so resilient and gravity-defying sagged flaccid like an old crone's, as I said, worse now than

Pandora's had been, criss-crossed by streaky white scar tissue, and not just her breasts - her body was covered in old wounds, her once perfect golden skin now looked grizzled and spent. The sight of so many lesions, and ugly blue contusions forced me to stand back. Karen just sat and looked at me. My only desire now was to cover her body, to hide the sight of it.

I quickly grabbed her night-dress and put it on over her head, and puled back the covers on the bed. She just sat there staring into space.

"Get into bed Karen."

"My body is a sacrifice," she said.

I put my hand on her shoulder and sensed the form of her muscle beneath the light satin material of her night-dress, and a fresh wave of desire went through me again. I wanted to crush her body against me, but the knowledge of how ravaged it was prevented me. Slowly she followed my urging, and got into bed. I rushed out to get Mersell.

I guess I must have looked pretty shook-up, because he asked me what was wrong. I told him to get in there and look for himself.

I glanced over at Rachine before joining him. Taking the cigarette out of her mouth she smirked. She knew all right, what I had seen, she had seen it herself, she would not have turned away from it out of decency, she would have indulged herself, used it, allowing her morbid curiosity to take over, she would have exploited Karen's vulnerability, perhaps she even helped to create it?

"I'm just going to take a quick look at you Karen," said Mersell, peering over her inert form.

She made no response when he asked her if there was any pain? did it hurt here or here? did she have any recollection of what had happened? She only muttered more stuff about sacrifice, of giving of herself her body as a living sacrament, or some such nonsense. I sat with my head in my hands. I heard him pull back the covers and I heard him sigh once more.

"Thank you Karen," he said, when he was done. He turned to me, putting his stethoscope away, I knew he was as shocked as me, by what he had seen. I followed him to his room, which was just down the hall from Karen's.

"Well?"

He shook his head. "Id say she was suffering from some kind of trauma. She's in shock."

"But her body! - did you see the bruises? - all over her!"
"Yes, some of the discoloration of the skin you saw is due to old trauma, which sadly may never clear up, but there are other fresh contusions on different parts of her body, her ribs her legs - all over in fact."
"That bitch," I said, eager to have it out with Rachine. "What did she do to her?"
"Not so hasty! They are consistent - at least some of them, with a fall. I listened to her heart, she's sound enough, she just needs rest and a few good meals inside her! I would have done a more *extensive* examination you understand..."
"Yes,"
"But not while she's like this..."
"No, of course."
"Well...there are what look to be bite marks on her neck, her breats," he gave me a searching look - "Other places too."
"You mean!....That bitch! She must have messed with her, taken advantage of her...God!"
"Look, I'm going to give Karen a sedative, just don't loose your temper Julian."
When I went back Rachine was making good still with the schnapps.
"Well did you enjoy yourselves in there?" said Rachine, gloating.
"What did you do to her Rachine?"
"Do to her! - perhaps it is I who should ask that of you?"
"The bruises? - all over her body!"
"She fell."
"Where? down a mountain?"
"She bruises easily. She falls a lot,"
Mersell came out of Karen's room. "I've given her a sedative she should sleep now. What happened Rachine?"
She looked a little perturbed. She knocked back her schnapps and poured another. Looking from me to Mersell.
"Is this an inquisition?"
"I would like to know how she came to get so weak and where did the bruising come from?"
"As I told Julian, she falls a lot, she doesn't balance well on ice?"
"What about the bite marks?" I enquired.

Rachine threw her head back exposing her wide throat and laughed a deep throated laugh. I watched it working up and down, I wanted to punch it in, to wrap my hands around it and squeeze.
"I don't know what you mean!"
"There are what look like bites on her breasts her neck - her thighs!"
Rachine turned her head to one side. She looked back grinning. "look at you, both of you, you are hypocrites. We all know what she is really like. We've all had her. Don't pretend you haven't Mersell. You've done stuff that could get you kicked out of medical profession - don't deny it!"
There followed a heavy silence. I got myself a drink, and wondered how she knew, or was she just guessing? She knew Karen well enough, better than anyone perhaps.
"And you Julian, don't pretend you didn't enjoy undressing her. I know you, I know how your mind works." She stared at me where I felt vulnerable. "I know all your sick little fantasies, how you love it when a woman, a strong woman like me or Karen dominates you - and I know you feel inferior sexually to other men - and not, I may add without a certain amount of good reason, I've seen you, all of you."
"That's enough," I said, moving towards her aggressively, but without any intention. Mersell put his hand on my arm.
Rachine never afraid of a fight stood up. Her eyes seemed to bulge - bull black, bull red, as the blood pounded through her choroid.
"Look at you, how touching, yes Julian - Mersell, I know what you two *boys* get up to."
I laughed in her face. "You're pathetic Rachine. Just stay away from Karen, I don't want you to mess with her again."
"It's not up to you. Karen had one of her turns that's all. She is a bit out of it at the moment, but I think when she comes round you will soon see who it is she wants to be with. Through me she found a new kind of love, a new way of worshipping god. She is too good for ordinary men - ordinary mortals. Her body! - did you see her wounds? yes of course you did, her tortured body, yet how strong it is, how *duro*, how *solide*, how *forte - puissant! intrépide! My gard* she shakes me cold, that girl! - her body is living testament to god, it is itself, a

sacrament, meant only for those that understand the true nature of sacrifice - something ordinary people such as you can never understand."
"All your fancy talk about sacrifice just hides the fact you corrupted her. You exploited her vulnerability. You are evil! - You are a monster!"

Rachine somehow put on an enigmatic look. "Through suffering there is love, though pain there is god - there is beauty in pain; Karen is beautiful because of her pain, her body is magnificent through its suffering. Her body is a sacrament, it...it is - sacred, because of it's suffering. Through it, lies the path to god's *true love!"* Astonishingly, tears were rolling freely down her face while her eyes, like a bull's, burned red, full of passion, full of defiance - hatred for all that was ordinary.

Her words, her conviction perhaps, more than just her words, disturbed me. I had never heard such things, never heard anyone talk in such a way, not even Karen, at her most Tanit zealous, came out with such convoluted logic as this.

My conclusion came, well, my response anyhow: "You're mad! - You're stark raving mad! You've been filling her head with this - this *gibberish* about suffering! She used to have such a good mind, a sharp mind, she would never have believed in crap about sacrifice, least ways not how you see it."

Rachine's face remained wet with her tears: she made no attempt to dry it, although the tears now had stopped. Her face was full of the disdain for humanity that I knew she was capable of.

"Is she really that different Julian? Think about it - she was on a path of self-destruction all along, except now she has found the true path to god, the one true god. Her suffering is all the more poignant for having trod the wrong path, but now her suffering has an even grater meaning. She is born to suffer just as the good lord was crucified by ordinary people, rather than set a criminal free. The pain she bears is all our pain - they did not listen then, when they crucified *him,* they will not listen now through her suffering. You are not worthy of her, non of you are." By the time she finished her tears had started up again.

She picked up the bottle of Schnapps and headed to her room. She was, of course the kind of person who could drink massive quantities of alcohol without it rendering her incapable.

"You think you know me," I said ranging round on her, "Well, I know you! I know how really sick and perverted you are. Your tears don't fool me - you, you can't *fool me!* I remember what you said at the hospital, how you would destroy her, well I'm not going to give you that chance."

She laughed: "Hah! - destroy her! I don't have to."

Karen again amazed us by her powers of recovery, a few days of rest and plenty of hot soup and square meals, and Karen, at least in body, seemed to recover sufficiently to make the return journey to Paris. Rachine was right about one thing though, Karen clung to her side as though she were her shadow. She was sullen towards Mersell and I, and only spoke in whispers to Rachine, in our presence. Sometimes she would glare at me, with icy silver eyes. I would plead with her: "Why do you look at me so, with such hatred? I've done nothing to you."

She would continue to stare at me. I don't know what it was I saw in her face, whether it was disdain or pity? After a few seconds she would look away. "I don't hate you," was all she would say. For the most part, this new Karen, born in the Alps and nursed by Rachine's cold hard Aryan will, was broody and as pale as a ghost. Her third resurrection, if one can call it that, and you are keeping count, was a persona, as removed from the common herd of humanity as it is possible to be without being dead: it wasn't like she was ethereal either, although I think she had begun to believe she was some sort of saint in the making. I guess she was just remote: truncated from the flow of life, she lived and yet seemed not to have any of the spontaneity of life. She was like a vessel, a pale coloured vase, into which Rachine poured her sanctimonious gurgling: tip the vase, and out spurted the same distilled, decanted twaddle: *god love - true love, beauty in pain, suffering and sacrifice.* I tell you, it was bitter tasting, foul smelling stuff.

Although Karen appeared to be Rachine's mentor, the truth was Karen was helpless without Rachine's presence. She was integral to her idea of herself, by validating her role as saint, and saviour to the corrupted, and nobody could play the part of a wanton and corrupted soul better than Rachine.

I had virtually given up all hope of winning Karen's love. It was torture for me to have her in my presence for any length of time. The girl I loved more than life itself could only look at me pityingly. No doubt Rachine was gradually poisoning her mind against me also. Judging by the way Rachine's mind worked, it is not difficult to conclude what she made of the close friendship I shared with Mersell. Not that I cared what she thought, it was what she said to Karen which worried me. Mersell was not fooled by her either, like Garcia and myself, he knew her for what she was. The friendship we shared perplexed her, she had to believe it was something more: it intrigued her, it excited her even, it frustrated her too, for there is strength in unity. Her nature required submission, and submission for Rachine meant enslavement to her sexual power, worship of her gargantuan ego; to this end she used all her seductive powers to drive a wedge between Mersell and I. He was the only one left out of the three of us left, who had yet not fallen under her power. If she could have him, then she would be able to dominate all three of us. It would have been such a victory that it must have put her into paroxysms at night just thinking about it. The climate between the sheets must have been torrid, the vapours she gave off, as dense as the Amazon, as she contemplated Mersell's priapic form, entering her tropical paradise. She knew enough from her audacious reconnaissance missions, to know that her victory would not simply be a symbolic affair. She would enjoy him physically, and then like a gigantic Praying Mantis, devour him whole. Yes, it must have been something like that, for she was normally quite cool and confident in her seductive techniques, but around Mersell she became agitated, always mussing with her hair, chewing her fingers, biting her lower lip, crossing and uncrossing her legs, sighing, scratching like a bitch on heat. This over eagerness for the dog, her impatience, betrayed just how great a prize Mersell was to her.

Of course Karen remained the focal point of her attentions, the campaign to win over Mersell to her affections was conducted in more subtle ways. Essentially she put up a barrage of the senses: a certain amount of subtle tactile contact was employed: a hand, the brush of a thigh. Then there was the look she gave with eyes that devoured. Then there was the visual aspect, the revealing of her flesh: the top of a broad thigh, and the red thong she had on, as her sarong, 'accidently', slipped open. Her round bosom, forced into a low-cut, tight fitting bodice; and then there was her voice, that she could make husky or deep, she would have made a great ventriloquist. Add to this, the content of her word spoken: how is long limbs, his long hands revealed so much more about 'the man'. How she was convinced he would make a wonderful lover. How he had all the signs of an alpha male, a superior creature like herself. How by comparison, other men, particularly myself, were weak and submissive. How it was that she could understand Julian being attracted to such a man - such a: '*Homme extraordinaire*'. Of course, I only caught part of her words spoken, as it was nearly always conducted in French. In this way it was more personal to Mersell, and it would not offend Karen, while at the same time it had the effect of alienating me. I had heard it all before. This half of the campaign she conducted continuously throughout the day, it went on, as I say, subtly - she saved the more direct approach until evening when Karen had gone to bed. She usually retired early, she still suffered from her 'heads'. A few glasses of wine, together with her pills, ensured she was gone to the world for several hours until morning. It was at night, after we had all had a few glasses of Chablis or some expensive champagne, that Rachine became more direct. He allowed her to take his hand and guide it to her bosom, or her thigh, or some other place. He allowed her to kiss him, to feel his crotch. At first his response to these advances was appropriate to their verve and audaciousness, perhaps he was even a little taken by her - one certainly could not blame him, she palpably oozed sex, not from just the obvious places, her whole body was suffused with sex, it came off of her as an effluvium. Gradually she became cognisant of the fact that he had not moved one iota towards falling under her power. The more she gave the less she got back from him; soon she realised it was *she* who had been taken-in. That the harder she threw herself at him, like the wanton whore that she was, the more the, *gentleman,* Mersell became. It turned into an humiliating defeat for her - and as we know, defeat was something unacceptable to a super-being of Rachine's calibre. Nothing vexed her more than his continued rebuttal of her dissolute advances. Nothing enraged her demon like rejection. On seeing him, it squealed and writhed inside her, flinging its wanton fury at the windowpanes of her mind. Then the dark centre of Rachine's eye would expand like that of a cat, that was about to pounce on a mouse, and the white that surrounded those two large fulminating black discs, became gorged with blood, giving the impression that they were about to explode. The temptation, if one was a mouse, was to run and hide from her obsidian gaze, but Mersell was no mouse. He would stay put, and smile at her, and act ever the the gentleman, which is not to say, given the right time and place, it would have prevented him from slitting her lovely throat. What horrors Rachine harboured for him is impossible to imagine. In the end she could hardly bare to be in the same room as him. Gradually the four of us became more and more polarised, Rachine and Karen living in one half of the apartment, Mersell and I living in the other.

As Karen faded out of my life Mersell became ever more important. I *owed* him my life. He became responsible for me. If it were not for him I would have gone over the edge - I'm sure I would, such were the depths of my despair.

In many respects it was *Kerkouane* all over again. I would sit with him getting pissed (this time on the finest French wines), reminiscing over the Karen I had loved and lost. I don't know how he did it - night after night? I'm must have bored him senseless. When I no longer made any sense, he would have to guide me to my bed, where for a time my torture would end. He filled the vacuum of the night. He was a man of great compassion, who gave freely of himself, without any expectations. He too understood the true nature of sacrifice.

As truly the '*Homme extraordinaire*' Mersell was, there was nothing he could do to take my mind off Karen for very long. He knew I was deeply unsettled, deeply unhappy.

"Why don't you get away from here? Leave her!" he suggested, one evening.

My reaction was one of frustrated anger: "No! - never! I'll never leave her."

"But you are so unhappy. I hate to see you like this."

"I have to stay. One day her memory will come back, and when it does I have to be here."

"You must consider Julian, the possibility that it may never return."

"Don't say that," I yelled, getting out of my seat. My glass went over.

He was so understanding. He just nodded and gently sat me down, and poured me a fresh glass of wine.

"Of course it will - one day!" he reassured me.
"She's got to come back," I said, sobbing. I felt his hand on my shoulder.

As it happened, it was Karen who left me. One morning, about a month after our return to Paris, Karen informed me that she was going away with Rachine. She said that Paris didn't seem the same anymore without Antonio. She explained that I could stay or go, it was up to me. Her words reflected her sentiment. If I liked, I could visit with Mersell, either way the apartment would be mine as long as I wanted it.
"But why Scotland of all places?" I said.
"She has friends there. I don't want to go into it Julian. Rachine thinks the fresh air and the change of place would be beneficial for me."
I no longer had any influence over her, I resigned myself to the fact that she was going, and that was all there was to it. But it didn't prevent me from tackling Rachine on the issue the first chance I got.
She gave me one of her bloodiest stares. "There are people there - good people, people who can give her what she needs most. They can offer her true love and support, " said Rachine,
Karen smiled. "Yes true love."
Rachine looked over to her. "That's right my sweetness. They will *love you.* You will find - *true love.*"
"True love." Karen smiled.
"*True love?*" I exclaimed.
"True love," said Rachine. She looked at me askance: "But I can't expect you to understand," she sneered.
She came up to me close, and stood in front of me leaning her body forward her hands on her hips. Looking at her like this I was reminded of just how formidable her body was, and how much she stunk of perfume.
"Stay out of this Julian, or I'll crush you," she hissed.
There was no doubting her ability to carry through her threat, and judging by her wide shoulders and big frame it did not have to be confined to the psychological. I looked into her jet eyes, I could see the blood rushing up to them truning them bloody-black. I shuddered inwardly.

She over estimated me, this intimidating show of her strength was no longer necessary. I knew I couldn't stop her. I was totally demoralised, any argument I had left was a futile gesture, a saving face, nothing more.
"You want Karen to make a full recovery don't you? It's for her own good."
I looked at Karen who seemed happy to be talked about in the third person. She smiled vacantly.
"As long as she will be well looked after."
"*Looked after!* They'll *luuuv her.*" Rachine marched over to Karen and put her arms about her and kissed her passionately on the lips. Karen carried on smiling vacantly, she looked up to Rachine, her face a little flushed. She took her hand and held it tight, and brought it up to her lips and kissed it.
"Rachine will protect me. Rachine knows the meaning of true love, she knows the true nature of sacrifice. Don't look so sad Julian," looking to rachine: "May be Julian needs to find true love?"
"No, I think it would be lost on him," replied Rachine. "He's not ready for it. He doesn't understand about sacrifice the way we do."
"Sacrifice be damned," I said, "You're taking the only thing I love away from me."
Karen suddenly looked sulky, and buried her head in Rachine's bosom. Her long bony hands ran through Karen's long golden locks. "It's all right my pretty one, "she said. Glaring at me:
"I told you Julian, *don't get in my way."* she said, through clenched teeth. "You're upsetting Natasha."
"Yes, you're upsetting Natasha," said Karen / Natasha - (whoever she was?)

Anyhow, it was done. Within three days Karen had packed her things and gone. All I found one morning were a few words written on a notepad in her erratic scrawl: The address of some farm in Scotland, and a few words to the wise. 'Try not to be sad. Best of all try and forget me. My prays are eternally with you. God's love Natasha.' Since I was far from wise, such advice was wasted on me. She knew me well enough to leave without waking me. That night, as she usually did, Karen just presented her cheek for me to kiss goodnight, being careful as always, not to get her body too close to me. Of course I knew it was possibly the last I would see of her, and of course I wanted to smother her with kisses, and crush her close to me and to plead with her to never leave me. But of course I did non of these things. Rachine had won. I was destroyed. I will spare you the details of the effect her going had on me. Eventually by around evening I started to come to terms with the reality of her going. On the second day I felt glad she had gone, on the third I felt terrible again, and so it went on, with my emotions vacillating between extremes. Without Mersell I doubt I would have been able to come through it.

"Why don't you just go after her?" he suggested.

"What's the point? She doesn't want me. Rachine has got her claws in to her good and deep by now."

"At least do something. You can't go on drinking yourself into an early grave the way Antonio did." He gave me a furtive look. "You know your blood pressure is up again."

"I don't care. What does it matter if I die!" Mersell tried to hide the hurt look in his eyes. "I'm sorry Mersell - it's how I feel."

"You need something to take your mind off her." He sighed, and looked at me helplessly. "I wish I could...."

"I know, but it wouldn't work now. There's nothing you can do. Nothing anybody can do."

Mersell looked grave. "You know I can't stay here forever," he said.

I looked at him startled. "What do you mean?"

"I mean, I shall have to go back to Algeria at some point. Probably very soon."

Suddenly I was gripped by panic. "But why?"

"I have a practice to get on with. A life to lead. I can't stay here forever, living off yours and Karen's charity.

I suddenly realised how selfish I was being. "I understand," I replied. I wanted to say more, but it would have been unfair to tell him that I was afraid to be left alone. I saw myself one night alone, confronted with that stark choice. A gun and me alone.

"Why don't you do the same?"

"The same?" I said, leaning forward.

"Leave here. Get a job some place."

"All I know is writing, I don't speak French."

"Then go to London. That way you will at least be close to her."

Almost immediately I saw hope, and within a week of Mersell's suggestion I was on the boat-train bound for Dieppe.

XXIII

I kept the apartment on in Paris as Karen suggested, it was a convenient bolt-hole if things did not go according to plan in London, but I knew as I bordered the ferry on that cold grey afternoon, that I could no more turn back towards the light, than change who I was. Ships and planes no longer existed for me. I moved as on tracks. I felt compelled towards some terrible destiny. I felt as though every movement, every gesture was preordained, and I often got that spooky feeling that one associates with déjà vu. Setting foot on that land to the north, marked the end of my life dominated by hope. This was a grey land - a land of monotones. A place where people had been ground down by circumstance. A place where doors were firmly closed in ones face. This was a place for me. A place beyond hope. This was a place where people buried themselves alive in their homes, others stiffened themselves against the climate, buried in a thick overcoat, their hands plunged into their pockets, their eyes cast down towards the grey pavement. Inside was the shell of the man: the body, twisted and bent, the character as brittle as bone. If you knocked it hard enough it would shatter into a thousand pieces. This was a bitter land. A mean land. Impoverished of spirit. It seemed as if people held on to what they had, with little to give. Even words, those feeble expressions of feeling, were given grudgingly: words of love, words of remorse, words of hate even, were in short supply. This was a land of impoverished hearts. There were no big hearts here. No great gestures made here. No unnecessary displays of emotion: 'no thank you we're British'! No sharing of ones feelings here. No sharing ones hopes or fears. No sharing! This was not Garcia's free and easy Greece, or Karen's beautiful and glorious Tunisia, there were no big hearts here. It seemed that, to even love would be impossible here. This was a place devoid of all hope, which is to say, it suited me well.

Landing on the shores of that fortress island could not have heralded a greater change in my life style, but there were some things that I was determined not to compromise on, and finding a good place to live was my first priority. I found an apartment in a part of London called *Hampstead*, it was an area that gave one the feeling of not living in the big city at all. I remembered what Garcia had said about certain parts of London where one could despair. Places with strange evil sounding names such as: Peckham, Walthamstow, Morden, Blackheath, names that made you shudder inwardly. I purposefully went well out of my way to find the most agreeable atmosphere and sounding name as possible. Hampstead sounded and was, kind of cosy. I learnt that the great psychologist Sigmund Freud had had a house there, so I guess I was on the right track.

Everything comes at a cost, and keeping an expensive property put a huge financial burden on me, which was something else I was not use to. Luckily I had kept up my contacts in the journalistic world, and a friend in New York was able to find me a place on an American based 'life style', magazine.

Every morning I would cram myself on the subway train, or 'tube' as the locals fittingly called them, along with thousands of other Londoners, as they headed to their boring mundane jobs, not that my own job was any less boring at times, you understand, and I would think to myself, 'you poor bastards, is this all you know of life? Are you honestly content with this - this way of being?' The truth was it wasn't even a life. It was an existence, a mad animal scramble for survival. I had become one of those strange creatures who lived in a kind of self-imposed exile. The faint ray of light was that I was not a native of this land, I could get on a plane at any time and go back to sunny crazy California, and never have to set foot on one of those terrible overcrowded little trains again, or have to look at those blank grey expressions on the faces of the people who squeezed into them every day. And then the glimmer of hope, if that is what it was, would fade away as quickly as it came, when I remembered why I was here. I had no choice in the matter. I was less free in fact, than those poor bastards I saw every day on the train. I was a mannequin, not a free thinking man. I moved as in a somnambulistic state. I moved. I ate. I laughed. I cried, seemingly without any volition. I was a being without reason or design, I just *was*. Intuitively I felt that this too was how Karen must feel. She was not connected with who she really was. She was just a blank slate for people to write on. Rachine was writing on that slate. God was writing on that slate. Christ knows who ever else was writing on it? The only thing I knew was she didn't want my name written there. Although this depressed me, and although I felt trapped at times, I derived solace that Karen and I were at least connected by the same piece of terra-firma, even though it was a long way from where I was.

How dare Rachine suggest that I did not understand the true nature of sacrifice! What was my life here if not a sacrifice? A person such as myself, who was a lover of the sun, someone who appreciated the importance of being able to express freedom of spirit; a person use to the *dulce vita*: to have given up all of this, in order to be connected, even in a remote way, to the one person they loved, more than their own life? Where had all those happy smiley faces gone? Karen still smiled in my heart, despite my surroundings.

Never had I confronted such a forlorn and worn out nation, that had become a slave to process. I thought my home town Los Angeles was full pretensions, but at least it had colour, at least it had panache. Here, it was as if people were afraid to live. They say the English are reserved, I'm sure Sigmund Freud would have agreed with my assessment, that they are not reserved, they are psychologically repressed. After about a month of having to quite literally rub shoulders with these people, I started to become like them. I began to grow into and away, not outward and towards my fellow man. I buried my head down in my thick coat and cast my eyes to the blank grey street, if only to avoid the inimical glare of the *passer by*. I became a passer by. You didn't stop and chat; you didn't linger here. To survive in this land, to survive in the *monotones*, it had to be this way. One had no choice in the matter. I could feel daily my heart muscles growing tighter, holding everything *tight* - tight to ones chest, until the heart itself became like theirs, hard, shrivelled and cold.

Not long after arriving in London, when I came face to face with the nation, I noticed that the people stared at me a lot. After a while I realised that they were looking at me because they noticed something different about me. I still radiated from my soul some of the purity of light, and vigour that one can only get from living in the south. But it was an aura that soon faded. Gradually my healthy inner glow became dulled down - my suntan lasted somewhat longer.

Perhaps my boss thought I could do with a break, whatever the reason, he came to my desk one morning with a brief on a story he wanted me to follow up on. It concerned a religious sect who lived on a remote farm in the North West

Highland's of Scotland. It was run by a crazy old priest who went by the name of *Saul,* who claimed he had died and been resurrected. As if this wasn't strange enough, he also claimed he could heal through the power of love. Well nothing wrong with that, except that it was only ever young attractive girls who were involved in these miracle cures, which lead one to believe that the kind of love this priest practised was not the same as that advocated by your everyday vicar; the whistle finally being blown on him by one of his own initiates, who didn't like the way, girls as young as fourteen were being lured on to the farm and ending up with more than just, 'hands on', experience of animal husbandry.

The fine web-like intricacies of destiny will never cease to amaze me, or at least they shouldn't, but when I discovered that the address of the community was exactly the same to which Karen had gone with Rachine, I was not as shocked or blown away as one might imagine. When one feels as though one is an actor on a stage, and that all the words one ever uttered in life, were just so many well rehearsed lines, then I guess one becomes blasé about yet another strange quirk of fate. In tones of one who had completely resigned oneself to one's fate, which is to say, 'unenthusiastically,' I told my editor that it was: 'just the kind of assignment I had been waiting for.'

I guess my first impressions of this land had been tainted by only ever having seen one tiny grimy part of it. On discovering the Highlands of Scotland, it completely reversed my impressions. To think that such grand scenery as this could exist in such a tiny little nation? OK so they weren't mountains of the scale of the Rockys say, more like foothills, but they were better than nothing in a landscape that was hitherto unremarkable.

Set on the shores of Loch Linnhe the *religious community* was idealy located on the fertile strip between the coast and the Morven hills; where all manner of crops that one would not usually associate with such high latitudes, was able to be grown, due in large part, to the warm currents of the gulf-stream. The community boasted a self-sufficient life style, that was completely benign to nature. I must admit, it reminded me a lot of Garcia's, island pagan community, except this was supposed to be a Christian outfit.

At its centre was a church and a large mansion, which in other times had belonged to the *Laird,* the English equivalent of 'Lord of the Manor' but was now termed: *The Vicarage.* The whole area of land run by the community covered several hundred hectares and took almost two hours of driving along narrow twisting roads, before arriving at the Vicarage. On my way I passed numerous small stone constructed dwellings, scattered throughout the hills and valleys, or *glens*, should I say, many of which looked to be derelict. I learnt later that due to something called the *Jacobite rebellion*, which had occurred several hundred years earlier, the Highland communities were completely decimated by the advancing *red coats*. The only buildings to remain totally unscathed was the Great Hall, and the church, although part of this had fallen into disrepair. Along the way I saw several fields given over to sheep farming and although I kept an eye out, there was no sign of either shepherd or shepherdess tending their flocks.

The vicarage was set among several outbuildings and a large paddock where there were horses and goats. An attractive stocky built girl, wearing jodhpurs and riding boots, strode over to me as I was getting out of my car. I told her I had come to do a story on the the community, and that I wanted to speak to the 'priest'. She smiled and seemed very friendly. I followed her into the imposing building, where she invited me to wait in the parlour: a large high ceilinged room full of antique furniture. She informed me, in a cute English accent, that the priest would be along shortly. She lingered a moment by the door and smiled again.

"I'm sorry for staring," I said, "but you seem strangely familiar. Have we met before?"

"I don't think so," she replied. She looked at me now, slightly suspiciously, "You're American aren't you?"

When I answered in the affirmative she smiled again. "I thought so," she said, as if this explained everything. She nodded towards a large ornate drinks cabinet opposite, "make yourself something to drink if you like."

"Thanks. Will you join me?"

The pretty girl smiled at me flirtatiously. "I would, but I have things to attend to. He shouldn't be long. I'll leave you to your drink."

I couldn't help but stare after her as she went away, waggling her cute bottom, and I got the feeling she was hoping I was doing just that. There was something about her that perplexed me. Again I had the fleeting sense of déjà vu when I reflected on the fact that she walked with a slight limp. Then it struck me: 'Bethany'! The statue on Garcia's island! - the beating she received! She had Christian beliefs and was friendly with Rachine. It had to be the same girl! I could see why Garcia was fascinated by her, it wasn't just that she was very attractive, her green eyes seemed to look out onto infinity: they had a dreamy quality. Those green eyes were the source of her beauty, and they could drive a man mad trying to get to the bottom of their mystery. 'A mystery, thankfully, that was not my concern.' I told myself. I had always wondered how I would feel if I ever met her. So much had been said about her. How courageous she was, the only girl ever to spurn Garcia, and for that she nearly paid with her life. Then of course there was the statue of her. I thought it magnificent, but it was obvious that the artist, whoever they were, had embellished her figure. Seeing her now, 'in the flesh', there wasn't that much to her. She was in fact a lot shorter than I imagined: a stocky five foot nothing. Then of course, the statue stood several feet higher, placed as it was on a plinth. I guess it must have been the lighting and aura created by the temple: the sense of mystery, as she stood out of reach in her golden cage. I might have wondered if it were the same girl at all but for her face. The artist didn't need to embellish that, he had captured her air of mystery perfectly - that same mystery that I saw in her eyes a few moments ago. I guess like most things in life that are given a big build up, they often disappoint. I was glad in a way that the spell her statue cast over me, (and, allegedly, over anybody else who saw her) was not further enhanced by her corporeal flesh and blood. Yes, her eyes were alluring, and she was the possessor of genuine beauty, and yes she had a cute ass, and she probably had a good body, strong thighs from all those outdoor activities: horse riding and hiking...But wait! - what am I I saying? I guess I'm only mortal after all? I had to admit Bethany was the first girl in more than a year to spark my interest in the the opposite sex. After loosing Karen I thought I would never be interested in another girl 'like that!' Now, to have these feelings! - it was discombobulating that's for sure! Perhaps the sculpture's seductive curves had not been an embellishment of an artist indulging his imagination, eager to please his patron. It was possible, that the kicking she received had knocked something out of her.

After all, hadn't Bethany too ended up by being put in a coma? And hadn't Karen's once splendid body also been unable to resist the ravages of violent attack and self abuse? "Karen!" I spoke her name out loud. 'Bethany was not my concern,' I told myself again. There was too much else to consider other than Bethany! As I sat with my Scotch, I contemplated what Karen might be doing.

My heart raced a little at the prospect that she might be only a few feet away in another room, or at most, working out on a field, perhaps tending to some sheep or goats. Another more wicked thought came to mind, one I quickly put aside. Suddenly a door at the far end of the room, which I hadn't noticed until now, opened, and through it sauntered Rachine. She was wearing a pair of tight fitting jeans, black knee-high boots and a white blouse that looked about one size too small, so that it appeared to be on the verge of bursting open. She really did have a fantastic figure.

"Oh it's you. Bethany told me a reporter was here?"

"*Ah..so that was Bethany!*" I said, nodding my head.

Rachine ignored my observation. "Look - what the hell do you want?"

"That's not very nice Rachine," I replied.

"It's not meant to be. If it's Karen you've come to see, she is indisposed, and any way she doesn't want anything more to do with you, or people from her *old* life."

"I haven't come specifically to see Karen. What Bethany told you is the truth. You should have got a letter from the magazine I work for."

"I never saw it? So you are a reporter?"

"Of a sort. I write for a small magazine based in London."

Rachine eyed me cagily. "Well since you're here, and you are what you say you are - I guess! What do you want to know?"

"Well I'd like to speak to the priest, the person in charge."

"You mean *Saul*?" snapped Rachine. "He'll be here in a minute. You can ask him all the questions you want, and then leave." Rachine walked towards me. "Don't make any trouble Julian." She stood a few feet away and bent her face towards me. "Do - you - understand- me?"

"I think so Rachine." Looking down: "I think we understand each other perfectly well."

Rachine went over to the drinks cabinet and fixed herself a large scotch, then sat down in a big leather armchair a few feet from me. She sipped her drink regarding me watchfully, like the predator she was. There was an awkward few moments silence.

"How is Karen?" I asked.

Rachine lent forward and stood her glass down. "Look Julian, I'm not going to..." At that moment the door opened again and in walked the priest. Rachine stood to attention as if in the presence of a commanding-officer. He touched her arm and she seemed to relax a little. For a man in his sixties he looked very fit. He had thick dark hair streaked with grey, his skin was sallow and he had pale grey, wolf-like eyes, that seemed utterly passionless. He came boldly up to me, with waves of superiority coming off of him. He extended a hand from the long black folds of his cassock.

"Ah! You must be the reporter? Very pleased to meet you," he said.

I stood my drink down and got up to shake his hand. His grip was firm. The feel of his skin, cold and unpleasant, like touching something subterranean.

"Pleased to meet you," I replied, perfunctorily.

"I see Rachine has already got you a drink. Very good."

Rachine laid her hand on the priest's arm and whispered something in his ear. He excused himself and went with her out of the room. He came back a minute or two later and sat down in the seat Rachine had occupied a moment earlier, and like his mascot, she took up the space on the arm next to him.

The priest cleared his throat. "Rachine tells me you know Natasha."

"That's right," I said, "except I prefer to call her by her real name - Karen."

He glanced up at Rachine and then levelled his cold gaze at me once more. "We know her as Natasha, and that is what she herself prefers to be called."

There followed a moment or two of silence. The priest's features remained still and composed. "What do you want?" he asked bluntly.

"I told you, I'm here to do a story," I said, opening my hand's

"Well I will endeavour to help you then," replied the priest.

I picked up my drink again. "What is the philosophy behind your sect?" I asked.

"Church, we call it a *church!*"

"Yes the church of *Saul*," put in Rachine, looking with admiration at her leader. "Our new Saviour," she added.

The priest touched her hand.

"Wasn't that Saint Paul's original name?"

"Yes it was," replied Saul. "Until, that is - he saw the light."

"And have you seen the light?"

"He *is* the light," said Rachine.

The priest gazed at me looking every bit the Saviour; his expression inscrutable, untouched by fear or worry, or doubt.

"Our philosophy is a very simple one. It is one of *love*. Love is all. God gave us love. He taught us to love our enemies as we love our neighbour."

"There are different kinds of love," I said.

"All love comes from god. Here we live with god. We do his bidding. All our energies are driven by *love*, the one true love. God said, go forth and multiply, spread my word. How else is one to do this without *love?"*

"So you advocate a kind of - *free love?"*

Rachine leered at the priest and he took her hand in his. There was something disgusting about their intimacy: the way they looked at each other. The way they touched each other. Together with all this talk about *love* - it was beginning to make me feel nauseous.

"All love is free, is it not?" he said.

"Is it?" I said.

The priest ignored my riposte and began to absently stroke Rachine's wrist.

"I noticed that there are mainly young girls here," I said

The priest made a strange laughing sound. "Julian, I may call you that?"

"If you want."

"I feel I already know you. Rachine has told me so much about you."

"All good I hope?"

Rachine shifted her lovely butt and glared at me. Parting her lips she made a kind of smacking sound. She raised her head a couple of inches so that she was looking down her nose at me

"They are my children. They come to me because they are lost. They need my love."

"Your love? Not *gods* love?"

"It is one and the same. God is with me. God is love."

"You are god?"

The priest had a good old laugh at this. "Not exactly. Not the creator. My body is just the vehicle through which god moves. I love my children as god intended. And what he commands of me, is to put love into them."

I took a large gulp of my drink, and nearly choked. "Do I understand you correctly?" I asked.

"Yes - yes I think you do," replied the priest.

"Love Julian. To feel wanted. To feel the warmth of another body. You know Julian," said Rachine. "And the priest has so very much love to give."

"You are talking about physical love?" I said.

Is there any other?" replied Rachine. She thrust her big chest forward as if to underline the point, and parted her lips, making the smacking sound again; moistening them lasciviously. I knew how long her tongue was, how wide her mouth could get: she reminded me not so much of a human being but rather some sort of lizard.

"What you have to understand Julian is that young girls find sanctuary here from the evil that is in the world: the world out there, "said the priest. "They come to me of their own free will. Here they learn how to express in a positive way, the love that is inside them. They lean to channel their energies - their passion towards god. Through god they find peace; through god they find love - *true love.* The only genuine kind of love. The coming together of two bodies, two hearts, two spirits, two minds."

Rachine seemed to be getting excited, she adjusted herself on her precarious perch, moving her big thigh so that it pressed against the priest's arm.

"God is love! Saul is love!" said Rachine in salutation, whilst looking at me sardonically and sticking out her big chest, until her blouse looked set to burst open.

"What you call *true love*, is just sex," I responded. "One could argue that you have sexually exploited these young people?"

The priest shook his head. "You are a man of the modern world Julian. Like so many of your type, you have become cynical. Sex, as you call it, is done without compassion, or love. It is empty. That kind of thing belongs out there. You see it everywhere. Women parading around half naked. It's disgusting. You see them in magazines and newspapers, cheapening their bodies, selling themselves like harlots. What is this, if not exploitation!" The old wolf eyes bobbled around in his head, his pasty flesh becoming slightly flushed. "Young women," he went on, wetting his lips, "young girls, are not safe out there. Young people are out of touch with who they are. All they worship is the body, and nothing more. *It's heathen I tell you, and I won't stand for it!"* He paused to regain his former wolfishness. "You see, the body has become cheapened - it has become commodified: put on the market and sold to the highest bidder, like so much prime beefsteak - when in fact it is something divine. When it is used correctly, it becomes an exquisite *conduit,* through which to feel god stir inside one - in here, in the innards..." he said, moving his hand around, in the folds of his cassock. "Why else do you think there is so much hate in the world? So much greed Julian! So much anger and ignorance, born of cold hungry desire? Lusting after the flesh is sinful when it is done in ignorance of god. To know god truly," he said, waving his finger at me, "can only be found through suffering."

"There is beauty in pain," put in Rachine.

"This is so," endorsed the priest rubbing his hand up and down Rachine's arm. "One must glorify in ones pain, love ones wounds, enjoy suffering as a benediction. Just as worship of the flesh is sinful when done in ignorance of *god love* - so too is suffering. The only way to feel god's love is to cleave open the flesh and put your hand into the gaping wound and hold it up bloodied, and cry: 'behold the blood of Jesus Christ our lord, God Almighty!' "

When the priest finished speaking he was salivating like an old wolf. His grey, cold wolf-eyes, were darting about his head like a mad thing's, and Rachine's chest was heaving. Her head was bent over, hiding her face. The old priest looked at her, and put his hand on her thigh, and she covered it with hers, pressing it hard against her. She went on breathing hard, making strange whimpering sounds - all the time, keeping her head bowed, as if in deep prayer, when in fact, I think it was more likely that she was trying to conceal the fact that she was on the point of orgasm.

I had heard this kind of ranting before from Garcia. The priest was good - no doubting that. It was easy to see how he could get the congregation swaying, and the young girls all hot and bothered talking about love and conduits and benedictions of pain.

What are we to do with fanatics? Fanatics of the worst kind: the religious kind? Should we perhaps treat them with fear or pity? Reach for the straitjacket and send them to the rubber room or just laugh in their face, then ignore them?

I looked down and swallowed the remainder of my drink, unable to suppress a smile. Rachine wasn't helping any either, although she had at last regained some composure, bringing her head up and putting her hands together praying - I imagine, that the orgasm had been averted - at least for the time being.

"Yes I remember Rachine said something similar about suffering, but don't you think there is enough pain in the world already without adding to it any?"

"Mankind suffers in ignorance of god. Mankind's suffering is therefore all the more because of his ignorance. One could say that mankind is born to suffer. Suffering is unavoidable - pain is unavoidable, especially when one considers how vulnerable these bodies of ours are, that we must carry about."

"It seems to me that the Christian church has only ever been concerned with perpetuating man's suffering: 'Glorifying in it', as you would say. Wouldn't it be more positive to focus on the good things in life - the joy in life?"

Rachine and the priest looked at one another and simpered in unison: a disgusting sight!

"Julian is one who will never understand the true nature of sacrifice I'm afraid," said Rachine.

"Hmm! - yes," said the priest nodding. "I think he will in time."

"It is said you believe yourself to be resurrected?" I said, with a wry smile. I would have loved to have laughed in his face.

There was a long pause as the priest and Rachine played with one anothers hands. They smiled at one another, *cognoscenti,* and then looked at me patronizingly. It was ugly!

"What can I say! I lived and I died, and lived again. What is this if not resurrection?"

"He *is* the risen Lord," put in Rachine.

"Let me get this straight - are you telling me you physically died and then came back to life?"

The priest got up and poured himself a drink. He swung round. "Quite so," he said, staring at me with his silver eyes.

"Did a coroner declare you dead?"

"I committed the ultimate sin by purposefully taking my own life. I came to with a rope around my neck. No doctor came - no coroner."

"You passed out!"

"I died. I saw god, and god spoke to me. He told me to go forth and prepare a tabernacle in his name, so that others, who, like me despaired, may come to know his love. He showed me the way. He taught me not to loose hope. Through my suffering I found a way though to: *true love! - god love!* In this way we reverence the body - reverence *life itself! - In the name of God the Father, and Saviour Jesus Christ our Lord!*

Like Christ before me, I was resurrected."

"Saul is the lord," said Rachine. "The living sacrament."

She looked at him with eyes full of adoration. You could tell it wouldn't take her very long to get herself worked up again. He took her hand as he sat back down again. It was a sickening sight to behold.

"I am sorry how neglectful of me," he said. "Rachine get Julian a fresh drink, his glass is empty."

She stood up, to do the Lord's bidding, first adjusting the crotch on her skin tight jeans.

"So, am I in the presence of the Messiah then?"

"The age of the Messiah is over. In this world even the voice of Jesus would go unheard."

"But surely if he is, or rather if *you are*, the son of God Almighty, wouldn't people listen?"

"You would think so wouldn't you! But it doesn't work like that. People have to learn to listen to god with their hearts. What he says is not uttered by word alone - you are like so many Julian, don't get me wrong, I think you are an intelligent young man, but you do not understand the question, so how could understand the answer? It must always be black and white. You see, what god demands of us is sacrifice. The true nature of which is something not easily understood by all."

"I tried telling him," said Rachine. "*Here!* - here's your drink," she said, thrusting the glass in my hand. She vauntingly swaggered off, her big heeled boots clanging over the wooden floor.

"What should I do then?" I replied. "Put a rope around my neck like you, and hope that god will resurrect me?"

The priest laughed, but I could see Rachine thought it an excellent idea. I would have loved to put my hands around *her* throat!

"I would not advocate that myself. But who knows what a man will do in desperate circumstances?"

The large French mantel-clock chimed the hour.

"Now is there anything else you wish to know? There are other matters, god's work - you know..."

I could feel my heart beating harder as I formed the words in my head. Barely able to speak: "Yes," I said - "Karen! I want to see her."

They looked at one another. "He wants to see his Karen...." mocked Rachine. "Well you *blardy* can't!" she said, on the verge of getting up. The Saviour had to put his hand on her arm to restrain her.

"You want to see Karen - *hmmmmm!*"

"You're too late," spat Rachine. She let out a sardonic laugh. *"Poor Julian.* You are out of your league. *Little man!* Don't forget I know you. *I know you! You are nothing! - nothing! you hear me? little man!"* The veins in her neck stood up, gorged with blood, her eyes turned pink, as she fulminated. Even the priest looked surprised. He squeezed her arm.

"Enough - Leave us a moment Rachine," he said firmly.

Rachine got up, her eyes fixed on me, firing arrows of cold black hatred. A dirty filthy scowl on her face. I believe if she had been allowed to, she would have launched at me with her feline weapons. She kissed the priest on the side of the face and walked out without a another word. The man cleared his throat.

"I'm sorry about that."

"That's all right," I answered, calmly, although my hands were shaking.

"She is very passionate. She can let her passions run away with her. She hates *you* - but to the matter in hand." He paused a moment as if searching for the words. "Look, I understand how you must feel," he continued, in a level voice, "I know that it must be hard..."

"I love her. I want her. She's mine. You have no right," I blurted.

"Compose yourself," he retorted, frowning, as if he expected better from me.

"The fact of the matter is that she is not *your* Karen any more, and probably never was. She has found her true path. She has come to me - at last."
"She lost her memory. She doesn't know who she is!"
"She came to me though. She found herself again. She found god. She found love *through* me. It has taken many years, but my Natasha has come home. I will *never* let her get away from me again."
"So - *you are the priest?* The one Garcia warned me about?"
"Hah! - *Garcia!* That old fart!"
"You know him?"
"Our paths have crossed, you could say. Let me show you something." He went over to a bureau and returned with a bundle of files which he dropped in my lap. There were newspaper clippings and a journal, some diaries, letters addressed to 'Paul' - all in the hand of 'Natasha'.
"Garcia no doubt told you all about her, and her unfortunate life."
"Yes - yes he did," I replied, "he showed me a few things he collected over the years, but he never had this amount of stuff."
"No, because he never knew her as I did. We were lovers you see. I have loved her all my life. I have been waiting for her return. Something Natasha told me once convinced me that one day she would come back to me. She always felt that she had not long to live. She was terrified of dying, yet she knew about death better than any of us. She told me to hold on. That if something happened to her she would come back. That one day our paths would cross again, and that I would know her when I saw her. So you see, I will never give her up - not now!"
"But Natasha - your Natasha, is dead. She died over twenty five years ago."
"Her body died. Her soul still lives on."
"Yes, in Karen."
The priest shook his head. "You do not understand."
"Yes I do. I know Karen as she really is. She's a happy girl. She loves the sea, and the sun. She loves life! She wouldn't want to be stuck out here worshipping some dead god."
"God is not dead," he said, condescendingly. He leaned forward in his seat and put his hands together. There was something about this act that transmitted an

underlying menace. "The truth is Julian, she came to me. Don't you see, that in loosing her memory she found who she really was. It was a sign that showed her the way to the one she always truly loved. In her previous life she told me that she would be famous one day, and that after a fall from grace she would find her true love. Well, don't you see! - she has had her fall from grace."
"She only came to you because that bitch Rachine was spying all along."
"Yes it is true. I owe Rachine much. Through her I was able to follow Natasha's every move. That old fool thought he could change her destiny. It is I - I who will save her. In me she will find God. I am the one who puts the love of god into her. Through me, through *Our Lord Jesus Christ,*" he boomed.
"As a sex slave?" I retorted, fast running out of patience.
"No - love Julian. Love between a man and a woman. You are a mere boy. Do you think for a second you could hold on to a woman like Natasha? I'm sorry Julian," he said, shaking his head and looking grave, "I don't wish to be indelicate but I think we both know that you are lacking in a certain department. Don't be embarrassed, Rachine has told me *all* about it. You had an affair, is it not so....? I take it from your silence that we both know what we are talking about?"

He paused a moment to study me closely. "In fact, both Rachine and Karen have raised there doubts about your sexuality. Isn't there some Algerian doctor you spend a lot of time with? I'm a broad minded man, I can understand how these things happen. All forms of love are blessed in the eyes of the lord, even with the same sex." He paused again, as if waiting for my reaction, which didn't come. "I'm not saying there is anything *wrong* with you - sexually! You see Julian, for women like Natasha and Rachine - well, they need a *real* man. You understand? Someone who is positive around them. Decisive. *Firm!*" He shook his head and had a little chuckle to himself. "These women Julian, they take a *lot* of loving. They demand so much love. It's not easy, even for me, I can tell you. Natasha! Now Natasha, well you know yourself how demanding she can be. *What a girl! Some girl that girl!* She always did need a lot of loving...So you can see how silly all this is. Go home Julian; go to your doctor friend or find yourself a nice quiet little woman, who will cook and clean for you. Leave the real women to those who know best how to handle them."

My response: I could hold out no more. I laughed in his face. "I don't know what Rachine has been telling you?" I said.
The priest put up is hand: "No! - no! - no! - It's all right, I understand. I don't wish to embarrass you."
"Who the hell do you think you are?" I said
"I thought we had already cleared that point up?" replied Saul. He sighed and shook his head again. "I saw the newspaper cuttings of Natasha, parading around in those silly get-ups, pretending to be some sort of ancient priestess. That's all Garcia's doing, filling her head with nonsense. And then you! - you call yourself a man? You say you love her! What were you doing allowing her to be attacked and beaten? Allowing her beautiful face to be scarred? that perfect body to be marred in the way that it has?"
"There was nothing I could do. It was chaos. I got separated."
"Nonsense! Allowing women to beat her, and cut her up? Why didn't you stop them? You have no answer do you? You see, a real man would have never have allowed that to happen. A real man would have taken the beating himself and put his body in harms way, but from what I gather, it was Natasha who gave her body, in order to protect your miserable hide."
To this of course there was no reply possible. He was right. She was braver than me.
"Well god moves in mysterious ways," he continued. "Your weakness as a man, your negligence, brought her to me. You damn well nearly got her killed, but god saw fit to resurrect her also. Don't you see the pattern, the symmetry? We were both resurrected. It is gods will that we should come together, in order that we may love one another, and do gods will: *as it is on Earth so shall it be in heaven* - In heaven Julian. Even god will not tear us asunder. Certainly not the likes of you. Look at yourself. Who are you? Rachine was right, you are really nothing! A little man who has stepped out of his league." The priest sat further forward in his seat, his tone growing increasingly derisive. "How could you indulge her in such fantasies? Allow her to go about dressed half naked? To be so prideful? You should be ashamed of yourself. You are as bad as that old pagan. God will judge you one day," said Saul, wagging his finger, "and when he does he will cast you down into the flames of hell-fire...And you can take that

smirk off your face me boy, or I'll do it for you." He paused, and for a second I thought he was about to become violent. He made a guttural sound, and waved his arm dismissively.

"I think you should go. There is nothing for you hear. My words are wasted on the likes of you."

"I'm not going until I see her."

The priest suddenly looked towards the door and Karen came in, closely followed by a fraught looking Bethany.

"I'm really sorry," said Bethany, "I couldn't stop her. You know how strong she is."

"It's all right Bethany. Leave us please, and close the door."

"Karen!.." I rose to my feet but the priest was there in a flash to cut me out. He took her hand.

"What's going on? I heard raised voices," said Karen.

"Nothing my child. We were just having a heated discussion."

"About me? You weren't arguing over me?"

"No," I said.

"I know who you are. You're Julian. What are you doing here?"

"He was just leaving."

"Why are you here? Is he here to take me away?" said Karen, backing away and suddenly looking very anxious.

"No. Not at all my child," said the priest.

She was incredibly thin and changed in some fundamental way. Her bloom, her vitality had gone. She was terribly wasted. Her narrow face looked gaunt, her cheeks sunken and dark. The scar dominated her features, a long deep livid fissure, that because of her drawn complexion gave the impression that it had been freshly hewn with an axe. Her lips were pale and cracked, and her skin seemed to have a sallow, dry appearance. She even had pimples and sores around her mouth. She wore no jewellery and was dressed in a simple green smock made of a course woollen material, that hung on her like a sack, which somehow seemed to accentuate her skinniness. Once she would have enlivened the most dreary form of attire, now though she kindled a different kind of fascination, one that was motivated by a morbid curiosity. The way in which the coarse material hung on her, suggested the presence of a figure, I shuddered to think though what the state of it was when laid bare. As I continued to look at her, I tried to work out what it was that had so fundamentally changed in her. It was something more than the physical deterioration. As I looked into her eyes it hit me. I saw something I had never seen in them before. There was confusion in them - there was fear in them!

"You have seen her, now go."

"Please just give me a few minutes alone with her. Please, it's all I ask." I begged.

At that moment Rachine burst in, and Karen immediately ran to her like a little puppy. She put both her arms around the powerful woman, burying her head in her big bosom.

"Is he still here? Can't you see you're frightening her," she balled.

"What have you done to her?"

"There is nothing wrong with her. It's you - you're frightening the poor girl to death," said Rachine, puting her arms about her defensively.

Karen puled her head up from her bosom and spied me with one eye.

"There!...there! my sweetling! *Mon petit chou! mon enfant miel!*" said Rachine, smoothing her long tangled locks. "The nasty man is just leaving. He won't harm you ever again."

"Now come Julian - don't make it hard on yourself," said Saul, putting his hand on my shoulder.

I looked at it, and he removed it. "Don't get any ideas," he said, "don't let my age fool you. I'm stronger than you. I'll break you up if I have to."

I looked into his steel-cold eyes, and I was left in little doubt that he was more than capable of carrying out his threat.

"Don't!" yelled Karen.

We both looked round.

"Don't hurt him." Karen had moved away from Rachine.

The priest put on a sickly smile for her. "I'm not going to hurt him, my child."

She came timorously up to the priest and he took her tiny hand in his great big fist. He looked over at Rachine, and some sort of signal passed between them.

Siezing the moment: "Please! please let me just have a second with her alone.

What can it matter? Then I'll go, and never come back. I promise."

The priest looked at Karen. "How do you feel about that Natasha? The man wants to speake to you for a short time. Do you want that?"

There was a pause for a few seconds, and then Karen nodded. "Yes, I know Julian. he is a kind man - I think," she said, putting her finger to her mouth in that cute way of hers.

The priest nodded to Rachine and she went out of the room. He lead Karen over to a chair and sat her down. He stayed next to her still holding her hand. She looked up at him with her massive lavender eyes.

"Now are you sure Natasha? You don't have to see him if you don't want to?"

Karen nodded frantically like a little girl. "I want...to....say....my good-by...to him...by..myself...please, if I may....please!" She looked at me and stuck her finger in her mouth and began to suck.

"Well if you're sure, all right then. Rachine and I will be just through that door - there the whole time, so you won't really be alone."

Karen looked into the face of the priest with big glassy doll-like eyes, and nodded again, somewhat too energetically.

The priest let go of her hand and walked up to me. The look in his grey eyes was the most potent force of pure will I have ever confronted. I felt he stripped me to the bone with those eyes.

"Five minutes - no more."

"Five minutes," I repeated.

"And if you make her cry, I'll kill you."

The priest turned back to Karen and smiled. "I'm going now sweetling, just through that door there. If the man upsets you, you just holler and I'll be here."

Karen nodded frantically again and kicked the leg of the chair with her heel as she swung her legs back and forth.

"He won't. Julian is nice man." she looked at me, her head a little to one side. "I think he is - any way?"

"Yes - well he'd better be," were the priest's parting words.

When he left the room I sat looking straight ahead of me and tried to compose myself. I swirled the last of my scotch around in the glass and knocked it back. My trembling faded slightly. I knew the one thing I must not let happen was for my emotions to come too much to the fore. I was almost afraid to look at Karen. I could hear her breathing and a sort of chewing sound as she sucked on her thumb.

"Well Karen - I mean Natasha," I said, looking at her. She smiled back at me. "Do you like living here?" .

Karen kicked the leg of the chair with the heel of her shoe. She nodded vigorously. 'Oh my god,' I thought to myself, 'it's like talking to a five year old!'

"Do you like the priest?" I continued.

Karen nodded, but not so enthusiastically this time. "You mean Saul?" she said.

"Yes Saul. And what about Rachine?"

Karen smiled, and nodded, and then looked towards the window, seemingly embarrassed by my question.

"You like Rachine?"

Karen nodded again - "She's lovely."

"How do you mean?"

Karen shrugged....."She's pretty, and she's all soft and cuddly." Karen pulled a funny face and giggled. "she likes to love me all up."

"Love you up?"

Karen laughed. "You know - *love!* True love. God love."

"I see. And what about the priest? Does he - 'love you up - true love?' "

Karen frowned. "Yeah!"

"Do you like it when he loves you?"

"Sometimes."

"But not always?"

Karen shook her head vigorously. "Some...sometimes...it...he hurt me, but don't mean to, he says it's god's love - god's love very very big and it hurt....because it's - go*d's...*"

"But you like it?"

Karen laughed like a naughty little girl, and put her hand over her mouth. "Yeah, I like it all right."

"Oh my god," I mumbled to myself, forgetting Karen's astute hearing.

"God!" she said, and laughed again. "God love, true love, *heee, heeeeee!*"

I just stared at her incredulously.

"What else do you do?"

There was a moments pause. "Ahhhh - spin."

"Spin?"

"Spin - *you know, spin,* with the wheel!"

"Oh...spinning-wheel!"

Karen nodded vigorously, indicating that she liked 'spinning' very much.

"Where do you spin?"

"In my room," she said, turning her eyes to the ceiling. "I like sitting in my room. I like sitting and spinning in my room."

"You like *sitting?"* I said, keenly.

Karen nodded, "*Yeah...* I like sitting. Do you like sitting down? I like sitting, sitting and spinning - *all'lll - day!"*

"What! - *all day?"*

"*Allllll* - day. Do you like sitting down?"

I laughed: "yes it's all right. But don't you get bored?"

Karen chewed on her finger and I noticed all her nails were bitten down to their quick's. "sometimes." Karen looked at me almost - one might imagine, coyly, as in the old days.

"What do you do?" she asked.

Her guilessness took me off my guard slightly. "I write - I write stories," I replied.

"Will....will you tell...tell...me one."

"I haven't the time my sweet," I said, fighting to maintain my composure. "One day though, I'm going to write a story all about you. And lots of people will get to hear about you - what a wonderful and beautiful person you are."

"*Gosh!"*

Karen turned her big lavender eyes on me. They seemed huge, I guess because her face was so thin.

"You're sad," she said.

Her childlike forthrightness was disconcerting...."Yes - yes I suppose I am," I replied, scratching my head.

"Don't be sad."

"I'll try not to be." I got up and went over to her: kneeling at her feet I took her thin, oh so painfully thin, hand's in mine. Holding them gently, lest they break: "You know - Natasha, you know I love you very much."

Karen looked around the room, as if looking for help.

"It's all right, I won't hurt you. I just wanted you to now that...well I love you."

Karen nodded, and smiled faintly.

I looked at her hands and morbidly I puled back the sleeve of her smock to reveal her thin forearms; feeling further along it seemed that her well defined musculature, that she had once been so proud of, had all but wasted away. I covered them again, I had seen all I needed to see.

"How did you get those bruises on your arms?" I asked of her.

Karen looked uncomfortable and hugged herself.

"Tell me. Nothing bad will happen. I promise," I persisted.

"God love," she said, reluctantly.

I turned away cursing the priest under my breath. I looked back at her; she was as weak and helpless as a child. I couldn't stop the tears from coming into my eyes when I thought about her plight, but I knew I must not allow myself to *crack-up:* 'Not now, not in front of *them,*' I told myself.

Staying with the maudlin sentiment I felt her arms again. "You're very thin my love."

"I don't eat a lot," said Karen, feebly.

I looked down at her legs, they too had wasted away. I wanted to touch them as I used to. To run my hands over her once strong thighs. But I knew that that would have been highly inappropriate.

"It's tragic," I said. "When I think how you used to look..."

"Saul says it is not godly to be conceited about the body...."

"So he - starves you?"

Karen looked around nervously and stuck her finger in her mouth again and started chewing. I gently pulled her hand away. Tell me - *Karen*?"

Karen's eyes grew wide and her mouth dropped open, and for a second I thought I saw the real Karen: my Karen return. Then she just closed her mouth and turned her face to one side and laughed.

"But my name is Natasha - silly Julian! - *Hi!- hi - hi! - heee! - heeee!!*"

Then almost straightaway she looked fretful. "Karen is dead. *Karen evil.....bad, mustn't mention name!*" said Karen putting her finger over her mouth and making a shushing sound.

Not wanting to run the risk of upsetting her I choose to ignore her words.

"What else do you do Natasha? Are *you* happy?"

She smiled cutely: cute like a child. "Yeah - kind'a..."

"Are you really happy - Natsha?"

"Yep.." Karen looked at the door.

"Natasha - what else do you like doing?"

She looked at me. "Not a lot. Sometimes....sometimes I go with Bethany to see the sheep and the goats. I like sheep *they're funny....*"

Suddenly the door opened and I jumped to my feet. The priest walked in with Bethany.

"Well - I've got to go now," I said, still holding Karen's hand.

"All right then," came the reply.

Spontaneously I hugged her frail body to me and spoke into her ear: "Julian loves you very very much, always remember that." I placed a kiss on her desiccated lips.

"That's enough," growled the priest.

Karen lent forward and kissed the side of my face. "Don't be sad," she said.

"I'll try not to be," I said, trying to smile. I touched her thin arms again. "Don't forget to eat all your dinner. Keep fit and strong."

"Come on, that's enough now," said Saul, and I could sense his menacing presence behind me. The last thing I wanted was a scene. I pressed my lips to her thin hand and let her go.

"You bastard," I said, as I went past the priest. He followed me into the reception area.

"Don't ever come back here. I don't have to remind you what will happen to you if you do!" he warned.

I ignored him. I could still see Karen in the other room sitting on the chair sucking her thumb, while Bethany dutifully held on to her other hand. I raised my arm to wave her good-bye, but I don't think she saw me because the priest walked into me, forcing me back. His body felt solid like iron. He stared me down with his wolf-eyes. "Bethany," he yelled. She came up behind him. "Escort this young man off the premises will you."

The priest turned and walked back into the parlour. "Sweetling, sweetling," I heard him say, as he slammed the door behind him.

Bethany stared at me, looking embarrassed. My impulse was to just run away, but I knew that would be wrong. Here before me was Bethany. The object of another madman's insane devotion.

"Will she be all right?" I said.

Bethany glanced over her shoulder.

"Yes. Now you really should go. The priest is not someone to mess with. Here, his word is law."

Time seemed frozen. What was it about this girls eyes? They were a perfectly clear green, as green as a cat's. They seemed to focus off into infinity. Insanely I touched her hand.

"And what about you, will you be all right? I asked.

Bethany glanced down at our hand's and then levelled me with an open countenance that seemed to say, 'yes we have connected. I am here now and not afraid.' We stood and just gazed at one another, neither of us making the slightest attempt to break the spell. Then Bethany heard a sound from within the room. She put her hand on the polished brass doorknob and opened the heavy oak door: ushering me under the porch, she looked anxiously over her shoulder. "Yes - don't worry about me, but you must go - really you must, you don't know what he's like - he'll kill you."

I looked at our hands, refusing to let her go. "I've seen you before..."I said, "or rather your likeness."

leaning towards me: "What?"

"On Garcia's island! The statue. It doesn't do you justice."

Bethany smiled cheekily, and then frowned. "Of course! You're Julian. I remember Rachine telling me. You'll know then, that I don't think very highly of that old man."

"I think what he did to you was terrible," I said.

"Oh well - it's done," she replied. "Now come," she prompted, pulling me by the hand. I became more strongly aware of her limp, as she escorted me to my car.

I looked nervously towards the big house. "Don't you see I just can't go? I can't leave her," I said, tightening my hold on her hand. "You must help me. Help me get her away from here."

Bethany looked at a loss. "You must love her very much?" she said, disengaging her hand from mine.

"I do."

"You have to understand - there is nothing that can be done."

"There must be something?"

Bethany looked fraught. "There is nothing!" she said, shaking her head. "If you knew what you were asking, you would see it is impossible. Now go from here - please, before he comes."

Not wanting to get Bethany into trouble with the priest, I got in my car. Winding down the window: Bethany leaned forward. "She belongs to them now," she said, "and anyway, even if you could get her away from here, she would never be the girl you knew. My advice is to try and forget about her."

"What have they done to her?"

"Nothing, you don't understand. She's been ill. It's nothing to worry about."

Reluctantly I started the engine. "Tell me, was it you who put us on to the priest?"

Distracted now: "Look...please, I..I don't know..just go will you..."

"Don't worry, they'll never know."

I handed her my business number and personal address. "At least keep me informed about her - how she is?"

"All right," said Bethany, moving away from the car.

'I had to be grateful for that much,' I thought. Bethany looked at the details on my card, she must have had some sort of change of heart, and came back over. "look, she began hurriedly, "sometimes I can get away from here - Saul sends me on errands now and again, sometimes to London, wherever there are waifs and strays...I know what you're thinking, but it's better than becoming prey to pimps and drug addiction. I'll get in contact, if I'm in town. I can't do anything more. Take Saul's advice, give up hope of ever getting *your Karen* back."

She looked at me again with that far off gaze, and smiled faintly. I nodded and smiled back. There was nothing more to be done, and this was more than I had hoped for.

As I drove off I looked in the rear-view mirror and saw Bethany, as she headed back to the vicarage. It was like a world apart, already so distant from me, as to be on another star. I past the farm buildings and abandoned cottages. I slowed down for a girl on a horse, who waved at me with a happy face. I passed the fields of sheep, and remembered Karen in better times, when she too had had a happy face, then the tears began to come, floods of them. I drove as far as I could and then had to pull over. I don't know how long it took for me to gain some sort of composure. I kept reminding myself of Bethany's words: the girl I knew as Karen was gone, I had to forget about her....'She was dead', I told myself, 'dead! Forget her, she's dead! Even Karen herself, had told me.' All there was, was this childlike creature, this shell, that called itself *Natasha!'*

The desire to put as much distance as possible between myself and that place of confinement, that stagnant world that housed the living dead, a body that was now only a sticky cloying memory, was the only reason I kept driving - driving almost non stop back to London. I suddenly wanted the people, the bustle more than anything, 'wonderful London, swallow me whole, please swallow me and make me forget.'

XXIV

I finished the article on the 'Church of Saul', comparing it with other examples of cults and sects, siting the brain washing effect on their followers. 'The cult of Saul,' as I referred to it, was just such an example of the power of religion when taken to its extreme by megalomaniacs and fanatics, who together with their co-conspirators, prey upon the weak and disaffected of society. Such individuals as Saul, rule their denomination through fear and ignorance. It was in this vein I went on to denigrate the priest and his mission, casting him in the worst possible light, as a dangerous *Svengali.* My power as a writer was all that I had to fight back with: the most I could hope for was that it might prompt the authorities to investigate such sects as his and find reason to close them down.

My editor had only praise for me: 'a great job Julian,' he said, 'well researched and written with true passion.' Of course he would never know the source of that passion. I took his praise, but it was nothing compared to the satisfaction it gave in getting back at those two rotters, who had taken Karen's life away - and in so doing that of my own.

At first I was hopeful of news from Bethany, but the weeks wore on and nothing came. Imperceptibly my sense of desideration evaporated as I got back into the routine of my job, and living in London. It had effectively swallowed me up just as I wanted it to. There was always another article to finish for the magazine, and my editor, impressed by my piece on Saul, gave me more interesting assignments; so there was never much time to look back, but of course there comes a point when what one has 'turned away from,' eventually comes to - 'face you'. How and why it happens, and when it happens, these are reasons that lay beyond our *ken.* But in the book of destiny everything is written, and someone, or something turned a page and read - and so I acted.

*

I had heard people mention the name Peckham, but I had never thought much about going there. Of course I knew it was that part of London that Natasha, (the real Natasha) had met her end. I remembered what Garcia had said about it: that it had been condemned. Places with names like, Peckham and Mordon didn't exactly inspire the soul, I was finding life tough enough in Hampstead. Why I went to Peckham I have not the slightest idea? but one grey miserable afternoon, which is to say, one indistinct day like all the others, I found myself standing on the platform of Peckham Rye station.

I had laughed at the time, when Garcia had said it had been condemned, but as I looked about me, at the squalor and degradation, the ugly tower blocks and council dwellings, I could see that he hadn't been joking at all. 'Places like this, shouldn't be allowed to exist,' I thought, 'its not good for the soul.' As I began walking down Peckham High street, looking for the road Natasha had lived on, I could feel my chest muscles constrict my heart, until I could hardly breath. I stopped and loosened my collar: some black kids ran past screaming and my head began to spin. 'How can people live here,' I thought. I had to rest a moment by leaning against an old brick wall, that looked all set to collapse. I looked up the long street, and the endless expanse of drab decaying buildings, and for a moment thought about turning back to the station. For some reason, as I said, I moved as an automaton, I carried on up the street, my feet falling heavily one in front of the other, with my hand firmly placed in the grip of destiny. The macabre instinct to find the place where Natasha had last lived came to the fore. Perhaps, in so doing, I was trying to get close to Karen: to the person she was when her soul moved about this world in another body. I remembered the name of the street and chuckled to myself at how cruel fate can be, but I couldn't be sure of the number; not that it would have mattered, one decaying Georgian terrace, one mouldering bed-sit, was much like any other. As I turned off the main street into Vestry road, then finally onto Dragmar mews, it was like passing through a wall of ice: the sense of déjà vue! I shuddered and took a sharp intake of breath. It was somewhere there, in one of those old terraced houses, that Natasha Tomlonson stopped living, and Karen Stockwell began. This drab indistinct little street was the genesis of Karen's soul, and the continuation of its tragic existence.

When Natasha had left her parents home in Stockholm, she was just seventeen. After travelling through Denmark she arrived in Germany, virtually penniless; her greatest asset though was her stunning looks and amazing figure, so she had no problem getting work in a strip joint in Berlin. It was there that she met Jon Kindell, the rich playboy who forced her into a life of debauchery: finally running away from him, to the love of her life, the priest, who in the end, put his ministry before Natasha. Weak willed and acting out of selfishness he allowed her to runaway to London, seemingly uncaring of the horrors that a place like that can hold for a girl like Natasha. Some might paint a picture of noble sacrifice, the truth was he was a coward, who hid behind his vestments, rather than stand up and be a man. His type saw themselves as martyrs to a higher cause. The pursuit of happiness was something altogether foreign, preferring instead to wallow in their own suffering. Again, I call it selfishness and cowardice, because he didn't care whether his suffering reached others. So typical of his type: the sick at heart - are only happiest when bleeding from their sick hearts, they love nothing more than to delve over their own festering wounds, nurturing a poison that is hatred and malice, which they regurgitate as righteous indignation. The truth was, the very sight of Natasha put him at odds with himself. It was no sacrifice therefore, to let her go.

And so, eventually, Natasha ended up living here, in this inauspicious part of London, in one of the mouldering bed-sits in the block of terraces that now stood before me. There are some places that you never really shake off the smell of, and this was certainly one of them. They represent a low water mark for the soul, and if it is of a moist disposition, as Natasha's most certainly was, then you will be drawn towards it, on the principle of like goes to like. It was here she was preyed upon by the sadist and sexual predator Steven Greythorpe, an associate of Jon Kindell. Greythorpe therefore had money, and indeed he lavished gifts on Natasha for sexual favours; it is not clear though why she remained on Dragmar mews? I suppose one will never know exactly the answer to that question, but I imagine that it had something to do with Natasha's perverse sense of justice: she felt that this was where she belonged. Just as she gave the food parcels sent by the priest to the Salvation Army, she didn't need to prostitute herself the way that she did, but her perversity of mind combined with her licentious disposition meant she would bring back men to her mouldering bed-sit, and on a damp stained mattress, she would give her beautiful body over to their sordid little fantasies, and all for just a few *quid.*

Her whole life was charted out: her fate sealed, long before she ever left Stockholm. And as I look at that dank row of decaying properties, I can only imagine the despair, the forlorn lack of hope she must have felt. I think she had decided that this was to be her last stand. She had been run to ground. She had reached her level: her low-water mark, all that was left for her was to gradually sink further and further into the squalor and filth that surrounded her and had become a part of her. Her violent death at the hands of a sadist like Greythorpe, was the natural conclusion to such a life as hers. Perhaps it even came as some relief.

I bowed my head and said a silent prayer for the life that was Natasha. I had lingered long enough: walking away from that depressing scene, I turned the corner, yet more dwellings of a similar sort lined the street. This place had all the trappings of despair, even in the most banal; such as the dismal looking gardens just around the corner, where I imagine, in twilight hours, all manner of horrors transpire. I imagine too, that Natasha was only too well acquainted with this little patch of green. And although nature is supposed to lift the soul, here the reverse was true. The feeling of danger, of decay, and of *strange goings on*, persisted, even in daylight hours. It was as if nature herself had been overtaken by despair, turned conspirator, waiting to trap the unwary and the too trusting. Such places as Lucacs Gardens bide their time. Little corners of London, that no one, not even the good old cockney: *gord blimey-lubaduck*, ever herd of; until that is, they hit the headlines, when some young girl is found strangled to death and raped, or some young *druggy* 'went a bit too far.' In the mean time, places like Lucacs Gardens remain very much a backwater to the hustle and bustle of the *big city.* 'If you are going to go there young lady, then be sure to take a very large dog with you.' In the mean time such places are home to rats, starlings and the odd stray cat, as well as the peeping-tom, who is sure to be watching you young lady, from out of the dark recess'.

For mile after mile the same scene met my eyes, until I became quite numb to the prospect of such squalor and filth and degradation. What disturbed me the most, was the knowledge that all around me were probably thousands of such condemned souls as that of Natasha's, slowly rotting away in despair, waiting for their own violent and ignominious end. One read about them in the newspapers: a decomposed body found in a bed-sit only after it had begun to smell. Death from a stab wound, or an overdose. It didn't even conjure up an image! The report was just so much space in a newspaper column. One didn't think of these victims as once being people with their own sense of sorrow and joy, even less that they all had mothers and fathers. And once they might have been loved - it was simply that nobody cared any more.

I kept on walking down the grey street, and it began to rain a fine drenching sort of rain. Looking about me, I could see how it could happen, how one could start to loose all hope. How one could start to - *slip.* If you started to, *slip-up* here, if you began to go the wrong way, on the wrong side, then you were finished: as good as dead. If you wanted to live anywhere in this hard hearted city, that was half descent, you had to be on at least fifty *thou* a year. I was one of the lucky ones, I had contacts, I had a descent job, I wasn't on fifty *thou* a year, but I had money behind me. I could get out of this stinking sess pit any time I wanted, so why did I stay? Had I, like Natasha, reached my own 'low water mark'?

Was it for Karen that I stayed? The strange thing was, as the months went by I thought about her very little. It wasn't a conscious decision to put her out of my mind, she just faded away. I had made a sort of life for myself. The routine was what held me together. I had to thank Mersell for the idea of getting back into life, otherwise this story would have had a very different ending.

One did not so much get used to living and working in London, instead one became increasingly *numb* to oneself and ones surroundings. The burden which I felt I carried around with me from the first day I arrived in this land, did not so much lift, I simply became less aware of it. That was how London sneaked up on you. You didn't notice the gradual slide - just as I didn't notice the gradual stoop of my shoulders. It was hard enough just existing on the good side, but if you were on the wrong side, of the wrong side - on the slide, as it were, you were finished. You wouldn't be aware of it happening but I saw plenty of examples, of those who had succumbed: bent and twisted out of shape, their minds twisted inside out and turned to mush, until all powers of reasoning ceased to exist, reduced to the behaviour of a rabid dog, who hunted simply to stay alive for the next fix, to make the burden a bit more bearable.

I had no time for those that were on the slide, I had my own burden to take care of - thank you all the same. That was the nub of the thing, everyone was 'taking care of themselves,' lest they too went towards the *slide zone.* Thank god, I say, for the 'English pub', the only salvation for the spirit, the only relief, momentary as it is, from the burden. During this period of my life I must have got through several cases of scotch, and several hundred barrels of ale.

On the weekend, if I wasn't working on a story, I would wander over to Hampstead heath, that bit of fenced in nature, that, like Lucacs Gardens, bides its time and I would sit, like other sad individuals, and blossoming perverts and watch the pretty girls go by; if it was spring time, then all the better. This was my other escape, true immersion in the oblivion of being oblivious, but still a part of humanity. One saw, apart from the pretty girls, the ugly faces and twisted shapes of those that were loosing the fight. You could see the dead look in their eyes, the dead look of modern eyes, drugged out, zonked out, finished! - sliding away as on some sort of celestial conveyer belt, on their way to the vast soul recycling plant in the sky. It was then that the words of Karen, (my Karen) would come back to me. Then, she had had hope, she thought she was going to live a good life, free of her demon. Karen realised that, she, like most people, would grow old. It had quite rightly frightened her. We all want to live, but we don't want to get old, and we're all terrified of death. But that was silly, when you spend long enough alone, just sitting, in this make believe bit of nature, looking around at everything, then you realise that death is nothing to fear because you - *already were!* London, and places like it, were nothing more than vast cemeteries for lost souls.

It is true that one only arrives at this conclusion if you spend most of your time alone, just thinking, thinking, about...about *everything.* I lived in my own world, although I contacted with others no one, and nothing, got through. This of course is not the way we are meant to be. There was something very fundamentaly lacking in this approach. I was not a complete person; I was a person only unto myself, but not to others. I existed too much for myself. What I had had to endure was not possible, without coming away with some fundamental loss of my humanity. But then thinking about it, and looking at you lot, I'm not sure it is so much of a loss. Quite how long I would have gone on existing alone like this, is hard to say, but one of those bastards up there, perhaps I should be more respectful - one of those sentinels of time: gatekeepers of the other side, turned to my page in the great book of destiny, and started to read.

It was on a Friday afternoon, I was at my desk making some notes on a tedious story about New Forest ponies, when I was informed that there was a girl at reception asking to see me. I looked at the scribbled notes on my pad and I felt my heart begin to flutter madly like the beating wings of a moth on a window pain. I remained motionless for several moments, as in some sort of somnambulistic state while asking slowly: "what did she look like?"

"Short, pretty, black hair," came the reply

"Well aren't you going to see her?" said George, when I remained sitting at my desk.

The truth was, I didn't want to see - any of *them*, ever again. Yet, reluctantly, I got up.

"You kept that one quiet," teased George.

"He's a dark horse, that one," put in another of work my work colleagues.

I picked up my hat and coat and went down to greet my guest. Bethany was looking pale and fraught, but as cute as ever, dressed all in denim. I decided to take her to the, *Dog and Bone,* a few blocks down the street. A quiet little pub that I sometimes used to conduct interviews, or else escape when work became too tedious. The journey there did not take as long as I feared, Bethany was good at small talk: good at avoiding the big issues.

The landlord eyed my companion with obvious envy. "Is it the same again?" he asked.

"Yes please," I replied. "It's been a long day."

It was late afternoon and the pub was full enough people and their chatter, so as not to be overheard. I took Bethany over to a quiet corner with the beers we had ordered. There was no doubting Bethany's ability to focus on the trivial. She asked me more questions about my job and my life in London. It became obvious that there were more important issues bearing on her mind than my own rather, humdrum solitary existence.

"So Bethany," I said, when she paused to take a drink, "what brings you to this neck of the woods - apart, I mean from saving more lost souls?"

Bethany looked at me demurely. "There's no need to be like that Julian. I am well aware of your opinions of the priest. Saul was furious over your article."

"Good," I replied.

"Excuse me," said Bethany, putting her hand on her chest and coughing. She took another sip of her drink. "Give me a second - that's better." She raised her green eyes at me and gave me that frank, disarming look of hers. "This is very difficult for me," she said.

I lit a cigarette and waited for her to muster her thoughts. "It concerns Karen," she began.

How Bethany described events, it seems that the following had occurred: Shortly after my visit, which took place over ten months ago, Karen's memory had begun to return. At first small things came back to her, which she choose to remain circumspect about, but after more and more of her memory came back it became increasingly difficult to disguise the fact from those around her, particularly Rachine, who knew Karen, probably better than Karen knew herself. So it didn't take long for her to pick up on the subtle changes in Karen's nature. It seemed that when her memory had come back fully, so too did the old Karen - at least in terms of her brave and obstinate self. When it became clear to the priest and Rachine that they were not going to be able exert their will over her, in other words reduce her to the shadowy creature of her former self, they decided to imprison her in her room. Only the sound of Karen's whimpers and moans, bore any testimony to the acts they perpetrated upon her, every day for several weeks, in the name of - 'true love'. Her nightmare captivity came to an interlude, when Karen managed to make her escape through a window and down a drainpipe. Even though she was in a very weak condition, from having to endure on a daily basis the perversion that was the priest's - 'love', as well as being virtually starved, she was still able to elude her captors for several days; eventually though they found her, several miles away, half way up Ben Nevis. After her attempted escape failed, her captors were determined she should not get away again. Her new prison was to be the church tower; situated about half a mile from the vicarage: most of the building was in a dilapidated state apart from the tower itself.

"I managed to get in through a concealed entrance in the corner of the vestry," explained Bethany. "They kept her chained up there, like a wild animal. God knows what those two had been doing to her? Apart from some filthy old blanket that she hugged to herself, she was naked - her body covered in bruises. It was terrible Julian, and so thin: they could have hardly been feeding her! There were no windows in that place either, it must have been freezing at night, it is a wonder she didn't die of hypothermia." Bethany suddenly stopped, and put her hand to her mouth.

"She is dead though, isn't she?" I said.

Her green eyes filled with tears. "I did what I could, honestly I did..."

Strangely I felt no emotion, instead I felt sorry for Bethany. I touched her hand. "It's all right," I said, "I'm sure you did! How - did it happen?"

Bethany took a large gulp of beer and tried to compose herself, before going on: "I told you they had her chained to the iron bars in the window, not knowing how to get hold of the key to the padlock, I managed to get a hacksaw blade from the workshop; the chain was really thick and it wasn't long before the blade snapped but Karen worked on it as best she could. Each time I went to the tower I brought Karen parcels of food and then worked away at the chain myself. I came one morning, I was squatting down, feverishly hacking away, we were nearly through, when Karen suddenly looked up and stared open mouthed. I looked round to see Rachine looming over me. She grabbed hold of my hair and pulled me up. She was crazy, like something evil..." Bethany shook her head. "I've never seen anyone look like that...so...so crazed - so mad, her eyes Julian! - they were bulging out of her head, I can still see them: black, the whites blood red...She called me a treacherous little rat and threw me up against the wall threatening to kill me. There was nothing I could do, she was too much for me, and I'm quite strong."

"So I've head," I said, aware of her sturdy little figure.

"Well I am," said Bethany, smiling in that impish way of hers. "Anyway," she resumed, with a heavy sigh: "she went on hitting me about the face - not being very steady on my feet - well anyway, I went down. I suppose you know what happened before - what Garcia had done to me? Well, although Rachine had not been a part of it then, she definitely made up for it this time round. I could hear Karen yanking at the chain and screaming for her to stop. I remember thinking, 'I had been lucky the last time: yeah, they smashed up my hip, one girl in particular, I can't remember her name got well stuck in, like Rachine, with those big boots of hers. I'm pretty tough you know but I knew that if she didn't let up soon I was done for. I don't know what happened - exactly, I lost consciousness at some point. When I came to I was on an intensive care ward." Bethany paused a moment and looked at me, as if trying to gauge my feelings. "I was *very badly hurt* you know!" She put her hand to her face, and I reached and touched her arm and she let her hand fall into mine.

"I'm glad you are here," I said

She smiled faintly, before resuming, in a matter-of-fact way: "I suppose Karen must have got free. Without her I wouldn't be here. She saved my life Julian!"

Bethany took a sip of her beer. "From what I can gather, there was a struggle: the balustrade gave way and they were found at the foot of the spiral staircase. Rachine was dead - the hacksaw blade was stuck in her chest.

"And Karen?"

"Well I haven't told you the full story. You see she was heavily pregnant at the time. She died giving birth. There were complications - what with the fall and everything."

"She had a child?"

Bethany laughed. I must have looked like I had seen a ghost or something.

"Yes, yes a little girl. Would you like to see her? I left her with a friend, its not far."

"Yes - yes I would." I lit a cigarette. My face darkened.

"What's the matter?"

"I suppose it's his - the priest's?"

Solemn faced: "I'm afraid so."

"What happened to him?"

"He went mad. I only heard about it later. He went up into the church tower and hung himself. I guess he couldn't get over the fact that both of them were dead.

He was very fond of Rachine. Together they treated Natasha, or Karen, I should say, like she was their little girl, but when her memory came back it was a different story. She became a threat to them. I had no idea Karen could be so forceful. I used to think she was simple or something - I thought..."

"You thought what?"

"Well, when you said you loved her, I suppose I just took it as pity, but I can see *now* why you would love her, and it couldn't be out of pity."

"No, she was a very special person. Those two took advantaged of her confused state of mind. Bastards! I'm glad they're dead. I hope they died horribly, for what they did to her, and that there is no resurrection for *him* again."

"No he did it properly this time."

"When did all this happen?"

"Well, let's just say the priest as been in the ground for just over two months."

"And Karen?"

"Yes I'm sorry I was in hospital at the time, otherwise I would have let you know. She was cremated."

I touched Bethany's arm. "I'm sorry. Were you badly hurt?"

"It was bad enough, I must have a hard head or something. They still had to operate." Bethany touched her side, and looked down, as if still in some pain.

"What did they do?" I said, my morbid curiosity spiked.

"Id rather not talk about it if you don't mind," said Bethany.

"I'm sorry - of course. That bitch! At least Karen got her in the end."

"Yes, in the end," joined Bethany, as if to infer that in some sense she was just too late. I guess she must have read something of that in my face. Jollying things along in a way that was unique to Bethany when things got too maudlin: "Don't think about it. Look - come on, lets go and see little Karen," she said, "I left her with a friend its not far.

We finished our drinks and hoped a tube train the few stops to Camden. Bethany's friend lived on a narrow boat moored not far from Camden Lock. I was not at all impressed him. He was the lean, shaven head, bonehead type, that one sees so many of on the streets of English towns. Usually wearing their Union Jack T-shirts, a can of beer in one hand and a *spliff* in the other. Thankfully there was no sign of the *sliff*, but it didn't make me feel any better. I liked even less the prospect of little Karen being brought up around such a species as him.

Bethany went into the fore compartment of the squat little vessel and brought out the 'little bundle'.

"I hope she hasn't been any trouble?" said Bethany, to the bonehead.

"Nar - not a peep," he replied, in one of those queer English dialects.

"So that's little Karen!" I said, automaticaly.

"Yes - well we weren't sure about what to call her. But Karen seems right?"

"She's very sweet," I said.

"Yes she's very good, isn't she John?"

"Yeah, good as gold, good as gold she is - a right little booty and no mistake."

"It was touch and go for a time - you know, when they brought Karen into the hospital. Of course there was nothing they could do for *her*. The fall you see," explained Bethany, "but they managed to save this little one."

I nodded solemnly.

"Do you want to hold her? Here, its quite easy, don't be afraid, you want drop her."

Bethany transferred the, 'little Karen' to my arms. I looked at her screwed up little face and wondered what she was thinking - if anything. It felt quite a dense little weight. Here she was, the offspring of Karen. I was as close as I would ever get to *Karen* - my Karen."

"I suppose it *is* the priest's?" I said, handing her back to Bethany, with a touch of distaste. She nodded, as she settled her down in her cot.

"In't amaze'n the things they can do these days! - er merther wus cl'se t'dith they say, when they brought er in. Bled t'death she did!" said John.

"Yes all right John! - Julian and Karen's mother were very close - well you were sort of married to her weren't you?"

"Yes."

"Sorry mate! Eer, grab ya'self a beer - if you want?"

I didn't want. I looked at Bethany and John, and sensed that they had been, or were, still lovers. And then I recalled the words of Rachine: 'she ran off back to England, back to the bonehead boyfriend. Well leave them to it,' I thought.

When Bethany came back I told her I had to be going. The conditions on the narrow boat were making me feel claustrophobic in any case. She eyed me suspiciously. "Well all right, if you must. Before you go there is something else." Bethany went back into the compartment and returned with a small blue envelope, that smelt faintly of Jasmine.

"It's a letter, " she explained, handing it to me, "It was written by Karen when her memory had come back to her. She was very adamant that you should get this. Somehow she knew she wasn't going to see you again."

I stuffed the letter in my pocket. Suddenly it all got too much. I was afraid I was going to burst into tears, or scream, or something. The only thing that prevented me from making a fool of myself was the presence of another man.

"I must go, I'm sorry," I said, heading to the gangplank. It felt good to be in the London air. Bethany followed me, running to catch up. She put her hand on my shoulder. "Hey! Stop a minute."

I turned away, ashamed of my emotions.

"Karen...my Karen, is dead," I balled.

I felt Bethany's warmth. I didn't want her to see me in a state. I tried to pull myself together, it wasn't fair on her. "I'm sorry," I said.

"Don't be. It's perfectly understandable. I'm sorry about what John said. He doesn't think..."

I went over to a wall and turned my face toward it, hiding my shame from Bethany. Out of frustration and an effort to regain my composure I kicked my foot against it a few times. It was a forlorn, if not pathetic gesture.

"Are you *sure* you'll be all right?"

I nodded, unable to speak. I felt her hand on my shoulder.

"You're not. Come back a while."

The thought of seeing her bonehead boyfriend again brought me to my senses.

"I'll be all right," I said, wiping my face roughly in the manner Karen used to do: so proud, so unremitting. I turned to face her. There was a genuine look of concern on her face, her keen green eyes fully encompassed my despair.

"Look, come back tomorrow. Perhaps the three of us can go for a walk along the lock?"

"The three of us?" I said, in incredulity.

"I mean - just you me and Karen." Bethany looked towards the long boat. "Oh John! He's just an old friend, I don't live with him or anything..." Bethany paused a moment. "There are things we need to discuss, little Karen's future..."

Bethany leaned forward and kissed the side of my face. "Don't be sad. Karen told me to tell you that - she spoke a lot about you. In the last month we grew very close." Bethany took my hand, "I only wish I could have done more. But she knew - she knew."

"There was nothing anybody could do," I replied. "It was destiny."

We wandered a little way along the towpath. I looked into the inky blackness of the Thames. "I suppose Garcia would say I failed?" I said, after a long silence.

I felt Bethany's hand tighten on mine. She would never know how welcome her presence was. How reassuring and warm it was, without it the Thames would have had me.

"You didn't fail," she said.

XXV

I got back to my apartment, and sat alone for some moments, just looking at Karen's letter. I picked it up handling it delicately, and careful opened it with my paperknife. Waves of emotion went over me, as I realised that the last time these words on this paper had been seen, Karen had still been alive.

Well my Darling! If you are reading these words it is most likely that I am no more. That is my body is no more. I know you will be upset and it will take you some time to get to the end of this little good-bye.

You will see that it is not really good-bye. I am in the family way. I carry new life in me. I expect Bethany has even shown this life to you by now. I entrusted Bethany with my offspring if I should die in childbirth, which is what I think will happen. I am in a lot of pain these days, but I am afraid the doctors will try to terminate my pregnancy. If I don't die giving birth, then those evil ones will get me. But it doesn't matter how I suffer, because I know now that it is only my body that suffers. The life that is in me, and which grows stronger as each day goes by, is the certainty of my own resurrection. Yes, that's right Julian. Resurrection! but a real resurrection, not the maniacal fantasies of the priest.

I trust Bethany with my life. That is why she has custody of me. You've seen me. I am only little, so I will need a lot of looking after. Bethany will make a good mother. And you, my dear, you will make a good father. I know you don't think much of yourself right now, but you are the strongest of us all. You kept on loving me, even when there seemed no hope, and when I was horrible to be with. You never left me. Oh Julian - we came so close to being truly happy. You know I always did love you. and always will. Be sure that I will come back to you. I promise that nothing will break us apart. You are my soul mate. You see I didn't forget.

Now about Bethany and you. She is a good person. I know you will like her. She will love you and take care of you in my absence. She is very sexy, don't you think? Well I know you always had a thing for her - well her statue anyway. Now you've seen her in the flesh, I wonder if you still feel the same? It's always strange when a dream becomes reality! In time you will come to love Bethany I am sure - that is as it should be. And you know I should like some company while I am growing up, so don't feel you can't on my account. I'm not the jealous type.

You know Julian you found the real me. We got my demon on the run. I was never happier than when I was sailing with you on the Aegean. I often think of the Hydra. I miss her, it seems like another life, especially here in this cold house in this cold country. But don't think of me like that, remember me as your own salty sea-lass. That was the real me, not Natasha the model, or Karen the incarnation of Tanit.

One day, perhaps when we are both free of our bodies we can join up with the One, which is the fountainhead of all love in the universe.

Now don't be sad Julian. I am not gone. My soul lives on in the child I gave birth to. You must believe it Julian. Look out for proof in the days to come.

My special eternal love to you Julian.

Your sweet Karen.

Ps, To Bethany.

Well my friend, it has happened just as said it would. Please do not feel obliged to follow my instructions. Taking care of a baby is a big undertaking for any one. I hope you get in contact with Julian. He is a good man, he underestimates himself. Likewise, there is no obligation upon either of you, it is just my wish and my hope that the two people I trust and love the most should be the ones to take care of me. My destiny will not be assured otherwise, but all is left to fate in the end. It is your choice in the end, both of you.

I know you will look after me. Good luck to both of you.

All my love, your Karen.

I met Bethany the following day as we had arranged. Until I had read Karen's letter I couldn't see what there was to discuss. As much as I disliked her friend, I had no intention of competing with him over the affections of, 'little Karen'. It was obvious to me that Bethany and John were on some level involved with one another. 'Let it be then,' I thought, 'let them get on with it!' It had not crossed my mind that I should play any part in bringing up Karen's child. Perhaps you might find this hard to believe, given my passionate love for Karen, but you must also bear in mind just how warn out I was by the whole thing. I longed only for the simple life. The idea of getting involved with anybody in a romantic way was not something I wanted, or more specifically, something that I felt I was even capable of. Yes, I was happy to accept Bethany's compassion. Anybody's compassion is better than non, and yes I found her physically attractive, but beyond that I had not considered anything like the intentions that Karen had set forth in her letter. Since Karen had included her, and they had been close friends towards the end, I felt I must follow Karen's wishes, at least in sharing with her the contents of her letter.

We walked along the towpath, from the lock, up to Kentish Town. Little Karen was snug in her pushchair. Bethany had brought some dried bread for the ducks so we sat a while watching them feed. Bethany as usual was good with the small talk, which helped a lot. She handed me some bread and we laughed at the way the coots scooted across the water after it. When it had all gone we sat a while encapsulated in our own silence. I handed Bethany the letter and said she should read it. The whole thing about reincarnation had raised its peculiar head again. I didn't know what she would make of it. Most people, I imagine, would think it the writings of a mad person, or a person who had a romantic idea that they could live on as another person. Such notions are not unheard of, but to consciously migrate ones soul from the body of the parent to that of its offspring - this was something else again!

Bethany read the letter, and then reread it. She peered in to the pushchair and waved at Karen. "Hello there, I've read your letter," she said, grinning. Little Karen giggled and gurgled kicking out excitedly. We both had a good old laugh at that.

"Well I don't what to say!" said Bethany, wiping her eyes.

"I know, it's not the sort of thing you hear about everyday."

Bethany turned to me, her deep green eyes serious. "Do *you* believe it?"

"I believe anything is possible. Karen certainly did. Garcia did, I know you hate him. I know the priest believed in reincarnation too."

"But do you?"

"Yes - I suppose I do - or rather, I want to believe it's possible. I've read everything I could find on the subject. There are a lot of interesting cases of people remembering their past lives."

Bethany looked back at little Karen, and pointed: "but her! Is that Karen? Is it possible?"

"I guess if you believe in reincarnation - that is, that the soul lives on after death and returns to earth again in another body...then yes, it's possible, that that little baby girl - *is* Karen! The Karen we knew!"

"I don't know what to think! It's not something I've thought a great deal about. I know when I was in Italy, Garcia wanted me to believe that I had been his lover in another life. I just thought he was some dirty old man trying it on, but after a while, I could see he really did believe I was this person he knew in another life."

"I know you have Christian beliefs?" I put in.

"It's not just that. You can believe what you like, and still be a Christian."

"Yes, that's quite handy."

"Its all right. I know what you think about religion, I read your article remember."

I smiled. "Oh that."

"Yes that! It was a very viscous attack. OK, Saul may have been mad, but not all priests are like that."

"I know. It was personal. I had had all I could take of religion, or rather, religious fanaticism - Garcia was no better," I said. "It's just I think human beings should stand up for their own self, their own, *humanity*, which they love to go on about so much. People use religion like a kind of crutch to lean on. It's about time mankind stood up straight, by himself."

Bethany mused a moment over my words. "It's an interesting point, but are we ready? is mankind ready?"

"He never will know unless he tries."

"Interesting." Bethany looked at me again with serious eyes. "You think an awful lot about stuff, don't you?" Bethany turned back to the, 'little one'. "Now I think about it, she does have a curious way of looking at you."

"She does, doesn't she," I said, peering at the little person lying there. "Almost like she knows something that we don't?"

We both looked at each other. "Don't!" said Bethany, sitting back. "It's weird! Sort of creepy!"

"She's just a little baby."

"She is cute. The thing is what are we going to do about her?"

"Well, look at it this way, she either is Karen, or just, 'little Karen', for the moment the question of reincarnation is neither here nor there. She is a little baby who needs caring for, just as she said in the letter."

"Oh yes, 'I'm only little'..." Bethany laughed, nervously.

"Look! - you don't have to do any of the other stuff she said, you know..."

Bethany gave me the look again. "Yes....Indeed."

"Why don't you and John take care of her?"

Bethany seemed exasperated; sighing heavily: "I told you, we are not together - like that."

"But you were?"

"Once, but not anymore."

We turned away from one another, falling under an unknown spell.

"We don't have to decide on anything now," said Bethany.

"No," I replied, still under the spell and feeling somewhat removed from her.

"If you really don't want anything to do with bringing up Karen, or even if you don't want t see me again - you know it's fine. Just say?"

Bethany's words ruptured my silence. "But I do! I do want to see you again."

"I'm not phased by what she said - about bringing up little Karen," said Bethany.

"You're not?"

"No..." Bethany smiled, shaking her head, "not by any of it."

I knew then that I wanted them to both remain a part of my life, and that I wanted to see Bethany again. During the weeks to follow we saw each other nearly every day. We would take little Karen with us, trundling her along in her pushchair, along the towpath and into Camden Town. Sometimes we would go up to Kentish Town and feed the pigeons in Belsize Park. From there it was only a short walk to Hampstead Heath. Despite her limp it was I who had to keep up with her: Bethany bounced along like a little terrier, except one day I noticed it was more pronounced than usual.

"Are you all right Bethany?"

"Yes - fine thanks," she replied, with a distinct note of irritation. There followed a short but heavy silence.

"I'm sorry," she said, slowing up. She went over to a bench and sat down. "I didn't mean to snap. You mean my leg don't you?"

"Well - yes, you seem to be limping a bit more than usual," I said, sitting down next to her.

Bethany stretched out her bad leg and began to rub her thigh. "Yes I know, some days it's worse than others. I should explain..." Bethany looked at me somewhat pityingly. "Poor Julian. I'm damaged goods I'm afraid. Garcia's mob mussed me up pretty good. Apart from other stuff, I had a fractured pelvis. I was out of it for two whole weeks. The main problem is the nerve damage," she continued, matter-of-factly. "I'm afraid the pasting I got from Rachine has made it worse. There are days when I just can't move it at all."

"I'm sorry..." I said, feeling at a loss as to what to do, whilst thinking of Karen, and the months she had been in a coma.

"Don't be sorry, I don't want yours - or anybody's pity. I'm only telling you how things are because you have a right to know, and so you don't have to ask about it again."

"I understand. You said you woke up in hospital?"

"Yes, that's right." Bethany appeared uncomfortable. She looked down and put her arm across her stomach. There was a pained look in her eyes. I felt tears were not far off, but this lady was far too proud to show any signs of weakness. She raised her head and gave me that open disarming look of hers.

"They opened me up - to investigate!" She looked away and rubbed her face. I touched her arm and she shrugged it off.

"Don't! - don't do that," she admonished.

"What is it?"

"I'm no good to anyone..." She sighed heavily "Oh Julian! don't you see, I may not be able to have children. There! - now you know. And don't look at me like that." She made a whining sound: "aww! - shit!" Bethany stood up and stamped her foot.

"Damn her - fucking Rachine...all of them. *Garcia!*"

I took her hand and she allowed herself to be guided back to her seat. She sat a moment, her head in her hands. "I'm sorry Julian. I hate getting emotional..." She sighed and took a deep breath. "It's my uterus. Hah! you should see me, I have been opened up, prodded, pulled around so much I look like a road under repair down there." Moving her hand down: "It's doesn't look very nice."

"I don't care."

"hah! - you say that! - you haven't seen me! Anyway I'm no good to a man. As a woman I'm all but finished."

I grabbed her arm, this sort of talk didn't suit her. I guess it reminded me of too much of Karen: her brave wallowing in despair.

"You don't know that for sure."

"They said I may have to have a complete hysterectomy. It could be too risky for me to have a child. There's a lot of other stuff wrong down there too. Like I say, I'm damaged goods Julian. Too bad hey!"

There was a silence. My burgeoning desire had been thwarted. Her phrase: 'damaged goods' repeated through my head. My own stomach grew tight, just as it had when Rachine had told me about Bethany's beating at the hands of Garcia's women. I had felt the same way then. Even though I had not met her then, for some reason it effected me deeply - I wished they had not gone too far, but according to Rachine Bethany had suffered internal injuries and was sure she would never be able to have kids. They, together with Rachine, had finally succeeded in inflicting the worst kind of injury a woman can receive. It was true, her pretty face had healed, but it was the damage that nobody could see, that was the more painful to bear.

There followed an awkward silence. After a time Bethany stood up and stretched. "Come on Julian, lets move on towards the heath."

"You know, there are all kinds of things medical science can do these days," I said catching her up. "You know, there are test-tube babies - surrogates..."

Bethany smiled at me sympathetically. "It's sweet of you Julian; I know you mean well, but it's not just about getting pregnant and having kids. If they take away what's left I won't be a whole woman anymore. It's a female thing - it's like castration for a man. You understand that, don't you?"

I nodded. "Well I guess you can understand what I mean," Bethany continued, "I've already been partially castrated so to speak, and now I may loose what is left - if it hadn't been for Rachine....Still there is no point worry now." Bethany fell silent for a few steps as we carried on up the hill towards Hampstead Heath. It wasn't long before she resumed her usual small talk again, as if all that she had said earlier was: 'by-the-by!'

Her frank disclosure of her personal injuries and the related fears that they held for her, had brought a new kind of intimacy to our relationship, an intimacy I was keen to deepen. And so, being close to where I lived I invited her over to my apartment for a meal. By the time we had finished eating, and had a few glasses of wine, it was getting late, so I asked her to stay the night. Judging by her response, I got the impression that it was what she had been wanting all along. I made a bed up for her in the spare room. It was strange having someone in my apartment. I had got used to living alone. For whatever reason I couldn't sleep, and neither could Bethany, even though Karen, as always was, 'as good as gold.'

I poured myself out a brandy and sat down by the fire. Bethany came through. She feigned surprise and apologised. I looked round, she was wearing just her blouse and knickers.

"Come and join me," I said.

"Are you sure I'm not disturbing you? It's just I couldn't sleep."

"I know, neither could I," I replied. "Sit down, I'll get you a drink. Is bandy OK?"

"Yes, it might help me sleep."

"How is Karen?"

"Dead to the world," replied Bethany, then she put her hand in front of her mouth. "Oh - what a thing to say?"

"But perhaps she's not," I replied, handing her her drink.

"No!.. " Bethany exclaimed. "Don't!"

"I thought you said you weren't phased by the idea?"

"I'm not. It just takes a bit of getting used to. We don't even know if it's true."

Bethany sipped her brandy and stared into the fire. There was a heavy silence. I looked over at her. Bethany crossed her legs. She had strong well shaped thighs like Karen, and like Karen, she was unashamed. There was something of the exhibitionist and the flirt about her. I knocked back my brandy and got myself another.

"You don't mind me staying do you?" asked Bethany.

"No, not at all," I replied.

"It's just you seem - well, agitated."

"Do I?..." I laughed nervously.

"What do you think we should do?....about Karen, I mean?"

"You mean, about bringing her up?"

"Yes," replied Bethany, a little breathlessly.

There was a long pause. "I mean, I wouldn't mind...."

"You mean us?" I ventured. Bethany just levelled me with her green gaze.

"I understand if you don't like me," she said, uncrossing her legs.

I could no longer resist. I put my drink down and knelt at her feet. She put out her arms and pulled my head against her chest. My hands rested on her knees. I moved them up her thighs.

"You don' know how long I have been wanting to touch you like this," I said.

"I've been wanting you to."

I kissed her mouth. Her neck. Her breasts were small but they felt good. With some trepidation I began to slowly undo her blouse, remembering her phrase: 'like a road under repair down there'. Bethany breathed in sharply, and turned her head to one side. I touched her face, and she looked round at me, her green eyes were without shame. I could tell she was at ease with her body, when she breathed in again I knew she was proud too - despite her lack of perfection.

"You're not put off?"

I kissed her mouth.

"You can do what you want, you won't hurt me."

She breathed in again making herself thin, and thrust her hips up. I sensed an eagerness in her to get the job done. We moved to the floor in front of the fire, and she lay back and spread her legs. She looked at me bemused. "You know if you want me, you'll have to take me."

I was momentarily frozen, captivated by her beauty. I had not to think too much of this - better to not think at all! So, I just roughly pulled down her knickers whilst staring at that amazing face. Her eyes grew wide, expectant, there was eagerness too. I was struggling to get myself free when Karen began to cry in the other room, which was unusual: she hardly ever cried.

Bethany turned her head to one side and began to laugh.

"It's no good," said Bethany, sitting forward arranging her underwear and buttoning up her blouse. "I'll have to go to her." She touched my cheek and kissed me, "poor Julian..." she looked down and raised her eyebrows.

When we looked in on her, she quietened almost straight away.

"Little terror. She's stopped!" said Bethany.

"She's even smiling, look."

Karen giggled and gurgled, and struck out with her little limbs.

Bethany looked astounded. "You don't think!...No!..."

"She said she wasn't the jealous type," I said.

I put my arm about Bethany and kissed her neck. Karen giggled again, making funny gurgling noises. "Look! - look!" cried Bethany, in astonishment. "She just winked at me."

"You're seeing things."

"No! - honestly, I swear!.."

"Come on, she seems fine, come back to bed with me," I said.

I took her hand and began to lead her to my room, all the time Bethany looking over her shoulder: "honestly Julian, she winked! she winked at me!"

I laughed. "Well at least we have her blessing."

"I'm not sure we should," she said, sitting down on the edge of the bed.

"What! - just because Karen made a noise, and you thought she winked at you?"

"No, not just that. You've seen what I'm like. I'm not a good person. I think before we go any further I should tell you about how it was with the priest. When I tell of the things he did - the things *I* did, you may not want to know me any more?"

"You don't have to. I understand," I said, trying to take her hand.

"No, don't! Please, let me speak."

And so I let her unburden herself of the horrors that took place under the name of what the priest called: 'true love'. How both the priest and Rachine used people to live out their sordid sexual fantasies. How they dominated through fear and sex. Like Rachine, the priest was a man who was used to getting what he wanted. A man who was admired by women for what god had bestowed upon him: his phallic potency, by all accounts, was staggering!

"I allowed Saul to seduce me," admitted Bethany.

"It wasn't your fault."

"But it was. I should have resisted him. He said he wanted to see me naked. That beauty like mine should not be hidden away. So, vainly, I did what he wanted. He made me kneel down and pray, and then...Oh how could I let him do those things to me, and in a church - of all places!"

"It wasn't your fault," I insisted.

"But it was! don't you see? I liked it. I liked what they did. I'm a wicked person, a terrible wicked person, Julian."

"There was nothing you could do, you were under his power."

"And Rachine? I gave myself up to her too. Oh god!" Bethany hit her head with her fist. "Stupid! I'm so stupid. How could I let her - when I detested her? She was the worst. Her conceit. I hated her," said Bethany, clenching her fists.

She was about to hit herself again when I restrained her. I had to admit I was a little surprised by this last confession. She didn't strike me as the kind of girl to submit herself sexually to another female. Perhaps she was just playing at being perverse. Perhaps she got off on it. Worse, perhaps Karen had told her a few things: that I got off on it?

"Its all right," I said holding her. I was getting frustrated. I wanted to push her down onto the bed. She was good at building up sexual tension, that's for sure! I was beginning to wonder how much more of this I could take when she looked at me coyly:

"What is it about men like the priest who can get women to do what they want?" reflected Bethany.

"I don't know," I said, thinking the same thing.

"I know you think I'm bad, but I Just couldn't help myself. I wasn't the only one. He had a strange magnetism."

"Perhaps it's some primitive thing that still exists in human beings, some animal thing: the urge to procreate? Survival of the species is a strong urge, perhaps even the strongest force in us, and the priest was the alpha male?"
"That doesn't say much for the human race - particularly women!"
"You're forgetting Rachine. As you may know, I too was under her control for a while: the alpha female."
"When she wasn't on the scene I was his favourite. I allowed the priest to do as he please with me." Bethany flashed her green eyes at me sugestively. She was too much!
"Wait!" she said, parrying my advances. "You are a better person than that. You broke free of Rachine."
"Only because Karen's love was stronger."
"She was an alpha female too?..."
"So are you."
"No, I don't think so," she said, but it was obvious to me that she was just fishing for further confirmation of her status. "It's not right..." mussed Bethany, "guys like you, good guys like you, just get pushed aside. I'm serious! You have a lot to give." Bethany looked up to me with her big green eyes, like some adoring cat. "I can't understand Karen, if I were her I'd never let you go. I'd certainly never forget a man like you."
I had a good old laugh at that.
"I'm serious," responded Bethany, "You have so much to give." Bethany moved her hands, "So very very much...."
"Come on, I'm nothing like the priest; from what I gather he was like Garcia - 'a big man!' "
"I wasn't thinking like that - but you're right, you're not like him, I doubt there are many who are - certainly not Garcia. Why do you think he's better than you?" She flopped down on the bed and stared up at me. "Are you going to let a silly thing like male pride get in your way. I don't need a man like the priest or Garcia - you'll see, if you let me! I'm here offering myself to you aren't I? What more proof do you need that you are as good, if not better than them?"
I lay over her propping myself up, my arms either side of her. She lifted up her blouse and breathed in sharply - sucking her belly in. She wasn't particularly fat

neither did she posses the muscle tone of a Natasha or a pamela Lloyd. What was obvious was that she wanted me to admire her; she thought her body good, that's for sure! Her eyes seemed to challenge me - audacious, in what they implied.

"Unless, it's that you don't want me? I can understand, especially after all I've said?"

I kissed her columnar neck. "I want you. I've always wanted you, from the very first, ever since I saw the statue of you on Garcia's island - perhaps even before then!"

She looked up at me, her eyes wide, showing her vulnerability. "I don't deserve a man like you."

"I'm not that good," I said, having a good old laugh.

"You are," she said, "you have no idea." I felt her hand like a feather glide over me.

I feverishly opened the rest of her blouse. Her broad ribcage swelled and decreased rapidly. She looked down opening her legs wide apart. Showing me the 'site of the investigation'. I saw the gynaecologist's gloved hand, the shiny surgical instruments: the laparoscope, speculum, dilators, forceps, and clamps that were employed to prod and prize apart her vagina: the insertion of the implements of their trade, the shiny surgical steel, the pneumatic drill, picks and shovels of the road gang. Then there were the scars of the invasive surgery across her abdomen, where they sliced and chopped bits of her away like so much liver on a butchers slab.

Something of this ran through my head at the time, enough anyway for me to check my stride, long enough for the sensitivity of the female to be alerted.

She laughed. She was similar to Karen in that she displayed distinct mawkish tendencies: a predilection to wallow in her own self-abasement. "Don't look like that Julian, I know what you're thinking - I know what it looks like, at least you can see I'm a real woman, not like some of these little girls. It still works, I'm still a woman, I still get aroused."

"There's no doubting that Bethany."

Bethany smiled coyly. "Oh Julian!"

~~"You're not put off by~~ it?"

"No, I'm not put off," I said, wishing I had the priests formidable phallic power.

"Do it then! - Take me Julian."

I looked at that beautiful face staring up at me, and nothing else mattered but to give her the pleasure and admiration she so ardently sought. Fortunately the gynaecological activity had in no way compromised the peristaltic effect of her smooth visceral muscles.

"Do it hard! - hard! Harder! - harder! - harder!" she called out, while all the time, squeezing and squeezing with her thighs.

Displays of tender affection were not a pre-eminent feature of Bethany's lovemaking; her foreplay was in the form of coquettish overtures, and coy looks, and subtly dropped in phrases of a suggestive nature, that got one quickly wound up like a taught spring, that when the signal was given, was released in the most direct way. Such an approach lead her into a very passive, submissive role, and the man into the dominant active position. At first I wasn't sure whether I could play that role, but she was good, in so far as she told you what to do every step of the way.

Apparently it wasn't easy for her to *climax*. It had no reflection on my abilities - she assured me. She was going to be hard work, for some reason it was always just out of reach, and then somewhere near dawn, after the fifth or sixth time of trying, her body stiffened and she let out a little whimper, and threw her hands over her head in a display of complete abandon. She put her head to one side and sighed a sigh of contentment.

"Did you come that time?" I asked, hopefully.

Bethany looked at me, and put her hand to her mouth and giggled like a naughty girl, she nodded and looked away.

I lay down next to her and in seconds I plunged into a deep coma-like sleep that I did not come out of until late morning.

As we got to know one another better I came to see that her whole idea of sex was tainted by her Christian beliefs: that is, that it was something a bit naughty, yet she couldn't help liking it. She saw it as a necessary evil, something that had to be done, got out of the way, like the ironing or the washing up. To this end she was fairly unimaginative: very orthodox in her technique. I came to realise that all her talk about letting the priest do what he liked with her, was probably just fiction: part of her foreplay. The idea that she would allow another girl to take advantage of her, seemed on the surface equally unlikely: that is until you consider just how dominant Rachine could be in bed. I don't doubt the priest did give it to her plenty of times the way she liked it: hard! She seemed too conventional to indulge in anything of a carnal concern with Rachine. It is possible she had allowed Rachine to: 'touch her up a bit,' but I doubt it was anything more than that. She was hardly the wild tempestuous creature: the sex goddess type, in the way Karen or Rachine were! The seed of the idea though was all that Bethany needed to plant, the imagination did the rest.

It wasn't long before Bethany had moved in with me permanently - and it was just as Karen had predicted: I fell in love with her. I was happy! - perhaps not as madly in love as I had been with Karen, but at least our lives were stable. Bethany didn't have that tempestuous side to her nature. Although her physical demands were equally enduring, due in large part to the elusive quality of her orgasm. In other ways she was like Karen, in that she was very proud of her physicality, although Bethany's figure was not as svelte as Karen's, in fact you wouldn't say she was model material at all really, except for her beautiful face. She kept a very strict regime of exercises, and worked out with heavy weights, so that her upper body, her shoulders and arms in particular, had very good muscle definition - perhaps she was even more robust than Karen in this respect.

I would ask her to flex her muscles; I loved to feel how firm her biceps were. When it came to arm reselling, which she loved to practice on me, she nearly always won. She hated it if she lost.

"You let me win didn't you?"

"I promise I didn't," I said, laughing at how angry she got.

"Come on, lets do it again," she would insist, putting her arm up. "This time really try hard."

I would put all my strength to the match, and eventually I would beat her. She would be equally annoyed in defeat.

"No, you can't..." she moaned, as her hand went down. Breathless: "But I am strong, aren't I?" She rolled up her sleeve.

"Let me feel."

She flexed her biceps for me. The muscle was large and solid.

"You're fantastic," I told her.

She looked at me coyly, knowing how it got me. She planted her elbow down, "Come on - let's do it again."

Eventually her stamina would win out and she would beat me every time. This kind of game was nearly always a preamble to yet more physical activity. Sex was always spontaneous, and just as competitive, with no room for tenderness.

It was Bethany who first brought up the issue of what to do with Karen's ashes. Seeing every day, the lapis-lazuli urn sitting on the mantelpiece, must have got to her a bit. For my part I didn't think anything of it, it was good to have both women I loved around me - in one form or another. Perhaps the truth was, that I found it hard to part with the last remnants of Karen's body, even if they were in a highly desiccated state.

"I didn't know it bothered you?" I said.

"It doesn't bother me exactly, it's your house - your wife's ashes after all," said Bethany, looking up at the mantelpiece.

"I'll move them then, into the back room."

"No don't do that - she'll still be here. I suppose I'm just a bit jealous."

"Jealous! - of Karen? she just ashes..."

"I know that! I suppose what I mean is you're still in love with her memory. You haven't really moved on."

This made me think. She was right of course; I had to make a break with the past, so a few days later I told her that I had arranged some time off from the magazine, and that the three of us, as well as Karen's ashes, would stay at the apartment in Paris for a few days. It would give me the opportunity of catching up with Mersell who was currently staying there. It would be good to see him again: the last tangible link with Karen's Tanit days. I usually received a letter from him once every two or three months letting me know how things were with him and the clinic. On a couple of occasions he had been staying at the apartment in Paris, when on business, and had invited me over, but I had declined his offer. I had decided to make a clean break of things after arriving in England: then, I had felt Karen was lost to me forever. I no longer wanted anything to do with her old life or the people she knew, but all that, was before I had met Bethany. Bethany had made me strong again, enough at least, to return to Karen's country. I also felt I should give Mersell the opportunity of saying his final farewell to Karen also. Very occasionally I also received a letter from Garcia, well three in fact, in two years. One was a reply to my letter informing him of her death. I felt he also deserved to say his farewell, but there was no way I was going to upset Bethany's feelings. The sadistic old man would have to come to terms with her death on his own - which, owing to his belief in reincarnation, was probably not that difficult for him.

What I proposed then, was, after Paris, to travel down to Marseille, where the *Idhra* was currently moored, and then sail out to sea and scatter her ashes off the coast of Tunisia.

"I think it's a wonderful idea," said Bethany.

"Yes, it was the only time Karen felt at peace, when cruising the open sea. I guess she felt safe then, away from people. She so loved the sea!" Looking up at the urn: "my salty sea-lass!"

Bethany could see that I wasn't far off from tears. She came over and hugged me: a rear outburst of sentiment for a girl who didn't go in for big emotional displays.

"You are going to chuck the whole thing in, aren't you, the vase as well?"

"It's an urn. Yes, it will lay at the bottom of the sea, along with her ashes, and those of other Phoenicians who used to plough those seas."

"I thought she was American, like you?"

"She was American, Swedish, Scottish, French, South American, Egyptian, Phoenician, Etruscan...She was all kinds of people."

Bethany looked at me leeringly. "Yes all right then - if you say so!...I think it's romantic anyway, what you propose." Bethany looked up at me, her eyes imploring. "Would you do the same for me?"

"Of course I would."

"I'm not sure I want to be cremated."

"No, me neither. We'll be buried together."

"Julian!" Bethany hugged me tightly and kissed me. "You do care for me as much as her!"

"Of course I do." We began to kiss and of course it lead to the usual aggressive sex that she so loved. One could very rarely be affectionate with her without it equating to sex. It seemed at times that that was all she knew of love or tenderness: that the only proof of my love for her was when she arrived at her brief climactic pinnacle, that lasted but a few seconds. Laying back in a reflective pose:

"I must say, I'm looking forward to Paris. I've only been once on a school trip. They say its very romantic."

"Karen seemed to like it." I laughed. "Especially the Notre Dame cathedral."

"Will you take me there?"

"Yes, if you want."

"I was reading about her in an old magazine I found lying around the other day, Time Life, or something like that."

"Oh yes..."

"Yes, she was very beautiful. Not only that but quite a famous model by all accounts."

"She was."

"You never speak about her. Is it because it's too painful, or that you just don't want me to know about her?"

"What is this about Bethany?"

"I don't know." She paused, looking pensive: "I mean...are you sure you want me along? May be it's something you should do alone?"

"I thought you were looking forward to it?"

"I am, the Paris bit...I just wonder that's all..."

"Wonder what?" I said, beginning to feel exasperated.

"Well, look at me, I'm hardly like her - am I? She was glamorous Julian. She had such an amazing figure..."

"You have a great body Bethany."

"I know I'm not like her. You don't have to pretend."

"No, you're not like her, just like I'm not like the priest."

"Don't Julian!" She turned her face sharply away from me and put her hand over her head defensively, as if she were shielding herself from a blow.

"What is wrong with you?"

"You wouldn't understand. I don't even think you love me - else you would know how I feel."

"You either believe I love you or you don't. I can't make you believe me."

She looked round at me sharply, her gorgeous sea-green eyes were magnified by the tears they held. It shocked me to see her like this. To hear her speak like this. The ice queen was melting, and Karen was behind it.

"God you're a cold fish Julian!"

"Me! - cold? All you know of love is a fuck. At least Karen was hot passion..."

"Yeah that's right! You're still in love with her."

"Karen is dead! - dead! dead! dead!" I yelled.

At that moment little Karen began to scream in the other room; Bethany gave me a searching look. "Now look what you've done!" Bethany slipped on her blouse. "I'll go," she said, she turned at the door: "Have you considered the possibility she may not be dead."

"I didn't think you believed in that stuff?"

"It's just, she has never cried like this before."

"We've never argued like this before," I replied.

Suddenly Bethany broke down in floods of tears. It was horrible hearing her cry, I'd never head her before. She set up a horrible howling: deep wrenching sobs from the heart. She cried in the way people do who bottle things up inside for years on end. I went over to her and she collapsed in my arms. I sat her down on the edge of the bed. Between convulsions that wracked her stocky little torso she began to confide in me how she felt.

"I just..sometimes feel...like I'm over..overshadowed by her...That everything I...I do I'm...being...being compared all the time...with...with her!"

I tried to reassure Bethany as best I could that I loved her, but I could not deny, that in some way I would always keep part of my love for Karen. There was nothing I could do about that! It was up to Bethany to accept that.

Those who find it hard to unburden themselves, are quick to recover their composure

"Listen....she's gone quiet," said Bethany. Starting to rise: "I should go to her."

"No, wait a minute." I pulled her hard little body to me. "Do you believe I love you?"

"Yes. It's not really about that. I'm not jealous exactly - it's not like me to be jealous."

"Then what is it?"

"I can't expect you to understand. It's me. I feel incomplete."

It suddenly dawned on me what she was eluding to. "You want a child - like little Karen?"

"Yes I suppose so, but it's not just that. I don't feel as though I am a complete woman. I know it's crazy - I don't feel attractive..."

"But you're gorgeous."

"Oh Julian!...Don't ! - you'll start me off again."

I sighed heavily, despising my fate, knowing that in injuring Bethany they had injured any chance of our finding true happiness together.

"There's nothing that can be done?"

Bethany shook her head forlornly, and looked down, putting her hand to her abdomen. "It's too late. It's gone - they took it! They had to, it was too badly damaged. I would have bled to death otherwise."

"But they haven't taken it all away?"

"No, they left my cervix and ovaries - thank god."

"Then you're still fertile. We'll get a surrogate..."

"Oh Julian, they cost thousands."

"It doesn't matter. Besides, Karen said she will need a little brother or sister!"

"Julian - you're such a good man."

"And *you*, are a good woman," I said.

"Yes - I am a woman aren't I? You do find me attractive - really, I mean as a woman?"

"Do you need more proof?"

Karen looked down. "Oh Julian!"

I started to undo her vest. "No - not yet! - I believe you. We'd better look in on little Karen first."

Bethany put on the light and we peered into little Karen's crib.

"She's sleeping."

Suddenly two large grey eyes were staring at us. "Not now, she's not," I said.

"How would you like to have a little brother or sister to play with?" said Bethany.

Little Karen suddenly gurgled and smiled and struck out excitedly with her powerful little limbs: the happiest, most content creature you ever did see.

"Oh Julian! - look at her."
"Yeah, she seems happy now," I said, putting my arm around Bethany.
She lay her head on my shoulder. "Oh Julian, let's not argue again."
"We won't. The storm is over." I looked back at Karen, as she lay in her cot, laughing and gurgling. "You know where we are going? Paris. Yes, that's right. To the Notre Dame cathedral."
Baby Karen began kicking out in frantic excitement with her little limbs. laughing in her way, screaming out excitedly: "Arggg! - ha!-ha-ha-ha! - heeee!!"
I looked back at Bethany. "Isn't she sweet!"
"Yeah she is sweet all right."
"I've never seen a baby be so happy and good," I observed, with mounting pride.
"That's because she knows she safe."
"What a little sweet'ms you are - aren't you! Yes you are! A little sweetling..!"
"You don't have to speak to her like that."
"You have to though, she's only a little baby," I said.
Karen went on giggling and gurgling, as was her way of showing us she was content.
I looked at Bethany. "She knows she's loved."
"She's not the only one."
I puled Bethany to me and kissed her. Karen giggled again, striking out with her tiny arms and legs.
"There..!Did you see it that time? She winked again."
"I did! My god - I did. Look! She did it again."
"Ha hee...hee....heee..ha..ha," giggled Karen.
I kissed Bethany again on her mouth and her neck. She smelt so fresh, so clean.
"You know what I love about you?" I said.
"No - what?"
"You don't wear perfume."
"You're crazy"
"Ha!..hee!..he!..heeheee!...."